UnHoly Pursuit:

The Devil on My Trail

A

Novel

by:

A. White

The first book of the "UnHoly Pursuit" Saga

Copyright © 2016 by Unholy Pursuit Saga, LLC

Written 1999, 2001-2003 by A. White, Published 2016

Jacket designed by A. White and Ann Harden

Illustrations designed Ann Harden

Library of Congress catalogue and publication data:

White, A.
Unholy Pursuit: The Devil on My Trail. A novel
by A. White.

ISBN-978-0-692-76482-4

All rights reserved. Published in the United States
by Muses' Port.

First Paperback Edition.

Table of Contents

Chapter 1

Blue sky above a red river of blood and tears.

"Hellions to the right, Hellions to the left. Hellions to the east, Hellions to the west, above, and below. The pits of hell must be empty by now for they're all here around me." 24 year old Ana BuFaye Wyett thinks while gazing at the streets one level below her window as the early morning heat waves dance before her eyes.

Augusta, Ga seems hotter than the foyers of hell. In the year of 2488, it seems as thus the ancient environmentalists have been proven right. It's now literally hot as the gates of hell.

At five A.M. with no air conditioner on at the moment, with only a folded newspaper bent into a fan to keep the heat from driving her insane, Ana stood at her window looking out on the streets. Her elegant profile is a lovely silhouette against the lucidity of the glass. She can't shake the feeling of being watched which is why she's standing back in the shadows. Since she has been on the run from who knows what she's often sensed unknown eyes watching her.

She stood in early morning's first light in the apartment's suffocating air recollecting the morning's events, wondering what did she do to offend the landlord? When entering the rental building to pay the rent this morning the landlord glared at her as if she had been touched by the demon Azazel and was rehearsing for a starring role in the movie "Fallen 4: Mad for No Damn Reason." To think things through she went back outside into the last dew of this day and paced the walkway while no one is up and about. The streets are deserted except for the early birds coming from or going to work. The rental office kept early hours for people like herself so there would be no excuse for not paying on time.

"I'm not taking your money." Shelia Jean sneered at her. "I want you and your whole shebang outta here."

Distress started escalating at an alarming rate but refusing to allow it to mirror in her eyes, Ana calmly asked "What have I done to violate the rental agreement?" Shelia Jean casually shrugged her thin shoulders and looked her squarely in the eyes and coldly but nonchalantly said, "Nothing. You're the perfect tenant. I just don't like you."

Sighing heavily from years of déjà vu with landlord's bullshit flashing through her mind, Ana asked for 30 days to find a place to put her ailing mother and 4 year old daughter. Shelia Jean chuckled nastily, turned, and smiled an even nastier smile. "I don't think you understand...I can't stand the sight of you. The sight of all of you makes me sick. I want you gone by noon today. Begone! Scat! Git! Outta my face, bitch! What more must I say to make myself clearer?!"

Ana was done being nice, deciding it doesn't get you anywhere but kicked in the teeth again and again. "Well, I hate to tell ya" Ana said, leaning in close and personal, her voice laced with fury, "That's just too damn bad you can't stand the sight of me. You know what...you aren't easy on the eyes either. For the past 9 months I've damn near gone blind from looking at your mug! But know this and know this clearly! You've lost your ever-loving, hell-bent mind if you think I'm gonna to drag my mom and child out in this delirious heat *ALL* because you don't like me. There's a whole lotta shit people don't like but they're mature enough to make up their minds to deal with it so you can scratch your ass and get glad about it for all I care!" Ana stood staring down at the seated woman, shifting her weight to her left leg with her arms folded tightly around her midriff to lessen the blow of the unexpected eviction as she glared at her with a burning hatred.

Flabbergasted and shocked at Ana's outburst which felt as if it snapped her out of a mean-spirited trance, Shelia Jean stuttered. "I-I-I had no idea you felt this way... about me. I-I-I assume something can be worked out..."

"So now you know that I think you're cow-ass ugly! But about the rent--- that's more like it!" Tossing the money on the desk, she sashayed toward the door.

6

As she turned to leave she said, "You better not call the police because remember I know where you live! I'll be out of here by August 1st."

Ana regretted the words the moment they left her mouth. But she was sick of taking an endless parade of crap off of people for no reason that made any logical sense. People insult and attack her for no justifiable reason. It makes no sense. It's the year of 2488 and you'd think with all the process and advancements made in the last five centuries a lot of what she endures would no longer plague the human race. But, sadly, it still does. As she sees it, sexism and racism haven't changed much from the 20th century. We'd like to believe it has, that we've evolved much more and are much more enlightened, progressive and tolerant than our ancestors but according to what she's read as to what went on back then and what she's encountered in the 25th century, she doesn't see much of a change from what she read.

Staring at the slammed office door, Shelia Jean dropped her head in her hands, dumb-stricken, wondering what diabolical mood came over her?! She searched her mind for a clue but found none. She shook with the realization she just come within an inch of her tenant beating her unconscious. Pondering what happened she asked herself, "*Why did I provoke Ana to attack me so viciously?*" as she input the payment in the system. "*I like the woman ok, she has been a good tenant; pays on time. She's quiet, easy going. Who was the creepy man on the phone this morning telling me to file an eviction? To get rid of her? Why did I even listen to the garbage pail of shit he was goading me with? I've never seen Ana with a date or a boyfriend let alone a john. I'll admit I don't like the way Dwayne looks at her but she can't help if a man have a roaming eye.*" Sheila Jean shuddered at the recollection of the strange thoughts and peculiar feelings the hypnotic voice on the phone set off within her. She thought to herself, "*But truth be told, as much as I like her I'll be glad to be rid of that family. There has been odd phone calls reporting devious deeds regarding Ana since she moved here 9 months ago.*"

Dwayne, having heard the argument between his girlfriend Shelia Jean and her tenant, watched the sexy, young tenant named Ana Wyett through the side window facing the streets and walkway leading to the Victorian apartment house. He watched her pace the streets in the sticky, dewy dawn of the early morning. She passed his window situated midway the property for about the third or fourth time as she paced between the

7

office to the complex as if trying to decide if she should reenter and apologize to Sheila Jean. He watched her hips seductively sway as she twisted back to her place, her over the derriere length auburn hair seemed to glow in the bright summer sunshine. Her dark bronze and brown skin looks exotic and sexy as hell. But he's glad Jean is evicting the stuck-up bitch. He offered to help her out if she'd see him discreetly. But she shot him down giving him what he felt was a sorry-arsed cop out excuse.

"I like Jean, she's a nice person. I wouldn't want to hurt her and you shouldn't either," Ana had said one day he propositioned her about the third or fourth time during at her lunch break at the local deli down the street from the bank where she worked. He had to find out where she ate lunch because she started avoiding him at home. Sore about Ana's blatant rejection, he started dropping hints to Sheila Jean she should evict her because something wasn't right about that woman. Jean would always say the woman had a lot on her plate; a sick mom and a little kid, she's probably preoccupied a lot. He stands firmly in the window and grins triumphantly at her when she turns around and look at him. It's clear in his evil eyes he is thinking. "*Who's sorry now?!*"

After trekking back to her apartment, subsequently crossing the already blistering concrete court, Ana entered the abode she shared with her mom and daughter and remembered to catch the door to keep from slamming it and upsetting her mother and child. She quietly surveyed their dwelling, taking in the worn cracked brown pleather sofa, the simple pine wood kitchen table, and the soft blue carpet all in a single optical sweep, thinking this ain't too bad considering where we've been and how much we've lost over the years.

Fannie looks up from the breakfast table where she's trying to coax four year old Breanna into accepting another spoonful of cold cereal. Seeing her mother Breanna hopped down from her chair, rushed into the living room, and hugged her mom's legs. Seeing her daughter is upset Fannie gently pulled the child away and looked at her daughter. Fannie sighed. "Honey, your job just called. Your boss said report to her office immediately upon arriving to work." Fannie carried Breanna back to the table to make her finish her breakfast. Bea isn't much of an eater and needs to eat as much as she can get. "Thanks, Mom." Ana said, leaning over to kiss the crown of her seated mother's head and then kissed Bea's turned up face, telling her to eat her food.

8

"Mom," Ana said sorrowfully, "We've to move again. Shelia Jean has a harpy in her bonnet and want us out." Fannie, drawing up to her full 5 feet 7 inches, pulls her daughter to herself saying, "That's alright, baby girl, the same God who bought us safe this far will lead us wherever the path leads next. Trust in the Lord, He'll lead us through." Shrugging her shoulders and pulling from her mom's embrace Ana didn't want her mom to see she really didn't feel like hearing about God right now. Where is He when you need Him?! He surely must be male. Sounds just like a man, never around when you need him. She doubt He even liked her very much let alone loved her.

Fannie hugs her daughter fiercely for she knows the stiffened back means "I love you dearly mother but I don't want to hear about God right now." While in her heart Fannie wonders. *"It seems to me, my Ana is one of those poor souls born and condemned to live a life of misery. She has always been quite distinguished from her siblings and I can not say her father and I have always understood her but we loved her no less. Seems as thus something have been after her since the day she was born. Her father said two men showed up at the hospital's nursery, one of the men----something indescribable and sinistral hung in the air around him, while the other man standing to his right appeared to be Native American was threatening the white haired white man on his left mentally. While looking directly at the hand on his left the white haired man vanished in the thin air and the young Native American man tapped him on the shoulder to get his attention and said "Even the spirits take care of their children." Jacob BuFaye, not knowing what just happened, nor what the man meant was not sticking around to find out. He rushes into the nursery, scoops his newborn baby girl into his arms and heads back to his wife's room, kisses his wife and delivers their baby to her arms. Telling her what the two peculiar men looked like and said.*

"Honey, we know everyone in this small country town and these men were no one we know." Jacob worriedly told his wife. Fannie, wondering at her husband's fanatical behavior in bringing the baby to her before feeding time, patiently says. "Dear...maybe they were visiting someone, maybe they were someone's relative? Some people just like to look at newborn babies." "Oh yeah! they were visiting someone all right!" The octave of his voice rising. "They were both visiting our baby girl."

Shortly after Jacob's sprint down the hall to his wife's room the prenatal nurses enter the room and demand the parents to return to the nursery. Citing to Jacob BuFaye "Your wife needs her rest and the baby is safe with us."

"I may be a farmer but I am not stupid! If my kid is safe in the that damn nursery why were there two sons-of-bitches standing outside the window watching her blow bubbles and rub her face with her fist?" The two nurses looked at each other in puzzlement and the red-haired nurse looking not much older than twenty said "Sir...there was no one out there watching little Ana but you."

"Well, now. I suppose I am crazy and seeing things too." He asked sarcastically. Fannie interrupted saying. "It's hot and muggy and my husband is exhausted from hard work and no sleep. Please excuse his outbursts, he means well. He's simply protective. I'm sure you ladies can understand." She said while smiling her award-winning Mona Lisa smile. A smile that she soon learns her baby girl Ana inherited.

Finally, the nurses resolved to leave the family alone when they saw in his eyes that Mr. BuFaye wasn't going to budge on his conviction that strangers were watching his kid and wanted to harm her.

On their way back to the prenatal ward the heavy set African American nurse whispered to her trainee "Does that baby smell like roses or some kinda flowers to you?" The younger woman replied in a returned whisper. "Yes she does. You know...I wasn't going to say anything because I didn't know if it was a perfume someone was wearing or but I smelt it again several times when changing her diapers. Maybe she's ill and the doctors haven't detected it."

Shaking her head no "The doctor say she's fine health-wise, well at least all they can do anything about it but they don't know why she smells like that. Now, don't get me wrong her poop smells like any other baby but sometime it doesn't." The nurse's assistant agreed, admitting she liked to hold her. The baby had a soothing affect.

Breaking into her mother's thoughts and putting on a facade of brightness Ana says "Come here, Breanna, and help mommy get ready for work. I've to be there in an hour."

Watching her daughter run as fast as her 4 year old legs could carry her Ana thinks to herself,"*Such a beautiful child. I pray her life be better than mine.*"

Standing at the closet with a dress in her hand, she asks Bea if she likes it. Bea nods and tells her to wear that one. She accepts Bea's verdict and lays out the outfit on the bed. Musing to herself. "*Kid has a great sense of fashion, a true diva in the making.*" Suddenly, she feels flustered and her ears start ringing with a horrible deafening roar. Feeling as though she's mentally being called or summoned, Ana looks out the window, across the street and sees a strange man looking directly at her window. Catching her eye he blows a kiss. She quickly stepped away from the window into the shadows of the room and ushered Bea back into the kitchen where her Nana is at the sink clearing away the few breakfast dishes.

Rushing back into her bedroom's closet grabbing her purse with her pistol and car keys inside thinking "*It's too early in the morning and too damn hot for their shit*", knowing he'll vanish as mysteriously as he appeared. Ana walked urgently outside to confront the peeping Tom, but it was just as she suspected. He was gone.

Deciding "Screw it! I'll wear what I already have on to work." She rushed back inside cracking the front door open telling her mom she'll see them this evening and to lock the door and don't open it for anyone and if the hospital calls tell them to call me at work. And to please crank the A.C. up, it's getting dangerously hot in here. But instead she goes in and turns the A.C. up higher in her mother's room and leaves the door open so the cold air can circulate all over the small place. She kissed them goodbye.

Once outside the car was nearly sizzling to the touch at 7:00 A.M. making Ana amuse herself by saying. "I guess today the Lord finally sent the fire and brimstone He been promising for nearly 2,500 years."

Thinking of the mounting hospital bills, Ana absentmindedly turned the ignition and nothing happened. The engine didn't turn over. Not even a click. She began hitting the steering wheel with the palm of her hand in frustration before she gets out to inspect the car. Stepping in fluids slowly seeping from the underbelly of her steel blue Toyota she knows the day just got worse. She kneels to take a better look and suddenly start

11

trembling, closed her eyes and shaking her head as if doing so would make all the events in the past 75 minutes a dream, vanish, disappear. But opening her eyes they were all still staring at her like a bump on a log. She wondered how much worse can the day get? A closer inspection reveals bullet holes in the transmission fluid pan and gas tank.

Sensing someone watching her rear end she cranes her neck around and sees the man from across the street has reappeared behind her in the grassy median. But he isn't hiding the fact he's lustfully watching her intensively. She leaps up into an erect standing posture and yells across the streets, "YOU PERVERTED RAT BASTARD! I KNOW YOU DID THIS." The mottled faced man stood still, staring extensively as a smirk slowly spread across his blotched face. He soundlessly mouthed. "Prove it."

The strange man with burnt blotched skin and nearly colorless gray eyes named Bjors smiles to himself. He's a stranger to Ana but not to local satanic cloister who sent him. He pulls out a cell phone and reports to his higher hierarchy: "Your highness. Mission accomplished! Another eviction is in progress as we speak."

The receiver of the call asks" Did the landlord say where she's moving to?"
Bjors replies "No, the dumb, simpleton landlord did not ask her."
Voice on phone: "You know what to do next."
Bjors replies "Yes, eliminate all witnesses, landlord, and military neighbor. Her elderly neighbor saw us."

Voice on phone becomes angry and says "You fucking idiot! How could you be so careless as to allow a military personnel to see you? Never mind, I'll assign someone to trail and kill him. You can't eliminate him without drawing suspicion!"

"Yes, Your Highness." Bjors humbly but resentfully replied.

Looking across the street, she wanted to shoot the bastard in the median so badly she swore she heard her pistol in her purse say "Do it! Do it! Shoot the fucked up face son-of-a-bitch!" Debating with herself if she had enough time to cross the streets and kick his ass and be to work on time she decides on the latter. Leaning against her car, she tries to decide if she should reenter the apartment and call a cab or bum a ride with a neighbor going her way. Charles from Apt. 6B pulls up beside her and asks "Do you know that fool across the street?" Charles, a military personnel officer at Fort Gordon, is dressed in his usual rigid attire. An officer and a gentleman, a dying breed.

"No," she said. "I don't know him. He has been out there all morning. Could you give me a lift to work?"

"Sure." He replied. Carpooling to work was something never occurred to Charles who asks, "Don't you think you should call APD about a stranger hanging around watching you? That's stalking."

Thanking him and pulling open the car door and hopping in she says "No, cause they ain't gonna do nothing but tell me they need proof." Charles glances at the security camera across the street. He knows how easily cities' officials can erase that which they don't want seen.

Relaxing in the cool leather interior of Charles' BMW Ana's mind replays series of events starting as early in her memory as age 3 of someone standing watching her from a field, from a junior high track field, from a neighbor's porch, a park, the edge of the yard and never knowing what they wanted. But she knew every time a stranger appeared bad things begun to happen, her life and that of her family suffers on-going bombard of problems that appear to have no real rhyme or reason. Death of a livestock, family pet found butchered, death of a grandparent, uncle, aunt or even her own father. Bills no one had any memory of creating start appearing in the mail. Lawyers getting absentee judgments on those bills. So she knew they'd eventually find her. Neighbors looking at you as though you suddenly grew a set of horns and don't know they're sitting on your head. Usually it's less than 9 months. She even remembered seeing a stranger at her wedding, when she peeked out the door of the luxurious hotel to see what was taking her new husband so long with the ice, she looked right into the face of a stranger peering at her from the far end of the hallway.

These strangers were always like some sort of bad omen. Like a bad moon rising.

13

The very aura around them seems dark and evil as a stormy night with banshees screaming in the wind. It always rings true. Whenever they appeared life-alternating destruction was soon to follow.

Mentally reliving two childhood events her mind drifts to an age of innocence. When she was a child, a few years older than Bea. She was at end of the porch of their farm house. Too young for school she enjoying the cool of the morning in the post-global warming spring. A boy a few years older than herself dressed in a blue velvet knickers suit and white stockings with neatly combed blonde hair across his angelic brow asked her would she like to see baby rabbits? Being an animal lover she excitedly said "YES!" This strange child led her to a spot and told her stand in front of the ancient red brick chimney, sternly telling her to wait here, he'd go get the bunnies. While standing, awaiting her new-found friend to bring the baby bunnies, someone yells, "Noooo!!" And startled her half to death, her little heart was pounding so hard it hurt. In a blink of an eye, an instant, she's sweep up by the lady in the beautiful white robe she met some time ago outside in her favorite morning spot. Upon being gently placed to the ground she heard and felt a very loud noise, so loud it jolted the ground. Something had crashed to the ground so hard it knocked her off balance. But the lady caught her before she hit the ground.

Instinct told her to look up. They both looked up and little boy blue was on the roof staring down at them. The boy's face was twisted in such rage it erased all his beauty. His face was downright ugly. He had pushed the chimney down. She then looked at the beautiful lady who was frowning up at little boy blue, when she disappeared the boy ran across the top of the roof and disappeared.

Since the age of three she knew someone sought to end her life but who or why she hadn't a clue. It was hard not to know that when knives and other sharp objects flew unaided through the air at you. There's no bones about the intention when someone is shooting at you, cutting your brake line, breaking in on you in the middle of the night- you're quite sure they're quite serious about killing you. The last 3 years she and her four year old daughter Bea have lived on the open road; somehow always one step ahead of the monsters gunning for them. They usually traveled back roads across state lines to avoid scrutiny by the local police or state troopers. Plus, she traveled with several loaded guns. She knew if pulled over with more ammo than the Marines had when they landed at Iwo Jima she would be definitely staring at jail time. Nothing made sense anymore not that much ever did.

Their lives had become a series of crisscrossing drives across the country to escape certain death. She'd worked various low-paying jobs, everything from a waitress, to a maid, to a short order cook. Although these jobs were far beneath her educational level. But who could complain when at the all the well paying jobs she applied for the interviewers took one look at her application and all but trashed it right in front of her because someone always called while she was still in the interviewee chair. So she knew she wouldn't get the job. But if the employer wasn't going to hire her was the dirty look on the way out necessary? As a result, she and her brother Jack created many aliases for her to use to gain employment. Potential employers acted as though her real name had a yellow plague circle drawn around it. But, even though using an alternate identity got her the job, once the mysterious phone calls came, her bosses would fire her for using the alias. Some even refused to pay her for her labor, arguing the name she worked under didn't exist, they didn't hire Ana BuFaye or Ana Wyett, and wouldn't have hired her if she'd been the last person on earth.

Even if she didn't know who was after them nor why she knew the diabolical forces were very real and formidable. She knew that better than most. She also knew anyone who denied their existence is a fool and will soon end up dead. She was determined that didn't happen to her, her daughter, and mother.

This is why twenty four year old Ana BuFaye Wyett was shocked when the bank in Augusta, Ga where she now works returned her call saying she was hired if she wanted the job. Hell yeeah! She wanted the job. She was a Cambridge graduate of the class of 2483, an accounting and business major, first year pre-law student. But after her former pro-football player husband was locked up by the feds for drug possession 3 and half years ago, finding a decent job become non-attainable. This morning marks the ninth month they've lived in this cheap, over-heated apartment. But it beats sleeping in an over-heated or freezing car.

She always counted the months because the harassment and murder attempts always took place in intervals of three, six, to nine months so it was about time the fools came fucking with her again. Their vivacious cycle of mayhem and madness is as reliable as the sunrise. Sometime the harassment got so bad they simply loaded their few personal effects in their small blue Toyota in the still of the night and hauled ass. Usually it took a few months for the mystery people to find them again.

She wondered how did her life end up in such a hot mess and none of it was a mess of her own creation. She did everything right according to the book of success. She even went to church every nearly Sunday. Before they were married, most Sundays Thad went with her. She completed college in 3 and 1/2 years. Got a well-paying job. Married the man she loved, they had the three story house in the right suburban neighborhood, all this was accomplished before Breanna was born. So whomever wrote that damn book about the road to success definitely didn't know what in the hell they were talking about.

She wasn't entirely surprised to learn about Thad's affair after his arrest, his behavior told her he was cheating on her, but she was surprised to learn about the drug possession. She'd never known him to do drugs. He didn't even like aspirin. And where did he allegedly get over 50 grand worth of cocaine from? All of their money from his NFL days was sunk into their home, the children yet to be born educational funds, and IRA accounts and other investments. She had to take out a second mortgage and fleece the IRAs and educational accounts to pay his astronomical legal fees. While many drugs were legalized in the United States centuries ago; such as marijuana, cocaine was not one of them. Her mother and older sister had said let his girlfriend pay the legal cost since that's where he was the night Bea was born. The judge released him on a cash bail of $250,000. But trying to be the good wife she and his best friend got him out.

At least he got to spend Bea's first year at home with her while she worked and supported the family before the trial and conviction sent him away for five years. The day he was convicted the accounting firm she worked for told her to clear her desk, she was fired. They couldn't risk the wife of a convicted felony handling billions of dollars.

16

The worst slap in the face was when a law firm tracked her down on the road and delivered a writ of divorce two years after his imprisonment. She was working as a maid at hotel in Nebraska under an alias which is why she didn't answer to the name Ana Wyett when the well dressed man walking toward her as she pushed a housekeeping cart down the hall called her by her married name. When he caught up with her he reached in his breast pocket and pulled out a letter. The letter was written in Thad's handwriting. Inside were two messages; he told her he wasn't coming back to her when his three remaining years was served; to do so would be a Mississippi move. She had no idea what a Mississippi move was. The second message was concerning their daughter. Citing their getting back together wouldn't be beneficial to Bea. She stared at the letter wondering what Bea had to do with this shitty letter? She was surprised she wasn't hurt. She was too tired to muster up the strength to be hurt.

The Birth of Bea

What was even more unaccountable or unexplainable happened during she and Thad's good years. And was still a mystifying event, or phantasm, or apparition. She wasn't sure anymore if she didn't dream it as Thad said she did, but she was almost certain after making love Thad returned home. She was upset he decided at 11:00 P.M. to visit friends after their love making. She was home alone in the big house. These were the pre-Bea days so the big house was quiet and often lonely. She was positive he'd returned in the predawn hours and made love to her again in the fading darkness as dawn drew near. But when she opened her eyes they rested not on Thad but on the most beautiful man she had ever seen. She felt her heart leap into her throat, letting out a bloodcurdling scream. Next, she heard Thad's heavy footsteps racing upstairs. Now the man was fully awake and looking puzzled; as if he was as lost to how he arrived in her bed as she.

"Sorry Ma'am, I took the wrong door," the stranger apologized. He was wearing nothing but pair of white silk boxer shorts. He rose and headed for the closet but paused half a second near her pale oak wood night stand and left a fistful of gemstones and winked seductively at her before walking fully into her closet. She couldn't believe she just saw that. Thad burst in the room, she pointed at the closet.

"Hey YOU! What in the hell you doing in there!?" Thad roared at the strange intruder and rushed in after him. But the man was gone. Poof! Just like that, it was as if no one had been there seconds earlier. After much rumbling around in there Thad stuck his head around the door frame and said, "There's no one in here..." Pulling the bed covers with her because she was still nude, she climbed out the bed and looked; sure enough the closet was empty.

"Thad! I'm positive he went into the closet!!" she cried wildly pushing aside garments and shoe boxes. They both searched the big walk in closet.

"I think someone just played some kinda mind game trick on us." Thad reasoned, hitting the solid wall at the back of the closet. She resumed looking for a secret entry. There was none. They had built this house.

She gathered the gemstones the stranger left on the nightstand. "If no one was here nor in here where did these come from?" she asked, waving them under Thad's nose.

Towering over her at 6'3", wearing a not very pleasant expression on his face he said "You tell me where they came from. The dude I saw was no one I'd ever seen before. Why was there this strange man in my house wearing white underwear and leaving jewelry? And why in the hell are you still undressed? I left here before 11:00 P.M." This was sounding an awful like an accusation to Ana. He roughly grabbed her arm wanting an explanation of why she was naked in their bedroom with a stranger who could disappear?

"Are you saying I know him?!" she asked, disbelieving Thad would think such a thing.

"What else am I to think? I can't explain how he got out but whomever he was I do believe he knows you," Thad said making more noise than necessary, angrily reinspecting the closet solid walls, "Perhaps he's some type of damn magician or we're both freaking dreaming." Thad pounded the walls hard enough to resound in the room before asking her point blank "Is he your lover?"

Frustrated, she yelled, "A man breaks in here while you're *supposed* to be at home protecting me and you've the brazen audacity to ask me if he's my lover? If I had a lover I wouldn't be dumb enough to bring him home!"

Dismissing her ranting Thad goes outside to further inspect the house structure for secret passages they were unaware of, but found nothing.

Later that day they met up for lunch. They each had lunch breaks at the same hour. During their lunch break he told her perhaps she dreamed it and her hysterical screaming caused them both to see an imaginary threat. She asked for the second time if that was case where did the gemstones come from?

He looked out across the plaza in the mild sunlight and finally back at her and asked what he'd been deferring all morning. "Did you make love to that man?" Not looking at her he asked. "Do you love him?"

"How am I to love someone I don't know?" She answered his inquiry in a surly tone. "No, I didn't make love to him. When I woke up he was there." She left out where exactly was he.

"Ana, I need to know, did you have sex with that guy? He didn't break in the house. Somebody let him in. This shit been lolling around in my head all morning. I think you know him but y'all wasn't expecting me back so soon. So did you sleep with him?" Thad asked, frowning at her.

She realized while they searched the house and what had been plaguing her all morning; if it wasn't Thad who she made love to this morning then it was that exceptionally handsome stranger. "No, I did not.", she lied to save her marriage.

After that morning Thad pretty much lost interest in her, their marriage, and their life. He was still polite most of the time but they fought more than usual. He showed marginal interest and excitement when she happily announced her pregnancy. By her 6th month he was rarely at home at all. Every time she called his best friend to ask had he seen him she got the same reply. "I haven't seen Thad in weeks." Antonia would always say.

So having no other close relatives in Boston she asked her married older sister to be the person to go to the hospital with her. "Where is Thad?", her sister had asked, saying she couldn't take time from the NYPD to do Thad's job. She finally acknowledged to her judgmental older sister she thought Thad was having an affair.

"I know he's cheating if he's gone for days on the end. You need to divorce his cheating ass." Helena advised. By the 9th month they were at least having breakfast and dinner again as a couple at home but her mom had came to live with them for the duration of the pregnancy but had to return home, coming back for the delivery and recovery. She wanted to tell someone about the strange morning visitor but decided against it. Who would believe her?

She felt a little queasy but thought that may had been from the tacos eaten for dinner the night before. But dinner at 7:00 P.M. had been over twelve hours ago. She knew something was wrong but Thad had been acting so weird lately she was reluctant to tell him she felt nauseated. She wonders what caused the 180 degree turn in him? He used to be so attentive and affectionate. Her lesser angel perched on her shoulder quipped: "So was Henry the 8th and you see how that turned out for his wives? Screw him. Get your ass up and call your sister or your mom. Helena might bitch but at least she'll be there." Mentally, she told her lesser angel. "Shut up. You're always starting some shit." Pushing Thaddeus Wyett's broad linebacker shoulder, she rouses him from sleep. "Baby, I don't feel so good." Ana said rubbing her round, heavy belly. The parturience of her condition seems to mean very little to him.

"Of course you don't, you're pregnant," Thad crudely replied without turning around in bed. She pushed him again. This time he turns around and look at her. "WHAT?! What am I supposed to do about it?" He grunted. "Are you in pain?" He asked a little softer seeing that his wife wasn't just nagging him to make him miserable just because she was. She shook her head.

20

"It's probably just gas. Where's your gas medicine? The one the doctor gave you?," he asked, got up, and started looking on her night stand for the pill bottle. After he found it he shook a capsule into his palm, went across the room to the water dispenser, and got her a cup of water. Handing her the pill and water he felt angry but didn't know why. He has been angry at her a lot lately, a-teeming under the surface; mean uncontrollable rage was building up inside. He knew he loved Ana and was happy about their coming baby. So what in the hell was wrong with him? Why was he mad at her? He felt couldn't control the rising ire he felt toward her. He had to let it out.

"Every damn time I turn around you're whining or crying about something! Women been doing this since the dawn of time and I doubt any complained as much as you. You and this one little baby is costing me more than either of y'all is worth!" The words out his mouth surprised and shocked them both. She glared at him and snatched the cup of water, splashing a little on her stomach and chest, took the pills, gobbled them down with water, and threw the cup at him hitting him in the chest.

"Baby, I didn't mean that. I'm just grumpy this morning." He humbly apologized. "I don't know why I say stupid shit. Want any breakfast?"

"No," She said curtly. "Remember you said my skinny ass wasn't worth feeding." She folded her arms across her chest and tried biting back tears. He sat on the side of the bed and apologized for those words too.

"Baby, you've got to eat. So what do you want before I go to work?", he entreated.

"You can't go work today. I don't feel so good," she plead.

"How do you expect to pay for all this?", he asked, waving his arms to emphasize his point. "We've spent all I made playing football!"

"You mean *you've* spend it. Remember, you told me *you* were the one out there taking those licks to earn it so, it's *"you"* who gets the say-so in how it is spent. Had you listened to me we wouldn't have bought this big ass house and those expensive ass cars.

21

My little car from my college days was fine."

"Whatever, it's done now, so what your ornery ass want for breakfast?", Thad teased walking out of the massive master bedroom heading downstairs. "Toast with no butter." She yells after him hoping he doesn't fry anything, it will only make her feel worse.

In the kitchen preparing his wife's breakfast Thad calls the woman he has been seeing for a while. "Sorry, honey I can't come today. Wife isn't feeling well," he whispers into the phone. He knows his wife can sneak up on you and you don't hear her coming. Plus, she got damn dog ears or something. She can hear shit he don't hear.

"Thad, honey. She's going to be sick until she pushes that baby out into the world. How do you know that's even your baby? I mean, she could be lying to you," Lola Wilson cooed.

"I know it's mine's. She was a virgin when I married her," Thad said through clenched teeth as he poured the orange juice and put a flower from the arrangement on the diningroom table in a bed tray vase.

Lola laughed. "So she said." But adds, "I can offer you a lot more than that inexperienced girl. When the child is born we can raise it as our own."

Thad exasperatedly sighed, they'd talked about this before. He told her before he wasn't leaving Ana. Why can't she get that through her damn head?

"Thad, I'm not playing with you. Get yourself here today or I'll tell that big-bellied bean pole wife of yours everything!", Lola threatened. Thad had tried before to break up with this woman but she won't go away. Now she's threatening to tell Ana everything. He'd to put a stop to Lola's madness. Tony was right when he said there was something evil about this woman. Sex with Lola was great, actually mind-blowing, much better than with Ana. Ana didn't know a damn thing about sex. Barely knew where to position her legs. He had to show her everything. Their first time, all she did was cry. He wondered did her mother and sister tell her anything at all? But still, she was his wife and annoying as she is right now, he loved her.

22

"Ok, Lola, I'll see you at noon," he finally said making up his mind to change their phone number today and break up with this woman. She'd started to really get on his nerves with her demands. Even had the nerve to ask him was he still screwing his wife. Of course he was, well until she got too big and he was afraid he'd hurt the baby. He wonders did Lola send the damn magician who disappeared in their closet? He took the tray upstairs to Ana who was still mad at him but at least sitting up watching a program.

"Here, baby. Eat up. I'm gonna get ready for work," he said putting the tray of cinnamon oatmeal and banana, dry toast, coffee and juice on his side of the bed. He kissed the top of her head before entering the bathroom and closing the door. He knew he wasn't going to work but to Lola's to break up with her. He don't believe in beating women but if she calls Ana while he's en route to her he definitely was going to beat her ass. Women have tried many times before her with him and haven't won. Nobody is going to make him leave Ana. He made that clear with the groupies that trailed him on the road so now he's making it clear to Lola.

Ana looked up at her handsome husband who bent over to kiss her goodbye saying he'd bring dinner home tonight as always since she got too heavy to walk properly.

"Call my sister to come sit with you today," he said, looking at her sulking face.

"That's your job!" She pouted. "I didn't do this by myself." He sighed and blew her a kiss from the door and asked what did she want for dinner tonight. He has eaten more oddities in the past eight and a half months than he knew existed. She watched food channels and decided she wanted it. Then he'd run all over town looking for it. His mom said all that will go away when the baby is born. Things like desert grouse and Amazon cat shit coffee, who ever heard of black folks eating that shit? And the shit is expensive as hell.

Ana calls Helena, her older sister, instead of her sister-in-law. "Ana, I can't come there right now. I'm in the middle of an arrest," Helena says. "Call momma."

"Momma is way down in Georgia." Ana whines.

"Where's Thad?" Helena asked. Ana paused a minute. "He's gone to work."

"He went to work knowing you were feeling bad? Suppose the baby is coming? Everybody don't have excruciating pain when in labor, some women feel really sick and nauseated when their time comes. Call a cab and go to the hospital. I'll be there around 3:00," Helena said, hanging up and calling their mother whose line was busy. Then she called their oldest brother's wife and explains she thinks Ana is in labor. "Ok, I'll fly up there," Frances said.

Ana is on the phone with her mother as to why the line was busy when Helena called. "Ok, baby--if you start feeling worse before I get there, go on to the hospital. I'll meet you there." Ana agrees. She pulls out her packed suitcase and calls a cab. She waits downstairs for an hour. None show up. She calls again, the phone is dead. Curious but thinking nothing of it, she goes to the garage and find her car tires flat. She click the keys' remote to reinflate the tires but the instant tire inflator had been disconnected. She hadn't been near this car in a while so, again, she thinks nothing of it because she hasn't driven it in a long while and tires do go flat after a long idle. She goes to the luxury car Thad brought her, the one she drove mostly at his nagging her, saying it was safer. The nuclear energy cell is completely drained. *Now* she is starting to panic. She calls Thad at work but his supervisor says he's out on the field. She calls his personal ISPAN phone, no answer. It clicks over to the voice message intake. Now, she's beginning to feel pain. Looking over their lawn over at their neighbor's garage she sees the neighbors' hovercraft car is still in the driveway.

She wobbles over to their house and activates their door chime. The wife answers, not very friendly. "Toanna, can you take me to the hospital?" she asked, holding her heavy stomach.

"NO, that's what ambla-buses are for!" The woman said, staring her chillingly in the eyes. Ana hadn't thought of calling an ambla-bus. She hopes it won't be filled to capacity. After making her call she sits and waits on her front steps. They assured her they'd be there shortly. But to be on the safe side she also calls a cab for the second time. Another hour later and neither of them are there.

24

Feeling the baby moving as if positioning itself to come out, she devises another plan. She knows there's a hoverbus stop about a mile from their house so she went back inside and put on layers of wet-proof clothing and underwear in case her water broke while she was on the bus.

A young woman, a college student going her way, fell in step with her snail paced tread and began walking slowly with her. "Ma'am, I think you need to be in the hospital," the young woman of about eighteen or nineteen said. She didn't feel like telling the young woman a year or so younger than herself she already knew that.

The hoverbus alit in front of them. "Ma'am, you can't get on here in that condition. I can't be responsible for what happens to you," the driver said as the young woman helped her climbed the steep steps. "You bloody pillock, shut the fuck up and drive!," the young woman said as she helped Ana lower her bulk into a seat.

Several older women on the bus ordered him to head to the nearest hospital. "That's out of my route," the driver informed them. They refused to take no for an answer and ordered him again saying if they have to come up front they were going to beat the hell out of him and everybody would end up in the hospital from a bus crash. Seeing they were serious he steered the big machine in the direction of the local hospital.

Three women helped Ana into the emergency room where all the doctors were pretty much ignoring her. The heaviest set woman of the three grabbed a passing doctor and told him this woman needs medical attention now. Ana knew her water had broken, it was dripping on the floor through her pant legs. Ana couldn't help but notice a woman who kept subtly but intentionally following, watching the four of them. She wondered why? Who was she? Their eyes met and the woman narrowed hers. By now she was in so much misery she really didn't care what the bitch's problem was.

Shortly afterward a nurse wheeled her to the maternity ward. She could hear the other mothers groaning and crying. "Don't you start that shit! You wasn't doing all that crying and screaming bloody murder when he was getting that baby!" The nurse said above her head. This was her last straw of dealing with rude ass motherfuckers this morning.

"Do you have any children?" She asked the rude nurse.

"No, I've better sense than to let some fool knock my ass up." the woman of indeterminable age snapped.

"Well, just remember this...some woman cried and moaned for your ugly ass to be here and I guess nobody wanted to knock your ugly ass up is why you ain't got no children. I'm not paying you to insult me! I'm paying you to do your damn job. And if you've a problem with that take it up with your boss." Ana insulted back. Another nurse, one who seemed to be both sensible and sane, heard the argument and dismissed the one steering the hover wheelchair. The mystery woman from the ER trailed them and followed them to Ana's private room on the maternity ward. At the room's entrance Ana put both hands on side of the door to halt the wheelchair and yelled at the woman following them.

"Bitch, what is your fucking problem?"

"She isn't with you?" The attendance room nurse asked, puzzled. Whipping her head around to get a better look at the woman. Thinking more along the line of babynapping.

"No, I don't know that freak!"

The woman approached them with her hand extended, wearing a bogus smile. "Hi, my name is Sister Etna, from the Montessori Adoption Agency. I was told you wanted to give your baby up for adoption being so young and all. You're Ana Wyett, aren't you?"

"Get away from me!" Ana screeched. "Hell no, I ain't giving my baby up! I don't know who told you that but they sure as hell told you wrong!"

"Ms. Wyett, being a single mother is harder than you think." The woman who was as much a nun as Lucifer's wife, Lilith, said.

"I'm not a single mother, my husband will be here soon." Ana replied as the nurse

26

helped her into the bed, telling the strange woman to get out the room.

"If Mrs. Wyett wishes to give her baby up. I'm sure she'll call you." The nurse said pushing the woman out the room, closing and locking the door. A knock was heard almost immediately. The nurse sighed and answered the door. Looked back at Ana and asked did she know a Frances and Fannie BuFaye? Ana nodded; they were her mother and sister-in-law. For those two to be here already she wonders just how long was she waiting at home and waiting in the waiting room? The two rushed in the room past the nurse saying they got here as soon as possible. Fussing over her, asking her how's she feeling right now? She ensures them the pain isn't so bad yet.

"Where is Thad?" her sister-in-law Frances asked, looking around the room for him.

"I've no idea," Ana said sighing from the pain that was building up and falling."I tried calling him at work, they say he's out on the field handling or evaluating a claim." She couldn't tell mom and Frances about this morning. They'd freak out. Mom already wasn't exactly a fan of Thad's.

"I knew he'd pull some shit like this," Fannie said angrily punching in her son-in-law's phone number on her ISPAN, only to be forwarded to his answering service.

"What's that friend's of his' name?" Ana's oldest brother Junior asked from the doorway.

"Tony," Ana replied and flinched. Frances rustled through Ana's purse until she found her phone and handed it to her husband and Junior looked through his sister's contacts until he located this "Tony". Listening to the phone ring a few times before a man answers, he barks, "If you know where your friend Thad is tell him his wife, Ana, is at Boston Medical Center having his damn baby! To get his ass here now!" Junior had a pretty good idea where his trifling brother-in-law might be, with another woman. He couldn't prove it but his guts told him that's where Thad was.

Ashton Cargill was dreaming, or at least he thinks he's dreaming. He's dreaming his mystery love is in trouble. He doesn't know who she is or how to find her again. But he can feel her sharp pains and muted suffering. He sense a great evil near her. He chuckles in his sleep. But believing it only to be a dream, he doesn't react. "*For once the great evil isn't him.*"

"Whatcha laughing about?" A female voice asked that he recognizes as belonging to Dawn, one of his many concubines as they call themselves.

"Dawn, you ladies go to another room. I want to be alone," Ashton said. In the sea of breasts, arms and legs, nobody moves for everyone is asleep. He gets up and goes into another bedroom and falls back asleep. The strange dream returns. He sees her in pain. He wonders what it's about or what's causing the pain until he sees her in stirrups, panting and pushing. He does a quick count of the last time he visited her. It's been about 8-9 months. The child isn't his; had it been, it would have been here 3-5 months ago. But he can't dismiss the fact she's in pain. He tells himself she'll be alright. Women are built for this. But no matter much he tells himself this is none of his concern he feels he's only lying to himself.

He finds himself in the hospital's corridors almost against his wishes. He sees the labor room and sees a male doctor about to go in. He feels intense jealousy and becomes enraged. He yells at the man in purple scrubs, "If you take your ass in there I swear I'll kill you." The doctor stopped and looked questioningly at Cargill, wondering what's he doing here?

"I want a female doctor in there. No males better take their asses in there." he orders the head doctor in the maternity ward. Of course, no one tells Ashton Cargill what he can and cannot order to have done.

"Sir, only the patient or her relative can order such changes," the head doctor tells him.

"Well, then you get your ass in there, you're a woman-in case you've forgotten that!" he said, pushing the female doctor toward the door as he heard Ana's screams and mumbled voices saying something to her he wasn't trying to understand. Ana's screaming is breaking his heart; he can't take it anymore. He wonders why her pain bothers him so much when he has been through this countless times with wives, girlfriends, concubines, and all else in-between. Not able to take it anymore he pushes the door open and yells at the doctor give her sometime to lessen the pain.

"Who are you?!" Fannie yells. "Get the hell out of here!"

The doctor feels that another dose of epidural will be too much for Ana's system to bear so she ignores Cargill's demand.

He ignores Fannie and grabs Ana's hand and absorbs a lot of her pain. Calming down, Ana looks at him and wonders why is the man from the closet here? Does he thinks this is his baby? "C'mon darling, relax and push when you feel the urge." He coached her. Ana stopped screaming long enough to make sure she wasn't seeing things.

Addressing the doctor he made attend to Ana. "I don't want a sloppy job done down there." Fannie and Frances are both totally flabbergasted at this man's nerve to barge in here and start giving orders. Who in the hell does he think he is? Besides, who is he anyway?

"Ana, who in the hell is this man?" Fannie asked pointing at Ashton. "Is he the baby's father as to why Thad isn't here?" Frances interrogates. Ashton ignores them both and get behind Ana helping her sit up, the doctor looks at him as if he is crazy.

Fannie pulls out her phone to call security to come get this guy out of a private family situation. No one comes. Fannie, Frances and Helena exchanged stares with their mouths agape. Fannie tried to push him out; it would've been easier pushing a huge boulder up a slippery mountainside than moving him. All his attention was focused on Ana and the baby. He utterly ignored Fannie hitting and pushing him and even Helena's gun drawn telling him to scat. Everyone forgot about Ashton Cargill when the ring of fire stage hit Ana. Ana realized her mother and sister wasn't lying when they told her this shit feels like your inside are coming out. "Don't believe that malarkey about it's a natural progress and yada, yada, yada." Helena had warned.

"This position is best," he tells the doctor. Soon the doctor sees the head crowning. "One more push, Mrs Wyett." The doctor says cheerfully. The fact that she's another man's wife registers with Ashton at the doctor's words. He climbs down out the bed and smiles down at Ana who is looking at him perplexed wondering why is this stranger in here? Why has the hospital let a stranger in here when he isn't anyone she knows?

"You've a girl, Mrs. Wyett." The doctor says, gleaming at Ana, handing the baby to the attending nurse who is terribly, truly afraid of Ashton Cargill. She knows who and what he really is. She was the witch who was supposed to rush out the hospital with baby Wyett the moment it was born but she wouldn't dare do that with Azazael standing there. No one was counting on him being here when they gave her this assignment! What's his relationship to Ana Wyett? The blood and DNA test shows the baby belongs to Thad Wyett. This is turning into an all-around bad day. Ana was supposed to have given birth at home so they'd be the only ones assisting her and they could easily walk off with the baby. How in the hell did Ana get to the damn hospital?! Mistress Lola is going to be royally pissed off when she learns someone helped her get to the hospital.

Azazael is looking glacially at nurse. He knows she's a satanist. The woman is wondering will he vanquish her? She contemplates as she quickly but nervously cleans up and hands Ana the squirming baby who is looking up at her with knowing eyes. She believes she sensed Azazael in this child. Now she understands why Shreveport wants the mother and child. This child is a spawn of something worse than demons.

"Ladies, glad I could be of service." He said, leaving the room the moment the delivery room attending nurse left. He knows why she's here. The nurse sprinted as stealthily as she could without drawing unnecessary attention, looking over her shoulder as she fled down the halls of the maternity ward. She ran into Etna, who expected her to hand the baby over so she could stuff the infant in a pet carrier and walk out unnoticed. Before either can scream Azazael vanquished them both into smoke, leaving no ashes behind.

Azazael is completely unaware that the heavenly realm sent him on a mission of the utmost importance, to dispatch of Ana's enemies quickly and efficiently. With his assignment completed the heavens erased his' and everyone else's memory of him being

30

there. No one in the hospital has any memory of him being there, not even Ana.

But he knowing something supernatural happened, he willfully muddled through the erasure and returned late in the night. Her pestiferous family is gone. He picked her up and cradled her in his arms and she finally fell asleep.

⌘

As their collective memory slowly returns the family discusses the stranger everyone in the hospital appeared to be afraid of before visiting Ana the next morning. They all knew he was there but can't remember what he looked like. Their mental image of his appearance is foggy. Their picturesque memory of him is being clouded. Their single thought is he's the reason Thad and Ana are having problems. Fannie makes a mental note to talk to Ana about this; boldly and blatantly bringing her boyfriend into the delivery room. Supposed Thad had shown up?

But when they arrived the next morning he was gone and a huge bouquet of yellow roses with a red trimming of silk bows is on the stand beside her bed. So Fannie stuffed the subject on the back-burner when she saw how hurt Ana was that Thad still hadn't shown up.

"What are you going to name her?" Fannie asked, looking at her latest grandchild. Ana had been thinking on her and Thad's great-grandmothers names but since Thad isn't here he doesn't get to name her.

"What about if I name her after your mom and dad's, her name was Beatrice Anna and dad's mom name was Analisa. Who you named me after." Ana said looking down at her first born smiling. The baby softly shrilled.

"No, I named you for my Mother, since my brother named one of his daughters her first name. I gave you her middle name. Jacob ain't felt a drop of pain so why should he get to name anything." Fannie corrects.

"Ok, I'm naming her Breanna Antoinette Wyett." Ana said looking up at her mom.

"That's a mouthful, hope she be able to spell it later." Fannie said shortening the name to her mother's nickname. Bea.

"She got your head of thick hair and beautiful but strange eyes." Frances said looking at the swaddled baby as Bea babbles and started making some kind of chirping sound. Her cries were more like shrills than a baby crying. Frances could see someone else in Ana's baby. Someone she didn't know. Then again, she didn't know Thad's people that well but none of them she saw looked like this child about the eyes. It was dark brown, amber and a blue jewelry stone mixed together making a beautiful combination.

Helena and Junior had been trying to reach Thad all night but he was nowhere to be found. "We got a little niece named Bea, after grandma." Helena had happily informed her brothers after leaving the delivery room. "She looks like me and mom."

No one, not even Ana, sees the angel who erased all their memories of Azazael having been there the night before.

⌒✱✱⌒

Fannie can't believe what she is seeing. No one else seems to see her but her mother Beatrice Prescott is standing near Ana and the baby. Her mother died before Ana was old enough to know her. She doesn't want to startle Ana for she has been through enough already.

"Frances, will you go see about Junior. Tell him Ana is fine. You know what a worrywart he is." Her daughter-in-law takes it as a hint Fannie wants to be alone with her daughter and new grandbaby. She isn't thrilled on watching the breastfeeding anyway. So she is kinda glad to leave. She isn't feeling alined, feels like she has lost time or something.

After Frances leaves Fannie asked Ana to look to her left and tell her who does she see?

"Nobody, ma. I don't see nobody."

"Fannie, darling, hand momma the baby." Beatrice says kindly.

"No, Momma." Fannie replied, shaking her head. Beatrice smiled at her daughter.

"Sugar, it's really me." Fannie doesn't think so, not if it's hiding from Ana who has the gift of sight.

"Momma, what do you want with the baby?" Fannie asked suspiciously. Denoting something evil showed up when Ana was born. Ana looks around asking who was her mom talking to? She still sees no one.

"Nothing sinister." Fannie knew her mother didn't say words like 'sinister.'

"I rebuke you in the Name of Jesus!" Fannie said compelling the Power of Christ. The apparition laughed that lovely, soulful laughter both Fannie and Ana inherited from Beatrice, even Helena had it whenever she really laughed and wasn't snarling at people.

"Get the hell away from my babies!" The real Beatrice Prescott cried coming through swinging her fists, grabbing her evil clone by the hair and pulling it back through the spiritual realms. They'd hear licks being laid but saw no one.

"Don't you ever try to trick my baby again! Do you hear me?" They heard Beatrice yell. Fannie sounded a lot like her mom when angry. Suddenly all was quiet and then a tender light brown face poked through the ethereal realms into the physical one and kissed Fannie on the cheek.

"Fantasia, Sugar, stay strong. Hell itself is after your babies." Beatrice warned. "They need you, stop worrying about me. I'm fine, I'm with the Lord, sugar." She looked at Ana and said, "You don't remember me but your baby is quiet like you was at that age. You didn't do much hollering. She's as beautiful as you and your mommy here was when y'all were babies. Fannie was so pretty she looked like a little cherubic angel, she was so sweet. Bea, here, looks a lot like Fannie. No matter comes your way, you can handle it.

33

You wouldn't be my daughter and granddaughter if you couldn't." Then she disappeared. Fannie quickly covered her mouth and wept quietly. Ana grabbed her mother's hand.

"Thank you, momma. She sounds like a heck of a lady. I wish I could've known her."

"She was one heck of a lady and could fight like a man." Fannie said laughing through the tears. "Hope Bea inherit that part of her, too."

⁓⁓⁓

Azazael wakes up knowing he has been somewhere but where? He can't remember and wonders what he did while there? "I've really got to stop making liquor and drinking it!" He chuckles to himself. "I probably killed someone for pissing me off."

His ancient mind muddled through billions, trillions of years and not giving a shit if he remembered what happened or not. But this time he cares. But whatever happened he can't remember. He feels it's important to him. Why? He doesn't know.

"Oh fuck it!" He says, giving up trying to remember and getting up pouring himself another drink, deciding it's billions upon trillions of years too late to start worrying about sobriety. He knows only up above can swipe the memory like that. He suspected they did.

"Ok, you guys upstairs if you don't want me to do something just come out and tell me. Just tell me! " Just say; Azazael stop it!" I'm not good at this hints and clues method of communication, Dad. You and I've always had a severe communication problem." No reply. He wasn't really expecting one.

His mind pans over to the mystery lady, he excogitate has she had her baby yet? He doesn't know how he knows she had a baby? It's been at least almost a year. He hopes she and her hubby are happy together for the baby's sake.

"Who am I kidding? Yea, I hope the guy is nice to her but frankly I can't stand him," he grunts, drains the liquid and winced not from the strength of the alien, unearthly

34

liquor in the crystal glass but from the fact he wants to be with the mystery woman and can not fully comprehend why? He decided months ago he wouldn't roam and search the spiritual realms for her because he didn't want to feel another man's child growing in her. He wondered was she the *one*? Whenever together, they always found each other irresistible. This whatever you call it; disresembled anything he can record feeling. Why can't he just screw her and move on? He doesn't like the influence she have on him. It feels too much like control. Her presence feels more like some sort of ignis fatuus, as though she really isn't there in his arms. Maybe she's an ideologue of his own creation? Whatever it is, he wished the hell it would stop.

When he looked at her that morning after they made sweet but wild passionate love before she started screaming like a banshee, she looked familiar to him. But he knows he never met her. Normally, he doesn't leave if a man catches him screwing his wife or woman. He usually gets up and beats mortal or immortal's ass and throw him out. But her screaming prompted him to leave. He cared enough to respect her wishes. But now he remembers, in the heat of their love making that night she called out his real name. He hadn't told her his name, so how did she know his name? He felt all the memories slipping away. He threw the crystal glass against the wall and turned and screamed at the angel standing behind him. "This fucked up shit has got to stop! Leave me the hell alone!"

As Ana nursed Breanna she looked into the child's eyes and she saw someone else besides Thad in her newborn baby. She pushed past the murkiness in her mind and her mind went back to the night of the midnight lover. Somewhere deep inside she knew whomever he was he wasn't Thad. Is it possible for a child to have two fathers? She never heard of such thing. Besides, she loved Thad. Right now, she didn't like him very much for not being where he was supposed to be. She knows he's long home from work. It's the next day. Bea is nearly a day old, so where is he? Why hadn't he came to see about them? Or did he come and she was asleep? She checks the cards on the flowers, they're from her family and friends. The big unsigned ones with the silk bow she suspect may be from her midnight lover. But there's nothing from Thad.

While pondering and feeding her newborn the phone on her night table rings. Thinking it's him and he has been in a horrible accident since she wished to believe that's the only thing keeping him from them, she quickly answers.

"May I speak with Mrs. Ana Wyett?" A sultry female voice asked.

"This is she." Ana says with abated breath, hoping this isn't an official personnel calling to tell her something truly horrible has happened to her husband. An intense pause followed her stating her identification.

"Ana, it's about time you learn the truth." The stranger said in a rather mean tone. "Thad and I are lovers. Been lovers for months. All those trips to New York City was to see me. We're in love. He has left you and Baby Bea for me."

Ana feels a deep burning pain in her chest as though she can't breathe. "Who are you and why are you saying such atrocious things?" Ana asked, after finally finding her voice.

She heard an impatience sigh on the other end. "You can't be that dense that you didn't know he's cheating on you! I know you knew. A wife always know. You're just one of those mousy women who will over look anything to hold on to him. Why do you think he started treating you like shit? He was hoping you'd have sense enough to take the hell on, instead you got yourself knocked up to hold on to him. He don't want your bony ass..." The unidentified woman said harshly.

"Who the hell are you? And let Thad come to the phone and tell me all this himself. If he loved you so damn much why haven't he asked me for a divorce to marry your funky ass? I ain't holding onto him! He just don't want you for but one thing."

"Oh, you'll be hearing a lot from me, my name is Lola Wilson. We plan to take the baby and raise it ourselves." Lola stoutly ensured.

"Like hell you will, you come anywhere near my baby I swear to God I'll kill you and Thad both if he tries any shit like this!" Ana promised. Lola knew Ana wasn't bluffing.

The steel in her voice told her Ana meant every word. Ana hung up the phone in Lola's ear. Baby Bea had started to cry. "Ssshh, my little darling baby. Nobody is taking you anywhere." She coos to the infant.

Resuming what they are doing, at nearly 5:00 A.M. her phone rings again and this time it's Thad. He doesn't give her a chance to inquire about anything. He tells her he's been in jail for the past twenty-four hours. He called his family and hers to tell her but both said she wasn't there but at the hospital. "Your girlfriend called and said you were with her. What are you doing in NYC?" She asked icily, thinking of all the things that woman knew about her when she knew nothing about the woman.

"What girlfriend?" He asked as if she were stupid or something.

"Lola Wilson! You damn son of a bitch!" Ana hissed at him. Bea started crying and shrilling again. "That's the baby?" He asked excitedly but noticed the child shrilled instead of cried. "Place the phone camera so I can see her."

"No, it's fucking elves in this damn room. The damn room is fill of the little fuckers! Of course it's the baby! Idiot!" Ana hesitated but placed the phone so he could see her. To him she looked like him, his mom, Mrs. BuFaye and Dreadful Helena.

"She sounds kinda funny..." He said but knew he had said the wrong thing when Ana started cussing him out. "Ana, I meant is she alright? Is she sick or anything. I've never heard a child sound like that."

"Fuck you!" Ana said barely above a whisper, clicking off the phone and continued rocking Bea.

A nurse entered and asked what she wanted for breakfast. Ana doesn't feel much like eating but knows she need to since seems as thus it's going to be just the two of them. She'll need all the strength she can get. The woman Lola was right, she did suspect Thad was cheating on her. But never had any evidence. She felt like crying but no tears came. She looked down at her sleeping baby and decided, "Looks like it's just you and me, kid, against the world."

Ashton Cargill felt her again. It felt like being hit in the chest with a steel headed sledge hammer. He panicked, wondering had she been shot her? Was she in danger? Was she dying? He panicky rushed through the realms to be near her before he could stop himself or consider the consequences. Damn the consequences! She's crying about something. He steps from through wall and asks. "Beautiful lady, why are you crying?"

She yanks her head up and around; he sees that she remembers him but she says nothing but continues to stare at him.

"Why are you crying on such a beautiful occasion? With such a beautiful baby?" He asked softly. She hugs the baby close and asked him how did he get in? Are you some kind of magician or magi?

"No, I'm not." He replies. "I walked through the wall." He saw her eyes widen.

"No, I'm not a ghost," he chuckled softly. She covered the baby nursing at her breast with a fresh diaper.

"I remember you the night I, ahem, uh, got pregnant. I'm sorry if I gave you the wrong impression that night. What happened that, er night...that isn't usually my thing. I don't know why I did it. She isn't yours if that's why you're here."

"Oh I know she isn't..." He paused a few seconds to collect his thought. He had reasons to believe otherwise but kept the information to himself. His security team has reported to him the husband is in the pen north of NYC.

"I've been wondering about you since that night. I knew the child was already conceived. But I'm not sorry about that night. It was beautiful as you are. How much do you remember from that night?" He asked moving closer to the bed.

She had started to feel a little effervescent and nervous around him. Was he flirting

38

with her? She was ashamed of her behavior with him. How can she be mad at Thad for cheating when she cheated on him with this man, demon, or whatever this supernatural being is.

"Thanks for the concern but I'm married," she said nervously. She really didn't like him being so close. She wished he'd back up. His closeness was making her very uncomfortable.

"Oh, I know that too, but where is he?" Ashton asked inquiring for the third time what was wrong, why was she crying?

"Oh nothing...just hormones fluctuating." She said, thanking him for asking. She nearly forgot to ask him his name. "What's your name?"

"I think you already know my name." He said, taking a seat on the bed near her legs which she drew up to keep from touching him. His touch was like something she had never felt before that night.

"Just call me Ashton." He said. She had not noticed the flowers in his hand until he put them with the others. "My husband may be in here soon. I don't think you should be here." She said in a weak, unconvincing voice.

The man pulled a rose from the bouquet and handed to her. "Why isn't he here now? No males have been in here." With those words the unwanted tears started falling again. He knew then why she was really crying. She was too hurt to ask this stranger how did he know all that?

"I'm sure whatever the reason he isn't here, it's beyond his control" Ashton said softly, trying to comfort her.

"No, it isn't. He's with another woman." She blurted out. It was so comforting to lean against him. She got a little worried when she looked closer into his eyes and saw her infant daughter had some of the same features. She found this disturbing but leaning on him for comfort was making her sleepy; apparently it had putting Bea to sleep too. She had quit suckling and was now asleep under the fresh diaper over her tiny face. He took sleeping Bea and laid her in the basset the hospital provided and gathered her in his arms as she cried until she fell asleep.

He awakened her when the nurse brought her breakfast, she knew she shouldn't be letting this stranger feed her like a baby but she felt so hurt and betrayed at the moment she didn't care if Thad walked in right now. When she woke up around noon, her mother was asking how was she feeling? She looked around for the stranger but he was gone.

"Who brought these?" Frances asked referring to the second big floral arrangement, a big bouquet of lilacs. Ana pretended she had no idea where they came from. They weren't there earlier. But she knew. She just had no intention of telling.

"I bet Thad sent them!", Frances cheerfully chirped. Trying to cheer Ana up. But Ana said nothing. Oh, she remembered who brought them and she knew it wasn't Thad.

Maybe she dreamed that guy showed up or maybe she is losing her mind? Mentally, creating a comforting stranger to cope with her pain.

"Your in-laws said they were here this morning but you and baby were asleep." Fannie said. Ana knew they were lying for she hadn't seen the Wyetts but didn't tell her mom. She wondered was Thad really in jail? Her brother Junior came and sat on the chair next to the side of the bed, "Thad could be here in a little bit, I think he has something really important to tell you," Junior said looking at his wife instead of his sister. But she didn't tell them she already knew because she didn't want anyone asking her question about what she plan to do about all this mess.

Analytically, she knew she owed Thad nothing. Had he not left her alone that night perhaps things would be different. They had just concluded a romantic evening, something they hadn't done in a long while. She thought the beautiful love making that evening was them returning to the love they once shared. She was hurt when he didn't want to cuddle but wanted go back out again. But this time alone. She was hurt their romantic evening meant nothing to him, it was only a ploy to get her off his back complaining he didn't spend time with her. He was cheating on her long before then.

40

Where else was he for entire weekends?

She wondered was she so starved for attention that she made love to a stranger who simply crawled in her bed? In her defense, she said didn't know it was the stranger at first until she felt the different body structure on top of her but by then she was so heighten by what he was doing, she dangerously didn't care. What in the hell was wrong with her? Why did she find this stranger profoundly soothing. She had heard of wives having affairs simply because they're lonely. Why does she always have to feel guilty all the time about shit when she is merely reacting to an injustice done to her.

The tall dark chocolate, spry, feminine like man who is proudly a self-proclaimed lady's man, named Rhode Adam Wyett. The younger brother of all-star football legend Thad Wyett decided on his late, predawn return home after a night of partying he'd swing by the hospital and say hello to his sister-in-law and new niece. Well, he had others but Thad the stud didn't acknowledge them so what could he say? This was the first one he acknowledged to the family. So, as far as mom knew this baby was her first grandchild. He heard the BuFayes are all bent outta shape because Thad wasn't there for the actual birth. What in the fuck could Thad do had he been there? Catch the baby? Her momma and sister was there so what more did Ana want? He and Dad told Thad a many of times your wife is spoiled. She been reading too many of them unrealistic romantic novels, no real man says the shit in those weepy, idiotic books and movies. But Thad wouldn't listen. Now he's paying for it, every time he don't rise up to that amore shit there's a crying fit outta her. She's hot and all but he couldn't deal with a woman so freaking Victorian. He teases his older brother saying he bet he has to be more romantic than fucking Lord Bryon before he gets any loving.

He goes to the nursery; they tell him baby Breanna is with her mother so he heads down the hall with intentions to try and smooth things over for his big brother. Try to soften the path to Ana's good grace so Thad won't catch oh so much hell when he gets here later today. But what he finds in the room with them floored him in his tracks, would've knocked his socks off had he been wearing any. Sure she's sleeping but another dude who looks like goddamn Hercules is propped up against the headboard with her

41

asleep in his arms. This ain't no freaking cousin. The man's hair remind him of a Rembrandt or somebody's painting called 'The Dutch Masters.' Except those old guys in the painting are bald in comparison to this big-ass fucker.

"Who the hell are you?" Rhodes asked angrily.

"Somebody who is doing your brother's job that he's too busy chasing after whores to do." The man said in his freaking mind without moving his lips. That freaked him out big time.

"How do you know Thad is my brother?" Rhodes asked mistrustfully. Replying again through his mind, the man said. "Your pictures are all over the place associated with your brother."

He knows the man is referring to Thad's house and ruminates when this man was there? "Stop that weird shit! Quit messing with my head!" Rhodes cried. The stranger smiled but it wasn't a good natured smile, it was more a like a predator smiling, about to pounce on their prey.

"You do know she's married, right? Sorry to burst your bubble but she ain't leaving Thad no matter how sweet your game is." Rhodes said picking up Bea, but when she opened her eyes and coos at him he saw why this fucker is here. He could see his mother in her, actually a lot. But somehow she had this man's hateful eyes. Then again, Thad had hateful eyes. So he couldn't use that alone as validation Ana cheated on his brother. He knew better than most that Thad was hateful, as many times as Thad had beat the shit out of him. But he believed the blue mixture of brown in this baby's eyes come from this man with the strange luminous eyes. That he was almost positive of. Or perhaps his brother and sister-in-law engineered this baby or what? That's all the rave nowadays. But he doubt Thad would've agreed to a designer baby. Knowing his brother, this kid was made the old-fashion way with all the fun, grunting and sweating.

"I'm aware she's married but does your brother knows he's married to her. His actions speak otherwise. She had a hard and difficult labor and is very tired. Your brother is supposed to be here to see her through it. There's no game he's attending so where is he?

42

I'm here to comfort her in her weakest hour." The hulking man said telepathically. Whomever this man is there's something very evil about him. It was like he had an otherworldly aura about him. He gave him the creeps. Rhodes snapped pictures of Bea and left the room but not before he secretly snapped pictures of Ana and her lover. Outside the hospital he debated should he tell his brother or not. Thad had stupidly got involved with that evil woman. Dad told him the first time he saw her, she was evil. To leave her alone. He complained about Ana couldn't satisfy him. She was totally bedroom illiterate.

"She was a virgin when you married her. So what did you expect? I know Fannie and her people from back in the day; all 'em people talked and think about is Jesus! I used to date Fannie's sister Gayle before I married your momma, not that your mom's people was any better about this Jesus shit. But Fannie kept that girl so close up under her until I doubt the poor child knew how to piss straight without her mommy when you married her. It's your job to stay home and teach her! I told you don't marry her but you wouldn't listen. The only advantage in marrying a virgin is she've no one else to compare you to so she'll always compare all men to you. That girl really loves you with all her little heart, I can tell it from the way she looks at you, she even find your stupid shit adorable, but if you break it, it can never be mended. That worn out heifer ain't worth losing Ana's love over. Women like her are common. Those like your momma and Ana ain't!" Thaddeus Senior had shouted at his oldest about Lola.

He remembers as a pre-teen boy he was half in love with her. Ana was always nice to him whenever Thad got after him, she made Thad leave him alone. Being exceptionally bright and finishing high school at age sixteen Ana got accepted to major schools like; UCLA, Harvard, Princeton, Berkeley, NCU, Purdue, Yale, UGA, and many others but she selected Cambridge to be close to Thad for he was in his rookie year with the Boston Minutemen. They were his epitome of what a couple could be. So no, he'd only show Thad pictures of Breanna. Thad had probably driven her into that man's arms. Thad damn near drove him crazy so he was certain Thad had driven Ana into this man's arms.

Thinking back on their wedding day; he was Thad's best man and Helena the hell bitch was Ana's maid of honor. Originally Tony was the best man but mom fussed until she got him that slot. Tony stood beside him. Neither could take their eyes off of

Helena's perfect chest, the woman may had been an engender of hell but she had a ten body. She was a brickhouse, she was a perfect hourglass. When Mendelssohn's wedding march started playing, Junior BuFaye appeared in the church's aisle with the sweet, little girlish looking Ana but nonetheless Thad was beaming like a lighthouse. So no, Thad would never see this picture, Rhodes decided, locking it away in his personal photo file.

Movie producer, investor, James Caldwell sits in his antebellum Arlington, Virginia mansion reminiscing over the kiss he gave Ana BuFaye in the back of his limo nearly four years ago. She didn't know who he was. She thought he was just a friendly neighbor. As far as he knows she still thinks he was merely a helpful neighbor who moved next door after Thad's arrest. He suggested to Vonderbilt it would much easier to simply kill Thaddeus Wyett than be harassed with him in the future. But Vonderbilt is convinced they may need him to learn Ana's whereabouts. She may reveal to him her location. But Caldwell doubts she will. She was acting. Anyone who saw the couple up close could tell she was peeved off at Thad, so baby's father or not she isn't going to tell him nil.

Relaxing in the ancient big chair sipping brandy he wonders what to do about the loose bull named Bjors. Bjors may be the Grand Wizard's nephew but he's still a fuck-up. He does things too boldly. Takes undue and unnecessary risks.

He had had the family next door to Ana and Thad Wyett evicted. In a few months he would be moving next door to her. He knew Thad wouldn't be home long, so he would patiently wait until the hearing.

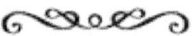

Back to the present

Reeling myself back to the present, the intense heat fain greeted me fully in the face. Southern nights are hotter than hell. I'd forgotten that. By the time it's cool enough to sleep; it's time to get up. The heat wasn't the only thing keeping me awake. I meditated in what form would my unknown harassers appear? I lay awake, worrying what would I do if they cause me to lose the apartment again? Bea hasn't had a permanent home since she was 14 months old and now she is 4. I can't ask for assistance with Bea, too many states had out bench warrants for my arrest.

From the window I could see the top of the so-called cursed pillar from my second floor apartment window and wondered the same about my life. Is it cursed? It certainly seems that way. My mother told me on numerous occasions something or someone has been stalking me all my life. According to mom, even as a newborn infant, strange people came to the small rural hospital to pay me a peculiar visit. They left before father could reach them. Mother also stressed there have been series of unexplainable mishaps all my life. Many I do not remember. I was too young to remember. Mom believes these latter day series of threats are a continuation of those from my early life, not that I've a clue as to who these people are nor why they selected me for their victim.

Yesterday, I took the incentive to visit a church a friend from work had recommended. I left feeling like a mega fool after talking to the pastor. I needed someone to talk to so I told him about all the horrors we had experienced in the last four years. I was even credulous enough to tell him about the stranger in my bedroom. I was hoping being a man of God he might have some answers. His repulsive, disapproving frown told me otherwise. I should've just gone straight home from work instead of driving through the boiling hot humidity and sun-glaring heatstroke inducing traffic to Sandbar Ferry Road. Maybella had told me the pastor was a very compassionate, understanding, and spiritually enlightened man. Evidently, he wasn't. He told me the devil was the source of my problems. Duh! As if I hadn't already figured that much out.

He lectured me about sins of the flesh, saying she inherited a demon through her ancestors as to why she had been plagued all her life. By the time I left I was feeling worse than when I arrived. Finally, he shortly before leaving, he said if I prayed hard enough and trusted in the Lord with all my heart all my problems would vanish. Oh believe me, I trust in God with all my heart! With a 359 magnum point blank in your face it would be foolhardy not to pray and trust in God. God is how we're even still alive. And I'm wise enough to know that. I patiently tried to explain these things have been happening to me all my life. He then said it was a generational curse. Some ancestor or my parents offered me to the devil and now the devil came to collect. That the man I saw in my bedroom was the devil came to collect. I told him no one in my family has even had any real wealth or fortune. Their talents were natural.

I don't know why I was dewy-eyed enough to talk about the night of the stranger visiting me. I told him I was hurt because Thad had a 'midnight rambling' habit. But the man showed not an iota of sympathy nor compassion to me, he was all on Thad's side saying I needed to have told my husband the truth, my lies drove him away. If I'm not mistaken, he was blaming me for Thad's affair! How obscure!? Just because a person has a dick doesn't make them always right. I was shocked when the man crossed himself when I rose to leave as if I were the evil source. The church secretary gave me a hateful glare when I passed her desk. Why? Maybe these people were nice to Maybella, this is her hometown but they definitely aren't compassionate or nice to strangers. I still don't know why his secretary glowered at me when I passed her desk.

⁂

While relaxing in the cool leather interior of Charles' hover BMW, I let my mind replay another series of events. Trying to put the dots together, trying to make sense of them. Trying to figure out how were they all connected to today's harassers?

The second ordeal occurred a few years later after the falling chimney. I don't remember my exact age but while swimming in the pond on the farm something tried to drown me. It was a clear, hot summer day so it was easy to see the bottom of the pond. My brother Jack and I were frolicking and splashing, enjoying the coolness of the clear water as only children could enjoy it. While absently floating on an inflatable raft looking through the clear screen at the fish swimming by something hits the raft with a blunt force and flips it over and I sank to the bottom. As I pushed myself up from the bottom of the pond a lichen covered hand reached out of the mud and grabbed my leg. My heart nearly stopped as I started kicking frantically at it but was unable to make contact with it. It wasn't completely solid but yet solid enough to hold onto me. Just as I was about to go in an over-drive panic a gleaming sword, blindingly reflecting the sunlight sliced through the water and cut the grotesque snot-green hand away from my leg. By now I was swallowing water by the pints.

46

A man in a white robe grabbed me; he was a spiritual being, that much I knew. He threw me back to the surface so hard I torpedoed out the water like a dolphin and landed beside my dad who quickly grabbed me and waded to shore. Jack was still underwater looking for me. But he soon popped up looking bewildered, asking how did I jump that high out the water? I told him a man threw me to the surface.

I nod attentively to show I was listening to Charles' ongoing dialogue about my stalker and to show gratitude for the ride on such short notice I (while covertly peering, stealing glances at him and admiring his handsome features) said, "No. The police won't find him. He'll be gone by the time they arrive so they'll say there's nothing they can do."

Shaking his head in disbelief. Charles says almost to himself. "*Isn't that unbelievable, waiting until he do something is too late to call the police. But I guess you're right. No one is fool enough to stand and wait until the police shows up.*"

Reminiscing back in her memory to the many towns, villages, and cities she's moved to in the past three years in futile attempts to escape their always watching eyes. To escape their, in general fucking things up for her and her child after she and her husband Thad split up she thinks to herself, *"I'm not a conspiracy theorist but there's something totally out of the ordinary happening here. No matter which way you look at it. Crap don't just pop up out of nowhere for no good reason."*

She's always had a nagging suspicion many of the local police departments knew these strangers were following her. What further ingrained her suspicion was that when she had what Thad always called her "paranoia moments"; usually the next day or so after arriving in a new place the cops started pulling her over asking questions like "where are you from?" and/or "you've any folks here?" (if it was a small town or village). One local alcoholic, bubonic-nosed sheriff told her "If ya here hiding out foam de law, girl ya cum ta wrong place. I don't 'llow no criminals here." Why did he automatically assume she was a criminal hiding from capture? Sure, she'd killed. But it's always kill or be killed. It isn't a crime to protect yourself.

That's how she know it's a load of buoyed bullshit the media feeds the public about the wholesome image and values of small towns and villages in almost every state. Most she had lived in were hellholes, some just had a prettier hometown main street than others. But nonetheless they were hellholes. And don't get her started on Tornado Alley. The Midwest. It was like the freaking "Twilight Zone." Some days were so weird you literally expected to see Rod Sterling from the old 20th century show step from behind a bush or convenience store welcoming you to the selective viewing of an episode of weird ass bullshit coupled with the eerie ass music softly playing in the background. But you could always be sure if a tornado did not get you, a racist yahoo would. It makes you wondered did the Civil Rights, the Feminist, and Gay movement skip this section of the country!? Gosh! That's been well over 500 years ago. They need to give it a rest! The only civilized city seemingly in existence in the Midwest was Chicago.

Charles pulls up at the corner of Telfair and Walton Way, (Walton Way, named for one of the Georgia signer of the Declaration of Independence who died under mysterious circumstances). She thanks him for the courtesy ride and turned and sprinted toward the bank's door where she works as a teller. Knowing her battle-ax of a boss is watching to see will she willfully go to her desk first, deliberately disobeying her order to see her the moment she entered the building.

This is the second time the woman wanted to see me first thing in the morning. I brace my emotions to face my sullen boss wondering where does this woman get the energy to be so mean and spite-filled with bitchiness so early in the day? I tried that and it's exhausting as hell. Wears you out before 9:00 A.M.. Is she a forgotten, long lost Tesla project designed to snatch meanness out the thin air instead of electricity?

"Good morning" I said respectfully to Mrs. Sandra Stevenson whom the employees refer (aka Mrs. Satan.) "I received a message you wanted to see me first thing this morning."

Aligning and shuttling papers on her desk and finally looking up at Ana from her highly polished cherry wood desk with matching chairs through stoic beady eyes inserted in a pale putty, dour face. The bank's junior manager eyes raked the auburn haired beauty over with disgust. All the while the air crackled with bitchiness around her too short neck and oversized bosom.

Ana thinks to herself. *"You-mean-hateful-need-to-pray-woman. I hope one day those up-to-your-neck-fat-tits reach up and strangle you. And choke the pure living shit outta you".*

Gesturing toward the empty seat in front of her desk Mrs Satan says. "Have a seat, Ms.Owego. I need to talk to you about the company's downsizing policy."

"Oh no, here comes another bucket load of crap! Can this day get any worse?" I silently dread.

"As you may know there has been an economic downturn, sluggish business affecting all businesses including banks. Please know *"We"* think your performance with us has been splendid and regret to inform you that unfortunately we'll have to lay off some employees and your name was decided be placed in the layoff group. Today will be your last day with us and your last paycheck will be mailed to you."

Ana is curious how this conclusion was drawn? Did they place her name in a hat with the others and let a drunk monkey do the drawing of names? Standing up fully, displaying her elegant figure and lovely African-American profile, and gesturing as if she is the Great Queen of the Nile, Nefertiti, Ana says "I'm sorry to learn of my soon to be unemployment but I fully expect to receive my full pay and all monies due me today, not two week from now. But today when I complete my shift at 6:00 P.M. Today! I expect to receive my pay and no later. Now if you'll excuse I've a job to perform." This is the second time this morning she's had to tell someone off. This is getting old real fast. But why bite her tongue? She's already fired so she can be as rude as she wanna be.

Mrs. Satan cheeks visibly reddened at Ana's audacity and brazen, impertinent attitude. She was pissed she didn't get the graveling-for-her-job response she was so gleefully hoping and waiting for and said "I understand your distress at the news but I'm sorry, Alana, that's not possible. You're free to drop by and pick your checks up two weeks from today!" The manager said whom the tellers dubbed, "Mrs. Satan" because of her petty, evil tactics. She was smiling as thus she held the secret to world's destruction. Evil as she is, she probably did.

But Ana felt it was her stink ass attitude causing her to smirk. Ana leans savvily over the desk and resorted back to her Southern root with a low, sexy drawl, in a laid-back down mellow monotone that was reserved only for people she can't stand and says in a whisper that only she and she-devil can hear. "Today has not been a very good day to piss me off. I'll be darned if I only had one nerve left and you've just pissed all over it. I knew when you called so early you were up to some shit. But if you don't have my check card ready by 6:00 P.M. you'll learn the true meaning of the word " destruction" because I'm going to go full-blown nuclear on your fat, dumpy ass."

"What do you have against hefty people?" Sandra asked with her plump hands resting on the desk, interlaced in front of her. "Nothing, nothing at all. I don't like you anymore than you like me. You disliked me the first day you met me. It wasn't you who hired me. It was your boss. You detested me so much that the dislike turned into pain. So why do you hate me so much? I haven't done a thing in this world to you." Ana said, getting up and turning before opening the door. "You hear what I say. I want my money today or I'll make you very sorry you ever fucked with me." Ana sashayed out the door hoping this woman didn't make her kill her before the end of the day. Sandra stared in disbelief at the closing door. She's totally shocked that meek and mild mannered Alana Owego just threatened her in such a bold, malicious, menacing manner. So, it's true---Ana BuFaye really is a murderess.

While still fuming from her wholly unpleasant encounter with Alana the phone on Sandra Stevenson's executive desk rings. Without checking the called ID on her private line she stares at the device a few seconds, waits to answer. She already knows who is calling; she licks her suddenly dry lips and breaks out in a cold sweat. With trembling hands and lips quivering she answers the phone in a barely audible whisper "hello..?" Evil seeps through the phone along with Bjors' voice. He greets her in an enticing tone.

"Good day Sandra, I pray for your sake you've done what I told you and don't forget to get Ana's forwarding address. Or did you forget that Alana Owego and Ana Bufaye/Wyett are one and the same? Regardless of what she calls herself, she'll be

50

moving shortly. Once she gets on the road it's hard to find her. Now, you wouldn't want me to lose her again? Now would you?"

Sandra whispers back although no one is in the office to hear her "Sir, I know Alana Owego is really Ana Wyett but she won't give me a forwarding address under any name."

"Stupid bitch! You'd better get it or else! We can't lose her whereabouts again! Do you know hard it is to find her when she's out roaming all over creation with those goddam meddling angels shielding her spiritual imprint from even our best clairvoyant and hougan? Do you enjoy living where you live and working where you work?"

"Yes, sir I do." Sandra sobbed. She knew the penalty for failure.

"If you do! Then get the damn address!!" Bjors Machiavelli snapped.

Upset at Bjors' tone and the impending possibility of death, Sandra Stevenson starts to wonder if the Coven's confederate aid was worth the hassle and headaches but calmly says "Mr. Bjors, when Ana leaves today I want no further contact with her, you, nor any more assistance from the Group." Little did she realized she just signed her death certificate. One on Bjors' level in the witchery hierarchy, a mere lowly member doesn't dare speak to him in such ire. The Grand Wizard's servant drops you, you don't drop him.

"You useless piece of shit! You do not tell me what you want!!!" Bjors screams, spittle was flying into the phone "I tell you what to do and I'm telling you to get the damn address and hold off giving her a cent of pay until we decide what to do next! Do you want to be the next one pulled out the Savannah River with eyes eaten out by golems?

"No" Sandra whispered, frightened. Actually, she's holding herself together fairly well for dealing with Bjors Machiavelli. She's terrified of this evil man.

Bjors hadn't turned on the camera on his phone so Sandra couldn't see him smiling his infamous evil grin which is the last thing so many have seen before their death."I didn't think so. You bitches makes me sick. When I called you with the nasty, juicy gossip you're all for bringing another woman down but when it comes time to put your words to actions you always whimper. You aren't dealing with the Christ here! Who is pansy and weak! I'm not running a fucking democracy. You're dealing with an agent of the Lord of Darkness and his commands are to be your only concern. Do I make myself clear?!"

"Yes sir, I understand and I apologize for my remarks. Please forgive me" Resorting back his earlier alluring tone Bjors says" Sandra..darling, you see...," Insincerely sighing and slowly shaking his head."You made me yell at you. It makes me unhappy to make you unhappy. You knew the demands of the membership when you accepted. By the way, sweetie, don't forget your dues, they're a few days late. Meet me at the Twain Hotel on the river front and I promise you daddy will kiss the boo-boo. But darling, there's no forgiveness in hell."

Nodding as if Bjors can see her, she hangs up the phone and start pondering how to complete her assignment. Or could she make a break for it? Run like the Valkyries are after her? No, she's seen what they do to defectors. Trembling, Sandra wonders "*What on earth have I gotten myself into? My boring, bible-thumping parents told me to stay away from people like Bjors. It was new, fun, and exciting during my college days when we'd do our little inept rituals and a few imps showed up to scare the senses out whomever our depressed Goth brood didn't like but now...whew, this is something different. This is the real deal. This shit is getting downright diabolic and scary! The Mafia aren't nothing on these clowns in the scary-as-hell category.*"

Near the electronic file cabinet hovering above her head a gleefully entity is watching. Unbeknownst to her, an evil ethereal being floats in the ceiling. A spirit, a demon of swirling, whimsy grey smoke pitted with red eyes, watches and waits to see if Sandra will try to escape or do the bidding she was commanded to do. The demon grins and rubs it semi-transparent hobbled hands together. It knows what's in store for the woman and it intend to have a front row seat to the show.

With closing time approaching the bank's branch president asks to speak with Ana, telling her to come in and have a seat. She sits elegantly in the available seat nearest the door. The office is modern with a sleek glass desk with numerous certificates and awards lining the wall. She once had an office like this one.

Mr. Bleeker says with false sympathy. "Alana, I'm sorry your name was submitted for dismissal, you're one of the best tellers we have. To show our appreciation for your nine months of service I'm giving your current week, final, and a small bonus totaling $2,500.00 and the letter needed to collect unemployment benefits. Your health insurance will remain intact for 6 months"

Ana still wasn't in a comfortable mood, she had an eviction hanging over her head like a hangman's noose, shot car, so no she wasn't in a mood to return his smile. Feeling angry and ornery she asked. "Where's the drunk monkey who pulled my name from the hat and influenced your scatterbrained decision?", not caring if she sounded pissed off because she was pissed off. This was one of those days she couldn't control her mouth. Shit kept flying out; left, right, sideways and upside down. A few more choice words was still pinging off the ceiling.

"Pardon me. I'm not sure I understand." Bleeker said looking at her as if she suddenly grew horns. She hated it when people played stupid. He felt that was a good severance package. He wasn't thrilled with Alana Owego's crude, mean-spirited attitude. Sandra Stevenson said she berated her this morning. But he dismissed Sandra's drama for that didn't sound like Alana.

In a louder decibel Ana nearly yelled. "I said WHERE's the drunk monkey who helped you came up with this bucket load of malarkey of an excuse for firing me?" Ana hated it when people have fucked over her and then try to justify it or patronize her.

The door opens and Sandra enters with a pleasant smile. Mrs. Stevenson protests, "Sir, I've already informed her these items would be mailed to her. I tried to explain to her, her short tenure with us is why she was chosen for downsizing. Alana is upset and taking the termination as a personal reflection on her performance while nothing could be further from the truth. I've also already explained to her that we need a forwarding address if she plans to move any time in the near future. I suspect when she calms down and sees the logic in my request, she'll abide." Sandra professionally and very politely

53

explains while looking down at an ill-natured Ana. Ana knew her boss could be pleasant when the agenda suited her. And this was one of those times.

With her arms folded tight across her upper stomach. Ana thinks. *"Like hell I will! Am I supposed to be some brand new kinda fool? That I can't see you're working with the man who shot my car."*

Mr. Bleeker turns to his manager slightly displease. "What's the point in mailing them when she's right here?"

Pretending she agrees with her boss Sandra goes to the file cabinet behind the bank's manger's desk and retrieved that which could've been prepared in the last eight hours. While standing behind her boss, pretending to search for the papers needed to complete the layoff, Sandra's eyes flashes hellfire at Ana. If looks could kill Ana would've dropped dead on the spot. Sandra is outraged this little skinny bitch doesn't care about anyone but herself. *"What about her? What's going to happen to her when she meet Bjors this afternoon? Those of that man's caliber don't visit unless there's something big going down. They can promote you or kill you and she suspect the latter tonight will happen tonight. But Ana doesn't give a fuck!"*

Sandra hands over the severance package, both shake Ana's hand, smile while neither meant it, and wish her well in next job. Ana quickly left the office. She had been promising herself all day she wouldn't cry and she hasn't but her eyes burned. Upon exiting the branch president's office several tellers gathered around wishing her well wishes and Godspeed. Unable to fathom why she's being fired while others whose erroneous work have caused the bank monetary losses and headaches are allowed to remain employed. All but Maybella offer their sympathy. But she shakes it all off and keeps on walking out the door with her head held up. This bank was no more of her concern. She has been through this countless times in the last four years.

Stepping outside into the smothering 100 degree heat Ana wonders for a few minutes how will she get home? Then is when a few tears started to fall, she angrily brushed them away with her thumb. Oh well, she has been fired many times before. This is no different. At least she got to give Bea a stable home for nine months. That counts for a

54

lot. She looks up and down the busy highway and up at the overhead traffic and pulled out her phone to call a cab but then she spots Charles bright red BMW glimmering in the hot sun. He pressed the button rolling down the curbside window. "Need a ride home?" He asked. She had forgotten since this morning how handsome he was. That's how bad her day had been.

"Sure and thanks for stopping back by."

"No problem." He smiled. "I remembered your car was disabled by a psycho."

Again sitting back, relaxing in the blast of cold air for the second time in one day, in a small voice she volunteered "I got canned today."

"WHAT?!?" Why?" Charles whips around to look at her small defeated posture in his passenger seat. "Some bull about the economy being sluggish." She exhaustively sighed.

"Oh! Pleasse! Spare me! You're one of the best they got. You want me to go in there and kick your boss's ass? You've a sick mom and small child to take care of! I don't know what's going on but it's like someone blacklisted you. In the normal flow of life all this crap doesn't happen in one day. Sure! misfortunes happen. But all in one day?! C'mon! There's some yellow-bellied coward behind all this. I can almost bet if were a gambling man. It's some rich old mook you told to get the hell out your face when he propositioned you."

Offering him a weak smile I said "No, Charles it would only cost you your career. But thanks for the offer. I don't know anyone with the kind of money and influence required to do all the things done today. "

Glancing at his lovely passenger, Charles says "You don't have to know them...you've no idea the evil which lurks in the hearts of men."

Ana sadly thinks to herself in reply to Charles last titbit of information. "*If only you knew, brother. If only you knew*" before asking him to stop by to an ATM to withdraw her earnings. She didn't trust the bank to be truthful. They might disengage the checkcard if she didn't get it out now.

After taking care of business they stopped by the local KFC, both ordered takeout dinners for the evening. The friends ride home in silence. He helps her to get her load indoors, she thanks him and again. He says it was no biggie, we all need help sometime in life. Once inside she was glad her mother hadn't turned the A.C. off. She drops her effects in the chair nearest the front door and places the KFC buffet on the simple pine table. The bright side of this day has been seeing Bea's smiling face when she walked in. She hugged and kissed her baby and sat her at the table. Fannie got up and got the plates. Bea loved drumsticks is why she requested four.

They ate in silence except for Bea telling her mom what she did today and how they played a card game. But Fannie knew something was gravely wrong the moment Ana walked in. For a child can never fully hide their agony from their mother. After Breanna was fed and safe in her mom's room watching TV Anna shoulders slumped, "Mom, I got fired today but the good news is I got a checkcard for 2,500.00, health benefits that are intact for 6 months, we can use the money to repair the car and move...and hopefully have enough left to pay a deposit upon another apartment but I think its time for us to leave this city. We done wore out our welcome here". Fannie reaches over and rubs her daughter's arm silently praying, *"Lord...I know You don't put more on one than they can bear but all this in one day is overwhelming my poor child and as a mother I am begging You to give her a sweet relief."*

In a whirlwind of activity the hours following Ana's showdown with landlord and bosses, they managed to get their belonging packed, the apartment cleaned of physical evidence of their having stayed there, and the car repaired. A friend of Charles miraculously agreed to work on the car all Friday night. Shelia Jean is revisited for a reimbursement of the security deposit but no one answers the door. Not that she actually expected to get the security deposit back but it was worth a try. They could use the money. Ana set sights on Atlanta, the state's capital city. During her lunch hour she had set up a meeting with an elderly lady whom she believes she'd seen before in a dream, to find her weary family temporary lodging. The name simply popped in her head and she doesn't question how she knows to call the woman. Now wasn't the time to search for logic.

While waiting for her car which Charles had hauled in she went and sat in the small park with her gun. She was hoping mottled-face show up again. The bench was still warm from the day's heat. It was sort of soothing, seeping through the fabric of her linen skirt. Her exceptional sense of Intuition felt something. It wasn't of this world, causing her to cautiously put her feelers out. She attuned her spiritual senses in the direction it was coming from. She sensed something humongous. Her extra senses felt the spiritual quake when it walked toward her. To her felt as thus the actual ground shook. She slowly eased off the well-lit stone bench and turned and headed for the house. Whatever was going through she didn't want to be here when it arrived. As she was running for the apartment she saw a huge lion-like creature blot out the overhead park lights. She ran faster. "My love, please don't run." A somewhat familiar voice pleaded. It sounded as if a lion may sound if it could speak. There was no ground traffic at such godless hour so she turned around in the one-way two lane road and looked. A large lion poked its face through the spiritual veil. The felidae-like being was towering over the trees blocking out the moonlight. Now, she really felt like screaming. In a nanosecond the being transformed into a humanoid.

I know the world outside will never ever resemble the one inside my head but I know, speaking for myself, that thing isn't human. I kept on running to my mother. She will know how to pray to keep it away.

Fannie looked up alarmed as Ana came running back inside. "I told you don't go out there. That boy is honest enough to bring your car back. All kinds of evil crap roams around at this heathen hour."

I could still hear the thing talking, begging me to come back outside. I looked out the living room window and saw a man. A very handsome man from what the darkness of the night revealed. Handsome or not, I wasn't going out there. It was the guy I was with a few nights ago in a spiritual world. I knew he wasn't human but he never seemed scary. I shook my head at him. His eyes kept pleading that I return to him. No, he scared the hell out of me. Why would I go back out there? What is he? A sphinx or something?

Ashton was terribly dismayed he'd frightened her. That wasn't his intention and knew he had to make her understand that. A legion of colossal demons attacked him enroute to her. He lost his temper and transformed into one of his original shapes. He spew limbs, body parts, and entrails far and wide. He was so anxious to get back to her he forgot to transform back to his humanoid shape and size. He can't come closer. Someone inside had put up a prayer barrier. The fright in her eyes broke his heart but since she's scared and isn't coming out someone has to pay for this. Disgusted with himself for allowing her see that form and with Lucifer for forcing him to reveal it he angrily steps back through the realm and transforms back and teleports to the bowels of hell, Lucifer's lair. He intends to beat him until his anger is spent. He teleports to the devil's palace, begun the long ascension up the wide curvy, scintillating walkway accented with hell moss and fungus, not bothering to step over the living stones slugging their way to serve their master, he kicks them over the ledge into the fiery pits below. He knows they'll be back on the path in a human's year or so. The billowing smoke and gushing fire nearly devours the entrance. The palace guards did not dare contest him, they step aside allowing their former master entrance.

He walks through the black, glassy hall littered with human souls and demons alike. The fire along the wall doesn't incinerate it, it simply burns forever. The stemless torches illuminate his way to the lair. He senses Lucifer's presence. He follows his instinct. Lilith sees him too late; she arises from her fun with her black cat-like pets pawing a living human who he knows they'll eat when they grow bored of playing with the man and attempt to distract his stride, to give her husband a chance to escape. But he shoves her out his way and steps through the walls of the richly decorated lair grabs Lucifer and start beating, plummeting his massive fists into his face until angels appear and pull him off, throwing him back into his carnal home. Back into the earthly realm.

In the pellucidity of daylight things always look different than in the cecity of night. She now felt silly for running. He was the only thing evil that wasn't trying to kill her. Somewhere hidden in her psyche...she is almost positive she knows him very well. She was getting tired of this mind fuck someone was committing against her. Tired of remembering some things in bits and pieces. While at other times, remembering nothing at all.

Giving the place a final look-over, bitter-sweetly recording the fun she and Breanna had in their barely furnished apartment. When closing the door of the apartment for the last time the Voice said to Ana as many time before when forced to leave her home; *"You've tested the spiritual nature of this place. I grant you power in Me if a place does not celebrate ME in you in MY NAME but have merely tolerated you. Withcall the blessing. I AM ALPHA and OMEGA."* She stopped, froze and looked around-she always thought it was merely her imagination when she blessed or cursed a place. She never took herself serious on the issue believing her bad mouth was enough to not to make her able to do such a thing.

⟶⟶⟶

The following morning after the car is packed and the trailer Charles insisted they take is securely hitched to Trusty. Ana leaves Augusta behind. Hopefully forever. She set out again for a new city, not knowing what it holds for them. She was lowly singing the ancient Robert Johnson's:

"I got to keep moving, I got to keep moving

Blues falling down like hail, blues falling down like hail

Mmm, blues falling down like hail, blues falling down like hail

And the day keeps on remindin' me, there's a hellhound on my trail.

Hellhound on my trail,

hellhound on my trail!!"

Whether the new city will be kind to them or a devil she didn't know but if the past was an indicator. It would be a devil. But she kept driving as the Richmond county local news station airs live coverage. Two seeming unrelated females and one male are found dead. A couple was found stabbed to death in their apartment off of Telfair St. The second victim was pulled from the Savannah River. Telfair was a fairly long street so she didn't conclude it had anything to do with anyone she knew. They didn't name the

59

victims but according to the family, which turned out to be Sandra Stevenson's, she never made it home from work Friday afternoon and was therefore reported missing around 1:00 A.M. Saturday morning.

The ancient warrior saint, Eugenia Harris

Eugenia Harris had received information from up above that the one she was sent from the past to teach will be arriving shortly. She'd waited over 60 years for this day. She didn't know what to expect. Eighty four year old Eugenia Harris was the last of her regiment who lived nearly 400 years ago. In the midst their final showdown at the Darktower her mentor threw her through the 8th day, body and soul. That's how she ended up here in the 25th century, unable to go back. She was lonesomely stuck here. She was only 23 at the time, she eventually married a modern man and raised a family. Her children used think she was crazy when she told them all after they reached adulthood she was from another time. Another century. The battle that caused her to be chucked into the future all happened before World War III, she hit the streets rolling in a strange time and century. But even in the future nothing had changed much, mankind was still an asshole and racism and sexism still existed. Much had changed technology wise but the basics of human nature were the same. But in many ways worse now than then.

In the heat of the battle, while their physical existences were fighting humans on earth who didn't understand nor care what was really happening on the other end of the spectrum of reality, their spiritual selves were literally fighting hell itself to keep the gates of the Darktower from being slung wide open. Back then, all nations had been convinced by the darkside that Nazarene warriors and warrior saints were the same as those crazed murderers butchering people allegedly in the name of God. Lucifer's followers used this misguided information to their advance. And waged a full-fledged war against her kind in every nation on earth.

The misfortunate causing her entrapment here was that several satanic groups had somehow managed to combine powers and open up the Darktower. Anyone with a lick of sense would be trying to keep it closed not open it. But no, not these psychos, they

60

wanted hell up and out, partying with them. A party that wouldn't have lasted the better of two minutes.

The lord of darkness was rising in all his hellish might, they succeeded in reclosing the gate but at a high fatality rate. She watched many she loved die at the hands of demons. Her mentors' kind was different than herself, they were the last of the ancient kind. She was of the new breed who didn't have to separate body and soul to fight in the spiritual world. The living proof she was there body and soul was the scrape marks and bruises from the battle and from hit-ting the streets rolling. While her superiors spirits were in the spiritual realms battling for humanity, humanity sought to kill their physical existences which was on the run from the very people they were trying to save from a fate worse than death. For this very reason she didn't care much for humanity. But did no malice to none who wasn't begging for it.

Speaking to them, her ancient mentors, spiritually through the Royal Telephone she called to their attention to the task she was about to engage into: "That girl is coming and I've no idea how to teach someone about spiritual warfare." She said aloud in her living room. For she was home alone. There was no one to eavesdrop.

"Teach her the way I taught you and you'll do fine." Saint Anne replied with a smile in her voice.

"I'm told she knows anything about spiritual warfare. She doesn't even know how to use her blade. That's an inherent ability. I can't teach someone a spiritual instinct." Eugenia explained to the disembodied voice.

"Eugenia, you've always worried too much about things you can't change. Simply teach the girl all you know and leave the rest up to God. That's all we all can do."

When the conversation was over Eugenia sat back and reminisced the last living conversation she had with Saint Anne. She had opened up the spiritual connection between herself and them and spoke to them through the spiritual network saying: "This is St. Anne....I've been contacted by followers of the darkside asking me to restrain my students." Her angry reply to the accusation was: "First of all "my students" are not

61

inflicting harm on you. They may not like the nature of your actions and no Law of God require them to like what you are but despite that they are not inflicting harm on you, contrary to popular belief."

Eugenia chuckled remembering the hell and brimstone sermon Saint Ann gave them because it was the young ones like herself whom the Grand Wizard was referring to as the dangerous, uncontrollable killers. But, hey, in their defense, the darkside followers had it coming. The young warriors had spent years watched those like Sts. Anne, Melissa, Cheryl, Thomas, Douglas, Gerald, Nehemiah, and many others try to reason with and live as peaceful as possible with those hell minions. There was no real peace to be had with them around and they weren't going to try. With this new girl coming she'd combine the two forms of teaching: Compassion when needed and bust their ass when it's begged for. She knew they were up against a new predator. One who strives clandestinely in the invisible ether of physical data and spiritual information. She had never seen him in the physical world but she'd heard enough talk of him to recognize him shall she see him.

Eugenia Harris was a little nervous, but not much. She's too old and have seen too much for that. She knew the girl named Ana was embarking on her most dangerous mission yet. Coming to her to learn the ways of spiritual warfare. She knew the darkside would do any-thing to stop her.

Standing out in the backyard in the predawn dew she felt the temperature drop to nearly freezing on a humid summer morning causing her to shiver. She was expecting the head satanist but there was something far more sinistral out here. Something even more sinistral and minacious than the wizard whom she did not record ever meeting. Whatever was out here was antediluvian, older than the earth and eviler than most demons. Yet it felt familiar. She had encountered it before. She wondered if it was the immortal who unrelentingly pursued St. Anne as a love interest? They drove him away several times. But he always came back. He was a real gadfly. He avowed she looked like someone he loved many years ago. They knew that was a lie. He was insusceptible to love, he may have screwed whomever he remembered but loved her!? Ha! But St.

Anne agreed to sit and chat with him a few times; she didn't mention anything about him scaring her or trying to hurt her. The time St. Anne fought him was because he was being charming, annoying, and wouldn't leave her alone. But whatever this is it is mad as hell. She knows she need to take this girl to the cave. She doubt she can handle this by herself. She'll tell Ana in the morning where they are going.

Through red eyed tinted with hate, the hatred was so great it cast red shades of rage over his eyes, the demon of rage which was sent to kill Ana BuFaye watched Eugenia Harris with intense animosity. He remained hidden, he wasn't dumb enough to show himself. He decided he would wait and slip into the house when the woman opened the door for Ana.

With a small trailer Charles retained for them hitched to the road and time-tested 2483 Toyota they nicknamed Trusty, the three generations head up Gordon Hwy. Detouring onto I-20 driving toward the Peach city. Looking in the rear-view mirror Ana noticed an excessively long line of cars pulling onto the expressway behind her and several quickly pulled up along side her while several sped pass them and slammed on their brakes, nearly causing her to rear-end them.

"We're being followed." Ana says matter-of-factly. Fannie turned around and looked behind, beside them, they're surrounded by faces brimming with hatred and malicious intents. She put Bea under the iron protection in the backseat and told her to stay there and don't peek out until they call her. All of a sudden Ana felt a white, excoriating pain in her head, it blurred her vision for a nanosecond, she knew it was the effect of the zapping gun the man beside her was using. He aggressively beckoned for her to pull her. She couldn't out run them. There were too many and the ones ahead had her blocked in so she had choice but ignore the pain that was giving her a nosebleed and keep driving.

Knowing what she had to do Fantasia BuFaye quieted her soul, bowed her head, and start praying. Suddenly, a white fiery whirlwind cuts in-between them and all the other cars surrounding them. Even those to the side are caught up in this precocious storm. They're riding in the eye of a radiant white tornado! They leaned over and looked up at the cars and people whirling, being crushed in the strange cyclone. This is the second time Ana has witnessed this. A few years ago this happened in Kansas as they were headed to Iowa. But this one was far worse. It sucked the cars up like a vacuum cleaner and crushed them like a winepress crushes grapes. As swiftly as it came down it went back into the sky equally as mysterious and disappeared taking their pursuers with it. Then the sky was clear again. Those who witnessed it seemed as perplexed as Ana. Regular travelers were left completely unharmed. Ana whips her head around and ask her mother in awe. "What did you do?"

With eyes still closed and head still bowed Fannie replied "Ask God for some peace and quiet."

While riding along, Fannie begin singing "The Old Rugged Cross" with granddaughter in the safety seat listening. While still singing Fannie's cellphone rings. Knowing who it is. There goes the peace and quiet. Fannie hates to answer but knows it won't stop ringing until she does. "MOM! Where are you?!" the caller shouts into the phone.

"Helena, it's good to your voice dear. How are you and the kids?" Fannie asked her oldest daughter, reminding her of her manners.

Obliquely ignoring her mother's hint Helena Wales frantically says. "Mom! the cops came here looking for Ana. They say her landlord was found stabbed to death in her end-condo connected to the Ana's apartment complex."

"WHAT! She was fine when she brought your sister her rent receipt Friday evening!"

"Well, she ain't fine now. She's dead. Dead as dead can be. They say two people were dead inside that place. They've been calling around to all of us asking where's our little sister. I told Junior her temper is bad enough to have killed the lady if the woman pissed her off. We all know Ana can't control her mouth or her fists. Junior said as always when anything pertaining his precious little sister 'no one knows who did it, with over 100 people in a complex how can they be so sure it was her or even if the murderer was a tenant. This is just a preliminary investigation. Standard police procedures.'"

Chastening her oldest daughter Fan angrily retorts. "Helena, don't say such a thing. You don't know who might be listening. I know your sister didn't kill that woman. She went no where last night. She went and tried to get her deposit back but no one answered the door. But that not unusual for Shelia Jean not to answer the door if it isn't rent day."

Second guessing it must be her overbearing, upper-middle class, Long Island residing older sister on the phone Ana glanced sideyed and asked her mom. "Can you pray *that* devil away too?" Bea sniggered at her mother's joke.

"The two of you stop it this instant!" Fannie ordered her two daughters for she knew the peace and quiet had flown out the window.

Again, ignoring her mother's command. Helena started raving over the phone. "Mom! I know a New York City's district court judge whose willing to help Ana if she turn herself in. Ana needs help. You can't go around killing everybody who piss you off. You and dad always defended her neuroses but the sooner you accept she's crazy and talk her into getting help the sooner everyone can breathe easier without worrying about what has happen every time the phone rings. I'm sick of being put under scrutiny because I've a crazy sister who likes to kill. I didn't ask for an insane sister. You and dad gave her to me. She has been making my life hell since she came home outta the damn hospital. I worked hard to get to where I am. I'm not about to let my little hard-headed, wayward sister destroy my life! Do you've any idea what will be said on my circuit if this get out? How can I lock up other people for murder when my own baby sister is dropping bodies like flies? Put Ana on the phone. There no one pursuing Ana, the only thing after her is her own craziness!"

Fannie scoffed, frowns, and hands her cellphone to Ana, "Here, take this phone before this smart-mouthed girl make me kill her." Smiling, thinking of a smart-aleck reply to give her big sister Ana says. "Hellooo."

"Don't hello me!" Helena snaps. "What in the hell have you done!? Can't you do anything without somebody dying? I didn't tell Mama but they found your former boss and your former landlord dead today. The cops are looking for you for questioning."

65

"WHAT!!??" Ana shouted. "Dead??? The last I saw of both of them they were still alive. Very much alive! Mean as hell but nonetheless alive."

"Calm down. Where are you?!" Helena asked, hoping if she remain calm Ana might cooperate. "Where do you think? On the road." Ana snapped. "I got fired and evicted all in the same day. Plus some fool shot my car but a friend of mine got it fixed last night."

Everything Ana said sounded like running and creating an alibi to avoid arrest to Helena's police trained ears. "Turn off and go to the nearest police station and turn yourself in. If you don't it will seems as though you are running."

"Sorry. Big Sis. Can't do that. All I know is I didn't kill them."

"And why not?"

I sighed. I couldn't believe my own sister was asking me to hang myself. To turn myself in for something I didn't do. As my general rule of the thumb. I don't share information with the police. Cops have an unerring tendency to turn whatever you say against you. From my experience, silence and keep moving is the best defense. "The mere fact I went over there this morning will be proof enough to them I killed her and you know it."

"ANA!! I'm not playing with you." Helen screamed into the phone. "Get your narrow behind to a station and tell them your story if it's as you say. Then you've nothing to worry about, nothing to hide. Not going in only make things worse! Think about mom and Bea even if you don't give a damn about yourself. If they catch you on the road they might open fire. It's said you're armed and dangerous."

"NO! I'M NOT GOING TO NO DAMN POLICE STATION AND TURN MYSELF IN FOR SOMETHING I DIDN'T DO. YOU KNOW GOOD AND DAMN WELL THEY DON'T WANT TO *TALK* TO ME. THEY WANT TO LOCK ME UP!!"

Seeing that Ana's mind is made up and when it's made up nothing can knock a notion

66

out of it. "Arrggrghh! Forget it. Put Mom back on the phone." I handed the phone back to mom.

Trying to sound reasonable and calm Helena says "Mom, wherever my demented, devious sister is taking you I've no idea but I want you on a plane headed to New York City the moment y'all reach your ardent destination. Let me know where's the nearest airport. I'm sending you a plane ticket and bring Bea with you 'fore Ana be done got that baby killed. Mom, as painful as it is---you gotta face the fact she's Bruce Manson kinda crazy and I'm not letting her drag you to hell with her. The next thing you know she'll be running around randomly hackin up people with chainsaws!!"

"Honey, you know your sister can't afford a babysitter. I stay with the one of my children who needs me the most." Fannie replied equally as calm.

Losing patience with both her mother and sister Helena retorts "Mom, all this stress with Ana agitates your health problems. Ana is always in one jam after another. You can't protect nor make excuses for her forever." Fannie bites her tongue and politely asks her eldest daughter "You're a mother, aren't you?"

"Yes." Helena answered frustratedly rubbing her brow. "If Rachael needed you, would you forsaken her?" Fran quizzed. "Of course not but I'd expect her to be responsible and keep her life in order. It's humanly impossible for one individual to get in as many jams as Ana without trying."

"I've lived with your sister off and on for nearly two years and have seen things fall out the clear blue sky into her lap. I've seen cops pull her over for merely driving along the road or stopping to buy gas. I know she didn't kill those people. All last night we were cleaning, packing, and loading. As much faith as you've in the legal system it would serve you well to apply some of that faith to your family."

"Mom, crazy people are stronger than the average person. I deal with them on a regular basis. You both say all these things were falling down around her all at once, she could've freaked out and killed them and not remember it." Helena said, clicking the button on the phone breaking their connection. She was in no mood to further listen to her mother rationalize her sister's bloodlust. Fannie heard a dial tone in ear. With no further ado Helena folded her phone.

Helena sat in her hovercruiser agonizing whether she should give them up for whatever happens next. While absorbed in her thoughts a man raps on the window. She doesn't let her window down, he maybe otherworldly handsome but there's something about him that put her on high alert.

The girl and her baby had finally arrived. The long line of satanists trailing them told her they'd been through hell to get here and were unable to completely shake those hell pestilences. She stood on the steps smiling with her invisible blade in her hand to make them feel welcome as the small car pulled into her off-the-street driveway and continued to the back as if the girl was already familiar with her backyard. A very pretty young woman steps out the car with more hair than she ever seen on a single human. It surprised her how much this girl and St. Anne looked alike. She sensed a lot of bravery and fight in this child, even the baby had gusto. Seeing her teacher's image made her yearn again for her own era. She made them as comfortable as she had available. She had prepared a feast of Southern fried pork chops, creamed spinach, chopped collard greens sauteed in fatback; mashed potatoes cooked with bacon and onions and a homemade peach pie. Eugenia knew she was a wiz in the kitchen. She was glad she was; that kid and her momma were nothing but skin and bones and her mother named Fannie wasn't doing too hot either. And like St. Anne, this girl had benignant eyes that took in everything. And like St. Anne this girl had a halo starting to grow. "Lord, do You have to advertise Yourself in those so helpless on earth?" She said secretly in her heart.

Watching the girl unload a few boxes that contained all her worldly belongings from her packed car, she knew they had been set adrift in a cruel world that cared nothing for their pain. Eugenia was remembering her teacher's words before her extinction, causing tears to cloud her vision. Those were some of the last words St. Anne said trying to convince a group of lost sinners to repent and stop fighting them. The exact time of the charge was: 10:43 AM 4/27/2073.

The world's lone mogul Ashton Cargill, shakes himself loose from the tangle of arms, legs, and breasts. He sensed something or someone unusual stirring in the nearby spiritual realms. Being an immortal has it advantages of being able to detect spiritual things mortals can not. The scent he detected smelled like a rose of Sharon. Damn! He wish his memory of spiritual roaming was better. Looking at his quickly healing, bruised knuckles he wonders who he fought and why? He always cursed himself for the lost of memory during his celestial imprisonments. He know he went somewhere several nights ago. Wherever he was the same scent existed. But he clearly remembers the feeling of whomever he was with. It was short of divinity. And he knows divinity having come from it. He records her soft touch on his rock hard muscles, her sweet lips on his mouth, his passionately making sweet love to her. He remembers everything physically about her but who is she and where in the hell is she now? But what puzzles him is whomever she is...she is human. Not an immortal. So how could he've known her for years? That doesn't make sense.

The oldest member of his Paris harem wakes and look at him. Wondering where is he going? "Baby, come back to bed," Dawn cooed drowsily, rubbing sleep from her eyes as several others awake to the sound of her voice. Dawn climbed over the others and scooped out the 16' foot wide bed and went to his side and begun gently rubbing his broad back.

"You having that strange dream again?" Dawn tenderly inquired.

"I told you it's not a damn dream. She's a real person. But Someone upstairs is keeping me from finding her!" He grunted and threw his head back, swallowing the brandy with a single gulp. His impressive, 6'5" muscular statuesque physique with its crown of a versicolored dark brown, gold, and black mane that flowed in perfect harmony and arrangement over his broad shoulders and down his back in cascading waves has stirred desire in many and he was fully aware of that fact. Down through the ages his inhumanely beauty have allured many to him, to their demise. But with this new woman, he doesn't believe it will be useful. She seems like a dream that always slips away when he wake up. She's like a dream lover which he knows is usually a succubus. But this woman isn't a demon. No demon smells like the Rose of Sharon.

Dawn Shepherd had been a member of his harem since age 21. His immortal substance prevents her from aging to her actually forty five years. She had a buxom figure, her deep brownish golden tresses, framed a face of an angel. The beauty of the Mediterranean blue eyes set in a face that Aphrodite would envy made her a total knockout and she knew it. So what if she used it to aid her progression in the world of the rich and famous?! She was duly warned by the harem members on their way out when she was coming in. "Do not fall in love with him. He isn't capable of giving love in return." They all warned. She intend to coordinate her position to her advancements. Dawn felt those before her were flukes and all flakes anyway so what did they know about capturing a man's heart? She intends to become Mrs. Ashton Cargill where others have failed. So what if he is immortal? Those who don't know that don't need to know and those who berate her for her choice are jealous and wanted to be in her shoes. She already has all the power of being Mrs. Ashton Cargill so she intends to get the legality of the name. It'll make her the most powerful woman in the world. That's a long way from her humble beginning in working at his seaside resort in Honolulu. And whomever this dream bitch is isn't going to fuck things up for her. She's way tired of the imaginary woman. But the reality is she believes the woman is real and is going to put an end to this madness once and for all. This shit been going on for four years now. He needs to snap out of it and come back to reality. While she's thinking, devising a plan to rid him of this Venus of a woman and rubbing his back, he cast a cold glance at her and disappeared.

"Aw, fuck!" She forgets for a minute or two he can read your open, surface thoughts. Oh hell, he already knows how she feels. She hasn't been timid about her demands. He has been avoiding talking about their future for quite some time now and she was sick of it. Every time she mentioned marriage he always said the usual.

He concentrates hard on retracing his steps and finding his way back the way he had traveled the other night. There's a stubborn, mental resistance. More stubborn and strong willed than himself. His head aches. "Ok, you Guys!" He says heavenward as he walks through the realms and dimensions finally exiting into the dusty, ethereal Neutral Zone. "I've done my time. So leave my freaking head alone!" He roared, not that he surely expected a reply. "Damn, I've gotta stop drinking. It's making my memory worse!"

Finally, after many detours through various portals, tracing his own steps he steps out the spiritual realm into the physical world in front of a big, rambling Victorian mansion that has been sublet into small apartment. The five hundred year old black shuttered, red brick mansion is swarming with police and forensic crew teams. "Sir, get back behind the line" a baby-faced, young officer ordered. Ashton Cargill raised his eyebrows, kicked the police laser tape out his way, and kept walking. All the veterans cops knew who he was. They also knew the rookie wouldn't be on the force much longer even if he remained alive. Which they sincerely doubted he would.

This man has more power in his pinkie than most kings, prime ministers and presidents had in their entire cabinet. But they're all curious as to why he is in their neck of the world? Why this murder attracted him? Whatever the reason was, they were certain they wanted none of whatever he intend to issue out at whomever. They watched him climb the high wooden steps to the front door and did not dare interfere. They let go sighs of relief when he steps on the wide porch and finally goes inside. At least they can go back to their work.

This isn't the murder victim's place. The victim's place is across the walk way. They know all there's to know about her. Her identity is no great mystery. This building houses the suspect's last known residence. They've firm reasons to believe this woman is their prime suspect. No one is paying much attention to the victim's place for it's the suspect who has burnt off her finger tips and those of her relatives. Which intrigues the police. What kind of mother would burn off a four year old's finger prints and what kind of grandmother would allow it? Her neighbors said she was quiet and rarely seen outside of going to and from work. But there's something ominous about that place. Normal people don't clean sweep evidence before leaving. They got a useful tip that she had a fight with her boss and landlord the same day. Now both women are dead. Now the place has been sprayed with an illegal cell deterioration agent and swept clean. There are reports of this practice listed in several other locations where it's believed she has once

71

dwelt. It's known the woman dwells in a place a short while, works low paying jobs, kills, sweeps the place clean, and moves on. But to where? No one knows for sure until another body drops.

From the appearance she left in a hurry, haste always create room for error. They found a microscopic DNA trace on the kid's bed. According to the world's DNA data base it belongs to a four year old name Breanna Wyett, the daughter of former pro football star Thaddeus Wyett.

They called the federal pen where Thad Wyett was being held under different charges than the first charges of drug possession with intent to distribute. This time he was given a six month sentence for assault and battery. The detective who spoke with Thaddeus Wyett didn't find the man useful. Thad was no real help at all. According to him his ex didn't have it in her to commit the crimes she's accused of. "Ana wouldn't hurt a fly. She's too sweet for her own good."

"If she's all that, Mr. Wyett...why did you divorce her?" The detective asked, looking at the court record of divorce proceedings filed from the federal pen housing him. "That's none of your damn business. Now is it?! Worry about your own ugly ass wife and leave Ana alone. You got real criminals running amok in the streets. Go chase them!" Thad had said.

"I'm chasing a real one. The sooner you accept that woman you married is dead. Dead, done! She doesn't live in that body anymore. A pint sized, bloodthirsty monster resides there now. The sooner you accept that fact and help us find her the sooner your daughter will be safe!" The detective said, trying to rattle Thad's cage. Urgently probing. Driving the mental blade in deeper and twisting it. "If and when she's caught, which she'll be. She'll be arrested but mind you- the cops have been given authority to take her down in a volley of bullets if they must. She's a coldblooded killer and knows very well how to use a gun. So it's your duty as a father to save your own daughter's life! She's with your ex! Did you know sweet, innocent Ana Wyett burnt off your baby's finger tips? What kinda mother does that to her own baby? That's how desperate she's to get away. Count yourself lucky to have gotten out that marriage alive. I make no exaggeration when I say the woman is a cold blooded killer", the man said shortly before the connection was severed. He slammed his desk hard with his fist, losing his temper for Thad hung up on him. At least NYC finest Helena BuFaye Wales didn't hang up on him. She simply lied, implying she didn't know where her mother and sister were. That her sister wouldn't hurt her baby. He reminded her that if caught aiding and abetting her sister who obviously needed to be locked away and given psychiatric treatment she will lose all she worked for. But the NYC cop vividly insisted she have had no contact with them. Her poker face stance told him she was lying.

⚜

The heavy oak door closed behind him shutting out the public clamoring and police radio cackling he looked around the dim sunlit foyer. The darkness does nothing in relieving the heat. It's hot as hell in here. He looks doesn't remember this part of his travel. Of course he doesn't. He was in the woman's bedroom not in her hallway. Instincts tells him the first apartment on his right is hers'. He pushed the door opened and he's right. He senses her spiritual imprint. The cheap furniture looked worn and old. The sparsely lit, meagerly furnished place looked sad without her presence. He keeps back to the bedroom. The first thing he noticed was the closet he used as a portal to visit her. It's empty. Plastic hangers are askew on the rod.

She left in a hurry. He remembers in a dreamy state her getting up out of this bed quietly as she looked back at the sleeping child and he led her back through the door he just came through to a realm he knew well, a world untouched. He led her via a route that wasn't so combative and evil. He remembered telling her as she laid in his arms in the purple greenery that he loved her. She laughed that high pitched, soulful, honey laced laughter of hers and said. "No, sugar, you *think* you love me. You love what we just did."

"I'm older than this world and yours combined. So believe me, I know the difference between love, sex, and infatuation. I know what I feel in my heart." He saw her eye brows knit while lying nude in his arms, then she looked up at him and asked what was his real name?

"I think you already know. But in due time I'll tell you." She rose off his chest and

73

looked him closer in the eyes, studying his face. "I hope it to god it's not Lucifer." She said half-teasing. He hugged her and smiled. "If I told you, you probably would run away."

"Probably not. You can't be any worse than the devils already on my trail." She said, contently sighing, snuggling back down to his massive chest. She felt his arms around her shoulders stiffen. He raised on his elbow and turned her to face him. "Who is bothering you? What devils are on your trail? Give me a name! I'll see to it they die a horrible, excruciatingly painful death!" Not sure if he was serious, she giggled a little to lighten the mood. His angry outburst startled her. She playfully patted his hairless, smooth, perfect chest."Pipe down, warlord! Calm down. I really don't know who has been pursuing me all these years. All I know is they want me dead. I wish I knew why."

Anger flashed and ripped through him like a nova star bursting. He shields her from it. He doesn't want to scare her away. Whomever is after her is going to be dearly, very, sorry when he get his hands on them. He'll find them. He always finds whomever he set his sights upon to find and kill. But inherent aptitude, something, tells him it's more than one person. "My love, they won't succeed in harming you. You've my word on that! If I've to kill a million to protect you--so be it" he said, softly rubbing her upper arm.

"I'd feel awful if you killed a million people to protect me" she said sadly into his chest. He wasn't thrilled with her sympathy for those trying to take her life. Take her away from him. "I wouldn't feel a thing." He replied, omitting telling her he had destroyed worlds before so a million humans was nothing to him.

Someone interrupts his reminiscence of their last night together asking may she help him? He turns and a kind faced, elderly woman is standing in the livingroom. He place an angelical smile on his face. "I assume you're her ex. The little girl kinda looks like you." The presumptive woman said.

"Yes," he lied. "I heard on the news what happened here and was wondering if my ex-wife and daughter were safe?" The elderly woman smiled a little. "You're as handsome as I thought her husband would be. It's a shame you two didn't make it. I think you two could've tried harder to stay together at least the little girl's sake. You young people need to learn to think of someone else besides yourself. That little girl needs her daddy as well as her mother."

"Yes, ma'am. We should've tried harder. I'ld say the same. Yes, she does need me. That's why I'm here." He respectfully agreed. Knowing he'll have to gain her trust before she'll talk to him.

The elderly woman side-eyed him with her clear brown eyes and scoffed as if saying "coming now doesn't help the baby's situation. Now does it?" but said, "I told the police there was a strange blotted face man, he looked like he had pits in his face. He was right outside on the streets watching this place Friday morning. If I ever seen a killer, he was one. But they haven't listened to a word I said. They said he was probably someone she was dating. I told them I never seen her with anybody. They're so anxious to get that poor thing they aren't considering other possibilities."

He gathered her fragile, thin hands in his own massive ones and kindly gazed in her wrinkled face, promising her the authorities would not get his ex wife and daughter. "Now, seeing how fond you're of them. Would you please tell me anything she may have said as to where she was going? Anything you can remember would be helpful. It's of the utmost urgency that I find them first!"

The elderly neighbor pondered a few seconds and slowly shook her head from side to side. "All I know is the landlady threw them out. Why? I don't know. I told Shelia Jean Friday afternoon when I heard about it from her mother, she should be ashamed of herself throwing a little child and an ailing person out in this kinda heat. God don't like ugly and ain't stuck on pretty. You see what happened to her? That's why you should be mindful of how you treat people cause you never know who serves God and who don't." The old woman lectured, holding onto his arm. He knew part of the speech was for his benefit. Refusing to let go of his arm she continued. "Somebody hurt that young mother bad. She tried to play it off as if she was alright. But I'm too old not to see the pain in her eyes. It was you---wasn't it?" She asked yanking harder than he expected on his arm. Now he was trying to unwind himself from her for he needed to leave and seek out other traces of this young woman.

"I'm not sure, but if I did, I didn't mean to hurt her." He said kindly, leading the old woman in the pastel blue floral housedress toward the door. Defiance set in her wrinkled face; she refused to be brushed off. "If you didn't then who did? You her baby daddy. You her ex so it's you who did it! I know it wasn't the young man upstairs for she had that painful, haunted look when she moved here."

Seeing the dark shadow of jealousy sweep cross his face, his gemstone eyes darken a shade or two at her mention of another man. Seeing he didn't like hearing about the young man upstairs. The old woman smiled complacently when she knew the jealousy in his face flashed across his heart. Meaning she had hit a nerve. He thinks he's so cool, so fine, calm and collected that nothing can rile him but that did. He paused, opening the door and tried to amicably ask about the young man upstairs.

"Oh, they were just friends. He helped her get her car fixed a few days ago. No, no, it was yesterday. Her mother said somebody shot it. Why would somebody do something like that?" She asked as he restarted leading her to the door and then into the hallway. "Some-times she'd go grocery shopping for me. She's a sweet girl." The woman added. He agreed, Ana is a very sweet person.

Now at the heavy oak door he came through, the old woman said as he stepped out onto the porch, back out in the horrible heat and blinding sunshine. "You still love her. I know you. I can see it in your eyes. So go get our girl and keep her this time. Let go of your damn pride. Pride ain't worth a damn if you ain't got nobody to love you and someone you love in return." She said in the doorway as he held it open. The police were frowning at her for talking to him when they told her not to open her mouth to the media or anyone. What part of shut the hell up didn't she understand?

"Miss, I'll do my best. I promise you we'll get back together if she'll have me. You've been very helpful." He said benevolently, instructing her to go back inside out of the deadly heat. She nodded and let him go.

Once the old woman was back inside he flipped out his phone and called the local branch of his security team to come guard the old woman in Apt. A4. He knows whomever killed the landlady is still out there somewhere and perhaps saw the woman talking to him. Not leaving things to chance for it could be a cop as far as he knows.

An archeia, a female archangel named Shekhinah, who is often called Lady Patience, one of the powerhouse female archangels is standing unseen outside the building among the police crawling all over the place when he came out. She was invisible to the mortals. He sighed for he knew she dealt with patience. Which he was all out of at the moment; patience wasn't one of his better virtues. He didn't have time to deal with her right now. Whatever she come to tell him would just have to wait. He didn't want to hear it. She fell in step with him as he walked to the blistering sidewalk to wait for his people.

"Azazael, leave that woman alone. She doesn't need anything you've to offer." Shekhinah, the Lady of Patience says looking sternly at him.

"What am I supposed to do?" He telepathically asked angrily. "Stand by and let those fools kill her?"

"Father has taken care of her all these years without your help. He can and will continue to do so. Leave this alone. This doesn't concern you."

"Oh yeah, I've seen how that usually turns out." He sarcastically replied."They usually end up a murdered, cold slab of meat. She won't be martyred on my watch."

He sees his people pull into the parking lot, many have never met him but knew what he looked like. Two men got out the first black SUV and approached their boss. He briefly instructed them on who to guard but don't scare the old woman and then he disappeared. He didn't have time for heaven's way of doing things right now. Heaven's placid way of letting the criminals carry out their deeds didn't set right with him. Not when it came to this woman and he really didn't know why. Hell, he should know all about heaven allowing criminals to run wild on the principles of their own free will for he was once the king of hell. But that didn't mean he had any intentions of letting hell kill his sweet lady love. Unlike immortals, once humans cross over the great chasm they don't come back. That's the end of their earthly existence. And he isn't idly sitting by and letting that happen.

He exited the portal in the police department not caring who saw him. He knew all about human's disbelief in the supernatural, so shall anyone tell what they saw they'll be deemed a nutjob. And in this day and age they locked you for malingering and just about anything. He walked purposefully down the hall to the sheriff's office and pushed open the door, he doesn't wait for anyone to invite him in. The well toned, brown haired, healthy complexion, sun tanned sheriff of about forty looks up, not exactly surprised to see the big man in his office for he had been told by his deputies Ashton Cargill was in their neck of the country.

"Call off your dogs. Or I'll kill every cop in this department starting with you." Cargill icily ordered without breaking eye contact.

Sheriff Haywood didn't flinch. He was a hardnose. He causally tossed an inch thick file across the desk to Cargill. "Read and you'll see why I can't do that," he said nonchalantly, leaning back in the chair and staring the ancient murderer in his arctic blue topaz, gemstone eyes that are quickly turning into gilded, dark sapphires. Not that he knows who he is looking at. He just knows when facing an opponent never let them see you sweat. Cargill perused the folder for a second, memorizing the woman's and her relatives' names. The rest of it means nothing to him. He tossed it back to the Sheriff harder than necessary. It slid across the desk and hit the floor with a dull flop. He places both knuckles on the polished desk, hands that have slayed millions, and intimidatingly leans across the desk and growls in a demonic voice as his face contorts from handsome to scary while forming a great ball of fire in his risen right hand, "I don't give a fuck who she has or hasn't killed. She can have killed your mother for all it means to me. If you don't want to join her landlady and boss I strongly urge you to do as I say".

Ken Haywood's eyes widened. He had heard much about this man but had never met him. The retired sheriff before him had warned him of this man. Saying it wasn't worth it to get into a pissing contest with him. He didn't know what he was dealing with but he did know whatever this man was he wasn't human. He pressed the button on his desk phone calling his people off the crime scene. To bluntly end the investigation but not taking his eyes off whatever the hell this thing was standing in his office threatening him.

78

"I can't do anything about the state troopers, FBI, and GBI." Ken said pressing the button, breaking the connection as Ashton Cargill extinguished the fire in his hand. "The woman is wanted in several states for murder or at least questioning pertaining those in her area at the time she resided there."

"Let me worry about that." He said confidently, referring to the other law enforcement agencies and disappeared in front of Ken Haywood. The sheriff gulped hard and quickly grabbed the bottle of Scotch in his desk drawer for he know he didn't just see someone with a big ball of fire disappear in his office. Of course he had heard stories all his life about people like that man but what kid in the south hadn't heard them?

Ashton Cargill picked up in the spiritual realms the life imprint of Helena Wales but first exited in his Manhattan office and called each of the law enforcement agencies involved in the manhunt for Ana BuFaye, clearly stating his demands. As he spoke behind closed doors, his ferocious temper roiled up into an insuperable rage. It swept him all over him like a wildfire as he yelled at the faces on the screen, making indisputable promises to show up if this wasn't resolved immediately. Everyone worth half their salt knew if you didn't do as he said, everything was over. The aura of fire around him told them it was best to leave this woman alone. He offered no explanation as to why they shouldn't pursue her. He clicked off the suspended air screen, fuming over the subnormality of a mob of people with weapons chasing a woman and a child. And humanity called him evil?

He next follows the spiritual trail to her sister. One of the relatives whose name he saw in the folder. That's the relative most likely to know where Ana BuFaye is. He doubts the brothers know. But most sisters are fairly close. He exited in an alley in NYC between Fifth Ave and 28th street. He has the woman's name and there's only one female cop in NYC by the name of Officer Wales. Being that his hearing is far superior to mortals the ground level and overheard noise of the city has always bothered him. He remembered when this place was a dirt hole in a wall. When these busy, crowded streets were a thick forest. He remembered when thick ice covered these grounds. He tracks the woman's sister since heaven is blocking him from tracking her. He finds her sister sitting in a hovercruiser parked by the curb, keenly watching the public for trouble. He politely raps on the glass, sees her hand rest on her gun as she lets the window down. The woman is beauteous, even the hideous the uniform doesn't squash her loveliness. But she isn't his type. He's in love with her sister and her eyes say she has too much attitude for his personal taste.

"Can I help you?" She asked through the slot of plexiglass glass. "Yes, I'm hoping you may be able to help me. I'm a dear friend of your sister Ana. I was hoping you could possibly tell me where she is?" He said, employing a 17th century gentleman's etiquette in speaking to the policewoman.

Believing him to be a Fed or a detective from her own department sent to entrap her into saying something incriminating, she begin to let the window back up in his face but not before saying. "A lot of motherfuckers would like to know where she is. When you bastards find her be sure to let me know!" The button stopped working. She stabbed it numerous times with her index finger before glaring at him over the window's edge believing he did something to the mechanism. Which he did. He snapped his finger behind his back sending an electrical surge charge to blow out the function.

"Mrs. Wales." He mellifluously said as a car passing very close blew at him, the driver yelling at him telling him to get the hell out the road. He turned, sending the driver a death look. Causing the man to freeze and cringe all in one motion and swallow the next insults like overflowing spit that were about to spill from his lips. Helena BuFaye watched him closely the few seconds his head was turned to glare at the driver honking at him. It wasn't safe to stand where he's standing but if he didn't mind getting hit---what was it to her? She quickly put the puzzle together. This man isn't law enforcement he's really another one of her sister's pretty boyfriends. How else would he know about she being Ana's sister if Ana hadn't told him. Hadn't her obtuse sister learned anything about pretty or handsome men after the way Thad Wyett treated her? Apparently not. She resumed her professional pose when he turned back around to resume their conversation. But something about him looked vaguely familiar...

"Mrs. Wales, as I was saying, I'm a very close friend of your sister's. Right now, she's in grave danger and if you can tell me where she is it would very helpful. It will be much appreciated and I'll be forever grateful."

80

"How many times do I've to tell everybody and their momma, I don't know where she is." Helena uttered as her phone rang. It was her mother. She knew her mom was calling back because she was angry at her. But that was alright about her being mad at her. At least she knew they were still alive. "Hold on a minute," she said through the stuck window to the man at the side of her cruiser.

Unbeknownst to Helen he could hear the mother arguing with her about pettiness in his opinion. He froze as tingles ran down his spine when he heard that soulful, honey-laced laughter from the other night trash talking in the phone. That squeaky, high, melodious voice, it's so unforgettable. He has heard many female voices much more beautiful and alluring than this one on the phone, even the sister had a more refined and elegant voice. But he didn't love them, this one belonged to the one he loved.

Forgetting his manners, he reached in to take the phone to talk to the sister on the other end. "Let me speak to her." He said more roughly than he intended.

Helena pulls the phone away from her ear and out of his reach realizing this man could hear them. She quickly breaks the connection in case he was who she originally believed him to be. She looked down a second or two to see if the light was blinking red on the source box meaning someone else was listening. It wasn't. The tiny orb was dead. She looked back toward the stranger but he was gone. Believing the sunlight was obstructing her view to the west she shielded her eyes with her hand. She then looked quickly in all four directions expecting to see him up or down the streets but it was like he never existed."*It's impossible for anyone to disappear that fast.*" She tells herself before pulling out another phone to call her ornery ass sister back. Ana will get their mother killed with her craziness. Why can't she stop killing? She know she killed those people in Pasadena. The bullet casing matched their great-great-great grandmother's gun.

He cursed himself for letting his impatience get the better of him. He knew blew his chances when he tried to take the phone. He attempted to ride the magnetic energy wave the phone emitted but it dissipated too quickly the moment the cop disconnected. So she does know where they are. Not that he truly expected her to tell him or anyone for that matter.

Seeing that riding and disrupting the magnetic energy waves are a lost cause he lividly returns to his Manhattan office to make sure the antics did as he ordered.

All circuits of his computer told him all warrants on the woman had been recalled. But he had to get a vow from each agency heads they wouldn't resume it as soon as he turned his back. The four faces in the screen vowed they wouldn't so he clicked off the screen, turned around, and bumped into his older sister Mikaela. Her blinding white radiance lit up the entire room. He shielded his eyes from her anger. With her fists planted firmly on her hips and pure white fire glaring in her beautiful eyes she scornfully said,"Azazael, I thought Shekhinah told you to leave that woman alone!? To stay away from her and stay out of this! This doesn't concern you! This isn't your world. You're on earth, not on AzazaeLand, you can not go around bossing humans around on Adam's world! Haven't your hardship taught you anything?!" She lectured. No, not really. Hardship, severe, rigid punishment and imprisonment, enmeshed in his psyche how to stay out of prison not how to stop doing what landed him there in the first place. He learned the rules better and how to skim around them. But he intended to find that woman and apprehend whomever threatening her life. Deep inside he knows he's pushing sensitive buttons and skating dangerously close to reimprisonment.

He waited to see if she was going to dispel her glory before replying. She did. "Ok, since you must know. I don't know why I feel the way I do about that woman. But I love her and you and all of heaven aren't keeping me from her. Perhaps you can tell me what's going on here? Perhaps you can tell me why do I love her when I don't even know her! Is this love business you all's way of tricking me into doing your bidding? Huh? I was happy just the way I was. I don't need love thrown in the mixture of my life. It complicates things. Yes, I know all about you all's plans or should I say, method of protection. They always get someone killed. Is that your plan? I fall hard for her and then she gets killed and then I follow her back Home and rejoin the army? Huh!?"

The archangel Mikaela, whose name is often spelled Micheala, stares at her younger brother for a few seconds before throwing her robed arms in the air in sheer frustration saying. "Azazael, we both know you aren't capable of loving anyone. Not even yourself. You've already lain with her. So why continue the pursuit? You've get what you want from any woman, mortal or immortal! Why can't you just leave her alone?"

"I just told you why!" He yelled. She grabbed him and hit his forehead with the heel of her hand, erasing his recent memory of the woman. She didn't have time for Azazael's temper tantrums. He might pitch them with Father and get away with it but she wasn't Father. A big burst of glory sends him back to his Parisian palace. This woman had God's work to do; she didn't need Azazael after her too.

⁓❧⁓

In the Heavenly War Room, Okinael aka Liberty, along with Freedom, and Justice had temporarily abandoned their physical existences to meet with their celestial counterparts. The twenty seven archangels took seats around the majestic table expanding beyond miles of any human comprehension or measurement. They met to discuss the situation with this woman named Ana BuFaye and Azazael. How his interference was distracting from the war plan.

"There isn't much we can do except erase their memories. She goes to him on her free will. But we all know love is the most powerful force there is." Lucidael, the archangel whom humans call Lady Clarity, said.

"Can't we just kick Nikola's rear end and make him take up his destiny?" Uriel asked around the table larger than many entire universes. But the question was meant moreso for Michael.

"No," Michael said. "We've to respect his free will."

"I hardly call it his free will what drove him to the darkside." Ratziel, the archangel of victory said. "He was forced into this just as they're now trying to force Ana into." Ratziel reminded Michael.

"That's truly the original case." Michael accurately reminded Ratziel. "But he's had ample enough time after the death of Orman or Oregon to return to God. To step down from the position of atrocity. He doesn't want to. He has willingly allied himself with Lucifer because he's angry at God. He feels God betrayed him by allowing his family to be slain and wants nothing further to do with heaven. But we still have Ana who is his equal. He should know better than most what it feels like to be forced against your will. And since she won't leave Azazel alone can't we petition for glory to be taken from her?"

"But for how long?" Mareia, the Lady of Virtues asked. "She's willfully going to Azazael whenever he can't find her. So how long will it be before she settles down with him and he tarnishes her? Turn her away from the Way of the Cross? I agree with Ratziel, perhaps it's best she give up the blade and go to Azazael."

"I'll make sure he doesn't." Michael ensured her. "We do not appoint saints their glory or abilities. Father does and He knows how things will turn out whereas we do not. He knows what He's doing. It's our job to keep order not question his judgment."

"Perhaps they truly love each other." Raphael suggested looking tranquilly around the table for support. His female counterpart Mareia, the Lady of Virtue, scoffed and folded her arms across her chest. "Do you know how many women Azazael has led astray? An entire city in hell is full of his conquests! What makes you think he'll change? Azazael only wants what he can't have. That's his only relentless attraction to this woman." His sister clarified. "I mean change enough to dwell in peace with her. Azazael is stubborn as hell itself!" She said, several archieas nodded in agreement with Mareia. Many once believed the mother of Jesus was named for her.

"How is this one little woman supposed to do what Nikola failed to do? Being so young, deprived, and hunted she's bound to eventually cave in Azazael's demands for the sake of the child?" Chamuel asked plaintively, pointing out Ana's predicament. "If he waves the wealth before her eyes, she might give in to his demands to give her child and mother a better life. I think there's too much at stake to be left in the hands of a woman." Several of the females looked at him in disbelief at what just came out his mouth.

"What?!" Aurora, the daughter of God who presides over the state of Grace asked and reminded her brother it was a woman who brought the Savior into the earthly realm. "That's the most chauvinistic thing I've ever heard you say."

Freedom agreed with her sister regarding Chamuel's chauvinistic remark but argued "She might be able pull it off. She's hard working, a woman of high virtues, kindhearted, and true. A true lover of the Gospel and practices it well, and to the best her situation allows. We need not write her off because of Azazael. We've all seen her fighting ability. She's far stronger and fiercer than she looks. Most would've given up or in to Nikola's demands by now but she hasn't. She has kept on fighting. Correct me if I'm wrong but I think she might be able to truly win Azazael back to our side. Maybe that's what he needs—someone as strong willed as himself. Sure, he accepted redemption but he hasn't practiced it. But if he loves her enough, which I believes he does, he'll follow where she leads him. Look at it this way; his wealth surpasses Lucifer's, but he doesn't care enough to gain any real sustained worldwide influence. He's only after pleasure. But with this woman directing him perhaps he'll care enough to help her do what she's appointed to do." Several nod and agree with Freedom, Raphael seconded it saying that's what he had in mind.

Tzadkiel shakes his deep purple-blackish mane, vetoing the vote, and in disagreement saying. "Have any of you forgotten the woman has a horrible mouth. Her choice of vocabulary is hardly suitable for one designated for such greatest. Her uttered words are as wretched as Azazael's. Hunted or not, she's not fit to wear a halo. She kills whenever cornered. She doesn't try to work things out with the opponents. She doesn't try a gentle approach, she opens fire."

Liberty voiced a sharp rebuttal saying. "I've lived among humans. You haven't. I do not feel you've curtilage to judge them. Had you had Lucifer and Nikola after you without your powers and might you'd be cussing, too. Humans are the cruelest creatures on earth."

Another archangel isn't sure Azazael will give up millions upon millions of eons of doing as he pleases for the love of one woman. In theory, it sounds like a great plan if only the chief character in question wasn't Azazael. Cassiel asked them all have they forgotten who they're talking about? "Do any of you hear yourselves? This is Azazael we're talking about. I say the woman must do her job without him. He'll derail the entire plan. Raphael, you must forget about love for once and deal with the grave principles of the matter. The AntiChrist is soon to come. We need to prepare her and the world for his dreadful arrival." Cassiel said firmly, looking at Michael for confirmation.

"Cassiel, you forgot...one thing." Raphael gently said. "What's that?" Cassiel asked, annoyed.

"That love conquers all."

"Yes, yes, it does. It conquerors everything but Azazael." Cassiel quipped. "Remember, he's so meticulously and willfully spiteful and hardened he didn't shed a tear when Michael clipped his wings. He didn't beg nor ask for mercy when chained to the rock and shut away into darkness. Have you all so soon forgotten he attacked Michael when his world was being destroyed?!" Cassiel shouted, pointing at the Chief Archangel whom they all have to bow to. To clarify his emphasis to those whose ideas opposed his own. "Have you all forgotten how he had to dragged through the streets of Heaven in chains due to his utter, total defiance?! If Father's Love, Patience, and Understanding didn't crack that cold, industrial shell around his heart I seriously doubt a mortal woman's love will crack it. Have you forgotten when he was released the first time he went a rampage of pure fury so insidious he had to be thrown into hell and once there he took over it. Ran it how he saw fit. He made hell out of hell itself! He was horrible...Father had to pull him out. No place is safe with him on the loose. No, I disagree. There's no hope for Azazael. He'll only upset the woman with his philandering to the point of rendering her useless to the cause. Just talking about him upsets me! So I can not imagine living with him."

Michael chuckled a soft laughter that resonated in the heavens. The others looked perplexedly at him. Only Micheala and Gabriel had an idea of why he was laughing. "Raphael, I'm putting you in charge of the position of supervising Azazael but shall I see that he isn't genuine with his feelings toward the woman I'll render them apart forever. Cassiel and others have made grave points. If Love could reach all mortals and immortals alike then there would be no need for hell. Dismissed."

Sunning on a Caribbean private island, location unlisted on conventional maps, Jim Caldwell, the South and mid-Atlantic states head warlock who answers to none other than the world's Grand Wizard summons a servant to bring him a phone. The male servant in vibrant white linen asks whom would he like him to call? "Bjors, the Grand Wizard personal henchman."

The servant dials the number and when Bjors answer, the servant hands the phone to Mr. Caldwell. Caldwell tell the Wizard's puppet he had better clean up his mess and it better not affect Ana Wyett. Bjors replies "Sir, the FBI is looking into the murders. I'll have to go above their heads." Caldwell sighed. He didn't know which were the most murderous, Bjors or Gianna. Vonderbilt raised both as sons.

Stoically, Caldwell says,"I don't give a damn who you've to talk to. Clean up your mess. Didn't you've enough sense not to kill two people affiliated with her in one weekend? I don't want her so traumatized she'll be useless to our purpose. I got a report everyone was swept off the road in their pursuit of her. Things like that mysterious whirlwind happens when she's frightened. The cronies you are working with scared her too badly!"

Bjors gritted his teeth and held his tongue. He hated his uncle placed this redneck over him. "Yes sir." Bjors respectfully replies. But makes a mental note to inform his uncle of the position James Caldwell took with him. Caldwell would pay dearly for taking a superior tone with him. After his last bloodbath his uncle has placed someone over him to supervise his actions. Caldwell, in his vote was a nagging prick. So what if he got a sexual release when a body expired. All killers got something from the act or they wouldn't keep killing.

The new houselady, Eugenia Harris, has waited her entire life for this day. It's hot outside but she's determined to stay out front and patiently wait. The tall, 84 year old woman with a flowing crown of stark white hair and sober but compassionate brown eyes had a secret no one outside her family knew. This wasn't her century. She was of the 21st century.

In the forge of a global spiritual battle to close the foregate of the very darktower of hell itself, which the satanists had somehow managed to open in an audacious attempt to free Lucifer and the princes of hell, she was transported to this time. All Nazarene warriors and warrior saints from all over the world were on the celestial battlefield that fateful night.

But in the heat of the battle she was grabbed and thrown into the 25th century by her regiment leader, Saint Anne. She came through the vortex of time spinning like a top and hit the hot, acerbic streets of Atlanta rolling.

She was bruised and battered but otherwise physically none the worst for the trip. She left behind all she loved. All she knew were long dead. So at 24 she found herself alone in an alien world she didn't know and never really came to like. She had no idea how to travel back to her own time. Had she known she would've left this time slot the moment she arrived. Seeing that they were all going to die, Saint Anne said someone had to live to tell their story, to teach future generations about spiritual warfare. So that their deaths wouldn't be in vain. Their deaths was not in vain for the world lived on under mankind's own idiocy and not that of Lucifer's.

Being the youngest of the regiment of Nazarene warrior saints she always felt her unit had abandoned her. But as she grew older she knew it was an act of love not abandonment. So perhaps when she passes the mantle to this young woman she can go home and be reunited with those she knows and loves. For she was sick of trying to teach the idiots of this generation about spiritual warfare. Everyone acted as thus it was a disease and she was the carrier. No one had enough common sense to see what was happening all over the world. No one could see the forces of evil moving in on the world in a way as never before. Her regiment member numbers of this century were slowly dwindling, so there was less and less of them with every four to five passing years.

Although today's life expectancy is 120-150, the years of a warrior are often cut short. They're the thin glowing line that's the last line of defense should a legion of demons break out of hell. This they had dedicated their lives to. Even the very same idiots who accused them of much horror are still protected by their work. So of course, demons want them all dead. There would no longer be a defense in any nation against them. Every nation that has killed off all of theirs' is presently up the creek without a canoe, let alone a paddle.

Silver bullets, salt, mojos, crosses, or none of the crap taught and believed can truly stop a demon or evil spirit. And she thought people believed any and every thing the darkside said in her original century but the imbeciles of this latter day got them beat by two long country miles! All you've to do is make something sound scientific or technical and they believe it with no questions. Demons and immortals can shrewdly manipulate both; science and technology, but it's impossible to get the birdbrains of this day and age to see that and she's long tired of trying to explain this to a bunch of idiots. These are the kind of people her mother and grandmother used to call educated fools.

People live in a false sense of security, they walk in total oblivion with their holograph phones, watches, televisions, and many other types of screens floating in the air ahead of them as they yap totally unaware they're talking to an evil spirit that has cleverly infiltrated the system. She has felt the urge many a times to grab them by the back of the neck, shake them, rough them up, and force them to look carefully at who they believe they are talking to. Often the evil spirit, recognizing her for what and who she is, will wink and grin at her.

The gulf separating mankind from hell is so thin now that plenty of days she has looked right over into hell shall she care to do so that particular day. But St. Anne told her this was a job of no respect; it comes with no earthly rewards nor appreciation, even those whom you protect often tries to kill you.

From her bullet-proof plexiglass walled in front porch she sees the midsize silvery-blue, chrome trimmed car towing a small trailer make a right onto her street. Her heart leapt with joy. Her successor had finally been born and grown old enough to take this tedious burden off her hands. She was long tired and had been ready to meet the Maker. All the houses on her block were at least nearly 500 years old. With loving tenderness and continuous care they were kept habitable and weren't dilapidated like many throughout the city. The overgrown elm trees gave the neighborhood a tranquility that made many happy to call this place home.

The bright bluish silver car pulled into the narrow concrete driveway that Eugenia Harris took extra care of to keep the weeds out the cracks. She saw the child; the woman asked about did she accept children. So many renter nowadays do not accept children. It's said their destruction equals that of pets. The beautiful child waves at her from the back seat. Smiling, she returned the greeting and patiently watched them disembark from the car. She's completely floored. The driver bore a striking, uncanny resemblance to Saint Ann. She was so stunned she grabbed the door frame to maintain her balance. Ana rushed to the steps and grabbed her elbow asking was she alright? "Yes, sugar, Mother is fine. Just this heat got the best of me." Eugenia lied, looking closer at the young woman. She felt the surge of power when the young woman named Ana BuFaye touched her arm. She sees the differences in them now that the woman is in front of her but still...they look alike. Saint Ann had blackish, sandy hair whereas this young woman has dark auburn hair extending all the way down to her knees. Reminded her of a black Rapunzel. She also sensed a different temperament between the two; St. Anne was meek and mild, but this girl didn't strike her as meek and humble. She was just her kind of girl.

Eugenia suggests they leave the car packed until it cools off and invites them inside out of the scorching heat. She hopes she makes them very welcome. She showed them their room and even offered the adjourning room to Fannie for free so she wouldn't have to crowd in bed with Ana and Bea. But Fannie politely declines. She knows it is best to let the woman rent the room to someone else for a profit rather than she take it for free.

Mother Harris, as the woman wanted to be called, had prepared a feast of a meal for the three guests (now boarders) and hopes they're hungry. She's glad they aren't shy about eating. After a hearty midday dinner she and Fannie sit on the porch while she calls a neighbor's son to come help Ana unload the car and put the trailer in the backyard's shed.

The day had been a harrying, supernatural one so by nine Bea was already bathed and put to bed. Shortly afterward, Ana joins her. Fannie comes in an hour or so later.

While lying in bed utterly exhausted, floating between the worlds of awake and asleep, Ana believes she hears someone singing. Cooing to her in the spiritual realm.

She hears a man with the most beautiful voice singing a smooth, mellifluous but yet so very sexy melody. "My eternal love, you thrill me. Yes, you do, yes you do! Darling, I love you. Oh! Yes, I do--yes, I do. My daring, I've given my immortal heart to you and pray we never part." She's partially awake, listening for the rest of the love song.

"Damn! That guy can sing! Even if the lyrics are corny" she giggles and thinks to herself while lying in bed exhausted, with Bea kicking her in the back. As she drifts, again into REM she believes she hears him again, singing. Cooing to her from a spiritual realm. She hears a man with the most beauteous voice singing a silken, mellisonant but yet ultra sexy melody. She perks up, she's positive she hears someone serenading her. "My eternal love, you thrill me. Yes, you do, yes you do! Darling, I love you. Oh! Yes, I do--yes, I do. I've given my immortal heart to you and pray we never part." She's now wide awake, listening to the rest of the love ballad. "Damn! That guy can sing!" She thinks to herself, "And here I'm can't carry a tune if came with a bucket and handle!"

The singing relaxes her and she soon falls asleep, but not for more than a few hours. Their first night in their new boarding room Ana hears ponderous footsteps in the hallway leading to their room. It sound as if the owner of the weighty tread is dragging something heavy and metallic across the hardwood floor. Or walking on hooves was more like it! Rising up from the bed shared with her mom and daughter she goes to investigate but sees no one. It feels as if someone is standing right in front of her. She calms her nerves and says an intense prayer, "*Father, give me the sight to see what's standing here*". Opening her spiritual eyes, she finds herself standing face to face with a red, dappled demon seemingly with fire bubbling beneath his crimson, mottled skin. The black cavities in its face houses what appear to be wriggling worms on fire. She gasped, swallowed hard, and stepped back. She was too scared to scream. It grins and steps forward, saying in a raspy, diabolical, hissing voice "You really thought you could get away from us by merely moving. We and our servants are everywhere!"

Suddenly Mrs. Harris, the new landlady, materialized in the hallway saying in a loud, clear commanding voice "I compel you in the Name of Christ to leave this young lady alone! To quit her presence this instant! To leave this house!" The demon vaporized in the air leaving behind a stench of sulfurous odor.

I must have looked rather foolish standing there gaping at Mother Harris for I certainly felt foolish. I've never seen anyone good able to do that. To appear out the thin air. All I seen able to do that were those on the darkside.

Mrs. Harris disregards the staring, invited Ana into the kitchen, put on an old fashioned coffee pot, and tells her to sit down. As Ana's knees were barely holding her up, she gladly sits. Turning to Ana she says "Dear, it's no mere coincidence you found me out of the hundreds of boarding rooms in this city. You saw me in a prophetic dream just as I was watching you in the same dream. I was appointed to teach you how to fight, spiritually. If you do not learn how to fight back the unseen they'll eventually kill all of you, including your mom and child. They want you alive is perhaps how you've evaded them for this long. Eventually, they're going to force you to make a choice and if you choose God's side they're going to kill you. I know you've experienced catastrophic physical phenomenons all your life and have wondered why. You're like me--a warrior saint of the Nazarene, a born enemy of the dark forces. Our kind are said not to exist but here we are. I see you know nothing of either who or what you are".

Shakily, Ana says "I don't know who you really are but you are much more than a kindly old lady."

Half chuckling to herself while pouring coffee in two mugs with hands as steady as the Rock of Gibraltar, asking if she preferred sugar or cream or both, Eugenia Harris says "Well perceived, young lady. But I just told you what we both are. Your spiritual eyes are keener than you think. You just never had anyone to teach you how to use them."

Ana replies "I'd prefer both. But please, tell me more about these warrior saints."

Handing Ana the streaming cup of coffee, Mrs Harris smiles and says, "I'm the same as you dear but my end days are drawing neigh, so it's time to pass on the mantle to the younger generation. First thing in the morning, I've a friend who is a priest I'd like you to meet. He can educate you in the ways of a warrior saint. You see... you've it within you, the ability to fight the unseen but you must learn how to access it. But for now...get some sleep. You look exhausted."

The new friends bid each other good night again.

❦

I wasn't thrilled about seeing another priest for anything. But I didn't tell Mother Harris that. I didn't want to offend her our first night in her house.

"What's wrong?" Fannie asked, sitting up on her side of the bed. "Nothing, Mom" I lied, looking at Breanna stretched out, legs and arms as far as her short limbs permitted, I smiled and rub the little feet that were earlier pitched in center of my back. Watching my toddler sleep, maternal protectiveness swells in my chest. I wonder how will I protect her from things I can't see. There's much I do not understand. They've plagued me and made attempts to kill me all my life. Perhaps now I can get some answers.

Seeing that mom wasn't going to let the issue go and that she knew I lied, I sighed heavily. "Mom, they've found us. I mean the big dogs. A scarred faced demon was walking the hallway." Fannie nods with a constricted facial expression realizing her Intuition was true. They want Ana for satanic reasons. Exactly what kind? She doesn't know. Turning to face her mother, Ana says, "I don't know what our new landlady is but she knew we were coming and said she's the same as myself. Mom, whatever am I?"

Fannie reaches across the bed and firmly grabs her daughter's hand. "Look at me. You're my beloved daughter. Yes, you've always been different. But being different isn't a bad thing. Nothing you've done created all the havoc in your life. I don't understand it all either but I do know God has been with you your entire life. Angels never stopped visiting you as they do most children after a certain age. How many people can say they're still visited by angels and can see them? So apparently God has something special for you to do." Fannie paused a few minutes. "Yes, I saw Emily was like you the moment I looked into her eyes."

"Her name is Eugenia." Ana chuckled at her mom's forgetting the lady's name so soon. It bothered her is why she tried to laugh it off. She wondered if all the stress was making her mother sick again.

"Well, whatever!" Fannie said, turning over to face the window to go back to sleep. "Whatever her name is I knew she was like you. I could feel it."

Ana was feeling safer than she had perceived in many months, she finally drifted off to sleep. Little did she know she had more than one wealthy, herculean pursuer. While she slumbered, Ashton Cargill paid Bleeker, her former boss, a visit. He had just left the house where Ana was now living but was unable to get through the prayer barrier Fannie prayed up. He had found her by following the kid's spiritual trail. He couldn't remember much else about the woman other than she had a kid. He walked back in the little's girl time line and found her boss.

The place where she lived in Augusta he could at least enter but this warrior saint's home was an absolute fortress. Perforating into Carlton Bleeker's upscale, upper-middle class home at such iniquitous hour, demanding the man to get up, was easy.

Bleeker was already troubled and uneasy about the minacious broadcast announcing his manager's death; he was on the edge and an early morning intruder wasn't bringing any of the much needed peace. He flinched when the police told him Alana Owego aka Ana BuFaye aka Ana Wyett was a killer. Ashton Cargill cared nothing for his discomfort; he slaps his sleeping face with the documents showing he is now the owner of Bleeker's bank, telling him to rehire Ana Wyett.

Bleeker mulls over how the man got pass the gated security and asks couldn't this wait until Monday morning? He sat up, fully awake, and reached behind himself to try to protect his wife who is peeking from under the covers' edge at the tall, muscular man, wondering if he's who killed Sarah Stevenson and have now come to kill them? The man has the meanest eyes she has ever seen. They're filled with awfulness. "If she's not back on the job by Tuesday don't bother going to work. You're fired!" Cargill said, teleporting out. The couple swoons from fear. The past two days finally took their toll.

Cargill suspected the firing was some more of Nikolai's fatuous mind at work for the things happening with Ana *aren't idiosyncratic.* So he calculates if he can get her back at the bank he'll have access to her. In order to find out exactly which morons were calling around about Ana, he sets up several decoy phones with false numbers. Knowing they wouldn't be unable to resist bad-mouthing her, he intends to kill whomever calls to silence them forever.

Using her alias Alana Owego. he enters into the national data base a bogus place of employment. Sits and waits and within ten minutes the fake job phone number rings. He answers as a potential employer. It was a man who worked for Bjors Machiavelli.

"What can I do for you?" Ashton asked, so ever charming.

"Sir, I don't think you want Alana Owego aka Ana BuFaye/Ana Wyett working for you. She's a scandalous woman, the lowest of the human race. She's a no good woman. A killer, a streetwalker of the lowest kind. She even prostitutes her child. No reputable employer such as yourself could allow her to grace your company's door. Eventually she will steal from you..."

Holding his temper in check to give himself a chance to latch onto the person's location, he says, "Sir, she only works in files. There's no money in the file room."

The man eagerly but angrily continues, saying "It doesn't matter. You don't understand how shrewd she is. She lies about everything. She'll find a way to worm her way into your company's bank account. There are trails of businesses she've left bankrupted. So to save yourself the heartache. Fire her now."

"Oh really?" Ashton asked but not from the phone. Hearing the speaker behind him the man freezes and slowly turns around. He knows he's looking death in the face. His Adam's apple moves a tab and his hands grow sweaty and clammy.

"Oh, do tell. Tell me more about this "evil, no-good woman. I love evil, no-good women, they really light my fire." Azazel said bemusedly as he scans for whom else this man is connected to. His scan lands on the grand wizard. Just as he suspected, Nikola aka Vonderbilt was behind all this. He quickly and brutally reached out and twisted the caller's head backwards, for a few seconds is the first and last time the man has ever seen his own back while his body faced forward without the aid of a mirror. Azazael knows every inch of human anatomy so he knows that humans live a few seconds after this diabolic trick which is why he performed it. The body flopped backward but face down on the tattered wooden desk.

Ashton Cargill finds himself back at the Parisian palace. But this time he knows he has been somewhere else again, doing something evil. So he made the harem members tell him what he didn't remember about his last departure immediately upon being supernaturally transported back home, much to Dawn's dismay. She was getting a wee bit tired of this imaginary woman. Sure, he has always chased women but this situation was begin to sound a little loony. She knew of his past to a degree. She also knew of his past suffering. But this was more than that. He was becoming obsessed with this woman. She has to find a way to end this craziness once and for all or he'll find himself desultory and take them down the drain with him. No one person is worth so much destruction and agony.

He was so angry no could tell him anything useful or wouldn't tell him. Losing his temper, he bellowed in a mighty rage and boxed the air sending claps of thunder and bolts of lighting throughout the house. Why won't they leave them alone? He had been hard at work, trying to remember almost immediately after his memory was erased. He felt with every step forward in learning who this woman is the heavens were pushing him two steps backwards.

Having returned to her master bedroom nearly expanding the entire length of the early 20th century house, Eugenia Harris knew the true paradigm is her successor isn't ready to take on the mantle and lead. The young woman knew virtually nothing about spirituality nor spiritual warfare. The mother, Fantasia, knows a little by trial and err. But in this agenda there's no margin for error. This girl didn't have a mentor like St. Anne as she had in her early life. She doesn't have a protector like St. Gerald or someone acting as a big sister, like St. Cheryl. She's footing this alone and afraid. It's little wonder she was even still alive, let alone in her right mind.

In the rental space in the back of Eugenia Harris' home Ana lay awake tumbling over in her mind their last night in Augusta. After packing and waiting for Charles to bring her car back she went into the park across the road after Bea fell asleep. Sitting, worrying and trying to find her way through all this. *"It looks as if things are turning out for the best in leaving Augusta"*, she drowsily thinks before sleep took her into its arms.

While Ashton was away from his Parisian Palace, the hottest international star in Hollywood named Caroline Caldwell called. The wife of legendary producer and film industry investor James Caldwell, one of the more prominent and sought after investors in the industry. If you had the name Caldwell on your movie chip, it was destined to be a blockbuster. Dawn Shepherd had been trying to get this woman's attention for years but Caroline, her idol, always shunned her unless she was standing right beside Ashton at a gala or social gathering and everyone wants to talk to Ashton Cargill. Therefore she had to talk to Dawn or Cargill would've frowned upon her ignoring his primary playmate. No one in the business world wanted to alienate Ashton Cargill. As easily as he made you it was equally easy or easier to break you.

"Listen up." Caroline Caldwell said with a great air of urgency and supremacy the moment Dawn answered the phone. "You Cargills' women had better keep Cargill away from a woman named Ana Wyett. He has been out on the scene chasing her and asking a lot of questions. I heard he even killed a few people. If he gets her...you all can kiss your posh little lifestyles good-bye."

Dawn's stomach tightened. So this Ana woman was real. Still in the picture. Not a figuration of his mind! She thought after the Honey LaSalle murder the woman would actually have had sense enough to disappear and Ashton was merely imagining things. She laughed and asked what did the woman look like? It can't be the same woman. Caroline forwarded a picture. Dawn sucked air through her perfect pearly whites and shows it to the others. "This is our competition?" Dawn laughed at the matronly dressed woman in a white blouse and black skirt. But those who had seen Honey's pictures of the woman all exchange a rattling, knowing glance. She wasn't gone. This is who Ashton was with when gone for weeks.

"OHHhh! Ppplease!" Another harem member cried, passing the photo around to the others "He's only chasing her for sex. She probably has her legs so clamped tight, it'd take a crowbar to pry them open them. But once he taps that he'll drop her like he has all the rest. Remember the woman who used to work in the NYC office who overdosed and damn near died because he broke it off with her. This is the same thing. Remember how he chased her until he got her. The thrill of chasing her will be vaporized the moment she sighs from the pleasure he's delivering. She's too homely and naive to be a threat to us."

"You think that one was a nut, what about the one who ran down stairs stark naked and chased him and he disappeared." Rashid laughed. "All the news showed was her standing there in the streets pissing herself. He was gone."

"Oh, oh, you all forgot the one who threw herself on the limo's windshield that night was we were at the annual gala hollering she loved him."

A belligerent chorus of snarkiness and giggles echos in the grand palace as the image of Ana BuFaye Wyett on Dawn's ISPAN Pad is passed throughout the group. All giggled and laughed at dark auburn haired, unadorned woman with no sense of fashion. "Comb all that wild weave over her plain face and she'll be a skinny, no tits cousin It!" another said, and all burst out laughing. Some wanted to comment on her dark complexion. But saw no room for that. Several of the harem members were dark. Ashton Cargill doesn't seem to be bonded by man's standard of beauty. He wasn't for he had seen man's standard of what beauty is change millions of times.

Exhibiting an air of preponderancy, Caroline Caldwell prejudged the women as preliterate whores. "Laugh all you like but you all need to take this seriously. You all need to devise a plan to keep him away from her. She's the type men like Cargill marry to give them heirs." Caroline ominously warns. "If she gets his full attention you all will be out on your asses."

98

Dawn snorts and reminds the persnickety Caroline Caldwell she has been with Ashton Cargill over 20 years. "Yeah, but has he married you yet?" Caroline shot back. "From the look of things---from what I heard about him you're about the age he trades his women in for a newer model."

The harem decides they don't like this bearer of bad news and click the screen off. But Dawn isn't so sure they've nothing to worry about. She has never seen him so hyped about a woman. She recalled his snipping at her the other day when she told him it was all just a dream, he was merely putting together bits of his lost memory. Now she isn't so sure anymore.

Deciding the only way to ensure her security is to kill the skinny granny dressing woman before she get her bony claws in his heart, she decided to ask Caroline back and ask does she know where this woman is?

Seeing the mean desperation in Dawn's eyes, Caroline knows what it means. "No, I don't. I want her dead as much as you. I'm not permitted to kill her but there's nothing standing between you and her life." Caroline encourages.

Lightly nipping on Foie gras Dawn courts the idea while musing, *"Why not send Cargill Security to do away with the annoying pest of a woman who threatens my security and chances of becoming Mrs. Ashton Cargill?"*

Without a verbal reply Caroline encourages "*Yeah, you do that!*" with eyes that gleam with anticipation at the idea of the nuisance disappearing. Not only does she threaten Dawn and the harem's security, she threatens hers, too. James thinks she doesn't know he's secretly in love with the woman. That she doesn't know he fell for her the few months he lived beside her in that puny little house. While she lived in her lovely small mansion. He thinks she doesn't know he gave her a very expensive bracelet the night he was supposed to do nothing more than screw her and gain her trust. Men are so easily duped. Can't they all see the look of wide-eyed innocence is a facade? Wyett, Vonderbilt, James, and Cargill, the whole lot of them have all stupidly fallen for it. Like a year ago when four warlocks showed on their doorsteps telling James what she had done to two of them. He wasn't worried about the dead men, he was more concerned with what Cargill might do to her for killing his whores. And Vonderbilt thought it was hilarious she killed so many in such a short interval. She could start World War IV and these idiots would still think it's cute.

Dawn summons Sewell to the Parisian palace. He has been the head chief of Cargill's security for over a century. The quarter of a demigod doesn't like her any more than she likes him. But she apparently means something to his boss so he pretends. He wishes she would put some decent clothing on. He stares at the wall above her head.

"I want you to find this woman and kill her." Dawn said, showing him the image Caroline Caldwell sent. It gave him much pleasure to say without retribution from his boss. "Sorry, Ms. Shepherd. I can't do that. She means more to him than ten of you" he respectfully said as they both watched the image fade into the abyss of wherever things spiritually erased go.

✷✷✷✷✷

Meanwhile, Ashton Cargill is standing in the spiritual realm closet to earth watching Eugenia Harris' house. He was able to track Ana through Bea. He saw the demon Mammon sent to punish the woman for destroying a healthy lot of his father's worshipers. He saw the red demon of rage fleeing the warrior saint's home. He reached out and placed it in a headlock, igniting its head in his arms, burning it to ashes. He couldn't see beyond the prayer barrier of the house but he could see the general area. He hoped she'd come outside the barrier as he watched daylight shimmer in the sky.

In the early dawn's light he saw a glowing figure walking toward him. He knew from the spiritual imprint it was the Archangel Raphael. "Azazael, do not torture yourself. She belongs to the heavens." Raphael said, standing beside his younger brother watching the house. Turning with an ornery facial expression to question his brother (for he believes his older brother knows the truth) Azazael asks, "When are you all going to stop bullshitting me and tell me who is she to me? Why she weighs so heavily on my psyche? Who is she really? I've searched my memory of exes and she isn't among them. Not even a one-night stand. I may not remember the woman's face or name but if I'm confronted

100

with her spiritual imprint, I remember our encounter. Things are murky with this woman. Hell isn't strong enough to block me; that's how I know it's coming from heaven. Inside, I feel I know her very well and then again, I don't know her at all. Tell Father and Michael to quit messing with my head. I need to know who exactly is she?!"

Raphael observes Azazael's unconscious unawareness that he's leaning against her car and the spirits incarnated into it have been instructed to attack those who threaten her and they haven't shocked him, at least not yet. This is a very interesting development here. So perhaps there's a slim chance for Azazael after all. "Azazael, you'll learn in the appointed time who she is." Raphael said disappearing, taking Azazael with him. And in the process erasing his memory of how to find her again. But he doesn't kid himself, he knows that if Azazael truly loves her he'll break through the memory block again and again. He, of all the archangels, knows the true, full power of love.

A little over a year ago

They traveled along the back roads of Indiana headed for the Kansas state line. She vowed she wasn't stopping in Missouri. The rain kept coming, as she looked ahead at the long strips of lonely road. She listened as the windshield wiper as they kept a steady whoosh of shrieking across the glass panel. The rainy night was no excuse for stopping although she was rawboned tired almost to the point of delirium. They had to put as much distance between themselves and the body she buried eight hours ago as possible. She knew she was taking a risk by keep driving at such a late hour but there was a greater risk should she get stopped and they caught.

Months ago we arrived in Richmond, Va. We never knew what to expect when we entered a city or town. Reading help wanted ads I learned early on was useless. They're mostly looking for local residents. I didn't chose to be a nonlocal. Someone else was always making the choice for me. But first I'd to find a cheap, affordable motel. Motels were better in case we suddenly had to run.

Canvassing the city establishment by establishment, by late that afternoon I'd found a job at an all night club-strip joint as a waitress. The owner at first balked at Bea being there by they served alcohol and had nude dancers, but I promised to keep her out of the customer's sight. I gave her my ISPAN pad to play with. It had basic reading and games on it. Nothing grandeur. I was glad this place didn't have a body type requirement as so many did. I didn't like the short skirt of the uniform but I guess that was to generate male customers which most of the patrons were. A few lesbians visited throughout the night. But they mostly came as couples and didn't stay long nor cause any problems. The first couple of days were normal, I had no problems out of any customers. But by the third day, a man who had been there that morning before I arrived (for I worked the night-shift) left a garnishment for me, to garnish my wages.

My boss showed it to me as I was situating Bea for the night in his office. Garnishing what? I haven't had credit in years! All the credit cards Thad and I had were paid out when the second mortgage loan was taken out on the house! So who is this fucker? How can he do this when I hadn't made anything yet! Except about ninety bucks in tips. I remembered the credit card I'd had with that company but I paid it off over three years ago. Their customer service was so rude I was glad to be rid of them. But the legal proceeding in my hand said the bill wasn't paid. I knew that was a lie. My boss told me if I showed him proof it was paid he wouldn't deduct anything from my paycheck. Great! This is just fucking great. Now I'm broke and sued. What a good work night this will be!

The next day I spent half of the day and the first half of the night upon returning to our room looking through our belongings for the receipt the bank sent me after the bill was paid. I had to go into bags I normally didn't take out the car. I found it just as the sun was midway in the sky, meaning it was noon. I was pissed off for I spent most of the night outside rambling through the trunk of the car, lugging in crap I normally didn't unload when I could've been inside sleeping. Today I was supposed to work the 3-11 shift. I needed my rest. This crap wasn't necessary and that bank knew it. I went inside to get some sleep for I had about an hour to rest before I had to get up and feed Bea again and just as I had crawled in bed and closed my eyes, I heard the room door open.

That's the thing about extremely cheap places; they invest nil in security. There was no chain to slide in a slot for extra security. I didn't know the man but apparently he thought I was asleep. He quietly pushed the door opened further and tiptoed to the dresser where the v-chip screen sat. I had a pistol under the cover, looking at his back through slanted eyes. I knew exactly who he was- the crook who obtained that absentee judgment. He had watched me all night digging in the car for the receipt and the thought that he was close enough to see that I found it sent a chill down my spine. If he was close enough to see what I found then he was close enough to hurt us.

The man carefully slid the next drawer open, and having seen nothing he turned to the night stand. That's when he looked into the barrel of my antique Colt 45. He slowly raised his hands and backed away as he gave me a crooked smile to match his demeanor. "Throw me your wallet or I swear I'll blow your brains to the ceiling." I snarled at him.

He cocked his head to the side and looked me boldly in the eyes, "Mrs. Wyett, it would be a lot easier to just pay your bills," he said, being a smart aleck, apparently not believing I meant to kill him. I was thinking of how to get the body of this long tall fucker out without detection. According to a card in his wallet, which I handed to Bea who was now awake and pointing her peashooter at him, he was a lawyer for a local collection agency. How in the hell had they found me so quickly? I put my jacket on and stuck another gun from under my pillow in the left pocket and told him if he valued his life he would do exactly as I say because if he ran or shouted I was surely going to blow a hole in him. I don't know what he saw in my eyes but whatever it was, it must have told him I wasn't bullshitting.

I made him take the passenger seat and kept my gun trained on him. I was pissed off like kings because I was still tired from the long drive from Arkansas. This was stopping today. They had already taken over two grand through garnishments two years ago. The last three jobs I had they found me and those bosses refused to tell me who they had given my paycheck to, I only got a lot of attitude when I asked. One told me if I paid my bills I wouldn't have to ask that question. I kicked him so hard in the sac my foot was aching and took the money from the cash register and hauled ass. We barely got out of Tuscon, Az. I drove like hell heading east. They thought I would immediately head for California but I waited them out in the dessert under the shade of a mountain and then headed back west. The further west one goes the less back roads there are. So I drove the car in between two mesas and waited in a shallow cave which was hot as the inferno during the day. I sat the portable fan in front Bea under damp motel towels which I constantly had to redampen with bottled water. At least we had three grand to survive on until I found another job.

"You're really a warlock, aren't you?" I asked as I headed out of town, back the way we came in three days ago. He laughed as if it was the most comical thing he ever heard. I knew then that he was. Only those truly in the occult ridicule the accusation so abstrusely. They always makes it sounds as thus you're totally nuts and a retard to boot for having the audacity to ask such a question. His caustic attitude told me all I needed to know. When I finally saw the road I was looking for about fifty miles out of Richmond I pulled off onto it and drove deep in the sparse pine thickets and made him got out.

"Ana, you can't be serious!" he said, giving me a cocky smile. "We both know you don't have the guts."

"You've made me serious and oh, have given me the guts." I said, shooting him in his upraised left hand. Walking upon him I said. "Motherfucker, for bullshitting reasons you've made my life living hell---moreso than it already is!" I screamed, shooting him in the right thigh.

"Please lady!" He went down to the ground on his good leg, begging and moaning. "I was only doing my job. I've a family to feed just like you."

"Oh please!" I cried rolling my eyes in a full arch. "You didn't give a fuck about what you took from me. That you what took caused my baby to have sleep in a cold car!" I yelled and shot off his right thumb. He howled this time in excruciating pain. So what?! By now I crazy with rage and I was pissed beyond caring and frankly didn't give a shit.

"I've kids." He whimpered, clutching his bleeding hands together between his thighs. "Shut the fuck up! My dad had kids, I was one of them but he didn't go around doing weirdo things to people. You heartless bastard! You don't give a fuck about my kid! Do ya?! So why in the fuck should I care about your ugly ass kids?" The next shot went into his right knee. I watched him thrash around for a while before kicking him, telling him

104

to be still. "Shut up and give me the code to your bankcard and I might let you live. Fuck me over and I swear on your ugly momma I'll come back out here and kill you!"

"Dear Lady" He panted, clutching his most painful bleeding parts. "...what turned you into such a monster?" He asked as he laid on the ground weeping.

"Sons of bitches like you're who turned me into this!" I sneered at him and shot him in the left foot for good measure. I cussed myself for making such a mess. He was bleeding all over the ground. Bea wrote down the code on my ISPAN pad as he rattled it off between gasps of pain as sweat poured down his face. I searched him for communication devices. I had one bullet left; my safety reasoning was telling me to put him out of his misery if I learned he hadn't lied about the code. But when Bea entered it his finances came up showing twenty eight grand, I told her to have a cash card send to the local supermarket under the name of Sarah Brighton, one of my aliases. Since I could easily use a cashcard that had less than $5,000, the supermarket presented no problem. The remainder would have to be put on a separate checkcard under a different name.

Now believing I intended to kill him he stopped pleading and started taunting. "You're a pisspoor excuse for a warrior saint. Your kind is supposed to be noble, gallant, compassionate, and brave but here you're swimming around in places I normally wouldn't set foot. Dragging your kid around with you. That's mighty selfish of you. Why don't you give her to you sister? What do you think she's going to turn out to be? Huh? Like the girls who dances on the poles, bitch!" He grinned through bloody teeth.

"Bea, get the rope out the car, a swift death is too good for this scum-filled bastard." I heard Bea moving objects in the trunk and a few minutes later she brought me the fresh hemp fiber clothesline I picked up in a hardware store in Vermont. The nylon kind picks up finger and palm prints. Although we had none I was still being careful. I bought several just for special occasions like this. I tied him to a resinous pine tree. I knew there was pine ants that bites the shit out of you on these trees. "Baby, go bring mommy face cloth and some tape." I said for I knew his mouth still worked.

"No, no I promise I'll be quiet." He was pleading again. I was pissed off because this was the fourth time he or someone like him attempted to take money from me and my filing status didn't allow bankruptcy. Nowadays, if you can't show proof of income you can't file bankruptcy. Not that it would've done any good. I knew this was no normal collection agency. This was a harassment agency and they kill.

"Hey Ana, there're ants on this tree. They're biting me!" He grimaced in the mid afternoon sun. "I promise you can have the money, I won't tell a soul." I smiled close up in the dark-sandy blonde haired man's face. I guess I must had looked pretty deranged. He recoiled from me and begun talking to Bea over my shoulder. "Lady, you're crazy. They told me you were meek as a lamb." He said wide-eyed, profoundly perspiring in the 91 degrees southern sun. "I know. But some lambs grow up to be rams." I grinned back at him searching his pockets again for keys. I knew he had to have them. I intended to ditch his car too.

Beseeching Bea he said. "Kid, you're sane, but your mother is not. Help me out here. I was only trying to do my job, talk to your mother. She's so far gone she doesn't even know lambs don't grow up to be rams. She doesn't know right from wrong anymore and in the eyes of the Lord, this is wrong." He looked frantically over my shoulder at three year old Bea. I slapped his face away from her direction.

"Suck SHIT and die!" Bea yelled at him and shot him in the left shoulder. I jumped back as blood splattered my jeans, for that shot came pretty close to me. "Gimme that gun! Go sit in the car!" I said taking the gun from Bea and resuming tying the last of the knots wondering where did I get the bright idea to give a three year old a Saturday night special? Suppose she had a tantrum one day because I said no about a candy bar and shot me with it? Oh well, that's just a chance I'll have to keep on taking. I can't leave her defenseless when I'm not around. Where did Bea learn such filthy words?

With his keys and bank card we drove back in town leaving him to die against that tree. I felt he would bleed out before the sunset.

Driving back in town at around 3:42, a little over two hours before I had to report to work for the 6-12 shift if I decided to go in. That depended on how much we got from the bank. The stout, stomping woman at the bank whom I asked politely to cash my checkcard (well his checkcard) walked to the counter and took my information. She kept looking suspiciously at me and the ID I presented. ATMs didn't dispense this large amount so I had to go inside to cash it. "That picture was taken in better days." I said as she scrutinized the photo and later asked for a DNA sample. I wondered why she had to pull up my credit report to cash a check card made out to me. The office was closed in, with no windows to the outside world and no visibility from outside. I knew she would find nothing under that alias so I threw my jacket over the camera and quickly walked around the desk and told her in a low drawl I knew she had figured out I was an obscurantist and was getting ready to alert the authorities. "I don't know what you're looking for but if your fat ass don't want to end up tied to a tree with the ants gnawing on you, it would be wise to just cash the damn thing and mind your own damn business." Having worked in three banks before I knew where the panic button was.

"Touch that button or scream, I swear as surely as there's a God in heaven I'll kill you. I'm tired of people like you and your shit. He wrote the check to me and his reason is none of your damn business." I was a wee bit tired of telling people 'I'm going to kill you'. That wasn't who I am.

"Ms. Dawson, there's nothing in your record. You've no accounts. It's as if you doesn't exist" The bank manager stammered. But nonetheless did as told. "Look bitch, if you want to go home to those little fat, dough-faced kids in this picture here this evening, you should stay the fuck out of my business. Just cash the damn thing and let's part friends. I'm not the one to make an enemy of." The terrified woman nods and opens the office safe and counts out the cash. I stuffed it in my plastic shopping tote. I pick my jacket off the camera and pat her face on the way out. "The less you know the better. Take my word for it. It ain't worth dying for."

Bea and I walked out perfectly calm. I knew the woman was going to call the cops so I called back to her office on the way to the supermarket, saying "I'm at your children' school with my gun trained on them. Call the cops I'll shoot all three of them and be out of town before they hit the ground." She gasped. My assumption was correct. She was waiting for the cops to arrive. But I had no idea where her kids went to school and definitely had no intention of killing innocent children but she didn't know that. She knew I had her address; I told Bea to write it down after I pulled her purse from the desk drawer.

When we hit the supermarket I told Bea to hit the button to send the other portion to "Sarah". The tattooed, gum snapping teenage girl at the customer service counter didn't give a damn what I was doing or why just so long as I got out of her face.

Once in the car we removed the wigs and other disguises and headed back to our room to make things look normal. When we returned to the motel to look for the collector's car I pressed the button on the keys to see which car beeped. An older land bound Ford signaled in the deserted parking lot. I opened the door for Bea; I remember passing a lake coming into this town. While riding out I pulled down the sun-visor and saw a picture of a family of four taped to it, smiling at me. I refused to let the normal pang of guilt grip my heart, "*No one cared about my family so why in the hell could I care about anyone else's.*" I think as I drove out to the lake. I put Bea out before I pulled up to the bank of the water, released the brakes, and let it roll into the lake. I made sure I took everything of value out before sinking it.

I walked about a mile to the highway with Bea piggybacking me, eventually a woman came along and gave us a ride. I noticed she had an odd tattoo on her left wrist. I had seen it before. It was an early Christian symbol. We rode in silence. The turns she was taking told me she knew exactly where we were living. "Who are you?" I asked wondering where are all these people when I need them? Without looking at me she said. "We're nearly three thousand years old. We formed an alliance to protect those we once killed. We once killed your kind. Did you know St. Peter actually soared over what is now St. Peter's Square? I mean levitated and flew through the air?"

"Why give me a ride? If you once killed my kind..." I asked to alleviate the tenseness of our situation. The woman must had sensed that I was uneasy around her and knew that when I'm uneasy bullets start flying. The dark brown haired woman finally looked over at me for I was slowly reaching for my other gun in my left pocket. "The Lord whipped our founder into submission." She replied. "Neither of them will be calling the police or anyone else for that matter." She let us out, recommending a safer hotel. With Trusty already packed we headed to the a place called the Yellow Abode. It was much nicer and had an inside security lock which we controlled.

Intuition told me to get out of town that night but police cars kept riding up and down the roads blaring sirens as well as flying overhead. I knew they were looking for anyone who looked suspicious. I went to work that night but only worked three hours. I knew things look would shady if I didn't. I knew it was best to turn up at work when the town was crawling with cops. Around 11:00 some cops came in the club but I kept my eyes off them and served drinks as if I was a normal waitress. I showed my boss the receipt showing "paid in full." He was satisfied.

The next morning while the local news talked about two murders. I looked out our new motel window, across the streets and saw a Talmart brightly lit by the rising sun. "A local, well known attorney was found tied to a tree approximately five miles outside of town." The plasma screen broadcast in the background as they flashed images from the scumbag's life. I wasn't paying much attention. I was plotting how to get the hell out of here. As we headed for the door, I heard the reporter say, "...And in a surprising twist, a local bank manager was found dead in her office. At this time authorities are not releasing the victim's name and have no leads to the killer's or killers' whereabouts but advise the public to be cautious and be on the lookout for any suspicious behavior."

To appear normal I took Bea to Talmart and we bought new clothing and other necessities we desperately needed. Having seen a Cargill restaurant in every major city we visited I decided for once I wanted to take Bea to a nice place to eat. We went downtown. I couldn't let the valet park my car. I didn't need anyone snooping around in it. The fine dressed patrons and attendants were all looking at us as if we didn't belong here. I waited a few minutes before a maître d addressed me. "Ma'am, the kitchen is that way," He said taking one glance at our new Talmart clothing. I almost told him I didn't work here. "I know, today is my day off so I decided to bring my daughter to know her where mommy worked," I lied.

"Very well, then. You know the rules. I do not remember hiring you. What shift you work?" He asked snobbishly. *No, I didn't know the damn rules*. He absently said. "Mr. Cargill may be here tomorrow, be on time. He's known to fire for being a minute late. So don't be late."

"Yes sir." I said and took Bea by the hand and led her to the back of the place. Where

109

we're brought menus which were written in every damn language but English. I pressed the button at the top for the English translation. I gasped at the unusual items like Ostrich egg salad, turtle soup, algae noodles and shark steaks. I'd just have beef steak and potatoes. I ordered Bea a cheeseburger and fries. I skipped the wine. I had to drive. I could see the porosity in my lie when the waiter asked why don't I go to the steak house down the streets if I merely want a steak dinner? I saw they knew I don't work here.

"Why don't you learn to be nice?" I shot back. Telling myself not to ruffle anyone's feathers. There were already cops looking for someone matching my description. I apologized when I saw a change in his face. "I didn't mean to insult you. I meant it's cheaper..."

"Oh, I don't mind the price. It's her birthday present." I lied again. One thing about being on the run—you've to lie a lot and I don't like lying and killing but it goes with the territory. Bea's birthday was a months away. I saw a satanist enter and they asked her to leave. I was glad, maybe I could eat in peace.

After dinner, I went in the back and asked the waiter who brought our food who could I talk to about getting a job here. "Depends on what your skills are. I'm the head dayshift waiter." He replied giving me a look over.

"I would prefer a waitress job," I said. "We don't collect tips here." He said obviously looking at my fresh Talmart clothing.

"I don't care. I like the atmosphere." What I really meant was I liked the fact that no overt satanists were allowed. He gave me an application. I completed it via the information of the alias ID. Made up several places I lived and worked. He stuck it in a machine and a red small flag appeared in the corner.

"You've no work history nor credit history." He said looking sternly at me. "Ok, here's the deal. I spend all my early twenties being a mom and housewife. I've never worked outside the home. This will be my first job since my divorce." He looked down at Bea, people usually melt when they look into her big golden brown eyes and she knew how to make them melt. I needed a job for if I'm spending money about town with no job, that's a big ol' red flag.

"Ok, I'll give you a probationary trial. Follow me." He said leading the way to the deep lavender and lime employee's locker and lounge. The lockers were metal with stained a dark wooden facade. I had never worked at a place that provided a get-up like this for employees to sit and take a break. My name at this job was Jan Dawson according to my brother Jack.

"When do I start?" I asked.

"Now. Tonight is crowded, we could use the extra hands." Bernard said. I left Bea in the employees lounge where she could lie down and watch the screen. One lady told me there was a nursery if I wanted to use it. So during my break I took Bea there. Bea didn't want to stay, saying these were babies. So I took her back to the lounge which was right outside the kitchen. The nursery sent her a snack which she didn't eat for I had trained her well not to take food from strangers. The employees were pleasant. Perhaps one of the nicest places I've worked. I was floored when they told me my salary was $80 per hour. I had never made that much.

The first night went well. I was due back in the morning at 7:00. I liked the daylight hours, gave me time to do things with Bea. But before turning in for the night I stopped by the bar/strip joint I worked at yesterday and got my three days wages. It was only $117.00 but I need it for who know how anything would go?

I was finally able to get some real rest, although I had to be back at work at 7:00 and it was now 1:00 A.M. I couldn't deny I was jumpy about the cop kicking in the door at 3 or 4 in the morning. It has happened before. So, of course I didn't sleep well.

The next morning we ate a quick bite at a local eatery down the street and I headed for work. I left early cause I was told the owner was expected today. I took Bea inside via the back door and sat her in the lounge, again to watch cartoons. I left a pillow and blanket so she could take a nap.

Nearly 11:00 A.M. a black stretch limo alit outside; everyone fell in place. Mine was

111

at the end, the last of the servers. I saw several men and women who looked like they were secret service get out and surround a tall man of indistinguishable ethnicity. I couldn't deny he was handsome but I also sensed he was the sort of man you didn't want to fall in love with.

"Is that the owner?" I asked the woman next to me. Which was a dumb question. She didn't reply. I looked down to see who was tugging my clothing; Bea walked out on the line and stood in front of me. Dragging her pillow and blanket with her. The daycare center aide rushed out and picked her up and rushed back to the nursery. Bea protested very loudly with a line of profanity that made me look straight ahead. My boss narrowed his eyes down the line at me. Thank God there were no customers.

"No, from what I heard that's one of the grandsons, Janus Cargill." The woman next to me finally whispered out the side of her mouth. The man named Janus was inside now, the managers were talking to the tall, handsome, bored looking man who was now walking down the line. At least he wasn't asking us to hold our hands out so he could inspect them for grime under the nails. I guess that's what the white linen/spandex gloves that were a part of our uniform were for. I was glad because my nails were in horrible condition.

When the boss was in front of me, I looked straight ahead but he tilted my chin up to look at him. I hung it cause I wasn't sure if he heard Bea's cussing.

"So you're the mother of the cussing baby?" He chuckled. "Only a mother would blush with such shame," he laughed out aloud. I saw my manager let out a sigh of relief that our boss wasn't angry.

"Yes sir, I'm her mother. I'm sorry, sir. I'll see that it doesn't happen again."

"You do that." He said and continued down the line to the cooks and so on. Next he went to the nursery. He stood and looked at down at little Bea Wyett, who stared back at him but no one understood why was he staring at the cute, foul-mouthed child. "Sir, I promise you she won't disturb the customers." The head caretaker said.

"She had better not or out the door she and her mother goes." Janus said firmly. The woman motioned in agreement.

Unbeknownst to Ana, Janus Cargill goes to the office and closes the door and calls his father Ashley Cargill. "Dad, I think you've a new sibling. There's a kid down here at the Richmond, Virginia restaurant that bears Big Papa's essence and mouth. If she cusses like this now I can only imagine what her mouth will be a few years from now."

"Oh well just so long as the mother isn't asking for money...who cares?" Ashley nonchalantly replied. "With my father's lifestyle. I'm not surprised."

"No, interesting thus, she isn't the type to live his lifestyle. She's kinda shy. I mean the mother. She's very pretty but I don't know where Big Papa met her but she isn't his usual taste, she isn't a professional cocotte."

An incident of long ago surfaced in Ashley's mind. An incident he'd never forget. "What exactly does she look like?" Ashley asked, suddenly alert, wanting to know; trying to figure out if his dad might be still seeing her or if she is impartially trying to force his father to acknowledge her child by working there. His sister told him there was a woman dad was smitten by but she said nothing about a child.

"Like I said she's very pretty, has the face of an angel. But not much of a body thus."

"Fire her." Ashley said with great finality. "Dad, I think that's a little harsh. I mean the lady got a cussing baby but the baby wouldn't be Big Papa's if she wasn't cussing. You cuss, Aunt Lavenica cusses and blame others for devising her to cuss. Cussing is a family curse." Janus chuckled, reminiscing the little girl's words.

Ashley sighed. His son clearly wasn't getting the message. "Janus, I think she's the woman dad has been trying to find. If he finds her think of what it will mean for us."

"So? How will that affect us?"

"Idiotic son! If he finds her he'll keep her. He's in love with her and that little girl and
113

others they might breed, will take our place in Cargill International. So fire the hussy before he finds her."

Janus flouted, his dad was being ridiculous. If she had meant that much to Big Papa she wouldn't be working as a waitress. What's new? Every time he turned around his grandfather had a new piece of arm candy so it's obvious he has already slept with the woman and cast her aside as he's known for doing. He thinks his dad is clearly overreacting. The woman most likely doesn't even know Big Papa's real name let alone how to find him.

Janus Cargill calls the new woman to the office. Her manager frowned at her again. Ana/Jan doesn't like being called to the office because it usually means you're fired. The man who hired her watched with nervous anticipation from across the huge elegant restaurant for it's he who will catch hell for hiring her. Ana walked professionally (or what she hoped looked professionally) to the elevators, took the staff one, pressed the button and watched the doors close. She doesn't relax for she knows these elevators have eyes. When it opens she maintains her professional stride and puts her ID card in the scanner to alert those inside who is entering. The door clicks open, she enters and stands before the huge antique designer desk until he invites her to sit. He gestured her to the seat in front of him, not one of those at the ends as she would have preferred.

"I see you and I name's are pretty similar. How do you like it here so far?" He asked and paused a nanosecond. "I see today is your first full shift. I've a position at the mansion here in Richmond. I think you'd make an excellent house staff member." He offered the position to see her reaction; to see if she knew who his grandfather was. She showed no recognition of his name.

"Thank you sir for the confidence in me but if you don't mind I'd like to remain here."

"Let's see, you'd prefer a room at a boarding house over your own room in a mansion?"

"Yes, sir. It's a motel room."

"Whatever, it's not safe for you and a baby to be in a motel room alone. Now take the job or you're fired." He ordered, looking sternly at her with those hard strange gemstone eyes she swore she'd seen before. The man in her closet had the same eyes, well not exactly the same but close enough. This man's eyes looked more human than the man from her dreams that she now knows is not a dream. But for how long would she know it wasn't a dream? Who knows?

An uncomfortable reality slapped her at that instant, sending a cold chill down her spine. She fought to control a noticeable shiver. The police are looking for her or someone fitting her image; if she's arrested Bea will become a ward of the state of Virginia at least until Helena retrieved and took custody of her. She resigns her dissent.

"Where do I report, sir?" She asked tightly. Her voice had a brusk she hadn't intended to reveal. "I'll send the employees' van to your *motel*." He said, a little icily. She had no intention of leaving Trusty behind and she didn't really need this job, she had just taken a large sum from a crooked collector.

In a nicer tone she said. "Sir, if you give me the address I can find the place."

"Maybe you can but you can't get in and I'll need the staff to train you. I'm giving a party shortly and I need you ready."

Before I left I asked my supervisor if I should quit after one day would he be held accountable? I only asked to be nice for I intended to ride out of town as soon as the roads were clear and never look back. I knew the cops had been to my old job.

"You can't quit. I hired you without a thorough background check." Bernard reminded me.

"I've been hired to help cater or serve at a mansion, at a party here in Richmond. I'm told if I reject the job I'm fired."

An ogrish shadow passed over Bernard's face lending it a grayish hue. He knew from one look at her she wasn't the type of woman who needed to be at such party. "Jan, forget what I said. Get out of here and get out fast. Don't accept that position. You aren't really wanted to cater at a party. Leave! I'll survive," he whispered so only she could hear him. He knew the men who attended these "parties" reputation. Jan was pretty enough to attract them but a little naive. Her big doe eyes told him she was stepping into trouble.

That's exactly what she thought, for at every residential domestic position she has ever had like the one she was currently asked, no told, to accept there was always trouble with the male residents unless they were under five. Even twelve year old sons, nephews or what have you, and ninety year old grandpas make indecent proposals. The day they hit on you and you say no is the day you're pretty much already fired. For they start to lie on you and their female relatives start to make your life living hell. The catty bitchiness starts. So I usually ended up walking off the job. Their lascivious behavior always costs me my job. But seemed as thus I didn't have much of a choice. It was either work for Janus Cargill or go to jail. His hard, cold, indigo steel eyes told me he wouldn't hesitate to turn me over to the authorities and would not lose any sleep over it.

When I arrived at the motel there were flashing blue, red and green lights all over the place. I thought the woman who picked us up said they had handled this? Apparently not for there was cadaver dogs sniffing my room. For what? I don't know. But anyway, the police were everywhere and the motel owner across the parking lot looked at me as if I were dirt on the bottom of his shoe. Those who escorted me back to the motel asked what was going on? The cops said a woman at the bank had been killed in her office and I was the last person seen leaving, a local lawyer had gone missing and my car was seen at the bank three days ago. And the day prior to the murders, the lawyer had delivered a garnishment to my job. The chief of household staff who drove back with me to the motel said that was impossible, I worked at the Cargill mansion over on Lees Street. I could see the cops was a little startled at this knowledge and didn't exactly believe him but I could also see they knew better than to dispute him. Whomever this man worked for much had a lot of power for the police to lay off a pursuit against me when they basically had me cornered. Right where they wanted me.

Ana had no way of knowing the satanists had gone behind her and killed these people to frame her for the murders. She didn't know the lawyer had wriggled out the rope and used the small phone tucked in his sock and called for help. She didn't know the wrist-tattooed woman who found them walking back to town, that her group listened over the airwaves for unusual activities is one of the ways they identify who they need to assist. She didn't know that with threats and intimidation they were working to clear her name. They had heard of her, she just never heard of them. She didn't know these people stood between her and the cops the very same night the woman told her where to find a safe hotel. She didn't know there were nooses waiting for her and Bea in the county jail. The story was to tell her family she was emotional distressed from staring at numerous counts of murder. Seeing no way out she hung her daughter and then herself. And when Helena questioned as to why was Bea even in the cell with her, the lie was to be told because her sister kept wailing and crying for her baby. She didn't know the satanists were watching her every move the entire time; giving her enough rope to hang herself via her own impulsive, careless actions.

We left the motel and headed toward the northside of the city and turned westward; the homes became grander and more lavish with each we passed. We finally arrived at gated estate with armed security guards. I followed the van inside when the guards opened the gate. I was halted for a few seconds. They scanned my car, using a mirror to discreetly look under it. I'm sure they saw my weapon sash but nonetheless waved me through. The estate's secondary entrance opened to a huge, well-lit, garden-like lawn. I bet it was even more beautiful in broad daylight. A woman was waiting on the large colonial style foyer and steps for Bea and I but I parked my own car for I didn't want anyone poking around in it. The same woman whom I had passed was now at the garage elevator waiting for us. I grabbed our beat up, worn overnight bags and headed for the elevator. The woman looked disapprovingly at our ragged bags but I ignored her and stepped into the elevator beside her holding Bea's hand tightly.

I don't know who these people are but right now it seems safer to take a chance with them than try and get out of the city. I could just kick myself for not leaving the moment we got the money. I figured if I ran it would prove me guilty. This wasn't a town that had a lot of woods to hide in. It once may have did years ago but not anymore and unless something divine happened like in Pasadena we would've been caught. I'll let this serve as lesson; always get out no matter how things appear. You're guilty before the crime was even committed.

Once inside we walked through the most beautiful home I had ever seen. I quickly rescinded the admiration when I remembered the main part of the house used to be a plantation.

We by-passed the kitchen, heading to another wing. We came to a kitchenette apartment with its own bathroom. "Put your things away. The party starts tomorrow at noon, I need to coach you", the woman said in an immodest tone after telling me to leave Bea in the room. I made it clear I never leave my daughter alone anywhere. She then called another woman and told her to watch Bea.

"I thought I said I do not leave my baby alone anywhere."

"Very well, then follow me!" She huffed, turning down her mouth. Her demeanour reminded me of the head of an 1890's English manor staff. I was expecting a uniform much like her own but she showed me evening and formal wear.

"You're to entertain and make sure all guests are well served," she said, showing me three sets of garments. Some looked a little suggestive to me.

"This is for the pool party" she said, holding up a two piece white swimsuit with a beige border. "I don't do swim suits." I said firmly. The woman sighed as if I were getting on her nerves. So what? She was getting on my nerves too and I'm sure mine were a lot more frayed than hers. She tells another woman to bring the matronly clothes. These dresses were ugly and gangly. "Don't you people have anything modest?", I asked. She showed me a gold sequined tube-top romper with a sheer cover.

"I can deal with that for the pool party. But black women have an ass and it would be hanging out that little bikini." This time she rolled her eyes and asked were I a former nun? "No, I just don't like showing the world my ass." The second woman giggled and the first one turned and her visage reflected her stern disapproval.

After Sour Face left me alone with the second woman for the fitting I asked her about closing up the top part of the two dresses. She agreed they would look better on me with

118

a closed top and jewelry. We didn't finish the fitting until around 2:00 A.M. and Bea was long asleep. It was nice of the woman who was told to watch Bea to bring her a sandwich and a glass of milk. I was told to be ready for the stylist in the morning. So I assumed I only had a few hours to sleep.

While they were inside hemming, tucking, and making plans for the party attire, unbeknownst to them a Richmond detective was inside, in another part of the mansion talking to Janus Cargill, punctually trying to convince him why this woman maybe a danger to his well-being.

"I ran her face through a recognition program. I find many parts missing so that means she has friends in high places; however as much of the puzzle I was able to put together proves this woman is a killer. So I strongly advise you to turn her over before she harms someone here. It's seems as thus almost anything can set her off. She's highly unstable!", the man vividly argued.

In truth, Janus Cargill didn't care. His whole damn family was highly unstable so what was that to him? When your grandfather is Azazel, crazy is normal to you. If she was brave and bold enough to sleep with his grandfather, he knew she had to have a lot of gusto, guts, or was just plain crazy. Whichever one it was, he didn't care just so long as she didn't kill anyone at his party. He was expecting the biggest event of the year for his company tomorrow.

※※※※

It seems I had just closed my eyes for a few minutes before someone was at the door telling me it was time to get up. It was the stylists. They took Bea on too since I refused to leave her with anyone. Sorry if they were offended. I didn't know these people. As far as I knew they may be working for that warlock who performed a black mass wedding on me about a year ago.

Bea looked so cute in corkscrew curls and a little, sunny yellow short set. The woman from last night tried again to get me to leave Bea in the nursery with the other children and I said no. But after entering the pool area I saw why she told me to leave Bea behind. I had no idea how everyone else would be dressed but most of the servers were wearing nothing except a pair of pearls and heels if they were female and a bowtie if they were male. I slapped my hand over Bea's eyes and led her back inside back to our room. The school- matronly woman from last night came charging in and asked what in the hell was my problem now?

"Those people are nude!" I cried. "Didn't you worked in such a place a few days ago?!", she snapped. "Yes, but my daughter was in the office. She saw nothing."

"You don't know what in the hell she saw. Kids that young don't give a damn about their own butts let alone anyone else's." While pedagogically speaking her phone bracelet rang. I heard the caller ask where was the last hostess? "In her room cowering at the sight of butts", the woman sighed.

The caller laughed. "Send her to the office." The caller said and cut the connection.

Janus was still laughing at this new-found woman when he broke the connection. She wasn't afraid of naked asses when she screwed his grandfather and he seriously doubted it was all missionary. He saw her step out outside as he was about to introduce her to some prominent businessmen and run back indoors. Several asked who was she? He almost said. "My grandfather's piece of ass and she's working on my last nerve." But instead he said she was new. They were right; she was stunningly, aerially beautiful when out of those drag, drab, and dull clothing.

I sat rigidly in the office chair awaiting for the boss to show up, we were there for at least an hour before he came in from a side door near the huge bookcase nearly covering the entire east wall.

"Ms. Dawson, I see you've never worked a pool party." He said patiently after taking a seat and looking at her and Bea for a short while. But his eyes were saying she was getting on the last decent nerve he had left.

"No, I've not."

120

"I see you told my manager you were recently divorced. What did you do before marriage?"

"I spent a few years in college and got married and had my daughter."

"Hmm, I see." Was all he said but a few seconds later added. "You know, several people have commented on how much your daughter and I look alike. I don't see it. Do you?" He asked, staring frigidly at her as an evil thought crept into his psyche: *"Had I known she would be this much of a pain in the ass I would've let the cops had her..."*

I froze. For now I knew he knew about the closet man, he's conspicuously and brazenly telling me he knows. Will that one night of pleasure haunt me for the rest of my life? Will Breanna hate me when I'm forced to tell her the truth. I smiled a nervous smile. This man was making me jumpy.

"No, I don't. You and my ex look nothing alike." I said, sensing this man was much older than he appeared.

"Relax, I don't like cops either, so your secrets are safe with me", he said, getting up and pouring himself a glass of scotch and using a long golden tong to drop ice in the glass. "We all have them." He said, referring to secrets while studying me over the glass' rim.

"How do you know so much about my life? Who are you really?" I bravely asked since I felt I had nothing further to lose. He was kicking us out because I refused to wear the swimsuit or appear in my birthday suit. I didn't like it; he could easily cipher so much about me when I knew virtually nothing about him. That was giving him the upper hand. And I don't like other people having the upper hand.

"I know nothing about you except your name isn't Jan Dawson, and your baby resembles me and I wonder why? I don't remember anyone who remotely resembling you from my past. But I've lots of male relatives so perhaps your ex is one of my brothers, cousins, nephews or someone closer, like my father", he said slightly smiling around the glass. When he smiled he looked more like the closet man.

This bastard is fucking with me. Making fun of my modesty. How does he know what I'm thinking? "Are you implying I had an affair on my husband?," I asked slightly aggravated but growing angrier.

"I don't know. Why don't you tell me?" He asked raising his left eyebrow; that gesture looked familiar, too.

"But if your ex looks nothing like me then the evidence speak for itself." He grinned. He's taunting me. He knows he looks like someone I know and is revealing it. I'm not good at the game of cloak and dagger.

"However, I thought I was paying you one hundred and fifty per hour but it's been nearly three and you haven't earned a dollar yet. So what could we do about you and my little relative here? I can't kick my little kin-person out when mom is in trouble. So I tell you what. Go change and work the evening party until twelve and let's see how that works out. You aren't afraid of evening dresses, too? Are you?" He asked, fully chuckling around the rim of the glass. His laughter sent chills down my spine. It sounded so much like someone I knew.

Sensing my distress, Bea shifted. "Eat shit and die!" Bea yelled from my lap. I hadn't realized she was glaring at him. I shushed her but he laughed heartily and pointed at Bea, "Lady, that's the kind of thing someone very close to me would say. So why don't you come clean?"

Determined to maintain my innocence. "I'm afraid I've no idea what you're talking about." I said surlily. He laughed again and said, "Ok, we'll leave it at that. But we both know you aren't afraid of much."

He teleported in while the party was in full swing. Janus' father Ashley wanted the mother and daughter separated to question the kid. He knows if she's like himself she's a lot smarter than the average child. He didn't see where he and this kid supposedly

122

resembled as Janus claimed. Sure they both had bluish brown eyes but that isn't uncommon. He gathered his pants up near crotch to make the squat comfortable and lowered himself next to the child drawing in a coloring book and asked what was she coloring.

"None of your damn business." The ill-natured child quipped. One thing Janus was right about; she has dad's bad mouth and lousy attitude for no apparent reason. He noticed the child's palms were shiny and without ridges. So her mother was aware Ashton Cargill was looking for them and to avoid detection she erased the child's handprints. Hmmm, he hadn't seen that done since the 1930's and 40's. That's an old gangster move. Most people today aren't strong enough to endure that. He touched the little girl's arm. She yanked it back so quickly it verified what he suspected. The child glared at him. He saw a small resemblance of his father's eyes in that tiny face for a few seconds. He was connecting to feel the essence. The substance he sensed was so much like his own he yanked his hand back as the child stared at him.

"Don't touch me. You don't know me." Bea hissed.

"No, I don't but I just might be your big brother."

He stood up, still looking down at the beautiful, angry child. "No sweetie, it's you who don't know you," he said and walked away. Bea gave him his own father's and sister's infamous, "Whatever" over her thin shoulder.

"Dammit... Janus! What in the hell does he think he's doing? Leading the bitch directly to dad. He hasn't found her in all this time so Janus is determined to help his grandpa out. Oh hell no! Not today or fifty years from now. He knew about his amnesia and the harems says it gets worse everytime he's near that woman", he thinks going to find his son.

He goes the security surveillance room asked the security team which of the servers is the little mean girl's mother? The man points to the woman with her back to him. He pans the camera and holds it until she turns around. When she does his heart jumps into his throat. She looks a lot like his mother. But this is the woman he remembered from

123

his childhood and that was over seven hundred years ago. That's the red haired heifer his parents fought over. One morning his mother caught her in bed with his dad. It's impossible to forget that hair. He is over seven hundred years old so if she isn't an immortal...then what in the hell is she? It's definitely her. She knows who dad is. There's no mistake as to why she is here! That bitch has got to go. She's the reason his mother is dead. The reason he grew up on the streets. After his mother was killed Azazael went nuts and started acting like who he truly is and heaven arrested him. He called his sister. "Lavenica, it's her. The source of all of our damn problems." He minced words into the phone with so much venom they stung his own mouth.

"Ashley, you need to let the past die. We've lived through it. We survived it. All who hurt us are long dead. Even that woman that supposedly broke up mom and dad. That woman is long dead. You need to face the fact that it was father's actions that created the problem. It was his negligence that drove mom to an affair with our youngest brother's father. He didn't have to go to that woman nor bring her home or however the hell she got in his bedroom that morning. Dad let her in. There's nothing you nor I can do to remunerate her for the past. The person you thought you saw is long dead", his sister said distinctly remembering the stories he told her as a child as to why their family was destroyed. Their father left them at the estate to go and get their mother. He brought her and their little brother both back dead and buried them in the cemetery on the estate. They both slowly watched him go mad. Ashley being only twelve was unable to make the staff do as he said so people begun to take advantage of them with their father not being around. And when he killed all those people in that village angels came and arrested him. That was the end of their sheltered life. Ashley always blamed the red-haired bitch as he called her for the next half of a millennium. But after her third husband introduced her to Taoism and she found peace, she eventually relinquished the past and wished her brother would find the peace to let go too.

"The bitch isn't dead. I'm looking dead at her," he fumed, getting angrier by the second. "Speak for yourself little sister. Had it not been for the red haired bitch I'm looking at right now you would've never been taken from me, captured after you ran and sold abroad a slave ship. Back then dad's powers were so weak we inherited very little from him. Unlike this little bastard of his in the nursery coloring a picture book. Maybe you can forgive and forget but I can't! But I'll promise not to kill them; this is the best I can do. Either way, they're getting the hell out of here!"

He teleported to his son's room. To wait for him, to cold cock him. To knock his ass out for going against him. He avoided the party for he knew Janus had disobeyed and had he gone near Jan or whatever the hell her name is, he would've kill her. Janus thinks she's beautiful. Of course he does, she's a seductress. A siren. She isn't human. He doesn't know exactly what she is but whatever she is, it's not of this world. He has always believed she's like Azazel.

The afternoon and evening half of the party went well, except the grabby hands which I had to constantly slap away. The only person I recognized at the party was James Caldwell; that was not the name I knew him by. Everyone else I didn't know them and from their fetid attitudes. I didn't care to know them. I recognized the movie star Caroline Caldwell from seeing a few of her movies. But frankly, to me the movies weren't that great. She's as beautiful in real life as on the chips. But I couldn't help but wonder did the woman know James and I had been on a date for she was definitely determined to make my life hell all night tonight. Had I not seen her foot over the edge of the tray of drinks, she would've tripped me and I would've crashed in front of all those people or fell into the pool. Every drink I served her there was something wrong with it. I was at the end of my rope when I threw the olive for the purple martini at her. She said the one in her drink wasn't fresh or something like that. My supervisor called me from that side of the pool. Janus thought it was funny. I thought he'd reprimand me for it.

I had finally left Bea in the nursery but periodically checked in on her. I got several offers that night to be someone's mistress, which I declined. I had enough problems. I didn't need to fish for more. I was wondering when would these people go home. Then I realized as some left others arrived. But when my shift was over I went and retrieved Bea and went to bed. Around four the matronly lady came to the room and called me again. I thought to myself, "*Dammit, it's four A.M. those rich drunks need to go home.*"

After Caroline retired, which was shortly after Ana threw the olive at her instead of bringing it to her, James decided he would let her know he wasn't ignoring her but couldn't acknowledge her with Caroline by his side.

"Whatever you've to say. I don't want to hear." I said heading indoors. I wasn't part of the cleaning crew for once.

"How about let's have dinner tomorrow night. I can take Caroline home and then we came have the entire evening to ourselves. I can hire a sitter for Bea", he said still holding on to her arm that she snatched away.

"You took advantage of my distress. You took advantage of me at one of my lowest points. You saw what was going on between me and Thad but my feelings didn't mean a damn thing to you. You even told your wife about the sorry ass dinner date. That's why she was picking on me tonight."

"Ana, I didn't tell Caroline about us. I'm not as stupid like Thad Wyett. Thad created his own problems. He had everything most men dream of but threw it all away for a two-bit whore. That isn't my fault. I won't accept the blame for that. All I was trying to do was be neighborly. Help you out. The whole town knew about Thad's Wyett's problems. Caroline and I were separated at the time. We were going through marital problems. Not knowing if we would get back together I reckoned why bother to tell you about her," he explained.

"What the fuck ever," I said and continued down the hall. Does this man think I'm some kind of desperate fool?

Her vociferously dismissing him and walking away set his teeth on the edge. No one walks away when James Caldwell is talking to you.

"Ok, since you want to be that way, I'll tell the police to come out here and pick your murderous, thieving ass up. Who do you think kept them off you at that rundown shithole of a room you called home. You've an awful lot of pride to be so poor. I know it was you who tied that man to that tree and shot him. I know it was you who killed that woman at the bank. That lawyer didn't write you a check card. You took it. I know it was you who massacred those innocent people in Pasadena." He said maliciously to my retreating back. But then reversed gear to the calm softening of his voice which was deadlier than a king cobra, "But Ana, remember I know the real you. This isn't you. I know how sweet and gentle your heart truly is. Look at what you've become! What have you become? A hunted animal? More or less a monster. A monster fighting to survive. So please, darling, let me help you revert back to the fine, upstanding Christian woman I know you are. Let me make you into an honest woman again. This isn't the life for someone of your attributes."

A sledge hammer hit me in the back. I stopped in my tracks, slowly turned around and looked, for at long last I finally I knew the identity of one of those pursuing me. I looked not at a man but at a devil. A pure devil. Another face had translucently covered James Caldwell's face, it was complete with antlers on top. He looked taller, bulkier and more flagitious than the physical man.

"Who are you?" I wanted to know. The whitish blue veined skin looked familiar but I couldn't place where I had seen it before. The deer antlers seemed to grow and expand toward the high ceiling.

"Ana, don't tell me you don't know who I'm. Surely you know me. The bible calls me Moloch. Had you been reading your bible then you would know 'who am I?'" The demon said as causally as this was an everyday occurrence. "You can run but you can't hide. I'll always find you. Make it easier on yourself and come do your duty."

I looked frantically around the empty hallway. Everyone was gone. There was no one here but me and the devil. "I'll never do the will of hell! You should know that by now".

He inclined his great head and chuckled a laughter that sent chills like nails grating a chalkboard down my spine. "A many have said that but we always win. Eventually, you will."

"JESUS!" I panicky called from the depth of my soul when he started flying toward me as I scurried down the hallway to Bea. I had to make sure no one was around her.

127

Midway to the room he caught me, something hard and squirming in his hand was boring painfully in my flesh and suddenly the black leather appeared, replacing the evening attire. The pain stopped, an inborn instinct took over my senses and instructed me how to swing the dagger in my hand at him. He shoved me hard against the wall; I bounced off and lunged for him with my all. I didn't know the blade was on fire until I saw his leathery hooded eyes widen as I was coming down on him. I had had it. I was tried of things and people fucking with me. I stabbed him in the right arm; much to both of our surprise. He fled the body of James Caldwell and escaped through the ancient iron wrought vents in the form of a whirling dark smoke. I don't care what happens tomorrow I'm not leaving Bea alone. I then ran to my room and saw she was asleep on my pillow. She seemed to be fine. I knee down and prayed God protected us from whatever that thing is. I can't outrun it for it's here in this house with us.

Janus Cargill wanted to talk to this intriguing woman without the kid staring at him. He had noticed James Caldwell seemed to know her. He saw Caldwell return to the pool after Caroline retired for the night. He figured the baby would be asleep by now. He didn't know if she's his grandfather's old lover or whatever but the woman is sexy as hell. It was understandable why the guys couldn't keep their hands off of her tonight. But nonetheless he needed to talk to her about her unprofessional behavior; slapping the guests, calling them names and throwing things at them. This is not a roadhouse honky tonk.

He was on the phone with his Aunt Lavenica when Ana rapped softly at the door. His aunt verified the same as his father had said but advised him keep it to yourself, the woman will wise up and leave when she realizes that Ashton Cargill has no intention of coming to her. According to Aunt Lavenica the woman showing up was no mere coincidence. She showed up in Richmond looking for Ashton.

"I'm not surprised she has a child by dad. But dad is better off the way he is," Lavenica said. "He went nuts when mom died. I can't go through that again."

"Come in," he replied to the knock at the door, leaving the phone connection open so

Lavenica could hear the conversation. Ana shyly entered in her usual timid manner. His Aunt had revealed to Janus the woman's real name but fortified herself to never make that information known to her father.

"Jan, you did good this evening except I can't have you slapping the guests and throwing things at them." Janus said. "Your shift tonight will be from eleven to six."

Listening to the conversation Lavenica heard this woman named Jan say. "I won't hit anyone who keep their hands to themselves. I'm not a lady of the evening. I won't throw things at people if they don't try to treat me like a slave. I know this used to be a plantation but this isn't the era you can treat employees badly anymore. If the woman hadn't started anything with me then I wouldn't have reacted negatively and embarrassed her. I'm not obligated to accept anyone's abuse." Ana firmly explained, jostling a wiggling Bea to a more comfortable position in her lap. She observed the rows of variorums on his mahogany bookshelf to avoid looking at him.

"Ok, I'll talk to the guests about no touching the attendants." Janus said dismissively.

"Is that all?"

"Yeah," He said a little grumpily. He didn't like the fact she made him think about making love to her from the snug fit of that robe around her shapely hips. He amusedly watched her hoist that big ass kid up in her arms and struggled to get out the door.

Lavenica waited until the door to his office closed. "Janus! Get that woman out of there before dad finds her. I'm telling you... that's her. I suspect she can go to him in her dreams and he can do the same. Dad is attracted to her because he thinks she looks like mom!"

He said he'd get rid of her but Ana/Jan didn't leave until two months later. He sort of liked having her around. He could see what made Big Papa fall in love with her; she was beautiful, intelligent, had a charming personality, and naturally sexy without trying to be. Security told him she said she was going into town and that evening she never came back. He hated to admit he missed her laughing and modesty and hoped she was well wherever she was.

His nostalgic feelings didn't last long. Two days after she left his grandfather showed up looking for her. He went straight to the room she had lived in for two months. According to Ashton Cargill, he saw this room in a dream and in his dream he saw the woman he was looking for. But Janus told him he was mistaken. No one has lived in that room since the days of the annual party which was over a month ago. Azazael looked at him, not knowing whether to believe his 187 year old grandson or not. He could smell her scent. So someone was lying to him. Why would Janus lie?

"Has your father been here lately?" Azazael asked suspiciously. He knew Janus was lying.

"I haven't seen dad since the pool party." Janus truthfully replied. Ashley was mad at him for keeping his archenemy as he called Jan around. But James Caldwell said her real name was Ana BuFaye.

Driving down the road in the loneliness of the night with nothing ahead but Trusty's headlights and more darkness, Ana wondered she did act too hastily? Did she make a mistake in leaving that job? They were safe for once. Neither the satanists nor police bothered her after the night of the pool party but she had a nagging sensation when the boss was bored with her company he'd let the police have her. He never directly asked her to sleep with him but made little suggestions. Perhaps he and the closet man were brothers and she wasn't about to sleep with two brothers. She made a mistake once and once was enough. She knew if she continued to stay there she was going to have to put out or get out. So she left before things came to that climax. At least they've enough resources for a decent place to live for at least a month or two. She mentally shook off the plaguing words of Moloch calling her a thief and a murder. Late nights like this is when hurtful things come back to haunt you but she started humming her anthem and kept on down the road in the darkness. *"Fuck Moloch!"*

We had taken a seedy apartment in southern Indiana, because I was trying to reserve resources. Sometimes months passed before I could get far enough ahead of the satanists to settle down long enough to land a job. This hick town had none but I was tired and beginning to feel sick and rundown so I had to stop somewhere and let my body rejuvenate or I was going to become seriously ill.

We had eaten and just retired for the evening after watching the screen which had nothing interesting showing. I was nearly asleep, again wondering did I leave that estate too hastily? I could've considered Bea's well being before I panicked and left. No one there was bothering me. I was drifter deeper into sleep when I heard a rapid muffed scratching behind the wall at my left, I knew from experience it was not rats. If they were rats I certainly didn't want to meet them. It was the height of the summer when we moved in so I expected vermin to be roaming freely but whatever was in that wall was no vermin. My heart was racing as I watched the walls breathe. At first I thought it to be an illusion. I was a novice in understanding these things but I knew I had to get Bea out of here, whatever was happening I sensed something about to come through that wall. I scooped Bea up in my arms and headed for the door. It was jammed shut. It wouldn't budge. I heard a swarm of bees and they came out the wall, attacking and stinging my back in small kamikaze like dives. They never lit on me, they just kept nipping my back and the back of my arms and legs. By now we both were screaming.

I don't know where it came from but I screamed. "In the Power of Jesus Christ! Stop! Leave us alone!" The bees stopped and began to form into a humanoid figure that was still buzzing. When the formation was complete it looked like a man. My heart was beating hard against my ribcage I felt I was going to faint but I didn't have that luxury; Bea was between me and the door whimpering.

"In the Name of the Prince of Peace, tell me your name!" I said firmly. I was pissed off, it had frightened my baby.

"Bitch, I don't have to tell you a damn thing!" The demon snapped. What is it with hell and the "B" word? I wondered.

131

"I command you in the Name of Jesus Christ to tell me your name!" I yelled back. It struggled, distorted, disassembled but could not escape.

"My name is Belpher," it said in a heavily accented English. "Your weak armor of faith cannot protect you, I've brought down much stronger than you." He informed, really lashing out at us. Now, I felt blood running down my face, back, arm and legs.

"FATHER! MY GOD! SAVE US!" I yelled at the top of my lungs and in my mind's eye I saw an old disused abbey, I had no idea where it was but this is where I was told to go. Obviously, it was nearby.

The apartment door suddenly unstuck. With Bea still in my arms I ran out the front door of my building wishing I had stayed in that mansion. I could kick myself for letting my whatever the hell this is going on in my foggy brain put Bea in danger. So what if I would have had to sleep with him to keep Bea safe. "*My stupidity will get us killed",* I think to myself as I struggled to unlock the car while this man made of bees runs toward us. I got in and slammed the door seconds before he crashed into the car revealing the most hideous face on the window and then dissolving into a swarm of bees again. They were covering the car. But they wasn't lighting on it. I could see sparks of fire flashing off the car, keeping them away. The smell of their burning ectoplasmic flesh was sickening. I backed out fast as possible and tore out down the road. As Trusty hit 75mph they formed into a large monster and headed straight for my bumper. Their swatting at and hitting it several times nearly sent me into a yard as I topped a hill going down. Before me was the building I had envisioned and I drove even faster toward it. I saw the moon; it seemed so close and big that I could reach out and touch it. I had never seen the moon this close. It was close enough to see the luna mare. I quickly forgot about the moon and looked back in the rearview mirror. They were still hot on my trail; they then leapt on top of the car, covering it entirely. I saw thousands of tiny, horrendous, harpy faces staring maliciously at us. Their tiny mouths were screaming hate and death at us. Trusty was burning layers and layers of them off but more were coming, blackening out every sliver of moonlight.

"God, it's in Your Hands, now," I said, taking an estimated turn into the old convent's court and driving all the way across an old cemetery into the ancient church. I heard the dreadful screeching of metal and stone marrying under the bottom of the car. The beast riding on top was shrieking like nothing I had ever heard. Suddenly, layers of grey dust covered everything. The ashes fell away as if they were being brushed off Trusty, now I could see in the darkness for the exceptionally bright moonlight lit the antique pews, altar, and cracked and broken stained glass windows. I looked over at Bea whose wide eyes were full with tears. I gathered her in my arms and hugged her tightly and slowly rocked her and hummed one of Mom's hymns. Hopefully, I was letting her know there's nothing I wouldn't do to protect her. All the while biting back my own tears. Times like these made me want to kill every single demon in hell and every satanist on earth. But I put on a cheery face saying. "Baby, we made it. So I guess it's time to hit the road again."

"Mommy, I wish we had stayed at Janus'," Bea cried, sniffling. I rubbed her head promising her that somehow I was going to make everything alright. Things wouldn't always be this way. "Sweetie, they had found us at Janus'. That's why we had to leave." I explained. Hoping that she understood.

With some cover of the night to travel under I decided to make the most of it. As I backed out the dilapidated wall, I saw we had bust through the ancient stone wall without leaving a scratch on the car. It's little wonder a heavy stone didn't fall and crush us. I saw we missed the tombstones. I saw the trail we blazed coming in and decided we were blessed. I left all the bed covers, clothing, and etc behind and headed out of town. I was making the Richmond mistake again. It was too traumatizing.

Back on the road again, heading west this time. The rain seemed determined to wipe out the road and us along with it. I guess the weather is a good indication of what lies ahead.

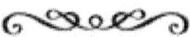

Belpher arrived in hell stinging and burning from foolishly clinging to Ana's car as it plowed through holy ground. Everyone in his vicinity knew the pain would last forever. Lucifer was at a loss in what to do about that woman. No demon was sent to spy on her while in Janus Cargill's home for they didn't want to alert Azazael of her whereabouts. He thinks Azazael still has allies in hell. He hasn't found the traitors yet but he knows they exist. Apparently, Janus didn't know what she was and they weren't about to tell him.

"Everyone fails in attacking her. What she must have? A band of angels on her side?" Lucifer wondered.

"That car has a spirit in it," Belpher moaned. "It burnt like brimstone".

"So heaven is sending her extra protection." Lucifer reasoned his thoughts aloud as he caressed his chin. Belpher was now useless to him. He kicked him into a river of fire. "Did the car burn like this?" Lucifer asked watching Belpher swim out the fiery river. "That's a reminder. Do not fail me. Do you know how hard everyone worked to find her?"

Leaving his lair, Lucifer continued on to Apollyon's chamber to see who may be connected to Ana BuFaye had arrived. He was looking for someone important enough to rain down punishment upon for failure. He propped on the corner of the black haired angel's massive desk. Apollyon kept writing in the life book of the soul damned, but he knew ignoring Lucifer didn't make him go away. He raised his cherubic curly head and asked what did he want?

"Oh nothing. I don't see why you write all that stuff down. You know I'm going to win this war. But thanks for upkeeping my library. Has anyone connected to that BuFaye woman arrived? I mean anyone in the last 24 hours?"

"No."

"Awww! C'mon Appy, learn to smile some of the time. It's not that bad for you and I here." Lucifer said playfully boxing Apollyon's rock hard shoulder. Apollyon looked perpendicularly at the smooth, pristine skinned fist and watched it return to its owner's side. Wishing he was allowed to break it off and beat him with it.

"Did I give you permission to touch me?", he asked, putting the quill that never needed refilling down.

"Ah, don't be so sore. You know most people think you are a demon anyway. So why not act like one?"

"If anyone seriously thought about it they would know what I am. Would anyone in their right mind give a demon or you the key to the bottomless pit?"

"Oh, I would love it if I had that key!"

"Everyone know you would, that's exactly why you don't have it because you would let all of hell out. You would open the pit out of spite."

"Oh well, no one can blame me for trying." Lucifer laughed and walked away.

Lucifer knew he wasn't allowed to hit him. They fought epic battles when Apollyon was first assigned this job. They fought all over hell until Uriel was sent to make them stop.

❦

Doing the right isn't always the same as doing the easy thing. Life has made sure she learned that lesson well. She wondered again had she made the right decision in leaving the only safe haven she had found in the past three years. Doubt was eating away at her confidence. Maybe the ascetic teachings of the bible, she believed, perhaps screw them royally. Her situations with men reminded her of St. Thecla. There's always some guy wanting to either hurt her, screw her, or kill her and sometimes all three. What about loving her for once?! Was she so unlovable? Bea had all rights to cry and whine, this nomadic life was very exhausting. If she were a child she'd cry too. She surely felt like crying right now. She glanced over at Bea who had finally calmed down and was dozing off to sleep. She pulled over at the next rest stop and put Bea in the backseat so she could stretch out and rest properly. Bea drowsily raised her arms to be kissed and hugged.

"Mwah!" Ana kissed her and covered her up with a thin sheet. The portable A.C. would keep her cool for about six hours. But she waited until Bea was asleep before covering her with the iron blanket which Bea detested. She ate a quick meal and rested a little more. Used the rest stop utilities to freshen up and walked around to stretch her legs. This place was empty but experience taught her that can be an illusion. They better get back on the road before next night fall. It's always more dangerous still than moving. She got back in Trusty, revved the engine, and started back the road again, hoping to make it out of Kansas tonight.

Jethro Manilow didn't want to rent the one bedroom apartment to the black woman and child but he had been fined a few years ago for discrimination. His bigoted belief was Blacks were destructive to your property. Knowing this and many other things about about Jethro Manilow, Gianna Machiavelli used the info to his advantage. He showed him the doctored picture of a nude Ana with her legs open.

"Is this the woman you rented to?" He asked and salaciously sneered at the photo. Auspiciously, the heavy set man looked at the photo, admiring the feminine attributes.

"Yeah, that's her. I thought she might be a slut. Most pretty women are," Jethro drawled. "Can I keep that picture?"

"Sure you can. You see, she ran away from her husband, that's who I work for. He loves her very much but you see this is the kind of woman she is. Sadly, my boss still love her regardless." Gianna said morosely in a heavy, beautiful accent.

"Them kind like this one ain't never learnt they place. They think they a damn man. Your boss got my sympathy. But your boss is making her worse by keep chasing her. He needs to leave her alone and go get a woman who do what he say. Tat lil' stubborn heifer ain't gonna never do what nobody say. I told her to keep that damn kid and dog quiet and she cussed me out. Them three bitches rides the road around here like they own it. Even the dog's siddity."

136

The gleam in the man's eyes told Gianna he had him on his side and he'd evict Ana with all ease when she turned the redneck down. He glanced at the shy, timid woman standing beside the big ruddy cheek man in a fresh washed and ironed t-shirt. One glance at her told him all he needed to know about this man. He could relax and let his words do the work. Gianna noted the woman living with Jethro, her fetal position, her body language told him Jethro had her completely under his control so she wouldn't warn Ana. From mere observation, Gianna knew that women in general hated other women. Especially if the woman was beautiful and every man's fantasy; the hatred was usually deadly. But no one they dispatched to watch her mentioned a dog. Well, that explained how she always seemed to know when someone was approaching her. That big mouth dog told her.

"You s-say there's a dog?" Gianna asked curiously, dropping the heavy accent.

"Yeah, there's a lil' yellow bitch about the size of my brother's dog here. It's a girl too. Snop, here been trying to tap that yellow bitch but the little bitch is as mean as her lil' owner. You know, the lil' girl with all 'em plaits in her head. The lil' dog is pretty as the sunrise but mean as a hellhound." The man laughed about the fight that sent Snop running back to them.

"I wholeheartedly agree with you. My boss should stop begging her to come back. But a heart wants what a heart wants." Gianna sighed to emphasize his sympathy. "You see, she left him to move in with Ashton Cargill. But Cargill dumped her after a few months. I'm sure you know of the man." Gianna lied adding fuel to the man's feverish anger at his own ex wife. Gianna had done his homework. He knew Jethro's wife left him for another man.

Jethro Manilow laughed. "No, I don't know the man, 'ever heard of 'im but it serves her right. Got herself a good man and don't know how to treat him." Jethro Manilow was totally unaware Vonderbilt was watching, listening, and planning to kill him for looking at the picture a second or two too long although it wasn't Ana's body just her face. He'd no idea he signed his death certificate when he asked to keep the photo. Vonderbilt was watching and listening through the camera on Gianna's diamond tie pin.

Jethro's own wife had left him five years ago for another man. After twenty years of marriage she was finally fed up with his chauvinistic, misogynist views and ideas in how women should be treated. So he had an axe to grind with the entire lot of the female gender.

Later that same morning he followed her when he saw her run out the building acting like she was scared to death of something. He and Sadie whose real name was Gemma heard them screaming that morning but figured her old man had finally caught her ass and was beating it. He didn't know Vonderbilt was back there trying to make her get in the limo with him. He didn't know the dog had bit someone and the kid razed him with her peashooter, giving them all a chance to run. Sadie saw them running and was secretly hoping they got away. She had left before the men in the limo but they saw her come creeping back later that evening. Unfortunately the men in the limo didn't leave an address on how to reach them.

He had asked her out a few times but she always declined. He knew her husband was some rich dude. He wasn't rich nor handsome so just as the stranger said. She was stuck on herself. Sadie called him on the road and told him they left a big hole in the wall. They wrecked the place. Dammit, he knew she was trash when he looked at her. He also knew she'd do that but the same damn law that made him rent to her ain't gonna make her fix it. Sure she gave him a 2,500 deposit but the hole and mess Sadie described is going to cost more than that to fix it. He reckon he could catch up her and take the rest out of her hide.

He parked on the side of the interstate watching her walking around the rest stop grounds like she ain't got a care in the world. He's curious as to where is she going? She been driving all day since she ran into the that old church this morning. She's fucking crazy! He had sat on the hill and watched her make a suicidal plunge into the old nun's covenant down the road. Wasn't nobody after her 'fore daylight this morning so what was they doing all that hollering for. He don't know what that man want her back for? She's batshit crazy. That rich man is better off without her.

He hadn't approached her yet because he wants to get her alone and beat the hell out

138

of her. Kill her if possible and carve the word 'hoe' on her forehead or tits to be warning to all others like her. Some women don't know how good they have it. He watched her start up the car and pull back onto the interstate.

I'm always alert so I sensed I was being followed. But they were too far behind to identify. So I pulled off the interstate onto a side road that headed toward Missouri instead of heading straight for Chicago as I originally intended. It had started to pour down again. It's been raining off and on for the past two months. When would it let up? It was raining when we drove into Richmond four months ago and damnit it's still damn raining. While my thoughts were on the rain and how tired I was of it, I heard a clunking noise under the car. Car trouble was the last thing we needed on this lone road in this down pour. I pulled to the narrow, weedy curb between the ditch and the road. I could hear the water rushing in the deep ditch before I got out to check the car. From the sound I knew it was the axle before I looked under the car. Night had come so I couldn't see under the car even with the flashlight in this Noahian rainfall. I stood up and looked both ways, hoping to see a friendly car coming down the road. Where are other motorists when you need them? Even the sky was clear of hovercrafts tonight. The green neon Roman numbers on my watch said it was 3:45 A.M., the last of the witching hours. I knew the myth about witching hours were between 12-4 A.M. was bullshit. Witching hour was anytime they felt like fucking with you which was 24 freaking 7. But a witch or warlock wasn't the source of this problem. It happened when I sped through that old church yard and hit a rock or tombstone.

Getting back in the car she drove slowly back the way they came, hoping the wheels held together a little while longer and there was a repair shop somewhere nearby the expressway. But a loud grating of metal dashed her hopes to the wet, soggy ground. She knew she had better stop before the wheel came off. Looking up data on her ISPAN pad, it showed a service state about two miles up the road. The rain wasn't letting up. She knew the longer they sat here the more danger they were in. She had to make a hard choice. Sit here and hope a satanist or another demon doesn't come along or they try and hike it to the service station. But she wondered could Bea walk that far? She knew Bea would be safer in the car, it offer more protection than she could give. She felt like a terrible mother when she had to make Bea hide under the iron blanket and give her the peashooter and tell her to stay there no matter what she saw or heard and if she isn't back

139

by the time the car alarm rings call her aunt Helena to come and get her.

Although, Bea Wyett maybe only three years old physically but she was much wiser than her mother knew. She knew the only way her mom wouldn't come back to her is if she were dead. She watched her mom hunch over against the rain and winds in a royal blue, short raincoat and prayed God protected her. The visibility in the silvery curtain of rain was making it impossible to see her. She folded her little hands together and prayed again that God protect her mommy. At least better than He had so far. She heard the silver hover-pickup truck before she saw it. It was the color of rain so it was hard to see it. She saw the distorted headlights through the windshield and somehow knew the driver was headed for her mom before the high beam lights trained on her. She squiggled from under the heavy thing her mom told her to stay under and opened the door and yelled for her mother. Ana turned to walk back toward the car, yelling and frantically waving her arms. Signaling Bea to get back inside just as the headlights, lowered like a bull's horns, aimed for her and the driver put the truck in a quick sprint. She saw her mom fly through the air and land in the ditch. She watched in horror as the man whose place they just left got out the truck and open a pocket knife. He looked at her through the rain and grinned. "Don't worry. You're next--little bitch." The slope to the ditch was steep and he had hold on to the long blades of grass to get down to mom. He was grinning like he had won the lottery.

"Bitches and whores like your momma needs to be taught a lesson," he said, looking back at her standing on the road near the left front of their car. He straddled Ana in the ditch, raising her head by pulling her hair, smoothing the dripping locks off her wet, soaked face and started to put the blade to her forehead after he kissed her fully on the mouth. He had been wanting to punish her since the first day he met her. He didn't take kindly to independent women thinking they're men. Before he could draw the first speck of blood he felt something like a hot branding iron in his back. He turned in great surprise, glaring up with a burning hatred in his eyes at the child with fireballs in her hand. He marveled for a few seconds what kind of child was this? The kid had bluish-red unquenchable fire in her hand. She threw another.

"Get off my momma!," Bea yelled, throwing another one. This one caught him in the face burning out his eyes, melting his nose and lips. He dropped Ana down in the rushing water to grasp his burning, melting face. She kept throwing them; watching the man howl and thrash about in shallow but strong current until he was nothing but charred remains. She had wanted to do that since the first day she met him.

Bea climbed down in the ditch and pushed him over into deeper water. Her mother was shivering but still unconscious. She lifted her mother's head above the water. She looked up at the early morning brightness and wondered who would help her get her mother out the ditch before the cold water killed her. She couldn't think of anyone able to do the things she could do but Janus and that's where she teleported after finding an old tire in the ditch to lay her mother's head upon.

Standing dripping wet next to his bed; there's a woman under him. *"Screw this! I don't have time for this!"*, she thinks, pushing his naked shoulder hard. The strength in that little hand surprised him. A very startled Janus whipped his head around to see a very wet, angry Bea standing there with blazing, fulgent blue topaz circles around the light brown of her eyes. Now, having his attention she begun telling him someone hit her mommy and she needed him to come get her out the ditch.

"Bea! Where did you come from?" He asked, shocked to see her standing there. He quickly covers his bedmate.

Bea yells as if he's stupid or retarded and asked her an even dumber question, "I said mommy is hurt bad. She's in a ditch. She won't wake up!" Bea yelled, frantically pulling his muscular arm.

"I thought you said you didn't have any kids!" The woman asked Janus, further pulling the covers around herself, up to her neck while glaring icy at Bea who frankly just didn't give a shit.

"I don't. This child isn't mine, she belongs to a close male relative," he explained slipping into his boxers under the white satin duvet since Bea wouldn't give him privacy to get dressed. He quickly turned the covers back and got up, found his pants and shirt and dressed with Bea follow him every step of the way. "Take me to your mother." He said taking her tiny, wet hand. "Show me where's your mother."

141

When they arrived on the wet embankment the water is just below Ana's chin, slowing inching toward her nose and mouth. Janus sees that someone had propped her head above the water; he also sees the charred body lying in the water by her and looked down at Bea who looked truculently back at him. Her eyes not denying she barbecued the man. He swiftly climbed down the embankment. The cold water reached above his ankles. He reached into the icy waters to feel for broken bones in vital parts. There appeared to be a serious injury on her right side. But no bones are protruding through the skin. Either way he has to get her out this water. The cold water had stopped the profound bleeding. He lifts her out the water and tells Bea to hold on to his pocket and teleports them to the nearest hospital. Being who he is they don't ask question as to who is the woman and child? He calls a tow truck to go get their car. He takes the dead man's truck too. It's his payment for the headache the charred dead man caused him. Now he knows without doubt Bea belongs to his grandfather and is his little aunt and is glad he didn't touch this woman. But he's curious as to what he sensed radiating from her. Whatever it was..it's beautiful and very peaceful.

He sits with the child until the doctors come out and tell them Ana has a crack in the right femur and ilium. They'd be keeping her for observation for a few days. But she was awake now and able to talk but still suffering from hypothermia.

He takes Bea's hand and they both go to see her mother. Ana is wrapped tight in silver thermal blankets which she's complaining are too hot. The nurse is trying to tell her her body temperature had dropped dangerously low so it may feel too hot at first until things evened out.

When she saw Bea wrapped in a child's thermal blanket she stopped complaining and trying to get out the bed to get to Bea. She held open her arms for the child who rushed into them. She looked over Bea's head at him; her eyes told him she wondered where did he fit in all of this.

"You two look like two little, wet, frizzy-headed birds."Janus joked. Bea turned and poked her tongue out at him.

142

"How you feeling?" He asked seriously.

"Like I've been hit by a sociopath driving a truck," she chuckled, trying to add humor to a humorless situation.

"The doctor said nothing is seriously injured. No full breaks in any bones but some hairline fractures which maybe painful for a while. Nonetheless, you're broken and pretty banged up so you need to listen to the doctors. Bea is fine. She's your little heroine. I assume the fool didn't put enough distance between himself and you to gather any real speed before hitting you," he said, beckoning for the nurse to leave them alone. The nurse nodded and left the room.

After the woman left them alone he drops the concerned friend, sympathetic disposition and turns to Ana with a serious expression on his face. "Now, Bea teleports and find me. So are you ready to be truthful with me. I already know your real name and know she's my little aunt. My father's little sister." He inquired, referring to the now exhausted and sleeping Bea. "So why did you run away? Was someone there bothering you?"

She looked down at Bea sleeping by her. She was thankful for her little heroine. Ana shifted uncomfortably and grimaced. She was hurt worse than she originally believed. She knew couldn't run and she needed this man's help to keep Vonderbilt at bay until she healed enough to continue.

She nervously licked her dry, parched lips. "Janus, when I saw you I figured you might be kin to the man in the closet?" She sighed. "I felt it was time to go. They had found me."

Laughter played in Janus' brownish blue eyes. "That's all you know about her father. He's a man in the closet. What in the devil was he doing in the damn closet? So that's who you running from? If you're running from my father or grandfather I can't say I blame you. There're many a days I feel like running from them, too." He teased her into smiling. She had to chuckle at the comical way he asked the questions.

143

To abbreviate the subject matter she says, "It's a long story. But my ex-husband is her father. But no, I don't think it's him who is trying to kill me. I don't know who I'm running from. All I know is they want me dead. There's one man who has a strange mottled face; he shows up everywhere I go."

"So how was running away supposed to keep them from killing you? Why didn't you tell someone at the estate about this mottled face man?" She squeegeed the question and moved to get more comfortable under Bea's weight. He took sleeping Bea in his lap. Her hip had started to ache and she was thankful he did.

"Look, Janus...I'm not used to people helping me. Most people I encounter help those trying to kill me. Not me. So when people are nice to us they usually have an ulterior motive."

"I'd no ulterior motive in hiring you. I saw you'd be asset to the party's scene and nothing more. Anyway, they said they're keeping you a few days and I paid for a place for you and Bea in Chicago, since that's where you were apparently headed. Here's the address and here is your last paycheck. Call me if mottled face show up again. Ok?", he said before calling his branch of Cargill's security team to watch this woman. He knew he wasn't safe around her. She just admitted she knows his bloodthirsty grandfather. "You can come back to the estate shall you run out of places to hide." He said kissing them both on the forehead before telling her he put the dog in a doggy hotel, the address was listed on the paper in her hand. He wanted to ask her about all the weapons the mechanic found in the car but knew she would dodge the question again.

She thanked him and promised she'd call him if the mottled face stranger showed up again but she could see from his facial expression he had no idea what having fear as a constant companion was remotely like.

Upon exiting the spiritual realm into the physical world again Janus saw his bedmate was gone. Not that he spectacularly cared. He poured himself a drink and sat at his desk and pondered a few minutes before pushing the airscreen phone to call his grandfather.

He was sorry about his father's feelings but he couldn't keep up this charade any longer. He felt his immortal grandfather ought to know where his mystery woman was. She is on the road to death and if Azazael walks the timeline and finds out he knew her whereabouts and didn't tell him, he will be on the same road. He didn't see the distaff's celestial finger reach from the heavenly realm closest to earth before she touched his temple, erasing what he knew about Ana and her whereabouts. He slumped over in the chair and fell into a deep sleep. Waking up a few hours later when a maid roused him. He couldn't remember where he had been nor why the airscreen phone was suspended in the air. He clicks it off and goes about his business for the remainder of the rainy day.

Janus had kept his word. Her car was repaired and delivered to the hospital and parked in the garage awaiting her release. Five days later nothing strange showed up but she could tell from the change in the nurses' attitude toward her there had been plenty of calling in about her. It was subtle at first because of who was footing her bill but the day she left her doctor handed her the home care slip and mumbled, 'good riddance."

No one brought a wheel chair nor came to see that she got out to the car alright. She leaned on Bea and the crutch to make to the garage. She knew they had called when she overheard a nurse laughing saying her hair looked like a balled up wool blanket that needed to be cut off. But she thanked them for their care and kept walking. It was a long, hard trip to the car and she was dripping with sweat by the time she made it to Trusty who started up without a glitch.

She drove through the small unknown town after picking up Bea's dog and was glad to leave it behind. About five miles from the pet hotel she saw the expressway she pulled onto I-65 N, headed for the new place already paid for and with her last paycheck in her pocket. She was alive with a little change in her pocket so she couldn't ask for much more. Three hours later she stopped at drive thru restaurant, they ate as she waited for the afternoon traffic to clear. She didn't feel like maneuvering all the traffic she knew was ahead. She drove further out and waited at the rest stop until 2 A.M., and then took side streets to get there. Bea was in the back seat long ago asleep. The place was located in the southwest side of Chicago. Janus had left a number to call when she arrived. She called the number but the person didn't show up until 8 to open the door for them. It was a nice spacious place. She liked it. It was in a nice neighborhood. The woman who let her in told her firmly. "We expect when you leave, you leave it exactly as you found it. Normally, we don't take your kind but since Janus called and said you were getting out of the hospital and needed a place to stay we accepted you but no holes in the walls, no tearing up the appliances, do not let your kid draw on the walls, and no pets allowed." She said looking in the back seat Bea's dog before handing her the key, leaving and closing the door more clamorously than necessary.

I searched and inspected the place, it was fully furnished. All I needed to do was supply my own sheets, towel and dishes. I sent Bea to the car to get them. I wish it was a downstairs apartment. But I know I wouldn't have gotten this place on my own merit. Bea and I dressed the bed and crawled in it and slept for three days. Only waking up long enough to go get food, eat, and use the bathroom. I know I shouldn't have mixed the pain relievers with rum but hell, I was still in pain. By the fourth day I felt better. I knew we wouldn't be here long for the place was $4,000 per month and I only made 8 in the past months of this year. So I knew I had to get well fast and go out and look for work.

Knowing they had only six weeks left before she would've to cough up another 4 grand she set out to look for work. By now the holiday season had rolled around and she had forgotten how cold and windy Chicago could be this time of the year. She had passed a help wanted for the holidays sign at a diner turning off the main boulevard and decided to stop in. The only thing they could say was no. She really didn't feel like carrying Bea but the hawk was nipping at their asses not their noses when they got out the car. She entered the crowded diner and had to wait a while before asking the waitress who appeared to be ignoring everybody about a position available. "Go talk to Veto!" the woman around her own age said above the clamoring of the holiday crowd. She walked back into the kitchen and asked who was Veto?

"Right here, babydoll," a dark complexioned, big brawny man said. She must have been staring at him.

"What can I do ya?" He asked, then she remembered her manners.

146

"Uh, I saw a help wanted sign in the window. I came to apply for a job." He looked down at Bea who was looking up at him.

"I hope ya got a babysitter, I can't have no babies running around here. We're a fast paced operation and children trying to follow their mommies around they liable to get hurt."

"I've worked before with her in the lounge or office. She knows to stay put."

"Yea, that's what all y'all mamas say." He scowled down at us both. "Look sir, I live right around the corner up in Cargill Ridge apartments. My mother is coming to keep her after the holidays. I promise-she won't be trouble." I said turning on the charm, adding eyelash batting for extra measure.

"You mean round there in Cargill Ridge. That's place's sky high. So I guess ya do need a job. Ok, tell Briggs to outfit ya and come in tomorrow at 9. I don't work mothers with babies all weird ass hours. I was raised by a single mom so I know the ropes. If everything checks out all right then you're regular."

I was a lot nervous about giving my references but was surprised Janus said I worked in the Cargill restaurant and didn't tell what I really did nor that I lived at the mansion the entire summer entertaining rich clients. Veto gave me the job.

Helena and Jack weren't happy that I asked mom to come and live with us. Things was going well again for the first time in years. I mean the satanists came to the dinner but Veto used to be a mob hit man and everyone knew it. So they didn't tarry.

One day Briggs Moulton, a savvy, sassy, sultry black woman of a paper-bag brown complexion, a little on the tall side pulled up a seat and decided to chat. She had a razor sharp wit; she missed nothing. We often reminisced about our college days and how things didn't turn out as we planned during our teen years despite all the careful planning and good grades. She strolled up beside me in the middle of my shift and asked me to walk down the street with her. She had our boss, Veto wrapped around her little finger so

I was safe to walk off if she said so. She wanted to take a smoke break, so I went with her, we walked up the streets all the back to my apartment complex and sat in the small, well maintained garden park for the residents enjoyment. It was a beautiful Midwestern early spring day, but it was still a little chilly, the trees hadn't sprouted their tender leaves yet. By now Lake Michigan had stopped trying to kill everything.

"It's pretty up here," she said looking around. "I see why you like it. I asked you to come with me is I could tell you were very well educated from the way you carried yourself. That's why I talked to you about my college days. You aren't like most of the employees at the diner. But the main reason I asked you to walk with me is somebody been calling saying a lot of nasty things about ya since day one. Veto don't have a moral stick up his ass like a lot of bosses. He don't care about the kind of shit they be talking about. They hangs up if he answers. He said whomever calling is who ya running from but we don't pay them no mind. But that ain't the full main reason I asked you to walk with me. Honey, I noticed ya aint' well. I don't know what happened to ya but ya need a job where ya can sit down. This work is too hard for someone in pain all the time and I know pain when I see it."

I thought I was hiding all this from her and everyone else. I told her about the crazy, insane attacks. About the harassment, about the evictions. "It's been crazy like this all my life." I said. "And I don't really know why." I told her about what I learned about James Caldwell.

Taking a long draw on her cigarette Briggs frowned as she listened and put the butt out on the ground near the concrete bench they sat on, "Caldwell? You mean the chip movie producer? Married to Caroline Caldwell?! Whew, girl those are heavy weights. But you know, I've heard the old folks in my family talk about something like that used to be quite prominent about 400 years ago. But I don't see how nobody is getting away with it nowadays. What's you describing is a crime called gang-stalking. They say anyone could end up a victim. You didn't have to do anything major to be selected as a target. Something as simple as cutting one of those egotistical people off in a parking lot for a parking space or one of them just didn't like the way you looked could get ya tagged. They're an underground network. They're a secret society that operated in broad daylight. They're all over the place. I heard they were mostly gangs of thugs, witches,

148

and warlocks. They served satan. I don't know if all that's true or not. But I had some ancestors who were their victims back in the twentieth century and the old people say they even turned family members against that person they picked out to harass. They said World War III pretty much put a stop to it being so standard. But I guess they started back up again after the big war." Briggs explained.

"Who controls the money bag? Somebody gotta be footing the bills. I mean, they can easily get anything done they want done." I cried.

"I heard a lot of people in law and those involved in court cases used them. Governments used them. Hitler used something like this when he was rounding up the Jews. Insurance companies used them. Just about anybody up to some dirt can buy their services. They're a bunch of sick psychopaths who already loved to hurt people so this sick shit is right up their alley for a career and yeah, you're right. I too, believe somebody is paying them to do it. A lot of them are in police departments. I'm not saying this is the case with you but it sounds like the same thing my ancestors went through 400 years ago. It didn't get no better until the family started catching and killing them. That's when they left us alone. Maybe you and your folks gonna have to start killing them."

I knew that would never happen, my family had too much 'religion' to do that. But at least someone finally placed a name on what's happening to us. I had never heard the term but it sounded about right.

After work, I finished dinner and washed the dishes. I looked up the term 'gang-stalking' and found it to be a legitimate word, it was illegal act of two or more stalking an individual with malicious intent. I read thousands of four to five hundred year old accounts sounding much like my own life. "Wow!", I cried out aloud after reading several reports from police departments and even psychologists. All these record became public after all the participants are dead. I read late into the night. While reading the strange reports I thought of Mom's strange illness. So I asked mom had she ever heard of it? She said she had.

But I think mine may be something different than these half a millennium old cases all over the internet.

The next day on our lunch break I resumed the conversation with Brigg saying, "C'mon, there's no way in hell the authorities could've concluded that tens of thousands of people were simply crazy or making this up!"

Briggs shrugged her shoulders. "People believe what they wanna until it happens to them".

At home I brought up the issue again with mom who had arrived after Christmas to take care of Bea while I worked.

"Well, yes and no, not really. Not to this degree." Fannie replied and read a few printouts. "It makes sense. I've known a few people who seem like their lives are bogged down in bad luck and nothing they try improve it made any difference. It's says here these people's situations and lives are deliberately orchestrated to fail. I guess in a way it's like Nazism, I guess it never really died out. It simply went underground."

Ana always liked her Mom's opinion on things. She's natty, charming and insightful. Through she and Ana are remarkably different in personality, as a team they had a wonderful chemistry to appears to transpire to the next generation. Bea. Which is why Ana didn't hesitate to call her and tell her mom she needed her help. Fannie gave her a healthy tongue lashing when she found about the second truck hitting her. Wanting to know why she didn't call her sooner or the day it happened?

I didn't call because I believe...no, I know Helena's and Mom's phones are bugged. But not all the time. You can feel the second connection when it kicks in. I always hang up. Nothing sounds different but the spiritual air changes.

"Aren't we lucky, it could've been much worse." Fannie sighed, shaking her head, trying to make sense of this madness.

"Probably would've been had not Bea saw him coming and called me. Allowing me enough time to leap out the way so he merely nipped my side." Ana said as the cheap wine and conversation flowed after Lady Bea was in dreamland. She has wondered about Bea's ability to instantly go to sleep if she wants. She've never seen anyone able to do that but didn't mention it to her mother.

"It's a blessing you two made it this far." Fannie silently sighed. She truly feared for her long-suffering, adorable youngest child and grandchild. Wondering what will become of them?

❧ ✦ ☙

The convergence in the Lundys' livingroom opened with Lambert Lundy, Briggs' great grandmother in her comfortable living room, talking about the subject of gang-stalking, saying they're ruthless, super competitive and all bound for hell and ready to bowl over anyone who gets in their way; they're very dangerous people and aren't to be underestimated. Do not underreckon the significance of the danger you face. If possible stay among a crowd as much as possible. The small, scooped spunky old woman lectured as she kept turning compulsively to her computer pulling up a bombardment of information on gang-stalking. Finally, she pulled up the reports her ancestors made to the police and their on-line blog, putting it all on a chip for Ana to read at her convenience.

I thanked her for the information. She gave a clearer picture of the psychopaths I were dealing with but the stalkers I encountered didn't care if you were among a zillion people they did supernatural and natural things to you. So maybe this woman's ancestors were dealing with a different type than mine. Those after me have shot through crowds at me, sometimes hitting someone. So I knew they would kill anyone who stood in their way.

So I explained the things that happens to us. I thought she was going to call me crazy as people usually do when I attempt to explain this madness. But Mrs. Lundy simply looked at me and dug up more information. She came across a group of people who once lived down in Kentucky who knew how to fight the kind I was dealing with.

"The site is in bits and pieces, somebody tried to erase it but you know you can never fully erase what's on the internet." Mrs. Lambert explained as I looked over her shoulder. Briggs explained her great-grandmother was an MIT graduate. I was

151

impressed for so was my brother Jack.

"Are these people's operation still in existence?" I asked excitedly. Hoping I had finally found someone able to make sense of my life.

"I don't know their last entry was more than four hundred years ago." The old woman sadly replied. "It just stopped, except a monthly constant called to prayer and I assume that was an automatic entry." The woman said, poking at the three computers surrounding her powered wheelchair which her excitement caused her to forget to use.

"I tell you what, when I retrieve their entire work I will send it to you by Briggs here. But you've remember back then people were named strictly by their gender, there were strict names for girls and boys that rigorously told if the author was male or female. Unlike today, a girl can so easily wear a name originally decided to be male and vice versa."

The price of the apartment and the stress of the job worked havoc on the new and reawakened old injures, causing me to seek employment and lodging elsewhere. Because the four grand a month was eating me alive. Janus' charity had ran out. I was able to live here longer than most places because I still had a lot of the money left over from that which I took from the man in Richmond and plus my salary from working at the mansion. I wanted to stay long enough for Bea to have her fourth birthday party in a nice neighborhood. I gave the party in the small park with the neighbors' children attending and of course my friends down at the diner brought their children Bea's age over that Wednesday afternoon. Veto and some of his old running buddies attended. I know Briggs made him to come to protect us.

I went around the city putting in job and employment applications, nothing panned out for a few months but by the fourth month when money start to becoming spare again I got a call from a bank back home in Georgia which had a branch in Chicago, asking did I want to relocate for a teller position? I was suspicious of the offer with it being from my home state. But I had no other choice, I couldn't use our last cent to pay other's month rent and not have the amount for the following month. Mom's health wasn't the greatest and I could just see my siblings bitching at me if mom was put in a homeless position again because of me and my problems.

The last day at the diner the satanists attacked with an all out assault on the place, one waitress and two customers were killed before Veto was able to come out the kitchen and blow away five of them with an automatic assault rifle. The rest ran and fled down south 128th street. After this ordeal I know what I had to do. I couldn't bear the thought of anyone losing their life for simply standing next to me. I ducked by reflex when I saw them coming in brandishing guns. I began firing at the first shooter after I was able to dislodge the gun from the Velcro band I wore around my waist. But it was too late; although I took him out the bullet intended for me hit the waitress standing to the southwest behind me in the back. She fell over on the table top, the customers begin screaming. Veto's friends caught several of them. They fled up the streets after shooting two more customers in the parking lot on their way out. There had to have been at least fifteen of them! The mobster hit men brought them back to the diner through the delivery door and tied them up and put them in the freezer storage. They tried in vain to get information from them but I told them they never talk. Veto took them all out one by one when he asked did they've anything to say? They simply stared hatefully at him but remained mute. He knew all about the street code of silence, so seeing he wasn't going to get anything out of the five they caught he put the Glock 53 to their head and pulled the trigger. I wasn't surprised at all when the police force didn't show up. They never do if the satanists kill someone. They only show up if you kill a satanist or your pursuer.

After the diner massacre I knew I had to leave and try to outrun them again. At least when I kept them after me so no one else got killed. I tried to send mom back to Helena's place but she wouldn't hear of it. So I accepted the odd bank job offer and packed up and moved back south. It was difficult to find a place willing to rent to me without a five year rental history and Cargill Ridge said I stayed there less than a year. Plus I believe that cranky old landlady told every calling rental office about the shooting at the diner. If that didn't kill my chances of getting a decent place then nothing would. I finally found a place that used to be a woman's boarding house. I wasn't thrilled with the age because usually old houses have a lot of bad history. Yes, I spotted a few ghosts round and about the place but they were nowhere near scary as the live bastards I deal with.

⁂

The big man wearing dark sunglasses inside smelt like money but Jethro Manilow's brother but he couldn't tell if he was black or white for he looked neither. He looked like no human race he had seen.

"Hello, my good man." Cargill said forcing himself to be cordial while slapping a thousand dollar bill on the counter. "I was politely wondering...has a woman with a child come through here?" At these words the man at the rickety desk used his spittoon before answering.

"I don't know, aplenty of women wit' chilluns pass thro' here. You gotta be mo' direct." The man said spitting again, this time was to show his distaste for the big man.

Ashton Cargill mentally grits his teeth. He knows the man doesn't like him for the color of his assumed human suit. But never mind all that for the moment; he needed to know if Ana passed through here.

"Ok, a thin woman. Very pretty with long auburn hair below her waist. She would've had a little girl with long hair like her mother."

"Oh, you mean this little slut," Jethro Manilow's brother said, slamming Gianna's picture on the counter and grinning a brown toothed grin at Azazael. He knew this woman must mean a great deal to this man or he wouldn't be here asking about her. But the spitter learned his err too late. That err was to whom he he was speaking to was a mystery. In the next few seconds he learned what he was talking to wasn't an earthly man. Azazael snatched the shades off, looked at the promiscuous picture. His eyes grew dark as fiery onyx before he let out a low hellish growl and reached across the decaying counter and tore shirt and skin from the body in one swift sweep. Leaving the man alive, but screaming and wishing that death takes him soon. He grabbed the picture and burned it in his hand. He knew it was a doctored photo but it was the principle that mattered.

Jethro Manilow's woman, who was hiding behind the door, waited until the big man left. She had heard the man screaming, calling her, begging her to take him to the hospital. She came out, looked down at him rolling on the floored in wretched pain. Her stoic expression told him she intended to let him die. She dainty stepped over him and left the way Azazael left. She was finally free. She went and sat outside to wait until he was dead to bury him out back.

The haggard woman with haunted eyes bloodshot from too many nervously smoked cigarettes and worry, sat and pondered. She wasn't in a hurry. Her hard and often slapped damaged skin looked older than her years. She was thinking of many thing but the man's screaming wasn't one of them. She was sitting and basking outside in the warm sun, thinking. She sat on the ranshackled, paint worn wooden flower trough that now only grew trash and cigarette butts. She was a world away, sorting out her plans in how to finally run the place to make some real money. Lots of traffic came through here heading to St. Louis or Indianapolis so she could make it work. Just lock up the room with all the stinky dead bees all over the place. Indianapolis is where she met Jethro five years ago. He made this place sound like a cute little country inn when it was really a dump. According to him, his recent runaway wife was the town's whore and didn't appreciate a good man. The first day she foolishly allowed him to sweet talk her into coming out here his brother climbed in the bed with him and when she demanded he get out Jethro started his abuse, saying they share everything. From that day forth his cronies kept their eyes on her and she wasn't allowed to leave town. Wasn't allowed to use the car nor the phone. He locked up everything when he closed the office. If women came in to rent she had to hide for he always said they'd get suspicious about her appearance.

The big angry man with a mane of hair had left the money, he had seen her peering out the crack of the door. But he wasn't after her so that's all she cared about.

She sat outside smoking a cigarette, recalling the days of yore when she was beautiful like the red haired woman Jethro and his brother despised so much because they both knew they didn't have a snowball chance in hell of getting in her bed. Not as much as a snowball. From what she heard, some parts of hell is cold. She listened until the thrashing and rolling inside the office stopped. She idly butted out her cigarette and went

155

back inside and he was nearly dead. She was indifferent. His dog was lapping the blood and other spilled bodily fluids. She gathered his bloody legs which was about the only part that still had skin and dragged him into the kitchen. The hard, old tiles were easier to clean than this new stuff. She decided a trash bag was too good for him, this bastard helped Jethro keep an eye on her which stopped her from running away. He helped his brother abuse her. So no, he didn't deserve one of her big trash bags, this is an animal. So he'll be buried like one.

No one ever came back there so she spent the next six hours gardening. All this fertilizer will surely make her plants grow. She rolled him slightly moaning into the fresh grave. His eye lids fluttered open a bit, he opened his mouth to beg her help; she threw a shovel full of dirt in it. He kept reaching for her. His dog kept trying to reach him.

"Gemma, please." He moaned with outstretched, bloodied arms, pitifully reaching out to her. This was the first time he called her by her name in years. It's usually "the ugly, toothless bitch, the whore, slut, cunt, the split tail." Why won't this damn ugly, tobacco chewing bastard die? She beats the dog back out the hole with the handle of the shovel as it tried to get the bloody skin and shirt she intend to bury in the hole with him. She didn't know which were the most annoying; this damn dog or the flies and gnats that kept biting her.

"Gemma, please—I need medical help." Dunson Manilow sobs. "No, you don't! What you need to do is go ahead and go on to hell! You stinking monster!" she said through clenched teeth as she jumped down in the makeshift grave, raising the shovel to finish him off. She heard her dead grandmother's voice.

"NO! Gemma. He isn't worth going to hell over." She peered anxiously up out the hole, afraid someone had caught her but she saw no one so she looked around the outback in the bright evening sunshine. She shuddered. Her sweat was chilling her soul. She was positive that was her beloved granny's voice. The bright light of the evening shimmered through the full leaved trees overhead and gathered itself into a human form. Her eyes widened as granny who she loved walked toward her and kneel down eye level. "Honey, you don't pray, but I know why you don't---this evil man isn't worth your immortal soul spending eternity in hell. Take him to the hospital. He'll behave from now on out. Won't you, Dunson?" The heavenly saint asked. Dunson nodded.

Gemma loved her granny but this was one thing she couldn't do. This... thing... she couldn't let live. She raised the shovel to bring it down on Dunson's bloody but clearly heaving chest. Her granny snatched it out her hand. "I'm not losing you to hell because of those two brothers. Jethro Manilow is already in hell. Do you want to spend eternity with him?" Her granny made her get out the hole and pulled the grimy, dirt crusted man out. The dirt had clogged the bleeding. She didn't understand how was he still even alive.

On the drive to the hospital. Gemma says."From now on out things will be ran my way. That big guy who skinned you left me his money and phone number. He said if you give me anymore troubles to call him. I got it right here on speed dial." She lied holding up Jethro's phone. "I put it on the voice activation phone. Give me anymore problems, I'm calling him and telling him everything you and your nasty ass brother said about his woman. I'm calling him to finish your evil ass off."

At the hospital Dunson lied, he believed Gemma really had the man's contact information so he told the doctors a gang rode through but when he refused to rent to them this is what they did to him. They buried him up to his neck but Gemma dug him up after they left. Gemma nods, verifying his story was true. He lied for he didn't know if Gemma had that big psycho's phone number or not and wasn't eager to find out. The small, dingy complex of apartments and boarding rooms rental didn't have security cameras in the office therefore all the local police had to go on was his and Gemma's word.

⁂

Her spiritual trail had grown cold, or heaven had erased it. Sometimes it was hard to tell the difference when they didn't want you to find something or someone. He knew he was close, oh so close but yet not close enough. A reasonable, sane man would've given up chasing a woman by now. But who ever said he was sane? Many days he himself didn't know if he was sane. Sure, he functions on a normal level but many days he

157

doesn't know if he's coming or going and others weren't helping his mental functions by pissing him off. He knew the picture was a propaganda doctored photo. He wish he had kept it to learn who gave it to the misogynistic pervert. But his temper got the better of him too quickly. The only conclusion he can scare up for Janus' lying is his grandson has fallen for her himself. If he find out Janus touched her he might not kill him but he'll make him wish he were dead. He makes himself promise to get a grip on his temper. He can't learn anything if he keeps killing everyone she has encountered. But that man deserved what he got.

Like when he asked the harem what did Caroline Caldwell want? They lied and said she called to invite them to a gala. He knew all sixteen of them were lying. The youngest wasn't able to hold his gaze. She tore her eyes from his and looked away out the harem's room window. But given time, he'll get to the bottom of the reason for their lying to him. He has all of his security people on the look out for this woman but the heavens keep erasing all images of her. Who else can erase something so thoroughly? All he's left with is the feeling in his heart. He had an image but stupidly, hotheadedly burnt it.

Alone, lying across his massive seventeen foot bed, with his feet dangling over the edge. He had allowed himself to grow a little toward his natural size. Well, not quite. This place couldn't contain his actual size. While in deep thoughts he felt someone standing over him. He opened one eye and peered up. It was his brother Raphael.

"Azazael, lets just say, hypothetically, you find this woman. What do you plan to do with your concubines? A woman like the one you are pursuing isn't going to share you with anyone else."

He slowly closed his eyes again, "Get rid of them."

"Ok, let's say you do that. How long can you stay true to one woman?"

"For all the days of her life. I told you I love her."

"Supposed she lives to be a 120 and become old and wrinkled? Can you still be true? She's mortal. She's going to age and die. So why put yourself through the pain?" The

158

archangel of mercy quizzed.

"Don't you've something else to do besides fuck with me? Don't you've some mercy to bestow on someone?" Azazael asked, grunting and turning away from the angel. There was no need for all the damn questions. Didn't Ralph think he had always thought about all those things? Why did he think he rarely marries and make a family? It's too painful to watch them all die again and again.

"Not at the moment. No, I don't."

"Well, go find something to do and leave me alone." Azazael said turning over on the bed. "Go get her and bring her to me."

"Sorry, I can't do that."

"Well, go away. I don't need a lecture."

The Black Mass Wedding.

While the doctor removed the small metal plug from Vonderbilt's arm he ponders on how to capture her and force her to do as Lucifer ordered. He grimaced and slapped the doctor more out of annoyance than pain. The pain wasn't so bad. He'd taken much harder blows than that fighting in Wizard Chess. He was more pissed off than in physical pain. Where in the hell did a kid that young get a gun and furthermore how she did know how to use it? With Ana being the only person in the world his equal in spiritual combat she seemed to have the same inherent knowledge as he; it's programed into her in how to block every blow he delivered. She's evolving. The daunting harassment is driving her. Is bringing her gifts to the surface in not a very good way. If they don't capture her soon, she'll be too powerful to handle. Right now, she can still be handled. But fighting that woman is like fighting a damn berserker! He was shocked when she took him down and ran. No one has ever taken him down. He was glad no one was around to see it.

159

And what were they doing all that screaming for? He was the one getting his ass kicked. He forgot. Woman and children scream for no reason at all.

After Gianna got the information needed from the landlord, as to which of the dumps was Ana's he came back to the limo and gave it to him. Vonderbilt got out and went inside the musty smelling building to talk to Ana. Try and make her see that running from him was futile. She peeved him off when he tried talking to her is how they got into a fight. He tried reminding her of their midnight wedding, their never begun marriage but she kept saying they were not married. She was divorced and didn't answer to anyone. She pissed him off for he knew she was pretending not to know him when she knew damn well who he was. He told her she was coming with him whether she wanted to or not. That's when the cat claws popped out. Ok, well, the cat claws popped out when he tried to back hand her and she inherently caught his hand and returned the blow. But still there was no reason for the outright fighting or the kid shooting him.

Dammit! Neither Lucifer nor Lilith told him that drinking the blood of a saint would have such profound effect. They told me this after the angels had taken her away that by her bearing the same gift as I once possessed I'd fall in love with her which was marvelous because that ensured I wouldn't kill her before she bore the physical vessel for Lucifer. I've been lying to myself. I can't shake my love for this wild, untamed woman no matter how hard I try. Lucifer is right, that is the only reason I haven't eliminated her and her whole annoying ass family.

Believing she perhaps had gone back to the place by now for she had no where else to go he summon imps to inquire. The trollish creatures appeared before him mirthfully grinning because Ana kicked his ass but knew to deliver aspiring news or they'd be sorry. They told him her car was back out in front of the tiny apartment. He was glad; she had upset the wrong man. He waved his uninjured arm and summon a powerful demon named Belpher. One made entirely of harpies that looked like flies, wasps and bees and sent it to kill her and that ornery child. Lucifer will just have to find someone else to birth his earthly vessel. There's no way in hell he's siring a child by that wild woman. She might castrate him. This was his first time being alone with her. At their Black Mass wedding his people held a knife on her baby so she submitted to his order

160

but today she wasn't submissive at all; she fought like a ninja. She reminded him of a movie chip he saw as a child, really old movies were popular in his country. It was about a child somewhere in the USA running wild with fire sparklers. As a child he didn't how she didn't set herself on fire running around with those things. So no, if Lucifer wanted that wild thing caught, he'd better bring his sulfurous behind here and catch her. He was now glad he hex-masked his face so she never clearly saw his features.

The night they captured her in that seedy motel and teleported her and the kid to his Alps' castle wasn't exactly a happy occasion. He had no real objection to marrying her. She was beautiful when in decent clothing and a lovely hairdo. He knew sending the demons he did to kidnap her would scare her stiff and it worked. They posed as rapists. Every woman's ultimate fear. They sworn they didn't touch her but they were demons and demons lie for fun of lying. This was the woman Lucifer chose years ago to bring him into the physical world to walk among men in flesh. They brought her to the castle, his women dressed her. Even Lucifer and Lilith made a rare appearance to see his future mother. She met his expectation in beauty, elegance and refinery, but most of all in the strength of the spiritual gifted she was endowed with.

By then Beatrice or whatever that ornery child's name is was about two. She held up two fingers when I asked her how old was she? A beautiful child but I knew I would've to turn her into furniture polish before she was five. She was a little firebrand and strong as a damn calf. They're right, the blood of saints is sweet. Not harsh and coppery as most humans, leaving a nasty after taste in your mouth. When the matrimony cup was passed to Ana with my blood, tears seeped down her face. She sipped only because the knife was pressing against the child's throat. She didn't flinch when the priest raised her dress to cut her inner thigh and caught the blood dripping into the cup. I saw the women had dressed her in crotchless black underwear to match her black wedding dress. Her eyes stayed on my men restraining her child.

I saw she expected Lucifer to look as human art depicts him. Hideous and horned with hooves. He kissed her before the ceremony after my women brought her to the altar. She turned her head in disgust when he called her "Mother." He chuckled and let it slide that time. I was surprised he kissed her so tenderly without burning her. He usually burns a person when he touches them. That's why I don't let him touch me if I can help

161

it. The idea was that Lucifer would stick around until a conception and enter the body.

As the ceremony concluded and the priest finally shut up and allowed Lucifer to commence to dignify the marriage a blinding bright light broke the dimness of the temple and she and her baby were stolen from us. Lilith said the two archeias were named Amethystia and Maryllisa. So in every definition she's my wife and I've every intention of bringing her home. A wedding in hell is as binding as one in heaven. So heaven will have do a better job than that to keep me away from her.

Chapter 2
Shattered dreams: The Betrayal

Thaddeus Thackeray Wyett hung his head between his massive shoulders, wanting to cry but too proud and tough for that. Flicked his tangled locks inherited from his Cree grandmother out of his eyes. Reasoned to himself, *"How did I go from being a high football scholarship reception, a Heisman trophy winner, a young man in love, a young father doting his infant daughter, an off-season pre-med student to an inmate in a prison cell in a matter of seeming minutes. How was a kilo of cocaine found in my car when I don't do drugs? Maybe a beer or two every now and again".*

Mentally reliving and relishing his life for the past 12 years. Starting with his meeting of his future bride, Ana. Remembering the pretty, doe-eyed skinny 14 year old frowning at his 16 year old attempt at being a Romeo. Telling him to go away. Get lost! Scat! Reminiscing friends' peals of laughter at her brutal dismissive of him. Determined not to be deterred by her rebuttal, he approached again, so sure of the self-indulgent fact he was irresistible to girls he strutted the ground around her group with her narrowed eyes following him. (Which she years later told him that move wasn't romantic, it remained her of a wolf stalking a prey.) Then deliberately ignoring him, turning to continue her chat with her friends.

Pulling aside a player from the opposing team he only knew from a tackle on the football field in a previous game. Pointing at Ana, he asked, "Who is she?"

"Which one?" The burly teen roughly asked looking at the group of pretty girls giggling. He wasn't too thrilled with a member of an opposing team interested in one of his fellow students.

"The one with the big eyes, long red hair, and lashes. She got a cute little keister."

"Why do you want to know?!?" The other boy asked. Making him wonder was he interested in the girl.

"Man, I think I am in love."

"Man, I think you are crazy. Stay the hell away from her," the slender but muscular auburn haired boy for the opposing team said, shoving Thad aside. Which resulted into a fist fight between the two teams before the game. Their coaches rushed in and pulled them apart. He knows now the shorter boy who put himself in the conversation was Ana's older brother Jack BuFaye. But how was he supposed to have known that then? He didn't look at the guy carefully enough to see the resemblance.

Thad smiled at this long ago memory. Thinking how badly he wanted to hurt that boy and get his chance on the field. The opposing team coach accused him of deliberately attacking his opposition's knees to put him out the game. Which he did do on purpose. But that's all part of the game. It wasn't fun at all when a 340 lbs man did the same to him after he went pro and ruined his knee forever.

Reeling his thoughts back from the past 7 years into the present. They both were college grads by the time Bea was born, she was pre-law and he pre-med. He studied during his off season. Both had been accepted in prestigious graduate schools, trying to decide if one could drop out and take care of the baby they named Bea before she was born and contribute more to the household income. He only played one season before his career ending injury. So he decided he'd drop out of graduate school and take a job.

To backtrack the speed of their progress, within a month after marriage the young couple was standing on the foyer of their first real home, a mini mansion he had built with his first check from the pro team he played for. They moved out of their cramped one bedroom apartment into a six bedroom Tudor-styled home of their own. He had started having the house built the week Ana accepted his proposal. He was walking on air. She was still in high school when he went away to college but was only in school a few months before a pro team drafted him. She encouraged him to stay the course, finish his education. He did it mainly to appease her.

He was glad he listened to Ana and put the remaining amount into an IRA and college fund for their children. Bea came along sooner than he would've liked but he enjoyed her. He sort of expected them to be married at least a year before she got pregnant. They spend their wedding night in their new home but it wasn't completed yet so they had to go back to the apartment. But they were happy and in love; it didn't matter.

His reliving the past soon started to grow dark. He remembered all too well the day he met Lola Wilson. Or at least that was the name she gave. She came into his insurance office regarding a claim she put in. Looking up the information she gave he saw she was a new widow. Her late husband was accidentally killed in his line of employment. But what was even more astonishing was a construction worker with a 10 million accident insurance policy. $250,000 was the usual limit. Knowing it was best to run this by his boss before approving the check he rapped on the opened door. Cecil Towne, the local Fidelity Insurance regional manager looks up and asked "What can I do for you, Thad?"

"I want to verify that this amount is correct."

Reaching for the papers Thad held, Cecile's bushy eyebrows shot up. Carefully scrutinizing the data on paper, he wearily exhaled after a seemingly endless pause. He handed the sheets back to Thad looked him in the eyes and said, "Unfortunately for us both the limit and the clause are correct."

"Whooa!" Thad exclaimed. "That's a lot of dough!"

"Close the door Thad," Cecil said.

He closed the door wondering what his boss wanted now. The client, Mrs. Wilson, was already cutting into his lunch break and now his boss. Didn't these people realize a man of his proportion had to have more than a Snickers bar to survive until 5:00 P.M.?? Taking a seat without an invitation wasn't Thad's style.

"What's on your mind, chief?"

"We can't prove it and heavens know we've tried but I think Fred Wilson was offed, killed for the insurance money."

"Chief..huh, that's a very serious accusation. The initial report says a beam was dropped on him from above."

Swatting the air as though swatting Thad's words away Cecil said with narrowing eyes. "Yeah, that's what they all say." Meaning the emergency medical attendants, the construction foreman, and the police. Cecil leaned in closer and said. "The high rise building being built is financed by Jim Caldwell. He is well-known for conducting questionable business. He is more slippery than an eel."

"OKKKKAYYY, Chief. You're beginning to sound like my wife. She see conspiracies, strangers, ghosts, demons, and little green men everywhere."

Realizing Thad is poking fun at him at the expense of his wife Cecil excused him to go ahead and authorize the hefty check. But gave a word to the wise before Thad exited his office. "Your wife sounds like a smart cookie, it's best you listen to her."

Walking back to the awaiting client with the confident step of an athletically trained man. Declaring with a brilliant smile and gesturing for Mrs Wilson to follow. "Come this way, ma'am," he said, pushing his claimant adjuster office door open inviting her in. Offering her a seat and turning to the his desk and thinking of what his paranoid boss just said. "Mrs Wilson, I'm terribly sorry for the inconvenience Fidelity may have caused you in your time of bereavement. But it's the company's policy to fully investigate a claim of this magnitude."

For the first time he noticed her expensive clothing, shoes and handbag. He knows he doesn't know a Gucci bag from a Tucci bag but he's seen his sister-in-law wearing an almost identical suit. Different color, though. Helena always bitched until Ana made him buy the latest whatever handbag to hit the high-end shelf. Plus, his own sister has dragged him to handbag stores. Crying about what she wanted. So he knew the items were real.

He remembered his uppity sister-in-law, who made it very clear he was not good enough for her baby sister saying as though it was Cecile's suspicious-of-everything-and-everybody voice buzzing a 5 alarm fire alert in his head. He was hearing Helena brag to Ana, telling her it was a Chanel suit, it cost over $12,000, and she had brought their mother one also with a matching handbag and shoes. Almost as though she expected Ana to turn green with envy. But Ana being who she is just said "That's great. I'm sure Mom will love it! It's a beautiful suit and you look lovely in it."

He felt there was much better usage of money than to put that much in clothing. Ana didn't buy expensive shit like that unless Helena bitched until she encouraged Ana to make him buy it for her.

It was as if she were aware he was watching her. Lola put the pretensions aside and said the suit and bag were a gift from her late husband. His own father was a construction worker and he didn't remember his father making enough to buy his mom expensive stuff like that.

Pushing his wife's and Cecil's paranoiac warnings out his mind he smiled. "It's nice to have someone who cares so much." Turning on the printer to print out the check and sign it and realized he must get Cecil's signature also so he excused himself again and trotted down the hall. Dreading to rap again for he doesn't want to see Cecile's sour, turned down mouth before lunch. But he needed to hurry and get the inevitable out the way to meet Ana for lunch. He raised his hand and knocked.

"Come in." the voice from the other side of the door says.

166

"Mr. Towne, I need your John Hancock on this check to finalize the approval."

Snatching the check grudgingly from Thad's hand harder than he intended but making no apology, Cecil Towne signs the check all the while mumbling something about a black widow spider.

Rushing to get this foul, bile-tasting case closed and over with and meet his babe at The Hickory for lunch he trots faster than before to deliver the check to the woman Cecil dubbed "The Black Widow."

He quickly reentered his office, handed Lola Wilson the check, and gently but firmly rushed her out of his office, wondering if Ana is still there or has returned to campus. He was proud to tell everyone who would listen his wife was a law student at Harvard. She really wasn't there anymore but nobody knew that but family.

Rushing, speed walking to his car, a hover Madza RX7, he bumped into Lola Wilson, nearly knocking her down. Catching her before she went crashing to the ground and wondering where did she come from? He thought she had left the premises.

He wasn't sure but he believed he felt something when he touched her arm. He wasn't sure what it was but whatever it was, it wasn't pleasant. Straightening her clothing, she breathlessly said as recovering from their near collision "I know I interfered and shortened your lunch break; I appreciate your assistance more than you know. So if you don't mind. I'd like to make it up to you. May I buy you lunch?"

This was his first time actually looking at her. She was an incredibly beautiful woman. Ana looked like a little girl in comparison. But a ten station fire alarm went off in his head. He said to himself, "*Great! Lady! Just fucking great! A great invitation if I want to die today. I'm already an hour late and if I walk in with a well-dressed, beautiful woman on my arm my pregnant pint-sized wife is going to kick my ass. No lunch in the world is worth facing Ana's wrath hyped up on hormones*!" But instead he thanked the sexy woman, declined the offer, hurried into his car, and flew out the parking lot. This was one of the fastest cars available without spending a cool million. Ana has been on him about selling it saying he isn't single anymore. He doesn't need it anymore. He'll soon need room for a baby's car seat. But he needed to enjoy it while he could. Having a baby is a terrible upheaval. He still needs to find a way to tell Ana he already has a child. Well, according to other women he supposedly has three children. He needed to find a way to tell her their baby isn't his first born. He doesn't want it to harm their marriage for she doesn't know about any of them nor does she know he secretly sees his son.

Declining the invitation and heading to The Hickory, a place he and Ana frequented when they were single he looked at his watch, cursing as time ticked pass 2 o'clock in languid increments. Downtown traffic as thick as thieves. He knew he should've gone airborne but the traffic above is worse. Thad's heart sinks as he knows he faces the un-Ana adorned cafe. Luckily he finds a parking space and has change to feed the meter. Running down the streets, bursting through the still-lunch hour crowded cafe's door, scanning the crowd he mildly swore in a sombre tone. Ana is gone. He wanted to have a serious talk with her. She needed to know the truth. There were many things he needed to talk to her about. The man he caught in their bedroom opened the doorway to speak in honesty. He was no fool. He knew the man was her lover but didn't protest much for he was feeling a little guilty for leaving her after such a romantic evening. He was feeling guilty for having just screwed another woman so shortly after making passionate love to her but that man still bothered him. He wonders how many times that guy been there when he was away on weekends? The man wasn't startled nor upset he caught him. He can't shake the man's cold eyes when he looked back over his shoulder at him. It was pure hatred in those strange eyes and he knew it was about Ana. This was so profound, something so deep he hadn't told even his best friend about it.

He couldn't wrap his mind around the possibilities that Ana had just screwed that man and only screamed to be perceived as innocent. Ana...was usually honest. But he can't fool himself and tell himself he didn't see the glance between the two of him. Unbeknownst to her he took one of the gemstones to a jeweler and the man said it was the highest quality gemstone he had ever seen. He never seen such a perfect one. Saying if he wanted to sell it, he'd give him 2.5 million. He angrily sold it on the spot but he needed to come clean and tell her about the extra income. So yes, there was a lot they needed to talk about. He's learning that marriage isn't deceptively simple but can be endlessly complicated.

Turning to leave before the waitress asked him where he would like to be seated, he nearly collided with Lola for the second time within an hour. She pretended surprised to see him. But unbeknownst to him she had followed him. He was her next target. The more suitable term was prey.

"We are going to have to stop meeting like this!" laughed Lola with rings of delight that rivaled the melodious tone of silver bells. "Sorry..ma'am. I was just leaving." Thad sadly said.

Slipping her arm into his she says, "Oh nonsense. You're joining me for lunch. You've got to eat to keep up all these muscles. I don't bite. Besides, I could use the company. Hardly any adults to talk to since Fred's passing and children aren't always good company."

"I wouldn't know." Thad replied absently scanning the bright sunlit streets outside the tinted cafe windows. Hoping to spot Ana wobbling down the street.

"Expecting someone?" Lola asked coyly, looking at him from under her long sooty eyelashes.

"Yes. my wife."

"I'm sure she'll be here in a moment and will understand your having a luncheon with a client," Lola ensured Thad.

"Oh well, I have to eat," Thad thinks to himself. Since this apparently lonely lady is hell-bent on paying. *I guess there is no harm in accepting the offer.* What harm can come of an innocent sandwich?

Outside The Hickory the new acquaintances bid each other farewell and good day. Thad was feeling good until he got back to work and the receptionist told him his wife had called. He knew Ana was in a foul mood. She had traveled all the way from her part-time job to be with him for lunch that day. They were trying to rekindle their romance. He had to admit to himself he didn't find a pregnant woman attractive. Moms to be

169

shouldn't be moaning and panting in his opinion. They should be practicing be a mom. Figuring he had better smooth things over before he got home, he returns Ana call. She answers on the first ring and asks "Where were you? I waited an hour and a half. Ordered lunch, ate and left because I had a to be back at work at 2 o'clock."

Not sure of why he felt guilty, he hadn't done anything but had lunch with the lady, Thad replies in a sweet melody reserved for Ana alone. "Babe, a client held me up. I got to the Hickory at 2 o'clock. See ya when I get home."

Throughout the remaining of the evening he couldn't shake the nagging feeling he had done something wrong. His insides felt like flummery. He kept no secrets from Ana, (well, not those kind). Told her his every thought since he was 16 years old. Well, not exactly everything. He hadn't told her about the few flings he had had since they married. He hadn't told her one night he thought she was gone to Helena's and brought home an old girlfriend. He don't know why he did it nor why he didn't hightail out of there when he learned Ana was in the master bedroom asleep. But they got out before she woke up. Thank goodness, their house was huge and well built. He had to slap his hand over the woman's mouth several times. She wanted Ana to know she was there. Ana doesn't know about their son. Chalice made as much noise as she could while he screwed her. He held her mouth as they snuck back down stairs. Ana's room door was still cracked. Chalice saw her curled up in bed. "Bitch" she said through his hand. He felt as if something wasn't right in that room. He had been in there a hundred times; especially since Ana was pregnant, he didn't want to be tempted to make love to her. He swore he saw shadows moving on the wall. But he told himself Ana had freaked him out with all strange ghoul stories so now he's seeing them, too.

His boys often ribbed him about his trait of telling her every-thing. Saying "Damn Thad! If we told you we were going to throw down a bank heist, the cops would come kicking in our door because you would tell Ana and she would turn us in." They called him "whipped." But there was a lot he didn't tell her and never intended to.

He was in anguish, reliving the past in the emotional darkness of his prison cell, awaiting transfer to the federal prison. Little did he know at the time, on that fateful day, that seemingly innocent luncheon would be the start of an illicit affair controlled by a succubus. That this affair would part him and Ana like Moses parted the Red Sea. He started lying, picking fights with Ana, and even back-hand slapped Ana once when she questioned him about where large sums of money were coming from. It came from the gemstone he sold. The slap snapped something in his psyche. He was enraged to the point of seeing blood red dripping, blinding his vision. Even played around with the idea of strangling her within the millimeter of a second of her life. Choking her until she was quiet and stopped haranguing him about the source the lipstick stain on his chest and the 50,000 grand she found stashed away in an old suitcase on his side of the closet. He hadn't noticed the stain when he left Lola's apartment. But Ana could cuss, fuss, and cuss some more. She didn't know when to shut the hell up once she got started. Like the time he yelled at her until she cried. He felt mean as hell telling her she was getting on his damn nerves and he hoped she dies having that damn baby. Once she asked him to go to the store late one night and he told her to go ask her big brawny boyfriend, it's probably his damn baby anyway. He couldn't figure out why were he being so mean to her? Once she came in the room where he was sleeping and started fondling him. He woke up and prudishly asked what did she think she was doing?

"You're my husband I can touch you if I want to" she replied stubbornly. As they made love he developed an excruciating headache. He rolls off her and tells her crassly to go back to the main bedroom. Again, there's a cussing streak out of her. He got up to keep from grabbing her around that skinny neck and squeezing. It was like something was goading him on to kill her, to choke the life out of her. He left to protect her that night. He fled their house and went to Tony's. Tony pulled on his pants at the urgency of the banging, getting out of bed with a blonde Thad did not know. He still never figured out why Tony's bed was in the front room. Tony opened the door but blocked the doorway. Thad pushed past him and barely greeted the woman standing in Tony's bedroom door way with a seriously disapproving frown on her beautiful face. Pacing the royal blue carpeted living-room with both occupants eyes followed his strait. The reality of what he nearly did was too much to hold in any longer.

Thad blurted out. "I wanted to kill her. I almost killed her!"

Tony's eyes signaled him they wasn't alone. "Thad, meet Gena," Tony introduced stubbornly. Realizing Tony intends that he properly greets his date Thad falls silence and shakes Gena's hand.

"Gena, meet Thad, my childhood best friend I was telling you about."

Tony's eyes were sending unsaid message saying, "Do not say anymore in Gena's presence."

Tony was aware of the "Thad-Lola affair" and thought Thad would reveal it in the midst of ranting in front of one of Ana's college friends.

Too distraught to accurately read Tony's eyes Thad continued his story, telling his best friend "An evil, scary thought crossed my mind. Something I never once considered doing. I thought of grabbing Ana's slender neck and squeezing until she stopped baraging me. Squeezing the life out of her. It scared the shit out of me when I actually hit her. But she hit me back. Slugged me right in the eye with her little bony fist." Thad softly chuckled as he absently rubbed the fresh bruise.

To diffuse what was quickly turning into an explosive situation Tony asks Gena can they continue their date perhaps tomorrow. Promising her a romantic dinner or any activity she deemed fit to remain in her favor.

Gena agrees to take a raincheck on the dinner and returned to the bedroom to retrieve her coat but while in there, she also to called her newfound friend, Ana. Ana's beautiful Scandinavian friend decided upon meeting Thad she didn't like him very much. She had seen him a few times with Ana but knew little about him other than what Tony told her. Ana's romantically arranged the meeting between she and Tony. So she further felt it was her obligation to get Ana away from Thad. She was remembering the years of abuse her mother suffered at the hands of her father as she dials Ana's number. Her mother said it started out with small slaps, pushes, shoves before escalating into violent blows with his fist or objects. The phone rings seven times before Ana answers.

"Hello, Anna. This is Gena. Are you ok? Want me to come pick you up?" Gena asked. "Your husband is here at Tony's ranting like a mad man." Gena informs, knowing that victims of domestic violence can't be trusted to tell the truth.

172

"Thanks. Yeah, I'm ok. He should be ranting for he been acting strange for the past three months."

"Strange...how?"

"I don't know... Thad is usually so sweet and attentive. It's hard to describe. He has been acting distant...like his mind is elsewhere."

Ana didn't tell Gena the horrible things he said to her. Waving red flags sprung up in Gena's mind, recognizing these characteristics from her own home life, her father. Gena knew Thad was having an affair. Chewing the inside of her of mouth; debating rather or not to make her friend aware of the source of Thad's strange behavior. But then, remembering Ana's pregnancy, she decides to keep this info to herself.

Leaning against Tony's Formica countertop, Tony tossed Thad a beer from the fridge and asked his friend, "What in the hell is wrong with you? Thaddeus!! Gena and Ana are friends. I saw Ana about 3 months ago at the Mickey D's on Independence Blvd and asked her to introduce me to some of her gorgeous friends. Hey! I figured you hit the jackpot in a spouse with her so I figured her friends would be women of equal ethics. Gena is worth keeping. So keep your voice down."

Thad's colour suddenly changes to a deep red brownish mocha. Rife with panic, he whispered urgently, "She's Ana friend?? Why didn't you tell me?! You haven't told her about Lola, have you?"

Tony softly scoffed, "No, I haven't. But you still need to get your shit together. Stay away from Lola. I told you the first time I met her she was poison. She had more experience than you and me combined. Now, wasn't I right? I think the bitch got roots on you," his childhood Italian friend said.

Thad made it clear he doesn't believe in hoodo, voodoo, or any other type of magic and was sick of hearing Tony and Ana talk about the supernatural.

Tony sternly pointed his beer bottle at his oldest friend saying, "I've seen you with more women than you could fuck but you never mistreated Ana for nobody. Ana was always your baby and everybody knew it. When you won the Heisman Trophy, you didn't ask Chalice to the ceremony--you asked Ana. You need to see a priest to get that shit up off ya."

"Tony, there's no shit on me," Thad scoffed.

"Well then how come you thinking about killing the woman you love? How come you're here? Something scared you mighty bad."

Before Thad could reply Gena appeared in the kitchen giving him dagger stares and leaned in to kiss Tony goodbye and let herself out the front door. Thad could tell from Gena's eyes she was going to tell Ana about Lola. She was going straight to his house if she must and tell Ana everything she overheard.

Resuming their conversation Thad says "Yea, you told me." Gauntly he admitted his friend's righteousness.

Tony begun boring down hard and lecturing his best friend out of genuine concern for his well-being. Thad hadn't been himself lately. Thad was acting peculiar and careless. He had even taken this strange woman to his home when Ana was in Staten Island visiting her sister. He knew Thad and Thad was not himself.

He was determined to be a friend but was feeling as though he had lost his blithe edge with Thad. Thad had changed, even with him. Lola didn't like him and he didn't like her. He knew she was encouraging Thad to end their friendship. But he pushed on in a last-ditch attempt to set his best bud on a blissful path again.

"Man...the last time I was in NYC..."

"I remember," Tony retorts. Draining the last of his now warming beer.

"She gave me a briefcase loaded with fifty thousand grand. I thought the gift was

174

empty until I got on the expressway on my way back to Boston and decided to see if anything was in it. I thought it may had been books for she often talks about I deserve to complete my medical school education. I called her on the road and asked her what was this for and she said for my education."

He shook his head in dismay and disbelief at the gullibility he's hearing coming out of Thad's mouth. These naive words have him worried. This isn't the Thad he knows. The Thad he knows would've opened the case and looked in before leaving the apartment. Tony asked "And you believed her?? She is buying you, man! Showing you how much more she've to offer you than your wife! She is turning you into her gigolo."

Thad chuckled and took another sip of his beer which was lukewarm by now, "Aw shucks, man. That theory is a little extreme even for you. I feel as though I am addicted to Lola; the lovemaking is so intense and electrifying. Like nothing I've ever felt before."

Tony felt like grabbing Thad and shaking him until his teeth rattled and yelling in his face. "That's what enchantment feels like!" But instead, he tries calm reasoning. "Listen, Thad and listen carefully, all women have the same thing. What is she? Fifty? And you're....what? Twenty-three. And where was Ana gonna learn to be *"electrifying"* as you call it? Who was there to teach her but you. All whores are exciting. That's how they make their money. No one would pay them if they weren't!"

"No, Lola is not fifty, she's only thirty eight. Besides, age ain't nothing but a number. Don't call her names. I don't call your women whores and you have deal with some down right skanks. She's a very respectful lady. She's just lonely and grieving. Her husband passed away a little under two years ago. Besides, I caught a guy in our closet one night I came home. So I'm not so sure the baby, Ana's baby, is even mine. He disappeared in the fucking closet. How in the shit he did he do it? I've no idea but that was freaky as hell."

"She looks fifty to me." Tony surly retorts pouring a stiffer drink and handing it to Thad. Referring to the man in question, he says with strong conviction "Ana ain't cheated on you. What you saw was a demon. It was a demon, man. I don't know why but

175

I can promise you Lola was sent by someone to break y'all up. Besides, despite the popular myths, demons can't make babies, man. That's a fact."

Pondering over when once he saw Thad and Lola together, Tony furthered his interrogatory point asking, "Why else would a woman who just got a windfall of millions off her dead husband chase you down in the streets and invite you to lunch? Tell me something I don't know? You said so yourself; she've bought you other gifts you can't bring home. Remember last month when I met you in NYC for a Mets' game against the Fox, you were wearing a Cartier 159 watch, worth over 30,000 grand? When I asked you about it, she proudly purred, 'Nothing was too good for her baby' and I corrected her, 'You are Ana's baby and I know that for a fact cause I stood as best man at the wedding.' If looks could kill I would be a dead man. My words shot down her claim like a birdie, and she didn't like the mentioning of your wife's name. Thad man, wake up. Something or someone been fucking with y'all since the day you said "I DO". It's been one problem after another. First, you break your leg...ending your sports career. Now all this Lola shit. Man, wake up before you lose everything!"

Thad had begun to feel Tony's avid defense of Ana was a little too zestful and started wondered did Lola have a vital point when she told him Tony was in love with Ana as to why he always defended her. Quickly shaking the rancorous thought from his mind, there was no way Lola could be right. There was no way either one of them would betray him like that. Lola's words came creeping back into his psyche, "A best friend is the one has the easiest access to your wife. I've seen it happen more times than I care to count. Tony is keeping up with where you are to make sure you don't catch him and Ana fooling around." He zestily rebuked her saying there was no way the two of them would creep behind his back.

"Tony...I only make twenty-four hundred a week at Fidelity and by the time we pay the bills, everything is gone. Ana clips coupons but that doesn't seems to make much different."

"Is Ana complaining about how little you make? Her part time job helps out and are you telling me you knew Lola was buying you? "

176

"No, but I think Ana deserves better than I can afford. No, uh yes... Tony climb down off my ass with all the questions."

Coming around the counter and joining his friend seated on the chrome high stool, Tony took the second high stool. He firmly grabs Thad's shoulder with a hard, manly grip to let him know he meant business. Forcing his wayward friend to look him eye to eye.

"Thad, your wife and unborn child deserve your full love and attention. Don't bullshit yourself about you're doing this for a better life for them. That's hogwash and you know it! The simple fact remains. You can't see Lola again. Give back the money. And pray to whatever god you serve Ana never finds out about this."

Thad nods, knowing what Tony's feelings about the affair. In recent months he had distanced himself from his lifelong pal. Lola and Tony were like sworn enemies. Both justifying their dislike and distrust of the other. Justifying his outlet of stress by the notion Tony didn't understand the stress and burden married life placed on a man. Life or even marriage to the one you love wasn't always a clear-cut pattern of black and white, there were plenty of gray areas. Tony's rigid Catholic upbringing left no room whatsoever for, affairs, relief, nor divorce. At least he owed it to Lola to tell her goodbye regardless of what Pope Tony said. If he listened to Tony and his back water primitive creeds he'd feel guilty about everything.

Returning home finding the art décor lamp on the nightstand beside Ana's side of the bed the only light on in the house. Shame washes over him when he looks into her angry eyes. She was propped up in the bed with the cover pulled over her swollen belly staring at the holograph scene. He could tell she had been crying. He sat by her legs and gently rubs the one closest to him, "Baby...I'm sorry for the horrible things I said tonight. There's no other woman in my life and heart except you and our little girl. You know I love you, so why you act like that? I don't wanna argue with you anymore." He tried to pull her to himself. But she shoved him off and told him to go to hell. He does loves her and not Lola. So why is he acting so impractical, like such a screwball?

Unspilled tears shimmered in his eyes. He groans when he bequoth the fact he was even with Lola the night Breanna was born. He was telling her good bye that night but sexually; things got out of hand. He made love to her to several times and lost track of time. He really did intend to come home at six. She became hysterical and told him she'd die without his love. Sure, he cared about her but he knew he wasn't in love with her. He was more fascinated by her than in love.

"Leave Ana, she's young and pretty. She'll find another love. We can travel the world together. I can teach you things she can't. We can move to another country and you come back to visit your baby...that is if the baby is really yours." He thought about the dude in the white shorts. So was Tony right? There are millions of men. Why had Lola opted for a married man when there're plenty of single men to date?

The night Bea was born his best bud, Tony, drove all the way from Boston to New and entered Lola's building in his trademark, old world movie star Al Pacino sway. He stormed up to Lola's penthouse apartment and banged on the door. Not caring if he embarrassed them. Telling him he kept his promise. Gena had informed him Ana was in labor and to get his behind back home. (Sure, Ana, had told him that morning before leaving for NYC she wasn't feeling very well. But he put it down to some more of her whining.) Yelling for all the listening world to hear, saying he had not told Ana of his whereabouts, forcing him to lie to another friend. The air-wave static cackled with cops' radios could be heard down the hall, for Tony had knocked the doormen out on his way up to the penthouse when they tried to deny him entrance. The doorman, according to Tony, tried to obstruct his path to Lola's Park Ave apartment by physically standing in the way. So he punched him. Well, that sounded about like something Tony would do.

Looking around the solemn dull gray walls of the sanitized cell, which was clearly pronouncing his fate, he tells himself, "Thaddeus Thackeray Wyett" If there's an opposite of kindness in life, this place was it. He'd beg, borrow, steal, or even kill to have his happy little family back the way things were in the beginning. Remembering how much Bea's baby angelic face looked like his own at that age. Back the way they were before he met his son's mother. Back to the days when he and Ana were happy and in love. Back to the days he patiently waited for her. He'd take on every burden in their world to have those days again.

He knows without doubt Lola's friends set him up because he broke things off with her. He had five years to plot how to kill her and get away with it and then find Ana. Win her back and put their family back together. He had to make her understand, believe that he still loved her, and always would.

Unaware of the spiritual activities surrounding him, Thad Wyett never felt the spiritual parasite dislodge itself from his psyche, having completed it's job. The one that was summoned to do it squiggled out of his left ear, inched down his back, and disappeared. It was free to roam the earth and look for another victim. But each victim's own life, beliefs, and actions open the barrier for it to enter.

Approximately a year and half, after his conviction, he was transferred from Rikers Island to the west coast. To California where Ana couldn't easily reach him. Creating greater distress. Although he told her not to visit him she came anyway. He was secretly glad she did. She always came with encouragement and the solid belief they could start anew when his five years were served.

Thad is supposed to be reading but isn't. He merely wanted time out in the library. He browsed and looked at some of Ana's favorite reads and smiled. He remembered her reading some of these books to him. She loved books. He simply tolerated them. There wasn't a day passed he didn't think about her and Bea, wondering how they're faring. His family informed him she lost the house. He was worried about them. Reading put his mind at ease. Reading some of the books she read to him while he used lay his head in her lap brought him closer to her. He was worried because he told her not to mortgage the house to get him out. Not to touch the money saved for Bea's education and their retirement to pay the legal fees. But she didn't listen and now they are out there somewhere. They hadn't gone to his parents nor Helena according to his mom. They had no idea where she had gone. And if the BuFayes know where she is, they are aren't talking.

Prisons today aren't as inhumane as those years ago, exposing the inmate's private functions to anyone who cared to look. The E-library was transported to him. He read or at least pretended to read until his four hours were up. It was easier and safer to walk back to the cell on your own with the android guard their a real one. At least the robots didn't ask no dumb ass questions. The robot opened the door , he stepped in, and the machine closed it. He was alone again with his private thoughts. While pondering and facing his predicament the door to his cell opens. He doesn't remember an appointment with his second lawyer. They had to let the first one go. He was far too damn expensive. The millions he had hidden had been taken from his hiding place which he told Ana about after his arrest so she could get the funds to pay the bail. Again, he dropped his head wondering what possessed him to take Lola to his house when Ana visited her mother and sister? A tall man wearing a custom-made dark gray suit with lots of well sculptured jet black curls walked in around the guard. The man sort of looked Italian like his best bud Antonia but not quite, much better looking. Actually, the man was beautiful. He narrowed his eyes at the man hoping he wasn't one of those 'funny men' for he didn't roll that way. He watched them enter and wondered what the man wanted for people don't come a-calling unless they want something. The guard closed the metal door and locked it. The stranger took a seat at his metal desk and looked at him for a few seconds from under thick, achromatic eye lashes.

"Oh lord, this fucker is funny." Thad thinks.

"Mr. Wyett, I've a proposition for you..."

"I'm not interested." Thad interrupted.

"Oh, I think you'll be once you hear me out. Hear what I've to say." Vonderbilt continued.

"Get the fuck outta here. You bastards have already taken everything meaningful to me. There's nothing left to take."

"I'm sorry about your plight but I'm here to offer you freedom and a new lease on life all in the exchange of your...how do you proud Americans say it. Your infallible John

Hancock." the stranger snapped his well manicured finger as if was an amusing adage. Vonderbilt turned around and turned to the computer on the desk, inserting a video chip. Powering up the machine. Thad hears Ana's voice and get ups to turn the thing off but he is frozen in mid step. A deep agonizing freeze seeps through to his bones. The man snaps his fingers again and pushes him back down on his bed as easily as a baby.

"Look and learn," the refined, elegant man said. What choice does he have? This man is something Thad has never encountered. He sat and rubbed his limbs in attempt to bring the circulation back to them. *"Is this man a witch? No, men are called warlocks,"* he recollects.

The video shows Ana in the backseat with a man dressed equally as refined as the bastard in his cell. He sees the man kiss her and gently fondle her breast. Ana shyly pushes the hand away and tells him she wishes to go home. He discourages her returning home but she insists. The video was insciently filmed without Ana's knowledge. She tells the man how much she misses her husband. How she tried to save him against all odds. The man clearly doesn't want to talk about Thad Wyett.

"You did all you could. The man cheated on you. Made a public spectacle of you so I think it's time to move on," the man said impatiently before pulling out a piece of expensive jewelry. By now Thad had stopped listening.

"What is your point in showing me all this bullshit? That cad is taking advantage of her sorrows and distress. What's so heroic about that? Where's the victory?"

"I agree," Vonderbilt said clicking to another scene. Thad narrowed his eyes at the vericolored haired man. That's the man he saw going in his closet. He had no idea the real culprit had been cropped out the holograph and replaced with the likeness of Ashton Cargill.

Seeing his acute reaction Nikola says. "That's the man wholly responsible for your being here. He set you up. He found out all there was to know about you and tore your family asunder. His name is Ashton Cargill. I don't like him at all. He thinks he's untouchable. That's why I came here. This is the man who had you moved all the way

181

across the country to San Quentin to make it harder for Ana to visit you. He took away her home to force her to come to him. Now she's on the run from him."

The next footage put him on the edge of his mattress. It showed Ana's little blue car whizzing by. She looked scared to death. Next, he sees police lights flashing all around her; he heard bullets flying and ricocheting.

"That's him having the cops to kill her because she left him. She was trying to get across the country to see you. He didn't like that so he would rather see her dead;" Vonderbilt calumniated.

"If she don't want him ---why doesn't he leave her alone. Killing her isn't the answer. Besides, why are you showing me all this? Yeah, I heard something about some of this mess from my family. But I know she still loves me." Thad said ascertaining from the information shown that the man in the footage wasn't the man his father described to him as he saw Ana out in the yard talking to over the hedges.

Now it was Nikola's turn to flinch. Thad didn't miss it. "*So this blackguard wants her for himself! That's why he's here. When in the hell did Ana become so irresistible to so many men? When did his mousy wife become a sex goddess? Seductress??*" The very idea seemed comical.

Clearly seeing what this man was doing Thad erupted into a roil of laughter. Vonderbilt knitted his smooth dark brow. This wasn't the response he was expecting from an imprisoned husband. Where's the jealousy? Where's the murderous outrage? Thad is really beginning to chafe him. What's so damn hilarious? To silence Thad Vonderbilt twisted his fist in front of him, using his power. Thad begin choking and gagging. But what he didn't know was this husband was hiding his jealousy and rage very well. That's what the laughing was all about. With sheer grit and determination embroiled in rage Thad Wyett rose like he used to on the football field when a four hundred pound player was on his back. He staggered to the smaller man and got his fingers around his neck.

"I let your shit slide the first time. But keep your goddamn roots offa me. If I'm going out so are you."

Willing himself to fight against a power unknown; this man totally underestimated the stamina that could be summoned by an enraged man with nothing else to lose. He hadn't counted on the sheer determination of a pissed off, jealous husband. Thad applied all his strength he could muster into his fingers on Nikola's neck. He squeezed from the shoulder muscles, flexing them as he had done so many times against as opponent. Vonderbilt clawed his forearm, drawing blood as he struggled to break the former linebacker's hold. Now he was seeing the rage, the jealousy he wanted to invoke. This sly dog was hiding how he truly felt. Three guards rushed in and hit Thad with an electrical charge baton. He turned, grabbed the batons and shocked them with it. Realizing these shocks were not working on the big man, two more arrived with their guns drawn, about to open fire.

"NO!" Vonderbilt cried quickly through spasmodic fits of coughing and wheezing. Lucifer wanted this man alive so they'll have someone Ana trusted enough to reveal her locations to. He waved the guards out. The guards reluctantly left, but they were determined to deal with Wyett later. The prison's psychotherapists had warned them he was a volcano waiting to explode. They were sick of his special treatment. People still remembered his days of glory. The public and people inside these walls still admired him. People treated him as thus he was the victim of a crooked system not a philandering crook.

Once alone again, Vonderbilt wonders how this man broke a spiritual hold? Duh! He's pissed off! Now Vonderbilt was ready to leave. To shorten his visit he pulled out the gold backed legal documents and the ten million check.

"I've a proposal. If you sign this divorce proceeding and kindly accept this check as a way to start a new life I can have you out of here by tomorrow afternoon. No, this afternoon, you can be a free man. But go another direction. Do not go back to Ana."

Thad conspicuously scrutinized the man with a woman's hairdo, in his opinion. *"This joker evidently hadn't looked around this hellhole. He doesn't seem to realize this is a penitentiary and clearly doesn't know what my charges are."*

"It will work to your best interest to sign or I can see to it that you never see outside these walls again. You attacked me. There's proof. There's no proof of what I did to you. Cameras can't record spiritual activities." Vonderbilt said snug as a tick on a deer. Thad knew by now this man and Lola were somehow connected. He didn't know how. It was all a scam to destroy his life. Now, he even wonders about the opposing team 415 lbs linebacker who took out his knee. Was it done deliberately?

"I'm not signing that crap! I'm putting my family back together when these five years are served."

"Idiot! Muscle headed fool! You've more muscles than sense! I don't see what Ana saw in you. You're an untamed brute! You aren't getting out in five years if you don't divorce her. I just told your dumb ass I was going to see to it you rot in here. I tried being nice to you but irksome animals you can't be nice to!" Vonderbilt shouted seconds before Thad leaped across the cell and tackled him football style. They both crashed hard onto the floor with loud clamoring of the metal in his cell falling on the hard cold concrete floor. He started punching him. Vonderbilt used his magic to throw him across the room.

"Fool! Your wife is like me! So is your daughter! That's what I want with her. I'm much more compatible with her than you'll ever be. Sure, I want her for myself. You were too stupid to realize what you had. You threw it all away wallowing in the mud with bitches and sows. I guess those are your proper mates considering the animal you are!" Vonderbilt said raising him to the ceiling and holding him in the vise of his power which felt like a steel cable around Thad's neck and body.

"Damnit!", he yelled unfolding the paper. "You'll sign this paper if I have to force your hand and you don't want to know what that feels like. There's much more at sake here than your sorry ass pity!" Vonderbilt let the big linebacker down to the floor again and loosened the spiritual cables.

"Here! Sign the damn papers!" Vonderbilt ordered retrieving an expensive designer pen from his suit's inside breast pocket.

Thad felt the thousands of dreams inside his heart die. He rehearsed many times the life of love they'd have when he was free. He learned from his errs what he had. He didn't know who this man was but now he believed Ana when she once told her people like him were real. So she knew she was like this man but hid all that from him. He thought he was imagining things when he sometimes saw a faint blue glow around her, you could see it well after the lights were off and sometimes when he watched her sleeping. In the darkness there was a glow about her. But when he turned on the lights it was less visible. That he and Ana had piqued the interest of a powerful warlord, warlock, devil, or whatever this man called himself was not good.

Thad looked him squarely in the face and clearly stated he would not sign those papers. Vonderbilt, who had modeled himself after Prince Vladimir the Great, also known as Vladimir Impaler, gave a fiendish smile equal to that of the one he emulated. He waved his arm and there appeared before them an illusion, a mirage, not that Thad knew that it was merely as illusion. Or was it? The boiling yellowish stew of human remains bopped with skulls and meat cleaned bones in giant cauldron under a roaring fire. A startled but stubborn Thad looked around the coldstone room. Lichens grew on the wall, climbing up to the ceiling. A small primitive window offered a pitiful ray of light and hope in this death room. A struggling child was brought in by a man whose face has been scarred by an unwonted source. But Thad saw a slightly older Bea, not the actual unknown child it actually really was. Scar Face held the screaming, frightened child above the bubbling brew and looked at Thad in a manner even more evil than the dude in the gray suit he dubbed "The Dutch Master."

"Now, which will it be. You keep your sweet Ana and lose your Bernice?" Nikola callously asked. The horror was occurring before his eyes. The little girl squealed and curled up like a rolly-polly and clung to the evil man's arm.

"Put that child down! You fucked up twisted, diabolical son-of-a-bitch! How can you be so fucking evil?" Thad asked, his exertion of emotions making him weak. The realization that this slick headed rat of a man really intended to drop Bea in that boiling pot if he didn't divorce Ana hit him like a four hundred lbs linebacker. The bastard really intended to put Bea in that funky-ass witch pot of his. His stomach churned. He couldn't

185

reach her in time before the bastard dropped her.

"Hand me the child and I'll sign the goddamn papers!" Thad said in a voice choked by anger. "If he drops her you ain't getting shit from me."

Vonderbilt smiled as thus he was his new best friend and patted Thad's wide shoulder. "I thought this would make you more reasonable."

"Bjors, bring Bernadine here. Give her to her new daddy." It would've been comical, Vonderbilt was calling Bea everything but her name, had not the situation been so perilous.

Bjors sneered. Disappointed he wouldn't be seeing this little cutie cook today. But he knew to obey. He knew better than most how cruel Nikola could be. He had doused scathing hot water in his face as a child for going in the ice chamber peering under his dead mother's dress. The gaping wound where he came from was still open, frozen in time. As a child, he used to steal away to the chamber to hold hand his beautiful, black haired mother's hand, begging her to wake up and they run away, begging her to reanimate and take him away from this creepy house. One day when around five or six his demented grand mother caught him in there. She had came to visit her daughter who she called "Slumbering Beauty." She told him how he was ripped from her womb and that's how she died. "Evil Oregon did this. No, Evil Orman did it."

"Is Evil Oregon my father?" He had asked looking up quizzically at in her shiny, feverish eyes soaked in madness as she rose the hem of the frozen expensive white lace gown, six year old Bjors Machiavelli asked. Back then he had his mother's beauty.

"No, I told you Jarvis is your daddy. I know you don't like him but he's your daddy. Nikola is your uncle and her brother. Making you his nephew. He loved his sister. Dotted on her. We all did. She was as kind as she is beautiful," Celdona Machiavelli said lovingly caressing her dead daughter's frozen face. All Bjors saw was a bluish frozen face with purplish blue lips silenced forever.

He hated that skull his grandmother carried around and often kissed. They tried taking

186

it from her but she did nothing but wail and lament for days until Nikola gave it back to her. She placed it close to his face telling him to kiss it, said it was his grand papa. The grinning teeth frightened him. He didn't want to kiss it. But nonetheless he pecked it on the top to make her take it out of his face. After the day Nikola scalded him he became determined to make everyone feel as much pain as he doesn't feel. He feels nothing. Growing up it was he who had to take whipping for Gianna, all because Gianna was Nikola's little brother and he was the little bastard who killed his sister. Like the time he, Gianna, and crazy granny ran away with grandpa's skull in tow the only person whipped when found was him. So dropping this kid didn't mean a damn thing to him.

He icily watched Thad and Vonderbilt conduct their business. He easily saw beyond the mirage. This wasn't Thad Wyett's kid. It was a kid from the village breed to serve the Grand Wizard.

When the papers were signed and the money exchanged hands Bjor was sent with Thad and the kid back through the portal Nikola brought him through. When back in the cell a man was awaiting with a suit of clothing. Thad gasped when he saw the child was white and not Bea at all. He realized the man had tricked him. The child on his hip cling to his neck like a leech. He rubbed her tiny back to comfort her. There's no way in hell he's giving this child back to those perverted psychos. He wasn't changing clothing clothes in front of this kid. She had been traumatized enough. Does these evil clowns have any sense of humanity in them at all? He guessed not when they had pots of boiled people.

Sitting on his bed with the child in his lap, everyone looked to the door when the heavy metal door opened. It was the warden. A bastard he hadn't seen the entire 10 months of his incarceration, at least not in person. He always talked to the prison population via screen or computer.

"Mr. Wyett, you're a lucky man to have friends that even the governors of two states listen to." Warden Jefferson said pal-like, sitting next to him on the hard, tight mattress, completely ignoring the child on his lap. Not even bothering to ask how she arrived. Or did he already know?

"One last thing you gotta do and then you free to go." Thad already wasn't liking this one last thing. Jefferson handed him a pretyped letter saying he must copy the letter in his handwriting to make it believable.

"Why? I've already signed the papers." Thad grunted as Jefferson handed him his copy.

"Your little lady is smart as Eisenstein and cleverer than Machiavelli." He paused and acknowledged Bjors who wasn't watching them but then again he was. "No, offense, sir." He said deferentially to Bjors who merely slightly nodded meaning continue and let's get this surreptitious business over and done with. He continued saying. "She isn't gonna believe you don't love her any more. She isn't going to believe you didn't sign it under duress if she doesn't read a letter from you saying so. Now, don't be difficult. Do as these nice people tell ya and freedom shall be yours. If ya keep your nose clean you will never see me nor these people again."

Thad looked up in Bjors' stone blotched face and for the first time saw the scalding marks and asked. "If I write this letter will you buffoons leave Ana and Bea alone?" In a crisp British accent Bjors replied, "We only want Ana. Breanna is yours if you would like."

"What am I supposed to do with this kid?"

Bjors lost his rigid compose and snapped, "How in the hell am I supposed to know? Throw her in the dumpster for all I care!"

The child whimpered and tightened her thin arms around the big man's neck. She understood enough English to know Prince Bjors was talking about killing her again. They had already boiled her parents for disobeying Vonderbilt's direct order and not freely handing her over. Thad patted her back. "I'll keep her."

Bjors shrugged his shoulders and directed Thad to the metal seat to write the letter they'd deliver to Ana along with the divorce writ. He sat the child on his lap and proceeded to write. The letter was cold and impersonal. He had no idea what in the hell a damn "Mississippi move" was but wrote it hoping Ana read between the lines and saw this wasn't his true feelings and wait for him. He indolently side-eyed Jefferson wondering how old was this beer bellied balding man? But kept Bjors in his peripheral vision as well. He had seen what this scarred face man was capable of.

By five that afternoon he and the unnamed kid were in a hovercopter flying over the Francisco Bay. Throughout the entire trip, Bjors said nothing except to direct his people to place at his feet a briefcase that looked like an old-fashioned medical bag. Bjor placed his foot on it and shoved it to him. "This is payment for your service. So I suggest you spend it wisely." By eight P.M., they were touching down in the middle of the road in front of his parent's house. As soon as he and the unnamed kid alit on the newly paved asphalt the unseen propellers emitted a burst of energy and rose back in the air as if nothing demonic and sinister had happened.

Twenty five year old Thad Wyett was interrogatively greeted by his perplexed family. He told them as little as possible as he kissed and hugged them.

"Where did you get that child from?" Thad Sr. asked following his firstborn inside.

"Her mother," Thad snapped wishing his parents would leave him alone. He'd just witnessed things he thought were myths and here they were asking fool questions.

"I thought they said you couldn't have conjugal visits?" His mother reminded him. This child was definitely older than ten months old. "They wouldn't let Ana see ya so how some old girlfriend managed to get in and how did you get out?"

His nerves were frayed, the kid still had death grip on his hand. The heavy bag of money was weighing his exhausted body down. He still felt achy and nauseated from what big-bad hoodoo daddy had done. He smelt shallots cooking which made it worse. He turned and looked kindly down at his short stout mother, who was looking up, searching his face for answers. Mrs. Wyett knew something was terribly wrong.

"Mom, I'll explain all that later. Right now, I need to lie down." He sighed heavily, bending down to kiss her good night. He and this kid had been through hell, they both

189

needed rest not food. Everyone could talk in the morning. But of course his mother and family thought otherwise and brought him and kid a banquet upstairs. He ate to appease his mother and didn't realized how much he had missed her cooking. The poor, too thin child must had been starving for she seemingly ate twice her weight.

His family finally left them alone after the four stood and watched them eat to their satisfaction. He asked the child did she know how to clean herself shortly before his sister burst in and demanded he hand the girl over. The girl looked at him with big frightened eyes, his sister reached over and tried to grab her. The girl dodged her. Finally she caught her and took her screaming and reaching over his sister's shoulders for him. He told her to go and let her auntie clean her up but his sister was out the door taking the child away.

"No niece of mine's is going around looking like a damn waif. What is she? " Nadine Ophelia Wyett declared. "She looks a cast member of Les Misery. You and her momma oughta be shame of y'all selves! Got this baby running around looking like a ragamuffin," she said shutting the door behind herself. When he saw the unnamed child again she was clean, wearing clean clothing, hair brushed into silkiness, with a cookie and glass of milk.

He stopped his sister before she left. "Have y'all seen Ana or any of her folks?"

Ophelia Wyett shook her head. "No, not since the sheriff put them out the house. Momma told Ana to come stay here until you came home, wasn't no shame in losing the house. But like we told you her folks were all bent outta shape. Her bossy sister whisked them off to New York. We heard a bunch of trash on the news about her supposedly killing people. But nobody believed that garbage."

Thad laughed for he had heard the sordid news too but told none of the other prisoners the alleged killer was his wife. "Ok, thanks," he said, waiting until she left to call Helena as his suddenly adopted daughter sat in the middle of his old childhood bed and ate Oreos and drank milk and laughed at cartoons. The child's laughing tugged his heart and made him wondered what did the real Bea sounded like now? She'd be about this age.

"Helena, is Ana there?", he asked the last person he wanted to talk to right now.

"Who is this?"

"Thad. Your brother-in-law." The phone went silent. He could hear movement.

"What do you want?" She asked ill-naturedly, reminding him of how Bea sounded when he wasn't getting her juice fast enough. Too bad Bea looks more like her aunt than her mother. She looks like him, Helena, and had a little touch of his mother and Mrs. BuFaye.

"I want to talk to my wife. Is she there?" He asked more aggressively but suddenly the connection was broken and another voice cut in. An unknown male warned. "Mr. Wyett, I thought we agreed no more contact with Ana BuFaye. We wouldn't want your little brother driving a black hover sport-car to have an unfortunate, mysterious accident...now would we?"

"Bastard, how in the hell else am I supposed to find my real daughter if I've no idea where in the fuck Ana is?"

The stranger laughed as if it was the most hilarious thing he ever heard. "Do you really think the BuFayes will give her to you? If so, then you're dreaming."

The phone went dead as quickly as it strangely and eerily came to life. But soon came shrilling to life again. It was Helena, she somehow overrode his phone's camera and turned it on. "Motherfucker, what did you hang up on me for?" She barked before saying, "Nah, Ana and Bea ain't here. I don't know where they at. And If I knew I wouldn't tell you. Whose child is that? When you got outta prison?"

There goes the industrious questions again. Questions even he can't fully answer let alone supply someone else with a sound explanation.

"Your crooked former boss bought your way out to play ball again. Didn't he?" Helena accused.

"Whatever, Helena. Well, if you happen to see her—tell her to call me at my parent's house." He said undefeated and broke their connection. He was no mood to debate his combative sister-in-law. The realization slowly but painfully sank in, as he remind himself she's his hellified ex-sister-in-law. He doubted after that shitty letter Ana would contest the divorce.

The no-name kid had fallen asleep and spilt milk on her side of the bed. But who cared. He covered the wet spot with a towel and her up and cleaned up her side as best he could before getting up hiding the money behind the secret compartment he rigged to look like a normal board in his closet. He rigged it when he first bought this house for his parents with his Heisman trophy award before he went pro. It's where he kept picture of old girlfriends and their love letters. Looking at the stash now, it all meant nothing to him so he tossed them back inside and sorrowfully picked up the picture of the teen Ana on his nearby dresser. His tear splattered on the digital screen as he flipped through the collage. He pulled himself together, turned the night light on, called his buddy Tony and asked him to come pick him up. Unlike everyone else, Antonia knew not to ask a serial of questions until Thad was ready to talk. They rode through the streets of Boston in silence. They stopped by their old hangout and ordered beer. Thad also ordered Jack Daniels. A beer wasn't going to erase what he just witnessed today. Ana and Tony were right. There are people who have magical powers.

Nursing the drink with both hands while staring into the dark gold liquor, "Your maw-maw and Ana was right all along. Witches and warlocks, demons and the whole nine yards worth of shit is real." He said. gulping down the entire contents in the short wide glass. "I used to make fun of her for refusing to go down certain streets here in Boston saying bad things happened there. That particular street was haunted but you know what? I owe her a grave apology. Man I tell ya. What I witnessed and how I got out today made me a true believer in the occults. That there's a whole 'nother world ruled solely by evil. Ruled by people with no scruples nor consciences." He said telling his Italian ancestral, childhood friend about his bizarre, ethereal day.

"Whew! Man, that's some heavy duty supernatural shit." Antonia whistled long and low. All the while surveying the place, especially the bar where two goths sat. When they flashed their blacked out eyes at him the hairs on his arm stood up. Sensing they were being watched by something stronger than those kids he got Thad the hell out of there.

Back on the streets again they were being followed from a distance too far to see the driver's face. "Take me by the house." Thad said. Antonia knew exactly what house. He pulled out his dark, tellurium Glock he earned with his first couple of kills for the mob from his jeans' concealed waistband holster and laid it on the seat beside him. They may be able to perform stregoneria, La Vecchia Religione but he seriously doubted their asses were bulletproof. The air in the car begin to feel heavy, telekinetic, and electric as if there was a dark passenger riding with them. He pulled from his designer shirt's opening the antique cross his maw-maw gave him as a child to protect him from demones and kissed it. The cackling of electricity stopped. So his maw-maw was right. The Cross did compel them. Damn, he wished he had listened more carefully to his nonna when she was living. He was now positive il sortilegio was being performed.

"Thad, I remember Maw-Maw calling Ana a saint, saying she was born with a velo soprannaturale meaning a supernatural veil, an ability to see and hear the spirit world." Antonia said as he pulled into Thad's old driveway. The beautiful empty house stood empty as a void reminder of young lives ruined.

Getting out the car as he so often did when he lived here, Thad sadly chuckled and said. "If so, then she's a cussing one. I don't think God will have her up there beside Him cussing people the way she used to cuss me. I'm going to turn the lights on. You coming in?"

"Nah, man. You go on in. Take your time." Antonia said for he intended sneak around to the back of the car which followed them and blow the passengers away. He watched Thad go around the house and saw the lights come on before he got out his hovercar, climbed the three neighboring hedges, crossed the street in the darkness where the streets lights didn't reach, snuck beside the car with his silencer already screwed on, and blew their brains against their car windows. The girl tried to escape while he was taking out the two guys in the front seat but he shot her in the back. He was back in his car by the time Thad came out saying take him home.

193

After turning on the light illegally, Thad slowly shuffled from room to room. Slowly, painstakingly absorbing what he saw in each room of the house that love built. The one that evil destroyed. It was once brimming over with love and affection, laughter and good cheer. They were happy, at least he thinks Ana was happy until he destroyed everything by foolish actions. He saw that Ana must had left in a hurry for much of their clothing and personal affects were left behind.

He visited the unlit dark garage. He used the flash light from his keyring to inspect what Ana told him. He knew the area very well. It was his trinket area where he fix things when he felt like it. He saw where someone had broken the thin layer of concrete smeared over the cement lined hole containing the money he gotten from Lola and the jeweler. He moved the heavy tool box back in place. It was a man who did this, this was too heavy for a woman alone. His brother told him he moved the tool chest for Ana and nothing was there. They both said saw a picket axe nearby. He knew it was taken when Ana was in the hospital giving birth to Bea and he was in jail.

At some point in life, most of us come across a person we're so enamored with that we can't help but go the few extra miles to impress them. Either we're hoping to ask them out or hoping to someday marry them. *I knew I wanted to marry Ana the first time I laid eyes her.* Sure, I remember the locker room talk about who could get the pretty little red head in bed first would win the bet. But we all soon learned Jack BuFaye was her brother. The pint size boy from Brunwick moved and attacked like a damn rottweiler. Outright fighting him as some of the bigger guys decided to do only granted you a humiliating beat down. The crazy boy took on three twice his size and won the fight all hands down. At our wedding, his way of welcoming me into the family was short slapping my face three times, pretty hard, hard enough to sting, at the reception. But when his baby sister, now my wife turned to hug him, he pretended he hadn't done a thing. But glowered at me over her head. All my old teammates whom Antonia invited to my bachelor party said congrats but Dashman, our quarter back told me he wouldn't marry a girl whose family oppose him so greatly. "Those people are going to make your life living hell. Always. I mean always if it comes between choosing them or you. Man, you gonna lose. And lose with a broken heart." But Ana proved Dashman wrong. She worked hard to hold our marriage together. It was I who didn't. I was high off the fame,

194

money, and women my career towed behind it. Never stopping to think how much I'm hurting the only woman I loved and truly loved me in return. With her it was never about money and fame. It was about love.

Chronicles was what the Wyetts demanded of Thad the moment he came down stairs the next morning. His parents wanted to know how he got his sentence commuted when they, along with his wife couldn't save him from prison. The judge even refused to listen the character testimony of his former team owner or teammates. Thad knew his parents wouldn't understand as Antonia did. So he kept the lewd account of yesterday and how he ended up with the child he named Marla to himself. Some horrors are best left untold.

Azazael followed the spiritual trail from the house in Boston he exited into a room of a sleeping man and child. He sees they aren't related. Perhaps his adopted daughter. The handsome specimen of a son of Adam looks familiar to him. The child doesn't but it's she who wakes up and stares at him as fear deepened in her tiny round eyes. He mentally projected,. "Fear not. Little girl, you've no reason to fear me. I didn't come for you. I came for your daddy. What's his name?"

The frightened, wide-eyed child violently shook her head and snuggled closer to her adopted father. The man who saved her life.

"Marla, don't get up roaming the house." Thad sleepily chastened her and returned to his slumber. But not before making a mental note he was going to have buy her her own bed tomorrow. The child wiggled too much. Maybe Bea wiggles like this too. Maybe all little kids sleep with their arms all in your face. Better yet, he'll add another room onto his parent's home especially for her. His mother told him she isn't going to sleep by herself until she overcome whatever she's afraid of. He knew that would be the next day after never. It's been two years and Marla still won't sleep by herself or with his mother or sister. He tried putting her in bed with them she does nothing but alarm the whole house until he opens the door and let her in or if he doesn't she cries until gets back and put her in her rightful spot.

"So, this is the man the mystery woman really loves," Azazael thinks to himself as he steps through the realm. He prided himself on never having to take on a husband's form to allure a woman to him. He stood glaring down at the Thad's sleeping form gambling with the idea of killing him in his sleep. Cloaked in the invisible realm he walks over to the maple wood dresser and looks at the pictures of the happy little family. The baby catches his attention. Everything else about her looks like the sleeping man but the eyes. She has his eyes. Even down to the killer expression in them. "Is this child like Aegeus' son, Theseus? Two fathers but one mother? If so the mother is more daring than she appears. It's said Aegeus and Poseidon was Theseus father. This is common among immortals but humans can not produce in such a manner." He smiles, he likes that. So that means the sweet woman in this photo is mostly angelic but with the right amount of naughtiness to make her very interesting. With his thumb over Thad's face in the picture he tells Ana. "My darling, I'll find you and make you mine's."

To a regular person it looked as thus the glass and silver digital picture frame was suspended in the air, unaided, like a magician's trick but not to Marla. Her innocent frightened eyes can see the spiritual being holding the digital photo and are watching his every move. He tries to hush her by ssshhing her with a finger to his lip. But Marla believing him to be Vonderbilt deciding to come kill her after all. She screamed a bloodcurdling cry and scurried upon Thad's face. Thad jumped up, disoriented, searching for whatever she's screaming about and pointing at. He, too believes their walking night terror is in the room. Picking her up after seeing the picture replace itself on his dresser.

"Vonderbilt! We had a deal! Stick to it! I know you are here! Show yourself!" Thad hissed angrily, he didn't want his entire family aroused and at his door. If Marla haven't already awaken them. Thad gasped and dangerously narrowed his eyes at the man who does step into view. The man is Ana's believed to be lover.

"What are you doing here?," Thad asked sitting Marla on the bed and walking to confront whatever this thing is. He clearly sees it isn't just a man with magical powers like Vonderbilt. He looks like a man but something tells him he isn't.

"Where is she?," Azazael asked returning the narrow eyed glare. Remembering what

196

Vonderbilt told him about a man pursuing Ana and Bea.

"I don't know and if I did I wouldn't tell you." Thad replied borrowing from Helena's sass. Azazael was way tired of that reply.

"How do you know Nikola Machiavelli?," Azazael asked. wondering if this man is a servant of the darkside.

"Who?"

"Vonderbilt, that's his real name." Azazael angrily informed him. He was very quickly losing patience with this man. "Do you follow him."

"FOLLOW HIM!?" Thad echoed louder than intended. "Are you crazy? I can't stand the Dutch Master looking rooty bastard. I'd kill him at the first opportunity." Thad said before he stopped to wonder did this man standing before him work for Vonderbilt?

"Well, that's one thing we have in common. " Azazael causally thinks as Thad stares at him. At least he was no longer delivering a saturnine gaze.

"What do you want with Ana? What in the hell were you doing in my damn closet?" Thad asked.

Azazael nearly replied. "What in the fuck do you think?" But instead says, "I've suspicion that Vonderbilt wants to kill her. So stop fucking around and tell me where is." Thad flopped down on the bed and looked up at the guy bigger than himself and said, "I really don't know. I do know Vonderbilt wants her for something unholy."

The big being froze at these words and disappeared, leaving Thad wondering what in the hell was wrong with these beings, people or whatever they are and why is Ana so important to them? Thad flopped down backward on the bed, discouraged because he realized it was he who left his backdoor open with his philandering and this thing came and in filled her loneliness.

Azazael disappeared because he knew what the Grand Wizards do a to woman once she gives him an heir or a gifted child. He kills them and preserves the body for the future generations of Grand Wizards to follow his example. The castle's catacomb is filled of their past victims. He exited in the vast tombs of decaying and disintegrating bodies. This particular location predates Christianity. He knows none of the skeletal remains are hers' so he makes his way to the latest ones. None of the latest ones he sees are her. So she is still alive or trapped somewhere in this haunted castle of pain. He rapidly teleports from room to room without the occupant's awareness of his presence and was glad he didn't find her. When he reached Vonderbilt's elegantly decorated bed someone had just hastily left it. It was still warm. He looked at the woman whom the mid-afternoon sun was beaming upon through the window, clenching the covers to her neck and staring at him much as how the child stared at him.

"Where's Vonderbilt?" He growled at her. "I don't know. He..." She swiftly shut her mouth like a bear trap but he read her surface thoughts which said "He sensed something powerful here so he fled."

He looked the woman up and down with disgust for refusing to tell him if she knew where Nikola had gone and said. "You're protecting a man coward enough to leave you to face me alone. If I had the time I'd kill you for withholding information. Now, one last time! Do you know where he went and do you know who I'm?" She shook her head truthfully answering both questions. He smiled his famous evil smile that even his Father chastised him for on several occasions and said. "I'm Azazel---live, in living color. Only chickenshit would leave you to face me alone." Her eyes widened at the mention of this unholy legendary name of utmost horror. One about which it's said in hushed tones that their master Lucifer does not dare to cross him.

"Please don't kill me. I really do not know where he went." She plead and clutched the covers with white-knuckled fingers.

"I won't have to—he will when he grows weary of you." Azazael said, touching the still tepid-warm bed and picking up on Nikola's trail. He took off through the realms after him. Nikola was going to tell him what he wanted to know if he had to beat it out of him. He encountered Zeus in the spiritual realms.

"Little brother, where are you in such a hurry to?" Azazael kept traveling without a reply. "Uppity bastard," Zeus mumbled and continued on his way to the realm of Olympus. "Always has been."

Azazael arrived in hell in Lucifer's lair but saw traces of the thin, faded line life emits leading elsewhere. "Azazael, what did I do to be honored with your presence?" Lucifer asked, grinning a handsome, loving smile. He knew Azazael was after Nikola who was long gone. He had pulled the line to himself, giving his valuable servant a chance to escape. Because if Azazael caught him the plan of his own incarnation would be over. Azazael said nothing. He shoved Lilith aside as she slithered up to him rubbing his massive chest. He followed the line exiting into a world he hadn't visited in over 900 billion years. It was a world of half reptiles and one of his many brothers. Many of those whose worlds had been destroyed kidnapped animals from earth to create life again. You couldn't kidnap people, Adam's offspring, or angels busted your ass. From what he heard the few who managed to allure or kidnap a human...it wasn't worth it. They screamed and cried to Father so loud and hard it was far better to have left them alone. After Adam was free, the few who were in other worlds and dimensions, he came for them and they gladly went with him. Even if it meant death and being placed in Paradise.

The twenty foot humanoid creature with scaled down T-Rex features approached Azazael and blocked his way as he walked his brother Cadeel's throne.

"Have you an audience to speak to my father?" The reptilian man with huge, scary choppers asked. Having increased his size to match his brother's creation Azazael said, "Boy, get out my way before I hurt you." And pushed passed the creature.

Cadeel knew the human warlock was hiding within his kingdom but the man promised he'd bring willing human females if he hid him from Azazael. Cadeel's main gift was the ability to erase a lifeline trace and that's what he did to protect the Adamite. He asked Vonderbilt what had he done to have to Azazael after him? The human explained they both were in love with the same woman and he was winning, so Azazael sought to eliminate him. Truthfully, that didn't sound like Azazael. For Azazael thought he was too pretty and sexy to have eliminate a competition to win a woman's heart.

199

Cadeel watched his proud, arrogant brother walk to the stone carved into a throne and take a seat, brushing his T-Rex wife aside. She growled but he told her it was ok. She lumbered over to his side and sat at his feet. He wondered how was he going to bring any human here without her trying to eat them.

"Cadeel, I know you hiding the bastard," Azazael accused.

"Hiding who?"

"That Adamite wizard named Nikola."

"Yes, I know of him but he's not here."

"Stop lying! I followed his spiritual trail here. So turn him over—I've a few things I'd like to ask him." Azazael's blue topaz eyes popped fire, making them darker.

"Azazael. Your bossy ass attitude is why nobody likes you," Cadeel reminded him.

"I don't care who likes or dislikes me just so long as they fear me!," Azazael said looking around trying to detect if Vonderbilt was still there. He didn't sense the trail had moved on. He wasn't in the mood to fight Cadeel but would if he had to.

Cadeel folded his massive arms over his emblem crested chest and looked peculiarly at his brother seconds before he went backward, breaking the stone throne. A black cape of smoke quickly swished from under the throne. The crash brought his children running. He held them off for he knew Azazael would enjoy killing them. Azazael took off after Nikola. Nikola looked back as Azazael was chasing him like a demon. Now he finally believed the legend about him being the creator of the race of demons called Cthulhu. Fear gripped his human heart as the big immortal was making gains on him. Nikola called upon heaven for mercy but that request only applied to saints. Azazael was in spirit so it was relatively easy to capture Nikola.

"Where's Thad Wyett's wife?" Azazael asked holding Nikola by the collar of the cape.

"I've no idea. She's Thad's wife so why don't you ask him." Nikola replied putting bravery in his voice he didn't feel in his heart. Some time ago he created an illusion cloaking his connections to Ana Wyett after Caroline Caldwell informed him that Cargill's said he was losing his mind over her. Several immortals with a beef against Azazael helped him create the illusion. Damn! Azazael made an awful lot of enemies and don't care. He felt the immortal scanning his mind for information.

Azazael let him go with a hard shove to the ground, satisfied he didn't know anything about Ana's whereabouts. "What in the hell were you running for if you didn't know anything?"

Getting up, straightening the materialized cape and clothing, Nikola replied. "You'd run too if you were coming after you. You feel like damn Godzilla or Cthulhu coming after someone. How was I supposed to know you weren't coming to kill me?!" Nikola grunted, trying to brush the gooey muck from the dead realm off his black wizardry attire.

"Why would I kill you unless you are messing with Thad's wife? Besides what kinda deal you made with him? Thad Wyett, I sensed and smelt your presence around him."

Nikola wasn't prepared for the inquisitive question but years of living with Orman's terrible temper taught him very well the art of lying and living up to his family's name. He sighed angrily and said. "If you must know---one of my witches begged me to get him out. Saying she's still in love with him. Promised she'd produce stellar results if I get him out. I gave him a hefty loan to restart his life and he hasn't paid a cent back." Vonderbilt lied wondering how Azazael knew about Thad and him. Thad's must have told him. Besides what did he mean by sensed and smelt his presence? "If that will be all. I'll be heading home."

Azazael called to the shadowy figure walking in this dark world with a black and dark wine cape billowing out behind him, "If I catch you fucking with her. I'm going to kill you." He knew the wizard was lying because true witches aren't allowed to love anyone, not even their own children, he doesn't care what bullshit the media spurts. And wizards on Nikola's level only deals with true witches not wanna-bes.

Nikola raised his hand over the back of his head with his palm upward in a dismissive gesture without turning around. "I know, I know. I may be evil but I'm not stupid." He half-expected to see Azazael's fist for the smart aleck remark when he did turn around. But no one was there except him and few wandering demons.

He stepped back through time and space back into the present day. Thankful to himself he arrived back home in one piece, uninjured after a confrontation with Azazel. That feat was almost unheard of. The moment he arrived he noted his generals and lieutenants are waiting for him, standing in a sentry line of dark capes shorter and less decorative than his own. Awaiting further instructions. His customary silver bejeweled goblet of fine wine is placed in his hand and next his black cat is brought to him and placed in his lap. He let the cape remain since he will be holding court in an hour or so. Everyone remained silent until he sat the goblet on the silver tray the naked blonde woman is standing by to receive. Knowing this signals court is in procession; Caldwell speaks first since he outranks the others.

"Your Highness, there was a setback at the restaurant where she works; we sent in fifteen but only two escaped. The owner was an ex-con named Veto. He and his people killed thirteen of our best. She has moved to Augusta Ga to accept the job I offered her but Lt. Bjors let his bloodthirst get out of hand and unfortunately she saw him. His eviction plot forced her to find Eugenia Harris."

All were quiet at the mention of the old warrior saint's name. From his throne Nikola rubbed his black cat with one hand and his chiseled chin with the other.

"I thought I told you twelve to watch Bjors to make sure he doesn't get out of control?" Nikola's piercing black eyes landed on each solemn face; leisurely languishing, abiding them each the same among of attention.

"What in the fuck were you all doing that you allowed Bjors to push her that far? Cause her to seek out the one person none of us is happy she found?"

No one replied for all knew what was in store for them. Nikola stared hard and cold at the men trying to decide shall he kill them and start all over with new blood or what?

"Ok, she just killed two Lieutenants in Pasadena, they never got the chance to celebrate the unholy day. The witches are doing better than you sorry ass, sons-of-bitches." Nikola fumed, quickly throwing green fire at Caldwell's feet, singeing his designer leather shoes. The fire burns away the toes of his shoes exposing his feet, causing him to step back in line.

Shrevenport knows he's next; Nikola throws fire before he can speak, burning his feet and ankles. The man sucks in the pain, hiss soundlessly, and bites down on lower lip to bear it. Nikola is still upset with him for allowing Lola Wilson to get out of control. The news coverage her affair with Thad Wyett didn't appease him. It pissed him off. He never said lock the man up. He wanted him eliminated. Shrevenport failed to do that because of his unnatural affection for the turned witch not born witch. Knowing the punishment for failure a black hooded couple walked up the line of warlocks demanding their clothing. All disrobed staring straight ahead. None look at their master nor their punishers. To do so only made things worse. The young ones having never encountered Nikola were surprised to see the welts on the backs on the older ones.

The open oil burning lanterns are cast eerie shadows across the walls onto the numerous crest banners unfurling from the lofty ceiling. The older ones know what the howling means. The younger ones glance nervously around when Nikola disappears and the servants vacate the rooms. They watched the older ones as they formed dirty fire in their palms; the room grows darker and darker until the darkness is all there is. Snuffing out the red flare of the open cask oil lanterns. Next...seemingly it lasts an eternity. There's biting, scratching, clawing, twisting and painful, hard pulling of penises, unseen things shoving taloned fingers into their rectums. Howling, screeching; terrible sulfurous breath being breathed into their faces. The foul breath burns their eyes. Pain is being inflicted on every part of their body, leaving not an inch untouched or unmolested. But they can not see their assaulters. They exist solely in a painful, pitch blackness that seemed alive. There's no place to run without running into a nestlian of attackers who bite them on the neck or face. The men feel their own blood making the floor slippery.

They wonder why the creatures appear to be sucking their blood from the floor or attempting to slurp it from their wounds?

In the thick darkness of hell they can not see the bubbling, swirling, fetid cesspool opened in the floor from which the creatures are crawling from. The odor fumigating the room is worse than the bites. The painful nausea is hindering their ability to fight back at their attackers. While throwing fire or creating a protective against shield at one group a hundred more are attacking. By now, all are upon the floor at the mercy of their unseen enemies. Each is certain this is how they will die.

Slowly, an eerie green light floats through the darkness, encircling each of the men. It burns like acid.

"That's enough." Nikola called out into the darkness. Light began to slowly return. Now, each see the battle wounds of their colleagues. Each is drenched in blood and unidentifiable substances but Nikola is nowhere to be seen. Caldwell, dripping in blood spots Bjors' mottled face peering from an ajar doorway smiling with contentment.

Chapter 3

Can't nobody hex like me!

Swirling the fine, 250 year old wine in a bulbous goblet made of borosilicate with small diamonds on the stem, he sniffed, inhaled and sipped, slightly swishing it around in his mouth to appease his palate. Tasting and savoring the wine as the true master sommelie, oenologist he is while admiring the medieval scene the sprawling on the rocky and flat terrain below. He long ago noted the carefully, militia steerage of the lay of the land, the rugged bare cliffs descending into the grassy knolls, and fields of crops beyond. The foreboding castle was designed to be impressive. The oldest part of the castle and village are said to be at least 25,000 years old.

Each Grand Wizard added to the grand castle to accommodate his own taste or removed that of his predecessor whom usually he defeated in a mortal battle of wizard chess. There are no friends at the top of the world. Here, one must stand alone.

The secluded, pastoral scene below has not changed much in over 2,500 years. The humble village of clusters of stone hamlets with graying straw thatch roofs was veined by traffic worn cobblestone streets that wove through the pristine design could be seen over the rise of the land that partially obstructed his view. He watched the houses as thin smoke whiffed from the ancient clean chimneys. Wondering who lives there. In his twenty years of reign he still doesn't know the names of the villagers and doesn't care to learn them. To him they are nothing more than cattle. He cocked his ear and listened as the soft, clamorous activities of the day floated to the Roman-styled stone arched window. This ancient village existed sole for the purpose of the Grand Wizard.

The clear blue sky on such a beautiful sunny day with a mild breeze rolling over the vast plains, fields and crops lent the well maintained village a perfect picturesque scene of peacefulness worthy of an old world Renaissance oil painting. It has graced the cover of many digital magazines and electronic post cards without the public having a clue as to what truly lies beneath nor within the lovely agrarian valley.

The Highness of the world wizardry turned to address his guests who have been waiting two hours for him to speak. Little has changed in the village below since the days of Eric the Red said to his minions "Behold the loveliness of these fine walls." Waving his arms to emphasis his point. "Did you know the furniture is kept in such vibrant state by being polished with nothing but the fat of infants? Some see obsolescence in this practice of preservation but we see beauty," the elegant man said, taking another sip and savoring the ambrosial flavor. "Besides, what in the fuck do we care?"

All in attendance mumbled in agreement and watched in awe as he flicks a single flame of dirty fire from his finger tip and lit a rich, drug laced cigar. Mixed slightly sliver and black hair neatly cascading to his shoulders added a distinguished quality to the high leader of the earthly dark forces. The world over regional leaders wouldn't dare cancel the invitation to witness their 2nd most highness in action. They cling to his every word and gesture as though he is a messiah...to them, *he is a messiah.*

Tourists visit the ancient village below seated among the mountains of northern Switzerland doting on its' ability to remain pretty much untouched by the march of time and industrialization. There appeared to be an elimination of the accessibility of electricity, telephones, computers, automobiles, private planes, and modern appliances which only Vonderbilt enjoys. The village is still much as was thousands of years ago. Luxury must be earned by the castle's servants and village's residents alike; it aren't something given on a whim nor allowed simply because of one's desire. It's granted through loyalty and paid for with the heart and soul.

Turning to adoring eyes gazing upon him with much admiration, in relevance and awe. The handsome man with looks even movie stars envy was once a designated warrior saint of the Nazarene, a regiment leader, the greatest of his nation, but that's another life. He hung up his bejeweled breastplate, golden sword and shield many years ago in exchange for uncontested earthly power and wealth. After the massacre of his family his nature drew darker and darker until he wanted nothing to do with God or any church.

Born forty-four years ago, Donte Nikola Machiavelli, but known to this group only as His Highness Vonderbilt. It's rumored among the highest members of the elite hierarchy he's a direct descendant of the famous Italian savvy mastermind, Machiavelli, the author of "The Prince." No one knows for sure if the claim is true, because no one with an ounce of self-preservation dared to question his claim nor dispute it.

Donte Nikola doesn't often entertains his subjects, even those ranking directly below himself, for he has no peers. The unforgotten lore of his origin is a mystery to most of group awaiting him to speak. The seven powerful figures representing the seven continents of the world and their own structural hierarchic broods respectfully stand silent as the beauteous archaic ornamented walls and wait. They know their master will address them at the appointed hour. These seven are only ones of his subjects whom he considers their superiority high enough to know his true origin and background. Recounting the ancient familial lore that once his ancestor was much like the young warriors they mercilessly pursue.

According to family lore, a Venetian coven of their kind drove him to become the world's greatest, most diabolical master-minder of devious plots, which they all exalted. It's said Leonardo da Vinci tried to save the young Italian engineer from this terrible fate. Knowing once the young man realized his full potential, life would become a hellish nightmare for anyone unfortunate or unlucky enough to cross him or his path. Da Vinci knew his kind; if they sunk deep into the forbidden abyss and turned to the darkside they became the opposite of their first nature. He knew this was the local coven's goal. To bring out the dark nature in the young man through relentless persecution. To erase all traces of God's characteristics in the person. They succeeded. But they lived to deeply regret their success. They didn't foresee he would turn on them; they were betting on him aiding them in their cause. But instead Machiavelli learned to breath in hate and exhale revenge.

While painting his younger friend's portrait (Da Vinci was one of the few who Machiavelli actually treasured their friendship without suspicion) and looking at the handsome younger man, DaVinci smiled to himself thinking, *"Be careful at what you create for you might not like it when its finished; for it might just up and kill you."*

Vonderbilt withheld his true identity from the remaining forty-eight admirers. He believed much as his ancestor' mentor Da Vinic once said. *"Simplicity is the ultimate sophistication. "* So without further ado, having spiritually scanned the group for disloyalty, he summoned his servants to escort them all to a large room resembling a college classroom. The personal staff, his closest aides, distributed black gold embossed binders bearing his emblem with the interiors printed on expensive, rare linen paper.

The attendees who had been called forth from all over the world by their twenty-four superiors knew this was an opportunity of a lifetime. Most of the satanic world never meet the Grand Wizard nor his Witch, their queen. The strength of one's natural gift or ability solely determines how far one can move up in this enigmatic power structure not wealth or social position. Those things means nothing here. In this secret society it is all about spiritual power. The very reality of it's Delphic existence is relatively unknown to the rest of the world. Some believe they are the Illuminati, with no clear understanding that the Illuminati are mere one sect of the seven and it is His Highness whom all branches and all the world answers to.

The well-tanned, well-toned, handsome man of about 6'1" of incalculable age with coasting whorls of raven black curls walked patiently in front of his silent, eager audience with his hands clasped behind his elegantly poised, well symmetrical straight, rigid back. He turn academically and performed another eye sweep over the group and begun teaching them saying; "All of you are quiet valuable to our cause. I called you here today because we are losing too many to the blades of the warrior saints. The turnovers and replacements are occurring too frequently among your ranks." Walking with his hands clasped behind his back, stopping at each pupil, forcing each student to meet his mystical glaze. He continues, saying;

"You and your subjects' trail are leading too many of the Archangel Michael's warriors to your lairs. I brought you here to teach you how to stay alive and how to control those under you. Covens are only as good as those who control them. Never hesitate to kill anyone exposing your world or work or anyone who refuses to do as you command them. Betrayal is an automatic death sentence. Yours and your subjects' deeds create a traceable trail in the spirit world. The warriors can pick up on these trails which will lead directly back to you! I'll teach you all for the next seven days how to create illusions and camouflages to throw them off your scent. Because there's nothing more terrifying than waking up in the middle of the night with one of those crazies standing over you with sword drawn and ablaze, asking if you would like to bow down to their master, whom they call "The Christ." He reveals to them if your answer is sincere, if it's not sincere, they behead you. The sword's fatal wounds can not be medically detected. And if it manifests physically, the wound is cauterized. No blood spills. Remember. Never look at them when they are in their master's glory, it can blind and even kill."

Continuing the perilous dialogue without interruption Donte teaches, "Always bear in mind we are at war. A celestial war. This war is as real as any mortal war. But it's also a war hidden from the eyes of men. Our greatest weapon has been the ability to remain hidden. To discredit the saints in their claims that we and the residents of hell are real. That we actually exist. The public's demands for logic and proof that can be analyzed by the scientific world have aided us tremendously and made the Nazarene warriors look like wild-eyed, zestful frantic, sword-wedging nuts on a holy mission against an enemy

208

that doesn't exist." Donte laughed ,throwing back his head while his black hair descend down his back below his shoulder blades. He heartily laughed at his own attempt at comedy, believing it to be witty and clever; the classroom erupts with laughter to match their master's. He bluntly halts the glee and resumes his lecture and not a sound is to be heard.

"There're many truths and legends existing pertaining us but no one has absolute, unwavering proof! Sure, such proof exists in the Bible, Torah and the Koran. It exists in the sacred writings of many cultures, the Buddhist, the Hindu, China, the Americas, but no one take these ancient oral and literary works seriously anymore. That works marvelously to our advance. Our forerunners ingeniously succeed in discrediting them which works marvelously to our advantage. Actually, we had not anticipated everyone would so readily believe our claims of the saints' mental incapability. Although we own all the major media outlets we never dreamed it would be so easy to dupe people and turn them against their own defenders. That people would be so utterly gullible."

 He chuckled to himself , shaking his head in disbelief at how easy it has been to hide the truth about their existence and discredit those who knew what they were and knew demons were real.

 Self-basking in his last revelation Donte says; "The veil, the chasm separating the physical realm from the realm of Hades is slowly but surely, coming down. However we, the faithful, the chosen ones, must masterfully create as much mayhem as possible to render the chasm open, to bring forth our master into this world. He is the rightful prince. The rightful heir. Not the so-called 'Prince of Peace'. The veil is down so low at this late date in the time that even I find it obscene that the herds of sheep called humanity can not see something spiritual is going on. But....who am I to question their stupidity?"

 Stopping to sip from wine his wine goblet brought to him on a silver platter, the high wizard spiritually scans the group to learn who is actually listening and taking notes and who isn't. He found no one guilty, so he resumes. "The ultimate goal is the make the warrior or warrior saint of the Nazarene life so miserable they eventually succumb to our desire. So in order to live in peace and comfort, have the comfort of a home, have food to eat, and be able to protect their friends and family they join us and aid us in our cause since in actuality, they can not defeat us. Their strength and might is priceless. "

The free flowing baritone of his voice resonated through the sound proof classroom as he delivered his elegant speech. The cadence of his speech rose and fell with vivid emotions. The crescendo and decrescendo of his graceful, refined voice rivaled that of any prophet. He had the gift of language and used it compellingly. Few knew he also possessed the gift of persuasion for he rarely used it. He always concluded why go through the tedious dance of convincing when brutal force worked better and was swifter?

"Attack them relentlessly, never let up, never feel pity, never let them enjoy life. Once the darkmaster finds one, never let him or her out your sight. Utterly destroy them—do not allow one to prosper or maintain a comfortable home. Follow them from the cradle to the grave if you must. Learn all there is about them. Learn their preference in a spouse or lover. Learn their preference in clothing, food, entertainment, their favorite color, all their family lineage. Dispatch your crews to move next door and befriend them of learn even the tiniest thing about them. Bug their homes if you can't spy spiritually. Relentlessly encourage your members to marry into their families so you'll always have ready access to all their function and activities. And if the gifted or saint figures out one of us has married among their clan, encourage your member to lovingly whisper, coo, whine or do whatever it takes, to solidify the said inconsistencies about spouse's their spiritual gifted relative. The goal is to drive an unamendable wedge between the gifted, warriors, or warrior saints and their family. No allies make them an easier target and easier to control."

Everyone was still spellbound by him after two hours. For it was rare anyone was privileged enough to see him other than for death or punishment. "You see...the weapons, gifts and abilities they possess are priceless. Are the most powerful instruments on earth, no man-made weapon can match them. But always be aware, bear in mind no matter how raggedy, downtrodden or skeletal they look in the physical world, they all posses the heart of a warrior and their God's law and orders are christened in their hearts and they'll behead you the first chance they get. They're of the order of warriors, eons foretold legions of saints which their saints Enoch and Jude wrote about".

"The Lord shall cometh with ten thousandths of his saints." Nikola quoted Jude :14. He knew the bible better than many ministers. He was taken to mass three time a week until age fifteen when Orman, his predecessor , decided he wanted him for a lover and a prodigy. "Most of them know nothing about their gifts and abilities. The church teaches them nothing but the Sweet By and By, teach them nothing about spiritual warfare. So we round up all we catch before they come of age, usually around age 12-23, they're much easier to control and force into doing our bidding," Vonderbilt states a tried and true theory. Grand wizards have been using the ploy for centuries.

"Every generation has legions of them. Every nation have its regiments of them. The nations who've killed theirs' off always ends up in a shit creek without a boat let alone a paddle because they no longer have a spiritual defense. Listen and listen very carefully, listen with great and grave intensity to my next words: Never, ever kill one, it is vital to our well-being and comfortable lifestyle that they remain alive. They are the thin holy line between humanity and hell. They are soldiers and it's their job to defend *all* of humanity. Nobody wants to return to the days of yore. The smelly, putrid, rodent infested, discomfort of the days of Merlin. Haunted by diseases such as the bubonic plague and the immortals."

The classroom is completely spell bound, listening to Vonderbilt's vociferation. "They're important to our well-being as well because through their master, the Christ, they can pacify the heavens into opening up and bestowing riches, and wisdom onto earth. Which we all presently enjoy. Us, moreso than they. And we aren't always sure which portal they guard. We can not control what comes through those portals they and their comrade angel buddy guards. Although we hate to admit it, and will never openly profess it, we all know Hades can be a rowdy, destructive bunch. And if one dies, whatever nation they're born to guard, well that portal is left open, destructive forces enter and the area they were guarding goes to hell in a handbasket. This realm is the domain of man, so humans were appointed to help guard it. The USA has more than any other nation on earth which explains their esteemed, lone status as the world's ultimate superpower. They're the thin holy line between earth and hell. They and their comrade angels are the spiritual police that beats hell back into the darktower. So we need them alive until the appointed time when hell is to let loose and our master arises to control it.

Then and only then shall we kill all of them when the Lord of Darkness finally walks the earth. Our kingdom shall then rule it until the end of time."

Voicing a falsetto of sympathy, Nikola says "Those of you from the USA, I sympathize with your plight. I can not imagine the turmoils you endure and gantlets you run to accomplish your missions. Your nation is ridden with do-gooders. They're everywhere, sticking their noses in every soup, pie and cake! Plus, you guys have this freedom of speech thing, which I think should be outlawed. The saints and warriors can say whatever they damn-well please and no one is able to silence them, no matter how crazy they sound! But we've found a way around this pesky law, we silence them through intimidation and fear!"

The three Americans, representing the Eastern Seaboard, the Midwest and the Western USA, look around at each other as though they share each other's pains and nod viciously in agreement.

⁂

Four hours later Nikola dismissed the special students and merrily reminds them to make the enemies miserable but never take a life, they are too important to their own well-being.

The properly dressed students wearing neatly pressed, crisp customary attire of black slacks or skirts accompanying white shirts and blouses are ushered into a grand dinning hall. Each is passed the sacrificial goblet containing the blood of a captured saint which make several severely ill and two drop dead. The dead are fed to the residential minotaur and remembered no more. This was Nikola's way of weeding out the weak.

⁂

He hated it but realized he was becoming obsessed with this woman. He didn't like to be ruled by emotion. Being older than this universe he never thought a human could engulf his mind, the very essence of his being. At some point, most of us come across a person we are so enamored with that we can't help but take a many extra measures to gain their love. In his case he needs to find a way to reach her. So he needed to pull off a great stunt, or get divinely arrested for trying. He knows she can hear him. The daring task was to sing like an angel. His pre-combat career was the heavenly choir. About five seconds of singing later he heard her across time, space and distance, timidly asked. "My immortal love...is that's you?"

He sung his reply back to her with all the love felt in his heart. He followed the emotions of her heart. He arrived in the backyard of Eugenia Harris' house. Mother came to the screened in back outer porch and glared at him. She could hear the serenading, too. She tore out back into the kitchen down the hall when she horribly realized it was Ana who opened a portal through the prayer barrier for him to enter. But when she pushed the door open without knocking it was too late, the room was all-aglow and an archangel named Haniel was blocking the doorway to the closet in the small by-room renters use as sitting space to read and whatnot. She watched in dismay as Ana and Azazel both reached around the Archangel and she walked with him on her own free will and disappeared.

Seeing he wasn't able to get pass the angel Ana reached out to his extended hand. She clearly heard Mother Harris yelling "No, don't do that! That's how Dracula gets people!" But her lover was here, that's all that mattered. Common sense was telling her she ought to scared to death of him but she wasn't. It felt perfectly normal when he put her tiny hand in the crook of his elbow and he teleported them both to another world.

Ana hadn't noticed she was still wearing her white and blue polka dot sleeping shirt until he called it to her attention after they exited into a house grander than anything she had ever seen. He handed her a much too large fine silk robe. After she put it on, he rolled up the sleeves all the while gazing lovingly in her eyes trying to remember where he knows her from?

"My love, what's your name?," he tenderly asked, pulling out a chair for her to sit at a breakfast nook table. It was daylight where they were. Following her gaze he said, "That's the Mediterranean Sea. We're in Morocco."

"My name is Ana BuFaye."

"Ah, sweet Ana." He smiled. She didn't know if he would remember her name or all he would remember were their times together. At least some of them. She took in his massive size and the flowing black, brown and golden hair beautifully blended together. His eyes looked inhuman. They looked as if made of a gemstone. Blue Topaz?... no, they were deeper blue than that. But totally unlike blue eyed humans. He's astonishingly, ethereally beautiful. *"I've never seen a beautiful man. I've seen many, many handsome ones but never a beautiful one."*

He was now standing by the chair holding it for her. *"Gosh, he has a killer smile."* She noted. She quickly regained her pose and paddle barefoot to the chair, when seated he kissed the crown of her head. Once seated she asked his name.

"On earth I'm known as Ashton Cargill." He replied looking deeply at her as professional chefs, she assumed that's what they were from their professionalism; entered pushing white cloths cover tables on wheels. This was old school. None of the floating remote control crap carts for their meal. She watched them prepare for a few minutes and asked, "What's your heavenly name?" He smiled that smile again.

"If I told you, you might scream and run," he joked.

"I promise I won't run," she teased and crossed her heart.

"You know me as well as I know you in my heart. Someday, hopefully soon. I can tell you my real name," he said. Hopefully they can soon be together without interference. As he poured a glass of champagne he informed her what each dish was. He sliced off a piece of Ris de veau and spooned in her mouth which was pretty good until he told her what it was. She politely spit it into a fine linen napkin.

"Sorry, but I only eat American food," she apologized. He told her there was no need to apologize, assured her that was no problem. He snapped his fingers for one of the people alined by the wall with their white gloved hands behind their back to step forward and told her to tell the woman what she wanted.

"I want fried pork chops, turnip greens, mac and cheese, and biscuits. Oh yeah, and a tall glass of sweet tea." The woman wrote it down as if the request wasn't unusual. There was no frown nor ridiculing her. She was surprised. They left the table at his instructions. He tried coaxing her into eating some of the other dishes.

"Where I'm from pigeons roam the streets and shit on cars. We don't eat them."

He laughed and remarked from experience. "There's nothing better than stuffing a bit of foie gras in a pigeon or quail and eating it with some wild mushrooms as these are prepared."

He laughed again, remembering more than he did when she first arrived. He chuckled because he remembered trying to introduce her new exotic dishes was like trying to coax a three year old into eating her vegetables. But if she didn't want it, well, she didn't want it. But somehow, somewhere in the back of his mind... in a part he couldn't quite pull to the surface... he already knew these things about her. It was like they both were acting on some inherent instincts. Spooning food in her mouth seemed the natural thing to do, it was as if she expected him to do so.

He knew he got pass the first stunt and the heavens were soon coming for her. So what was one more stunt?! While they waited for her dishes to arrive he got up and walked across the room and pulled out the jewelry set he had made for her long ago. He walked back to where she sat as lovely as an auburn haired angel in his oversized robe and knealt before her, opening a velvet box containing a matching jewelry set of a necklace, earrings, and rings and said, "Whatever your reply is I'll have to accept it. I know you don't know me. But I feel in our hearts we already know each other. This is why I brought you here. Will you marry me?"

She was flabbergasted, but somehow felt it was natural as sitting here with him in a bathrobe. Nothing seemed out the ordinary.

"Yeah, just so long as your name isn't Lucifer," she nervously said.

He chuckled softly in that sweet melody of a laughter of his. "You've no idea how happy you've made me. But no, it isn't Lucifer. When I'm sure you love me enough not to scream and run away, I'll tell you my name. My real name," he promised her kissing her nape as he lifted the single long plait to place the necklace alone worth over a million on her slender neck. Now was time for the second stunt. He already had a priest standing by in case he was able to get through to her. He rang for him. He hated to rush her but he knew heaven was holding off for a reason and what that reason was---he didn't know but he knew Haniel had reported back by now on how he had serenaded the woman out. He'd found her. He saved the ring to use in the ceremony. The man rushed through the ceremony as Cargill had instructed. He was placing the ring on his finger as the kitchen was bringing in her dish.

The robe was so overflowing on small her frame; it might as well had been a gown. She wondered were her reasons for accepting this proposal honorable. She was tired of being chased, tired of being rawbone exhausted, scared, homeless and broke. He loved her. The tenderness in his eyes told her he did. She loved him too; as stupid as it may have sounded she knew loved him. It was a different type of love than what she had for Thad. It was a mature love. Not the starry-eyed, teen puppy love. When the priest pronounced them man and wife, the staff members clapped and welcomed her. She was so dazzled she didn't know what to say.

"Everyone look at this face and memorize it. This is your new boss lady." He informed the staff. After all left he said. "If I can help it, you will never go back to your old life. No one will ever touch or hurt you again." He beckoned her to cut the small two-tier white cake with the silver serving knife. She did it and fed him cake and he the same to her.

They were finally truly alone; by the adoring look in his gemstone eyes, she knew he meant it when he told her he loved her like none other. She felt the pull of their mutual addiction. Ana sipped her champagne to hide her nervousness. But boldly did something that even surprised herself; she leaned forward to him loosen his his belt. The band of his was in her way. She placed her small, delicate hands on the button and snapped it feel revealing the silken undergarment he was wearing. Next she slowly unbuttoned his shirt. Kissing him as the fabric gave away to each inch of his brownish bronze flesh.

216

"Gosh! He's handsome." She thinks. Ana released, freed him from the confinement of the shirt and thrust Ashton's shirt aside on the floor.

He didn't want to seem impatient but he had to know. As the sunny, bright Mediterranean sun beamed through the glass wall of what was now their bedroom, reflecting a sheen blue tint on the richly adorned wall he hungrily lowered his mouth to hers and found he was right, there was love and passion for him in her heart and body. The heat of her love and desire poured into him like hot lava; they seared right through his core into his heart. "I love you," she mumbled around his lips, entwining her finger into his thick mane of hair and fiercely pulling him to her.

"Thank God," he thought, before his hands slipped over his oversized robe, over her curved, tight derriere, to draw her closer, to mold her to his frame against his aching hardness.

"My sweet, cherished Ana, the love of my life. Death, hell nor the grave will take you from me. I'll love now and until the end of time." He said cupping her beautiful face in his massive hands. "I've waited since before creation to hear those words spill forth from your lips." He kissed her tenderly as one would kiss an angel. For to him, that's what she was. A precious sweet angel.

Perfect, his hand cupped her perfectly, as if they were made for each other. Standing nude before his new wife he pressed her firmly against the rigid length below. He glided his hands over one breast before slipping his robe off her shoulder. He slowly and gently pulled the night shirt over head before gliding his hands over the smooth skin with many blemishes he wondered where they came from?

He lifted her for to him, she was light as a feather and carried her to their bed and laid her on the massive bed as gentle as one would a new born baby. To him, she was his baby. He gathered her in his arm and gently glided his fingers between her soft silken thighs. She jumped and tried to pull the covers up, he eased them out of her hands. Again he glides his hands over her hips to relax her before moving to the center. She thrust her hips toward him, almost against her will. They lifted to his loving touch as his fingers sifted between the auburn curls. He knew it had probably been a long since she had been touched this way. Despite the fact he pulled off this marriage against heaven wishes he had to be gentle and not distress her. He gently massage her perky breasts to put her further at ease. He was determined to make love to her. He covered her slowly, all over with hot kisses that caused her to arch her back to him. He kissed the sole of her feet as well as the palm of her hand. She wanted him to enter her. To fill her. But he refused.

His kisses trailed down to her triangle as her naked heaving breasts obstructed her view of what he was doing. The nipples were hard and taunt, and the aureoles against dark bronze skin added beauty he hadn't expected. Her narrow waist flowed out to curvy hips. His perfectly sculptured fingers gently pinched the nipples, making them more rigid. The triangle of her vagina was warm and inviting. There was a radiance glow in her beautiful face, making it so beautiful it was nearly painful to watch. Then he reached behind her and loosen the long plait as he kissed her and the locks and tendrils of the dark auburn hair spread out from around her like a dark red crown of glory.

Not knowing if she had ever had cunnilingus performed before he gently pulled her clitoris between his lips. Whatever he was doing was driving her mad. She wanted him to stop and then again she didn't want him to stop. She tried to shut her legs, he held them open, she tried to pull the cover over her shame but he gently pushed it aside. Softly ensuring her she was beautiful and had nothing to be ashamed of. She knew she was at his mercy. Her response told him this was somewhat new to her so he took his time. The off-white silk bed covers glided with his muscular body to heighten his pleasure along with her soft moans and sighing and trying to get away from him. The soft touch of her small callous hands in his hair and back made his penis ache in such intense agony that was all the more pleasure. He applied all his skills of erotic knowledge along with the caring with his every touch. He was, deliciously dedicated into pleasuring her.

Now she was emitting a soft rose scent, it was driving him insane. He didn't think she was aware she was screaming and begging him by his real name to enter her. He decease the delicate touches, he didn't want to overdo it, since this was her first time being at this height of ecstasy. Rising from between her shapely legs, kissing her all the way up, he traveled up until his naked body hovered horizontally inches above her, his massive chest was scattered with goose bumps across every pore. It had been ages since he seen this reaction within himself. With eyes closed and heaving breasts she reached down and searched for his penis, he guided her tiny hot hand to it, around it. His erection making it pulse when she squeezed. Her gentle grip told him she loved him and was ready for him. Ashton moved Ana's fingers to the soft head of his erection where she let them lingered a few minutes and explored, running the tiny, callous pads of her fingers over the surprisingly not heavily veined skin. He cupped her soft but firm bottom in his hand as she guided him inside, the warmth and love felt from her caused him to pulled a moan into his throat. It felt like warm cascading waves of love coasting over him everytime he thrust into her, the oscillating motion was driving them both beyond the border of madness. No longer able to restraint his feeling, an animal like growl escaped his lips. He felt fire and bolts of electricity convulsing his body, intensifying his senses. He had never made love to a saint before and especially not one heighten to this degree of ecstasy, so he did not know what to expect. He knew the heavens would get him good for this act of deliberate defiance but so be it. She was his wife and he loved her.

Ana lost track of time and reality, she kept telling herself she had gone too far. But another part of her brain was telling her she had just married the man, so how was this be wrong to feel this good? If loving him was wrong, then she didn't want to be right. Because at the moment there was nothing in her mind but Ashton's kissing, touching, and enjoying his exploring every inch of her body with his mouth, lips, tongue, and hands. For the first time in what felt like eons she was able to forgot everything troubling her. She felt his love for her in his touch, now his thrusting in her with expert skill was sending rapid temblors through her loins, causing her mind and body to teeter on the edge of the divine.

She and Thad had made love many time but nothing in limited her experience prepared her for the new heights she was experiencing, the agony but yet blissful, pleasure in her neck, arms, and hands felt as through live fire was coasting through them; the tightening of her belly when a wave of passion engulfed it send her in uncontrollable shivers; the escape of her moisture as it saturated them both was sexy as she had never experienced sexuality before. Bashfully, she realized that once unrestrained, her passion was fierce, strong and unbridled, but Ashton had gently forced her to yield to his slow but loving pace, his leisure touch, bringing her repeatedly to a climax so hard it nearly hurts and then built her up again. All this was even before penetration. She started to feel if he kept this up, she would go mad.

While he speed up his lips devoured hers; his tongue explored her mouth, her neck, and her ears. His tongue skillfully tortured her lips as she moaned in his mouth. She

219

pulled him as close as possible everytime he told her over and over he loved her. She felt she couldn't pull him into her deep enough. She had to hold on to the covers when he took them to a higher plane. She had no idea there was one.

Lost in the fabric of time, it was now dark. She had no idea when they wedded nor when they started making love. They lay in each other's arms and watched the stars from the glass wall. Hell, she doesn't even remember when he closed it. She was glad he had sense enough to close the heavy curtains for she certainly didn't. His hands opened her again, she wasn't sure if she could withstand something so intensity again. He slowly, gradually, insistently caressed her with his thumbs, he spread her softness, the moistness, as he talked to her.

"My love, all of this is yours. So what would you like to eat. You mortals have to eat." But somehow she wasn't hungry. He explained he radiated his essence into her but they hadn't been together long enough that she no longer needed to eat." She wrapped in the bedcovers and tried to get up. He pulled her playfully back into the bed.

"Mrs. Cargill, you do not attend to yourself. There's a staff here to attend your every need. That food is cold, no longer consumptive," he said asking again for a second time, what would she like? She had no idea what she would like so she said Beef Wellington.

Thirty minutes later it was there, so she assumed they must had already some food cooked. It was succulent. She hadn't realized how hungry she really was.

After she finished eating, several shopping bags were brought into the room. Most were of places she had only heard of. They were left outside the door on a serving cart. She was still hungry so she ate again but is still bashful about changing in front of him. She doesn't know why when she has just had her legs as wide as they would go before him. But that was just her. He didn't question it.

He admired her dark bronze body, all the richly hued contours and shades were beautiful to his eyes. His hand slipped between her thighs again and she let out a small cry, a half sob of pleasure as he gently touched her already hotwired, delicate, supercharge, aching flesh. There was no point in getting dress, he simply removed the luxurious gown and proceeded to making love to her again. The heat that started to move through her again, reawakening the need. She was almost speechless, nearly mindless when she heard Bea calling her. Her daughter's voice brought her back to her reality hard and fast. She quickly covered herself; fear returned as old companion.

220

"*Supposed something terrible happen while I'm here enjoying myself. If so, I'll never forgive myself,*" she frantically thinks.

"Well, it's time to face the music." He chuckled softly getting up and getting dressed. "Do you think your daughter will mind having a stepfather?" He asked casually but she knew it wasn't. "I'm sure she won't mind. She never had much of a father of any sort," she said wondering how did she get back to Bea?

⁓⦿⦿⦿⁓

After we quickly finished getting dressed he took my hand and teleported us back to Mother Harris'. In Atlanta it was daytime, a still, very warm mid afternoon. There wasn't much air stirring. Mom and Mother Harris were sitting on the front porch. Bea ran out to meet me, I picked her up and started up the steps. Mom yanked the door open, nearly causing me to lose my balance. Ashton held me steady with his hand at my waist. "Get your narrow behind in this house!," Mom said, opening the screen door wider. I looked back at Ashton and shrugged my shoulders.

"We all thought you had killed her!"

"Mrs. BuFaye...why would I do that?," Ashton politely asked.

"Because Mother Harris say you're Azazael and that's what Azazael do!," Mom said, snatching me the rest of the way into the house off the steps and quickly locking the door. I set Bea down and turned and let him in. "Mom, before you and Mother scream at me I married him yesterday," I said showing them the ring. It flashed fire in the brilliant early September sun.

"Oh Lord!" Mother Harris lamented, slowly shaking her head from side to side. "Child, what have you done?" She asked shortly before a burst of light brighter than the afternoon's sun appeared on the porch with us. It was that angel named Haniel, again. But another one appeared with this one. An angel no one knew but Azazael. He quickly flashed everyone with a blinding light, erasing their memory and took Azazael with them.

The three brothers exited in another world. The people and creatures watched them from afar on an island with it's base extending out the water. The inhabitants watched with great curiosity.

"Azazael! I've had it with your stunts and tricks!" Cassiel yelled shaking the small rock island. "We stood back and let you consecrate your marriage but unless it's heavenly it's deemed a black mass wedding! It isn't official, she isn't your wife! Vonderbilt married her in a midnight ceremony nearly two years ago."

Azazael scoffed. "You know good and damn well a satanic wedding under duress isn't binding on earth let alone in heaven! I didn't take her from Thad Wyett. Records clearly show he divorced her. I'm so tired of all the damn secrecy until it sickens me. Will you all tell me what going on? Why is this one woman so important to heaven? She's my wife and I've every right to be with my wife. I didn't force her to do anything. She loves me and I love her."

Cassiel had grown very aweary of repeating the same reasons to Azazael. Tired of hearing Azazael talk about how much he loved this woman. Azazael wasn't crazy. He understood perfectly well what they were repeatedly telling him. He was just that spiteful.

He aggressively swung for him but Azazael ducked and caught him with an uppercut to the chin. Cassiel staggered back a few steps and came back at Azazael and hit him so hard it crumbled the island and the houses into dust, knocking Azazael into the waters below. Azazael shook his head to clear his mind and leap back in the air taking Cassiel down into the waters with him. Haniel called Uriel to pull them apart. There was no way he was getting in the middle of fists sounding like thunder. Uriel appeared underwater and tore the two apart, sending Azazael back to his normal earthy resident without the memory of his few hours old marriage.

Azazael arrived back home furious, knowing his memory had been erased. His

222

brothers had stripped away so much this time that the familiar coldness was filling the hole left in his heart by removing the woman's name, love and memory. Giving him back his old self. He knew Cassiel had given him a royal mind fuck but didn't care. He looked down at the diamond accented wedding band on his left ring finger and quickly removed it. He wondered who he had been dumb enough to marry? It didn't matter. Whomever she is he is annulling the marriage as soon as he finds her. She will surely show up asking for money.

Dawn watched in horror as he stood looking at the ring. Caroline Caldwell was right. He has found and married the woman. Well, that's just too bad. She didn't tell the bitch to up and marry her man. Not knowing his memory had been erased Dawn asked. "Have you told her about us?"

Her seductive voice brought him out of the trance of trying to figure out what had he done? "Told who about you all?", he perplexedly asked.

Dawn wasn't in the mood for his playing dumb crap. "Your goddamn wife! The homey redhead you just had to chase down and marry! That's who! Does she know about your harems? Of course she doesn't. She's too precious to know what you really are!"

He moved so quickly she didn't see him coming. He gripped her face between his thumb and index and snarled, "What do you think gives you the right to question my personal life? You knew what our deal was before you accepted. My personal life is none of your damn business."

Dawn's clear blue eyes stared bold and audaciously back into his inhuman ones. "Yeah, I know what the deal is. But your end of the bargain isn't being held up. If you're married, which you are, your pixie of a wife owns this house, too. She can and will throw every single one of us out. I know women, for I'm a woman. So yes, your personal life is my business. You're who broke the contract not me. Your actions have jeopardized everything, everyone, and you don't care."

He smiles nastily and asked. "What's the problem? Have you tripped up and fell in love with me? Didn't those before you warn you not to fall in love with me? Mmm? Didn't they tell you I don't give a shit about anyone's feelings but my own? You knew I would never love you in return so why torment yourself?" Dawn tried to shove him off but knew he'd tear her face off before he let go.

"Azazael, I'm not giving up the power of being Mrs. Cargill. You can do what you want. But I'm not budging. I bet you didn't bang her brains out like a stallion in heat?!"

Truthfully, he doesn't remember what he did. He only partial remembers the emotions of it but nothing else and that was quickly fading. He remember there was a sweetness and kindness that he missed and hadn't let his guard down to savor in many centuries.

"Dawn, I'm kind and patient but you've never had the power of being Mrs. Ashton Cargill. Keep talking and my wife won't have to thrown you out. I will."

"My severance pay is fifty million," she said, poking her chin stubbornly in the air.

"It's twenty four million. I know how long you been here getting on my damn nerves," he corrected, going to a nearby desk to pull out a checkcard book and punch in her pay. She strode angrily across the room and slapped it out his hand. Put her hand in his pants waistband and yanked him to her. She sees what his problem is. Why he's so testy. That homey ass woman can't satisfy a man like him. The little stupid girl named Ana doesn't know what she got herself into. This isn't a mortal man. She honestly believes she can handle him. She can do the work of 56 women. Poor gullible child. He'll have killed her in a week. Dawn wonders why is he wet but doesn't ask. She isn't sure she wants to know. She helps him out the wet clothing and sits him down in a chair. While relaxing in a huge leather chair she knee in front of him, spread his legs and begun kissing his inner high. His penis is already erect so she need not work on that. She brushed her tongue several times across the tip then pulled it hard into her mouth. She knows he rarely show emotions when being pleasured but she knows he's enjoying it. He laid his head back against the cool leather of the chair to let her do what he hired her to do. Yes, she's right. He doesn't remember his wife pleasuring his him this way. Not that he would ask her. He listen to the sucking sound of her mouth against his immortal flesh, the sweet smell of her juices mixing with his own exotic cologne scent, the feel of those hot soft lips caressing the sensitive flesh as they slid over the head of his cock, and the strong grip of her warm hand, all fought for his sole undivided attention but his mind was a million miles away. He had to find this woman again.

She doesn't mind sucking him, he isn't nasty with this like most men wanting to squirt off in your mouth and face like you ain't shit. She knows why he doesn't release without a condom; it's so none of them can collect his semen and take it to the fertility clinic. He doesn't want children by any of them and doesn't trust them to always use birth control. But with that red-haired bitch she can safely bet he didn't use a condom with her.

"Dawn, what's the woman's name you believe I've married?" he absently asked. She smiles around his cock but doesn't stop licking the side of his penis which she has found different from any other man she've known. He pushed her away. "How in the hell am I supposed to know who you married?" She said grumpily, standing erect over him.

Realizing he's suffering another temp memory lapse she sits in his lap; for years he could only remember bits and pieces of his past and it seems to be getting worse and worse. She kisses the side of his face and feels something like a small electrical shock. Determined not to be deferred by whatever hex that little witch put on him she encouraged, "Take that ring off and let's forget this whole tumultuous marriage business. If she let you left her then that means she doesn't want you or wants to come here. Let's put our happy home back together. You don't need her and her flickery when you've all you need here."

"I remember she said she loved me. That's much I do remember." He pondered. She sighs, rolls her eyes angrily, lecturing him saying, with his magnitude of wealth any woman will say that but that doesn't make it true and he's beyond old enough to know that.

"I love you." Dawn cooed. "Don't you believe me?"

"Hell, nah. The only thing you love is wealth."

"Why don't you believe me?" Dawn teased kissing the side of his neck and was

225

steadily growing frustrated with whatever this woman did to him.

"Because you're bullshitting."

"See, that's my point. I don't care what you think you felt on your wedding day or night, the rendezvous may had been minding blowing but the question is? Where's she? If she loved you, she'd be here." She said, gussying her way into his psyche.

Believing him to have calmed down she attempted to remove the ring. He balled his fist up so violently she wasn't sure if he wasn't going to hit her. Despite what's said about him, he rarely ever hits one of them. That's why so many are drawn to him. He takes well care of you, doesn't beat you, and set you up for life when you leave or your contract expires. How many so-called respectable wives can boast they get all that?

He teleports out the chair leaving her to hit the chair's seat. She pounds the heavily cushioned armrests with her fists. What more proof does his antediluvian dumb ass need that this coy little hussy married him for the money? She called her good frenemy Carol Caldwell. The moment the international star answered, Dawn lamented. "Would you believe his dumb ass has up and married that homey, skinny hussy?!"

"Who?!" Carol asked dreadfully. Praying it isn't true...

"Ashton Cargill!" Dawn shouted and half sobbed. "He done fucked everything up."

"Calm down, Dawn." Carol pleaded as the muscles in her stomach clenched like a rebellious fist. Her job was to primp the women to keep him from marrying the woman. Marrying her means death to their agenda.

"I'm sure there's a logical explanation for whatever you believe he has done."

"Sure it is!" Dawn retorted. "The bitch is going to show up one day and kick everybody out on their asses. We don't have the power to legally fight for our pay against the Cargill empire. You know she isn't going to let him pay us another red cent."

226

Carol swallowed her anger , thinking very hard, *"This is so typical of air headed bimbos. Think of nobody but themselves. What will Nikola do to me when he finds out I failed to keep his wayward wife from marrying Azazael? If I had nuts he would string me up by them!"*

"DAWN!" Caroline shouted. "Shut up and think! Think where he might be. You know him better than anyone else? Go to him and talk some sense into him. Get him to annul that silly marriage. He's merely infatuated with her," Caroline desperately offered. The desperation sparked a twinge of jealousy in Dawn. She was now curious as to why Ashton's business was so important to this woman.

Everyone ducked for cover as sizzling hot, green dirty lighting ricocheted throughout the castle down into the village below setting the thatch roof cottages ablaze. The commotion below was further pissing him off as well. He materialized a dragon in the sky to make the people run into the houses not aflame. So they'd shut up and let him think. He sit down hard on his throne, the lighting from his finger tips left them smoking unharmed like a fired gun.

"I told Lucifer this game playing crap of breaking her will wasn't going to work with her. She's my oppose and my equal. That's how I know how she thinks! Our wills are tougher than steel. But he thought he could play with her like he does most saints. We needed to go after her hard and furious because heaven is helping her. That's the only way to capture those like me. But knowing Azazael he has knocked her up by now."

Through the hellish grapevine news travels fast. A huge black billow of smoke appeared in front of Nikola. Lucifer glared down at a stoic looking Nikola. Satan hates these damn wizards who are born this way. They're much harder to control than those whom he bestows power upon. Nikola is as stubborn as Ana. They are like good and evil twins. If he didn't need this arrogant bastard he'd kill him and his whole dysfunctional shebang.

"Knowing myself, I duly told you you were gravely underestimating her strength."

Nikola said without looking up.

"That's the beauty of this." Lucifer grinned shoving Nikola out of his seat and taking it as his own as everyone bowed their foreheads to the floor before him.

"Fidget not. This is even better. She still bears my mark so I can find her. Just think of it--When Azazael impregnates her I will drive out the soul of their child and inhabit the fetus for myself. Imagine how strong I'll be with Azazael as my father." Lucifer's clear angelic eyes said signaling to Nikola to come closer. Nikola felt like shaking his head no.

"I don't need you anymore and you know what happens to those I no longer need." Nikola didn't flinch. He knew Lucifer still needed him for the human side of the operations of hell.

Lucifer watched Nikola beat and kick the Caroline Caldwell for failing her mission. He yawned, the beating started to bore him, watching the woman twitch and scream from the blasts of fire from Nikola's fingers. But that was the punishment for failure. Everyone knew that. He halted Nikola for he needed her beautiful. She was useless to him disfigured. Naked and bleeding she tried to crawl to her dress that Nikola made her cast aside but a sneering demon pulled it out of reach.

Lucifer didn't tell Nikola he knew he couldn't find her again if she hit the open road for she no longer bore his mark. Those pesky archeiaes had erased it but Nikola didn't need to know how often heaven derailed his plans. He couldn't afford to appear incompetent in front of his subjects. Without further ado or instructions he disappeared in a fiery blaze causing every one in the dim room but Nikola to shield their eyes.

After Lucifer disappeared with much flair, Vonderbilt beckoned his servants to clean the sulfurous resumes from his throne. They quickly did so. He reclaimed his throne. He didn't care who Ana BuFaye slept with. He was peeved off she embarrassed him before the whole witchery world by marrying Cargill, openly displaying her disloyalty to him by marrying another man. No one embarrasses him without stern and harsh retributions. Orman learned that the hard way and so will she.

He teleports to the backyard of the house across the streets from Eugenia Harris and make himself comfortable in the overgrown Chinaberry tree. He knows she doesn't work so he will probably have a long wait before sees her exit the house. Sure, she doesn't have to work now or ever leave the damn house with access to Cargill's trillions.

He looked afar up the streets; he sees many dark shadows stirring around in the park at the end of the street. They are moving around like thick cream in black coffee. They lack faces and mouths. They usually appears when a tragedy is about to strike. He wonders which of their homes are about to experience a catastrophic event? Their presence send a brilliant cognitive content through his mind. Why not create the event? Ana had the audacity to embarrass him. Lucifer's idea is crocked filled of shit so why is he listening to him. He isn't immortal. He doesn't have years to play cat and mousee games with her. She has capriciously chosen which side she's giving her gifts and loyalty to; her body and gifts to Azazel and her soul to heaven and as Lucifer said when someone is no longer useful to you the only recourse left is to eliminate them. This is a job for Bjors; he drove her here so let him drive her out. His evil mind smiled at the diabolical idea of pliers pulling her teeth and ravishing her cloying screams and sobs with every extraction. Let's see how beautiful she'll be to Azazel. Oh, well he'll probably then fill her mouth with gold ones or whatever kind she desire. But at least he'll get the pleasure of pulling them. His eyes pops open when it dawns on him Azazel would do the same to him.

Chapter 4
The Kidnapping of Little Queen Bea

While sitting on the large enclosed plexiglass front porch enjoying Mother Harris delicious iced tea I spread my fingers before my face and stared at the beautiful diamond, ruby and sapphire ring wondering where did it come from? Who gave it to me and why? Whomever gave me this must like me an awful lot! I'm not accustomed to people actually liking me. If any friendship is shown it's usually to gather information or get close enough to hurt me.

Somehow I sensed there was some time missing from my life. Being a Timewalker you keenly notice such things. Everyone say today is Thursday but we arrived here over a week ago and I don't remember the past Tuesday and yesterday. Nor what I did. Mom say I was here all day but I don't think so. But she nor Mother Harris can explain where the very expensive clothing, shoes or handbag came from? I'm kind of used to lost time for I learned I had the gift to see the past when I was eight, learned I had the ability to visit it when I was eighteen and often did so to escape the realities of the present day. Especially during the year Thad was waiting for his trial. I often time traveled. No two realms and dimensions were the same. Some were alive and beautiful while others were dead, barren and ugly. They looked like someone had scorched the entire realm let alone the worlds within. I saw everything from the birth of supernovas to the birth of my world. NO, I haven't heard God speaking yet...at least I don't think so. I try to be careful as to where I go for I'm not the only passenger on the highway of time. It's as crowded as downtown New York City. Some I met were good and others evil. But sometimes I go so far back in time that the sense of time of is lost. It's almost like a loop of time. I know then I'm into the 'Indefinite' but still there are giant angels guarding these doorways.

In the immeasurable Indefinite there's a blue crystal like door, the first time I saw it I was drawn to it. Rarely am I drawn to a door. I travel with my feelers out to know not to open certain doors. If it feels like something messed up behind that door then don't open it. But behind this blue door I never clearly remembered what happened while there. I always left when the angel called me saying it's time to go home. But once back in Boston I felt I had lived many, many years in another world when I had only been gone a the few hours while I was asleep. Once I felt very hurt and couldn't remember what I was hurt about but I ceased visiting that world. Someone there had broken my heart and the last thing I needed was another heart break. Thad had already wrecked it. But then I found another door similar and was happy for a while but it didn't last.

Mother Harris wasn't pleased at all when I told her these things. "You've no idea what might follow you back home. It's like walking a lone, dark street at night and being surprised a mugger or rapist follow you home! I mean for you to desist and cease that as of this day!", she ordered. "I know it's an escapism from reality but those worlds are a reality too. Ones you know nothing about."

I tried to tell her I'm not alone. There's always someone unseen with me. I can hear and feel them. But rarely do we converse. But she wouldn't hear of it. I tried to explain to her how majestic it was to watch the angels change the guard of time. How if you didn't slip back through at the change of the guard you had to wait until the next earth hour. And no one wanted to be present when Michael stood guard.

"So I guess the next thing you will tell me is you've a spirit guide." Mother Harris asked rather surlily. Ana didn't know the tone of voice was the woman biting back the urge to ask Ana to take her with her. Back to 2059. The last time she truly happy.

"No, no, no, nothing like the New Age stuff. This I believe is an angel who walks me to the present and leaves. He answers a few questions if I'm so astonished with what I see. Did you know there were millions of universes like ours'? There are many of other worlds like ours', these people looks like us? I mean some have unearth-like hair and skin coloring but nonetheless they are people like us?"

"Of course they look like us when all the immortals came from the same source as us. God. Adam and Eve were the youngest brother and sister of all the other immortals. All the so called ancient gods and deities who looked human were Adam and Eve's older brothers and sisters and some their nieces and nephews. But I don't think they viewed family the same as we do. That's why you shouldn't be over there. They didn't like Adam and Eve so they ain't gonna like you. Lucifer is the most notorious enemy we have but not the only enemy we have. Personally, I think it was with Adam and his siblings as it was with Joseph and his. They all got tired of Father bragging on him and decided to show God he wasn't all that."

"Is Lucifer a son of God?"

"Hell nah! Thanks be to God he isn't. Imagine if he was able to reproduce as offspring of God can. Just imagine how many half Luciferian and half human people would running around. Despite what the popular satanic media preach he isn't a son of

God. He was once from the highest rank of angels, one whom God loved like a son," Mother Harris explained.

"What about people who say they're sons and daughters of Lucifer?"

"If they're truly descendants of anything from hell they're descendants of one of Lilith's children. Most likely Mammon. But they don't know the difference and can't nobody tell them. The only thing Lucifer can create with Lilith are demons. But stop roaming around the spirit world. You don't know what's out there."

I promised her I wouldn't do it again but I'm sure after raising three children and several grandchildren and foster children she knew I was lying. Because she promised me as an ass-cutting if she caught me doing it again and I'm learning from all those she reared she doesn't make idle threats.

⁂

Dawn Shepherd watched the two figures sitting on the porch from afar through high-powered binoculars from the comfort of the short luxury limo. Caroline Caldwell warned her this woman was dangerous. She had better hire a hit man to kill her rather than take matters in her own hand.

"I paid you. What are you waiting for?" Dawn grunted. She wanted to watch her anarchic rival die. To be sure she was dead. The man raised the high powered rifle and positioned it in the narrow slot of the open window, trained the gun on his target's head, and pulled the trigger. Nothing happened. The woman didn't slump forward or jerk backward. Her head was still moving in a very lively manner.

"I thought you were supposed to be the best there is?" Dawn hissed looking through the binoculars, gravely disappointed Ana was still alive and running her mouth.

"Ms., do not insult my expertise. I kill with the first shot. I did not miss her. That glass is made of something that even the best bullets in the world can not penetrate. What? I do not know. Pay me. If you tell Ashton Cargill about me, I've an unknown partners," the hitman threatened.

"Pay you? You haven't done a damn thing! I could've taken a shot at her and missed." Dawn's blue eye flashed fire like a blue diamond. How dare this lowly killer for hire threaten her? She's the main mistress of the richest and most powerful man in the world. "Yeah, and if you harm me all of your associates will be dead before their next morning piss. But listen here, Neanderthal in a suit. That's the bitch standing between me and Ashton Cargill's purse string. That's how I'm paying your dumb ass. Do you get the gist? Fuck your one-shot reputation! Now shoot the bitch again."

The hitman angrily grunts and reposition his gun on his shoulder, using a different, more powerful one. Designed to penetrate five feet of steel. It would kill the elderly woman too but so be it. It would take the woman's head completely off, saw it off the upper shoulders. He hated to make a mess of killing women. Especially beautiful ones like this one. This time when he pulled the trigger they heard a loud explosion.

"What was that?" ,he calmly asked himself. This ammunition made no sound. Beholding this woman beside him wasn't worth going to prison over he takes the long black gun case and exit the side of the limo next to the park's border hedges. This job didn't feel right with him from the beginning. He doesn't ever remember having bad dreams prior a kill. He dreamt this woman on the porch came for him and massacred his entire family with Cargill's help and made him watch.

Ana and Mother Harris quickly retreated indoors at the second ping and looked out toward the streets from the door frame to see who was shooting at them. They saw no one. They had no idea the assassin was a mile away. Something very powerful hit the glass and rocked the house. While standing next to Mother Harris Ana says, "It's time to hit the road again. I know who that was."

Mother Harris sternly pressed her lips together and asked. "Are you gonna to run everytime they fire a shot at you? You are a Nazarene Warrior saint. We don't run. We fight back."

"Yeah, that's kinda the idea. If I don't they'll kill you, too. I couldn't live with myself if

233

you got killed because of me." Ana was thinking of how they hurt and maim all who dared help her.

"Did you know a warrior saint's motto is "Never call retreat!"" Mother Harris said.

"Might be. But it isn't mine." Ana replied moving out the doorway and to the east window and peering through the heavy drapers, telling her mom standing in the diningroom with Bea to start packing. We're leaving. Mother Harris froze them both. So they had to listen.

"Listen up girls. I can't teach you to defend yourselves if you gonna run everytime they say "Boo!" I've taken care of myself and hundreds of others for over sixty years. This ain't the first time they shot at me and I doubt it will be the last. But to be a warrior you've to learn how to fight back or you'll be dead in the next five years or so. You can't run forever. Learn to fight back for little Bea's sake if not your own. If they kill y'all, she's next. They don't cease. They pursuit you to the grave and then kill everyone who's alive to tell what happened to ya. Now, this is how it's gonna be. You, Ana, are going to learn what you were sent to me to learn if I have to hogtie ya. Fannie, you're gonna learn how to direct the power of prayer better. Both of ya'll are some of the spiritually strongest people I ever met but you ain't had nobody to teach you how to use what you got. That's what Mother aim to do."

Several cars came to a screeching halt outside at the curb and on the driveway as Ana and Fannie were let loose from their frozen state. Having never been frozen before Mother Harris took them outside in the parching hot sun to warm up. It was Mother Harris' brood. Recognizing that shiver Horatio Harris Jr. chuckled and said, "Mom don't freeze you unless she loves you."

"I told your mother we were leaving because they tried to bomb the house because of me." I explained.

Horatio and his sisters dismissed my claim. "Mom got more weapons in that room than the military had at Cape Cod," her oldest daughter laughed. I knew she was referring to the famous World War III battle.

"They've been shooting at us for years. But momma sometimes get so hot behind them, so bad and mean, sometimes she scare the hell outta us. If you come after her you better finish the job for she doesn't rest until she gets you."

"I hate them!" four year old Bea shouted, snuggling up to her mother and burying her face. Ana and Fannie affectionately ran their hands over her head to calm her down.

"Amen!", one of Mother Harris' great granddaughters seconded Bea's motion. "We all hate them blankety-blanks!"

The Harris children all knew how the little girl felt. She had their utmost sympathy. They all knew all too well how it felt to the child or grandchild of a warrior saint. Their mother desperately tried to teach all of them never to hate anyone but it was impossible to love people who are repeatedly trying to kill the one person who meant the world to you. Maybe Jesus could do it. He was God in Three Persons, but they weren't Jesus. Mother Harris glanced around the crowd gathered out back, sending everyone a strict look. (No one knew she had just knocked a warlock out the Chinaberry tree across the alley behind the house.) Everyone knew it meant shut up with the hate talk. It will take you to hell. She rose slowly from the many times repainted iron chair not from old age but from the seriousness of what she was about to do. Everyone fell silent and watched her. She raised her still muscular arms despite her age, heavenward and cried out in a loud clear voice. "Thus says the Lord God in Ezekiel 25:17-And I will execute great vengeance upon them with furious rebukes; and they shall know that I am the LORD, when I shall lay my vengeance upon them."

Suddenly a loud clap of thunder pierced the stratospheric air above, so loud it resonated and vibrated through the body cavities, then a second not quite as loud clap of thunder followed by a white-hot bolt of lighting flashing across a clear blue sky made Fannie, Ana and Bea jumped but Mother Harris' children were unfazed. They were used to it. They all saw a lighting bolt come out of the clear sky without a thundercloud in sight; flash southeast ward. The heated bolt plunged so hard into the ground behind the thick tall trees of the public park frequented by druggies and criminal elements that it shook the entire block. Then Mother Harris sat back down, looked calmly around at everyone and said, "According to playwriter William Congreve, I think he lived in the 1700's. I'm not sure. But anyway he wrote, "'Heaven has no rage like love to hatred turned, Nor hell a fury like a woman scorned!' And it doesn't do well to scorn me."

Mother Harris' family burst out laughing. Ana and Fannie looked perplexity at each other. They didn't catch the joke. They saw nothing funny about terrible swift lighting flashing across the sky.

Dawn's psyche was deeply rattled seeing such a huge lighting bolt come so close she could smell the burnt air and sizzled hair on her head, the leather of the limo was fried. She was frozen stiff with fright. The chauffeur quickly beckoned her to get out the hover limo, they ran for the nearest house. But the assassin she hired wasn't so lucky. He and his car was struck and burned to a crisp in the middle of Memorial Drive as he reached over to turn on music and forget the failure of the day.

Unbeknownst to her an unexpected and unobserved person smiles as he watches the event unfold. Sewell didn't think Dawn was evil enough to carry out a hit against the woman his boss was in love with but he sees he sorely underestimated her. Being sick of having his mind swiped of memories pertaining his boss and this woman he crossed himself. He may be a killer but he knows the work of God when he sees it.

"Oh well, she showed you who has the biggest guns," he chuckled, turn his ignition and rose into the air.

❧

The following morning Mother Harris took her three guests for a ride in the agrestic country side. Her old car arduously tried to keep up with the fast moving traffic whipping up and down I-85 but she didn't let the speed bother her. She stayed her steady pace until they reached the provincial area surrounding the glamourized city. Mom sat upfront beside Mother Harris as Mother Harris chatted about her own hometown being further south toward Macon. They passed farms and other bucolic scenes as trees whizzed by. The annual seasonal change was in its early stage, making the landscape a patchwork of colors. It made Fannie a little homesick for Brunswick which she knew she could never return to. Her top priority was keeping her children and grandchildren alive and Brunswick offered no shelter.

Ana told Mother Harris she didn't want to meet an egregious religious person because her experience with them had been rather spotty. Mother wanted to show her all weren't like that. Then she wanted to know if she could go Elijah on people what did she need to take her to this man for? She could tell her all she needed to know. But no one tells Mother Harris what you don't want to do; she's everyone's mother and does not care what you don't want to do. You shut up and do it and be happy about it.

After about a two hour drive outside of Marietta they turn offed onto a short well-used dirt road leading to a box Georgia red ranch-style house surrounded by a just mowed dead lawn. A few happy, yappy dogs started barking (Ana felt a tinge of guilt for having to send Bea's dog to her oldest brother) as Mother's old car pulled up. A man and woman a little younger than Fannie come out on the front scoop and wave. The couple came down the cement steps, met mother, and hugged her. The dark man was huge and impressive. The heat caused his smooth dark skin to gleam like wet black marble. The man had a friendly face and his much shorter wife had a pleasant smile.

"Ana, Fannie and Bea, this is Rev. Blackwell and his wife, Savannah," Mother said, making the introductions. The powerful man shook all three of their hands as he lowered the decibels of his powerful voice. The Reverend leaned down to Bea's level and shook her little hand as well. Telling her what a pretty little girl she is. His paper sack brown wife hugged them instead of shaking their hands and cordially invited them inside out of the Autumn heat. Ana felt guilty for having a twinge of jealousy; for this was what she had once wanted so much for her own family. Something like this was how she romantically pictured Thad and her twenty years in the future. But now, that will never be the case.

"I heard the roar yesterday and wondered who had upset you."

Mother gave a short version of what happened for she quickly wanted to get down to the real reason she brought this young mother out here. She wanted to show Ana all minsters aren't self-righteous, judgmental assholes. To learn how to distinguish those called by God from those called by man. Their kind often have to work alongside them and Ana needed to know how to find the real ones. A real one, a true man or woman called by God, knows what their kind does and why they do it and accepts the fact that each person has a different job in the body of Christ without the petty jealousy that so often is the real reason their kind are so violently reprimanded by the established tradition of the church.

Enroute back home they were suddenly surrounded by a swarm of troopers and local police. Mother politely pulled over, but waved her hand in an odd fashion resembling an "OK" with the index and thumb connected. Three cops approached on her side and two more on Fannie's. Ana and Bea were invisible to them. All they saw was an empty backseat.

"Ma'am, you're driving far below the speed limit. If you want to drive this slow you need to go airborne," the woman in blue said, looking into the back seat as she wrote Mother a ticket. "We saw you when you passed but thought enroute back home you'd realize what a hazard you're to the public."

"I know you saw me when I passed. I wasn't trying to hide," Mother Harris quipped, freezing the whole squad of them and pulling away from the grassy roadside back onto the highway. The cars whipping around her started to move in slow motion. Every car near them was like moving in a thick invisible syrup until they passed. The three passengers watched in amazement as Mother Harris drove on, chatting about one thing or another. Bea stuck her tongue out as she poked her thumbs in each ear and wagged her hands at the vehicles they passed as the drivers and passengers watched them passe. None realized the others weren't moving in slow motion, it was they who was moving at a supersonic speed.

"I did it because I'm not paying for another ticket. Over the sixty years I've been here I've spent at least 250 grand on tickets and fines. They'll bankrupt you with them high-assed tickets. I've been arrested over six times and ended up having to pay to stay out of prison. Once, I did a six month stint in jail, but Horatio held the fort down for me. A wizard before your time named Orman had me locked up since he couldn't beat me in the spiritual realm." Mother Harris laughed and glanced in the rearview mirror at Ana

238

who was staring out the window as excited as Bea but keeping it in check. "So yes, I froze their asses," Mother Harris explained to her awed passengers as she pulled back into her narrow driveway and proceeded into the backyard and parked beside Trusty. The spiritual ambiance felt different so she knew hell was awaiting them inside or coming.

Ana got the call while at work at a major P.R. firm downtown Atlanta. Helena had gotten Bea accepted in a prestigious private pre-school which cost a small fortunate which she agreed to pay for. She felt her niece was nearing five so it was time Bea received a formal education since Ana was determined to settle down in this hellhole of a place. But Ana knew Helena was like that. Always out to impress.

Helena's visit to mom at Mother Harris' wasn't going too well. Mother's house didn't meet her good housekeeping seal of approval. She said the house and everything in it was old and passe. She said it was cold, spooky and drafty. Which it wasn't. While in truth, it was sturdier than most modern houses. Mother Harris fostered a warm, cozy, loving environment; there was nothing spooky about the ambiance of Mother's house.

I'd lived in many spooky places in the past four years so I knew spooky like Helena would never guess. Sure, the neighborhood was centuries old. But I knew my sister; if Helena was in heaven she'd find a way to tell God what He did wrong with creation. Helena's constant belittling caused her and Mother Harris to developed a mutual dislike for each other. In the middle of one of her berating-Ana rants Mother Harris spoke sharply saying. "I can see you're accustomed to bullying your little sister. But I don't allow bullying in my house. Tragedy can strike anyone at anytime so be thankful for all your blessings. Even having a little sister is a blessing you aren't wise enough to see."

This set Helena's teeth on the edge; she inauspiciously asked "Pardon me?! Mrs. Whatever-your-name-may be...is that a threat or a command?" Helena walked closer, approaching the woman old enough to be their grandmother.

Mother Harris didn't back down; instead she rose to her full height which had to be at least 6 feet and said, "Little girl, take it however you want, you can take it with a cup of tea and an aspirin for all I care. No, save the tea and aspirin for me. You're giving me a pain in the ass." Mother replied looking her straight in the eyes.

Helena squinted her eyes menacingly and spoke as if speaking to an imbecile "I'm a decorate detective of NYPD. I made detective faster than anyone in the history of the NYCP history. It's a crime to threaten an officer of the law."

"The only law I respect and obey is God's Law. Man can't keep his own business straight so how in the devil he can create a law telling me how to conduct my business? Them people you hollering about don't know their ass from a hole in the ground. But yet they supposed to be able to tell me how I should run things. You ain't Jesus Christ nor the Holy Mother of God, you're just a first class little bitchy girl who likes to bully people." Mother shot back. "You come up here in my house complaining about everything you see. If I ain't doing good enough for your family, then you do better. But no, you can't cause they might embarrass you before your siddity ass friends!"

This was one of the few times I've ever seen Helena speechless. Helena gasped and turned to me and said "Ana, are you going to just sit there and let her talk to me so disrespectfully?"

I stifled a giggle before letting out a howling laugh. Helena screwed up her face and marched through the big rumbling house calling mom as she did when we were kids and I had bested her in something like wrestling, tree climbing or racing with my tomboyish ways. Although, she was eight years older I won at a lot of things.

Mom, wearing her Mona Lisa smile, entered the old-fashioned living room decorated with heavy dark wine velvety coverings and curtains that Mother keep in immaculate condition with Bea holding her hand. I knew that smile meant she had heard the argument.

"Honey, I'm in here." She called to her oldest daughter in another part of the house seeking her. She knew better than most how much of a pain Helena could be if she set her mind to it. Helena reappeared, her light brown honey toned face flustered with rage.

240

Helena BuFaye Wales was an exceptionally beautiful woman and had a figure most only dream of but only if her attitude was beautiful as she was.

Mother Harris and I suppressed our laughter as Helena stood looking at us with her hands on her shapely hips. Glaring at us as a mother might glower at naughty children.

She mentally positioned her mind to ignore the two sillies as she dubbed them; she tells her mom, "I was telling Ana about Buckhead Academy's pre-school program. Friends of mine pulled strings to get Bea in and not on the waiting list" She showed Fannie the letter of approval. "These two don't feel it's safe for Bea to be around other children. Then your landlady called me a bitch for wanting the best for my niece. Everyone agrees with me, Bea needs to start formal education. Studies have proven the earlier, the better. Bea is already four nearly five. She's a year behind most children her age."

"Who's everyone?" I asked curiously. "I've no problem with Bea attending school. But it just isn't safe. I know without doubt someone is out to harm me and they'd hurt her just to hurt me. Bea is only four but can read at a fourth grade level, I teach her a lot while we travel."

Helena rolled her eyes, "Here we go again. With you and your imaginary stalkers. Everyone in the world and their mother is after you. If anything happens to you it will be left to me and your two brothers to raise Bea. Plus, mom is too old to be raising your child. That's your job."

"Hmmm, is that right?" Fannie asked with her eyebrows raised in the perfect imitation of Helena's.

"Of course that's right, you're 54 years old!" Helena cried.

"I know how old I'm and now so does half of Atlanta." Fannie snapped.

To deescalate the building tension that was about to explode, Mother Harris interrupted Helena saying "Your sister didn't say no, she wouldn't let Bea go. You were trying to bully your sister into letting her go. I told you to stop badgering your sister. She was trying to explain why it wasn't safe for Bea to be away from home."

"I heard her the first time." Helena retorted. "I just wasn't in the mood to listen to her paranoid, crazy person rambling about strangers following her, spooks, ghouls, and only who knows what else is in that head of hers. I've been listening to her craziness since the day she could talk. Nothing is going to eat Bea. I'm not going to stand by and let her ruin this child's life based upon unsound, unfounded fears that exist only in her mind."

"Those things are real," Mother Harris said, pointing a stern finger at Helena.

"Oh Lord, you believe that craziness too?!"

"And you'll too before you leave this world." Mother Harris promised..

"One thing you forgot Helena, Bea is my child. Not yours." I reminded my overly zestfull sister.

"If you continue to neglect her proper care and education I'll be forced to report you." Helena threatened. "You aren't qualified to teach elementary education. What criteria do you have to properly educate Bea? Bea needs to learn to socialize with other children. Or she'll grow up with an antisocial personality disorder. Doing weird things like hurting animals, setting fires, unable to carry on a normal conversation with people and then moving on to hurting people; from there moving on to killing people, destroying property. Someone has to take the reins from you to make sure she grows up healthy and well-adjusted."

"Yeah, you do that." I said narrowing my eyes as I stood up to my sister who was bigger and taller.

"Both of you sit down and shut up before I take a switch to your behinds." Mom warned staring sternly from one child to the other. We both claimed a seat for we both knew she wasn't kidding.

"Ana, if it's ok with you, we can go take a look at this place and check out their security before Helena makes me kill her."

"Sure, mom" I agreed hoping I didn't live to regret it.

"Come on, mom." Helena's facial expression said she preferred Mother Harris not to come, she wasn't family. But she remained silent as Mother Harris got in my car with me and Bea. Mom rode with Helena.

Bea was tested and passed with flying colors and was accepted but it came with a whopping price of 20 thousand every per quarter. I wanted to know what kind of nursery school charged damn 80 thousand a year? This isn't college. Helena signs the promissory note for the tuition. Afterward the four women and child dine at an exclusive restaurant in Buckhead called Cargill's and everyone behaves civilly for Bea's sake. But another bombardment of dagger stares from my sister are fired when I asked the maître d' what is Langue de boeuf. He explains it's cow tongue saying. "The trick to cooking the tongue is to slice it into nice thin slices and it will really melt in your mouth, I promise you won't notice it is cow tongue."

"Sorry, but we aren't eating that." Mom said, asking the man does they have regular food? Helena is now roiling furious with all four of us vowing to never take us anywhere nice again. We had thin sliced steak smothered with brown onion gravy with a side order of succulent fries while she ate cow tongue.

Ana takes Bea in on her first day. Bea's a little nervous having never been away from her mother. But seeing the other 3 and 4 year olds she soon lets go of Ana's hand and joins them. Seeing how well Bea is adapting, Ana heads to work. At approximately, 11:00 A.M. Bea was kidnapped. The classroom security camera capture a man in all black appearing out of the thin air; he baffles everyone, teachers and students alike. Bea attempts to run as he trained his eyes on her singling her out from among the other children. He takes a few long-legged steps, scoops her up, and disappears all in one single swoop. The children are crying and screaming, one of the aides fainted. Bedlam reigns for several seconds before the teacher frantically calls APD and the kidnapped child's mother.

Ana's phone on her desk rang. The air cackled in her trained psyche. Somehow she knows this isn't a normal call from the number showing on the ID scene. She answers. She can barely understand the unintelligible words of her daughter's sobbing teacher. She hears screaming, terrified children in the background. Her heart sinks painfully to her lower guts; she knows her worst fear have come true. She hears police radios cackling mingling with the children voices. She doesn't give the teacher a chance to finish. She already knows something horrible has happened to her baby. She grabbed her keys and handbag and rushed home, picking up her mom and Mother Harris who were both in the backyard hanging freshly washed laundry on an old-fashioned outdoor clothesline. She needs them for what she is about to face. She drives her old style, which means driving like hell, hitting up 90-100 MHP, expertly maneuvering through the crowded streets as she has done so many times escaping pursuers and takes them for the ride of their lives through the streets of Atlanta. She runs every red light she encounters and there seems to be hundreds of them. At one point she resorted to her old trick of riding the sidewalk.

Ten minutes later she came to a screeching halt in Bea's school's parking lot; four patrol cars were right on her ass, chasing her as she ran toward the school's door. She was moving with a speed she didn't know she possessed. Fannie and Mother Harris stood between her and the six cops saying, "She's the mother of the child an alert has just been issued for!"

"That doesn't justify her putting the public at risk," explains the officer writing the ticket.

Seeing that the child's mother had arrived the FBI shows her the footage and asked does she know this man? Fannie and Mother Harris are standing behind Ana trying to console her as she tells the agents she has never seen that man before in her life.

"I know him," Mother Harris volunteered. Everyone turned and looked in astonishment at the tall, silver-haired woman for her new revelation.

"Who or what is he?" the agent questioning Ana asked.

"He isn't American, he's called Vonderbilt but his real name is Donte Nikola Machiavelli. He's the world's Grand Wizard," Mother Harris says with a sober, straight face.

"You mean like Niccolo Machiavelli, the author of "The Prince?" another agent asked.

Mother Harris slowly nods.

"Can you explain how he just appeared and disappeared?"

Mother Harris doesn't like their condescending attitudes. She doesn't insult them because she wants them to at least try and find Bea, but in truth, she knows they can't. She further doubts they can if they aren't willing to listen to a supernatural explanation. "If I told you, you wouldn't believe me," she said wearily.

"Try me! After seeing this I'm about ready to believe just about anything." The head agent said.

Taking a deep breath and exhaling audibly, Eugenia Harris explains how he did it. The two men looked at each other and then at the lone female agent who hands them a note the teacher found on Bea's desk. It read:

> Beautiful Ana,
> I asked you nicely to have dinner
> with me but you declined. Come enjoy a glass of
> fine wine with me and I'll give you back your
> *Precious* little bundle. That's all I ask. No
> tricks. No Mother Harris. Just you.
>
> Signed your husband,
> Nikola.

The female agent suspiciously asked Ana "I thought you said you didn't know him?"

"I don't!" Ana cried.

The agent hands the note to Mother Harris and asks, "Is he crazy? Or dangerous?"

"No, he isn't crazy- he's evil and yes, he's very dangerous. He's perhaps the most intelligent person in the world," she replied, passing the note back.

"Are you Mother Harris?", an African American agent asked. He was curious as to why this child had no finger prints nor school record? And who are these women?

"No."

"Then who is Mother Harris and why is it important to the abductor a person named Mother Harris doesn't accompany Ana?"

"I've no idea." Mother Harris lied with a serious expression. " You would have to find him and ask him those questions."

"Ok, your name is what?"

"Sherre Gibbs." Mother Harris lied.

"Ok, Sherre, you say this man is a warlock? A magician...a magi, or whatever?"

Mother Harris angrily interrupted. "He isn't a magician! What he does is real. He is humanity's leader of the darkside. This is no parlor trick. In this world he's one step above Lucifer."

The second agent interrupted the barbs with an exasperated sigh "Lady, we know he's evil-he just proved that. Only evil people kidnap four year olds. What we need to know

246

is how to find him."

"I don't know how to find him. Most than likely he isn't still on this earth." Mother Harris blatantly lied for she knew had she revealed his location Bea would be dead the moment he learnt Ana had betrayed him and sent others. For they'd have to gather authorities from another country to search the house and who knows where Nikola is by now. If he's anything like his mentor Orman, he'll kill without blinking an eye and she wasn't taking that chance with Bea's life. Ana was their best hope in getting Bea out alive.

The agents begun to feel they were wasting value time in finding this child by talking to this old woman who was talking about witches and wizards, dungeons and dragons.

"If no one knows how to find him, how is he inviting the child's mother to dinner? Mrs. Wyett, your phone has been tapped. In case he calls keep him on line as long as possible if you have to promise to meet this nutjob for a glass of wine," the woman advised.

Ana nodded she understood as her whimpering grew louder. Fannie pulls her head to her shoulder and rock her if she was Bea's age.

The women are escorted back to Ana's car. The local officer who pursued her earlier intercepted their track and handed Ana a fistful of tickets which the FBI snatched from her, balled up, and tossed back to the officer. "A child's life is endangered, we don't have time for this!", the man said before telling Ana when this is over she needs to turn herself in.

"Mrs. Wyett, we're holding off placing you under arrest for the suspicion of several murders but know this. If you run, our aid in finding your daughter ceases." The head agent severely warned her as his cold eyes stare icy into her teary amber ones.

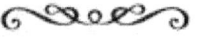

The high lofty latitude of Vonderbilt's castle caused the air to feel crisp and chilled. Bea was cold and frightened but was determined to be brave so she remained quiet. She carefully watched her captor's every move.

"You're cute. Did you know that?" He asked her.

Bea remained mute.

"Beatrice, I assume you're old enough to talk." he said trying to engage her in a conversation. "You can talk to me. I'm your real father. Your mother ran away from me, taking you with her when you were a baby. So you don't know me."

Bea simply stares at him but says nothing.

"You're cute but too skinny to boil down for furniture polish. Lucky for you , you're mine." He chortles when he doesn't get the aghast response expected. He produced a rigged birth certificate and ask Bea to read it. He watches her read his lies.

"You see, Thad isn't your daddy, I am. I had to get rid of him. Sure, he was your mother's husband and all but he was in my way. Your mom, who is now my wife, got upset and ran away. Do you understand what I'm saying?"

Bea narrows her eyes at him for talking to her like a retard. Vonderbilt sees the fire and defiance in them and smiles. "Like Mother like daughter." But thinks, "*What an unfortunate surprise.*"

"Are you cold?", he asked. "You're a brave little one. I like that in a kid, most kids would be snotting and crying by now".

Bea shakes her head.

"Of course you are, you're shivering. Mommy wouldn't like that-no, would she?" he says, ringing a bell and a man in a black and white tux appears. To Bea he looks like a penguin but isn't cute nor good like penguins.

248

"Bring the child, a blanket, warm milk, and cookies."

The man bows stiffly at the waist and turns sharply on his heels.

Bea giggles.

"So Jarvis amuses you? We can have him to do that again." Nikola giggles with Bea. Again Bea says nothing.

An excruciatingly thin woman quietly enters the room, encircles Bea, watching her with sharp birdlike eyes and says," Your Highness, I do not think it was wise to have taken this special child." Nikola's eyes grew dark and stormy like an approaching southern thunderstorm. "Do you enjoy living?" He asked the woman.

"Yes, Your Highness...I enjoy it very much."

"Do you want to keep on living?"

"Yes, Your Highness...I'd like very much to continue to live," the woman shakily replied.

"Then don't interrupt me or question my actions!" He snapped, dismissing her with the flip of his hand. He have a love-hate for the thin woman. He hated her for not dying as his sister did. But yet he loves her for choosing life even if it meant being strapped to that sex chair and fucking the whole castle. That image was branded on his brain, this is how he saw her when Oregon and Orman had him dragged in like an escape convict, as thus he was a captured run-away slave.

"Yes, Your Highness." The woman said, kissing him on the forehead before skittering away as quietly as she arrived.

He noticed Bea paid no mind to the angry outburst. This strange tyke was beginning to exhaust his patience. It hit him like a ton of bricks. Her silence meant she was sending out SOS as to her whereabouts. He grabbed her, shook her hard, and yelled in her face.

"Stop that! Stop that this instant! Before I send only your head back to your mother!"

Bea smiled an evil smile that was not of a child. A smile which reminded him of someone else. She finally speaks saying, "Yeah, motherfucker, you do that and my mother will cut off your head and send it to your mother who was just in here."

He was unmistakeably impressed. How did this tyke know that woman was his mother?

That voice was not that of a four year old child speaking. Someone else said that! Nikola leans away from her. Wondering if his mother was right. What is this thing? It wasn't a child talking to him. It sounded like an archaic male. And cussed like one too.

"How did you know that was my mother?" Nikola asked, since he got his proof this child was highly gifted. Frustrated and angry he wonders what he brought home? Can he control it? He also wonders what kind of entity dwells in that child? What on earth did Ana roll around with to create this devil-child?

Jarvis returns with the milk, cookies, and blanket. An unseen hand pushed the glass across the table, it crashed to the floor, shattering. Shortly enters a woman dressed as Jarvis who cleans up the mess and exits as quietly as possible.

In Nikola's reasoning, he ponders should he lock this thing Ana gave birth to in the horror chamber to teach her what happens when you piss him off. Snatching the blanket from the child's tiny shoulders he barks. "Jarvis, take this thing to the chamber!"

Jarvis reaches for Bea; her tiny hand presses the air knocking him across the room.

Seeing what she did to Jarvis, Nikola says through clenched teeth as his jaw muscles flexed, "Forget it! I'll take her myself." He roughly grabs her thin upper arm but is unable to move her.

He doesn't know Mother Harris is telling Bea to sit heavily like a rock. He realizes too late her hands are glowing.

"Oh shit!" Nikola whispered to Jarvis. "Look at her hands. They're glowing. This is a fucking nephilim!"

To combat Bea's attack he throws a glowball formed from dirty fire, which hers' dissipates in midair. The thin woman tries to sneak up on Bea, armed with an ancient battleaxe. She rises it, prepared to murder the child. An unseen hand stays the axe and that strange voice says, "Don't make me turn you into ashes!"

Bea rise one thin arm toward the mother, and the other toward the son. The axe is ripped from the woman's hand with such a force she is pulled face down into the expensive carpet. The velocity in which she fell knocked her unconscious. Nikola rushed toward the fallen woman and a blue glowball struck the floor between them. In that strange cherubic voice Bea says, "Since I can't go to my mother. You can't go to yours."

"Go to your crazy ass mummy!" Nikola yelled. Bea threw another one, this time so close it scalded his shoes and burnt hole in the carpet. Sensing this child is drawing on an unholy power stronger than himself Nikola raises up the residential legion; they black out all slivers of light. Bea closes her eyes tightly and remembers the prayer her granny taught her. Behind her closed lids she sees a brilliant brightness. She hears shrieking, screeching, the shuffling of feet, the stomps of hooves. In the middle of all the commotion she hears her mother scream. "You bastards get away from my baby!"

Someone scoops her up and takes her upstairs. She hears her mother walking through the house of horror looking for her.

"You be quiet or I'll shoot her." A different man said, roughly clamping his hand over mouth. She had seen him before in many places. She can feel her mom near. She hears her calling the man's name who kidnapped her. Mom is really, really extra peeved off. She has seen her mom kill enough times to know what tone means.

She sees the fortress, a dark gray stone castle in her mind's eye; she sees the open flame oil lamps burning outside illuminating and casting ghastly shadows against the walls. She see humans dressed in medieval clothing milling around as the Papal *Swiss Guard*. Ana felt she had entered Pandemonium itself. The fortress of satan when she walked through the castle. She followed the trail of Bea's kidnapper to this fortress of horror. The guards don't challenge her. They let her pass as if expecting her. This was her first trip through the spiritual realms in a long time. She entered the 8th day without thinking, her precious gift was stolen from her. She knew she had to remain calm if she was going to be successful but her heart had rent in two. Walking the smooth foyer with her blade at her side but not yet aflame, she realized she had seen this place before, she believed so, in a dream. But these days it's getting harder and harder to tell dreams from reality. They're starting to appear as one and the same. She also realized she should've kept Bea in home-schooling and not listened to her know-it-all sister. She knew this would turn into a security debacle. She didn't know the man from the security chip but Mother Harris knew him. Now this man has left a message on Bea's desk asking, no ordering, her to come to him and join him for a glass of wine. She's here and intends to make him choke on that wine bottle.

Her boots heels echoed on the antiquated but expensive marble floor. The place seemed void of life. The black and white chess patterned floor shone with incandescent, evil brilliance. She've seen this pattern before. She remembers the black and white asymmetrical floor design made her dizzy. Where? In a dream? The aura of place attested to being completely void of love. At least a good kind of love. For all its evil auras and arcades the castle was not without physical beauty. In a grandiose sense some might say it was magnificent, Appealing to the palate of one who had a taste for the excessive. It appeared that the present and previous occupants and their staff worshiped every inch of the place, from the nude goddess painted on the highrise ceiling to the scintillating, vibrant sparkle of the chandeliers to the pure gold framed baroque mirrors. Every where there was gold decorative figurines.

To her left stood a great sweeping, black gold-veined marble staircase designed so the occupant could make a grand entrance. And there stood the man she was looking for.

"Hello wife, welcome home," the incredibly handsome man said as he descended the staircase. "Sorry, I had to kidnap our daughter to make you come home. But that's only person you truly care about." The man said, still descending toward her she clutched her blade that still sort of intimidated her even her at times. His slightly olive skin blended with his jet black hair highlighted with natural dark brown. Loose strands of hair perfectly framed his handsome face. Wide apart, greenish brown eyes brought out his natural beauty.

I couldn't help but stare but not for the reasons another observer might assume. His well sculptured eyebrows showed contempt, but friendliness at the same time. He might be the man of someone's dream but he most definitely was not my dream man. He's my nightmare. This is the source of my troubles. I reserved the instinct to attack for I knew most likely Bea was being held at weapon point. The spiritual scan tells me this is the same man who attacked us about a year ago; somehow he created an illusion over his face at the time.

"Where is my daughter?!" I hissed in a low deadly tone.

"Now, now sweetheart there's no need for all the drama and hostility. Beatrice is fine. She's in her room where she belongs. Not trotting all over the earth. And put that thing down before you hurt yourself. It isn't a toy," he said walking pass her to a woman Ana hadn't seen earlier. The woman held two heavy crystal glasses of wine. He takes one and hands the other to Ana who yelled, "Where in the hell is Bea, don't make me ask again!"

The woman's eyes widen when she held up the sword. She have no idea how she knew his name. "Nikola Donte, or Donte Nikola, or whatever the hell your name is! I'm talking to you! Where is Bea?!"

Her calling his name made him turn around slowly with a grin she didn't like. "Sooo, I see you remember my real name. You're one of the few people who know that. So you do remember the wedding. But my name is Donte Nikola, Mrs. Machiavelli." He smiled like a king cobra if a cobra had lips. "You can call me Nikola. You are the only person allowed to call me that. Between the sheets you can call me whatever you like."

He studied her through hooded eyes framed by sooty thick eyelash and mildly chuckled as her eyes flickered in discomfort at he references to the bedroom. "Your angel buddies took you away before we got to the good part, the consummation of our vows." He said making another crass reference to sex to watch her become flustered again. *"Surely, she's unskilled and untrained if she took her eyes off me in embarrassment. That's the last thing you do when facing a gifted enemy. Luckily for her, I do not want to kill her at the moment. I merely want to consecrate our vows."*

"I've no idea what you're talking about and don't care. If you don't hand over my child. I swear I'll kill you," she warned.

A white haired, elderly woman whom this Renaissance man bore a striking resemblance appeared in the broad doorway to her left, walked swiftly to Nikola, and stood between him and Ana while looking hawkishly and hatefully at Ana.

"You kill my son, I'll kill your child." She vowed, staring hard and icily at Ana.

"Calm down, dear Mother," he said soothingly. "We're merely having a spousal spat. We disagree on how Beatrice should be schooled. This is your wayward daughter-in-law," Vonderbilt said. At this, the woman's personality did a 180° turn around.

"Oh, you're little Beatrice's mother!" the thin woman cheerfully cried as if she hadn't heard Ana screaming at her son, threatening him and demanding their release for the last ten minutes...

"I expect many beautiful grandchildren as pretty as the one up stairs. You're so pretty and my son is so handsome you two will make stupefyingly beautiful children. Then I'll have many more grandchildren besides evil ass Bjors." The woman gleefully clapped her hands like a two year old. That's when I noticed the disturbing imbalance in her eyes.

Ana thinks to herself *"And you are so 'stupid-fied' if you think I'm letting your evil-ass son touch me."*

Pushing Nikola closer to Ana, the skeletally thin woman clapped her aged spotted, bony hands covered with parchment paper thin skin together. Her skin is so think the bones are visible. Recalling general lore and knowledge about warlocks, Ana thought it's said warlocks have no weak spots. This one has one. It's his mother.

"Donte, Nicky! Feed your wife she's nothing but skin and bones." His mother chastised him as if is a still a child. Not a grown man old enough to know better than the crimes he commits. "She is too thin to give me many grandbabies!"

"These people are straight-up tripping!" I think as the elderly woman led the way to an even more elaborate dining hall.

Waiting for me to catch up, the thin woman turned aside from her son before we entered a massive dinning room, "Honey, if you do what he says, you'll last. He cares about you." The woman pulled me down to her level and whispered in my ear pretty much telling me I was trapped here. Everyone rose when they walked in, Bea was sitting next to a younger version of Vonderbilt. A man whom the crazy woman said was her son named Gianna. I recognized the other man with scarred face at the table as the man from Telfair St. in Augusta. He's the man who shot my car, Trusty. I saw insanity doesn't run in this family; it gallops through it like a Triple Crown winner.

"Now, that you know we're family as to why I did the things I did." Bjors said with a half sneer and half smile when he saw Ana recognized him. He and the little girl next to Bea but younger than Bea looked alike. She was surprised to see Bea had not been crying. Bea was calmer than her mother. Her eyes held the confidence of *"Mom have gotten us out of tighter spots than this so I'm not worried."*

Vonderbilt appears behind Ana's chair. "You and I are eating alone." He said pulling her and chair from table. Now she saw a hint of fear in Bea's eyes. "Relax, Beatrice. I'm not going to hurt mommy if she be good." He said leading Ana away. They passed through several doors before coming to an ancient unremodeled part of the castle. She could sense an enormous amount of pain and suffering had occurred in this area, the downward spiral took them to a basement. The blue-glow light revealed rows and rows of disemboweled bodies in various stages of decomposing. Some were frozen mummies while others looked like the victims were asleep except their frozen entails were piled

255

upon their midriff and some seemed as they were strangled with their guts. Most appeared to be women and children.

"There're thousands of others further back, they're completely skeletal, they died long before the days of refrigeration." He said as casually if as one was talking about a rose garden. "You're like me. We're cut from the same cloth. I used to be good like you but it brought me nothing but pain. You're my spiritual equal and opposite, but together we can build a better order."

"So this is where I'll end up if I don't do what you say?" I asked as equally casually as he was speaking. He slowly, nonchalantly nodded.

"So this is what all the chasing and harassing me all my life has been about." Again he nods.

"Well, did so many people have to die and so many lives have to be ruined?" I asked.

He shook his head. "People don't have to die just so long as they do as I say. I'm a man of great mercy. Had your family handed you over when Orman came for you, a lot of lives would've been spared, including your father's. But, they like you, were stubborn. Had you came home when Bjors found you, again I would've spared lives. But you kept running. I control the whole world, so you can't outrun me. You're my Grand Witch so I expect you to act like you rule the world beside me and stop embarrassing me. Milton said, "'millions of spiritual creatures walks the earth, both when we wake and when we sleep.'" But that's a vast understatement. Billions upon billions are here. You and I are powerful; together we're unstoppable. You can keep fighting me and end up here or you can rule the world at my side. The choice is yours. Either way. I win."

Looking around at the translucent spirits and hideous demons roaming the horror chamber she sensed this room as well as this entire castle was rigged, hexed or whatever, supposedly against the usage of her gifts and that these souls were trapped here.

"There is one problem-I'm not a witch." I said.

"You'll be when I'm finished with you. I wasn't born a warlock, I made myself into one," he said leading her back up stairs and turned to the right to a grander room than the dinning room. There was a table was set for two. Again more wine. She noticed one of the solemn women standing in attention was holding lingerie. It looked very sheer, she could see the woman's arm through the garment. Her mind was scheming how to get to Bea and at least get her out even if she had to sacrifice herself.

Seeing her looking at the translucent lingerie, "I'm not into the courtship routine." Vonderbilt says, prodding her to eat. How could she eat when she knew Bea was under the guard of those men? One whom she knew one was a killer. But to show cooperation, she nipped at the food in case it was poisoned.

Pointing his fork at her to emphasize his point. "You and mom are the only two people who have pissed me off and lived to see the light of day. I've had numerous opportunities to kill you but I preferred life. So don't *make* me harm you. Like mother said I do care about you."

If this was how he treated people he cared about she hated to see how he treated those he detested. He was eating a dish unfamiliar to her. She wondered if the gift of love worked on one with the same gift who had turned? She knew her gift was their only method of escape. She wonders why Mother Harris doesn't follow her here?

Deeply inhaling and exhaling, letting go of her hatred for this man, she lets love rise to the surface, it was a bitter pill to swallow but a necessary one. She had to save her baby. Bea shall not end up in that horror chamber a frozen piece of meat and nor does she plan to. She sat in his lap and ran her finger along his strong chisel jawline and cooed "Donte, before we consecrate our marriage can I get a real tour of the place, you know since you've spoken and explained things to me I didn't understand before. I thought you wanted to hurt me is why I ran. Now I see that you don't I feel safer around you."

All inherent instincts tell him she's lying. But something stronger than his own power is pulling him and encouraging him to believe her. Lying to him is punishable by death. But she doesn't know that so he will have to teach her about loyalty and lies. She has been mingling with the deplorables too long.

Knowing what she's doing and fighting it, he laid down his fork and looked at her. "Dear, I've the same gift, it doesn't work on me. But you're welcome to see where you'll spend the rest of your life."

Even as he spoke the words he wasn't so sure it wasn't working on him but didn't want her to know it perhaps was. She smiled Fannie's Mona Lisa smile at him.

"I swear, I'm not trying to hoodwink you, I've accepted my lot in life. I'm tired of running" She said kindly in the most seductive purr he ever heard. It went to the core of soul and next to his cock.

He mentally fought back, but emotionally, she was getting under his hard, tough skin. "Even to the point of renouncing Christ as your Lord and Savior?" He asked looking directly at her. She knew he saw her lowered her eyelashes in saying that was more than she could bear. Her heartshaped mouth said "I renounce Him."

Vonderbilt laughed softly, playfully patting her outer thigh. "You little liar, my sweet little liar, you haven't renounced him in your heart, your heart still loves Him above all things. The halo is still there." He chuckled and pointed at her head.

She was startled, she didn't know he could see it. "I can't undo a lifetime worth of training in a few seconds." She mildly argued.

"True that. But I thought considering all you been through you could give Him up easier. Exactly what has He done for you to make you love Him so? But I see I was wrong."

She wished she understood more about making this blade work..she would burn him to a bacon crisp. She loves the Christ but she was definitely not Him, she would've annihilated those who were cruel to Him had she been Him. She reaches out and touch his hand. She doesn't know if you would honestly call it emotions or currency but she felt something flow from herself to him. He quickly snatched his hand back from hers. She quickly figured out she was spiritually stronger than him. Much stronger. His hand sounded like a whip across her face

"Don't ever do that again. Your job isn't to control me. You've me confused with Thad Wynett. I'm not your lover and will never be your lover. Tell me, do you know a man named Cargill?"

"No, I don't."

"Is he Beatrice's father? You can tell the truth. I won't get angry." Nikola coaxed. "No, he isn't." Ana said, not quite sure who Nikola was talking about. He slapped her again and called a liar.

She saw what she was doing *was* working on him but for the worse. His eyes had changed from nonchalant to jealous. "Stay away from him. He's a satyriasis. If he touches you, then you leave me no choice but to eliminate you. Did Caldwell touch you?" Vonderbilt watched her with narrowed eyes, waiting for the answer from her he has waited three years to hear.

"I don't know either of them. What's a satyriasis?" This was the first real smile she had seen all evening. Well, all night for evening had long passed.

"It's someone, a man, who can't get enough sex. A sex addict. James Caldwell lived next door to you for a few months after Thad was sent to prison. I understand you had a few dates with him."

She knew her next answer was critical. Bea's life depended on it. She wondered what this man didn't know about her.

"Oh Teddy, well that's what he said his name was. No, we were just friends, uh, we had dinner once—that's all and the other man I don't believe I've ever met him." Vonderbilt flicks on a large wall screen.

"Did "Teddy" touch the titty?", he asked jealousy, thumping her nipple through the black leather uniform that was soft and supple not like leather at all, which shocked him.

This angered him. "Him? You don't know him?" He asked pointing at the screen. Ana shakes her head. Truthfully she didn't know him.

"That's Cargill! Ashton Cargill." He said pointing at the screen.

"Didn't you go behind my back and piss all over our marriage to marry and fuck him?" Before he could slap again, she grabbed his face and did the unthinkable. She kissed him long and hard, had to swallow back vomit for only God knows what this man been eating? With her mouth on his she pours her gift into his mouth to get his mind off killing Bea.

When she finally let him up for air he hoarsely waved to his servants as he called them and the women came toward her with the gown. "Dress her." He commanded.

This was the part she dreaded and had hoped to escape. The women begun removing her clothing as he watched. It was hard to tell if she turned him on or not. He saw her chassis was well formed. Not too muscular and she definitely was a cream-puff. He took in her battled scarred otherwise flawless brownish-bronze skin accentuated her slightly almond shaped amber eyes in a small pixie-like face. Long semi frizzled, curly locks of dark auburn hair hung loose down her back, down to her calf. Shrouding her like a cape or the painting Venus De Milo. But it was something about her full luscious lips that just phased him. He wanted desperately to kiss them again. To drink in the nectar of her soul. It was beautiful. Her lips tasted of honey. Like sweet honey in the rock. He had no idea where that description came from. It wasn't his own thought. Requisite, needful things were roaming his mind like a gentle fawn as he drank in her ethereal beauty. He fought, clawed his way out of this comforting nestle of gentleness, peace and light she was drawing him into.

"The mark is gone." He cried when his eyes traveled to the site of the Mark of the Beast. "We'll have to redo the marking first thing tomorrow." He said walking to her and kissing her neck and moving further down over her breasts. He wasn't prepared at all for the consequences in touching her. Desire stirred so strong, it weaken his knees. He took a sip of the muscatel nearby to steady his insides.

Standing behind her kissing her nape with his penis rubbing her backside he said. "Don't run away again or you'll make me hunt you down and kill you. I don't want to but I can't stand the thought of somebody else doing this." He said backing away from her. He was glad the servants were gone so no one witnessed his moment of weakness.

There was no doubt, she's far too strong to allow come to her fullness on the path of good. He felt incongruous and consequential. He didn't like not being in control of his emotions. He had to get away from her or she would engulf him.

"Donte, can I got check on Bea, she sleeps better if I kiss her goodnite."

"Sure, sure, go ahead." He said dismissively, struggling to regain control.

"Wait, a minute!" She freezes in her stride to the door.

"Put this on. One of the slaves will show you which room is hers." He said, tossing a thick silk robe to her. She smiled cozily at the tent in his trousers.

"I expect you back in 20 minutes." She smiled that charming smile again and blew him a kiss. It gently, so lovingly floated on the air like a wisp of a white puff of opaque air and slapped him as hard as he slapped. He tried to dodge it but it chased him down and slapped him, bitch-slapped him in the center of his psyche, the third eye. Leaving it blind for a while.

He wearily took a seat wondering how could he control her if her gifts were the strongest between the two of them? What talismans can be used to use to bind that power?

A woman waiting patiently outside the door took her to Bea. She prayed hard all the way through the castle. She was begging to be let back through the 8th Day, apologizing about the bogus renunciation.

Bea was still under guard. She prayed those freaks hadn't touched her baby. Bea had been crying. Ana's heart went overdrive into the maternal mode when her daughter

261

reached up for her. Bjors jumped up startled the moment he saw her pointing a gun at him. A gun she had hidden in her boots that she thought she lost traveling through the 8th Day.

Bjors is caught totally off guard. He doesn't remember seeing a gun on her. Why is she back in uniform? Where are the guards? Why is Nikola letting her freely roam around like a sneaky house cat?

He drew his gun but she was faster. She shot it out his hand. The next bullet goes through his shoulder, spinning him around. Although, the bullet lodged in his shoulder burnt like hell, his determination to kill them was stronger. He had been wanting to watch her die for years. He lunged for Bea with the six inch knife he had been holding at her throat. With a karate kick Ana's foot met his midriff, sending him flying backward away from them, sending him flying into a chair; the crash resounded throughout the room and was heard outside in castle's hallway.

Knowing their time to escape was limited for she felt others coming, spiritually and physically. She took Bea in her arms and yells to God with all the worth of her soul. "Visions of Rapture, Glory Divine!" She wept with relief as she heard a gun fired as glory engulfed them.

Nikola looked over at the ivory scroll end dressing chaisse and saw the uniform she willingly took off was gone, "Damn! That bitch is gone to fight her way out of here!" He quickly teleported into the girl he called Beatrice's room; he fired into the starburst of glory as it eclipsed the room. He is furious at Bjors and himself for letting her escape.

She was right, this house was rigged to prevent her escape into the 8th day. His blasts knocked her over but she held on to Bea. She was able to move from room to room but not teleport out. When she exited in a red carpeted him she had to sit Bea down and face him.

"Now, little liar, you're in my domain. Why couldn't you behave yourself for five fucking minutes without trying to escape?" He asked, menacingly advancing on her with his blade drawn and challenging her to a battle.

In the nanosecond of traveling through the 8th Day, Ana hears Mother Harris warning her Nikola has called up reinforcement. She didn't care what she had to do to get her daughter. All she knows is Bea is here with her and alive and she wasn't leaving without her.

There are ashes everywhere in the room. Where Bea was sitting is the only clean spot in the room Bea was originally in. So apparently he already called the army and something or Someone defeated it.

Somehow Nikola managed to pull them back through from the lower level of the 8th Day unto himself. But that was a grave mistake on his part. Ana burst into the demon dark room. Stench was thick as the goo of hell's floor in it but she came back swinging with all her might. She wasn't as skilled of a fighter as he and missed him for she was fighting with emotions not skill. He swung for her midriff, with the intent to disembowel her but the diabolical blade resounded with a hard bing when it hit the invincible metal of divinity. He switched hands and tried from the left aiming for her neck. She threw up her shield blocking him in a split second before it was too late. He did a leg sweep knocking her feet from under her. She fell on her back but rolled out the way of his blade coming for her heart, it stabbed the floor instead. Her sword is fully ablaze this time; now that Bea is in her possession she didn't fear fighting back in full force. She held the mighty blade with both hands swinging and burning everything in the arch of it's trajectory. A gash of radiant light broke through the cauldron-blackness of the room created by demons packed in like sardines in a can. Her insurmountable rage cause the sword to whoosh to a towering flame, burning many of them and scattering others.

Focusing on behind them, on the fact there was more of the same than not; she swung backward in defense mode bring the blade to a full circle, encasing them in a ring of fire and sliced through his blade like a hot knife cutting through butter. He dropped the molten metal for it was on fire. She took advantage of his momentary distraction and knocked his legs from under him. As she raised the flaming sword and was about to deliver the death blow, the boney, stark white-haired woman threw herself over Nikola and begged God for mercy. She curled up on her son as if expecting the blow; that stopped Ana dead in her tracks. A warrior saint always had to show mercy when sincerely begged for it.

Ana blasé facial expression told them both; it was God's Will they live. Not her own. Seeing there was nothing she could do she took Bea, who was behind her throwing fireballs at demons trying to sneak attack, by the hand and disappeared back into the 8th Day.

The second Ana was gone Nikola shoved his mother off and sounded a world wide satanic alarm; ordering every single member of Ana BuFaye's and Eugenia Harris' family killed but bring those two warrior saints and that biggety kid to him. He wanted to enjoy the luxury of making the three suffer a painful death.

After their satanic version of a family dinner Bea senses her mother coming for her. The man watching her doesn't feel her. Her mom gathers her lovingly in her arms, now she's warm again. The hard material of her mom's armor even feels warm. She and her mother go through a wall of light. When they exit, she can hear Mother Harris' prayer. Her granny is kneeling beside their bed praying when she looks up and see them. A smile spread across her pretty granny's face. Now she's back home and happy.

Opening her eyes Ana saw her mother who immediately thanked God they were back in one piece, hugging them fiercely. She looked around quickly remembering she was back at Mother Harris' house and what Vonderbilt promised her he'd do if she left him.

"MOTHER HARRIS! WE'VE TO GET OUT OF HERE! NOW!" Ana yelled slipping on a pair of jeans and a t-shirt, ripping the satanic version of a romantic attire off; that's what was under her uniform. They heard the elderly woman coming. She joined in the hugging of Ana and Bea, and started pulling the three toward the closet in their room.

"There's a secret door behind that wall" , she said sliding a normal looking wooden panel aside. "My husband built this for times like these. It opens out in the sewer." Suddenly a loud blast rocked the house, throwing them all against the wall of the passage. Something sounded like legions of hell were roaring through the house. Smoke was smelt before seen. Another blast brought the roof down in their old room. Where they stood seconds ago was fire. The smell of old wood burning and dust seeped under the iron door. They heard the wooden panel automatically slide back in place to give them more time to escape. Mother Harris led them through the steel walled room equipped for living at least 6 months. She unhatched the heavier door leading to a city built tunnel.

"My sweet prince, Horatio, was a construction worker." she volunteered. The thick damp walls of the sewer prevented them from hearing the third and final firebomb that leveled the house. The three women walked along in semidarkness while Ana carried Bea on her back. Their hands were feeling the damp slimy walls for guidance and balance along the narrow concrete catwalk above the fetid and moldy liquid below.

"There's a manhole a little piece up ahead." Mother Harris pointed out. "Ana I didn't follow you because they warned me if I did they'd kill my children and grandchildren."

She didn't hold it against the woman. She's a mother too so she had to do what she had to do to defend her own children. Bea was her concern, not Mother Harris'. This was the farthermost thing from Ana's mind right now. That man was cruel enough to kill anything and she had regretfully added more ire to his already deranged mind.

"I'm so sorry we brought so much trouble to your door." Fannie said as they slowly followed behind the flash light in the dank darkness.

"This is what I was sent to do." Mother Harris replied shinning the light ahead. "My children and husband knew about these people. I taught them how to protect themselves." She said stopping to call someone. "Meet us at the park behind the house. " She told the recipient of her phone call.

Half a mile to the south they climbed up a metal ladder. They saw the lid slide back and they begun crawling out the manhole as a man's hand reached down and pulled them up one by one. Ana passed Bea up to him as he held onto the iron ladder. He had a friendly face.

"Everyone, this is Silas." There were three people up top. One was a woman, thin like Ana with a round, pleasant face. The three ushered them into a landvan. Ana's heart was wretched as she watched Mother Harris watch her house burn. Years of loving memories lost forever

"We must go to Florentine's", Mother Harris cried frantically over the distant but loud clamor of the sirens and roaring fire.

"No, I've already sent them there, they'll meet us at the cove," Silas said gently urging Mother into the van. Ana felt her heart sink to her stomach. She felt nauseated for she knew *why* Silas sent whomever to Mother Harris children' homes.

"God please let them be alright", she prayed as they pulled out the park. She squinted her eyes and two winged beings were standing at the front and back of her car. It was untouched by the inferno of Nikola Machiavelli.

They had to hid from those looking for them until Silas decided it was safe to pull out and head for the safehouse. By then it was afternoon in their part of the world. Ana watched the amassment of agrarian dockets of land pass swiftly by her window. All this may had been avoided had not she let Helena talk her into a trial run of Bea at a nursery school. She'd love it if they lived a normal life. She yearns for Bea to have playmates but that isn't going to happen, and from Donte told her; one Grand Wizard continues the work of their predecessor. So even if one dies another one would easily replace him and pick up the unholy pursuit. It was someone named Orman was who started the harassment against her and he continued it.

About two hours later the rambling van turns off onto an unbeaten path. The ride becomes bumpy. They are now slowly inching into the Kennesaw mountain range. This is historically known the last stronghold of the confederacy. It's also the route of the Trails of Tears. Being a sensor Ana hated places like this for she could feel the emotions of those before her, branded on the spiritual walls of the place and there was nothing good here. It appeared they were nearing the end of their harrowing escape from Nikola induced hell. At first she saw nothing but woods and a mountain but slowly a settlement came into view; it was like it slowly emerged from the thin air. She saw a gate with armed men standing guard. But she got the feeling they were there and then again they really weren't there. Fannie said saw nothing. There was nothing there but wilderness.

❧

Having heard about the bombing via his security team Cargill rushed to the site and sees the house where Ana once lived in flaming bits and pieces. Knowing no human could've survived that his heart fears she is dead. Dead before he ever came to truly know her. But his mind refuses to believe nor accept she's dead. He ran into the fiery remains of what's left. His emotions are skewed. He follows her spiritual imprint to a back bedroom. He noticed a gaping hole in the flaming debris. He pushes aside the burning roof beam and continues to follow by instinct until he reaches a manhole. Here her spiritual trail ends. He laughed aloud in the darkness, relieved she's alive. He hunkered down hard on his memory. He vaguely remembers her sister. Tonight his emotions are so raw he's shedding his polished modern persona. Ashton Cargill is reverting back to Azazel of old.

He walks through Helena's house demanding to know where is the rest of her family. He isn't Ashton Cargill. He's pure Azazel. He intends to find all of them tonight; he knows Ana is safe.

"I do not have time for your shit. Tell me what I need to know or I'll kill you myself."

Helena gives him her answer; she empties her service revolver into him but he merely takes the gun and comes within a hair's split of hitting her but calmed himself down for Ana's sake. Ana loves her even if he can't stand her. He's afraid if he strike her he'll kill her. David Wales nervously doles out the information he demands. He dispatches several teams to the houses instructing them in where to take the families. Dave omits Fannie's sister Gayle. Mainly because he thought the man only mean his wife's siblings.

When Nikola's third and fourth teams of assassins arrived at their designations they find unexpected company; they recognize the dark vehicles awaiting them and know they won't escape if they open fire on the residents. They leave without a fight. But the fifth team send to south Georgia completes their assignment and murders the last reminding members of the Prescott family beside Fannie Prescott BuFaye. The son trying to protect his mother was dragged body and soul into hell as a personal offering to the Lord of Darkness.

Azazel is there when Helena gets the call from her mother. She's vexed with sorrows for not heeding Ana's prognostication. Fannie ensure her they are safe but is inquiring of her two brothers and their families. Helena informed them a stranger came and said he was helping them for Ana's sake. This time Helena doesn't break the connection so he follows the electronic magnetic waves of the phone to the location Ana is hiding. Upon arriving he senses she isn't there. He senses her in hell and descends into hell to look for her. By the time he arrived in hell very little of Ashton Cargill is left. The only thing on his mind is learning what happened to Ana and why is she in his old domain?

It was late September, the few deciduous trees' leaves were turning various hues of gold and burnt orange and it was still fairly hot but these men wore long sleeves shirts. The gate opened and they drove through. Everything appears to be antiqued; it was they drove into 400-500 years in the past. The temperature here was pleasant and cool. Much cooler than on the other side of the gate. The outside looked like an old settlement of Colonial America with its unpainted log and plank houses, but Ana could see the residents had the comforts of modern living. Several crowded around them to offer condolences for the tragedy. Ana liked it here. The atmosphere was quiet and peaceful and the people were nice and easy going.

Everyone turned toward the sound of engines approaching. Six landvans loaded with armed men and women accompanying the arrival of Mother Harris two youngest children and their offspring. Her son and daughter who looked about Fannie's age hugged their mother and told her something. Mother went to the ground wailing in lamentation. Her oldest daughter and grandchildren had been killed. A petite blonde woman of about 35 years old rushed out of the mouth a cave and lowered herself to the ground to help Mother rise from and led her inside; she beckoned for them to follow. The petite woman was much smaller than Mother Harris. That wasn't the unusual part; she was wearing a long white robe and glowing all over so brightly it was difficult to make out the features of her face.

Ana hadn't realized her mother's face was glowing until she looked around after hearing her mother pray aloud. She panicked when she realized Fannie was ahead of her in thinking they were going for the entire family. "Can we call our family?" Ana asked Silas. "Yes, out here but not inside when Saint Cheryl is taking Eugenia. Fannie listened carefully as Ana called her three siblings. They all swore they were fine. "Get out of the house, go hide somewhere," Fannie ordered. "And do it quickly." Fannie yells at them fearing for their lives.

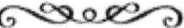

Some of Cargill's people were already watching Ana's siblings homes and jobs at the order of Sewell, not Ashton,in case she showed up they could contact their boss. They'd heard about the bombing in Atlanta and were told not to leave their posts. They saw Vonderbilt's people when they arrived to kill these people. They'd been instructed to kill on sight. They surreptitiously carried out Sewell's orders. No one heard nor noticed anything. Although Sewell had already acted without his boss' authority, Ashton ordered that to be done just in case that old Warrior Saint had saved her boarders. So that Ana wouldn't be so depressed she was incapable of doing what he needed her to do. Not that he cared about her family. He believed the love for her had died. He wanted her safe to heal his emotional wounds.

James Caldwell saw this as an opportunity to prove himself to Nikola, and get back at Fannie for her not welcoming his visits to Ana in Boston. He summoned hellhounds and sent them to Fannie's sister in Georgia. Secretly, he wanted to punish Ana for refusing to have sex with him on their last night out and refusing to be his one night stand. He felt he had wasted time on her for nothing but a feeble grope and half-hearted kiss.

Upon his arrival to his destination at infuriating Fannie's sister's homestead, he gleefully watched the mayhem unfold. After today, he bet the old cow will wish she had welcomed him with open arms.

Gayle Prescott Preston could see vaguely what was pulling her son through the cesspool but didn't know how to stop them. They clawed they carpet and furniture as they pulled Ana's first cousin, body and soul to hell. There appeared to be smoke coming from the opening they were dragging Clyde Preston through. Who was screaming from the pain. The stench was overpowering everyone in the house. Determined not to lose her child, Gayle grabbed his arms and pulled. One tore into her flesh to make her turn him loose. When Clyde was pulled through the portal closed, but the overpowering stench remained. Gayle knew since they were children Fannie was the stronger prayer of the two of them. Hysterically, she called her older sister and sobbed her story into the phone. This was the last time the sisters talked for James Caldwell was entering the foul room and broke their connection.

Ana grew furious when she heard her favorite and only aunt crying.

"Enough is enough!" She said. "If I'm a warrior saint, it's high time to start acting like one." She disappeared into the 8th Day. Mom, Bea and Mother Harris was safe now. So she could fight without fear of retaliation.

She didn't know how to find Clyde but she concentrated on her aunt and what she must have seen. She found herself in an area of blackish gray area surrounded by jagged stone walls. The dirt floor appeared to be covered with the feces of unknown creatures. The stench was enough to kill you if the beasts didn't. Clyde was unconscious, his breathing was sporadic. He was badly injured and blood was seeping from the deep wounds on his legs and abdomen. She hurried to him to see how serious his injuries were but soon heard several beasts growling.

"We'd hoped you'd come," a hulking shadowy beast said, seemingly growing larger as it red glowering eyes bored into hers. She stood up and unsheathed her blade from her side to protect her cousin and herself. She then held up her hand palm up, and beckoned the beast to attack. She had no idea if her skills were honed enough to defeat it but she definitely was angry enough to kill a hundred of them. They made her mom cry.

Therefore, they had to die! When they charged she started swinging like a madwoman. Her enraged screams of anger married their horrendous snarling and both of their angry growling and screaming wildly bounced about the enclosed in space, a cacophony of sound that could be heard quite a distance away. The torrid flame from her blade was casting incandescent light, causing figures to dance against the ancient wall. The sword was quickly incinerating them but more were coming as she quickly as she sliced those around them. They retreated a few seconds and moved in on her for the kill. Those above her were positive she didn't see them. Calculating an accurate position to pounce down on her, they waited. She kept swinging and rotating the blade again and again. By now, they stopped charging and started encircling her like the predators they were. She looked to her right and saw someone coming. It was a humanoid form so she assumed it was a man. The man was wearing a black outfit similar to her own except his was studded with spikes and loaded with an array of knives of which she didn't know the origin of. Even the arm braces were studded with razor sharp spikes. His finger tips were wearing razors of some sort. She quickly held an arm toward him, clutching her dagger in her right hand him telling him not to come any closer. The dim light showed her a somewhat familiar face. He yelled at the hounds of hell, "GET OUT OF HERE!" She was surprised when they stopped and glared at him.

"Get whomever you came for and get out of here," he said pulling the realm's veil back with his hands as easily as one would open a closed curtain. She didn't trust his help. She looked before she stepped through with her 190 lbs, 6' tall cousin across her shoulder. She came out on a mountainside. She started running with Clyde and ran into the man from the hellhound den. He caught up with her and tried to take Clyde off her shoulders.

"Leave me alone!" she snapped brusquely as Clyde started to slip from her shoulder. She struggled to hostler his dead weigh comfortably on her narrow shoulder.

"You're a real firecracker to go there alone, you could've asked Heaven for help." He teased her.

"Thanks for helping me but would you please let me pass.

"Not until you agree to sit and have dinner with me." He smiled, a smile that could be a woman's undoing in a private situation. She tried to brush pass him but he refused to move. She materialized the dagger and swiped at him. He easily dodged her and laughed. She didn't see anything funny. Her cousin was dying and this thing is talking trash. She had been nearly killed three times in one day, her family was under attack, she nearly had sex with a man she despised to save her daughter, had to walk through a sewer to escape killers, friends had been killed, and now hellhounds dragged her cousin into their den. She saw the skeletal remains of their victims so she knew what they had planned for him had not she shown up and this man is asking for a date?! So no, she definitely was not amused.

He reach out and shifted Clyde further on her shoulder. With her cousin secured she continued to walk at a faster than normal speed. The climb down from the mountain was steep so she had to lean back to keep from going down too fast. She looked around, the man was gone, if that what he really was...a man. She knew that was no mortal man. She tottered down the mountainside the best she could, holding back her feelings until it was safe to let them go. Soon the village came into view as a small silhouette against the dark mountain. The high, long fence forced her to go to the gate but before she got there she noticed the devilishly handsome man was ahead of her leaning against a metal post. She had never seen boots with straps like those he wore. They were adored with some sort of silver gargoyle creatures with glittering black eyes.

"I see you made it in one piece," he said, still teasing her as his luminous bejeweled eyes twinkled in the sparse moonlight.

"Who are you and why are you plaguing me? I've enough on my mind without this stress."

"Why not let talk about it, this stress over dinner? Then I'll tell you who I am," he says seductively leaning closer to her. He tried to remove Clyde again but she batted his hands away. Telling him to leave her and her cousin alone. His kind had done enough harm already.

"Ana!! Is that you? Who are you talking to?" Silas asked opening the gate. She saw the edge of the blade gleam in the light. Two men exited and took Clyde from her, carrying

272

him inside. Her arms were now free, she was intrigued by her pursuer. So she turned to face him.

With a face filled with distrust Silas stood and looked the gem-stone eyed man.

"Thank you for your help. Why did you help me? What are you? Why were those things afraid of you?", she inquired.

"Because he's a devil like they are," Silas drily answered for the stranger. She giggled to keep from crying. Silas demanded she come inside as a father would a teenaged daughter he caught kissing her boyfriend goodnight on the front porch.

"Hey, we aren't doing anything but talking," the studded leather stranger said in response to Silas' suspicion.

"I'll be in shortly.", Ana replied, determined to find out *why* this man keep pursuing her. She remembered his face but never seen him dressed to kill. Turning to face him, her eyes fell on his lips. She found the light mustache as intriguing as him. She somehow felt she knew him and knew him well. When he gently pushed her hair over her shoulder she felt this was a very familiar gesture of his. She felt something from that simple act. Apparently he did too. He slowly drew his hand back. The white gleaming moonlight highlighted his handsome features as it reflected off his face and black glossy hair.

He adored the thread of gold in auburn hair and the way the silvery beams of the moonlight made her dark amber eyes to shine like the precious gems they were to him. He bent down and kissed her. She wanted him to but now wasn't the time for reminiscing emotions. She had been kissed by too many mystic men for one day, men she knew nothing about their esoteric abilities.

"Somehow I feel connected to you and I know you feel the same. I don't know you but would like to know you better." He said respective of her wishes and reclaiming his position leaning against the post, towering over her. To her dismay in a very sexy pose.

"I don't know you but thanks for your help. Uhhh...how did you know I was there?", she asked suspiciously.

"Somehow I can feel things pertaining you like I can none other. I heard you screaming in distress so I followed the sound to see what was ailing you. I know you but from where I do not know. That's why I want a date with you so perhaps we can figure out where and how we know each other."

"What are exactly you?" She wanted to know. "I'm your father Adam's and mother Eve's older brother." He replied matter-of-factly.

"Adam and Eve didn't have any brothers." She laughed nervously at his attempt to confuse her. At this he laughed "Oh, that's where you're wrong. He had billions upon trillions of brothers and sisters he just didn't know it." The stranger patiently pointed out her misinformation.

Now she was confused, the Bible says nothing about Adam having many brothers and sisters. She reasoned if he's a brother of Adam then he's a son of God.

"I keep feeling we were once very much in love and happy together and somehow, I don't remember how...I messed things up between us." He added before kissing again her and whispering in her ear "I know you so well, I know every inch of your body. I know your every pleasure, I even remember you've a heart-shaped birthmark on your vagina."

She gasped and pushed against his massive chest, struggling to break away from his kiss and embrace. This man had a vile mouth. But how would he know that? His kiss brought submerged memories forth from somewhere deep inside she didn't recognize, a time of long ago she couldn't identify. She gasped at this very private newsbit, again, wondering how did this stranger know all this. He wasn't moving. He was mercilessly teasing her. She forcefully pushed him away but he held onto her like a drowning man.

"Ana, please don't leave me again. My life is meaningless without you." He plead. "We were once happy together. We can be happy again."

She had enough of people knowing too much about her as if her life was an open book for anyone to view and study.

"Get away from me. I don't know you and do not care to know you.", she hissed as she slipped into the gate Silas was earlier trying to make her enter. She heard a sob break from his lips as he begged her not to go. She leaned breathlessly against the wall and listen to him cry, her heart ached for him as her loins desired him. She wondered what spell had he cast? Whatever the case may be she had to worry about survival first and love later.

"I know you are still there. I know you remember. Do not be afraid to remember. I know you remember how much I love you. I know you remember your love for me. I can feel you standing there." She placed her hand against the wall made of wood and felt the warmth of his hand through the beveled logs. She snatched her hand away and ran to find her family; this was more than she could handle all in less than twenty-four hours.

He placed his hand on the wall and bowed his head, he knew he was losing himself in this consuming madness and knew only she could bring him back. He didn't have the strength not to love her. He has tried with his all not to love her. She's too flickery and fickle. But for right now, he had to go kill Nikola.

⟡

In the spiritually ghastly but carnally beautiful castle across the sea Bjors Machiavelli paced his room and pondered how would he tell his grieving master/uncle what he had done? He had killed the High Witch, his Queen. Nikola said kill her but apparently he didn't mean it. But had Nikola done as he suggested and poisoned the food she would be here, unconscious or dead. Either way she would be incompetent and inept of running and fighting. He listened to Nikola's wails as he wept on his mother's knee, "She's gone, she ran awaayyy again!"

He heard his grandmother. "Dear, she'll be back, she's simply scared right now. You gonna have to stop scaring her. Your daddy didn't teach you that. Evil Orman taught you to be mean."

Yes, his grandmother...he knew he was Nikola's son. His mother's body and his own eyes had told him. Nikola treated this damn Beatrice better than he ever treated him and his mother. He knew Nikola hated him because of his incestuous origins. He knew Jarvis was made to say he was his father to erase whatever happened years ago. Why didn't he save his sister? Yeah, he hopes the bitch is dead. That's what Nikola gets for letting his true gift surface. She is, well was, gifted in love and compassion and so was Nikola. He of all people should've known better than to try to restrain one like himself. Love is the strongest gift of them all. As closely as he followed her he never allowed himself to touch her, he knew she'd fuck your mind up. He was also pissed that Nikola didn't allow him to strap her to the sex chair.

Nikola was waiting for him seated behind the desk said to be polished from infants' fat. He could see the fires of Heliopolis in his eyes.

"Who gave *you* the authority to shoot at and order an assassination of *my* wife and stepdaughter? You sanguinary bastard!"

"She was escaping, your highness." Bjors grovelled with spite in his heart. He was so sick of that woman he could just puke. "You, your highness, was the one who gave the order to kill her, her mentor, and their families," Bjors reminded him.

Nikola hated it when someone was right. However right or wrong, he wasn't accepting responsibility.

"Did it ever occur to you I let her escape for my own personal reasons. That maybe I enjoy the chase. I accomplished more in one afternoon than you and your infantile muggins have been able to do in 3 years. They haven't found any bodies in the ruins so perhaps they somehow escaped."

Bjors was hoping to hell she hadn't teleported out before the bombs got her. But he knew the news, the retribution for his actions was bad when he saw the household executors standing by. A grand wiz could execute rectification for even an order he issued should he change his mind about the creed.

276

"Take him and lash him and lock him in the dungeon for three months."

"Oh well it could've been worse like ripping your guts out." Bjors thought as he turned to quietly follows the muscular man in the black iron mask. Nikola has had done it to other sons of his born nongifted; his gift of astral projection is what makes him invaluable in a hunt. When one proves useless to Nikola he eliminates them. This isn't his first punishment and probably won't be his last. But this is the first penalization about a damned no-good ass trifling woman. Nikola is lying, he didn't let the bitch escape. She bamboozled his ass.

"Father?" Bjors asked sarcastically, not caring if Nikola killed him. Which he was sure he would. But he didn't care. He was tired of being punished for how he came into existence. "Why do you project the detestation of your own act on me? I didn't do anything but you hate me. Why? My name is not Bjors or Bjorn, but you hate me so much you shorten it to anything to erase whatever happened. "

This was the first time he had ever seen Nikola lost for words. He wasn't throwing fire or summoning monsters. He simply asked in low tone,"How long have you known?"

"Since about twelve" Bjors replied, standing defiantly between the two black masked guards, staring at his father/uncle.

"How could you have let that woman live but didn't protect my mother-your own sister? I killed Ana BuFaye and I'm happy to be rid of her."

Again Nikola sighs and say in a deadpan voice. "You exist because I was a fifteen year old trying to save my sister. Jarvis is ☐☐ ☐☐☐ ☐☐ ☐ Orman and Oregon were lovers but wanted gifted children. Jarvis was one of his partners. As you know, regardless of how useless those like Orman and Oregon may find women and love fucking each other you can't reporduce without them. Somehow Jarvis couldn't get her pregnant so Oregon was threatening to kill her if she didn't come up pregnant with a gifted child. So I did it to save her life. But it didn't because Orman wasn't entirely into men, he had started to fall for her and Oregon didn't like so Orman allowed Oregon to

277

kill her to prove his affection hadn't strayed. That's why when I turned to the darkness those two were the first I killed. It had nothing to do with their sexual perference as it's whispered around the castle. I didn't give a damn where they stuck their dicks as long it was nowhere near me or my family. Sure, I was tired of their raping me but I killed them out of revenge for killing my family. You had another uncle and a aunt. They were children when Orman raided the farm. Mother and I are only two survivors. Your grandmother was used as a sex slave for many years because of her once great beauty, she went crazy, that's why I let her carry skulls around. So no, Jarvis isn't your father. I am." He said knowing Bjor didn't understand all the words. He didn't speak Aremenian nor Romanian. He looked up at his incestous son and asked. "So, what do you want?"

Seeing Nikola was showing weakness, he moved in for the kill. "I want my face fixed. I want to be an equal memebr of this family with the same authority as Gianna. I want my daughter to remain alive. After all I'm the last living link to Sophana. Grandmother said my daughter looks just like her." Nikola said nothing.

As he was led away by the men in black leather mask he teemed with hatred for Ana BuFaye, vowing if she wasn't dead when he found her again he would make her wish she was.

"Let him go." Nikola told the guards who immediately unhanded Bjors. "I'm willing to meet his demands." Nikola said exhaustedly. While thinking *"Between Bjors and Ana he didn't know which was wearing him down worse."*

Caroline Caldwell got the news of Ana's death while soaking in the tub; she felt exhalation that everything had finally returned to normal in her life. She felt back in the driver's seat again, her heart angina was now gone. She paid a terrible price for her betrayal of the Grand Witch whom dumb ass Nikola can't see really isn't a witch. He took away her celebrity status. But you can't turn saints into witches no matter how hard you try. They've some eldritch obsession with the Christ. Nothing works in the abscission of His influence over them. She sent a demon to make the bitch sick and that didn't work. She figured if she was sick she wouldn't be screwing her husband.

Taking a seat on the relaxing couch chair in Caroline's bath chamber, her personal assistant Helga brings in a glass of champagne and proposes a toast. "Our troubles are over. But you can't deny she had a regal and statuesque disposition about herself. It's a pity it was wasted!" Helga laughed. "I like my women small."

Caroline screwed up her face. She had tried the girl on girl thing in her early Hollywood days but she didn't like it. Helga was addicted to it. Helga was a pussy hound and made no apology about it.

"What in the hell did you and James see in her? I mean, she had a pretty face and all but Hollywood is full of pretty faces. I mean, she had no tits that I could see. She always worn big baggy clothing. So what was damn special about her?! I just don't see it. I looked at her Thad Wyett days pictures and she's rather plain. What in the hell did an MVP star marry her mousy ass for when he could have had any upcoming starlet he wanted."

Helga laughed and said "You aren't attracted to women is why you don't see what we saw. Some women have to practice at being sexy, she didn't. It came naturally to her. She oozed with a sexual magnetism and mysticism that made everyone want her. All lesbians aren't attracted to big boobs anymore than all men are. I love a woman with a big ass. All men do, they'll say they don't but they do. They'll say they don't if the one they love doesn't have one but let a big one come in their view they'll crane their necks until they choke looking at it sway."

Caroline listened carefully to her philandering female friend and abruptly laughed. "That's the biggest load of shit I've ever heard. You're justifying why you play around so much. The woman was plain as home-made sin and you didn't get a chance to suck and dump her." Helga shrugged her shoulders and swallowed down the last of her champagne in a single gulp.

"Oh well, you asked. If you didn't want to know then don't ask."Helga quipped. Caroline rose up from the tub, the bath is beginning to become boring to her. She feels

279

the water running in rivulets from her pubic hairs "Let me call Cargill's bitches and tell them their adversary is dead. Like it or not, they're my only real connection to the snobbish mogul. James need that deal."

She's a tad bit jealous Helga found Ana Wyett attractive and not her so she is giving her a full view.

The one named Dawn answered as usual. "That Wyett bitch Ashton was chasing is dead. You ladies have him all to yourselves again. Remember to talk to him about financing James' Jupiter project." Caroline said hanging up the phone without waiting for a reply. She hated talking to those empty headed sex dummies.

"Arrrgghh!" Caroline screamed. "I hope I never have to talk to one of them again! I hope I never have to deal with this again."

A staff member came in and told her James wanted to talk to her. She pulled on a robe and threw the towel to Helga. The staff member looked sentry-like at the wall.

"Did he say about what?" Caroline looking perpendicularly at Helga as she tied her silk robe, who shrugged her shoulders in reply.

"No ma'am. He did not." The woman wearing a black dress and white apron maid uniform said.

She was highly displeased with being called from her leisure time; this had better be important. She walked merrily on air, as freely as her injuries allowed without wincing, to the antebellum southern living room where her husband sat. They were an odd couple. Some years they had an open marriage and other years a closed one. Them being about the same height she walked up and kissed him on top of the head. His hair was thinning a little on top but with his money, power and infallible influence --- who cared? He was still as handsome as the day she married him. He wasn't unnecessarily cruel like a lot warlocks such as Warren Shrevenport, who gave even her the creeps.

He looked up at her wearing an unreadable expression with those pale blue eyes and said. "Our man with the fire department team said there were no bodies in that house and there was a steel enforced tunnel leading from the back yard into the sewer. No bodies were found in the sewer. They did find a child's toy dropped on the walkrail. So they are alive."

Caroline agitatedly thought, *"No, this can't be happening! She has to be dead. I can't take anymore. The woman is a constant thorn in the ass."* She dropped, completely enervated, in the seat opposite of him. This can't be happening. What is that woman? Their findings must to be a mistake. No one could've survived all that fire! Frantically, her eyes dart all over the room. She doesn't know where to rest them. She finally rest them on her husband's face. What she sees angers her. A small smile tugs at the corner of his mouth.

"You're happy there's a slim chance of her surviving? Aren't ya?" She accused. "I don't know." He honestly replied. "But since you asked. In some ways. I'm glad if she survived it. One might say...I'm a little hopeful."

"How dare you say since a horrible thing after what Vonderbilt did to me for not carrying out my mission? Don't tell me you're still in love with her?!" Caroline cried. She felt like pitching the stained glass antique Tiffany lamp at him. He looked curiously at her and asked didn't they've an open marriage this year? "Well, it just closed again." She retorted, narrowing her eyes at him.

Looking down at the primitive village below as the sun rose over the straw thatch roofs casting a palish yellow tint over the simple house. Nikola knew now that Bjors knows who he truly is; he still may have to kill him after all. Bjors was a bad seed no matter how you look it. Unlike Gianna, Bjors was a natural born killer.

Chapter 5

Saints in the Cave: The Teachers

No scientific theory has yet come close to fully explaining why some people when dying few see things while others do not — which can include visions of tunnels, bright lights, angels, heaven, hell and meetings with dead relatives. I've seen these things in near-death experiences is how I know the person aren't confused and distressed.

I somehow knew Aunt Gale was gone when a disoriented Clyde said his mother and father was with him. I didn't have the heart to tell mom, so I left the room.

I nervously sat indoors and watched the nuns and monks move quietly around the oddly lit place. There was no lighting system that I could observe. Clyde was in a hospice with mom attending him. I wasn't much use. I kept seeing a glow down the hallway, well actually a tunnel because this place was hewed out of a mountain. Wondering where it was coming from, I tiptoed toward it and peeked around the door. I saw several people praying around my injured cousin's bed. They were all glowing like the woman who helped Mother Harris inside. This woman was among them. A woman I had never seen looked into my face; I was startled in how much we looked alike. The woman looked up and invited me inside.

"Hello, my name is Anne, the English version of your name." The tranquil eyed woman said, introducing the others. "This is Cheryl, Gerald, Melissa, Gerald, Nehemiah and Thomas." All nod gracefully toward her and smiled. She noticed they were all wearing golden crowns. Their exquisite white habiliments seemed to breathe as if it were alive.

"Are you people heavenly saints?" She asked feeling aerroneous for asking this question when their clothing told plainly what they were or at least she thought.

The woman named Anne asked, "What do *you* think we are?" Leading her out the room away from the others.

"I don't know. You somewhat fit the description in Revelation of what the saints will be wearing. But you're alive, here talking to me."

The one named Gerald said "I'd assume God would have updated the fashion since John the Revelator's time."

Ana's eyes widen. "You been here since the time of Saint John?" The one who helped Mother Harris pops the one named Gerald on the arm with her tiny fist. "Quit teasing the child. We're old but we aren't *that* old."

"Ana, you're here because we're to pass our knowledge and mantles on to you and a new generation. For that same reason we're here too. We're here to teach you all we know about spiritual gifts and spiritual warfare. The veils are coming down more than ever. Time is running out. Your generation is very late in time. If you'll wait outside a few minutes longer I promise you we'll be with you. I advise you to eat a full meal. Our training is a lot more rigid than Eugenia's." Anne said.

After seeing she hadn't moved and that silent tears ran down her face they all moved toward her, formed a circle around her, pulled her into their embrace and hugged and kissed her cheeks. "Dear child... it's all in God's Hands now. I know you're severely traumatized. I know what you've been through. But things will get better. You aren't alone. There're many others out there like you. You'll find them someday. When the appointed time arrives. They'll come to you as you came to Eugenia." Saint Anne said adding that her mother and daughter were fine. Mother Harris had returned to bury her children. The woman glowed brighter and brighter as she talked and walked her back to the eating area where a full meal and her family was waiting.

"She's a smart, brave little girl, and as pretty as can be." Saint Melissa said complimenting Bea as she rubbed her small back. Bea blossomed immediately among these people. She looks up at the woman and says in a four year old voice. "Thank you, pretty lady." Without Ana having to remind her to say "thank you."

"That's it!" Helena screamed at her brothers. "I've had it with Mom's craziness in following her insane daughter all over hell! Some black clad nut job comes up in my house and started ordering people around. I swear I emptied my gun in the bastardization. He must had been wearing bullet proof clothing. I've had it! Enough is enough! This foolishness stops now. After Aunt Gayle's funeral Mom is coming home with me! I don't care what excuse she gives to remain in Ana's madness. Ana knew you don't fuck around with rich men like James Cadwell and walk away from them. Our baby sister knows some really dangerous characters. Hell! I'm a cop and she know more dangerous people than I. She can leave Breanna but she can't stay in my house with all her craziness. The little sneaky thing think I don't know the real reason she took Mom and Bea and left with no explanation. Junior, you and Frances can take her in. She gets along with Frances, pretty well. Don't she?"

Jacob Jr. knew his oldest and youngest sister never got along but he had a hard time believing Ana would harm any of them as Helena said.

"Junior, you don't know her like I do." Helena snapped. "Ana has always been a weird, evil little thing. She doesn't live in the real world. She lives in a fabricated world that exist only in her silly head. In her world, she can do as she please and there's no serious consequences. I'm beginning to wonder were the Wyetts correct in saying she's the reason Thad's life is destroyed."

J.J. wasn't thrilled about taking Ana in. Ana disrupts people's lives. Where ever is Ana, there's bound to be some strange, far out trouble. It has always been that way with her and he enjoyed his serendipity at the university. Life in the small college town was good but if his sister comes...everything there will fall into shambles. He didn't want men hanging around his house, around his wife and daughters. And everywhere his sister goes there's surely to be guys sniffling around. She seems to draw men like a lantern draws moths.

"I'll help her to get her own apartment and a job on campus." J.J finally said.

"I'm all maxed out," Jack quipped thinking of the expensive equipment he had to buy to keep Ana's identity a secret and how close he came to losing his job a few times when the feds suspected he was somehow helping his sister but couldn't prove it. How his wife been bitching at about where all his money is going. He lied about his real salary to help his mom and sister. He secretly resented the fact Junior never puts out anything to help them, it's always him and Helena.

"They shot missiles through the place and then went and fire bombed someone else she was associated with on the southside of Atlanta." Helena said breaking into Jack's thoughts.

"Where are they now? Did mom say how they got out?" Jack asked.

"Yeah, some mumbo-jumbo about God and how He saved them." Helena answered rolling her eyes in a full arch. "I don't know where they're right now. Whomever they're with, won't let them come to the phone. The lady said Ana was gone to get cousin Clyde when I called mom back after she called me telling me to go hide somewhere but when I called Mom's phone a few minutes ago she said Ana was outside talking to Ashton Cargill."

"How did Clyde end up in Atlanta? I thought he was still down in Brunswick with Aunt Gale?" Junior asked. "Who in the hell knows." Helena sighed.

"The Ashton Cargill I know is a billion times trillionaire, the single more richest person in the world. How in the fuck does Ana knows him?" Jack cried.

"See, that's exactly what I'm talking about. She should've had her skinny ass indoors seeing about mommy and Bea but she's outside trying to hook another man. That isn't the only one. One called here a few hours ago wanting to know had I heard from her. He had a foreign accent. He said his name was Vonderbilt."

Jack whistles "Whew, I know of a man named Vonderbilt but never seen him nor

Cargill but the Vonderbilt I know controls all of Wall Street that Cargill doesn't. Why is she so broke if these two powerful men are interested in her?"

Helena sighs and says "Jack, you know people like that merely use people like us for toys. They probably are lying to her to keep her strung along. Neither of those men are serious about Ana. I thought she learned her lesson with Caldwell. His wife called me and told me to keep my sister away from her husband. And like Caldwell they're probably already married. Let's face it; Ana's stupid. They probably dished out a thousand every so often to keep her happy. You see how she put herself in the alms house for Thad."

"Maybe these are others by those names." J.J. inputted.

"With Ana, I seriously doubt it." Helena scoffed

"Our little sister is troubled and we know that. Whomever these people are they're taking advantage of her tumultuous life." J.J. said asking Jack how do you find these men?

"No one really knows where they live." Helena sighed. "If they live on earth I will find them." Jack vowed.

ᑲᑲᑲ

It had been nearly five hundred years since the legendary St. Anne had walked the earth. Coming back before all was done and said brought back the pain of their final battle. She had requested that Heaven not send her and her officers again. Their existence was peaceful now and she wanted it to remain so.

A rupture of moonstone-yellow light appeared in the carnal-black sky. The moans and screams of the injured but living were heard ascending to the dark dome overhead. When they broke though the gates of the Pandemonium, the forces of hell were waiting, the fiery heat roasted their faces but they felt no pain. Her final speech to her regiment was all who wanted to turn back do so now. There's no shame in being afraid. No one

286

retreated, this broke her heart looking at young Eugenia's stubborn face as they stood looking across the smoking, fiery plains. She didn't have good feeling about this raid, she didn't feel they would come out alive. She didn't feel they'd see their families, let alone God's green earth again. They were fighting two enemies on double front. In the heat of the battle, their physical selves were fighting humans who neither understand nor cared what was really going on on this end of the spectrum, while on the other end their spiritual selves were literally fighting hell itself to keep the gates of the Darktower from being slung wide open. She watched from a smothering boulder the multitudes below as they bleed themselves to use the precious power of life to open the foregates.

Back then all nations had been convinced by the darkside that Nazarene warriors and warrior saints were the same as the crazed jihads butchering people. Lucifer's followers used this misguided information to their advance. And waged a full-fledged war against her kind in every nation. Several satanic groups had managed to combine powers and open up the Darktower. Anyone with a lick of sense would be trying to keep it closed, not open it. But no, not these psychos, they wanted demons up and out partying with them. A party that wouldn't have lasted the better of two minutes before hell would turn them all into a bloody pulp. But the popularity of the darkside as being something cool and fun and child's play was fueling the flames against them as being over-crazed religious zealots. Most of their kind in other nations were dead. So her regiment was pretty much the last left standing between earth and hell. Many of her superiors wanted to walk away and let the darkside have the fools. But she kept seeing her and many other of their descendants falling prey to the darkside as punishment for their ancestors' actions. So they had to fight or millions of the generations yet to be born would perish.

All the regiments leaders of all nations looked down the human line at their comrades from every nation on earth and in unison signaled a charge and rushed among the Gothic worshipers at lighting speed. Mowing them down like blades of grass. They heard a mighty rumble inside and regrouped their warriors in a battle stance mode. They knew who was coming through. The first gate had been resealed, the second gate was opening. They had no idea there were so many devoted satanists sacrificing themselves to let Lucifer out. They were greatly outnumbered, thigh deep in hell's slimy creatures. As one turned to ashes ten more appeared.

They saw the lord of darkness was rising in all his hellish might, racing out the narrow slot like an angry lion. His hateful eyes were deadly trained on her. But they succeeded in reclosing the gate but at a high fatality rate. She watched many she loved die at the hands of demons. When face to face with Lucifer, he grinned triumphantly at them for he knew they were doomed. As he reached for her she used the last measure of her existence; she separated herself from that of divine which protected her, her sword and shield by throwing her blade leaving herself vulnerable to close the gate in his face. Next came her shield, which she threw like a disc. The brilliance light lit up downtown hell like high noon. His painful roars soon sounded as thus they were coming from a long dark tunnel and then she saw light. She heard the whooshing of the air her weapons made returning to her, she looked around and knew none of them were on earth anymore. They had beaten them back across the gulf. Eugenia was the only one she was certain had lived because when she threw her blade so hard at Lucifer it ripped a hole in time and space she got a glimpse of the future and grabbed the stubborn girl slung her through the time slot before it closed.

But she noticed those like Ana was different from her kind. Those like herself were the last of the ancient ones who had existed since the early days of the Crucifixion. Ana was of the new breed who didn't have to separate body and soul to fight in the spiritual world. They had the ability to bring their gift much more profoundly into the physical world than herself. Eugenia was like these future warriors and warrior saints. The entire day before she spoke to her people from 10:43 AM to 6:30 P.M. on April 27, 2073

Speaking to them in spirit through the divine connector called Royal Telephone she called their attention to the task they was about to engage into: "This is Anne. I've been contacted by followers of the darkside asking me to restrain my students.

Her reply to the accusation was; "First of all "*my students*" are not inflicting harm on you. They may not like the nature of your actions and no Law of God require them to like what you are. Despite what is said and contrary to popular belief they're peaceful people."

(The satanists were unable to hear the warriors giggling. But she heard them and silenced them.)

The reply came back: "We don't think you understand. These people are using their gifts to hurt, maim, and even kill. And we need you to stop them, they'll listen to you!"

St. Anne replied, "Remember a short while ago I was collecting and teaching all the strongly gifted people who came to me to learn about their gift(s) but you people wouldn't rest until you until destroyed every method I established in teaching them the proper and Godly way to use their gifts for the betterment of mankind. You all killed my family, you destroyed my home, household, told lies on me, vandalized my home and car, created bogus bills that you were given legal authority to collect, killed anyone or anything living close to me, even my pets. And you expect me to care about some people whom I don't know spiritually stalking you?! I bet you can't call the cops and the use the courts on a person's whose existence you can't find! Can you!?"

They replied; "They're doing much more than stalking! They're terrorizing and killing!"

"Isn't that's what you people do?! Terrorize, stalk and kill. So maybe whomever they're---they've learned well from the examples you guys set. Isn't that's what you all have done to them and millions of others who didn't want to serve your lords and masters? Maybe they just got tired of running and hiding and decided to fight back the only way they knew how. So now...you realize you can't control them because you don't know who they are and what their gifts maybe and you think I'm dumb enough to tell you. If I knew I wouldn't be stupid enough to care what they do to you. I tried for years telling you people there were groups of gifted people, so strongly gifted in the world, whose gifts couldn't be controlled by means of man nor hell, but only by God. Your incantations aren't working? Huh?!? How do you know its isn't your demonic masters attacking you? You know the veils are down a considerate bit now so they don't need you to come into this world."

She wasn't sure if it wasn't a trick to get her to let her guard down.

They replied; "You're a saint, haven't you been commanded by your Lord to care what happens to all humans? We know your primary gift is Love and compassion."

Anne replied; "Yes, to care about humans. You're no longer human. You all have made yourselves into demons in a human form. My Lord didn't instruct me to care about demons. You all shredded every ounce of your humanity years ago, so you no longer belong to the human race. So don't try to use the "love card" with me."

Then a lone male spoke out saying: "I saw you in a library in Indiana in 2061, you knew who I was just as I knew you. I came to talk to you about the keys we believe you have, only a saint would've such powerful keys. But you ignored me, I even sent my servant to get a luxury room for you and yours' but you refuse to accept it, you preferred sleeping in your van. I see you're asking to be compensated for your loss. I can't bring back the dead but I can refurnish your life in a greater portion than your wildest dreams. If you agree to do as we ask I'll send a courtier with a special check to you for 13 billion dollars, honoring the 13th warrior of your kind. I'll even provide the transportation so you can go to check it. Call off all your harassers and I'll call off mine and they'll never bother you again. Do we have a deal?! I'm a world renowned businessman, I'm known for going through with any deal I conjure."

She laughed, a bitter hostile sound, and replied; "I really must look like a new kind of fool to you. If I could do something about your I-don't-give-a-damn-'bout problem, which I can't, I wouldn't, for the moment the problem abated you would call the bank and swear the check was stolen and it would become the world evening news story. Your driver, banker ,and courtier service would disappear as witnesses to the transaction. No one would know anything about it other than I, who cashed the check!"

He replied, "OK, then what about cold, hard cash? Think of the goodwill you could do with it."

"Hell no! Leave me alone!"

Seeing she wasn't budging and a black leather attired warrior was sitting here in his office at this very moment looking underbrowed at him, cleaning his nails with his dagger but threatening his assistant which he really didn't care if the man killed. The angry, dark eyed young man jerked his thumb upward, meaning ample the ante. He raised it to fifty billion. But she still said no. The young warrior shrugged his shoulders. Fearfully, his eyes darting to the angry student of St. Anne, he asked. "Just why would I do that when your clan would sneak into spiritual world of the night and kill me!? I'm trying to save my life, not take it! What's your price? Everyone has a price."

"I cannot be bought."

"Why not!? Think of your children! Think how much better their lives will be for years, no centuries to come." The man pled to them both. The nail cleaning young man grinned. "I don't have any kids," the young warrior whispered. Hoping his mentor didn't hear him.

Anne replied as her students listened in, even those out right now fathoming murdering someone: "Because your father is the father of lies and you're his son, nothing you say can be trusted. I nor my service can be bought. Nothing your kind would do for me wouldn't come without a price attached. Yes, I knew who you were years ago when I saw you, I received the message from your person. I'll not serve you or your master for all the gold in this world, for my in Father's House the floor is paved with gold."

He angrily sighed, seeing his offers and pleas were falling on deaf ears. But also seeing no further need for niceties he chuckled and said, "Then it appears to me your father isn't a very good dad. Has a floor made of gold and won't give his daughter a single bar. A good father takes well care of his kids. To me your father isn't a very good dad. But then again you wouldn't know for yours died when you were just a little kid. What good is all that self-righteous bullshit when you're broke as a field mice without a pot to piss in or a window to throw it out. I've personally seen to that. I held the mortgage to your house years ago. I came to you in good faith but you with all your stupidity spit in my face! Now you and your four kids are sleeping in that rundown, patched up van. So what in the fuck has God done for you? He doesn't give a damn about your pain nor heard your cries. At least Lucifer answers and answers well when we call him! Can you say the same about God?! You know what else sweetie, I told the doc to kill your old man. He was a real pain in the ass. He was getting too close to the truth."

291

(The students saw and heard St Anne gasp)

She replied; "You know....remarks like that is exactly why people in their spiritual forms are after you and your crew to kill y'all. Y'all talk to everyone as if it's your birthright to speak to them like chicken droppings! At least I can sleep at night without worrying whether whether or not someone in their spiritual essence whom I've teed-off will ambush me in my sleep. Because my Father protects me from such. You know...those fatal wounds show no outward signs so all your CSI buddies will never be able to prove what happened to you. So go ask your *loving good father* in hell to deal with this issue and leave me alone."

He then screamed at her, "My very fucking life depends upon *not* leaving you alone! If I knew who they were I wouldn't be talking to you!"

He stole a glance into the feverish, grinning eyes of his visitor. He saw madness. He knew this man was one of those who had been visiting them in the night and offing them. This man had been driven mad. He glanced down at the electronic Identifier on his desk and saw the face recognition program wasn't working on him. This man was blocking it. So no, he doesn't know who he is but is positive he's one of hers. The man said she wouldn't believe he would do such a thing.

"We thought utterly destroying you would make them stop! Instead they got worse. Worse with the nightmares, worse with the stalking, and they have finally started actually killing. We know it's one of your kind, those of us who they didn't out right kill said they saw their spiritual garments and weapons, so we know they're Nazarene warriors! You're their regiment earthly commander! Do your fucking job! You do have some control over them, you're just pissed off about what has happened. We're so very sorry we hurt you. So will you please talk to them and convince them killing us is not the answer!? Do you realize what is at stake here? If all of us dies?! I don't think you do...if we all dies the world economy will plunder into worse darkness than the fall of the stock market could ever create, every nation in the world will fall. The visible world leaders are mere figure heads, we're the real world power. The real leaders of the world! Do you want all this suffering brought down on your head. Because if you do nothing to

292

control them that's exactly what will happen!"

She solemnly replied; "Rather I care or not care is totally irrelevant in this situation. As I've been telling you for the past 25 minutes or so. I don't know who they're, from all the evil you all have done, it could be a group of avenging angels for all I know. If you aren't sure they were warriors of the Nazarene, then you're speaking to wrong person. Go talk to the Nazarene Whom you crucified, they're His warriors. Not mine."

Cutting his eye nervously at black floor-length coat wearing, blade wielding lunatic in his office (he notices the blades at the edge of the coat) the man replies, "I'm positive that's what he is. He's wearing a black leather dress coat with blades in the hem. I'm looking right at him. Christ will not answer us is why we're speaking to His servant in hope you can get Him to answer!"

(St. Anne was thinking, *"Gee! Good luck with that for a lot of times He doesn't answer me.)*"

The solo male, seemingly the leader of the group sighed and said to the others; "She doesn't know who they're and if she knows, she isn't talking." (Apparently he forgot they could still spiritually hear them.)

Finally, in defeatism, he addressed her again saying. "I tell you what---to show you we aren't all evil, I'll send you payment for your time."

A lone lady's voice asked; "Saint Anne...What do you suggest we do? I can't take this anymore. I'm afraid to die."

St. Anne told her to repent, if the Lord sees fit He will stop them.

She asked, "Will repentance stop them for sure?!"

"I do not know but it will save your soul from hell."

She scoffed through her tears and said, "I should've known it all would circle back

293

around to repentance, grovelling to God on your hands and knees! He's going to let deranged terrorists kill me in my dreams just to make me repent?!? What kind of God is that? What about what I want? I want to continue to enjoy life on earth without the destitution He requires! Everything is about saving my soul! What about my life now!"

St. Anne thought, *"Lady, God doesn't appear to be much in the business of caring what you want. I want a lot of things but I ain't got them."* But knowing her students were listening she said to all of them: "You people are getting on the last good nerve I've left. And heaven knows I don't have many left. I'm not your servant, and refuse to be spoken to in such abusive tone; one more rude outburst from any of you and you won't have to worry about the strange persons in the night. For I'll do their desire for them! Woe! You've some audacity. The audaciousness to ask me for help after all you've admitted you've done to me!? I told you about salvation because my Lord requires that of me, I don't care if you're in heaven or hell. I gave you the only answer there is for no one can bargain with God and only He knows who they're and can stop them if He chooses to do so! I've no more control over how He operates than any other creature He made! That's His Choice alone if He stop your afflictions after repentance. I'm obligated to tell the truth of what He will do. Even when speaking to demons such as yourself I'm still obligated to tell the truth if there is the slightest chance of your salvation!"

Another voice which she had not heard earlier timidly spoke up saying; "You're a saint. You're supposed to forgive, forget, and help us?"

St. Anne replied, "I'm not after you. But no one asked me for forgiveness. All I've heard from you all is you're sorry because some spiritual thing(s) is walking down on your hides and you can't control it. There's a real difference between genuine remorse and asking forgiveness cause your sorry heinie is in a bind!"

The first lone male said; "You know we can not ask nor beg your forgiveness. It must be granted to us on your own free will. Asking your forgiveness would show weakness. We're never to bow down to the likes of you. It would destroy all we've accomplished in this world to ask even a mere lowly saint for forgiveness. You've to voluntarily grant it and all will remain intact."

She finally said; "I'm aware you can not ask forgiveness and remain in your lifestyle. However you've made your choice. There's nothing more to be said." Saint Anne said before breaking the spiritual communication and turning furiously on her students throughout the nation via the Royal Telephone. She knew those people spoke the truth about them.

"How am I to convince people we're affable and helpful if you guys are running around killing and hacking up even satanists? You all are making their accusations true!"

The young warrior sitting in the satanist's office lazily got up, perched on the corner of the man's desk, and said, "I told ya, she wasn't going to believe we're capable of such atrocities as you call what we consider Justice. You wasted my time. I could've killed you thirty minutes ago and been back home by now. But you think my time isn't valuable." He drove the short dagger through the man's hand pinning him to the desk and beheading him in a flash of glaring silver and caught the assistant before she had a chance to make it across the office to the door. She ran right into his extended blade.

"Sorry, darling. It's a shame to waste someone so fine." He said kissing her on the mouth as she looked up at him in disbelief he would actually do the deed. He watched her life drain from her body and pushed the corpse off his blade and stepped back through the Neutral Zone.

Enshrouded in grief, she looked around at St. Cheryl, and then at their mentor. Wondering if St. Anne was right? Peace can't be won nor accomplished by the blade. Through tear blinded eyes 84 year old Eugenia chuckled at memory of the serious hell and brimstone lecture Saint Anne gave the young ones because it was the young ones like herself whom the Grand Wizard was referring to as the dangerous uncontrollable killers. But hey in their defense, they had spent years watching those like Sts. Ann, Melissa, Cheryl, Thomas, Douglas, Gerald, Nehem, and many others try to live as peacefully as possible with those hellions. There was no real peace to had with them alive and they weren't going to try. With this new girl coming she would combine the two forms of teaching: Compassion when needed and bust your ass when it's begged for.

She knew all too well they were up against a predator that strives on the invisible ether of spiritual information.

St. Melissa comes and sits beside St. Anne on the stone bench, interrupting her thoughts. Anne cast a wary smile. Melissa knew she was comprehending something difficult to do or accomplish.

"I've been praying for our baby Eugenia. That God give her strength to endure." Patting Melissa's callous, knotted hand. "I'm more than sure He will."

"Have you noticed that new girl and her mother looks like you, your mother and your daughter Hershana? How much the little girl named Bea resembles your Hershana? Do you think they're yours or one of your siblings' descendants? I mean, we don't know what happened to our families after that fateful day."

Knowing they all shared the same fate, St. Anne has always felt responsible for their lives even thus they were immensely out numbered.

"Yes, I noticed that the moment I saw her. But that's not what we're here to do. We were send to teach her all that we know." St. Melissa nodded. She knew her friend well enough to know the reply meant she didn't want to talk about it. And she was right. They were here to do a job not reminisce about the painful past. No matter how the past is now romanticized, she was there and knows in truth, it was pure hell.

Chapter 6

Ode to a Memory: All's Fair in Love and War.

It had been more than seven hundred years since Azazael shed a tear. After leaving the camp of saints he resolved more than ever to give this woman up. The chase wasn't worth it. There were too many other women, mortal, immortal, other worldly ones too, to invest his whole heart in one so traumatized she'll never be able to fully love anyone. He stands and looks out the window of the castle. He wanted to be alone. He's ending this mad pursuit of this disheveled woman.

"Sure, you say that until the next time you hear her crying", his own conscience told him.

Reasoning out aloud. "The woman is beautiful as an angel, it's a pity Vonderbilt has driven her bat-shit crazy."

"Can she help that?" His conscience asked roaring in his ear as he roared at people. Talking to himself, he felt as pernicious as Ana. Determined not to listen to his own insanity he calls his personal staff to throw an all out party so he can listen to the mindless chatter of others rather be here alone listening to his own nonsense.

While at the party he dissolves his corpuscles and molecules and goes totally spiritual. It hurts less this way. He could feel himself slipping away. He felt there was something he wanted to hold on to but was unable. He fought hard to hold on to why he was looking for this particular woman and why he needs to kill that damn wizard. His mind drifts to his future which he saw nothing there except a hole in the a celestial prison cell somewhere deep in the unknown.

He watched, uninterested; even the frescoes of the fundamentals of the elaborate and airy party bored him. Naked and toga-clad men and women milled around. His harems had gotten together to throw him a party to shake him out the funk has he been in for the past 3 years. Dawn, being her usual self, invites people he doesn't care to know.

"C'mon darling let's dance." the women say pulling him up from his askew postilion position on the lounge chair. He didn't feel like dancing. He felt like killing a wizard. He dances a few steps and then reclaims his alcoholic beverage before sitting down again. Dawn pushes the nude woman off his lap who hops on him the moment he sits back down.

"C'mon, stop being a sourpuss," she purrs at him in her special seductive manner that made him bring her home years ago. The woman she pushed off his lap refuses to go away.

"This ain't no damn ancient Playboy mansion." Dawn snaps at her guest.

"Well you coulda fooled me!", the woman snapped back at Dawn who had been with him the longest, over 25 years. He usually changes up every 30-40 years. Gives the harems their stipends and lets them go, bringing in new ones. Sometimes some stay on staff as a secretary or something if she had the skills. He noticed this group isn't aging the way they normally do. Only his girls must be dressed, the others do what they want. Many had wandered off with a rich oiler or banker. He didn't care just so long as they didn't give away what he was paying for.

He really didn't care for all of them being here at once. It was starting to feel overcrowded in here. He learned eons ago that when all are in one place they're apt to bitch over who he bought what. Like Delores had been sugaring up to him all night saying she want a Cartier watch like Dawn and Cindy has. He told her she wasn't living with him when he gave those watches out. All 56 of his group knew to stay in a group during a party like this or it would be hell to pay. Dancing with a guest was fine but no cornering off with one. He didn't tolerate disloyalty. He has had too many unfaithful wives to tolerate infidelity.

He also knew Dawn had called a meeting with the others to discuss their future. He told them when and if he fall in love they'll be the first to know. Until then, chill the fuck out. Dawn isn't the type to chill out if she feels threatened. But there's really no reason to feel threatened. That woman is definitely not his type. She isn't a threat to them. But why does he keep seeing fragments of a memory where he made love to this woman. He can trace back to all his latest conquests and she isn't one of them.

As the party wears on until the wee hours of the morning Dawn pulls him into privacy and begin to make love to him. He stops her.

"What's the matter, baby?" She purrs. For some reason her purring annoys him. Dawn is also the only one he can talk to. Exasperatedly he said, "When I saw her... I think I know her from somewhere. Where I can't exactly remember. I mean like somewhere in the recent past."

Dawn really didn't care to talk about their archenemy. Caroline Caldwell said the woman is a powerful enchantress who bewitched men. And that's what wrong with Ashton.

"Baby, just maybe she was a one-night fuck and you did your business and left. I mean since you can't remember her, apparently she wasn't that important to you. I mean, why don't you let that wizard have her, she is more suitable for him than for you. I mean you said so yourself she isn't your type."

"No, she isn't the type to have one-night stands," he replied although he didn't want to admit Dawn had a point. She didn't exactly arouse him. She was dressed in a bunch of baggy clothing and that definitely was not appeasing. She had an exceptionally beautiful face but it took more than a pretty face to arouse him.

"Well, why do you keep at this madness, everyone is on the edge wondering what will you do when you find this woman."

He carefully takes her on his lap to try and make her understand, "Dawn, you know I'm immortal. I don't die, sometime my kind needs something a little extra, it's like a balm to the spiritual part of me." He said trying to explain the makeup of his spiritual self to her and what he needed that woman for was nothing sexual.

"And you feel she can give you that?" ,Dawn asked, not sure what to think. "Uh, supposed she doesn't want to. Had you thought about that!?" He smiles and says "I'll just have to sweet talk her into believing she does. That's where I need you all to stay out my way."

"So your plan is to seduce her into believing you love her?"

"Yes, if I must." Ashton replied lazily. He knew he was lying to Dawn and to himself.

"Supposed she go all felo-de-se on you when she finds out you don't love her? I've seen them go nuts before." Dawn asked giggling at the thought. Maybe he can demise Miss Pain-the-Ass whereas she failed.

He shrugged his shoulders."Christians don't commit suicide, she might be heartbroken for a while but she will get over it."

But Dawn cautions. "That's a bad idea, those church women don't believe in birth control nor abortions. At least the ones I know don't. Suppose you knock her up and then what will you do?" Dawn lectured on precaution. "They expect men to marry their holier-than-thou ass if they get knocked up."

Ashton laughed at Dawn's precautionary advice. The last time women expected that was over 400 years ago. "I'm sure she isn't living in the stone age. Plus, she already has one child. From the look of things she's barely taking care of that one so seriously I doubt she'll be eager to have another. But if that happened as you're warning me---I'll just send her money to take care of the child. She doesn't have to know who I really am." Dawn snugged under his arm and sighed, although, she doesn't think it will turn out the way he believes. Caroline said James wrote the woman love letters and bought her expensive jewelry.

To test his true feelings, for she believes he's lying,. "Are you going to leave that wizard alone about her?" His luculent eyes darkened. Seems as thus lately his mood changes quicker than usual.

"What is it to you if I don't? He has already killed her." Ashton said, ill-natured and crude. "I'm on him because he took away from this world something I need. I've very ancient wounds which need healing."

Dawn sat up quickly off his chest and reminds him. "She's dead!" She's forgetting to hide the excitement in her face and voice. He nods but doesn't reveal he knows Ana is alive and doesn't want him and he's doing his best to forget that fact.

"Yes, Nikola firebombed the house killing everyone inside; her kind come into this world maybe once every 400-500 years. Now do you understand why I'm so pissed off and why I want to kill him?"

Hugging him in exhilaration she says, "I'm sure there will be another one in the future." In reality she feels like singing "Ding-dong, the bitch is dead." She leapt up and said she was ending the party and calling all the girls in the room. "We're having our own private party!" She vowed, prancing out the room.

Dawn kicks every one out except the nonresidential harems members. She tells the harem their troubles are over. Nikola killed that witch for defiance. All walk toward the room Dawn left Ashton in carrying champagne and caviar. But they're surprised he's gone.

"I thought you said the bitch was dead? Then where's he?" Delores asked. Dawn looked around and saw Ashton was gone. There would be no celebration orgy."He was lying on the bed a few minutes ago!" Dawn cried.

"He lied", Deila said "That witch or bitch or whichever one she is ain't dead. He lied to make you stop badgering him." Several of the 55 others agreed.

Believing Cargill is taking them all for a ride, Delores speaks up, "I say we send an assassin after her ass for trying to fuck up our good thing." Again several others agreed. "I mean, if she's powerful as Carole says she's going to hex him into marrying her and he'll throw all of us out of his life. Then we can kiss this grand lifestyle good-bye." Delores preached waving her shapely arms to emphasize her point. "Sure he might give us the 10 million each but if she has her claws in him deep enough we might not get that."

Suzie nervously implores, "Suppose he finds out about the kill-for-hire plot?"

Dawn winces internally, knowing she already tried to kill Ana but failed and the memory of the lighting bolt and its heat was still fresh in her psyche.

"Then what do you suggest?", Dawn asked with her hands on her hips impatiently tapping her foot. "We all sit around and wait until he marries the bitch and she kicks us out on our asses?"

"Does anyone know any assassins?" Sapphire asked.

"No, but with 10 million it won't be hard to find someone willing to do it. People have killed for a whole lot less."

Making up her mind to try again, Dawn said, "Let me call Carole, she probably knows somebody." The others listens as the phone call dials through. A very high or sleepy Carole Caldwell answers. Carole told them about the injuries she suffered because of that woman.

Frankly, Dawn didn't give a shit about her lamentations. She was still alive. "The last person I sent to you is dead. No, I don't know anyone else!" Caroline lied and rambled on about her injuries at the hands of Nikola. She was suffering a splitting headache.

Everyone gasped almost in unison when they saw him in their far peripheral vision and realized he was still there all along but cloaked. He was sitting listening to their plans.

He walked in the center and took a seat on the ancient ottoman from the days when he lived as a sheik. Stared at all of them hard and cold. He didn't like their plotting to eliminate a person who could possibly help heal his wounds.

"Ladies, I never lied to any of you about the kind of arrangement this was. I never promised any of you marriage nor you'd live with me the rest of your life. The only accomplished lie is that which goes unseen and unspoken. So, if I cared enough not to lie to you then consider yourselves lucky. My personal life is none of any of you all's business. Don't get so comfortable with me in basic cognitive process that I won't hurt you because I haven't. Now HANG UP THAT FUCKING PHONE! I swear if any of take out a hit on that woman, I'll hurt you really bad. No, I promise you I'll kill you. How dare you all insert yourselves into my personal life like that?! Years ago I would've simply killed you and that would've solved my problems. But here I'm trying to be a nice guy for once and you all are taking the advantage of it."

He stopped ranting and chuckled a really nasty laughter, bearing his teeth in a ferine manner when he read Dawn's mind calling him a manwhore.

"Well, you knew that when you agreed to live under my terms." He responded to her name calling. "I never lied and said I was anything else."

Dawn thinks, for she knows he can read minds, "You're a chauvinist pig and an asshole, too."

He stops again and stares at her. "That's enough with the name calling, Dawn. I haven't called you the whore that you are so let's be mature here." He said abrasively. Dawn tilted her head upward and angrily wiped away a tear. "The rest of you are excused", he said motioning his finger to open the door and closing the door behind them. Then he turns to face Dawn whose face is damp with tears of anger.

"Dawn, I think over the years your feelings have grown into more than a business contract I think you *believe* you're in love with me. But I don't think you are__I know you're in love with this lifestyle not me. You haven't a clue what it would take to love me."

Dawn angrily wiped the tears away and yelled "Has it taken twenty-five years to see I was in love with you? If it did you haven't learned a damn thing in your long life." He sits her on his lap and wipes away her tears. The next move puzzled them both. He rose and sit her in his seat. "Dawn, I noticed it long ago and thought you'd have given up on that notion by now but I see you haven't. I'm not capable of giving you the love you want from me. I care about you- if that's love, then I guess I do love you in a way but I'm not in love with you." He said softly. "Can you understand the difference?"

The agony of seeing the life she has lived slip away before her eyes swept through her. "Unlike you, I've feelings. I can't live with someone for years and not give a damn about them like you can."

He kneel in front of her and gently tilted her chin to look at him. "The way you feels right now is why I don't allow myself to love. Mortals don't live very long and most immortals are bitches and bastards so to keep from feeling this way time and time again, I've kept my feelings to myself. It's safer that way. I hope when you leave here you find a mortal man who can give you the love you obsequiously need.", he says extending his hand to help her to stand.

"So you throwing me out?" She asked sourly, crossing her arms and firmly planting her bottom in the chair as if saying she refuses to go.

"No, but if you can't handle this anymore it's in your best interest to leave."

She folds her arms tighter and stubbornly across her ample breasts and tells him he isn't getting rid of her that easily.

He tells her to send the other girls back to their respective residences and quit plotting against him. That he has no estimation of the whereabouts of this woman nor if she is even alive. She nods she'll carry out his instructions but she likewise noticed he has changed into the black leathery outfit and excogitates why. She knows wherever he's going, it have something to do with this Ana Wyett.

∽◦◦◦∼

Nothing seems to be going right for Lola Wilson, it has been five years since she did as Shrevenport ordered but one relationship after another has fallen to pieces. She heard Thad was out of prison. She called him but he hung up on her again and again. Old friends shun her. Her own children are behaving strange. None of past four husbands are alive. She killed them all for Shrevenport, the head of the satanic order in her native area.

She heard through unreliable sources that Thad Wyett had a wind-fall of millions. That's why she is in Boston. Thad once cared deeply for her. She knows he did. She watched the site; he's building a new home. He's as handsome as ever. She knows the only thing saved his life was he refused to divorce Ana and marry her. So had he died all the money on his life would've gone to Ana. Shrevenport didn't see that as productive.

There was a thick built woman out there with a small child on her hip. So what if she's his whatever. Ana didn't defer her with all her finery then neither would this ghetto fab woman. This isn't a fantasy or romance empty headed movie chip; this is real life and in reality it's everyone for themselves. Wait a minute? She sees a dark outline around the woman. Meaning only one thing. She's into the occult. Haven't Thad gotten enough of the darkside?

She onerously got out the rented hovercar and sashayed in her best walk to the couple. Thad was startled to see her. He recovered rather quickly and stepped between her and the woman.

"Lola." He said angrily. "I told you to leave me the hell alone!"

"Thad! She's a witch! Get away from her." She said, pointing an accusatory finger at the young woman. He looked back at the woman holding his son and snidely asked, "It would take one to know one, wouldn't it?"

The woman smirked around him at her. Oh, she knew how to slap that smirk off her face with a single strike. She knew who he really loved. And it wasn't this woman.

"Smirk all you like. But the day Ana comes back that smirk will turn to tears. He'll drop you like a hot potato." Now it was Lola's turn to smirk when she saw the woman had heard of Ana and how much Thad loved her. Turning to appease the woman he said. "I told you I divorced her. I gave her up long ago."

"Yeah, sugar--he told me the same thing. But it never happened. I don't care what he says. She left him. He didn't leave her and will take her back. So if I were you I wouldn't get too comfortable in that house because Ana and Bea is coming back to throw you out."

The woman looked questioningly at Thad and asked. "Who is Bea?"

Lola didn't give Thad the opportunity to reply. "Oh, that's his beloved daughter. The *real* apple of his eye." The slap came so hard and suddenly it staggered her before she fell back on her ass.

"Keep my wife and daughter names out of your damn mouth!" He growled. He was so angry his dreds looked mad. Blood seeped down the corner of her mouth but it was worth it to see this ghetto fab bitch twist away with that baby on her hip. He ran after her but she kept yanking her arm out of his grasp, all the while cussing him out. Ah, so that was the button to push with him. She knew it! She knew it! But she took this opportunity to run to her car for she knew he was coming for her next; which he did but she was a mile in the air watching him from above run for his car to catch her. Knowing he'd follow she led him to her hotel room in Boston. "He's now a free man and open game." Lola thinks as she watched in her sensor viewer his hovercraft lift off the ground to chase her.

❧

She was born forty two years ago as Lolana DeWitt, in the Delta Bayou of a poor but loving, die-in-the-wool Christian family. Which is how she knew so well how a woman like Ana BuFaye mind worked. She was raised by such a woman. Her father was a shrimp farmer to a major seafood company. Her mother, a fancy New Orleans restaurant maître d'. Every year the glam of Madras Gras further stirred the impressible, unbridled imagination of the young Lola. Harvesting a yearning and longing for riches out of her reach. Being the eldest of seven children, often the burden of the six sibling's upbringing fell to her.

A honey toned girl of sixteen, with flowing tresses of golden-auburn hair, a genuine Creole beaute, one of exceptional attractiveness, her charm never failed to escape the notice of many patrons of her mother's place of employment. Little did the DeWitt family know they were in the presence of pure, unadulterated evil. Being a God-fearing clan, they were the DeGaults' supernatural enemy.

Jon Cherver, the Northeast USA regional leader of the most powerful ancient occult, often bestowed his presence on his servant Jeanque DeGault's famous restaurant. The

DeGault family have been servants to this ancient cult from time immemorable.

"Who is that honey toned beauty?" Jon Cherver asked DeGault.

Following his superior's eyes. "Oh. That's Lola. Mildred's daughter." He said disinterested pointing to his loyal maître d. His place catered only to the rich and famous. It wasn't for the regular New Orleans partygoers. Just then the pearly laughter of a woman twinkled in the restaurant's elegant atmosphere, the men looked around to see who possessed such an enticing laughter? They spotted Ashton Cargill with her. Another great beauty. "What's he doing here?" DeGault asked, frowning.

Reaching for his glass of water to hide his nervousness. "Probably hiding from some of his women. He has a whole harem of them." Jon Cherver said. He noticed Shrevenport wasn't nervous sitting within striking distance of Ashton Cargill.

"I want her," Shrevenport flatly declared. Cherver believed him to be referring to the woman at Cargill's table and being a warlock of equal rank Cherver could ask him had he lost his mind?

'Why isn't he at his own place?" DeGault whined. "I know, he knows he doesn't serve authentic Louisianian food and is here scouting. They serve that stellar high morsel from France. There's a big difference between American, Creole French cooking than what's served on Rue Saint Roch in Paris!" Cherver cast him a glance to silence his nervous rambling.

Shrevenport frowned. "No, I'm not talking about Cargill's woman. I'm talking about the pretty girl, there. She can be a great asset to us. Start her out now there's fifty good year or more to get out of her. She's pretty and endearing. Marry her off to some millionaire buffoon and collect the fool's money." Shrevenport reasoned his evil plan aloud.

DeGault looked at Cherver for defense. He knew it was Mildred who brought in all the famous blacks, if she was gone they'd cease to visit. Cherver urged him to comply. "Her, you shall have" vowed DeGault dishearteningly.

"Invite her to my table"

The elegantly dressed DeGault strode across the massive dinning hall and carried on a short but private conversation with Lola who peeked questioningly at the man in the Armani suit DeGault was referring to and shakes her head saying. "Mom and Dad would never allow me to date someone that old."

His voice lowered into a gruff voice Lola had never heard Mr. DeGault employ, he says "Lola, you don't say no to a man like that. That man has more power than your backwater parents have ever seen. If you don't grace his table, who knows what he'll do to them. May I remind you, remember..you've a house filled of siblings to think about too."

She knew a threat when she heard one. She'd been around this place long enough to know many inscrutable characters passed through its doors. Fearfully, she takes a deep breath and another peek around DeGault at man and begin nervously entwining her fingers. The stranger is watching her if she were a prime Kobe steak not a girl.

"I don't know...Mr. DeGault. That man gives me the creeps." Lola whispers. He roughly grabbed her upper arm and stealthy squeezed it hard enough to hurt. He knew Cherver wasn't going to protect him from Shrevenport if the local head warlock whom he had always boasted he didn't have to obey decided to hurt him. He heard from others that Shrevenport was a real nasty piece of slumdog's shit. He intend to escort her over there if he had to physically carry her. Mildred stepped in their path and demand's to know what is going on?

"Nothing" cooed DeGault. "A long time customer wanted a closer look at Lola. He thinks she is model material."

Hearing the urgent voice of a dead woman, warning of her husband, Mildred's employer. DeGault's deceased wife speaking ambient in her mind saying, "*Mildred..you mind that girl around Jeanque. He likes them young and so does many of his porn-freak bastard friends.*"

Mildred snatched a bewildered Lola from her employer, placing her behind her back and even psychologically bracing to be fired on the spot, she says "Sorry Mr. DeGault, we aren't interested in parading our children around in front of strangers. Lola ain't gonna be nobody's model."

"Ah! C'mon Mildred." DeGault said jovially. "It can't hurt to at least talk to the man. See what he have to say!"

Pushing pass DeGault with Lola in tow, Mildred retorted "I've nothing to say to your friend."

Aware that Shrevenport is threateningly watching DeGault returns the gaze, shrugging his shoulders in defeat. Shrevenport eyes begin to glow red as if he'd been swimming in a too strong-cholrine sauteed pool for too long. DeGault knew the meaning. Otherworldly, unseen, menacing shadows slink from under the elegant, Swiss tat lace tablecloth and grabs the ankles of Mildred Dewitt, sending her sailing, headlong into the eloquent array of steaming, exotic foods and heirloom silverware. Creating an unbecoming noisy bedlam and distraction.

Warren Shrevenport grumbles, "If you want something done. You best to do it yourself." Masterfully strolling across the room, ignoring DeGault's pleading eyes, directs a demon to choke his associate's servant unconscious.

He smoothly approaches the hysterical Lola, guiding her out the path of the waiters frantically attending to her mother and their boss, summoning an ambulance. Making Mildred as comfortable as they can until medical help arrive. He expected no interference from Cargill and got none. He didn't meddle in human affairs. DeGault's incoherence and the girl's refusal had peeved him off. He was being as nice as he gets. Cherver was too lenient with his people.

He gently lowering the sobbing woman-child into the antiqued red-velvet chair opposite himself. Cherver has a shark's voice and knew how to use it to intimidate, seduce or even throw one in a trance deep enough to cause them to commit suicide if

309

that was his muse at the moment. He was seductive enough to enchant a starving, homeless man into giving away his donated meal. It's a voice Lola grows to love and to hate, years later.

Cherver handed her a fine linen napkin from a scrolled engraved silver napkin holder to dry her tears. Called his chauffeur and limo to ferry them to the local hospital behind the ambulance. All the while, saying."Your mom will be fine, dear. Shhhh..hush, hush, you'll see. It's just a minor occupational accident."

The blood spurting from Mildred's head wound looked worse than it actually was. Head wounds always do. The doctor wanted to keep her overnight for observation but Mildred protested, not knowing the whereabouts of her beautiful daughter, attempted to rise, only to be pushed back into the bed and told to rest.

Shrevenport had instructed that Mildred DeWitt be kept overnight, to allow him abundant time to sink his claws to her daughter's young psyche.

Driving to the hidden-unknown location outside of northern New Orleans, Louisiana, Shrevenport offers Lola champagne to put his plan in motion. Receiving the exact response expected, he phones ahead to tell the servant to prepare a room for a girl. They antecedently knows the preparations to make. This isn't the first girl or boy their superior has stolen and they know she won't be the last.

They arrived in a room of more sophistication and luxury than young Lolana had ever seen in person. Everything a poor girl from the backwaters Bayous could possible dream of owning was littering her appointed guestroom. Lola gasped, unbelieving her eyes. She was too distressed to even think of enjoying what was laid before her. She had no idea what was going on with her mother. Looking out over the dark terrain, a chilly shiver travels up her spine. To her, the artistically trimmed hedges looked like monsters in the dark. Realizing she may have landed in a situation too mature for her to handle, she started stepping away and questioning her seemingly knight-in-a-shining-armor. Who seemed determined to save her from old red-glowing-eyes standing in the doorway. She knew perfectly well what he wanted.

"Why?", she surly throws up the question like a reinforced stone wall.

"What do mean, dear?" Cherver smoothly asked. Alluring her into his trap. Shrevenport's right. She has style, taste, and glam. Too elegant to throw in a whorehouse. She's Paris, Park or Fifth Ave material. A diamond in the rough. All she needs is a little polishing and she's good to go.

"Why are you being so nice to me? Mama warned me about men like you."

Softly pulling her into a gentle embrace he placidly says "Your mother was right to warn you about men who will do anything to befriend and use a beautiful girl like yourself. But I am not such a man. I simply saw you and appreciated your beauty; I own a modeling agency and am always on the look-out for new talent. I dearly regret the misfortunate event that occurred in the timeline of my visit to the DeGault's establishment. I do my best to help anyone in need. That's my nature. And about the designer attire..if you accept my contract, these items will be yours to keep."

"Ok, but do you kidnap all models you want to work with?", she nervously asked, gnawing her lower lip. He prompted her to stop that, saying it will lessen her chances of finding work.

"But I must visit my mom in the morning." Cherver agreed they shall visit her mother first thing in the morning.

Lola wasn't stupid she knew these men were both evil but DeGault said they'd harm her family if she resisted them. She had heard of men having strange boating accidents in her father's line of work and now wonder if men such as these were behind the accidents? For she was positive she saw a decaying, fleshless skeletal hand trip her mom.

At the mention of her mother, a dark, evil shadow of pitch darkness crossed Shrevenport's brow and dissipated quicker than Lola could believe she witnessed it. His rummy eyes continued to inspect her over the heavy crystal tumbler of imported cognac. His churning mind at work, he was undressing her with those evil, odd reddish golden eyes.

"Sure, sure...we must always attend to Mom. We shall do that immediately after breakfast. " Cherver lied. This other man was proving to be a complete durpee.

Lounging in a silk smoking jacket in his Edwardian quarter of the mansion. Shrevenport reasons "The mother will prove to be a problem. Lola is too attached to her. But I can remedy that with drugs if I instruct a higher dose than usual to be administered. The girl will become brainsick and fall apart with worry, becoming useless to me. It's better your way. We need to put her in some rich dude's house quick. Orman's demands and expenses are bleeding me dry, killing us. He's trying to appease his fagboy."

Snapping his finger, a manservant appears. Ajar, a tall cafe au-lait hued man. Shrevenport's personal aide steps to his side. Shrevenport likes to run this place much as it's said his ancestors ran the place, as plantation it once was.

"Tell the hospital to induce a coma." The white suited man bows slightly and says in crisp, clear Queen's English. "As you wish, sir."

Cherver angrily wonders why in the hell are these black people here? Being a Northerner, and his people died to free them, and they voluntarily going back into this shit. But then again when in the occults you've to do as your regional leader says or else. No matter how sick or degrading it may be. That's the part they withhold during recruitment. And this man is obsessed with the ways of the old south. He wouldn't be surprised if he saw hoop-skirts flaunting around here.

Getting ready for bed. Shrevenport smiles and congratulates himself at his accomplishment. Another secret weapon against the male warriors and warrior saints.

Lola never arrived at the hospital, instead she is mastermindedly persuaded to board a Lear jet headed to a private airport in New York with the reasoning that her mother is in a coma and her father would never let her leave if she returns home or visits the hospital. It's like the thoughts and ideas are her own but again they aren't. Laying out a plan of her

312

providing hospice care her mother is sure to need in the near future. Cherver doesn't authorize it because he has grown a heart. He does it so the distress and worry about Mildred DeWitt doesn't break his hold on her daughter. Nothing can break a spell like love and concern for a loved one.

A sore and bruised Lolana looks behind at the dry dusty field as she boards the jet leaving all she have ever known and loved behind to begin her years of valuable service to Jon Cherver. But not before being deflowered by Shrevenport. He felt she was his prize so it was his privilege. To protest Cherver would be cruising for a bruising battle with another warlock on his home turf surrounded by his followers. He knew that was suicidal. They'd all defend Shrevenport and then his people would arrive and they'd battle it out in a battle of wizard chess which Orman Vonderbilt would get wind of and come kill everyone involved. He has seen what Vonderbilt does to the disparaged warlocks for fighting among themselves.

Paul Dewitt returns home from a shrimping expedition and find his house in shambles. Paul Jr. struggling to keep his siblings in line and in school. Dodging the children protection service by lying to the elderly neighbor Mrs. Harlow who keeps inquiring of his mother and older sister. Eying him suspiciously as though she knows he's lying. Mildred nor Lola would leave those kids for a week unattended.

A distraught, nerve wrecked Paul DeWitt Sr. questioned each of his remaining children. Sternly asking how long have they been alone? For Mrs. Harlow, the next door neighbor summoned him to her porch and told him before entering his house. She haven't seen Mildred nor Lola for a week. They've been missing since the last day of Mardi Gras. He visited the local hospital and find his wife in a coma. But doesn't find his daughter. He goes to the local police department but they're useless in helping him; saying kids run away to big cities every year with a visitor to the city. But he knew Lolana wasn't the type to run away.

Mildred's sister, Lolana's aunt, had an idea where she might be but knew no one crossed Shrevenport and lived. Her date and all the other restaurant patrons acted as if they didn't see or care that this man was leading her niece outside. Oh well, the place was in a festival mood. They probably thought she was leaving willingly with him.

313

Seeing Shrevenport maneuver her niece through the place she left Cargill's table and tried to follow but two men pulled a gun on her warning her if she knew what was best she'd go back inside and forget what she saw. In the rudimentary feasting mood of the early dusk she saw Lolana's scared eyes looking back at her. She saw him shove her niece in the back of the black hoverlimo and rose in the air. No one even noticed the men holding a gun on her. That's the kind of city this was this time of the year.

∾✺ၜ✺∾

Flustered and scared she reentered the place to find another woman in her seat. Her date didn't follow her to the hospital when she walked out with her sister stretched out on a gurney. Not that she expected him to but she at least expected some sympathy. She heard he wasn't quite human but she wondered was he made of black-hearted ice?

She and Paul met up at the hospital, the sight of his wretched soul pulled her heart in so many directions. She desperately wanted to tell him where she believed his daughter was but she knew that would invite death to the entire family, children and infants included. She was once one of Shrevenport's girls. He let her go past age thirty when he couldn't get a hot price for her anymore. Mildred and Paul will just have to deal with it. She did. But she went to him on her own free will. Lolana didn't. One year while working the Mardi Gras scene for him he did something to her mind, she could hear him.

While plumping her comatose sister's pillow she heard him and froze. "Haven't I've been good to you." he asked in her head in his heavy Louisianian accent. "If you want me to keep on being good to you and your folks you better not push Cargill up to come here fucking with me. Long as the dumb girl do as I say she'll be fine. Y'all wasn't gonna do nothing but waste all this beauty on some hick boy and a bunch of hollering babies."

Knowing she could hear things, spiritual things, like his wife Mildred, Paul Dewitt asked what the matter?

"Nothing." She lied.

314

If Lolana is in New York with that clan, perhaps its for the best. At least it's better than remaining here being rented out to high rolling freaks. Who horde all kinds of sick fetishes. Paul would only get himself killed going up against Shreveport. Who would wipe out the entire clans; even those who moved away would be in danger because she've seen how their networks operate. It expands far and reaches wide. Unlike churches who are separated and laden down with pettiness. These satanic bastards stick together and help each without judgment. So yes, he'd easily ask his buddies to kill their relatives outside the immediate area. The others never ask why another want someone dead. They simply do it. They'd probably have a fucking decathlon. To see who can kill the most of the two families; the DeWitts and the LaSalles? So how she sees it, beauty is a bigger curse than plain women realize. There's always a freak who want you but ain't willing to treat you right.

Remembering her own days of working for Shrevenport. Remembering when she used to work the holiday month as Shrevenport called Mardi Gras. It was living hell on earth. He set his people out male and females to bring in as much as possible during the festival. If anyone failed, it meant a severe beating or death. She still cries for the girl brought from somewhere a pervert paid good money to choke to death while screwing her just to see what it felt like to have someone's life in your hands. The males didn't fare much better under Shrevneport's rule. So many needed anus surgery after the holiday was over and often times died if the evil bastard decided that particular guy wasn't worth keeping alive. Kidnapping was how they kept attractive, fresh supplies for the tourists. She used to try to signal people something was very wrong with their set up but the so-called, uptight, conservative assholes merely looked the other way and allowed Sheboygan, Shrevenport's main driver, to treat them all like animals. That's how she met Ashton Cargill, she and two other girls were sent to his hotel room. At least he wasn't a freak who wanted to beat or cut you to get off. He gave them nice things and lots of money but evil ass Sheboygan found out they had these things, accusing them of taking them as a way to get out of New Orleans. Cargill told Shrevenport he better not ever see any more bruises on her is how she got taken to a better position. She decides, yes, it's best her niece is gone from this place. She hope the one from New York was better. She heard he was.

Chapter 7
Ana and the Saints of Ages past.

It had been two weeks since the bombing. Mother Harris was painfully coming around. Everyone knew they would have to let her grieve at her own pace and that they did. Everyone else from the outside had been taken to a refugee part of the cave and given a permanent home. Ana was the only new arrival still daily sitting at the table they came in near, close to the door covering the mouth of the cave. She didn't like the closed in space.

Bright and early one morning the Saints asked her to follow them immediately upon arriving for the breakfast the nuns she couldn't quite figure out had loving prepared for her. They spoke with the urgency of now! So she left the plate she really wanted and followed.

"Ana, you're being charged to command the greatest fighting forces on earth. The warrior saints and warriors of the Nazarene." St. Anne said. "I called you here to begin teaching you all I can and am allowed about what you need to know. So you can teach and lead others." St. Anne literates walking back and fro in front of her. Making her wondering what happened since yesterday evening and this morning?

"Every religion in the world talks of spirits, devils, and evil entities. I'm sure you've already encountered what many say isn't real; the western world is supposed to be the most advanced in the world. For in most of the western world the etheric or spirit world isn't real, to some it doesn't even exist in any reality, so they think! But they're all WRONG! It's real and all things come first from the invisible then transmute through into this visible world of solid matter. Not believing they're real is how they've wrecked havoc on the world for so long".

"There's a universal law no one cannot escape, we're all part of it, start to understand it and become aware of it and its effect upon the body, only then will you be able to conceive the effect other dimensions are having on man in and around us on a daily basis. There're far too many inaccurate definitions floating around as to what a warrior saint or warrior of the Nazarene is. Too many conjure the image of a wild-eyed zealot who is out to bomb, kill, and maim anyone who disagrees with him or her. Yes, we kill if we must but that isn't our first notion. Our job is to protect mankind from the darkside. We're those who stand guard against the darkside while the other saints do their jobs, whatever it maybe."

She pauses a few minutes to see does Ana understands. She sees understanding and eagerness to learn in those dark amber eyes so she continues. "Just as every nation has a physical army, they must have a spiritual one as well. What's physical can not see nor fight that which is spiritual. You're going to receive a lot of ridicule and rebuttal from the world because of *who* it belongs to. Some are going to say you are trying to force "religion" on them even thus you're trying to save their life."

St. Anne pauses again, her heart aches for this wide-eyed child whose life has pretty much been cursed. Whose head is asked to wear such a heavy crown. "Some who know of us view us as too harsh. Nor are we the people who have gone to other cultures, societies, and nations and looted and plundered their way to great wealth in the Name of Jesus Christ. These were simply thieves using the Gospel for their own gain. A true warrior or warrior saint goes and teaches the Gospel; if the people accept, they gladly welcome them into the Family, but if they rejects it, you move on. That is the satanic version of what we are. In reality that is not what we are and has never been. Jesus gave the apostle most like us the authority to spearhead the Gospel into the world.

"And which Apostle was most like us?" Ana asked.

"Saint Peter, he was given the key to the kingdom." Saint Ann replied. "Had he been as the world has painted us, he would've confronted Caesar and killed him the entire Roman army and *not been* crucified."

"Why are we being gathered now?" Ana inquired inquisitively.

"The spirit veil separating the physical from the spiritual is being torn down by the evils of the world and the actions of the darkside. When the going gets rough, God has always called up His Warrior Saints. We're the earthly extension of the heavenly army. The first of our kind was Jared, the father of the 1ˢᵗ Enoch and the son of Mahalaleel. We're the guys who beat hell back so the others can do the goodwill."

"I read Genesis before coming here. There are two Enoch listed. What's up with that?" Ana asked flipping over her bible.

"One is the son of Cain and the other the son of Seth. The first Enoch had a city in Nod named for him. The second Enoch is the ancestor of Noah." St. Ann answered.

"Since you're familiar with the Bible, I'll start you out with the basic first. Turn to Genesis 6:1-6." She read aloud. Genesis 6:1-6 New King James Version (NKJV) Now it came to pass, when men began to multiply on the face of the earth, and daughters were born to them, 2) that the sons of God saw the daughters of men, that they *were* beautiful; and they took wives for themselves of all whom they chose. 3)And the LORD said, "My Spirit shall not strive with man forever, for he *is* indeed flesh; yet his days shall be one hundred and twenty years." 4) There were giants on the earth in those days, and also afterward, when the sons of God came in to the daughters of men and they bore *children* to them. Those *were* the mighty men who *were* of old, men of renown." St. Anne stopped and asked had she heard of the ancient men of renown. Ana nods, she had. St. Anne continued. "5) Then the LORD saw that the wickedness of man *was* great in the earth, and *that* every intent of the thoughts of his heart *was* only evil continually. 6) And the LORD was sorry that He had made man on the earth, and He was grieved in His heart."

She closed the book and looked at me, saying they still exist. Those mentioned here, still walks the earth. Saying she once met one who was half snake. All aren't giants as the Bible say. There're so many different variations of them that it's impossible to know them all. "These descendants of mankind and the fallen sons and daughters of God were called Nephilim. They're half mortal and half immortal. These Nephilims, were the ancient men and women of renown. These people once walked the earth. Their actions are remembered through myths and legends."

"What happened to them?" Ana asked, amazed at what she thought were mere folklores actually had truth to them. But she also sensed this was the woman's way of telling her she knew about Bea.

"The generation mentioned in these verses were destroyed by the Great Flood. Their immortal parents tried to save them by dipping them into the spiritual realm Jordan River or by trying to take them into the heavenly realm both body and soul. But there were many born afterward as it plainly says here."

"Are they even human?" Ana asked not sure if she wanted to know the answer. This was hitting too close to home.

"Some are and some are not. Some are part animals. I'm sure you have heard of many lores where existed a half animal creatures whom the local served such as Pan?"

"Yes."

"Well some are half dog, cats, crocodiles, squirrels. and just about every animal to have ever existed, some are even half insects and worms."

"Eeeww! That's disgusting!" Ana proclaimed swallowing back the bile rising in her throat. "No wonder God destroyed them...who would create a half-human and half-worm?"

"The fallen sons and daughters of God did so and did so for millenniums. Their offspring terrorized the descendants of Adam and Eve for centuries. By correct definition some had to chose between which parents they'd ally with if one parent was human and the other a fallen spiritual being. Of course some chose to dwell among the gods but a few did not."

"Are they all evil?"

"Most of them are, but you may meet a few who aren't."

"Are you telling me these things still exist?" Ana asked in shock.

"Yes. And I think you know why we need to discuss this subject. They're back plenteously again as they were in pre-Noahian days."

Yea, I knew why but I wasn't admitting it. So I moved on to the next question. "How will I know one if I meet one?"

"Allow your spiritual sensory to scan their nature just as you'd anyone else. Listen to your gift, you can pick up on their origin. Test them as you'd a spirit. If they refuse to confess Jesus is the Christ and Lord of all, then arm yourself and do so quickly. Do not trust them. I've a deep ominous feeling you've already encountered one or two but was unaware of their origin. Some call them aliens, some call them spirit guides, some call themselves demons. But they aren't any of these things."

Believing the girl to be a child of Azazael and seeing that Ana already knew what her daughter is Saint Anne moved on and further instructed "I am quoting from work not of a Christian source but nonetheless effective in spiritual warfare; the words of ancient Chinese military general; Sun TZU *The Art of War*:"

"*Sun Tzu- Therefore I say: Know your enemy and know yourself and you fight a hundred battles without peril. If you are ignorant of the enemy and know only yourself, you will stand equal chances of winning and losing. If you know neither the enemy nor yourself, you are bound to be defeated in every battle.*"

"Why do we need to know them and their warmongerous ways? We already know they're evil. Isn't that book talking about killing people?" Ana grasped, skeptical that a saint in a white robe is quoting from "The Art of War"!

Seeing Ana's shock she knew such literature. Saint Anne smiled a sweet, placid smile. "Yes, its talking about war, defeating your enemies. The enemies know the Church far better than the Church knows them. Our job is to guard the Church along side our appointed angelic comrades and we can't do our job if we don't know ourselves nor the enemy or what we're supposed to be guarding. We didn't start this war. It was started

320

before Adam drew his first breath, but by the Sword of the Lord of Hosts we'll finish it! At Pentecost we were given abilities we didn't posses before. The Prophet Joel foretold of these abilities years before the birth and death of Christ. Through the way of the Cross we were empowered against an unseen enemy. It's our responsibility to use what God gave us to protect ourselves. And if killing them is how the battle ends.... Sadly it must be done. As in any war; it's kill or be killed."

Ana was not really enjoying all this talk about killing. This woman white,glowing eyes felt as thus she was looking through her, into her core, seeing her dirt. "I was taught to hold your peace and let God fight your battles." Ana quipped.

"He fights battles we can not fight." The saint recounted. "But those He has given us the power to fight, He doesn't fight those for you. We're a part of hundreds of millions of our kind. We're mentioned in "The Book of Jude" verse 1:14-15: *"14) And Enoch also, the seventh from Adam, prophesied of these, saying, Behold, the Lord cometh with ten thousands of his saints, 15) To execute judgment upon all, and to convince all that are ungodly among them of all their ungodly deeds which they have ungodly committed, and of all their hard speeches which ungodly sinners have spoken against him."*

There're as many different types of saints as there are people. But as I said our kind have existed since the fall in Eden. We're mentioned through out the bible and many other works such as "The Book of Enoch," and " The Book of Joel" Biblical figures such Joshua, Ehud, Judge Deborah, Gideon, David, and the mighty men of David were all warrior saints.

"What about Moses?"

"He was a prayer warrior."

Cocking her head to the side, Ana asked what's the difference?

"A prayer warrior works strictly through prayer. Many often work alongside the army with prayers of encouragement and beseeching of blessings. A warrior saint works through prayer too but have the authority and means to fight if they must. In our hands the Words become a supernatural weapon. A sword in most cases. Most battles are fought on spiritual planes but the outcome have a great impact on life on earth. They can wreck havoc on earth if they breach a portal or open a vortex. The darkside counterattacks in the physical world because they're no match for us in the spiritual world. Their methods of attacks on us are numerous. I know you've already experienced many of their modes of attacks. They use the governments of the world to shield their evil deeds and legalize their atrocious. Their brand of criminal and immoral actions have the local, state, national and international seal of approval." Saint Anne said, staring me hard in the eyes, making sure I understood I can expect no help from anywhere but someone Heaven sent or Heaven Itself before continuing, "Our weapons are the Word made into a reality. Our shield materializes by faith." She said, materializing hers. I noticed her uniform was different than my own. Mine's looked akin to a gladiator's uniform while hers' was bedecked with three rows of stones, four stones in each row. She worn a long tunic under a golden breastplate, her sword was bejeweled as well. She explained she started out like me. The stones represents the walls of heaven.

"I know Eugenia has been practicing with you so get up and show me what you know. Throw your blade."

I looked at her and wondered. "Throw it where?"

Reading my surface thought, she shows me how to throw it. She kept her arm extended and It came roaring back into her hand so fast I didn't see it coming. "It harms nothing that means you no harm."

At her urging I copied her and when mine returned to me, it came in so hard and fast it flipped me backwards out the chair and stood suspended, floating in the air. "Take it." She instructed. Well, this was getting better than my running from it.

For the next seven days, different saints taught me different things. They were cramming me like a student studying for a final exam. The actually combat reenactions were still mainly taught by St. Anne. I was getting tired of getting my behind kicked. I tried matching her every move in hand to hand combat but still got my ass kicked. With every error she duly reminded me a devil won't give me a second chance. I learned her ankle length tunic was deadly as sharp razor blades, she had blades and dagger tucked everywhere. She showed me to run through higher level of the 8th Day so the darkside can't reach in and pull you out. She showed me how to use Glory to my defense. She showed me to properly command them in the Name of Christ.

I had started to feel as thus I was at a combatant church service. But I liked her. No matter what we talked about she was never judgmental and I told her things I never told my own mother. Now, I understood why Mother Harris loved and missed her so much.

Over the weeks my training continued. The others were encouraging me to tap into the inherent knowledge already within. I lost my head at least ten times every day. Mother Harris said Saint Anne was hard but firm, hard doesn't describe this woman.

Ana and the numerous saints pored over many volumes unfamiliar to her. The aged leather binded tomes had been out of circulation for centuries and many were uncanonized. Ana didn't notice she had been indoors for a week. But yet she didn't feel the pangs of hunger nor the dryness of thirst nor the constant worry about Bea. She did inquire of the saints were they heavenly or earthly residents. They never revealed their habitation so she resolved to quit asking. Wisdom poured in her spirit and mind as water into a vessel. Her abilities became keener, her insight was sharper, even the ability to feel for sounds one can not hear was developed. They taught her to see better with her spiritual eyes and hear with spiritual ears. Taught her how to separate her body from spirit in an instant to prepare for battle but cautioned her greatly never to do this for thrills. It was way too late to warn her in that area. She was a Timewalker so she did it all the time.

They taught her how to use her sword and how to weld it against an enemy. They taught her to how to watch for signs of what's going on by watching the signs in nature and in the sky.

"Through Grace, mankind through salvation is brought into divine harmony with the demand of God through the Spirit of the Living Christ, Christ serves as passing over the dark waters of death, destruction and mortal distress as on a Bridge of Light over whose radiant arches hovering angels draw neigh." St. Anne read one evening after her studies.

Saint Gerald

"The Way of the Cross served as a divine opening up to mankind many gifts of the spirit. Through the Cross came the Holy Spirit into our world as never before. Even the world of technology, medicine, and science as we know it today came into the world via the Way of the Cross. How? The Holy Spirit poured out wisdom onto mankind as never before. Some may say God had nothing to do with the destruction visited upon mankind with these inventions! True! He did not." St. Gerald taught her outside on a stone bench. "God did not create such things as bombs, the use of hackers stealing vital info, the use of the telephone for means of destruction, the use of medicines and biological weapons created to maim and kill. All this is man's misuse of what God allowed to come through via the way of the Cross.

She listen carefully for he was a great orator. "God granted the wisdom and skills to create many wonderful things but it was the evil nature of mankind which used these inventions and discoveries for evil purposes. Each person, no matter rather their gift is spiritual or manifests physically, decides how they'll use it.

"No, that is not to say there aren't serious consequences and repercussions for misuse of any gift because there is. Yes, even those with the gifts of wisdom who create things intentionally to cause destruction will have to pay the same price as those who use a spiritual gift to create destruction. There is no difference. A gift from God is still a spiritual gift no matter which avenue it manifest. They all came via the same Spirit."

He explained to her how it was Donte Nikola Machiavelli who was supposed to be here in her place learning from them but the sheer harshness of what was done to him turned him away to serve only himself.

"However, always be on guard; that all one has to do in order to establish spiritual contracts of entrapment with the invisible world is merely wish, desire, demand, or insist

324

and immediately soul personalities or entities that are always close at hand rush in and complete the agreement of contract. They aren't nice about it as Jesus is, who knocks at the door of your heart. They're already there looking for a way in, so beware of your thoughts as they create universes of reality. Being offspring of God we've the ability to create beings, realms, and dimensions that are all our own. Just as the immortals can do this so can we".

"When you look outside yourself you can become lost if you don't firmly anchor yourself in Christ. When you venture into the created universe of others, thus you become a co-creator of another's creation, and all this is done through intent and free will."

I can't say I understood fully all he was saying but I was getting the gist. Don't think weird shit or weird shit of your own creation might bite you in the butt.

"The mind consists of many dimensions, thought is by itself a dimension, and it is different from the dimension of sight, sound or feeling. There's a dangerous realm called "WHAT IF" it contains another reality of what would've had happened had you made a different choice in life. Many get struck here and can't move forward for it will constantly remind you of your "What IF" Choices. I'm sure you figured it out to be a bad place." He said, smiling before continuing. So they had a heavenly projector watching me all these years. They know much more about me than I about them and their earthly lives.

"Sight, apart from being a dimension of its own, is individual in its interpretation with each person, some may be colour blind and all they see is of a bluish colour or maybe brown, some may be simply without colour, in the way that they interpret what they view within their sight. All of us will see and interpret in a different and individual way but arrive at one Truth. Man's created universe shall be what he desires it to be, for man is the construction of his own temple, through the intent of his own thought; mans thinking is his thinking, mans thinking has created all there is, that occurs in his life."

I'll admit St. Gerald lost me with the discussion of colors and a few other things but I kept my mouth shut and decided to ask for a greater in depth later.

Saint Thomas

This was one of the ones I hadn't said much to. I want to answer a question openly that was asked of me privately. No, I won't reveal who asked the question. But it wasn't a saint, at least I don't think so. Sometime the nuns and monks sit on a class but mostly I'm alone. The question was; is it a sin to use your spiritual gift to defend oneself? Thinking, knowing I used the gift of love against Nikola to pry Bea out of his grip.

The answer was no it is not a sin to use a spiritual gift against a known or unknown enemy if you're in danger. No you don't have to know the name of the enemy for the Lord to allow you to protect yourself. He knows who they are and that is all which counts.

My next question was: It is only a sin to use a spiritual gift against someone when no one is bothering you and you simply decide you want to hurt people for whatever reasoning that's valid to your mind?

St. Thomas cautioned. "Yes, it is. I've said this time and time again; be sure you can mentally withstand the result of using a spiritual gift against an enemy because oftentimes than not the result is far worse than you imagined it would be. That's why God often does not allow His children to use them against their enemies for the results are devastating."

I listened carefully to his humble speech. To me, he was the most Christ-like of those whom I had worked with so far. Although, he was a warrior saint. He wasn't combative as the others. St. Anne and St. Gerald could be downright scary when they wanted to be, I hope no offense is taken if they know what I'm thinking. St. Douglas, his best friend, always interpreted St. Thomas' messages in a layman's term that I could understand. He was the fun one of the group. I like the way he always greeted me with, "Are you having a happy day, kiddo?" I felt like a little kid again around these people.

"Most people imagine a mild consequence such as God changing their heart so they no longer desire to do evil deeds. Sorry, but rarely does that happen because we all have

326

a God-given free will to choose our path rather it be evil or goodwill. In many instances the offender(s) have carried on their crusade of destruction against the Child of God for so long the offender has grown to feel confident and cocky; actually believing within their heart there will be no divine punishment for their actions. In many cases the ordeals goes on so long the victim feels as thus God has abandoned them and have taken their gift back unto Himself. But that is not the case! The gift(s) is still there and nor has God abandoned you. Oftentimes He is giving the offender a chance to repent and change their way of life because His Actions may cause such destruction that it ends their life and their immortal soul will be lost to Him without repentance."

"The second reason nothing may happen when you attempt to use your gift for self defense is you may not be ready to deal with the result of letting loose the Power of God. The same applies today as God instructed Joshua leading the Israelites through Canaan; you can fault nor waveringly, cry, feel sorry for them or ask Him to retreat when He fights a battle for you. Sometime the manifesting of your spiritual defense may manifest in a way as devastating as the falling walls of Jericho. That is why I always emphasize be kind to everyone for you don't know who serves God and who don't. If your heart is too tender with Love to withstand His Result, pray and ask Him to give you the strength to stand. He will give you the gift of stout-heart if asked".

Saint Melissa

"The world would have us to believe the gift of stout-heart is the same as an uncaring, callous heart. That's not true; a person with the gift of stout-heart in normal everyday situations is a very caring, kind, and loving person. Only when needed does this gift manifest. Faith, hope, and charity are a part of being a warrior saint as it is with any other saint. But as you know the greatest of these is love.

But it's important we take things beyond the physical into the metaphysics for that's where our enemy cometh".

"Luke 11:17 & Matthew 12:25: "Every kingdom divided against itself is brought to desolation, and a house divided against itself will not stand." If you and your soul are not in agreement, then your house, your temple will not stand; there will be discord within your body, which will through time manifest through into the visible physical world, creating in your created world of reality what you've chosen, confusion, illness, disease, an imbalance of the free flowing Kinetic energy, which flows through the three subtle bodies in harmony. Those against us expect this."

Ok, the saints were losing me again. I had heard of these things but never fully understood them.

"Awareness is the name of the key, you must develop an awareness from a duality standpoint, understand that you're multi-dimensional. Man must learn to acknowledge his own spirit within, I sometimes call this his genetic entity as man's spirit is an entity, it's the same entity that has traveled through time and space taking on different vehicles, sometimes entrapped in bodies to experience different games on different dimensions. Hopefully I one day get the opportunity to show you how to possess someone for information if you must. But it's better to use the blade against them than take over their private thoughts. In MATTHEW 18:19: "Again I say to you, that if two of you agree on Earth concerning anything that they ask, it will be done for them by my father in heaven." If two independent naturally occurring frequencies join together in a single phase, then a resonance occurs as their high and low equal opposite are reached simultaneously, both frequencies oscillate in unison and under these conditions the waveform created by the two frequencies, will exceed that which either could produce autonomous results. But keep in mind that the intent of its created universe was of the joint intent of the individual intentions. In another word. All things are connected. The physical world came from the spiritual world. Not from some big bang in space. We're merely spiritual beings enshrouded in flesh".

Saint Cheryl

"Many teach that Christians aren't to defend themselves against adversities. That unfortunately is a false teaching. Surely Jesus proclaimed to us to turn the other cheek when smote on one cheek.
So what did He mean? Surely, we all know Jesus never advocated violence of any sort. He meant avoid all violence possible and never instigate and turn all issues we can not handle over to Him in prayer. Let the other cheek they smite be His".

328

"You might say: Suppose the offender continue to cause harm? Is a person being abused or harassed supposed to simply stay presence and pray the abuse stops. By no means! No, are we to remain in harm's way? If you see someone harming another, it's your job to make them stop. Sure you can pray for them but I seriously doubt there will divine intervention to make them stop. Jesus instructed us to be as sly as a fox and harmless as a dove. Meaning if the opportunity arrive to avoid confrontation with the offender do so but if not He intended that we defend ourselves".

"God wouldn't ask more of us than He have accepted for Himself. He defended HIS KINGDOM and expect us to do the same if we are able. When we becomes a child of God our home, dwelling and personal space becomes an extension of His Kingdom. You carries the Kingdom of God within you everywhere you go. God doesn't just protect the parts of the Kingdom which houses HIS Throne. He protects all of IT. Yes, even the tiny piece of the kingdom of God you occupy".

"They'll try and trick you saying things like he who lives by the sword shall die by the sword. But pay them no mind. If you lived by the sword you would have no problems. Deliver the blow if needed. Do not hesitate".

Saint Nehemiah

Most of our lessons were strictly from the Bible. He taught me a few Hebrew letters in case I needed to read ancient Hebrew. We spoke a lot on uncanonized saints. He took me to practice on performing exorcisms on demons. Not that we were lack in supply. I thought it was funny when he showed me how anything natural could be made holy and used against them. He consecrated rocks on the mountainside and told me to throw them at them. Saints Cheryl, Melissa, and Gerald were who secretly taught me how to make demons cry. I didn't know they were capable of shedding tears. Yet they warned me many can turn on tears as easily as a water faucet to be on guard for the kind who might appear as a weeping long lost soul. They warned there's no such thing. All humans are in heaven or hell. It's a demon and be aware it's a trick.

Saint Anne

The most astonishing events of them all was when all the saints took me from the room in the mountain and showed me how to travel to other worlds, galaxies, realms, dimensions, the allotment of time, and time travel. Reasoning to myself and trying to decide if my teachers were living or deceased. Most spirits are warm to me. I knew that the feelings from the spirit is dictated by their true nature and whence they cometh. Not all are warm to my touch; some are cold as ice, some feel slimy, some feel like a fiery furnace. I knew these were demons not human spirits, While many I've touched were peaceful and offer a sense of serendipity. These were usually heavenly or other earthly saints or angels. But these people felt like living humans. So exactly what were they?

Although most are solid and warm to my touch they don't feel quite like the saints in the cave. These people felt like living people but they supposedly lived over four hundred years ago. But I'm not always solid to them for their hands often passed right through me. But to some I'm so solid they can playfully ruffle my hair, plant a kiss on my cheek, or strike me death blow. "It's the latter ones are the ones a warrior saint must always be on guard against," Saint Anne warned.

I felt like a solely different person, an enlightened person, when I finally emerged the from illuminating room of the secret monastery. I knew I'd never be the same after encountering these people.

Besides my mother and Mother Harris, I've to say St. Anne was the most intriguing woman I'd ever met. This is whom I wanted to model myself after as a warrior saint. I know it will be a tall order to follow but I'll try.

On her final day she asked Saint Anne could Bea remain with them. Her kind eyes brimmed with tears. "Sweetheart, we're not of your era, we're from your past. We'd love to keep Breanna, she's a delightful little bundle of joy. But honey, when you leave we'll all return to our own appointed time. The veil to the future will close, I don't know enough to tell you if you will ever be able to retrieve her again. You would send her back to the past. By the time she is due to be born she'll be long dead, can you live with that?" Anne asked.

"If it will give her a life without fear. A normal life, yes, I can."

Saint Anne shook her head and said "I wished and yearned and even prayed for the same for my daughters. All of us here are parents. Our lives were in many ways worse than yours. We haven't always been here in this sanctuary. No one was sent to aid us but God will send one of His sons to aid you. I know it's scary right now when someone surely promises to kill you but God will protect you because He wouldn't have sent us from the past simply to allow Vonderbilt to kill you. I think you already know whom He'll send. Plus, you need Bea as much as she needs you. She'd be more traumatized by not being with you than anything the satanists can do to her. Be patient, dear child. Wait upon the Lord. If trust Him, which I believe you do, He'll provide a sanctuary for you and your people."

"But you don't understand, this psycho guts people while still alive." I cried, truly afraid of losing Bea after what Vonderbilt pulled. "I saw children too, in that horrible ice crypt. I believe you're one of my lost grandmothers so it won't be like I'm giving her to a stranger. I'd rather her be with you all and know she's alive than be with me and I'm not sure I can protect her."

Ana had finally said what had been weighing on Saint Anne's mind since the first day she met the three. But nothing had been divinely verified and saints can't scan each other. Ana's plea and tears were breaking her heart. She too had wondered if Ana and Fannie were her children's offspring.

"Don't cry, sweetie, I can promise you Bea will live to become an onerous, very old lady just like my baby Eugenia. And so will you. Everyone was put here on earth to solve a problem. You've a job to do. It won't be easy but you won't die by the hands of this cruel demon named Vonderbilt. Fannie and your siblings will all be fine. I do have authority to tell you that much." Saint Anne said, hugging her and wiping away tears. "My advice is go further South and wait until Spring to head North. There's a major winter storm raging in the North and Midwest right now. Dear, as far as I know...I'm not your ancestor. Perhaps we share a common ancestor as to account for the strong resemblance but if I am—I'm proud of you."

331

Ana nodded and pulled herself together. She felt she was being kicked out the only safe place she had ever known.

"I'm gonna miss you all." She sniffled. Now she knew why Mother Harris loved and missed them so much.

"Then you're promising me I'll see you in the Army, in rank and formation in Rapture, honey, and then we shall never miss each other again." Saint Anne said, disappearing, taking the others and all the ethereal brilliance with her.

Nuns stood by awaiting her. This was her first time seeing these particular nuns. Without speaking a word they silently beckoned her to follow, ushered her down the stone corridors into a simple decorated room with high windows. Glints of sunlight gleamed through, she was unable to discern neither the day not hour. Feeling disorientated, the nuns directed her to a hand hewed wooden tabled adorned only with a ceramic bowl of soup steaming on the worn table and an ancient green grape-embossed depression goblet serving as a water vessel.

"Sit and eat, you've fasted for seventeen days. A light meal of vegan soup and sourdough bread has been prepared to help you regain your strength before returning to the outside world. When you finish, I will lead you to the toilette to freshen up." These were the first and only words by the nuns before leaving Ana alone with her thoughts and sanctification of her experience.

Now I could hear the merry conversations of the other occupants. I could hear Bea and Momma laughing and talking from somewhere in the cave. I wanted to continue to hear those merry laughs and to the hell with anyone who felt I was being a wimp. They could kiss my ass. Let them take their sorry asses out there and deal with Nikola and then come back and tell me how they liked that crazy apple. I ate as instructed but when I finished I dropped my head into the crook of my arms and cried.

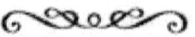

Here we're on the road again. I knew they would take drastic measures to get us out of that house. I must go back someday for Mrs. Harris. She is the kindest person I've ever met. I don't care what she says; her family would still be alive were not for us. It was me they were after not her.

But I didn't think the homicidal bastards would actually bomb the place to smoke me out. The years of attacks have taught me how to move inside of violence while keeping my wits about myself and ignoring the potential for harm. If you panic or freeze, you're dead. In spiritual warfare you learn the ways of your enemy more than you would from any church sermon.

And speaking of church, the woman in the cave monastery told me God would send one of His sons to help me out with all this madness. Saint Anne laughed when I told her me, and preachers, and priests, or whatnots don't get along too well. Why? I wish I knew. I dated a few church guys before Thad got serious about marriage, mainly because Mom thought I needed to date someone stable but we never clicked. I remember one plainly told me I was too boring and opinionated. I wouldn't make a decent preacher's wife. Another criticized everything about me. Please don't get me wrong. I respect ministers and the work they were called to do. But I can only speak from experience. The ones I've dated were not very nice people. Most were rude and made not the least attempt whatsoever at romance and acted as thus I was supposed to fall down and kiss their ass. So I've to disagree with Saint Anne on the son of God prognostication. Being on the road at all weird hours you talk to yourself about all kinds of weird shit.

Now getting to a cognitive content I've experienced. No one knows better than I that what we call reality is far more complex than the five senses can discern, see, touch or smell. If it wasn't there would not exist the need for "gift of discernment". Our world with all its mysteries and hidden knowledge is a mere smaller planet to much larger spheres that intercept into each other's path. Usually one passes through the curve of the other with no harm to either but with strange effects. Such examples are crossing into the 8th Day (Eternity) temporarily or traveling through realms and dimensions like bi-locating or teleporting. Few humans have this ability but to beings of other worlds and realms in the spiritual world it's as common as weeds.

The actual passing of one world through the another is whole another level of seriousness. You had better be sure you know what you are doing or another being can hitch hike into your world or your life and make it pure living hell. The veil or chasm that separates the Spirit world from the physical world has slowly but surely eroded.

In my travels I've seen spirits and supernatural beings that if I were to openly admit I saw them I'm more than certain I would've ended up in an asylum. There are already more spirits on earth than humans but with the veil holding back the worse kind. Thanks be to God for that but with worse kind easily and steadily crossing over; they're bringing with them mayhem and destruction. Dealing with havoc created by spiritual beings has always been the job of the warrior saints and spiritual warriors. We and our comrade angels are the last line of defense before they make into the physical world. So I guess we're really celestial cops. The thinning of the veil is why we're witnessing mythical creatures walking around in Central Park and many other places.

It puzzled me as to why this and many other things, nothing is written about them. Perhaps we may have thought ancient generations must have had a very active imagination or were high on hallucinogenic ceremonial drugs to have penned or orally passed down having seen such a creature. But lo and behold, they may had not been high but were sober enough to know they actually saw Pan or Zeus and bright enough to know these beings are a nasty piece of work.

The spirit world remembers what mankind has deliberately chosen to forget or plain ignores and uses it to their advancement. Which is why some spirits enter without the aid of a human and can only remain here a short time span. Which would explain the Minotaur galloping down Interstate 5 along the Pacific Ocean leaving smash-ups in its wake. Everyone thought it was their bad driving causing the pile up. Not that flying down the road at 120 MHP in light fog was aiding their cause but I saw fog wasn't the culprit.

I'd hate to learn if Medusa is real or not, oh well, there're far worse and uglier things out there than she. But to all myths and legend there are threads of truth.

I wonder sometimes why those who theorize, study, and analyze the human mind can so easily dismiss the belief in the existence of things they can not see, touch, smell nor hold in any real or meaningful manner but yet believe such as the Id, Ego, and Super Ego exist? Where's the logic? You can see neither of those with the naked eye. But yet they regard the notion as superstitious that the body has a soul. That the body is a cover for an ethereal life-force that animates it. This life force is who we all really are. We are souls; we're not an energy force separate from ourselves, our souls.

Most spirits are affable to me. At least some are. Yes, I've felt the cold-hearted bastards too. I've seen the vaporous, transparent kind too but no matter how much they weep I now know they're not lost or whatever they say their problem is, if you talk to them then you'll have a haunting on hand. These aren't human spirits, they're demons or other malignant spirits. Many spirits I've came in contact were peaceful and offer a sense of serendipity. These were usually heavenly or other earthly saints or angels. These aren't the ones to worry about.

Hauntings can be created mainly evil deeds done in a place and the demon that caused or influenced the deed is trapped there by God to make them see what they have done for all of eternity or at least until someone sends them back to hell. Or the evil spirit is conjured and specifically sent to that person usually to watch and spy on them for the conjuror. Some are familiar spirits and some just like to do bad shit to people. Most satanists think this is all fun and games until one of them gets hurt.

Since living with and learning from other Warrior saints I now know there're many whole other worlds we know very little about. I now know that my TimeWalking was as real as walking earthly streets. Even if I remember very little about it. The saints taught me to believe in what I see and let no one convince me otherwise. I've learned our world is rather small and insignificant in comparison to what I know to exist. And I also know that 75% of what goes on in our world has its root in the spiritual world. I can't say I have ever seen the devil; well, not and known who he was but I know he exists and I know the devil is never true to anything he says. He wouldn't be the devil if he were. It's not a pretty story but a pretty classic one.

Now, my job is to learn what the darkside really wants with me. Ostensibly, I'm very valuable to them for them to have followed and spied on me my entire life time. If they're expecting me to someday bow down and say "Hail, Satan!" they're out of their ever-hating minds! Sure, I hear the heavenly realm all day long every day. They're a genuinely clamorous and communicative bunch but at least nobody is crying and screaming as I've heard in hell. Now, why would I want to talk to a place where people or beings are crying, screaming, moan in pain all the time? I can hear enough of that listening to myself when Bea is asleep.

I've yet to understand why would anyone serve Lucifer? He doesn't he own anything anymore than I. I've learned he and warlocks, wizards, or whatever you'd like to call the human males in the occult don't like women at all. My gender is totally and utterly despised by them. So I, being female, would be an ultimate fool to serve something or someone I know hates me. Plus, I'm not ending up in hell for no one. My hell wouldn't be the scorch of the fire but being in a place condensed with a bunch of bellowing, screaming idiots.

Oh, there's a service station; I do pray they're open at this hour. We're down to a 1/4 tank of gas and I don't like to hit lone country or back roads on so little gas. There aren't many gas stations in the boondocks.

Done talking to myself, I pulled under the eaves of the late night station and the clerk looked out at the security window at me; I can see him shifting off all the antiqued pumps. So I guess I've returned to reality after all. At least mom is safe and comfortable with Helena. Junior said we could come live with him but no thanks. With the minions of hell at his service it won't be long before Nikola learns I'm alive.

Chapter 8
The first solid clue they wanted me dead.
The Mack Attack

It was the 5th of September, a bright and clear early autumn morning, no harbor fog lingering that morning to obstruct anyone's view when I got in my husband's 2484 BMW on my way to cash in several saving bonds, stocks, and shares Thad and I bought years ago to fatten our unborn children's college funds. I had been fired a week ago from my first real job after college graduation. Money was tight and my nerves were tighter. The resources from the second mortgage had gone to cover Thad's legal fees.

I hired the best defense lawyer in Boston to handle Thad's case and the best came with a pretty price. A fat of good it did for Thad was still convicted. Ask me, I don't think either law team really tried. All they both had was bad news, recent bad news, and fees to help themselves to our money. Even as a first year law student I could've put up a better defense than that. But by the 25th century the days of representing yourself or an inexperienced person representing you were long over.

Traffic was smooth and free flowing that morning. With none of the usual congestion. Despite my financial peril I was in a fairly decent mood. I proceeded with caution to the intersection of Lexington and Concord, following the car ahead. A black, hummer-like vehicle was coming from the opposite direction. I proceeded carefully into the intersection and waited under the green light for the approaching vehicle to pass. I wondered what was taking the driver so long to get through the intersection. Hovercrafts have been around for centuries but still only the very wealthy and well-to-do could afford them. Most people still drove land confined cars. A few passed over head. Thad used to tease me about proceeding with too much caution. Saying once the light turns green, it will have turned red by the time I make it through the intersection. It was still early but most of the morning traffic was sitting in an office cubicle by now.

I turned left to go up Lexington; in a matter of seconds I saw my entire life flash before my eyes. A huge industrial mack truck carrying a load was boring down on me. The driver was staring hard eyed and coldly at me with a deadly determination totally was uncalled for. Next thing I knew the airbags were inflating, roughly compressing my chest and sides, the seat belt tightening as it yanked me back into the seat. The enclosed space of the car amplified the deafening sound of crunching metal. It was gut wrenching to feel death's cold hands reach for my soul as I spun in confusion and my body painfully contorted. It felt as if a Boeing jet had slammed into my left side. Before all consciousness evaded me and all turned into darkness I said a quick, hopeful prayer "Lord, please remember me as I come into Your Kingdom!" I was certain I'd never see Bea and Mom again.

The deep, graveyard quietness scared me a little. I was sure I was dead. I didn't feel pain when I at first woke up. I wondered where was I? Was I dead and they're embalming me? I drew this conclusion because my legs wouldn't move as my brain commanded them and the only thing I could see was an office-like ceiling.

When my eyes adjusted to the light I peeked out the slit in the bandages at the blinding. bright white walls realizing I was in a hospital. When I attempted to move that's when I felt excruciating pain all over. The pain was so bad I felt nauseated, I was sure I was going to choke on my own vomit overflowing into my throat. But my stomach must had been empty for nothing but spittle rose. The strange person nearby who was screaming sounded like a morbidly wounded animal. Mom's face came within my limited visual range. That's when I realize it was I who was screaming.

"Sweetie, be still. You're severely injured." Mom said, rubbing my head but it felt like I was wearing a helmet. I felt as if every bone in my body were broken. There was no way I could still be alive and hurt this much.

"Someone is awful bright-eyed and bushy-tailed for someone just coming out of major surgery," a nurse said cheerfully out of my vision range. "I'm readjusting your IV drip." The nurse informed me, stating the doctor would be with in here shortly.

"Momma, uh so it wasn't a dream...I saw people in hospital scrubs standing over me...trying to make me go back to sleep."

Mom shook her head, telling me to rest. She wouldn't answer whether or not I dreamt those things. But I knew it wasn't a dream. I knew I had died. A mack truck had totaled Thad's BMW leaving me with only one car, my little car from my college days.

"Where's my purse?" I stiffly asked as best my lips could move. I think my jaws are wired shut. Mom mildly protested but brought the purse and Bea to the bed and opened it. While one year old Bea is on my chest trying to look into my eyes through the slots. I hope they're smiling at her.

"Mom, how long have I been out?"

"About a little over a week."

I emotionally flinched. Wondering had anyone paid the mortgage I was on my way to pay that morning. "Mom, there's saving bonds, stocks, shares and certificates in there, go cash them and pay the mortgage." I could hear mom rifling through the bag, "Honey, there's nothing in here except bills, even your wallet is gone. Your electronic wallet is gone as well."

"Well, take my wedding ring set and jewelry and pawn them." I instructed as I tried to ward off sleep. I didn't know it was possible for a fourteen month old baby to look worried but Bea's tiny face looked worried. When I tried to smile at Bea I realized the left side of my mouth felt immobile. My upper teeth felt as thus there was wire holding them in place. The pain was subsiding; I tell Baby Bea mommy will be home soon. I saw Bea reach for me but mom gently pulled her arms down and picked her and lowered her just enough to kiss my forehead.

The doctor enters and casts Fannie a disapproving look that Ana can not see. He had forbidden Bea to be there and threatened to call DFCS if Fannie didn't find a sitter for the infant. In return Fannie had threatened, no promised, an old-fashion country beat-down if he so much as looked at the DFCS' phone number.

The doctor pulled up a chair beside the bed and showed me my extensive injuries on the plasma pad he carried under his arm.

"Mrs. Wyett, you're very fortunate. We lost you several times. Had not the world renown surgeons Dr. Louise Merriwether and Dr. Angie Cotten been here teaching that week we probably would've lost you." He updates her on her medical prognosis.

Fannie angrily cleared her throat. The doctor ignored her and continued. "Your ribs pierced your left lung, we're grateful it wasn't very deep and missed the major heart artery. As you can see here, the left pelvis was crushed. We had to go in and rebuild it to support your internal organs. However, you may not be able to bear children in the future but that will be determined after your healing. Your recovery is going well. Your estimated recovery time is six to nine months and if you do well with physical therapy you could be able to return to work in a year. You've been in a coma for the past nine days. I'm puzzled about some of your injuries, they aren't consistent with your type of auto accident. We found fist imprints in your face. Can you tell us who assaulted you?" The doctor asked staring curiously at her, waiting for an answer. She was as surprised as he. Her mind traveled back to the accident, if she wasn't mistaken...that man deliberately hit her. When she tried to speed up and get out of his way, he changed positions too. The murderous, determined expression in his eyes flashed in her mind like a night terror. Yes, he intended to hit her and the car lolling around in the intersection was setting the stage.

"Dr. Muriel, I've no idea where fist marks could've possible came from." The tall pale, middle aged man nods and pat my encased arm while forcing a smile.

"Perhaps you were mugged after the impact." He concluded.

"*As if I didn't already have enough woes.*" I tried to joke causing Bea to giggle and clap her hands.

Apparently Dr. Muriel contacted the police department regarding the assault bruises. While he was standing there evaluating my chart a young, nonchalant officer entered.

The man looked royally pissed off to be here. He seemed to be inflamed and angry about something. And whatever it was she was the center of it. He turns her face disinterestedly to the left and writes on his plasma pad before saying, "Lady, I've never heard of anyone being mugged after an auto accident. If the truck driver had mugged you I do not believe he would've waited for us to get there. Besides, a mugger would've taken that wedding set. You ran a red light, plain and simple. That's what the traffic light is there for, to prevent people from killing themselves. Here's your tickets." He clanked out several tickets from his ticket issuer.

I can't believe it's I who is getting the ticket when I'm positive the mack truck driver ran the red light when I attempted to turn under the green light.

"Sir, you need to carefully review the traffic camera again. I did not run a red light. The light was green. A huge car, a hummer was preventing me from turning. Leaving me directly in the truck's path. Someone ripped me off while unconscious," I said listing the contents missing from my bag.

"I don't need you to tell me how to do my job. I've already checked the camera twice. It shows you're at fault," the man huffed and asked about my auto insurance.

Still puzzled as to how on earth could I possible had been in the wrong I cried. "Officer! The man in the mack truck deliberately hit me. The light was green on my side. I had right of way. After I saw him I canceled the left-hand turn. I decided to keep straight, he came within a few inches of hitting another car, speeding and wildly crossing lanes just to hit me."

The fair-skinned African American officer smirked as if something was really funny and asked "If you saw him why didn't you get the hell out the way. You saw it was a mack truck. Lady, you're lucky to be alive."

"I just told you a big ass hummer was blocking my way. It moved and took off seconds before the truck plowed into me!" I cried aloud grimacing from the pain in my jaw and the pain in my ass he was stirring up.

Fannie sharply sucked in her breath and spoke up, refusing to be intimidated by the gun and uniform.

"What in the fuck of unadulterated hell is wrong with you!? If your breeches are too tight you need to take that up with your supervisor. If my daughter say that fool deliberately hit her, then he deliberately hit her and you ain't giving her no damn tickets!" Fannie wadded them all up in a ball under his nose, looking him defiantly in the eyes as she threw them to the floor at his feet.

341

The officer nuanced the issue at hand and unceremoniously drops more tickets on my leg and angrily walked out wishing it was still the good-ole days when a cop could arrest or beat the crap out of citizens for such misconduct as this old biddy just pulled.

Fannie hadn't told Ana when all her siblings were here earlier they argued as to who would pay her mortgage so she would have a home to go to when released from the hospital. She hated letting Ana know these things. But she knew her siblings were bound to tell her as soon as they learned she was awake.

"Y'all baby sister is in there fighting for her life and all you guys can worry about is getting back to work and to your spouses?? The three of you together can pay it until her insurance kicks in!" Fannie had argued in the family waiting room.

J.J. looks at the other two sheepishly and say "Mom....Ana put herself in this dire financial predicament. Their house was already paid for. We told her not to hire that expensive law firm for Thad, he's going to prison anyway. But she wouldn't listen. Those charges were hard to beat. We don't feel it's our obligation to put ourselves and our families in a recession because she's being stubborn, thinking more about Thad than herself and Bea."

Helena and Jack mumbled in agreement. Helena's husband Dave said, "Mrs. BuFaye, we need to realistic here and brace ourselves for the seemingly inevitable. She has already died twice. What's the point of paying for a house when by the end of the day we may be paying for a funeral?" Helena elbowed him hard in the stomach and told him to go to the nearest chair, sit down and shut up. And he'd better not move and better not say a damn thing else.

"Get out!" Fannie yelled tearfully. "I'll call you all if she dies and after I've arranged the funeral. Be sure to ask your spouses can you come and if you can't let me know." Fannie slightly sobbed, Baby Bea begin to whimper because the loud voices and her grandmother crying frighten her.

J.J. hates more than anything in the world to see his mother cry. He tries to appease

342

their mother but yet make her see the situation from his and his wife Frances' standpoint.

Fannie stared icily at her oldest. "Well, where am I and Bea supposed to live while here in Boston? In the streets?!?" Fannie snapped. He sighed and hung his head and slowly punched in on a checkcard for the stated amount of $1,500.00.

"Mom, this is the best I can do without dipping in my IRA account."

Fannie doesn't take the check, instead she sent him to Ana's bank to pay the mortgage. Junior tells the other two they'll have to pay the next two months, hopefully Ana will have figured out something by then or have come to her senses and sold the house. With Thad being a football star it won't be hard to sell it.

A man, according to Jack, had contacted him about buying the former NFL player Thaddeus Wyett's house but said his wife won't sell. The man did not tell Jack BuFaye he only offered Ana 25% of the market value. And had Ana sold to him, she'd be deep in the hole with this half a million dollar loan.

Helena had to cuss her husband David out before she left this morning. He was riding her hard about her irresponsible sister. "I'm sorry she's hurt and in the operating room, but according to the bank's notification system you just took five grand out of our joint account. Ana needs to learn money doesn't grow on trees and she'll never learn that if everytime she cry you're rescuing her. She isn't a little kid anymore!" David lectured, following Helena around their bedroom as she rushed around the room throwing clothing in a Louis Vuitton duffle bag with the phone to her ear talking to her boss.

"Yes, I'll let you know how she's faring," Helena said in the phone, super embarrassed for sure her boss at NYPD hears what David is saying. When she snaps the phone shut she cusses him out belligerently, the way she's heard her mother cuss people out. Good and righteous when they so desperately deserved it. He storms out the house, go into the garage, gets in his luxury sedan, and burns rubber heading up the road from their three story Long Island suburban Tudor-style home.

She catches the next flight to Boston praying her little sister is still alive and all right and she doesn't have to kill her husband when she returns but Dave comes back and catches the plane with her.

Twenty-three year old Jack BuFaye is an honor MIT graduate. He works night-shift at Cisco Visata Technology. He had long suspected his wife cheated on him while he was at work but has never been able to find evidence. He had just came in the front door of their upscale Woodburn Apartment when the call came. The phone was ringing ominously so he rushed to answer it, it was ringing the minacious ring that let you know there's bad news on the other end. When he answered his mother was crying so hard his heart leapt into his throat as he tried to make sense of what she was saying. His mother was sobbing so hard he was certain Ana had been killed. Then he heard his 1 year old niece crying in the background. He started to freak out.

"Jack, Ana has been in a terrible accident," Fannie gasped loudly. "The doctors say they aren't sure if they can save her."

For a few seconds he was speechless. When he found his voice again he asked. "Mom, when did this happen?" Was all he could think of to ask.

"About 45 minutes ago. A huge mack truck simply bulldozed into her, right now they're working on her head, earlier they pulled a rib out of her lung. They say her back is broken in three places. They're mending it with cartilage I donated."

He didn't like the idea of mom being cut on to save Ana but he would've done the same had it been one of his children that needed his body part. He was raw-bone tired but told his mother he'd be on the next flight out heading for Boston. As if he had the money to spend on a spontaneous ticket. His wife spent money like a fish boozed water. Maybe Helena will tide him over until payday.

Lesheiksa Walker BuFaye stood in the doorway and stretched lazily; she was wearing a babydoll lingerie and he could see she was wearing nothing under it. Suppose one of the children popped back in? They were all at school, but still he was certain the lingerie wasn't for him. She strolled over and kissed him good morning.

"Your drama queen momma called about 8:30 or may had been 9:00, babbling something about your Ana, I told her I'd tell ya when you came in but I guess she already told you..." Lesheiksa said, yawning as she poured herself a fresh cup of coffee before adding. "If she's calling bout money-we ain't got none to spare. This household comes first."

Jack was already in a bad mood. He was angry and scared all in one accord. His emotions didn't know where they wanted to settle; so he couldn't feel worse. So he distinctly picked a bone with her. "Why do you dislike Ana so much? Is it because you fucked Thaddeus Wyett months before he married her? I know now, you dislike mom because she always said you never fooled her."

Angrily, Lesheiksa sizzled and slammed the cup on the counter top so hard coffee splashed on the floor."I'm sick and tired of your dogging me about that. I can't stop people from lying. I don't care what his teammates say. I never visited the damn training camp. For what? He was engaged to my sister-in-law. We just don't have the money to spare. Maybe 500 years ago an MIT job was the shit but today they don't pay that much. You already help take care of your momma. How much more they want?"

Jack yells, "My sister is dying and all you can talk about is damn money!" He storms out without packing an overnight bag. He heard the mug when it slammed and scattered against the closed door and the pieces rained to the floor. Hell, he'll wear some of Thad's clothes. Just his luck, Ana would have another one of her freak accidents when his cash flow is low. If there's a freak accident to be had Ana will have it. She has always had some of the most weirdest accidents on earth. She has mended bones and battle-scars all over from trips, falls, and strange things caving in on her. When she was small she used to say demons attacked her until mom and dad made her hush talking about them. But who ever heard of lighting striking someone's footsteps as they race to outrun it? In the old rumbling house where they all grew up, there was one mishap after another with Ana. She's lucky to have lived this long. He never admitted it, but some of those odd attacks against Ana he saw what happened but to avoid being scorned by the adults he remained silent about what he saw.

345

He ran into Helena at the airport. "J.J. is flying out from Rochester," Helena informed him. He should see she was angry and tense. Dave was with her. That was enough to make anyone tense. But he didn't feel like talking so he asked no questions as to why? Unlike Ana, Helena doesn't express a lot of emotions which made her an excellent police officer. They purchased adjoined seats. Basically they rode in silence except Helena ignoring regulations and talking to mom over the phone getting a minute by minute update on Ana. She had pulled through the first operations, although, she crashed a couple of times. "Calm down, mom. She's going to make. She's tough as nails. You know that!" He heard Helena tell their mother, consoling her.

Fannie calls her sister in Brunswick, Georgia and tells her to sell something from the hundreds year old book collection. The books have been passed down from one generation to the next for the last 300-400 years. The family started collecting them in the mid-twentieth-first century when paper book begun to phrase out of en vogue. Gayle asked if she need her to come to Boston? Fannie declines the offer but she wonders where did her sister get the thousand she sends a few hours later? No buyer can be found in two hours.

"I know y'all think what Ana did was stupid and irresponsible but she was inherently following what Jesus said about doing good even unto those who spitefully use you. She was only trying to keep her family together." Gayle said, guessing her big sister's thoughts. Fannie smiled, remembering her sister always had a biblical answer for everything. She could definitely use one right about now. But little did these two close sisters know theirs' weren't only ears who heard their words. Gayle Sinclair Preston's phone was bugged. And the listener were not please about the sisters' plot to save Ana's house nor life. They silently vowed Gayle Sinclair would pay dearly for her interference.

"Mom...you and Bea can go home. I'm sure they'll call you if there are any major changes" I said for I saw mother dozing off to sleep. Fannie heard her but ignored her. She wasn't going anywhere until she took Ana with her. Several strangers had shown up at the hospital inquiring about Ana. One was the creepy guy who recently moved next door. She wasn't taking any chances. That cop's callous attitude confirmed what she suspected. This was no accident, this was surely as the sunrise attempted murder.

346

Something ethereal has been after her daughter since the day she was born. They let up for a while when she was living with Thad but she isn't convinced whomever or whatever is trying to kill her is gone. She believes they've merely shifted gears.

They know she's alone now with an infant, that makes her extra vulnerable. So no, she isn't going home. She is going to sleep on that roll out bed tonight. Somebody have to watch these devils. And speaking of the devil; here's Ana's new neighbor who has been visiting nearly everyday leaving flowers. And Fannie has been throwing them out everyday. She directly can't place her finger on what it is but something about that man is downright creepy. He feels like he bathed daily with creepy vibe soap. He is obviously important for a limo picks him every afternoon, he rarely spends the night in that house. A few times he had dinner with them. She didn't care to ever sit at a table with him again. He made the hairs on the back of her neck stand up. God gave us all the gift of intuition and she believes He hopes we will use it along with the common sense He gave us. Listen to that little voice that tells us when danger is around or nearby.

"Oh! How marvelous?! You're awake. You gave us all quite a scare a few times!" Teddy/James Caldwell exclaimed, bent and kissed her bandaged forehead. Ana smiled a small polite smile the best she could. He placed the flowers on the table beside her bed. "Oh no, dear don't try to talk. Don't worry about a thing but getting well and coming home. By the way, the sheriff came to tack a foreclosure notice on your house but I gave him and the judge who signed the meatless writ a piece of my mind. I told the court you had suffered a terrible tragedy and was unable to attend court. Poof! It disappeared, I can't have my three favorite girls homeless, now can I?"

Ana glanced in her mother's direction. She was certain by now the bank had foreclosed and she intended to use the 90 days grace period to catch up.

"Teddy, may I speak to you for a moment in the hallway?" Fannie asked ever so sweetly. Ana knew that was her mother's I'm-about-to-tear-you-a-new-hole-in-your-ass voice. The moment they were secured in the hall Fannie leans in close so no one nearby can hear, "Ted, I don't know what you are up to and don't give a shit but my daughter is not for sale."

For a few nanosecs of a second James Caldwell's light hued eyes darken.

"Mrs. BuFaye...it was obvious Ana needed help. If she didn't the sheriff wouldn't have been at her door. I only did what any real friend would've done." Teddy/James Caldwell said politely.

He was a charming, silver-tongued man, Fannie had to give him that much credit. And by most standards he was very attractive, well dressed, she could tell his suit and shoes cost more than most people's one month's salary. But why was he living in an upper middle class neighborhood when he obvious could easily afford a large mansion?

"Maybe the case but whatever it is we will handle it when Ana is released." Fannie ensured him.

"Do whatever you feel's best, but please do not make things difficult for Ana. She has enough to be agitated about without worrying about where she will live. Don't make your daughter suffer because you're paranoid." Caldwell advised pushing the door to Ana's room open to bid her goodbye and to let her know if she needs anything else to feel free to call him. When he closes the door and his eyes meet Fannie's, their message is "*You've been warned.*"

Six weeks later on a cool, partly cloudy late October day with the leaves on her street in full versicolors for the season, Ana is taken home in an ambulance because her legs are still encased. Her old college friend Gena and Thad's best friend Tony are there to welcome her home. Her mother-in-law had left a message Fannie quickly erased. She was volunteering to keep Bea until she is better. Fannie deleted the message because that's whom she called to look after Bea when the hospital first called about the accident. The chameleon of a woman had said she shouldn't be bothered with an infant but she could be bothered with the insurance policy she had taken out on her daughter-in-law's life. The woman was genuinely surprised to learn Ana was still alive and there would be no insurance payout when she called Fannie at the hospital to offer her consoling on Ana's passing. Passively, she claimed she heard Ana had passed away. She'd such a policy on Thad and Bea as well, saying her son could be irresponsible at times and she wanted to make sure if anything happened to him Bea would be well taken care of. Had

Fannie known that she might have killed the cheating bastard herself.

Several friends and neighbors joined in the light celebration. Teddy/James Caldwell was one who invited himself. He showered her with gifts; everything from bathrobes to slippers. He handed her the deed to her house. She was astonished but told him she couldn't accept it.

In her den alone with him she told him she liked him as a friend but their relationship would never be nothing more. "Never say never, my dear friend." Caldwell replied, refusing to take the deed back. She had to find a way to make him reclaim his money. She was in no emotional state to attempt a relationship with anyone. There was an emptiness in her heart. She felt it was flapping aimlessly in the breeze from the winds of distress. She had several letters from Thad. His mother told him about the accident. He wrote he may get out early on good behavior. She felt he may had omitted asking how was she due to the stress of his own situation. Either way she felt hurt and neglected. She still couldn't accept why Thad had been neglecting her every since she got pregnant with Bea.

"Ana, if you holding out expecting to pick up with where you left off with your husband... As a word to the wise I advise you not to place your life on hold. For heaven sakes the man cheated on you! Why should you be serving a sentence too when you've done nothing wrong?"

She hadn't forgotten Thad's arrest was a big media circus here in Boston being a former pro and all. So everyone and their mother knew every shoddy details. "Won't deny I think you are perhaps the most beautiful woman I've ever seen. Few are beautiful inside and out." She laughed off his comment. Her head was looking like a wild person's, her left arm was still in a cast, she was wearing a body cast, and her legs were sticking out like dead bird legs. "Teddy, you need to take some of this money and get your eyes examined if you think I'm 'beautiful'. I'm sitting here looking like the damn Bride of Frankenstein." She teased him.

He refused to be deferred "Ana, there is more than one type of beauty. You've an inner beauty that even time can not erode. When you are well enough I'd like to take you out to dinner."

Fannie had left Ana's guests downstairs; poor baby Bea had been asleep all afternoon. She wanted to talk to her children about how did Ana's neighbor pay for the house if they had paid as they told her they would. That man was in the den where they set Ana's hospice care equipment up. Sure her daughter was very beautiful but no man really wanted to court her right now. Especially not a complete stranger.

"Mom, when I went to the bank the mortgage was already bought out in Ana's name." J.J. said. Helena tells her brothers to hang up she wanted to talk to mother alone. The two screens closed and Helena decided to have a heart to heart talk with her mom. "Mom, I don't care what lie Ana is telling you she knows this guy. No man is going to pay that kind of money for just a friend! I know Thad only been gone something like 5-6 months. But think about it, he moves next door a few days after Thad is sent away. I'm wondering if Ana isn't the reason Thad was cheating and if this guy is who set him up. His family knows about this guy, how? I don't know but his sister called me angry saying her brother hasn't been gone six months before Ana steps out on him. She hopes we are now happy for we never wanted her to marry Thad."

Fannie finds it hard to believe Ana knew this man prior to his moving next door. She talks to him over the fence and he has been over a few times for dinner but Ana never goes anywhere so when and where does she see him? "Mom cheaters don't do it openly, apparently he's enamored with her and wanted Thad out the way." Fannie searches for the right words before expressing her opinion. "Helena, there's something off about this man. I sense he's very dangerous to know. He never spends the night in that house. A hovercraft limo picks him up every morning. I mean, he's friendly and all, but I sense a viper beneath the skin."

Helena laughed "Mom, he wouldn't be attracted to Ana if he was sane. Look at Thad. She seems to attract the love-to-hurt-people/ serial killer type. Adversity, you know, is a state which one can easily became acquainted with themselves, so maybe by the guys Ana picks tells us a lot about her true inner self."

Ana's recovery is swifter than medically expected mainly because she is determined to
350

pay Theodore/Teddy/ (unbeknownst to her) James Caldwell the full amount back. She doesn't like being beholden to anyone for anything. But she still hadn't figured Caldwell out, why he still pursues her after she has made her feelings clear?

The mack truck driver wasn't told to beat the woman in the face, the man whose car was blocking her way told him to let's go before regular people started paying attention. But it felt good to hit her. Women like her didn't give guys like him the time of their day. He remembered her from Thad Wyett's football days and thought how he'd like to fuck and beat her. Now was his chance. Guys like Thaddeus Wyett had it all. Good looks, women, and the media loved them; a pretty wife, a beautiful child, a lovely home. No one person deserved all that luck. He tried out for the Boston Minutemen and was told he didn't make the cut. But Thad waltzed in with all ease. Of course, that was fifteen years ago and Thad was probably wearing diapers back then but still, he didn't deserve all that fame just for doing some thing any man their size could do. He intended to give the jewelry he took off the woman to his wife. She didn't need all this jewelry.

With no one at the Wyetts' home, no one had been there for days, James Caldwell entered through the garage door a locksmith had opened for him. Having been in before he knew his way around so he goes upstairs to Ana's bedroom and looks around. Had she not been so picky she wouldn't be laid up in the hospital now. He looks out the side window and sees the two men arriving. At least they had enough sense to leave the pocketbook in the car. He slithery reentered the rented house and asked the men would they like to see the home of Thad Wyett? Sure, who wouldn't. Caldwell is pleased neither man is exactly a fan of Wyett.

Once inside they go through everything they think may be of value and take it. Caldwell encourages their theft.

Downstairs, sipping Ana's wine from her holiday collection, Caldwell peruses the papers and other loot; he's rather surprised at the nest the couple built with Wyett's football earnings. This mini-mansion is paid for. Their cars and furniture the same. He didn't see much designer clothing in Ana's closet. Thad's closet was loaded with designer items. He took the expensive watches, rings, and cuff links. Wyett won't be needing them anytime soon. The couple's debts were rather low in comparison to the four million they had tucked away. Combined with what Lola gave Thad, which she found after his arrest by the money was tagged. By any standard, the couple was siting pretty; they had enough to live comfortably for the rest of their lives. So his call was correct, she *was* going to cash in all these stocks, bonds, certificates, and off-shore accounts and pay off the second mortgage and therefore remain in this house and wait for Wyett's release in five years. Ah, the good wife. Thad Wyett didn't deserve such a wife.

The traffic security camera showed the truck driver took Ana's jewelry. He wants it to have something personal of hers' as a trophy so he calls the man and made the man hand over all he had taken off her person. A personal trinket made it easier to summon things and sic on her.

He heard a crash in the livingroom and frowned, he didn't want to kill any of her family but he would. Perhaps, it's the two starry-eyed underachievers working for him.

"A beautiful place, isn't it?" A female voice asked aloud. He recognizes the voice as belonging to the Bayou warlock's main lady Lola.

Lola walked in after the men, she knocked over a fragrance bowl of dried potpourri Ana had neatly arranged by the entrance. Her mother did shit like this so the sight of it pissed her off. She hadn't told Cherver nor Shrevenport about the money she found in Thad's garage so who told them? Caldwell. He was the only person who saw her go in the garage while Ana was in the hospital having Bea. The Wyetts normal next door neighbors paid no mind for they had already been conditioned to accept nothing Ana said to be true. She came to retrieve the expensive gifts she had given Thad since Cherver took the three million, the big-mouth named Caldwell told Cherver she had the money.

"Dammit." She softly hissed. Rifling through the closets, seeing the jewelry was gone. She surveyed the room and saw Thad had lied about moving out the bedroom with Ana, his things were still where he said they wasn't.

"I think these are what you're looking for," Caldwell said from the master bedroom doorway, holding a huge, highly polished wooden jewelry chest. Pushing off the doorframe he walked further into the room.

"You know you aren't to own anything without your superior's approval or knowledge. Luckily for you, I stopped you from a dreadful fate. Supposed Cherver or Warren had later learnt you were keeping wealth from them? I shudder to think of the consequences."

"I needed those gifts to bait the next husband. You know the rule. You only keep them as long as the relationship lasts." She reminded him, demanding the expensive chest be placed in her outstretched hand.

"All of this didn't come from you. I see some came from Ana. His rings came from the NFL. So no, I'm keeping them. They live in Cherver's jurisdiction so he gets the say so in who this goes to. Not you or Shevernport."

All had been lost. There was no retaining a thing. The sheriff barely allowed her to pack her old college days car with all it could hold. She didn't know what happened to Thad's jewelry chest and many of other pricey things the papers was accusing her of hiding. Like Thad's MVP ring. They said it was worth millions. Saying it could be used to satisfy the debt. But she swears she doesn't have it.

Nothing was clear about the foreclosure. Teddy left the deed in her name but someone else decided the agreement wasn't binding resorting it back to the original second mortgage company and refusing Teddy's attempt to buy the house stating it along with the inside possessions were worth far more than Teddy paid. That Teddy was under minding the bank. Getting an estate worth six million for 400,000. She tried desperately to show the courts the papers were in her name but the judge refused to listen. Instead she banged the gravel telling her to get out.

We were shortly outside of Boston when I smelt a soiled diaper. It smelt like an upset stomach. I had to stop and clean my baby up. We couldn't keep on down the road like this. I pulled in to a parent station which, thankfully, are public places designed for these types of incidents. I went to the women side where several women sat breastfeeding. Bea had long been weaned from the breast and trained to a bottle. Now, I was thankful for that.

With a fresh diaper on her bottom and a smile on her face we exited the stall heading back to the car where mom was waiting. But first I stopped and picked up baby snacks and some soft beef jerky for me and mom.

Suddenly I felt heat drive hard and deep in my left shoulder, spinning me around. I crashed to the floor but somehow managed to hold on to Bea as I fell to the fresh moped tiled floor. I was quickly losing conscious. I saw black steel toed boots trolling near my head when I looked to my left, the screaming and clamoring was drowning out his words. The black gum-metal Glock was pointed in my face with the trigger finger squeezing as he smiled wickedly down at me. I was sure this was the end, I closed my eyes and prayed. Next I heard the strawberry blonde man screaming. I heard an old familiar sound ring out, I recognized voice the swearing. The man spun as hard as he caused me to but being much larger than I, it didn't immediately take him down. Before he could hit the floor beside me a thin pale blue fire quickly traveled up his legs, he twitched and jerked trying to extinguish it. He was fighting two forces at once. I watched in horror as opulent blue fire traveled from his knees upward turning him into ashes. Clutching Bea with my uninjured arm while blood seeped from wound forming a puddle under my shoulder, I watched in awe as the man crumbled. Nothing remained of the shooter except his boots, all else was dust.

Fannie rushed in and quickly gathered her granddaughter Bea in one arm and her daughter in the other. Helping Ana off the floor she supported the weight of her daughter and granddaughter as they made their way to the car. Ana's wobbly legs could barely hold her up. Ana wasn't fully healed from the accident that nearly killed her and this was the last thing she needed. Another injury. All the while her husband's old ivory handle, which yellowed centuries ago, Colt 45 was tucked neatly in her jeans waistband in case there was any more trouble. She had hit him in the forearm to stop him, she didn't see nor cared what incinerated him and wasn't sticking around to find out. She quickly loaded them both in the small car and tore out of the parking lot as mortified bystanders watched.

Fannie swiftly cut through several old neighborhoods until she found a quiet, isolated spot under an old elm tree and pulled out the first aid kit I'd argued we didn't need. But this hot lead burning in my flesh was telling me otherwise. We needed it. Damn it, I was just getting over a nearly fatal hit and run, so why had guy just added more insults to my injury?

"We're blessed it's just a flesh wound. It's gonna leave a nasty scar but it will heal," Mom said trying not to show her distress as she applied the liquid skin application after cleaning the wound. Bea hadn't cried or screamed as the other children. She sat placidly watching her grandmother work and when finished she kissed my bandage as I've kissed her mishaps and falls. I saw mom curiously watching Bea. Yes, I noticed she was too calm, too.

Chapter 9
Unlawful Pursuit-Dangerous to know.

Agent Augustine Pembroke watches his partner and another regional agent sandwich the woman between them and begin groping her. The woman pushed the child out from between the two men. He sees her reach for a knife and so does Manson. Cerberus Manson grabbed her hand and shoves her against Agent Bender who begins humping her. He gets out his car and yells at the two. The frightened woman and even more frightened child looked in his direction. When the two left her unbracketed she grabbed the child in a running sweep and sprinted toward her car. She's a merchant at a local fleamarket. He sees her head go down; apparently she's putting the child in the floor of the car. But when she raises up, she firing a semi-auto gun out the window at her gropers. She sprays the crowd aiming for Manson and Bender but they use customers as shields. Pembroke wonders what just happened.

Pembroke thought it revolting, those nearby saw what Manson and Bender were doing and no one tried to stop them. Had he not yelled at them they probably were going to publicly rape that woman! A disgust sunk to his stomach. The crowd seemed to be egging them on. He had a clear shot at the back of her head hanging out the window but something about looking in that kid's eyes... Looking at him from the back window stopped him. He couldn't just blow her mother away when that's all she had. Manson and Bender were in the wrong.

Somehow that kid knew that's what I was considering as to why she held me with those strange, haunting eyes. I knew within my heart had I killed that insult shouting woman, I would need to kill the kid also for that child's eyes plainly told me she was coming for me when she grew up. Another reason I couldn't shoot her is Manson and Bender were perverts and dead, shamefully wrong. They were a disgrace to the badge. They had no right to grope that woman trying to pass between them headed toward the women portable toilet section. We were told to capture her and bring her in for questioning, not rape her.

Manson makes a mad dash through the crowd as the rat-a-tat-tat-tat-tat of multiple rounds of gun fire sounded off and somehow made it safely back to their car by running through the multiple concessional stands. He didn't see Bender among the running crowd. Perhaps she hit him. If so, he had it coming.

"Shoot the crazy bitch!" Manson frantically yelled at me. His breathing was coming in rapid gasps as his fleshy face perspired from fear and having to move excess weight very quickly. He reached over trying to take my gun, for his clip is empty, to return fire. The dark, red haired woman turned around and aimed for us. Now it she who has the advantage. Her eyes are saying, "Do not make me kill you because I will!"

Manson stupidly ignored the warning in her eyes and raised his hand and aimed to fire after reloading and she sprayed us with bullets. E-e-e-e-ow e-e-e-e-e-blaow!!; the powerful gun is heard seconds before all hell broke loose. We both ducked down under the dashboard covering our eyes and head as glass showered the hovercraft as the volley of bullets shattered all the glass. She had illegal bullets able to break bullet-proof glass and pierce armors. I know those are illegal in civilian possession. Those are my grounds for arresting her. But hell! I can't get out the car. She had us cornered. It's said she's a killer but I haven't seen the evidence enough to arrest her.

Manson is screaming he has been hit. "I'm going to kill that fucking whore. I'm going to destroy that bitch!" He yelled, holding his bleeding face. When the overhead and panicking ground traffic was clear enough they rose and saw red taillights brake as she was making a sharp left turn onto Hill Street. I revved up the engine and quickly rose higher into the sky above the bedlam below. I intended to cut her on Route 66, that was the only way out! Looking below, the little blue car was nowhere in sight! Where did she go? Where in the fuck did she go?! That's impossible to disappear that quickly.

"You could've shot the bitch when you had a chance. I told you she was a witch!" Manson groaned, wiping the blood and glass from his face. I looked at his wound made by flying glass, not a bullet. One of those illegal bullets would've taken his face off. It was only superficial, nothing serious.

"That's no lady. That's a lying scumbag, a killer."

"We're on a stakeout not a killing rendezvous. You and Bender had no right to grope that woman."

"The bitch flirted with us both at her booth. She was asking, no begging, to be fucked," Manson justified while watching for the woman's car in the traffic below on the screen.

"So, you two were going to fuck her in public? Manson, what in the hell is wrong with you? Our agency has a greater preterit legacy than that! People already say we are nothing but a bunch of freaks and perverts who use the authority of our badges to get our rocks off. You prove the public to be right! Where in the hell did Bender come from?"

"I called him, he's alright. She's a whore! Everybody verified that! Fuck the public! It's us who put our lives on the line to protect the gullible, infantile public. They don't do shit for us! Where in the hell is she?" He groaned brushing glass out his lap.

357

Augustine Pembroke firm jawline tightened, he really doesn't want to work with Cerberus Manson, the man is a certified social psychopath. He never evolved past his juvenile years nor above the misogynist notions of the past. His mother's brother is a powerful senator and the current Speaker of the House so he can get away with just about anything-including murder. Once he murdered a hooker in Miami because she wouldn't perform fellatio him saying he hadn't paid enough for all that. He is an ultra conservative who really doesn't like women very much. To Cerberus all women belong one of the two categories. They are all either the knuckle-under-a-man-kiss-his-ass June Cleavers or the whores. There's no normal working women trying to make ends meet. His kind tolerates the June Cleavers but doesn't really like them. According to Cerberus Manson all women living an independent life are all whores, even our boss, Madame President. Manson is one sick as hell puppy.

We check the radar for the tracker I put on the car but that car seems to eat them and there's no ping nor blimp. Nothing. The car had disappeared like a phantom in the night. My phagocyte of a partner says, "That's the fifth or six tracker we've tagged her with. I know she didn't remove it. She was at her booth. That's proof again, she's a witch like they say."

I can't explain how she knows a pin size tracker is on her car nor can I explain how she vanished in broadlight.

Neither of men knew they were sent to find this woman even after Ashton Cargill strictly forbade anyone in the upper level of their agency to look for her. They didn't know there was someone else equally as powerful as Cargill in this world looking for her and they were merely pawns in a deadly game. To appease both forces their bosses sent them in order to keep the peace with both of the powerful houses.

Seeing that continuing searching for her is a loss I turn the hovercraft around to head back to the fleamarket bazaar. Maybe she'll return to pack her stand. We inspected the stand. It's mostly junk one might find rifling through rich neighborhoods trash piles, public trash bins, and dumpster diving. Seems as if all the best items are already sold. Her cash is gone, she only left the trash. She isn't coming back.

"What did you and Bender talk to her about?" I asked.

"Nothing special. Bender asked her out for dinner tonight but she shot him down. I know her type. They want you to pay for the pussy. I look too damn good to pay for pussy. Besides, a good woman don't ask for anything but your time and your love," Manson said dialing Helena BuFaye Wales who has recently been promoted to detective at NYPD at his recommendation.

Pembroke didn't feel like explaining to this Netherlander that the woman was selling second-hand goods, she smiled at every potential customer and it didn't mean a thing. That women by nature are gentler than men. Women smiles, it doesn't mean she is into you. That's just their makeup.

The screen rung several times before Detective BuFaye-Wales answered.

"Det. Wales, your sister was involved in a recent shoot out with the Feds in downtown St. Louis a few minutes ago. Has she contacted you?"

"No, was anyone hurt?" the honey-toned beauty asked. She was beautiful, far prettier than her dark, no-tits sister if you asked Manson.

"No, but she caused a public panic. Only sheer luck saved everyone. We would appreciate it if you could tell us where she might be headed next. She's hazardous to herself and the public. She lost control of the powerful gun and shot her daughter. If isn't already dead, the child needs medical attention." Manson lied.

That's when Helena knew he was lying. Ana hadn't lost control of a gun and hit Bea. Momma would've heard about it and beside Ana was a better marksman than she. If she didn't hit you it was because she didn't want to. It wasn't because she missed.

"No, she haven't said a word to the family." Helena truthfully replied.

"You'll let us know if she calls??" Manson asked knowing the woman wouldn't. But that was alright; they had all her phones at work and home bugged. Even the mom's and brothers; were tapped. He clicked off the screen inside their hovercraft.

"I'd love to fuck her! The woman has a helluva pair of knockers and an ass to match and the face of a goddess. She's a lot prettier than that wild, bony thing we just saw pointing a gun at us." Manson sighed in such ecstasy that it made Pembroke wonder did he just come over there in the passenger seat. He frowned and reminded himself to never sit there.

"I mean, grabbing the woman I felt nothing but bones, she ain't got nothing a woman supposed to have. So what in the hell Cargill want with her? He would've to fatten her up to fuck her unless he's one of them freaks who enjoy banging bones." Manson laughed. His uncle had confided in him of Ashton Cargill's interest in the woman.

Manson disgusted him, all his talk is gross. His personal hell was having to sit for hours and listen to this pervert.

"You'd fuck this car if it had a vagina." Pembroke lazily annotated turning toward the place with rooms reserved for them at the Cargill Hotel. He dialed the local headquarters to key in his report. Manson saw too late Pembroke ratted him and Bender out.

"What in the hell you do that for? You trying to get me fired?" Manson bellowed.

"No, I'm trying to save my job. You two fools groped the woman in front of hundreds of witnesses. Some feminist is bound to think it wasn't cute nor funny and tell the truth and if I put in a lie and they pull up the public surveillance cameras then my ass goes down in flames with yours and Bender's."

Manson laughed because he knew nothing would come of it shall anyone report it.

"Pembroke, following the rules is why guy like you'll always be plumb broke," Manson laughed at his own joke. "You're forgetting. By the time we go after someone we've tarnished their rep so badly that no one will sympathize with them but a fool. So let a Nelly say something. We'll go after them too. Pembroke, you don't realize the power we have. We rule this fucking country. I mean several men and women have testified she is a deranged woman so what harm was a little fun? I'll safely bet a john picked them up and hid them. She'll surface again tomorrow. Wait and see."

Something unholy snapped in Ana when those two guy sandwiched her between themselves. She wasn't surprised some bystanders thought it was funny or even got excited by it. She would've been beyond stupid to go out with that freak when his eyes told what was in his mind. The man had "I'm a freak" mentally tattooed across his forehead. If he showed it so boldly in public she could only imagine what being in private with him would be like. But the one calling those two off had an opportunity to shot her, she wonders why didn't he? He definitely was as brittle as his partners. She saw it in his eyes. Because anyone who will run down a mother and baby is in one serious state of coldhearted bastardization.

The angry rise of the windowless, huge official black hovercraft was the last thing she saw before the blinding light of heaven's door opened up and they exited the 8th Day in an unheard of place called Sinkhole, Wyoming.

She had to jump out the car and start shooting in her traditional style of walking toward her attacker and firing. She thought Bea was down in the floor of the car as she leaned out the window, firing off rounds at the perverts who had the gall to put their murderous hands on her. (She picked up on the spiritual fact they were killers the moment they touched her. They were no better than those who worked for Nikola.) When she turned around and looked in the back, the heavily jowled one was aiming at Bea who was up with her head visible through the back window. No, she didn't feel sorry for what she did. They could've been ashamed of what they did but they weren't.

The weather wasn't quite as hot here as in St. Louis and there was a cool, gentle wind stirring through the early summer trees. This wasn't where she would've gone but at least it's miles away from St. Louis. She hated to leave their camouflaged canopy behind. She used it to cover the car when hiding in the woods but it was either that or go to jail or worse; get them killed. Those hell dogs got the reaction out of her they wanted. Her reaction was normal. Besides, what were they doing over near the women's public toilet? What made her lose complete control was the guys in the public grabbing themselves and shaking their penises at her. She was greatly offended at the females laughing. Stupid bitches, if they'll do it to one woman, they'll do the same to you. We're supposed to be in the era of female equality but the more things change the more it remains the same.

We had exited near an unknown clear lake. The sunlight sparkled lazily on the soft waves in the midday, as if millions and millions of diamonds were floating on the surface. I don't know if it was private or not. But it was bordered in by a graying rotting fence. We got out and walked around. I figured perhaps it used as a cattle pasture so I told Bea to look out for cow pies. She thought the idea of cow shitting pies was funny. I was too glad we got help from up above to lecture her on obeying. She may be only a child but this shit was hard on her, too. So I let her enjoy the beauty to calm her nerves. Neither of us are some callous automatons.

Surveying the area, we saw no houses nearby. So we drove a little distance down the road surrounding the large lake and came to an estate. I noticed the altitudinous layout of the land and knew we were somewhere in a mountainous range. The Rockies, I presumed.

Going back to the car to see what we had left I saw our armamentarium was low. It had been steadily dwindling with Nikola's incessant attacks. They had little time to refurnish their supplies. So she knows that quite contrary to the popular belief that all monsters are hideous and lurk and hunt in the dark that some are handsome and hunt and hurt in broad daylight.

"Oh fuck," I said under my breath when I saw an estate which was surrounded by a high wall, like a fortress or something. I saw tiny hidden cameras pointed in our direction. Let me get the hell outta here! I did a backwards turn around and someone appeared behind me standing in the middle of the dirt road. I knew this had to be a satanic hideout. Who else can do that but a satanist? The man put his hand on the back end of the car as I slammed on brakes to keep from backing over him. I heard him calling me but to the hell with that; there was no way I was stopping. But he teleports

362

again.

"Ma'am, please stop. I mean you no harm." The dark brown man said. He looked and spoke as if he may be from the South Pacific.

"Move, or I will run over you." I yelled. He teleports into the car. We both got out and ran around to the front. "Get out of my car!" I yelled reaching for my pistol but damn! It was under my seat.

When the chief of security lazily looked into the camera after hearing a car outside the premises. He bolted upright. He couldn't believe his luck. That's the woman the entire security teams on all seven Continents been looking for! And she wandered into his jurisdiction! He knew he didn't have time to call his boss for she was quick. She could disappear in seconds never to be seen again and their boss would then thunder at them as to how did they let her get away?

Waiting no time, for he had no time to lose, he alerted the others with a yellow code accompanying her picture and teleports to the area on the north side she's trying to get out of. He startled her. Dammit, she's afraid of him. Maybe he shouldn't have teleported, but she spotted the hidden camera where most people wouldn't have thought to look, inside the hand of a marble sculpture. He quickly reached over into the car and took the keys so she would have to stay and talk to him. Now she has a knife in her hand and grit in her eyes. What kind of madmen have this poor woman encountered?! Forcing her to behave so febrile? She went out one door and the kid out another after he teleported inside the car to try and talk to her. They took off out across the pasture. He got out the backseat of the small four door sedan with both hands raised.

"Ma'am, I mean you no harm. My boss would like to see you." The man said called after her as she and the child sprint across the pasture toward the old section where cattle still grazed. Ana stopped running when he teleported in front of them and started swinging the knife at him. She was wondering where in the hell was her uniform when she needed it? He was dodging her swings. He could've easily taken it but it would've broken her thin, frail looking wrist. To him, she looked so tiny, fragile, angry and scared. It was the proper thing for a man to do, to simply dodge her and not add to her already

363

hyped state and mentality. He could see clearly, something very harrying had already put her in such a terrible fright.

"I know Vonderbilt would like to see me. Who in the fuck do you think I'm running from?" She replied. At the time she had never met the man. She had only heard the name mentioned in the dream world. Schickel had to think for a moment who was she referring to. Although his mother was an immortal and his father a mortal his father taught him real men do not frighten women and children. His father treated his mother like a Tahiti Rose even thus she was strong enough to cast boulders into the sea. Nonetheless, somehow, his parents made things work. Among the ancient Polynesian Deities her name was Papa or Po who was the supreme creator, goddess, their mother earth. So when his father passed, in her tremendous grief she took him away, and he and his siblings still don't know where she took the body.

"Oh, no, no, that isn't my boss," he said smiling, still holding up his hands but keeping his distance from her. For she meant business and the mortal side of him could bleed blood.

"How do I know that!?" ,she snapped, gripping the kid's hand tighter and walking further into the pasture as Schickel carefully approached her. He tosses her her keys as a gesture of good will.

"You're a satanist so Vonderbilt is your boss."

"No ma'am. I'm not a satanist. I hate the whole shebang of them," the man said with his hands still in the air.

"Yeah, right. Tell me another one. How did you do that then?"

"If I told you, you wouldn't believe me." He smiled. His ultra friendliness wasn't fooling her. The devil can smile a pretty dazzling smile.

"I tell you what if you don't trust me..."

"Hell naw, I don't trust you. I know what you are. You're a warlock." She sneered and

364

looked him up and down in total disgust. The whole lot of them disgusted her. She may not know them by names but the past years had taught her well what they can do.

"No ma'am. I'm not a warlock. I'm half immortal," he replied.

I stood and stared at him. Now I knew he was lying. Immortals like the ancient gods and goddesses and half immortals like Hercules didn't exist. They were myths and legends so I knew he was really crazy and dangerous. He didn't look crazy. Most serial killers don't look crazy cause they aren't. They are simply evil. I glanced over at the flock of killdeers and wondered could I use them to fly into his face as I ran through them toward the woods. *No dummy you never go into woods with a potential killer on your ass.* That's their home. He reached in his pocket. I threw the knife he effortlessly dodged it.

"Hold on, Ms. BuFaye. I'm not trying to kill you. I was reaching for a card!", he cried going to pick up the knife. But changed his mind and stepped away from it.

"How do you know my name?"

"I told you my boss has been trying to track you down!"

"Who is your boss?," I asked as Bea handed me her knife.

"I'm not at liberty to say but he is crazy about you. All I ask is you go into town. There's a place called the Purple Closet. The owner is a friend of his; buy something nice and fix up. I know you're tired cause I'm tired from chasing you. Wait at the Germack restaurant. He'll meet you there in an hour. I promise you he won't kill you. There's a hotel right up the street. It's small but nice. You can check in and stay as long as you like. No one will dare touch you. It's all at no charge, it's for free. No charge!" The man begged with both hands in a praying position to prompt her to please listen to him.

Standing in the middle of a pasture looking for a way to get around this man, I probably did seem odd but fuck it, if I did. "I must look like a red-headed fool to you.

365

Nobody does nothing for free. I bet your boss is crazy about me. Crazy about killing me! So what does this man really want?"

"I believe he wants to take you on a date."

I felt a tug at my arm, "Mommy, are there cow pies out here?", Bea asked looking down and around at where they're standing.

"I don't know.", I replied out the side of my mouth. But addressed this man taking me to be gullible, I burst out laughing a cruel, mean laughter. All this because some guy wants to ask me out on a date. I gotta tell ya; this one is a new low.

"Why don't he come out that big-assed house and ask me himself? No, because he's up to some shit. That's why. I've had my full of sickos for one day. Leave me the hell alone."

"Sorry, ma'am, I can't do that," The man apologetically said.

"Why not?"

The man patiently sighed and kindly says, "I've already told the others you're here and if I let you get away he'll be very unhappy."

"Oh, I'm sure Vonderbilt will be very unhappy. But that's just tough shit. Now move!" She ordered. He was standing between them and Trusty.

The man stepped back as I ordered him. He laid the card on the ground folded in a bill. I couldn't see the denomination. I was too far away.

"You think my life can be bought?"

"No, ma'am..."

"Then why in the fuck are you paying me to come to you?"

The man grabbed his medium length black hair and pulled it. His mouth opens and then closes but no sound escaped. She watched him walk around in a short semi-circle and stopped and looked at her, sighed again with one hand on his hip while the other beseeches her but nothing comes out his mouth. She had seen Thad do something like this when she bombarded him with hard questions when he was at loss in what to reply for no matter he said she had a clever counter reply toppling his answer. He was even doing the rubbing of his brow thingy she had seen Thad do when she frustrated him. Is this a man's thing? Or just a black guy's thing?

Finally, he stopped pacing and looked at her pleadingly across the pasture, "Ms. BuFaye, I swear on my own someday grave, I'm not trying to harm you or the child. I swear, there's has been a massive search for you for months. My boss is in love with you."

She raised her eyebrows at the profession of love. Cocked her head to the side and glared intensely at the man who the sunlight highlighting his blemishless brown skin. She sensed he was being truthful. Her resolve begun to melt. She doesn't quite know why she believes the man but she does. "Ok, if I agree to meet your boss...will you stop chasing us and let us out of here?" I asked, shrewdly watching the man.

"Yes, Ms. BuFaye, I swear to you. You have my word. I'm sending someone with you to show the way. She'll catch up with you."

I eyed the card and money on the ground for we only made eighty dollars at the bazaar and left more than half of our merchandise. When I walked toward the car with the other knife from inside my socks in front of me. I used my foot to draw the currency to me so Bea could pick it up while I kept an eye on him but I then thought otherwise. It might be poisoned. I used the tissue in my pocket to handle it.

"Step away from my knife!" I said beckoning him to move with my pistol now that I had reached the car and retrieved it. He moved further away, his hands were still up. Bea was already in the car and aiming her peashooter at him. He stepped further away as I revved the engine and made a swift turn, opened the door and snatch up the big bowie

367

knife and kept going. Soon, I heard a hover craft above us and looked up. There was a smartly dressed woman driving. Her clothing looked like a woman's version of the man we just left. I didn't know the way out, she alit in front of us. I stayed behind and followed through the mountainous road. It wasn't long before we reached a small town.

"Mom, are we going to meet this bossman?" Bea asked.

"No, sweetie. I'm trying to see a way out of here."

"Won't the Big Guy open the bright door again?"

"I'm not sure if He will just in case He doesn't, I need a way out," I said as the expensive vehicle pulled in front of specialty shop that looked rather expensive. The woman was out her hovercraft, on the driver's side before I had the opportunity to survey the streets. It looked like a one Main Street town which had only one way in and one way out. But this one had an exit on both ends. I still wasn't sure which way was out.

"*Duh, dummy!*" I told myself. "*The way you just traveled leads back into the mountain, straight ahead leads out of town.*"

"Sorry, but I need to take my daughter to the bathroom," I lied to the woman waiting for us to get out the car.

"Ok, your room is ready. We can go to the hotel first and then come back and shop." The serious woman said. She definitely didn't wear friendliness very well. But at least she was putting forth the effort. When we took a side street I spotted another black SUV hovercraft down the road at the other exit out of town. I saw they had no intention of letting us leave.

"The fricassee can be prepared however you all would like to eat in case you are hungry now," she said as we checked in the hotel. It was small hotel but much nicer than our usually abode. The room was on the seventh floor. I thought it was unusual for such a small area to have a luxury hotel.

"Skiers use it during the winter months." The woman explained, as if she read my mind while waiting for Bea to use the bathroom. "I wondered *did* she read my mind."

"Look lady, I need to know who am I meeting. I'm not meeting a stranger whose name I do not know." She smiled a curious smiled and said, "Ana, you know him. So don't pretend you don't. He is the man from your dreams." I was a little nervous now. This woman unnerved me more than the man down by the lake.

"I do not know what you are talking about." I replied. I did know but I didn't fancy anyone, especially a stranger knowing about my sex dreams. "If you people aren't occultists then how do you know all that?"

"Occultists are those who use the darkforces to do supernatural things. People like you and I are born this way. We don't need demons. We were born with our abilities. I used to be like you. Didn't trust no one but sometimes even when you've been hurt and betrayed you've to learn to trust again. Everyone needs someone who cares enough to go the ends of the earth for them. All I ask is you meet him. He cares for you a great deal."

I couldn't tell her there was something chilling about this man. It was the same feeling I got when I once looked at painting in the New York Metropolitan Museum, a painting about the second coming. And the artist wasn't referring to the Second Coming of Christ. The few times I sensed him coming the feeling was very ominous, horrifying. The man or whatever it was felt very minacious, overwhelmingly menacing. So no, I wasn't meeting him. But oddly, he didn't feel maleficent at all in my dreams. It's guessable due to the dreams are my own mindwork so I made the images felt however I pleased.

"He isn't as bad as he feels," the woman said. Now, I knew for sure, she could read my surface thoughts.

"I'm sorry but the man scares the crap out of me. I can't meet someone I'm afraid of."

"Ana, look at it this way. Just like he scares you he scares a lot of people and things, including this Vonderbilt and all else who is trying to kill you. I'd safely say he loves you

369

and would never harm you. You've more to think about besides yourself. You've Bea and Fannie to think about. He'll keep those agents away from you. So which would you prefer? Living in luxury with a man who adores you or continue on the dicey road to certain death? Because we both know that's the inevitability. We both know that Vonderbilt is going to one day kill both of you. And when he does he's going to purge your entire family from this earth. They always do."

I knew the woman spoke the truth. But her words sent chills down my spine. I couldn't run forever. She was right. I had been given a hand to play and must play it to my advantage. And speaking of Bea, what on earth is she doing in the bathroom so long? It doesn't take this long to pee.

"Breanna, what are you doing in there?!" I asked through the door. I opened the door to find Bea sitting in the middle of the luxury bathtub blowing bubbles. The sweet, fragrant white suds covered all but her head.

"Mom! Close the door! I stepped in a cow pie!" Bea yelled. I looked at her shoes encrusted with dried cow shit in the middle of the floor. I sniffed the virile odor I had not noticed and looked down at my own manure encrusted sneakers and closed the door back. I hadn't told her to take a bath. I told her we weren't staying here.

"Leave the child alone, she is tired and worn out. I heard a bath being run. She is taking a bath. It would do well for you to take one too. You look seconds from collapsing from exertion. I tell you what, I'll instruct the chef to prepare a meal and have it delivered here to your room."

Why was it so important I meet this man? What does he really want with me? Oh...because he *loves* me. Yeah, right! He doesn't even know me so how can he love me? I concluded he wants the same thing Vonderbilt wants but is just nicer about asking.

"Bea, get outta that tub, dry off, and get dressed! We're leaving!" I yelled when I didn't intend to but my nerves were frayed, shot, and fried and Bea wasn't cooperating. She could sleep in the car. I went in to get her out and dry her off and put some fresh clothing on and clean her shoes. Hell, I would just clean mine on the grass.

"Mommy, I'm hot, tired, and hungry. I'm thirsty." Bea whined as I dried her with the soft plush towel. The woman looked smugly at me from the doorway. "Ana, why are you pushing that child when you don't have to?"

"Mind your own damn business. How much he pays you to say these things?", I snapped. I could hear Bea quietly sobbing from exhaustion. The day in St. Louis had been dog days hot and muggy. We had spent the forenight in the woods under the portable AC, but it wan't a very comfortable sleep. It was too hot to rest comfortably. So we kind of woke up tired. I had planned to use the proceeds from the sale of the merchandise we scavenged from trash bins at the curbs of affluent neighborhoods to get us a nice, cool room for a few nights. Hopefully there would be no dead bodies lodged in the walls. Now, I was torn in what to do. Bea was in the bathroom crying from sheer exhaustion and mind was telling me the appropriate thing to do was to let her rest a few days, she's only a child, little more than a toddler. But on the other hand, I don't want to get us killed. She can sleep while I drive. I pulled the money-clipped bills out my pocket and looked down at my hand, the man in the pasture given us a five grand bill.

"Bea, we are getting out of here! Now!" I said pulling her fresh clothing, we didn't know these people. They could be cannibals for all I know.

"No, Ma!" She yelled back. "I'm tired."

I looked closer at her face and my child's young face looked old and worldly worn. "Mom, had they intended to do anything bad to us they would've done it by now." Bea said, sounding much older than her years. "A devil don't wait this long to hurt you."

"Wisdom from the mouth of a baby." The woman said, ordering a meal and asking what would we like.

"I want hamburgers, ale soda, hot dogs, pepperoni pizza, seasoned french fries, apple pie, cheese cake, a cherry soda, orangeade, and milk." Bea yelled through the crack in the door. She looks at me in defiance as if I protested she couldn't have it.

371

The woman was talking to someone she called a 'fricassee'. "Just add iced tea." I said and Bea broke out in a smile. Knowing she had won. I heard the woman order a full course meal. I assumed she intended to dine with us to make sure I didn't run away.

Ana was observing the heavy potted agave near the window wondering if the pot was heavy enough to break the window and allow them to make a break for it.

"He's here." The woman whose obviation was keeping them from leaving, said, adding. "Will you please put these on? My job depends upon it." She went to the sliding door of a closet Ana hadn't noticed and pulled out a dress. It looked her size and all, it still had the retail tag but she knew it was there for the unfortunate woman he intended to bed in this room for whatever night. It wasn't bought especially for her.

"No, I'll not. I'm not wearing that dress." Ana said feeling a tad bit jealous of whomever the dress was bought for. Marian smiled at the fact Ana didn't know she instructed the boutique to bring the dress over while she and Schickel were out in the pasture bickering and fighting. They had no intention of her getting away again. Cargill would have their heads and asses for it should she escape them again.

"Let's go shopping then."

Marian escorted her and a squeaky clean Bea back outside to her hovercraft. She didn't trust Ana to her own car. The mother was as defiant as her daughter. Ana knew this was the type of hover caddy that could morph into a mini-airplane.

The shop owner was waiting for them. She already had an array of clothing laid out. Normally, she would've ignored someone as sweaty and ill-kept as this woman or asked them to leave. Her shop only catered to the rich and well-endowed. But since it's Cargill who sent this sweaty, smelly woman who had cow shit on her shoes, she had to exempt her normal protocol. They dressed her and had called in the local beauticians to see if she could do something with her looks.

In Hong Kong Ashton Cargill was in a business/pleasure meeting with Hong Kong's most influential woman, Ming Tekco. The affability of their meeting amply lent truth to the relativistically that business and pleasure can mix if one knows the right ingredients for the recipe. Ming commanded the respect of any man she took to bed. That was her endgame for this late night meeting of the two business powerhouses. Her wealth neither equaled nor surpassed his but lagged not very far behind. He sought after Ming to convince her to surrender the pharmaceutical company her father built in exchange for a cool fifteen trillion. The opium drug her company produced was no longer in high demand by the medical field as centuries before due to the creation of a much cheaper, less addictive synthetic drug.

"Lady Tekco, I'm honored you agreed to see me on such a short notice. I concatenate you've seriously considered my offer." The elegantly dressed man said. Ming noticed he have always reminded her of a lion. Maybe it's the flowing hair. The man stands and walks as if he's king of the jungle. She heard his cognition in the bedroom are a duplication of his outward motility. She knows he could easily drive her to sell so why the cordiality? The ominousness in him is sensed the moment he enters a room. Perhaps that's the allure. Other than he is devilishly handsome. Unlike the days of old when it was considered unladylike to proposition a man for sex, today's time is different. In those days women weren't believed to even possess sexual urges.

"Mr. Cargill, I took you seriously at your first instigation. A man of your calibre is always taken serious but I'm curious as to why? The present market isn't lucrative for medical opium." Ming inquired.

What she didn't know was he knew it may not be at the moment. He had been around long enough to see fads fluctuate, die out, and return so the present generation thinks it's a brand new thing. So in a hundred years from now all the present comprehensibility could change. He have seen it happen many times before. But of course she wouldn't be around to see it and can only predict by what her limited sight, existence, and knowledge can perceive.

They were seated on a white arch designed sofa facing each other. Openly appraising each other over a glass of monk wine. Which has been all the rave in Hong Kong's elite circle in the recent years. He noticed Ming Tekco was one of the few modern women who possessed the old world beauty. Had she lived in another century she would most certainly had been the empress or the favorite wife of the emperor. But her boldness and sharp tongue would've gotten her killed. She doesn't conceal the fact she is sizing up his crotch. Her hand slides smoothly and seductively over the seat next to her, but they both are accustomed to a potential lover coming on to them so neither makes the first move. In houses of power and prowess the one who make the first move is the loser and is to be conquered. The screwiness of this game has built and destroyed a many empires.

While playing the game of conquest his personal phone rings at the worst possible time. His chief of security from the little town of Sinkhole, Wyoming is on the phone. "Sir, we found her. She's being retained at the hotel in Sinkhole!" Schickel said. He wasn't thrilled to hear that now. He knew he was winning when Ming crossed her beautiful legs and uncrossed them only to repeat the feminine gesture. He pocketed the phone and said, "Milady, my people will be forwarding the acquisition forms. When all is signed, I can ensure you the sale will be of your best interest. If you will excuse me I've an urgent matter to attend. One which is demanding my utmost attention." He rose and she extended her hand. He bowed over it and kissed it, looking her seductively in the eyes. Letting her know this wasn't over. She knew he would be back and she had won the match. She slowly smiled a small victorious smile.

"The conclusion between our businesses is finished but between you and I, it has just begun." She said in elegant English. He returned the smile. He knew she wouldn't be able to handle him in bed if he put himself fully into making love. She possessed many black belts in various martial arts and it's rumored she's very, very selective in her choosing her lovers; that she once beheaded a lover for not pleasing her.

"Indeed, milady." He nobly replied, and walked out the room. Her guards planked him on each side to escort him to the door. The door that was once his about four millenniums ago. He used the door for she did not know he was an immortal. He isn't generous in others knowing his true nature. As he walked he called Schickel back.

"Keep her there until I get there."

"Yes, sir."

Once outside in the fulgent but mild summer sun he teleports to Sinkhole, or at least that was his intended designation. But he finds himself standing before the Archangel Raphael. The Archangel who dealt with romantic love and courtships.

"Azazael, I brought you here because we need to talk. From your intents a few moments ago you're not ready to be what this woman needs. Her heart is not to be trifled with. Your wanton behavior will break her heart. So I can not permit you to pass."

"I didn't find her. She found me." He argued. "The security team remembers more than I. I don't even clearly remember her and what do my actions with Ming have to do with her?"

"No, she was merely bilocated into your backyard."

"Why did you all bilocate her into my backyard if you didn't want me to touch her?" He asked, crossing his arms across his massive chest.

"For protection. Nothing would follow her onto your property." Raphael explained.

"So let's get this straight. You all send her to me for protection but I can't touch her?!" He chuckled for the ways of Heaven never ceased to amaze him. "I'm not interested in being her babysitter. You know my interest in her."

"Yes, and that's what bothers me." Raphael knew Azazael wasn't going to stop until he gained Ana's love. But he also was afraid he would do as he has done to many others he pursued. When the chase was over he lost interest and moved on to greener grass. Leaving the woman wondering what she did to drive him away. Ana's life was far from normal. She didn't need his kind of distraction, putting her in further danger but one of his estates was the only place on earth the hordes of hell wouldn't dare to tread.

Azazael teleported into the next town over from Sinkhole to avoid Raphael's blockage and called his people to come pick him up. Schickel is there within fifteen minutes.

"Marian is with them, sir. They are still at the hotel." Schickel said, also informing Ashton Cargill of the unusual circumstance of Ana simply appearing on the security screen out of nowhere. He gave a full account of their stand down in the meadow.

Ana wouldn't go in the back and let them dress her hair. She felt white beauticians rarely knew anything about black hair. In her opinion it wasn't a racial thing. Just difference in culture and physical make-up. Now she was the one who was forestalling by looking at dresses the shop-keepers preferred she didn't touch with her dirty hands. While she had her head bowed looking at a dress a large hand settled on the next dress on the display rack and a mellifluous male voice said, "I think this one would look better on you." She turned quickly around and looked into the man's face she was being held hostage for. She didn't exactly remember his face. But he had the voice, face, and body that could easily get a woman in serious trouble. She wondered why she didn't sense him coming.

"You know it's illegal to hold people hostage," I said turning back around to let the dresses absorb my attention.

"It's also illegal to trespass on private property but you did. I treated you kinder than I treat most. I usually shoot trespassers. So holding a trespasser accountable is not kidnapping, my dear!" He nonchalantly and casually said but temptingly added, "Some women think it's romantic to be held hostage."

It was hard to tell if he was joking with the last part, so she didn't reply to it. "I wasn't exactly trespassing. I just happened to have landed there." The fluidity in which he could switch moods was somewhat making her nervous.

"Enlighten me. Elaborate. How did you and your kid just land there? Did you two and your car magically fall from the sky? Out of a plane? Off a chariot being driven across the sky?"

"No," I said wondering where were he going with this annoying ass conversation. He

376

was making fun of her.

"Well, then you were trespassing and I've a good mind to have you arrested."

Ahhh, ah ha! So now I understand it all. They were retaining me for trespassing and awaiting the owner to determine shall he or she turn me over to the authorities. I knew it, I knew it. I knew something was amiss. I knew no one was really that nice. I should've ignored Bea's whining and ran when we had the chance, even if I had to shoot my way out.

"However, I'm willing to let all be forgiven and forgotten shall you have dinner with me this evening," he said, offering a truce.

So this is how gets the women those dresses in that hotel room were meant for; they were trapped in this hellhole!

He chuckled a low throaty laugh, "You really do have a vivace and wild imagination.", he said in his normal, deep speaking voice, pulling the dress from the rack telling the shop-keeper to pack this one.

"I do not. You've a room full of dresses for unsuspecting victims who have the misfortune to wander onto your property. You offer them either dinner and afterward or jail." This time he laughed out aloud at her accusations. He do wish he could remember more about her than he does. This woman doesn't feel nor look like the beautiful woman he visionized. Maybe it's somewhere underneath all this grime. Right now, she looks like she been out in the desert making bricks for the Pharaoh. He snapped his fingers ordering the women to fix her up, a new dress isn't going to do the trick. She needs a whole makeover. Plus, she stinks. There's remnants of cow shit on her shoes. If she wanted to repel him, it's working.

I didn't like the way he bossed people around, as if everyone here were his servant or something. I followed the women only because I could use a bath. Hadn't showered in over a week cause we been sleeping in the car and living in the woods and couldn't find a public place in or around St. Louis to bathe or shower. The local YWCA required membership to use its facilities. Now, I wondered if is he really the antichrist? I mean he befits the description.

I did my own hair with Bea's help. I replaited the single braid going down my back and wrapped the long plait around my head like a crown. I guess I looked presentable. But frankly didn't care. I was tired. If I were a child I'd cry. The woman named Marian takes us to the restaurant. He rose when we entered. This was awkward for I didn't know this guy's endgame. The waiter seated us and Cargill reclaimed his seat.

"Order whatever you like," he said. So far he had shown no overt interest in me outside of teasing me. So perhaps Marian was wrong or lying. This man isn't truly interested in me.

Laying the leather binded menu beside his empty plate, "Ms. BuFaye, I understand the devil himself is pursuing you. Do you plan to be on the run for the remaining of your days?" He asked, leaned back, sipping wine and looking at me in that intense way of his.

A light bulb goes on in my head. Oh yes, nnnow, I remember him well from the closet of my old house in Boston. He was a lot nicer then than now. I was now a little bashful because we'd already had sex, so he wasn't interested in alluring me anywhere. So from what avenue was he really coming?

"If I have to. Yes, I do."

"That isn't much of a life. How will you outrun him when you grow old and feeble?" He asked. I mulled was his words for a few seconds. He was patronizing me?

"No, I'm not patronizing you nor ridiculing you. I'm inquiring of your intents. On the road like this is destroying your body. You won't last much longer. So here's my proposal. You and your family can stay here as long as you like. I rarely visit this place."

"Where will you be?" I asked, surprised again at unexpected jealousy rising in my nature.

"I do not live here. This is a resort town," he replied flipping his napkin out as the waiter brought his dinner.

"Where do you live?" I questioned a little too abrasively, displaying an emotion I was fighting to keep in check.

"I see you're an inquisitive little bee," he said looking around as if awaiting for the waiter to bring our plates before he begin eating. We had already eaten a big meal a few hours ago and weren't very hungry.

"No, she is not. My name is Bea." Bea quipped. "And you're a lovely little Bea." He smiled at her and blatantly turned to me and asked was he her father? I nearly choked, the impertinence of this man knew no limits. Now he turned those intense eyes on me again.

"No, my ex-husband is her father."

"If you say so," he retorted as if it didn't matter one way or the other to him.

"Why are you being rude? I mean, you hold us hostage. Threaten me with jail time and now insult the paternity of my daughter. What do you really want from me? Why have you been chasing me all these years? Your employees say you have searching for me for years? Why? To insult me? I've been insulted enough to last ten lifetimes. I do not need anymore vilifications."

Ashton Cargill has wondered that very question himself. He has already screwed her so why was he still chasing her?! He was testy because he wanted to get back to Ming. This woman was pretty but she was no Ming. Somewhere in the back of his mind he sensed he knows her from somewhere. Where? He can not remember. He wonders was she as annoying then as she is now?

"Lady, that's an excellent question...why am I chasing you when you don't want to be caught? I think you enjoy the chase. But shall you leave here. I'll leave you alone."

"ENJOY THE CHASE??!! DOES THIS MAN REALIZE THOSE AFTER ME WANTS ME DEAD?!

He saw a hurt shadow of sadness flicker in her amber eyes. She mentally brushed it aside and stabbed her food. Poked a piece in her mouth and violently chewed on it. He remembers that move of hers from somewhere else prior today. She only did that to hide her true feelings.

He heavily sighs, lays down his ornamented, decorated silver knife and fork and looks at her a few minutes. "Ok, it's obvious you're upset so what do you want me to do? Chase you until you die?" He asked. His voice was laced with sarcasm. He was not quite comprehending why he cares what she thinks. She's a pure royal pain in the ass.

"Do whatever you want. Something tells me you always do."

"Look lady, I don't know you and you don't really know me. I'll admit I was interested in finding out where I knew you from. Finding out why the darkside has such a keen interest in you. That heightened my interest as to who you really are." He was getting angrier by the minute. Now, that he sees she isn't very interesting. He wants to end this dinner as quickly as possible and get back to Ming Tekco. A far more interesting woman. Why are the archangels making such a ruckus over her and don't want him to date her? Of course he has no intention of marrying her or anyone else.

"Ana, I'll tell you what. Let's just forget this dinner and go our separate ways. You don't want to be here and nor do I particularly want you here. So get a good night rest and decide what you want to do with the rest of your life. But if that's my kid, send me the bill." He said, asking were they finished? Ana kept her head down. This is the first meeting and real remembrance she have had of her midnight lover and after seeing her in person he doesn't want her let alone love her. She has been living with this crazy fantasy for far too long. It's time to face reality which isn't beautiful at all. She feels like she just used an online dating service and was the reject. Where the profile was better than the live person.

"No, I'm not." Bea said biggety, looking intensely at him as he was looking at her mother a few minutes ago. He saw something dangerous in the little girl; she was like him. Capable of being a real first class bitch. He lit a cigarette and waited for them to finish. He swore the kid was prolonging the dinner for it was now nearly 9:00 P.M. and they started at 6:30.

"C'mon honey, we need some rest. We have a long day ahead." Ana said softly. Bea's eyes didn't soften as she glared at him. He knew his own ways enough to know perhaps Ana didn't know the girl was his but he knew. Could he force her to stay to keep the kid safe? Or could he simply take the girl? No, that kid would grow up with raging hell in her and kill him if he did that or force him to someday kill her.

Finally at 9:30 Bea was getting sleepy and leaning on the table. She had eaten so much she was falling asleep. Ana picked her up but he claimed her, the girl was nearly as big as her mother. He got them both in the limo.

"How old is she?" he asked. "Three nearing four." Ana replied. "She's awful tall for a three year old. I thought she was about six." "She took after her dad, Thad is big and tall." Ana said.

While escorting them back to the hotel and carrying a sleeping Bea inside, somehow this felt right and comfortable. He felt this was where they belonged. And where he belonged, with his family. His mind wasn't totally on Ming Tekco anymore. He knew he had hurt Ana's feelings. He didn't totally understand the feelings that reemerged when around this woman. She did something to him to tame the inner beast in him. He put the girl on the bed and kissed her forehead. Ana was still standing near the kid.

"Would you care to stay and talk? I don't know anybody here and I spend all my time talking to a child. It would be nice to talk an adult every now and again." She said rather timidly.

"Ms. BuFaye, I think it's best for the both of us, I shan't spend the night. You already have one child. You do not need two."

"I'm not offering to sleep with you. I'm merely offering a simple conversation. Maybe a cup of coffee. You've lots of people to talk to but I don't."

"Don't you date?" He asked surprised at her insisting he stay. Her request was a little puzzling. Ah, he sees, she can't handle the conspicuous rejection.

"It's very difficult to date when hell is after you. I'm afraid if I go out with anyone he'll be found dead the next morning. So no, I do not date."

I agreed to stay against my better judgment. Old skills were telling me to get out of there as I watched her prepare the coffee in the tiny kitchette. Her movements were very familiar to me. She moved like the motion of a soft wave. It was intoxicating. So I stopped watching; it appeared to be making her nervous. If I remember correctly, that plait wrapped around her head extends down below her knees. I feel like teleporting to her and gathering her in my arms and never letting her go. But since I can't have her why bother with the effort? She serves the coffee. It tastes better than expected to be instant. She asked about the latest movies, books, and music. I'm a multicultural individual so I really cannot say much about the things she knows about.

"Ana, where do I know you from, other than the night in your home three years ago?"

"I don't know. I think I know you from dreams. But dreams aren't reality." She said doubtful they can be real or if they are even dreams but another plane of reality.

"Sometimes we think we're dreaming when we're not. We're actually in another existence. Another realm as real as this one. There are billions upon trillions of other existences. I believe that is where I know you from." She smiled because she was wondering the same thing.

"The woman you were to see tonight. I'm not sorry you didn't..." She said out of the blue, letting him know she knew the reason for his earlier rudeness. She knew she interrupted a date or other social function. "Because in this other realm or existence... You belong to me." She made that clear with a shade of meanness, no jealousy.

He was vexed by her suddenly boldness. "Hmm, is that right?" He asked, curious as to where she was going next with this jealousy that seems to be embroiling and emboldening her right now.

"Yes. In this other existence we're husband and wife." She explained things as they slowly seep from some unknown place into her brain. Looking him boldly in the eyes to let him know she was serious. She sat the cup down and continued seductively but threateningly, "Yes, that's right. But I get real nasty when I sense you seeing other women." Now he was wondering if she was mental. He had met a few women who were but she didn't look it.

"Ok, since you remember that much...where is this so-called other existence? Where did we live? Reincarnation doesn't exist so I know it couldn't have been another lifetime." He had heard many lovers tell him they had lived and loved in another life time. But he knew reincarnation didn't exist. But he was curious about her explanation.

"I didn't say I knew all that. I just remember bits and pieces. Sometimes you were dressed differently from seemingly from one day to the next or from when I last saw you. Why? I don't know. I remember once you were in prison and it was pitch dark in there. I couldn't see you but I could hear and feel you. I could feel things crawling over my hands as I touched you. Your skin felt tough like tree bark. I remember I told you to keep the faith that one day you'd be free. Another time, I remember you were in a land of snow and ice with two dragons behind you, your hair was yellow and black then not mixed colored like it is now. Another time, I remember a huge planet made of some sort of blue glass, it shone a blinding glare for miles. It was so beautiful. I remember another time, you took me for a walk in a strange bejeweled park and picked a fruit....." she stopped talking when it seemed to be upsetting him.

I nearly dropped the hot liquid in my lap. I had to get up. I sit the cup down carefully. My hands had begun to tremble; that's a very rare thing for me. How does she know all this? This shook me to the center of my very confident core. Sure, I remember a woman visiting me in the darkness of prison because I was going mad. That's a place I never wanted to visit again.

"I'm sorry if I upset you." She said with genuine compassion in her voice. "I was only trying to cipher all this other existences crap. We can talk about something else."

"No, no...please do. Continue. I've thought for years that was all a dream. Wishful thinking." I said totally astonished. "I've spend years, eons dissecting those visits. I'd admonished it to merely wishful thinking of a fervent, deranged brain. "You told me you loved me and always would. That time, death, nor hell would keep you from me." I said, knowing I had to get away from her. She was a stark reminder of the painful past it took billions of years to bury within. But in just minutes she ripped the scab off leaving a festering boil.

I walked out on the balcony overlooking the large pool. She shyly followed me.

"I don't remember exactly what I said but I do remember fragments of the visits. I can't fully even remember what you looked like. I mostly remember your clothes were different everytime I saw you. I sometimes feel that something is missing. That somehow we offended someone and are being punished." She rapidly explained.

I, too felt we were being punished for something we don't clearly remember. I doubt we would remember tonight once it ends. I know I had a lot to be punished for because of what I had done but why was she being punished? Did she say something offensive to the heavens?

Turning to look down at her, he figures what's the hell? They won't remember beyond tonight anyway and grabbed her and kissed her. She kisses him back. The kiss ignite a long dead fire in his soul. This fire was real, nothing like the seductive emotionality he was feigning and anticipating with Ming. He remembers kissing her on the banks of the Nile, oh so very long ago. He remembers the cool breeze off the water, her taste, and the warmth of the African sun and how it heightened the bronze in her skin. He remember the chattering of the shocked servants. He guessed the people were servants, he can't remember for sure. But this he did know, that whatever satisfies the soul is the only truth. He also remembers the pain of her leaving.

"Are you sure you want to do this? This time it won't be a dream," he hoarsely asked her. "You know...we won't remember in the morning."

She looks deep into his gemstone eyes (his eyes are what she remembers most) and nods.

He prays she doesn't get pregnant. He doubts she's using contraception, so that part is up to him. He thinks back; when was his last vasectomy? She reenters the bedroom to check on Bea, to dress her for bed, and put her under the covers. The room is a bit chilly, cool enough to sleep comfortably under the covers. While she is attending the kid he calls the security and tells a woman to come sit with the child in case she wakes up while they are away.

I feel like a new bride on her wedding night. I'd vowed during my teen years never to sleep with anyone whom I'm not married to but that was another life making a childish pledge. With the life I live, I do not know if I'll be around from one day to the next. Now, I fully understand wartime lovers, meeting as two passing ships in the night, never to see each other again. I do not want to part with the pretense notion of seeing him again after tonight. I do not look forward to any type of future, in the past three years I've learned to live for the moment. For that is all I'm certain that is mine.

He takes her hand and leads her out the door as the nurses walked in. The women sees a worried look on Ana's face when she looks back at the sleeping Bea. "She will be fine." One of the women smiled and closed the door. He teleports them to a much larger room with a spa. He pours them both a glass of champagne and make a cheerful toast to what they remember and have forgotten.

"I believe you're a timewalker." He says.

"What's that?" She asked, sipping her champagne. Drinking was a luxury to her. She rarely drinks for she must always stay alert.

"A person with the supernatural ability to walk into other era or eon through a rip or portal in time. However, in your case I don't think you came through a time rip by the length of time you were able to stay. Time isn't exactly a straight line. There're many curves and many different linears. How long have you been doing this?"

"I'd say all my life. But it didn't become very intense until recently. After we hit the road. I've no memory of you prior these road adventures if you omit the closet episode." She chuckled softly. "What you're describing I've heard it associated with witchcraft. I don't think I'm a witch. Apparently, this Vonderbilt, whomever he is.... seems thinks I am. I don't even know how I know the name Vonderbilt but somehow I do. Sometimes, I suffer from a weird type of amnesiac lapses. I can remember things for a moment but don't know how and then they go away. I know the name but do not know the man. Perhaps I've met him. I do not know." She knew she was nervously rambling but what else was there to do when such a handsome man brings you to a private room in preparation to have sex with you?

"Sound like fatigue amnesia to me. Sometimes one can become so exhausted you become forgetful. Which is why I think you should stay here or at another mansion and stay off the road because that man is going to eventually seriously hurt you"

"Do you know him?"

"Yes, I know of him and he isn't a pleasant character. He's a very dangerous, eccentric man."

"I feel there is a reason I'm out there, that I'm supposed to do something..." She said, crinkling her brow.

"Other than get yourself and that baby killed?"

"Yes, other than that." She laughed softly. He didn't seem to find it funny. "I feel I'm much like the prophets of old. I'm supposed to do something very important. What is it? I do not know. But I feel it will be revealed to me." She didn't know where all that came from. She never felt she was supposed to do something important. "Do you still love me as you once did?"

Her question took me by surprise. I don't remember telling her I loved her. Yes, I've strong feelings for her but I wouldn't exactly call it love. Right now, it's called lust. I've heard this too many times. This woman is harboring an illusion of what she believe I'm to her.

"Ana, I should lie to appease you, simply to get you in bed. But I won't. I don't remember this great love you speak of. I don't think...I know I'm not your husband. Never have been and never will be. I remember all of my wives very well and you aren't one of them." He knew he had to correct her on the subject of love and marriage right now before it got out of hand and she start fostering the idea that he's going to marry her. The route she was taking was quite disturbing and led only to illusions and heart aches.

She refuses to accept his stance, "Yes, we were married. You told me you loved me like none other."

"Uh, Ana, a man will say anything to get you in bed. I thought you knew that. So, at any given point if I've relayed the impression I was in love with you, I'm sorry. I'm very apologetic. I care a great deal about what happens to you. It's obvious a lot has happened to you. Distorted your thinking but I can't say I love you because of it. I can't say it only because you wish to hear it."

"Then why are we in this room if you don't love me?" She asked, wiping away a tear.

"That's a good question but I thought you wanted to make love, not talk about love and marriage."

(*I felt like my hand was telling me to slap the shit out of him. But I told my hand no, we have to stay here tonight, we can't get out of here yet. We will slap him in the morning*).

Now she was making me feel like a first class heel. I've left many a women in tears and not gave a damn so why do hers bother me? Maybe I did tell this crazy woman I loved her. I must have if I care about her crying. That makes me as crazy as she is. I knew I was making things worse by saying the truth.

Squatting in front of her, believing exhaustion is causing her to cry, "Baby, don't cry. We'll find away around these mental blockades and discover what really happened to us.

If we really loved each other once it will shine through again. Love always find a way."
I felt like a corny heel now.

"Oh, that's ok, go to your other woman. You don't owe me a thing if you can't remember what you told me." She cried, wiping her eyes with the back of her calloused hands. This was his first time noticing how rough they were. The dried, cracked, rough cuticles of her nails told him she had taken some seriously hard jobs. He noticed there was old scars on her knees and legs. He knew battle scars when he saw them.

I apprehended it was nearly morning from the slowly lightening of the sky. I distinctly decided let's go ahead and do it and get it over with so I can go on to Ming and she can go wherever her crazy mind is leading her. At least that's what I told myself, but my heart wasn't listening. I kissed away the tears and intended to make it quick so she would go to sleep and quit bugging me about love. But I found with every kiss, touch, and caress, I was remembering things trillions of years forgotten. She was right; we did once share a great love. We were once married. When I entered her it was like a time warp opened. This woman was once my queen. How could I've forgotten that? The love making was so slow, tender, and compassionate. I remembered her hair shrouding her whenever she saddled me. The feel of her soft derrieres in my hands. I felt a foretaste of what I lost many years ago. I wanted to hold on and never let her go. Now it was my turn to cry. The pain of losing her came flooding back like a fusillade riverdam.

"Sweetheart, what do you remember?" Cupping my face with her tiny, toughened hands she asked ever so tenderly, caressing my face.

"I immensely remember how much I loved you and you were sealed away from me forevermore. But I don't know why? I remember we were husband and wife, we were very happy. How is that possible when your world didn't exist then-I can't explain it all. But you are right. We were once married. Why did you leave me? It broke my heart."

Then it was her turn to kiss away my tears. I wondered had my bellicose nature separated us? I became a monster after she left. Were I a monster is why she left, never to return?

"My bellimissia, I'm sorry for being such a Rabelaisian, such a satirist. I'm sorry for hurting you. I think deep down inside I knew you were telling the truth. But didn't want to bear the pain that truth would bring."

I made love to her a fourth time. Secretly, I was hoping she got pregnant so she would have to stay. Her responses told me she still loved me and never stopped from all those years ago. I see now that love really does transpire across time and space.

We spent six happy weeks together before people started questioning her whereabouts. A month and a half of blissful making love every night, playing with Bea during the day. The rest and fresh air were giving the two a divine makeover they needed. Now, she was looking again like my beloved Ana. I knew the Feds had been in Sinkhole looking for her. The last agent they sent... Well, let's just say he's still here.

In their merry weeks all has been well, but he keep expecting divinity to show up and whisk her away. He knows better than most men for he have lived longer, loved, and lost. That a good woman is someone you never want to lose. She will take you above the average to the greatest. She will be the peace that calms your angry soul. She is your better half. If you have her heart cherish it because if you let her go, you will never find another whom you love as much as her.

⤷✣↶

Augustine Pembroke and Cerberus Manson had to find a way to flush Ana BuFaye out of the Cargill haven. The place was a fortress and the owner a monster. They first hear of her whereabouts via an anonymous caller. A local agent was sent to the estate but disappeared. That was two weeks ago.

"Pembroke, I suggest we use her family to flush her out. She's from the backwards deep South. There, the people still believe in shit no one else cares about anymore. You see, she's living in sin with a renowned playboy. So tell her family of his lifestyle. And I can promise you they'll root her out into the public again. You're better at talking to mothers than I. You tell her mother."

Pembroke never liked anything Manson suggested for it was always somehow laden with deep deprivation. "What am I supposed to tell this woman to make her get in touch with her daughter?"

"I don't care what you tell the woman's mother. I tell ya what. You can pretend to be jilted boyfriend who believes in the Lord and say she left you for this rich guy who she's now shacking up with. Tell her the man is loaded is why she left you. Tell them that you asked her to marry you but she prefers to live in sin rather than marry a decent, honest, hardworking, God-fearing man." Manson said laying it on thick as he laid out his entrapment plan. "And I can guarantee you they'll find her and give her hell."

"Manson, everybody shacks nowadays before marriage. You'd be a fool not to."

"I'm telling you man, these are my people so I know how they still think. Yeah, I know everybody's shacking nowadays but try telling Southerners that! You from the north. You don't understand how serious they take this shit."

"We told her sister her niece has been shot and got no useful response." Pembroke reminded him.

"I'm telling you man, to those people who a woman give her pussy to is far more significant than a brat getting shot. I know what I'm talking about."

"If so, then all of you all are batshit crazy!"

Manson shrugged his shoulders. How can he explain to a liberal like Pembroke that the ghost of the feudal lord system still lives on in some parts of the world? "I didn't make the rules. I simply know they exist."

I reluctantly go along with Manson's harebrained scheme and was absolutely flabbergasted it actually worked. We listened through the bug as her family ranted about the sins of fornication and how dare she dump a good God-fearing man for one who will never marry her. They violently lecture her on her recalcitrance, even demand since she is with a man of wealth she pick up the entire tab in supporting their mother.

"Ana, that is not how I raised you." They heard the mother say, "A man is never going to marry you if you shack with him first."

"What's wrong with your real boyfriend? He's respectable, a nice guy, and wants to marry you but you dump the man for a playboy who is going to treat you just like Thad Wyett treated you. Didn't you learn anything the first go around?" Her brother Jack asked.

"What other boyfriend? I don't know who called you all but he emphatically is no boyfriend of mine for I don't have one!"

"What are you going to do about helping us with mom?" Her sister asked.

"Helena, I'm still not working. Nor do I've a permanent place to live." The four way embattled Ana cried. "I sent something up there a few weeks ago. Didn't you get it?'

"It sounds permanent to me. Yes, you do have a job. It's done on your back." Helena snapped. "Nah, I ain't got nothing from you but some guy calling here crying over you. That ain't nothing new."

"Helena, keep it clean. Mom is on the network." The oldest brother chastised on the phone.

"I'm here hiding out from those who want to kill me." Ana says to her family.

"Ana, I'm beginning to wonder if all this talk about people trying to kill you; are they really excuses for avoiding the reality of life? How come they haven't come after anyone else in the family but you? What makes you so special that all these people want to kill you? So this guy is rich enough to buy off the killers? Huh? Seems to me if he cared so much he'd help you with your mother." Jack BuFaye asked. "Yeah, by the way... a fat dude showed up at my office saying you shot a fed. Ana, you have got to learn to control your temper."

391

The constant bickering back and forth had become tiresome. I wasn't listening to a lot of it because a lot of it was plain stupid. I knew Manson would tell me I told you so. This was his kind of amusement. Little wonder the man is so fucked in the head if his own family is anything like the people speaking. I became alert and sat up and paid attention when Cargill himself got on the phone.

"I'm sending a payment of 200 grand, that should cover the cost of a home-care provider for years. Any excessive medical bills for Mrs. BuFaye send them to my office in New York City. Ana is safe here. This is where she and Breanna needs to remain. The threats aren't fabricated they're real."

"All that is well and good," Helena says. "But how's that gonna save her soul from hell? If you cared so damn much about her you would marry her. Throwing money around is the easiest thing in the world to do."

"I'm under no obligations to discuss our personal life with any of you. Ana is an adult fully capable of deciding how she wish to live her life," Cargill replied. I could tell he was angry. And he thought his in-laws were meddlesome?

"I'm her mother and I've a right to know your intentions toward my child." Fannie BuFaye cut in on the barbs between Cargill and Det. Wales.

"If she wishes, whenever she is ready we can get married." He informed her mother.

"Ana, what's wrong with that one? Since the other one wasn't rich enough for you?" Jack asked.

"Aarrgghh! I told ya, I don't know who you talked to but whomever it was he was no boyfriend of mine. I don't have a boyfriend. I told ya it's *them* you was talking to and don't talk to them. They're liars. They'll say anything. Just like they told ya'll where I'm hiding out from them at!" Ana screamed at her brother.

"Sure you would say that with the rich one listening." Jack retorted. "But that guy came here all broken up about ya and you expect us to believe you wasn't paying him no attention? That he's just some crazy guy who came here asking for help? He said he helped you out as much as possible but you said he wasn't doing enough."

"What did he look like?" Ana carefully asked.

"I don't know, some white dude, neat cut dark brown hair, dark blue suit, dark lime, or gray eyes. Not hard on the eyes. Why do you ask?"

Ana knew perfectly well which of the men from St. Louis it was. The one who had the chance to kill her but didn't take it. Knowing what she now knows, it wasn't his heart that prevented him from blowing her away, it was his fear of Ashton Cargill. They were fully aware of what she meant to him.

"Yes, I expect you all to believe whomever you talked to, some lying scum. That's the kinda shit they pull. Fuck you, Jack! Ain't everybody like Lesheiksa and I'm sick of you trying to make me fit in the same category!" Ana's end went dead. Someone quickly called her back. Cargill answers her phone. "One of you all can pick the money from Ana at any Marathon Nation Bank, all you need to do is show ID."

"Where is Ana?" Fannie asked.

"In her room. You all have upset her a great deal. I'll not forward any upsetting messages to her."

"That's fine. Tell her to bring her skinny butt to Brunswick and see about mom." Helena said and cut the connection.

Manson and Pembroke watch the routing network of the Marathon banking systems take in the transaction. They see the payment from Cargill International Bank placed in a dummy account and retrieve it. Knowing this will make him look like a liar and make her family put more pressure on her to leave him. I must say this is much easier and profitable than chasing her all over the country.

We listen as her family discloses her secret phone number saying there was nothing

393

down there. Her rich lover is a liar, and is simply using her, and when he gets tired of her (which will be soon), he will dump her for someone new. She defends him saying he sent it. They call her names like fool, stupid, gullible, and says she doesn't have the sense God gave a gnat.

"*It's little wonder she has any self-esteem left at all.*" Pembroke thinks. I could tell this is their accustomed method of talking to her. Cargill vows he sent the said amount and someone picked it up.

"I'm sorry." Fannie said sincerely. "It wasn't any of us.

"I'm sending another 200 grand and I want one of you to be down at the Brunswick local bank to pick it up." He said, calling his security team in the area to see who is listening and who picked up the payment. "There will be two increments for 200 grand each." He said. "Mrs. BuFaye, it shall be in your name."

He hung up and waited until his team was in position and clicked the button twice.

Pembroke and Manson weren't in Brunswick; they were catching the payments under an anonymous code for alleged tax evasion. They were physically in Spokane. Cargill Security was viewing the transaction and reversed it from Spokane. They contacted their co-worker telling them where to look for a man or woman pretending to collect for tax purposes. The Spokane branch of Cargill International was waiting when Pembroke and Manson arrived. The two had been joking Cargill was dumb enough to send a second payment in the same day. They entered the bank; unknowingly they were being watched. They use the same tactic as they used earlier. The teller informed them then the money had been reversed. That's when they realized it was a decoy. That Cargill is onto them. They turn and walk briskly but professionally out of the bank behaving as if it was they who have been grossly wronged. As they approach their hovercraft a black hovervan pulls up beside them and yanks them inside. "We have them." The two men heard one of their captors say. The four men of considerable size didn't bother to hide their faces which both men knew that meant they intended to kill them.

"We're both federal agents and to erase us will bring the entire agency down on Mr.

Cargill." Manson threatened. The agents nearly fainted when Ashton Cargill appeared out the thin air in the back of the van with them.

"I'm giving you two disgraces an hour to collect my money. I already have people trained on your loved ones awaiting my signal to kill. Manson, your senator uncle can not help you and Pembroke, you knew my profile well enough to show repudiation of the scheme. You should know Manson's family has been in the occult since they hit the shores in the late 1700's. Had you researched him instead of hounding and harassing my wife you would've known that. But freaks like you two prefer to harass innocent women and children than go after real criminals."

Manson scoffed at the *innocent* part, feeling he had nothing else to lose. Manson grinned and told the most powerful man in the world what he and Bender did to the woman he loved. Pembroke was horrified Manson thought that would help their situation.

"I've a wife and two children." Manson plead when Cargill opened the air compressed door. "You should've thought of them before you decided it would be fun to try to rape mine". He slung him out the door so hard he soon appeared as nothing more than a black dot in the sky. The man's eyes were flames of fire when he turned to question Pembroke.

"I've never put my hands on her."

"But you have thought about it, haven't you?" Cargill asked. He was walking Pembroke's timeline. He saw the man call his colleagues off Ana. It was a distressing thing to watch her surrounded by them. He projected the image in the minds of the four men in the back with him. They knew he meant find those jeering and laughing and slaughter every single one of them. Kill them all.

"Pembroke, I'm letting you keep what you stole. Tomorrow morning you will be the new director of your agency. You'll weed out those who work for Vonderbilt. I own your ass. You work for me. If not, you'll end up in the Tombaugh just like Manson or if you double cross me I'll destroy you and your family. You'll keep track of all shady requests to track, stalk, or harass Ana BuFaye. Have I made myself clear?"

The only thing that saved Augustine Pembroke from death was Cargill saw where he had a clear shot at the back of Ana's head and had a change of heart about killing her. He saw him look into Bea's eyes and lower the gun. Which meant the man had some decency left in him.

Pembroke nods. He's too stunned to reply. He has no idea what Cargill is but he is certainly, positively not human. These men were more stealthy than the secret service when they took him home. No one saw them arrive or leave. It was like they vanished as Cargill did. He was home less than thirty minutes when he got the call from the vice-president to report promptly at 5:30 for his swearing in ceremony. He swallowed hard. He didn't realize Cargill had so much power. He feels he has sold his soul to the devil.

⁂

The tellers looked at Fannie with deep resentment when she walked out the bank carrying an antiqued carpet bag containing almost a quarter of a million. The president of the bank called everyone he could think of to justify not delivering the money but it came up clean. He and the guard constantly sent Fannie acrimonious glances as the machine counted the money. The guard walks her through the small lobby and opens the door; "Fannie, you better careful toting around that kinda money. With people, you never know." Fannie said nothing. She felt if she opened her mouth vomit would spew out. She hurried to her car and drove home as quickly as possible and locked all door. She firmly believes Ana sold sexual favors to this man for this sort of money. He now owns her stock, lock, and barrel. How can she do such a thing? Fannie's sister Gayle told her the man is obviously deeply in love with Ana, no one pays that kind of money for sex and especially not to the woman's family if he doesn't love her a great deal.

"Gayle, that's besides the point. He owns her now. He's never going to marry her and she will never be able to marry anyone else who might really love her."

"Fannie, y'all should be glad she found somebody wants to look after her. Y'all know something been after her all her life. Y'all really shouldn't give her as hard a time as you do. If y'all treat her badly so will others." Gayle argued with her older sister.

"So you're telling me I should condone what she's doing. Going against everything decent she was taught!"

"No, but life isn't always a straight line, clean cut black and white, there are many gray areas. Sometimes one have to do what they have to do. Maybe after Thad she doesn't want to get married again so is she supposed to live a loveless life? Fiddle with herself for the next 50-60 years?"

"Gayle! Watch your mouth!" Fannie warns. Her other lines rings as she and Gayle debate rather than talk. Gayle hears Fannie says to the her other children she needs them to come pick up the money. She doesn't feel safe with it.

"How much, mom?" Jack asked.

"400 G's."

"Ok. Mom, stay indoors. Keep the doors locked. Don't let nobody in. We'll be there in approximately four hours." Gayle listened but waited until her nephew was off the phone before speaking her mind. "Fannie, Ana sent that to take care of you, not her siblings extravagant lifestyles. If you don't feel safe with it, Clyde and I will go with you to a bank in Atlanta or Savannah to deposit it but that's meant for you to live from not your other children. I'm sure she don't mind your sharing but I think you are doing the wrong thing."

Fannie explained the bank ordeal as to why she told the others to come pick it up. She knew Ana was always Gayle's favorite of her four children. She guess it was because they both are baby sisters. Some-times Ana reminded her of Gayle. They both possess the same whimsey, cutesy way of doing things.

"Gayle." Fannie said.

"Yes??"

"Mind your own damn business. These are my kids and this is my money. I do whatever I want."

"But Fannie, you've always been unfair to Ana. Why? I wish I knew. She can't help she was born gifted or different from the others."

Fannie sighs, this is just like something Ana would say, "Ana is like her Aunt Gayle. Doesn't think of the consequences before she acts. She's like you. She doesn't consider what her actions will do to others." Fannie replied.

"What harm have her actions caused you?" Gayle stubbornly retorted.

"The list is so long it will take until next week to label them all."

"Fannie, those things aren't her fault. Those evil people fix things to make it seem as thus it's her fault. She need you all to love and support her so she can stay strong against them."

Fannie sighed for the third time during this conversation, she expected that kind of remark from Gayle. "Gayle, everyone in town will be asking me what kinda job Ana have that pays this kinda money? I know she doesn't have a real job or career and what am I supposed to say! Lie??"

"You ain't got to say nothing! Those busybodies are who you need to be telling to mind their own business. That ain't none of their damn business. They need to be worry about their own rugrats and not yours! You've always worried too much about what other people think. Their opinion ain't paying no bills for you so it don't matter. The bank had no business sowing your financial business all over town."

Looking out her front livingroom window she sees a black hovercraft alit at the curb, the sleek black exterior sparkled brilliantly like stars in the bright Georgian sunlight, telling everyone in the whole damn neighborhood serious money just lit in front of her house. She tells Gayle she has to go, for Fannie knew with Gale this conversation was going to turn into a debate about civil and social liberties. Gayle has never conformed to anything asked of her. Just like Ana. Fannie peeked outside between the heavy white panel curtains. There appeared to be two seriously mean looking men just sitting there in the dark tinted windows SUV, not really watching the house but watching the streets and neighborhood. Her house phone rings. This is something her children rarely used. She looks at it and out at the vehicle. She knows the caller is in that sinistral official looking SUV. She debate should she answer. But decided to let it ring. It stops. About fifteen minutes later it start ringing again. This time she answers. "Look here, you creeps. Leave me alone!" She said pertinaciously.

"Sorry, Mrs. BuFaye. I didn't mean to cause dismay. I was sent by your daughter to make sure you are well." The male caller politely informed her. "I humbly apologize for the disturbances our presence may have caused.

"Oh, my daughter's boyfriend sent you. Well, you tell him I don't need him sending nobody to sit in front of my door."

"Mrs. BuFaye, Mrs. Cargill- your daughter sent- us not Mr. Cargill." The man said. Fannie laughed.

"You mean he got y'all calling her Mrs. too, when she's really just his girlfriend for the moment. What is he gonna tell y'all to call her a few months or years from now?" Fannie retorted and hung up the phone. She shook her head about her wayward daughter. She had no idea what to do about Ana's free wheeling lifestyle.

Jack BuFaye could use the money. Lesheiksa has been riding him hard pertaining the lack of money with all the children they have. He asked her to cut back on some of the salon visits, designer clothing, and trades in for a new car every two years but she balks and says that he knew she was high maintenance when he married her. She doesn't wake up looking like this, all glamourized. It take a lot of work and effort to look this way. Now that their youngest is four and in preschool he asked her about taking a part-time job. But she says being a mom is a full-time job and more work than he realized. And working will make her looking old and tired like all the other working women. But Junior said dump her and get a career woman. But he does love his wife and has no intention of listening to his older brother's advice. He doesn't see Junior dumping

Frances. But it is slightly irksome how he busts his butt to make a living while his little sister does absolutely nothing but whine and complain but yet ends up with some fool willing to shell out half a million all because she bats her eyes at him. He loves her but he's the first to try and tell all these nutty guys; his sister is a fruitcake. But apparently, from Thad, to her former next door neighbor, to the curly haired dude with the funny accent, to this latest fool...they all love themselves some fruitcake.

I decided to give it a whole day before calling mom. The security people said she got the money and was shut up in the house. I hope she turned the air conditioner on for it's hot down there. I know those damn agents who took the first payment are who told her about me and Ashton. Maybe mom is right. Maybe I've sold my soul and body for protection instead of toughing things out. Perhaps I've taken the easy way out. But it doesn't feel that way. Besides I'm tired of being afraid all the time. At least here Bea and I are protected. He has mentioned maybe we should go ahead and get married since we obviously love each other. But I don't feel ready for another marriage yet. I intend to see how things work out between us before I take another plunge. I don't think he's eager to wed, either. We did seriously sit down and talk to see if we both have a memory of a wedding but neither of us have one of an official divorce. Does that means we are still married? If so, then that means my marriage to Thad wasn't valid. Shit! All this thinking is giving me a headache. This is why we try to stay away from that other existence/reality because it makes no sense at all.

Twenty four hours later Fannie is on the phone with Bea. She knows Ana is mad is why she hasn't called. The room Bea is in looks like a place for royalty. "Grandma, I've a pony now. I named her Fancy."

Fannie noticed Bea seems to gain a few lbs. She doesn't look tired and hungry as she did the last time she spoke via screen to her.

"Oh, that nice sweetie. But you know you have a first cousin named Fancy?"

"I do?" The three year old asked.

400

"Yes, your uncle Junior's daughter. Where's your mother? Who is that lady in the room with you?" Bea turned and looked at her nanny.

"That's Rikki. She's my nanny. Mom is in her room asleep."

"Bea, uh, does the man you live with... does he sleep in the room with your mommy or does mommy have her own pretty room like yours?"

"Grandma, this house is really big!" Bea said, holding out her slender arms, expanding them over her head.

"Sweetie, you can tell grandmother anything. I know your mom probably told you not to tell me. But you can tell granny." Fannie coaxed, rising her eyes above Bea's head to meet the eyes of the man's employee, the eavesdropping nanny. She knows the woman really work for Ana's boyfriend and not Ana. She knows the woman was employed to keep Bea out of the way. She can feel the ephedrine of her morning medication kicking into high gear as she waits patiently for her young granddaughter's reply. The child's eyebrows knit in confusion as to which one to obey. Mom or Grandma?

"That's ok, sweetie. Grandma shouldn't have put you on the spot. You're to obey your mommy." Bea is smiling again. To her, Bea looks like Helena and someone else, but who? She doesn't know. She can see Thad's annoying ass mother in the beautiful child but she can also see someone else. Perhaps it's a long-dead, distant relative. Suddenly, Ana is in the screen dressed like a movie star.

"Hello mom, I intended to call you," Ana said, turning to tell the eavesdropper she is dismissed and to take Bea to the playground.

The moment they are alone Fannie lets her have it, "Ana what on earth do you call yourself doing? Don't you see everybody in that place is spying on you for him? You don't own a damn thing there. When that man gets tired of you he's gonna kick y'all out on the streets. And you can't get nothing from him. You ain't married to him."

"Did the nurse come?" Ana asked, already knowing Helena turned the woman away at the door saying Mom wasn't an invalid. She also knew this was Helena way of incapacitating anything she did for Mom.

"What kinda example you setting for Bea? She will think it's OK to shack up with a man." Fannie said ignoring Ana's question.

"Well, can you tell me if you got the money?"

"Yeah, I got it. I gave it to your siblings. I don't want nothing you made being dishonorable." Fannie quipped and tilted her chin upward. Ana sighed and shook her head. "Mom, that was given to you so you could stay at home. In your own house. Hire someone to come in and do your cooking and cleaning. We're taking care of the medical bills. It wasn't meant for my siblings."

"So now it's *"we"*, it's *"Mrs"*. Ana, get your ass outta that man's house. Come home! I mean now!"

"Mom, you know why I stay away from you. To keep these people chasing me. To detour them from you. I told y'all these people are dangerous. Do not talk to them. Talk to them once and they never leave you alone."

"If you got killed do you know you would go straight to hell? You ain't never seen me with nobody but your daddy." Fannie said, again ignoring the topic Ana was discussing.

"I'm glad things worked out for you and dad. I really am but what was I supposed to do? Stay by myself the rest of my life because Thad didn't want me? I'm sure Thad would love that! That's every man's dream come true."

"Had you listened to me you never would've ended up with that player. But just like now. You aren't listening. Bad things happen when you don't listen to your mother."

"Mom, it doesn't matter what I do. It's never good enough or honorable enough for you. So why bother? Why can't you for once be proud of me for just being me. I tell Bea everyday how proud I'm of her for just being Bea. I don't compare her to nobody else! Cause ain't nobody else like Bea." These words infuriates Fannie. *How dare this little shacking-up hussy talk to me that way?!*

"Maybe for once if you did something to make me proud. I'd be proud of you. But what have you done? Got a degree and don't use it. Always got the law at my door. Run all over the country shooting people like you done lost your damn mind, always on the run from the law cause you done killed somebody. Now, you shacking up with a rich man and you want me to be proud?! What have you been smoking? I don't know how you turned out so different. All the others have good jobs and are settled down. But you are like sumthin wild outta the damn woods!" Fannie said as her eyes popped fire on the screen at her perceived to be wayward daughter.

"The rest ain't got psychos after them messing up their every plan in life. If they had these people on their hineys believe me, their lives would be screwed up, too! Mom, you were in Boston. You've seen what these people do. I don't have the power or resources to stop them. I've hardly escaped with my life."

"Maybe if you prayed some of the time God would protect you from them. Have you ever thought about that!" Fannie asked. She was still furious at the tone Ana had taken with her.

"Ok, Mom. I'll come home. Although it's not safe. I know I'm gonna to end up dead or in jail or one of you all end up dead but since honor is dearer to you than life, I'll come home and I hope you are happy when these people end up killing somebody or everyone! Some people have to see things to believe them and I thought you had seen enough to know these people are dangerous. You saw the man shoot me in the Parent's Pit for no reason. "

"I've seen enough to know they're dangerous but you can't run forever. You gotta stop and put your faith in God. Let Him fight your battles. They can't do no more than God lets them do."

Neither knew Bea had sensed something wrong indoors for she had defied her nanny

403

and was back in the room listening. Both looked behind Ana when they heard a child's voice say. "No, mommy! I don't want to go back out in the hot sun. I don't wanna sleep in the car no mo'! I don't wanna go live with grandma. I don't want to leave my pets!" The little girl cried running and poking her small face in the screen and screamed at her grandmother. "And you can't make me!"

"Bea, honeybee. That isn't your home. None of those people are your family. We're your family. With your family is where you and your mom belong." Fannie tried to placidly to explain to the tantrum throwing three year old.

"I don't care! Daddy Ashton said I can stay here as long as I want to, I can stay here until I'm old and grown if I want to. You can't make me come to you. I hate you!" Bea shouted, bursting into tears. Her nanny came and picked her up and took her out the room but Bea ran back in and jumped on her bed.

"Ana, Bea is a child," Fannie patiently explained, it hurt her to see the two of them so deprived they were depending on this stranger who may or may not be there for them in as little as next week, "Children can easily be bought with toys, fun, and games. But you're the adult and you know it's best that you get out of that house and come home."

Bea sat up in her bed and yelled. "Go away and leave us alone!" Fannie told Bea she loved her and wanted what was best and decent for her. Sometime adults don't make the best decisions. She'd see them when they get home.

Ana didn't see her sister standing out of the camera range with a smug expression on her face. Once again she was doing better than Ana. She had researched the man and he was Ashton Cargill, the single most richest person in the world. She knew if they kept on after mother she'd make Ana leave him. Now that Ana was leaving him, things would be back to normal. The pecking order was restored.

"Mrs. Cargill???! Ha!" Helena cried after Fannie clicked off the screen. Fannie saw Helena's reflection in the screen and wondered had she done the right thing, this was her first time seeing that jealous visage her husband Jacob had warned her about in Helena. He said it was an evil, enviousness in Helena pertaining her little sister. But she rebutted him saying Ana was his favorite daughter that's why he see something amiss in their oldest daughter. It's obvious whomever the man is he wants them or he wouldn't spend this ridiculous sum of money on them. The evil expression she saw made her heart heavy with sorrow.

None saw the demons surrounding Helena, fanning the seed planted years ago. Nor did anyone see those in the back bedroom of Fannie's home, egging her on in a negative temperament toward her youngest child. They had been lurking outside for years but were unable to break through Fannie's prayer barrier. They saw their opportunity to get inside when a man with a very dark soul arrived; they rode into the BuFayes' home on the back of Augustine Pembroke.

In the Sinkhole, Wyoming Cargill mansion the nanny Rikki was among the other employees for lunch. She had seen to it that Bea had eaten. Bea was angry at her mother and refused to eat.

"I've to tell you, that woman has the craziest damn family I've ever heard of! Do those people still think this is the Victorian Age or what?" She asked the others after gossiping bout what she heard on the screen between Ana and her mother. Rikki wasn't thrilled at prospect of losing her job taking care of Miss Bea as they were told to call the child, but they only call her that in front of Ashton Cargill. He was such a stickler for formality.

"Rikki, keep that to yourself. If it gets around you're gossiping, that's an automatic dismissal. The chief of household said glancing at the chiaroscuro of Ashton Cargill in the hall way leading to the main diningroom. It had been years since he last stayed here. The rooms were usually rented out during the ski season for those who could afford them.

"I mean the woman is beyond stupid if she doesn't stay! Heck, I would stay and be his lover if he asked me. Did she get beat with a stupid stick growing up? Bea has more sense than her mother." Rikki cried. "It's so close to Christmas, Mr. Cargill have sent me Christmas shopping for the kid. I say the woman's family don't love her. I say they're a shogunate, a tyranny. But if she jumps everytime they say move they're always going to do that. Shit! If my sister hooked him, I'd beat her ass for trying to leave him."

Santayna shushed her for she heard someone coming. Santayna knew these people could hear better than humans. Her mom said they are what their ancestors called demigods. Marian appeared in the doorway and asked was everything ok.

"Yes, everything is fine." Santayana said, smiling. Marian didn't return her smile. She never does. Her people say Marian is really over 200 years old. But she looks about 38. They believe the woman heard Rikki ranting and raving. "Rikki, shut the fuck up before you get everybody fired. I like my job here, where else you gonna find a job you do what you wanna and only actually work about 3 months out of a year?"

"I like it here too, that's why Bea's dingbat mother is pissing me off. I've had other nanny positions and those little bastards were imps from hell. Bea is a very well trained child. She is polite and obedient. I'm going to talk to Mr. Cargill. He'll straighten that woman out. It's evident she's in love with him. Anybody with two eyes can see that!"

Seeing that Rikki's mouth and actions are about to get the whole staff fired the pastry chief says, "Rikki, mind your own business and keep your nose and opinions to yourself."

"But the child doesn't want to leave and neither does Ana really wants to leave, somebody's got to have some sense about all this. That child is terrified of something out there."

"Rikki, you aren't to fall in love with the children you supervise. Remember you're nothing but hired help. How they raise her is none of your concern." Santayana said. Rikki turns up her nose and grunts. "*We shall see about that!*" she thinks.

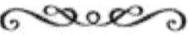

"Mommy, can we get Fancy in the car?" a charily eyed Bea asked, wiping away tears as her three year old mind devised a plan to take her pony with them. They were planning a trip for the holidays. Ashton said the big Christmas tree downstairs was hers. She never had a tree of her own. They always went to the places where lots of other cold, smelly people were for Christmas. At this moment she really didn't like her Mommy and Granny very much. Who will feed her pets and Fancy if she leaves? Ashton said they were her responsibility. They'll die if no one feeds them. This horror and stark reality to her, irked her three-year-old mind. The image her young mind conjures of her pets slowly starving to death sends her into another fit of rage and high pitched lamentations. She wails and throw herself back down on the white and pink fluffy bed that was all her own. Falls to the floor crying. She knows very well the pain of hunger.

"Bea, cut that out!" Ana firmly ordered. But Bea gets louder, hops off the floor, climbs into her pink and white ruffled canopy bed and kicks and screams. Ana has a good mind to get up and spank her but Rikki is watching very carefully.

"Hey, hey, what's going on here?" a voice asked from the doorway across the expansive princess room. Bea jumped up from the bed on the other side to avoid her mother and ran to him, grabbing him around the leg. He picked her up. They both stares frigidly at Ana as if she is the villainess here and is making them both unhappy. Ana is a little disturbed in how much Bea's eyes looked like his when she did that.

"My goodness, you two are fighting World War IV up in here!" he exclaimed, bringing Bea back to into her room, back to her mother.

"My daughter is acting like a spoiled, little rich brat. That's what's wrong."

"*Our daughter is* a little rich princess. I thought you knew that by now," Ashton replied sitting on the bed beside Ana with Bea on his lap since she refused to go to her mother. His eyes told her he had her tested and wasn't letting her go anywhere. *Maybe mom was right. Maybe he did have an ulterior motive.*

"Everything is set for her to enjoy a wonderful Christmas so why ruin it? Your family will be fine. They're welcome to come and see that I'm not mistreating my girls." He tickled Bea. Ana knew that was a great idea but also knew her mother wasn't coming. And if mom didn't come neither would anyone else. The family dinner was usually held at Helena's house. Seeing her face drop he says, "I've a palace outside of the Hamptons, close to your sister's home. How about let's move everything there for Christmas and you two go on a real shopping expedition?"

"Can Fancy and Mikey come?" Bea asked with glowing bright eyes as only a child can. "Sure can." Ashton assured her. "We'll load them up on the jet and they can spend Christmas with you. How about that?" Bea wrapped her little arms around his neck.

I couldn't compete with that and he knew it. So I agreed for Bea's sake. I had to relinquish my desire to go home and then maybe those two will stop looking at me in that creepy way.

The next day the three of us and Bea's pets, including Fancy and Mikey, headed to the palace. He did say palace not mansion. So I was thinking something along the line of the antiquated Caesar or Trump Palace in Vegas but I was wrong. This things was a true work of art, built with agility, grace, and beauty. The place looked more like a small town encased in a granite wall. I could see the smoothness of the highly polished granite reflecting off the fresh fallen snow. It was beautiful here. Light snow was dusting the place making it look like a true winter wonderland. Maybe Bea was smarter than I. No, no, no, I can't let myself get sucked in by all the gold and dazzling lifestyle. I don't know what my goal is but I know this isn't it. But I can hold off long enough to give Bea a Christmas she will never forget. She's right, she doesn't remember her first Christmas so that doesn't count in her book.

A snow mobile built like a limo comes and takes us to the house, well, city. Inside was decorated like a Christmas Fictitious place. The Nativity had real people and animals. I had to greet these people. I thanked them their wonderful service. This tree was bigger than the one at the mansion. I had to crane my neck to see the star on top, the bottom was completely surrounded by gifts.

"I made plans for the three of us to see *The Nutcracker*," he said as Bea and I both stood dumbfounded, staring at everything. "I think she will like the Sugar Plum fairy and etc."

We moved on to the outside that wasn't really outside. The garden was covered. The decorations were splendid. It looked something like a medieval courtyard turned into a garden. As we walked and talked he explained how the dinner would be served tonight. I was still reeling; just a few hours ago we were in the western discussing these things and now I'm surrounded by things I didn't know existed.

I knew it wouldn't work but I didn't tell him. I didn't want him to know some things about my family. Everyone was cordially invited but no one came. Instead they all were furious at me for not coming home as promised but Bea's happiness buffered the blow of the harsh words and accusations. I owed it to Bea, I'm sorry if my family disowned me for trying to make my daughter happy. But she comes first before whatever anyone thinks of me.

⸎

The BuFayes minus Ana and Bea had gathered at Helena Wales' home for the Christmas feasting. Fannie couldn't let go of the reoccurring dream for it refuse to let go of her. The nightmare always started the same. Ana in a massage spa, on the table awaiting the masseur to come but instead a bunch of strangers arrive, pull away the sheet and riddle her nude body with multiple bullets. In the dream Helena comes in afterward and look down at her sister's dead, mangled, bullet ridden body and snickers, "I guess he won't think you so pretty now." She walks out with a faceless man on her arm who is said to be Ana's boyfriend. Bea is shot in the back of the head as she kneels beside her mother's dead, bloody body trying to wake her up. The man who shoots Bea says he has to so she won't come for him when she grows up. The dream is so disturbing it wakes her screaming every night since they had the terrible argument regarding Ana returning home. She goes in Helena's bathroom and tries to make the call one last time. This time on Christmas Day a happy sounding Ana answers.

"I'm at Helena's, I need to see you, send some of your people to pick me up." Fannie whispered into the phone. Screw it if some of those people are listening. She has to warn her child not to come back to Brunswick. They're waiting there to kill her. She can't explain how she knows back home is where they are waiting but she just knows and is sticking with her intuition.

"Sure, Mom. You ok?" Ana asked, concerned over her mother's deep whispering. "They could be there in fifteen minutes."

Fannie stood in the thin snow on the side of the house adjourned with a red-bricked patio where Dave and the other men were drinking and supposedly barbecuing a turkey and waited. From here she could clearly see the streets. She was there less than ten minutes before a black hovercraft alights with a driver that is staring straight ahead. She strode briskly toward the aircraft as the soft snow sucks at her shoes which aren't designed for this element. She heard her sons calling her and even Helena calling from the patio door. She turned her head and shot them all a look that could curl paint off a wall. Everyone is puzzled as to what the look was all about? Helena sends her daughter Rachael to retrieve her wandering grandmother, believing her mother is suffering a sudden bout of Alzheimer's. Fannie brushes her granddaughter off her arm and keeps walking. She yanks the car door open with such force that everyone watching knows she isn't sick, she is angry, and slides into the front passenger seat refusing to look at the others. The vehicle arises, engages, and sprints off into the semi-cloudy December sky.

"I think Ana just kidnapped you all's mother," Dave chortled. His father joined in. "I know she did." Helena replied, cussing her sister for every sneaky bitch name she could think of. "She did it to show off."

"Do you all know where the place is?" Jacked asked, worried his mother got in the car with a stranger going only God knows where.

"Sure." Dave's mother said immodestly. "It's so exclusive that you've to be a very important person to be invited in. That's why I told Dave we should go. Who knows how long Ana will be able to hold on to that man?"

"Well, then let's go!" Jack cried. "Ain't no cocksucker gonna sent his folks to pick up my momma and think I ain't chasing his damn ass down!" He beckons Celestine Wales to follow so she can show him where Ana has whisked their mother off to. Dave holds his mother back. He knows she only wants to go to be able to brag to her Garden Club friends she had been invited inside the most extravagant palace in the world.

410

"I'm sure Ana will bring her back when she finishes showing off." Dave said. He didn't want Celestine there for he had heard the owner was a very dangerous person to know. Everyone heard Junior on the phone with Ana. He put it on speaker.

"Mom is fine. She wanted to come so I sent for her." a cheerful Ana said. Celestine Wales, the Manhattan socialite, turned sixty shades of envious green hearing that countrified Ana and her bumpkin mother were sitting in a place where kings, queens, presidents, and nobility has sat and haven't the sense to recognize the significance in being there. This was so not fair. Life is so unfair.

"Ana, send momma back here this instant!" Jack demanded.

"You ain't daddy. You don't tell me what to do! Screw you! I've as much right to momma as the rest of y'all. All y'all can go to hell." She yelled and broke the connection.

"That went well, Jack!" Celestine said drily. "Now, he isn't going to let anyone in. You don't show your ass until you get what you want!" Celestine groaned, wondering how her fine etiquette trained son ended up with such backward,troublesome in-laws. "Come here Rachael, call your grandmother and tell her you want to come over and give Breanna her Christmas gift."

The nine year old does exactly as her grandmother Celestine says. She calls her maternal grandmother and says exactly as instructed. But she wondered, *"What present? We haven't bought Bea a present!?"*

Celestine Wales knew Fannie would be delighted in seeing her two granddaughters exchanging gifts. So she rushed and rewrapped one of Rachael's leather accessories promising to replace it. While unbeknownst to them all Ana had gifts for everyone while no one had a gift for her except Bea, Ashton, and several staff members trying to persuade her to stay. Her presence made working for Ashton Cargill so much easier. Ana was so excited to see her family. Their not having a gift for her didn't matter. The fact they were all together again was gift enough for her.

"Sure, darling. Aunt Ana would be happy to see you and DJ, tell your uncles to bring their kids too."

Celestine sat triumphantly in the front seat of Junior BuFaye's car showing him the way. She doesn't ride backseat. His wife Frances had better get used to it. Celestine Wales knew the way out there like the back of her blue veined hand, the president of her Garden Club lived about twenty miles down the road from the extravagant estate. One had to gross at least fifty billion to live in this community. It didn't accept mere millionaires like she and her husband.

Meanwhile Ana informs Ashton her family is coming. He wasn't surprised since they captured the queen bee, Fannie.

"Dear, that's fine. What is Christmas without family? But I'm not tolerating the verbal abuse. I've heard how they berate you. So if you think I'm going to standby and let them belittle you then I need not attend the shenanigan, for the devilment in me is bound to surface. I think it's obtrusive the way they talk to you."

To Ana, this was very embarrassing. She was remembering once she and Thad were arguing and he cussed her. She told him she'll not stand for him swearing at her. Thad told her if her family talked to her like shit how did she expect him to talk to her? It was like a sore slap in the face because it was true. She explained to him the same she is now explaining to Ashton.

"Honey, I know they can be abrasive at times but they only do it because they honestly believe they're doing what's best for me. They do not mean those words. There's always something going on to upset them and this is how they deal with the frustration. It's not done out of lack of love. It's said out of love. We as a family have been going through this madness created by outside forces for years and it rankles everyone's nerves."

He listened and when she finished he kissed her forehead. He had seen this many

412

times before. The abused don't know they're being abused for it has gone on so long it is normal to them. But no one is abusing her in his presence. He doesn't give a shit what they think of him.

Pulling Ana aside before the others arrive, Fannie privately tells Ana why she came. She tells about the reoccurring dream.

"That's a bad omen if I ever seen one." Fannie warns. "Don't come back to Brunswick. Whomever they are, they're waiting for you there. This guy ain't half bad. I can see y'all being well taken care of. Both seem very happy. Sometimes a mother gotta do what she gotta do. Bea is delirious with joy as any child would be in this wonderland of toys and candy. At least you two will always have this Christmas to cherish." Fannie said, affectionately watching Bea not able decide which toy or ride she wants to play with, watching her run from one to the other.

"Your boyfriend, ahem, what's wrong with his eyes?" Fannie carefully asked watching Ashton operate a rideable old fashioned train model indoors with Bea and several other children in the open cars riding and laughing. The tracks had been laid in the beautiful marble floor. Ana didn't think he should have defaced the floor that way but he said it could easily be repaired.

"He has iris implants." Ana unknowingly lied, repeating what Ashton told her about his eyes.

"Why would such a handsome man want to mess up his eyes like that?" Fannie wondered aloud, not knowing that above all the laughing and clangorous noise the children and their toys were making he could hear them. She laughed at the fact the pony was wearing a shit bag strapped to its ass. Even Ana had to chuckle at Fancy following Bea around the track. Everytime she was near her mom and granny she grinned and blew the whistle.

The chef soon came and announced dinner was to be served and instructed the children to go wash up saying that pony was not coming to her table. Fannie was floored to see how long the table was. This thing could seat at least a hundred people or

413

more. Each setting has at least sixteen utensils. She had to reminisce on what was each utensil's function. Her mother and grandmother taught her these things. She taught them to her children but the opportunity rarely arrived to use them.

Celestine Chalice Wales was stunned beyond her wildest dreams when they entered. Even the president of garden club had never been inside here. All this extravagance spent on one little girl!? She was certain the BuFayes would be shown up for the country bumpkins they really were when they entered and were seated at the ball-like dinning room. She carefully watched her daughter-in-law and her birth family arrange everything in the proper manner for a formal dinner. How they ladled the soup served in decorated personal soup tureens from the correct side with the correct spoon. How they knew what the finger bowls were for? She watched Jack constantly instruct his wife and kids in which utensils to use. Even Bea knew what to do without her mother instructing her. She never knew Fannie was trained in fine and elegant dinning. *"If they know all this...then why are they so damn loud and rumbustious? Helena never showed an iota she knew all this. Even when I was tirelessly teaching her. Her bored look and disinterestedness was driving me crazy! The bitch already knew! I see my son watching Helena wondering what else about his wife he doesn't know."*

"I'm happy everyone decided to join us," Ana said, smiling, after about thirty minutes of silence. Trying to retain her joy of seeing the people she loves and haven't seen some in nearly four years. "Everyone, this is a very important person in my life. My second greatest love." Ana giggled like a silly schoolgirl but Cargill didn't seem to notice.

"Who is your first?" Jack asked curiously. He was taking Junior's advice in controlling his temper. "It's me!" Bea quipped from beside her mother and Celestine knew enough to laugh. Whether she liked his choice of companion or not she knew this man was powerful enough in the business world to make or break anyone.

"Of course it's you, sweetie pie." Jack smiled, pointing his fork across the table at his giggling three year old niece whom he hadn't seen since she was an infant. Turning to Ana who was seated next to Cargill, "I just thought Mom would be your second and he your third. You've been knowing her a lot longer."

414

"Jack, I'm certain Mrs. BuFaye comes before me in Ana's heart." Ashton said, attempting to nip the mayhem he foresee arising while it's a mere eddy.

"Dude, I gotta bone to pick with you. If you love my sister oh so muuuch...how come you haven't married her?" Jack asked the question he's been wanting to ask all evening. Ana flashed the engagement ring Ashton gave her on Christmas Eve. The thumbnail sized diamond sparkled like fire under the fine chandelier lights

"I want to be sure this time around. I don't want another divorce." she said. Helena was besides herself with jealousy. She wasn't expecting this. She had to find a barb of some sort to launch an attack.

"Well, I don't see what's the hold up. A good friend of mine is a justice of peace; she can come out here right now and perform the simple ceremony." Helena said looking at Ashton knowing or at least believing he will back down, that the ring is a dupe he is using to pacify her family.

Ashton surprised them all saying. "Baby, what do you say? Your family is here. The mood is fete and fusible." Knowing she wasn't going to see any peace unless she agreed. She timidly agreed although it wasn't in heart to wed him yet.

"Okkkk," Helena slightly stammered, dialing the person she spoke of and explaining who was marrying whom.

"Obtain her address. I'll send for her." Ashton excitedly says, again to Helena's dismay. "Oh, never mind, that's ok. My people will find her."

That trap didn't turn out as expected so she tried another barb. "What are you gonna do about Bea here? I mean, are you going to adopt her? I doubt Thad will let you." But taking it further saying, "You know what? Bea kinda looks like you." She turned and asked her husband Dave doesn't Bea look like Cargill. Dave mumbled he didn't know, he wasn't looking at them.

Helena had found her prodigy nail to drive into Ana's perfect little world. Bea's paternity. "How long have you two known each other?" she asked, almost sneering. Causing Fannie to look at her and frown.

"About six months." Ana replied.

"Six months is awful quick to get engaged. What do you know about him? Unless you've known him much longer than you two are letting on. Let's say like four or five years."

"What is it to you how long she has known me?" Ashton asked angrily. His devilment he warned Ana about was surfacing and showing.

"It matters a lot. Are you Bea's father or not? I think you know you are why else would a man she just met months ago be buying millions of dollars worth of toys and gifts for another man's child?"

"Maybe, unlike you, I enjoy making people happy not miserable. I bought your kids nice gifts so am I their father too? If so, perhaps you should explain to your husband how we met and how I banged the fuck outta you. But you don't have that to worry about. I wouldn't touch you with a ten-foot pole!"

An aghast, heavy silence fell over the elegant diningroom. Jack threw a carving knife at him. Ashton caught it by the blade and loured at him. Ana grabbed Ashton's fist clutching the blade and lowered it as Lesheiksa grabbed Jack's arm struggling to pull him back down. He didn't reclaim his seat until Fannie made him sit down. He slowly pulled his chair under himself again but all the while giving Cargill a knowing glance at his sister's inherent reaction to a threat against him. He smiled a little, daring Cargill with all his martial arts. He dared him throw that knife back at him, his hard dark amber eyes said. "Go ahead. Hit me. Throw it back. We both know if you do, my sister will leave you so fast all that hair will swoosh up on your head. Then we'll gotten what we came for." Lesheiksa looked from one man to the other and exploded laughing.

"Yeah, right...like Ana had enough sense to have an affair when she was with Thad. Maybe had she had enough sense to cheat on him he woulda treated her better! That guy

416

and Thad kinda look alike to me. That's how come Bea kinda looks like him. Try another one, Helena. Miss Squeaky Clean here ain't had no damn affair." Lesheiksa shakes her head, giggling at Helena's foolishness. "Give it up, your sister finally tops you and you can't stand it." Lesheiksa slapped her hands and leans back laughing louder than necessary. Still clapping her hands she wipes tears from her eyes. She knows Helena loves putting on airs and doing better than her sister. She knows Helena has never liked her. So she is happy Ana is able to outdo her older sister. She doesn't like either of her sister-in-laws very much but she can at least half-way stand Ana.

"Jack, there's nothing compared to how I love momma, so there was no need for that love to be explained," Ana cried.

"In my opinion, you making a fool of yourself sitting here telling this man how much you love him and he hasn't said one time how much he loves you." Jack grunted and shoveled a forkful of creamed spinach and parsnips in his mouth while looking across the table at this muthafucka his sister is hanging all over as if he is a source of life.

Ashton gravely wonders can he ever grow to like this mean man who keeps putting Ana down? Maybe it's these people's way of expressing love. He already knew they had come to take Ana away. The man didn't have to profoundly think it. They aren't simple nor stupid people. They're very intelligent and highly trained in proper etiquette. So maybe it is as Ana said. Stress has driven them to behave so ugly.

"Jack, I love Ana more than I love myself and I love me a lot. I show her that love every day and not the way your churning mind is thinking. I want to protect her and Bea from harm. Give her all she deserves and more. There's nothing I wouldn't do for her. I would kill for her shall anyone dare to harm her. The ring wasn't given to appease any of you. I asked her to marry me the second night she arrived. It was she who has taken so long to accept it, not I who have taken so long to ask."

Junior, trying to defuse the anger building between the two men, says, "All we wanted to know is if you love her, we aren't asking you to go out and kill anyone." That sort of lightened the mood as the room belched scattered chuckles.

"Thank you all for the beautiful dinner." Lesheiksa says. She is good and ready to go see what's under that monstrosity of a tree they passed coming to the dinning room. Let Ana and her super rich man handle their own business. But the judge arrived before the gift exchanging starts. Junior walked to Ashton standing under the arch of mistletoe and thanked him for looking out for Ana and Bea.

"You are welcome, Monsieur BuFaye." Ashton politely replied for Ana's stake.

"Shall we?" he asked Ana, extending his hand to help her rise from her seat.

"Aren't you gonna put on a bridal dress or something?" Helena asked.

"No, what she is wearing is fine." Fannie said. Seeing the uncertainty in Ana's eyes, she pulled her aside and whispered, "You don't have to do this to appease us. You are who will have to live with him not us."

Ana wanted to snap, "Y'all coulda thought of that before you raised enough hell to bring down the walls of Jericho." But instead said, "I do love him and have no doubt that he loves me. This is who I coulda and woulda married the first time had I known him."

Fannie nods, content with her daughter's answer. Rikki, Bea's nanny, ran and grabbed a floral
arrangement from the living room and gave it to Ana as a bridal bouquet. Junior and Frances loaned the couple their wedding bands after Junior walked Ana to Ashton standing under a massive red and green live holly arch twinkling with tiny white lights that led to the covered garden. The justice stood patiently as "Have Yourself a Merry Little Christmas" played in the background. When the vows were exchanged they learned Junior's band was too small for Ashton's hand but Ana placed it as far as it would go; Frances' band was too big for Ana's slender fingers. The simple ceremony was over in fifteen minutes and then the gift giving began. Ana tried not to show her slight disappointment that none of her relatives had a gift for her except Celestine Wales and she could see it was a re-gift and so was Bea's gift. But she told herself it was the thought that counted. She swallowed the petty thought and was determined to enjoy her

418

wedding/Christmas Party for with her life who knows what tomorrow would bring?. The Christmas/after wedding party lasted until after 2:00 A.M. She insisted everyone spend the night since it was so late. After all, she was now officially the lady of the palace.

Ashton was glad she didn't go to her sister's home to be with her family. In his eyes they have no concern whatsoever for her feelings nor happiness. Sounded a lot like his own family. How did they think she would've felt had she and Bea gone to them and sat there with pasted on smiles and no gifts? As he saw it, they were only going to spend the entire holiday berating and belittling them, making them feel worthless and small. But his new in-laws might as well accept that those days are over. He doesn't understand, why does the mother allow the other children to treat her horribly?

Oh well, this is their wedding night, he wants to make it a night to remember. He thinks she deserved a wedding ceremony with much more grandeur.

She spent the first couple of minutes of their wedding night/morning explaining to him her family has been through so much is why they appear rumbustious at times but they have her best interest at heart. He didn't try to explain to her or make her see what was really going on for he wanted to make love tonight not stay up until dawn's early light arguing about her family.

❦

Little does anyone knows this happiness won't last. Ana has been called to do something of epic proportions and the Council of Law and Order in the Heavens firmly believe Azazael will stand in the way. The Heavenly Council of Law and Order votes that when the earthly sphere thaws to erase the memory of everyone involved in this feat of love, so that the nuptials will not remember the months of bliss in each others' arms, their wedding, the Christmas party, nor will the couple remember they are, husband and wife. It shall be done to send Ana on her way to finish what she is called to do. To finish what she was created to do. This must be done for the greater good of all mankind and beyond. A very important prophecy is about to be fulfilled and nothing must stand in the way.

Raphael protested saying. "They won't forget each other and won't be happy apart. I believe it can be done even with Azazael at her side."

The others knowing how romantic and quixotic Raphael is don't debate him but all vote in favor for the separation because of Ana's role in the prophecy fulfillment. Denzuiel reminds him that what has already been ordained can not be changed even if they are in love.

"If their love is true and strong enough they'll find each other again. But you're forgetting one thing. No matter how beautifully attired that being is, he is still Azazael the destroyer. He hasn't been truthful with her as to who and what he really is. He's starting the marriage off by lying just as he did in antediluvian times. Brother, we know you yearn to see the Azazael of yesteryear again; so do we. He's our brother, too. It's a beautiful, whimsical, nostalgic idea but that Azazael died eons ago before the creation of humans. All is left is this chimerical version of what once was a glorious being. Who in my opinion will only behave a few months before he returns to his ancient way, interrupting our process with his madness."

"We preach to humans about forgiveness and giving one a second chance. Where is it among us? Love can blossom in the most unexpected places and who are we to snuff it out? That makes us no better than the ancient gods whom we detest. I say it's her decision to make if she wishes to be with him or not. I do believe she can change him and bring him back to our side." Raphael argues. "Show me a man who has been totally truthful with his wife as to who he is! If they were there would be no marriages and humanity would've died off long ago. All husbands lie."

"Are you now upholding falsehood?" The angel of Law and Order asked.

"No, I'm not but I'm upholding the sanctitude of love. Perhaps in due time he'll tell her the truth. How often do two meet and love each other immediately? Very rarely! Many lust first and then love and think it was love first! Have you all forgotten the giving and upholding of the Law abides in pure love? I think it should be left up to Ana to decided whether or not to forgive him for lying to her. You all can see clearly that he loves her very much and she loves him. "

420

"Ok, Raphael, since you made your point when her goal is completed then he shall find her again and we will not erase the memory but shall she reject him when she learns who he truly is and he behaves badly we'll imprison him. For her safety he must be imprisoned again." The Council agreed.

"But it's Father Who will have the final say. He isn't trying to harm her. It's Lucifer who is trying to kill her since she won't bow to him." Raphael said, leaving the grand Halls of the Council.

Around 5:00 A.M. one morning early in March she woke up with birds chirping outside but also with the nagging urge to be on the open road again. This was about the time she woke up and started moving to make sure no early birds found them asleep in the car. It was a puzzling but scary yearning. Why in the hell would she want to subject them to that danger and hardship again? They barely made it out alive the last time.

"I don't understand it, it is like I am weary of married life already. Truth be told, I was never sure about marrying him to begin with. I love him very much. Sometimes I think I love him too much. I love him, that I'm sure of, but there seems to be a calling in the depths of my soul inducing me away from the luxury and comfort he has given me".

She knows it is stupid. What more can she ask for? She's happy and doesn't have to lift a finger if she doesn't want to. Bea is happy and really filling out, finally gaining some weight. What's wrong with her? Why isn't she deliriously happy? She has a super rich, handsome husband who totally adores her. She knows without doubt she loves him. What in the Fuchs is wrong with her? Maybe Helena and Jack are right. Maybe she is nuts.

They've been trying to conceive a child of their own but with no success so far. She hasn't voiced to him how she feels restless. Perhaps it's the hormonal therapy a world renowned fertility specialist prescribed her. He agreed to go back into the woods of Wyoming to appease her. The staff was happy to have them back. They liked her much better than the harem they occasionally saw him with. That was one of his fears. Someone would secretly tell her about the harems he kept in Europe and around the world. But so far everything was good. He knew he needed to get rid of them before someone who knows about them told her. His overall security chief named Sewell asked what does he plan to do about them? Mrs. Cargill may someday decide she would like to visit the other properties. He knew he loved Ana, no contest about that but he also knew his sexual appetite and he has been holding back with her. Ironically, even to himself, he hasn't contemplated cheating on Ana not once in the entire months they have been together.

"Move them to Cape Verde and wait until I give further word." he said. This was his first step in pushing them all out of his life. He also knew these women were not as easy going as Ana, they were going to fight to maintain the lifestyle they had grown accustomed to. But Ana has been acting weird lately. She gets up early to pray, uses excuses as to why he can't touch her. Finally, one morning in late March when she got up to pray, he grabbed her arm and asked her to tell him what's wrong?

"I don't know. It's like something is pulling me away from you and our life together. I love you more than I tell you but it's like there an inherent calling within me," she sadly said.

His innards turned to ice. He knew Who was calling her and now he knew why she wouldn't let him touch her after praying.

"Baby, I'm sure it's nothing. A new marriage can be a major adjustment. Give yourself some time to get used to the lifestyle." He said, cuddling her in his arms but he knew he was only kidding himself. He knew the calling wasn't going away. The heavens were calling her away from him. He wondered why? There were 12 billion people on earth; over half of them single with no spouse so why did *They* have to screw with his baby? What had he done this time? He was faithful, he hadn't touched another woman since the day he kissed Ming Tekoc's hand! He treated her well. He was attentive, he even stopped roaming the spiritual worlds. He barely had a drink and certainly didn't get drunk. He expressed his affection everyday. So why are they alluring her away? He waits until she falls asleep again which she always does after morning prayer. He goes into the back woods outside the walls and calls Raphael.

"What have I done this time? I know you all are up to the memory erase game again! Why won't you all let me be happy with her?! I'm happier than I've been since the fall of AzazeLand. There comes a time when gold loses its luster; without love, it gleams not as bright nor does the gemstone sparkle as stars without my beloved. Tell me what I must do to keep her in my arms. I love her as I've never loved anyone. There are billions here who can do what she's being called to do. By the way, what is she being called to do?"

"Azazael, I can not tell you now, but her calling... when it is over I voucher for her return to you." Raphael ensured him.

"How long shall that be? Human years are short! I've seen prophets and prophetesses separated from their loved ones for the remaining of their lives. I've seen them killed, driven into destitution, I can not stand idly by and let her be killed. You know they seek to kill her."

"She will not die. What can she do if she's dead?"

"I'll not remember her nor will she remember me?"

Raphael shook his golden head. He knows that they both will remember each other. A love as deep as theirs can not be erased.

"I love Father but I cannot accept this predisposition bestowed on me. Marriage was created in heaven so why do you all seek to dissolve mine?" Azazael asked.

"So was thundering and lighting but they still serve a purpose as frightful as they are. Just as what I'm telling you will happen, yes, it's frightful but when it bears fruit... eventually, you will see why it must be."

"I do not and can not contemplate what you are saying. At least let us bear a child. So I'll have someone that's a part of both of us." He laid down his pride and begged.

"Azazael, she is not being taken from you. Try to understand that her calling will affect all of us as well as humanity. It will even effect you and how you operate in this world and beyond. When it is completed or the appointed time arrives you will encounter her again and resume where you left off. You will have your children then but not now. Be patient." Raphael knew Azazael would continue to seek her out as he have done down through the ages. "She is a born saint. Do not attempt to corrupt her believing that the heavens will release her and leave you free to be as you please."

The idea did cross his mind but he let it pass. Right now he was too distraught to go through the motion of converting anyone to evil. He loved her too much to do such a thing to her. He looks afar off into the mountains, at the healthy sunlight filtering through the trees after his brother was gone and cast his mind back to the ancient days. When things seemed simpler in the olden times when he rode the lands on horse's backs and chariots as a king, warrior, sometimes as even the winds as a god. His mind recalled the many times when he led his followers into battle or taught them how to defend themselves. He knew the blood offerings were wrong but did not care. Is all that what he's paying for now? If so, he deeply regrets every ounce of blood spilled in his name. Sorrows always revisits. Back then he didn't care. He wouldn't allow himself to care. Now that he has put his heart back into his soul, it ends up broken in a million pieces. He has been a prince, a king, a warrior, a watcher, a god, the king of hell, a demon, a lover of millions but one thing he has never been and that's in love. At least not a love this strong. He debates, is it a marvelous thing or a curse? To him it seems as thus it's both. He suspires, his the sound of his heavy heart. But he knows there nothing else he can do but give her a divorce and set her free and they go their separate ways. But that isn't what he wants. As if heaven ever cared about what anyone wanted. It's all about keeping the Law and fulfilling prophecies. He does something again; something he haven't done since before the fall of his world and before the creation of this one. He sits on a boulder and cries. He has shed more tears over her than anyone he has ever known. He knows she will walk away with his heart.

Ana wakes up wondering where is he? She doesn't feel like checking on Bea right now. She feels like laying in bed and crying until no more tears are left. Perhaps she should give him a divorce. Jealous as a child pitching a tantrum, a mighty conniption swelled up in her. No, she won't give him anything. So what if she won't remember him!

The heifers would love for her to divorce him. Well, she's not and they all can kiss her ass! She got up and grabbed a bottle of his liquor, deciding to get drunk so heaven will quit talking to her. At least she will be unconscious and can't hear them. She turns up the bottle and gags and coughs. This shit is strong! It's like drinking acid. She tries it again, this time it doesn't quite feel like liquid fire. She turns it up a third time and kept drinking. Suppose she give herself alcohol poisoning? So what?! There's a doctor in the house. She stands up in the bed and jumps around the way she's caught Bea doing and starts yelling at the top of her lungs. She has no idea why she is yelling. It just felt like the right thing to do.

"Can't you Guys up above let me be happy for once in my miserable life?! He ain't no worse than the other dogs out there! I've seen truly evil people! I'm sick of being a pawn in something that ain't got shit to do with me. I was born into all this mess, so how am I supposed to clean up anything when I spend all my time trying to stay alive? Trying to keep Vonderbilt from turning me into one of his collections. Yeah, I've seen his trophy of bodies in some giant freezer. I ain't no prophet of Old. Maybe they could handle all this but I can't. My faith ain't that strong! I ain't nobody important enough for all the crap I go through. I'm sick of being chase like a fox running from hell-hounds! Do you hear me!? When I get to heaven you people will have eternity to talk to me but for right now leave me alone and let me be happy! I been on the road for nearly three years scared to death most of the time. What do you want from me? I don't know what to do with these so-called gifts. They feel more like curses to me."

I stopped; the bouncing was making my stomach hurt. I felt like I wanted to puke. I had never been drunk before so I didn't know what to expect. I hear so much raving about it but what was there to rant about when you felt sick as a dying dog? I tried to leap down off the bed and run for the bathroom but my foot somehow got caught in the tangled bed covers and I hit the mattress so hard I bounced right off flipping straight toward the floor. The high bed made the trip down a long one. I braced myself the best my fogged mind would allow, expecting to bust a few teeth for I was falling face down first. I felt someone catch me and that's the last thing I remember.

I decided I wouldn't mention it until she brought it up. I took a slow stroll back home. I heard her screaming and yelling from the other side of the property boundary wall. I quickly teleported inside and saw her sailing through the air, the bottle flying one direction and she another, the position she was falling I knew was a fatal one. Her neck would bearing the impact of her weight. It stopped my heart as I rushed and caught her; when I did she vomited all over us both. I saw she had nearly drained the bottle of my liqueur which I never gave her because of its potency. Normally, I would've dropped anyone who retched on me but instead I took her to the shower and cleaned her up. I ordered a hangover spray for I knew she would need it when she woke up. I called the house doctor in to wake her up and attend her headache after she slept longer than eight hours. When she woke up the first thing out her mouth was. "I'm not giving you a divorce. Crazy or not. You stuck with me!"

"Honey, that's not what I wanted to talk to you about. I wanted to ask why were you jumping on the bed with a bottle of whiskey?"

She looked like her puppy had died and she had lost her best friend all in the same day.

"I don't know how to explain it but I'm not supposed to be here with you. Whatever I'm supposed to be doing is out there. I wonder how many times we been through this? Perhaps more than we know as to why you felt so familiar to me when met. Have you ever heard of anything like this?"

"No, I haven't."

He knew it was time to tell her he wasn't exactly human but felt she could only deal with so much. Or perhaps she had already figured out he wasn't simply a gifted human. "Ana, I know you won't remember after you're gone but there's something you need to know about me."

"What's that?" she asked, watching him curiously as if looking for something physical she had missed.

"I'm not human. Not mortal."

426

She blinked twice and stared perplexedly at him. "I'm an immortal. I'm older than the earth. I'm a celestial being." She listened but I could feel her tensing.

"Which one are you and please don't tell me the scariest one of them all."

"Since you are leaving me does that matter?" I asked, "And just who do you think is the scariest one of them all?"

"Everybody knows Azazel is the scariest motherfucker ever to grace this earth." She cried, looking at me wide-eyed. "You aren't him are you?"

I couldn't rather decide to lie and let our last few days together be peaceful and loving or to tell the truth and have her grab Bea and run away screaming.

"No, I'm not but Azazel really isn't the any worse than many of the others. He just was stronger and the others did a lot of lying on him."

"If you aren't him how you so much about him?" She asked inauspiciously. And also drunkenly. He wanted to laugh at her fighting to keep her eyes from crossing but they were having a serious conversation.

"He's my brother. Just as your original parents were my brother and sister. Adam and Eve are my brother and sister. Humanity is related to the immortals. You all are the same as us just made mortal."

I could see the cogwheels turning in her brain. "Have I ever met Azazael? I mean, has anyone you took me to meet... were any of them...him?"

"Why are you so interested in him?" I asked in mock jealousy.

"I don't know. I just heard so much about him."

"Hearing about him and meeting him are two totally different things. I don't want to talk about him anymore." I said, slightly irritated.

427

"Ok, ok, I'm sorry I mentioned him. But which one are you?"

"Does it matter, since I'm not as exciting nor famous as your *Azzzazzaell*", he mimicked her incorrect pronunciation of his real name. "But supposed I told you I'm Azazel or Azazael."

She covered her mouth with the back of her hand and bust out laughing. "Yeah right, you aren't him. I know you aren't, you're my sweet prince. Beside we're still alive, so you can't be him." She grinned and kissed me with liquor tainted lips.

"What makes you say I can't be him or I'm not him?" He toyed with her liquor fogged mind.

"My darling, you're too sweet to be him. You're kind, loving, generous, you ain't fucking with my head or scaring me to death," she replied rubbing her temples. The hangover spray was slowly ebbing the dopiness away.

"Honey, a lot those are myths about us, we've always been among humanity, undetected."

"So you telling me all those crazy, diabolic things the ancient gods had people doing aren't just myths? Humans were so primitive they couldn't distinguish reality from their imagination!" She asked with raised eyebrows.

"Ana, you knew I wasn't human. Didn't it strike you as odd, I never talked about my mother."

"Do you have one?" She asked wondering why she never asked about his parents and family. She then realized how little she knew about him. She had spent the last six months so engrossed into herself that she really hadn't asked him much about himself.

"No, not in a sense as you've Mrs. BuFaye. But what we need to discuss is what are we going to do about us."

428

Her eyes clouded up before a single tear spilled. "I don't want to leave you. Immortal or mortal. Sinner or saint, you're the best thing that ever happened to me and my daughter. I feel I'm being forced out of my home." One thing true about being drunk, she was learning...you speak the truth. In vino veritas indeed.

"Baby, then don't go! Just because Heaven called doesn't mean you've to listen."

"If I don't go they're going to play a Jonah number on me. You know like the man who didn't want to go tell the people of Nineveh to repent and God sent..."

Azazel interrupted, "I know the story of Jonah and the whale. That was a behemouth. Yes, Father can be One of hard countenances. But if we band together they'll have to listen."

Even in my drunken state I knew heaven didn't bargain but nothing beats a failure but a try. We stuck it out, clung to each other until Raphael showed up three days later saying God wasn't playing with me and if I didn't get going Michael was coming next. There was too much at stake for us to only consider what we wanted. He advised the sooner it was done and over with, the sooner we could get back together.

"I promise I won't interfere," Ashton pled.

"Some of the adversaries she'll face, it's only natural that a husband intercedes to protect his wife. Nothing will happen to your love. Someone will always be there. I'm more than confident you two will find each other again."

By May I had made up my mind it's better to go on do as I'm told before "Mike" shows up and pulls a Jonah on me and locks Ashton up away from me, never to let him out again, at least not in my lifetime. I'd been given the ultimatum. The last night we made love before leaving, after we finished he gave me an a leather bag stuffed with money. There was twenty million there. He had had a secret compartment built onto Trusty's trunk and had redone the iron blanket so it was easier to pull over Bea if I had to. He wanted us seated in and driving an armored hover Humvee but the instructions from up above forbade it. So we had to leave just as we came, in Trusty.

"I pray you remember shall the going get tough you know you can check into any of your hotels and rest. There's a list in here of all the places you can go for refuge," he said showing me the huge bag was filled with small bills. The next morning I went around and said goodbye to the friends I made the pleasant months I spent as their boss. I walked Bea out to say goodbye to her numerous pets. That was the hard part. Ashton promised her he hired someone to look after them. That calmed her down somewhat but not completely. He had never ridden in my car, I must say it was quite compact for him. So he rode off the steep mountainside with us. Now I saw why they called it Sinkhole, it was really like you going down into a big hole. About midway through town we noticed the usually quiescent, sleepy town seemed militarized.

"Who are they?" I asked.

"Your harassers called in reporting threats saying the people up in the mountainous estate were terrorizing the town," he replied drily as a man in military gear walked into the middle of the road and halted for me to stop. I did, although I wasn't totally puzzled as to why. The moment I did, he came to my side and did the motion for me to roll the window down. I did. Trusty had old fashioned roll down windows because I didn't want something that operated by electricity that could easily be disabled or jammed by an electronic magnetic sensors disruptor. Then he pointed a facial recognition scanner at my face.

"Get that shit outta her face," Ashton groaned.

Looking at down the result the soldier sternly, but professionally said. "Ms. BuFaye, step out the car."

I looked worriedly at Ashton.

"Son, I see you don't know who you're talking to. This is Mrs. Ashton Cargill and if you don't step away and tell your people to stop pointing their guns at my wife, I won't be responsible for what happens to you and many others." Ashton said in a voice, deep,

430

menacing voice I had never heard, it was like it belonged to an animal. More like if a lion could talk.

"I'm sorry sir, but Ana BuFaye, uh, your wife, is wanted in several states for several murders, fraud, prostitution, and a whole array of other crimes." The young man said as another soldier approached introducing himself as General Shankshaw.

"Step out the car, ma'am, and I'll let your husband and kid continue their way. No one in this car is wanted except you," the hateful frowning man named General Shankshaw said.

"Go to hell!" Ashton hissed at Shankshaw, while directing me to the curb. "Baby, pull over there while I deal with these fools. I'm already having a pissy ass day and now these bastards are shitting all over the grand scale piss of it all."

I did as told, but I didn't know Ashton had such a terrible, foul mouth. I watched him turn into a man I had never seen. He got out and slammed the door so hard the entire car rattled and began balling up his fists as he walked toward the general and the young solider. Both were wearing protective gear. He shoved the soldier out the way so hard the man flew over the building near the ancient railroad track. He looked as if he was growing larger. He grabbed the general and slung him on the other side of the tanks as if he were a rag doll, yelling at me to get out off out here, go back up the mountain just as a shower of bullets pelted him. It was all happening so fast I didn't have time to analyze why the ammo was having no affect on him.

The car was idling so I quickly backed out and made a right turn down the short street. I intended to use my back alley trick and come out behind them but the moment I was about twenty yards into the side street four soldiers stepped out and aimed at me. The one in the middle harshly ordered me out of the car. I reversed and started backing up at a high speed. They opened fire. I had just made it out the narrow side street with the volley of bullets swept pass. I ran over one man behind me firing and pierced the bullet proof back window. The others were aiming for the gas-tank and tires. I heard the bullets ricocheting off the car body. I made a wild, wide back turn onto Main Street and saw several security officers from the estate security team in the streets with my husband.

431

They had guns and were shooting back, I noticed the bullets were having no affect on Ashton. He pressed the air in such a force that sent the bullets back to the shooters, blowing over cars parked along the streets along with the militarized vehicles and tanks. A helicopter above shot a bomb at him, he caught it and the threw it back at the copter. The explosion was a roaring, red ball of fire in the sky, the flaming debris hit the top of the local hardware store. People rushed out screaming. This was the most intense fight I had ever been involved in so I think some of the screaming I heard was myself. I saw fire shoot from his hands, incinerating the tanks and other vehicles into heaps of ashes. But they didn't seem to have sense enough to stop shooting and run! He beckoned for me to come on. I crept behind him as he walked out front pressing the air making the bullets fall to the ground. The sides of the streets were littered with burnt out cars, tanks, militarized police cars, and bodies. When he looked back at me his eyes were orbs of fire. I must have cringed for he softened them for a split second.

"Baby, keep going!" He yelled. I had to stop and kiss him one last time. I noticed two SUV were right on my tail. I saw Marian was driving the one right behind me.

"Drive safely, baby," he said but I could see the pain in his eyes. He told Bea, who was frightenedly peeking from under the iron blanket, to be a good girl and obey her mother. Then he looked around to make sure everyone was incapacitated and reached in and hugged me hard.

"I love you. Hold on to that," I tearfully nodded and kept on rolling through the red light out of town. I watched him in the rearview mirror until I was out of the sight range. I passed Shankshaw being attended by a medic. The man glared at me with so much hatred, his pale blue eyes gleaming in the hot June sunlight. The hate was so intense it ought to have been ultra violet rays glaring at me, burning out my corneas. The place looked like a war zone. The others beside the road plagiarized Shankshaw's gesture. One shot me a birdie, another grabbed his crotch and shook it at me. The guards in second SUV behind me shot them both dead. I saw the general knew enough to not let them see his true feelings.

We continued down the state road side planked with thick evergreen trees leading to a side road with more woods before reaching the road leading to the expressway. I saw there were snipers all along the first road waiting for command to fire. I heard several helicopters above, I looked up and saw it was our own shooters aiming for those on the ground.

"Daddy Ash, are you going with us?" Bea asked from under the iron blanket. I was stunned. I didn't know he was here.

"Bea! Where is he?" I asked, looking around.

"Here, there in the seat beside ya," Bea said, pointing her tiny finger at the empty front passenger seat. I looked over and he materialized out of the thin air. He was wearing something totally different than that which he had picked out this morning. It looked, well resembled, the uniform of an ancient Roman general but yet was vastly different. I had never seen anything like it. I quickly pulled over and hugged him long and hard, inspecting him. He had not a scratch on him.

"No, my Little Bumble Bea, I can't go with you and mommy. I wish I could. But I'm seeing you two safely out," he replied.

"Why not?" Bea wanted to know.

He looked at me and this was the first time he spoke to my mind. *"That's a good question, isn't it?"*, he asked telepathically, looking at me to explain to Bea why we are out here in this hot ass sun getting shot at when we could be home relaxing in safety.

"Sweetheart, we'll come back someday when all the bad people are gone. Daddy Ash gotta go back and fight the bad people." Bea's young but intelligent eyes told me she didn't believe me. That she knew we'd never come back.

"Don't try to make this drive all night, pull over, get a room and some rest," he said, disappearing. Shortly afterward we heard a copter come flaming down behind us, shaking the ground. I heard bloodcurdling screams behind and beside us but couldn't see who was doing the killing. All I saw were bodies splattering like a watermelon dropped on a hard floor and then all was quiet.

I kept my eyes straight ahead but I was like Bea. I wanted to cry. Bea was a child so she had the freedom to cry. The survival instinct had kicked back in. I knew we had to keep going while the coast was clear.

I drove down the road after the harrying escape from the darkside forces with a pouting and sulking Bea in the back seat. Every time I looked in the back seat Bea was glaring at me. I was praying I made the right decision by leaving. Seemed as thus the farther I got away the less vibrant he was in my memory. I begun to sing a song I learned as a child. "Oh Lord! I want you to help me! Help me on my journey. Oh Lord! I want you to help me. Help me on my way!"

⧼⧽

Ralph Bender had escaped the Cargill hit men so far but didn't know how long he could keep it up. This being on the run thing was exhausting and disorientating. He knew the phones to his mother and wife were bugged. He couldn't call them. Unlike Ana BuFaye he wasn't dumb enough to disclose his hiding place based upon stupid relatives' whims. Manson's uncle warned him the moment he suspected his nephew was dead to get the hell outta Dodge.

Ralph Bender still had the agency issue equipment and could periodically tune in on Ana BuFaye's family. He had a sneaking suspicion these people were toying with him the same way they toyed with Ana. But even if he had to die he was killing her first. They were only having fun with her. Couldn't she take a joke? But no, she had to tell Cargill about their harmless pranks. Manson didn't have to die for it. He don't know how Pembroke became the agency's director. Probably through betraying Manson. Pembroke always thought he was superior to them, anyway.

Hiding in one of the many dim, dark allies out of the range of the dull illumination of the rusty, old-fashioned, yellow fluorescent lights in an undisclosed city, he semi concealed his face from the men passing. He knew they were elements of the night. The alley he lurks was so much like the ones he had so often chased down a pleading victim, showing no mercy. He teems with rage, avowing he'll show the uppity bastard.

434

Pembroke he knows all his moves so it will be hard for him to gain access to him but he knew a man who owed him a favor. A man he caught red-handed years ago killing someone. He and Manson let the man go if he promised to be on-call shall they need him. Over the years the man had perfected his skills. He would use him to track down and kill Ana BuFaye too once her family bitched her from under Cargill's protection. He had already planted the seed of badgering saying she was sleeping with a married man. He knew her folks were a bunch of holy rollers so they'd force her to leave Cargill to allegedly save her soul.

The notorious hitman was known simply as Travis to all in certain underworld circles. A world where fear was not known. But there were a few who feared there was a hit out on them and suspected he had the contract. With Travis they knew death was inevitable. To make matters worse, no one knew what he looked like so there was no way to evade him or plan an escape.

The Hitman

He was relaxing in a luxurious penthouse suite when he got the obligatory call from Ralph Bender to take out Augustine Pembroke. He wasn't thrilled with the disgraced g-man being at his place but the man had information on him that could put him under the federal pen not in it. He also knew Bender was as crooked as a barrel of fishhooks. He was as much a thug as himself, the only difference was Bender had a badge and the authority to commit his killing whereas he didn't.

"He's a snitch and a traitor. He broke the sanctity of our brotherhood." Bender said carefully watching the nude women in Travis' penthouse. He knew no one could be trusted when on the run.

"They cool," Travis said following Bender's questioning eyes and answering the unasked question as to whether or not his guests would repeat what's said. "They know better than to talk." Travis assured him, following Bender's now lustful eyes. He also knew of Bender's fetish to inflict pain certain women. He knew Bender once strangled a

435

young prostitute to death just for fun saying she was a thing; not a person. But no one could report him for he was untouchable. He found the alcohol -ravished faced man despicable.

With his little au revior, the rendez-vous over. It was time to get down to business. Bender downed his drink in one hard, forced gulp. The dirt he and Manson had on him was they were on stakeout at a federal judge's home, a high profile criminal was about to walk. The man had killed Travis' sister along with several other women but the prosecutor was unable to prove it. Travis didn't see it that way. He killed the defendant and the judge and would've faced the death penalty had not the three agents been impressed as to how he stealthily got passed them into the judge's house. That was ten years ago. He has honed his skills considerably in the past decade and was one of the best. Plus, he owed them. He knew if he were to go against them every national agency in the land would be on his trail like a hellhound. That these men promised him with no uncertainty.

Bender pulled out a picture of the intended target. "Have you ever heard of Ashton Cargill? Of course you have. Well, she's one of Ashton Cargill's whores. I assume his main one by the way he hasn't let her surface in the past three months."

Travis took the electronic device from Bender and studied at the picture. To memorize her face and features, her gestures and moves. These were things people were rarely able to hid. He guessed she was pretty if one were into black women. He was into blondes as evidenced by the two naked women. But the fact he had heard so much about Cargill made him think twice about killing this woman. In his profession, you knew who to accept a job on and who to leave alone. If not, then you didn't last very long. Ashton Cargill fell in the "let alone" category.

"She's a sharpshooter and doesn't miss so don't let her get you in her sight. She has an uncanny ability to sense another's presence," Bender warns.

Travis knew about that ability. He, too, possessed it. Looking at the picture, studying it, he knew one could tell a lot about a person from small things most people didn't notice. Like the way they carried their head or shoulders. They way they look at you and

436

this woman didn't know this picture was being taken so it captured her in her true essence. One glance told him she's a killer; have killed and will kill until she's stopped. Whatever her reasons for killing are...she's an expert at it. Don't let the sweet, angelic face fool you.

Handing the ISPAN pad back to Bender, Travis asked, "Isn't Cargill the world's renowned business mogul? Said to be the richest man in the world?"

"Yeah," Bender said from his kitchen where he was fixing a plate from the party platter the caterers left earlier. He was broke and hungry. He hadn't eaten in days. It was hard to go anywhere publicly and get food. He wasn't going to romance a woman with a houseful of kids just to eat. He didn't consider himself *that* desperate yet.

"How important she is to him?" Travis wanted to know.

"I assume pretty important for him to protect and support her entire greedy family." Bender said, stuffing a slice of honey glazed ham into his mouth. He was so hungry it hurt. This was his first time experiencing hunger pangs. He hadn't eaten decent food in quite a while so the food was causing a tumult in his already acidulous stomach but he kept on eating.

Travis mulled over the relationship between Cargill and this woman. He knew for a man to go to that length this wasn't just a fly-by-night rendezvous. He wondered how much Cargill cared for this woman? That determined how much time Cargill would invest into hunting him down and killing him.

"Why do you want her dead?" Travis always asked these questions before a kill. He didn't accept everyone who came to him. Some wanted someone dead because they beat them to parking space at the mall. He didn't take such trivial cases.

"She told him about Manson and I groped her at a shabby-ass fleamarket. She didn't have to tell it but she did; it was only a joke, nothing worth dying for. He killed Manson for it. That's why he's after me."

Bender brought the platter into the livingroom, sat on the luxurious sofa, and leaned in close to make sure Travis understood he was in no position to ask questions. Travis could smell his bad halitosis and body odor. He knew Bender had been on the run for weeks if not months. Waving a thick packed sandwich at Travis, Bender explained his only lucrative position was to take orders. Bender patted his chest, "If you don't stop her and him, I'm sending in the footage of both murders live in living color. I've an implant; shall my heart stop beating the images go live. Then the world will know who and what you are. Now, what's it going to be?" Bender asked in a tone Travis didn't care for. The cold gangster stare, the fashion in which he chewed the food clearly told Travis this was how he was going to chew his ass if he didn't kill this woman and avenge the wrong committed against him and Manson.

Bender saw in his eyes Travis wanted to kill him but wasn't sure if the threat was true.

He was trying to hide his distaste for this man, he really didn't like this man and was as of this moment weighing the consequences of killing him. He knew Manson and Bender were lovers and that's the real reason Bender is so upset about Manson's death.

"I thought the deal was only to kill her."

Bender shrugged his rounding shoulders, "What's the point in killing her and leaving him alive? He's coming for you and I doubt he'll toy with you as he has been toying with me. Take them both out and I'll think about having the implant removed."

Travis knew the man was lying about destroying the evidence but pretended to believe him. Nowadays, it much harder to be a hitman than it was before the days of ready images streaming constantly from every corner of the globe.

This was too easy. It was just as Bender told him; the woman, stupidly, was out in the open. He followed her all the way from outside of Sinkhole, Wyoming to Flagstaff, AZ. He knew how to stay hidden and after seeing that attack on the group waiting for her to emerge the estate he was cautious almost to the point of paranoia. He saw something explode human bodies like a child bursts a water balloon. He didn't know who did it but the thing he got a vague glimpse of didn't look human. It looked like some type of

438

demonic lion. So he knew it was best to stay out of sight. Supposed that thing is still around her? He saw Cargill in the car with her one moment and he was gone the next. This was no ordinary kill. There was something ethereal about the entire mission. He was nervous for the first time in his life about a hit. He saw that man-beast pull a man's head off and smash it like an overripe muskmelon. The hulking man-beast was Cargill so what was that other thing in the woods? He didn't know what Cargill was but he definitely wasn't human. And Bender was off his fucking rocker if he thought he was going after that thing. Bullets don't do shit to him. What is he? Damn Superman?

After seeing what he saw outside of Sinkhole, Wyoming he decided to do more research on this man. That thing he saw was definitely not a man. He needed to know more about this couple, together they commanded a forte that not even the US military could penetrate and defeat. He wasn't going in there half-cocked. He watched them beat the hell out of an army unit. After the woman left the commander called in a unit of Marines. The quick and furious battle was like watching a group of kindergartners engage professional street fighters. He saw many of the people in that town were not human. So what were they?

To learn the word on the streets he visited his PI friend whom he had been using for years. He got down on to 42nd Street a little after 11:00 P.M the Saturday night after catching up with the woman in Flagstaff. Standing on the stoop in the darkness he urgently rang Henninger's bell and shouted his name in the unseen mic over the noise of the hovercraft above and the ground traffic. NYC never slept so it was nothing unusual about a late visit. Henninger charges ten grand a research but he's worth it. That way you didn't rush in blindly into a tight spot you can't escape. You have a lucid idea what you are dealing with.

Henninger lived in an old pre-World War III apartment that was once sumptuous before the days of sky-high rent forcing everyone but the extremely rich into the outer suburbans. Even upper Jersey's rent was ridiculously high nowadays. The low ceiling was decorated popcorn plaster, it was spacey for the amount he knew Henninger paid. There was an amoir'e, a dark leather sofa, and a coffee maker sitting on the table in the front room. He doubted Henninger ever used the tiny kitchen, he probably ate out all the time. He took a seat and went straight to matter of the visit.

"Can anyone find a trail of this data gathering leading back to you?" Travis asked. Knowing if they can find Henninger, they can find him.

"Discretion is my specialty," the man of German descent said, affirming his reputation. "Before I show you this information, I need you to swear on your mother's grave you'll never breathe a word of it to anyone."

"Sure, I don't talk to people. I don't like people enough to talk to them. You know what I do."

Henninger nodded, accepting Travis' word before continuing. "Ok, the woman..there's nothing unusual about her. She's just a run-of-the-mill Southerner. But it's about Cargill that I don't want you repeating what I say outside this room. I've strong reasons to believe he is an immortal. That's the only conclusion I can come up with to explain what I found and what you said about him being invincible." Henninger picked up the bible and showed him the verses about the sons of God and their offspring with mortal women.

"I think he goes all the way back to in the beginning." Henninger excitedly said laying out pictures matched by face recognition. "What you saw was an ancient god. I'd advise you well to leave his woman alone. I'd rather face prison than face him." Henninger consulted, arranging the photos by dates, going all the way to pictures of bas reliefs of the gods of ancient Sumeria, the Mesopotamia. "I've strong reason to believe he was around long before these images were carved. But mankind wasn't drawing back then or the images have been destroyed."

"Do you have any idea which one is he?"

"I'm not certain but I strongly suspect he's Azazael better known as Azazel." Henninger moved his pointer to illustrate the vital places in the life-like facial relief, matching the present day face of Ashton Cargill. "His face matched the craving of Draco, the dragon. He can be any race he chooses to be so you can't go strictly by ethnological attributes and traits." Henninger said, looking intensely at his friend to

440

make sure Travis fully understood the magnitude in going after Azazael. Travis heavily sighed. He couldn't do jail nor living on the run. But he didn't want to die and facing Azazel was begging to die.

"What in the hell has this Bender done to get messed up with an ancient god?", Henninger asked.

"The sick bastard groped the wrong woman. She told her old man and now he's out killing everything that moves. I saw him take out an until military unit as easily as slapping a baby." He recounted Bender's dire threat. "Can you hack a federal agency to retrieve after it has been released?"

Henninger knew about the two agents who were blackmailing Travis. "I can but to eliminate the entire extension after it has been released and viewed is difficult to accomplish. If you let me know exactly when to catch it then I stand a greater chance of eliminating it." Henninger explained after Travis relayed more of the ugly conversation with Bender.

"If we can find the central connector that would be vital in stopping him but the system today isn't as primitive as years ago when you could so easily hack and shut down everything. A quantum, cold fusion powered system doesn't exactly have a set location. But something tells me he doesn't have it routed to go through the central brain at his job nor his home. The dead one, Manson, was he heart-wired?"

"I think so. But I think Bender kept it from going live. To keep his bargaining chip from exposure to keep his hook in me."

"Here's my solemn conclusion, if you kill her Cargill will come after you; if you don't kill her Bender will release the footage. But I say you stand a greater chance of escaping the legal system than Cargill. It will take God, Himself to keep this ancient demon off your ass and you aren't exactly a praying man. I suggest kill Bender instead and we go from there."

Travis didn't like the verdict he was hearing. He knew he was stuck between lower and deeper hell. He didn't like the idea of living on the run as this Ana BuFaye was apparently doing. Hiding from the authorities is difficult to do nowadays. Everywhere is digitally connected. Even small, once third world nations were now connected to the global system and often turn in criminals and fugitives from richer nations for the reward money.

Bender let him listen in on the recording he made of the woman arguing with her zany family so he knew she was on her way to Brunswick, Ga. He needed to find her trail again and catch her before she reaches there. There's no point in killing her in front of her family. Besides, it's harder to kill someone surrounded by their home-town folks. They may not like the person but they aren't going to tolerate a stranger coming in killing them. But unfortunately, killing her in front of the kid can't be avoided.

After leaving Henninger, he employed his gifts and tracked her down through the spiritual realms to San Antonia, Texas. She obviously hadn't pushed for many miles. Three days ago she was in Flagstaff. So she doesn't know there's a contract out on her. Or she would have at least tried to hide. Three days was enough time to have made it to the east coast.

⚬⚬⚬

Around 1:00 A.M. one morning, late May, early June she woke up and they were on the road again. She didn't try to figure out where they had spent six months out of the elements; all she knew she was weary of this open road life.

In the cool of the morning I heard the radio say; "It's said we choose our joy and sorrow long before we experience them. " I reached over and clicked it off. Whomever said that didn't know what in the hell they were talking about. Who in their right mind would choose my life? I dislike philosophic bullshit that ain't got shit to do with reality. It all sounds like someone who has never been through any real trials and retributions, someone is living well and comfortable sitting in the cool or warmth spurting off at the mouth. No, talking out their ass. Let them bring their ass out here and live my life and then see if they still think we selected this shit. How about them and us trade places and let's see if they still feel the fucking same?

442

The past three days been hitting over a hundred degrees so whomever blabbering off at the mouth should come sit in this hot ass car with me and tell me they'd chosen this experience. If I let the windows down the mosquitoes will open-pit barbecue us. The small portable AC was struggling and humming hard to override the Texan heat.

She had the oddest dream the last couple of nights. It seemed like nearly a year was missing from her life. Last night she had the same dream. She dreamed she was married to an awesome, sinfully handsome man who was sexy as all outdoors. She laid her lazy ass around all day and did nothing but eat and screw him. And the best part of it, he totally adored her. Showered her with gifts and kisses. Now, *that's* the dreamy experience; given a choice that's the one she'd prefer. She knows it's all wishful thinking. In her dream she and Bea were deliriously happy. Bea had nannies, a pony, a dog, and other children to play with. Oh well, it was a nice fantasy while it lasted. She turned her attention back to the task at hand for she knew that's all it was. Just a wishful fairy tale.

Truth be told, she was never sure why they were out here like a couple of nomads begin with. She has heard the name Vonderbilt whispered in the still of dreams but has yet to learn who is he or she?

She loved her daughter. That she was sure of, but there seems to be a calling in the depths of her soul calling her away from the best decisions as a mother. She knows it sounds stupid but she must have robbed a bank. Where did all that money and jewelry come from? Why was she wearing a wedding band? This isn't the band she and Thad bought for their wedding. Plus, she long stopped wearing that thing. She looked back at a sleepy Bea, her cheeks were chubby, not shallow and thin as normal. She became alarmed. Yesterday Bea was a healthy thin. Why is she so plump this morning, sliding toward baby chubby? Is she ill? She doesn't look sick. Where did that Burberry kiddie clothing come from? Damn, she's really losing her mind!

She reached in the back and awakened her sleeping child. "Bea, honey how do you feel this morning?" she asked putting the stuff she had dragged from the trunk into the front seat aside on the floor of the car. She got the camp breakfast out. She didn't trust her mind to go into a town yet; with all that loot she must have flipped out and robbed

443

someone.

"I'm fine mommy. I had a dream I had a pony named Fancy. I'd my own room. I'd a dog and lots of friends." she said, rubbing her sleepy eyes with her dimpled fist as I reached back and wiped her chubby Raphaelian face with a damp handiwipe. I froze, I had the same dream. Maybe someone is playing Jedi mind tricks on us. But a mind trick wouldn't explain the money, the updates to Trusty, this ring, or the bag of money in the compartment below the trunk. I found it when the hotel room cost more than I had on me and I was scourging the car for the two dollars short the clerk wouldn't let pass which I thought was kind of mean. The last thing I clearly remember was us outrunning a hovercraft in St. Louis after I lit up the streets with gunshots after those two guys groped me.

Those guys were no ordinary police. What agency did they work for? I didn't know but I knew they were far more dangerous than any local police. That's why I prayed so hard we escaped them. Maybe they dosed me with an hallucinogenic drug when they touched me because none of the halliard of my life is making much sense. Where did all this money come from? I didn't rob any banks. At least, I don't remember robbing anyone. So who likes me enough to have given me this sort of money? I'm positive I saw a list of addresses in the bag the night before. It's gone. I was afraid to spend the night in a hotel in case I did rob a bank in the middle of my madness. I didn't want a swat team kicking in the door and filling us with bullets. We were right outside San Antonia so I decided to take a chance and take Bea to a doctor. She is obviously swollen with an illness or allergy. I took out a hundred grand in case she had to be hospitalized and drove around looking for the children's hospital. It wasn't hard to find.

Bea protested all the way to the glass enclosed emergency room. She resisted and refused to cooperate with the doctors saying she was not sick. After a battery of tests the doctors informed me there was nothing wrong with Bea, she was a normal healthy child who just happened to be growing. Bea frowned and looked up at me and crossed her arms. Her set face clearly illustrated had I listened to her before dragging her in there I'd have known that. Sure, Bea swore she felt fine but I'm a mother and all kids say they feel fine. I felt a little sheepish. The doctor looked at me as if I were neurotic, over protective mom or something but rescinded her glare realizing all mothers are neurotic.

444

We had used the open parking space because the garage was filled. While walking along the sidewalk aligned with the hospital, I suddenly felt a strong sensation of being watched when we exited the final glass tunnel onto the streets. I put myself between Bea and the threat, mentally drowned out the traffic, and attuned my senses in the direction the deadly sensation was coming from. I stepped quickly toward Trusty but kept Bea sheltered. In my guts' intrinsic pit, I knew a sniper was aiming for my head. How? I don't know but I just knew. I pinpointed his location and when he was in my line of fire I raised my arm at lighting speed with a powerful gun at the end. Looking up on top the parking garage I couldn't see him, the harsh sun glare was blinding me but in my mind's eyes I saw a medium built white guy with short dark brownish-black hair. I knew it was him, I branded his face in my mind. He didn't know I wasn't looking at him with my physical eyes but with the occasional spiritual ones that kick in when needed. I saw his shocked expression that I saw him as he looked through the scope of the high powered rifle aimed at my head. He knew should he pull his trigger, I was going to pull mine and did. With the second shot he realized my spiritual eyes were looking deep into his physical ones. He knew if I die so would he, he knew I was missing on purpose, so he quickly reconnoitered the notion of killing me seeing I could've taken him out but something was preventing me from doing so. He left the tripod and ran, leapt off the huge concrete ventilation pier gleaming in the hot afternoon sun, physically blinding me, and headed inward off the roof. A few seconds later I heard an engine inside the parking garage being revved. I knew he was trying to escape. The damn scum-pit was getting away. I quickly hauled Bea in Trusty's back seat, telling her to get under the iron blanket. I intend to kill this motherfucker for aiming a gun at me while Bea was walking beside me. I ignored the machine asking for payment and broke the traffic guard of the parking lot exit gate and headed across the street, darting right in the middle of traffic after him. I was pissed off. I broke the parking garage entrance bar and revved Trusty up into high pursuit. Over the mighty the roar of her sports engine I could hear him ascending as I was descending. He was gunning for the roof; he was driving fast as I cut the bends in the overcrowded space. The sound of the engine told me he had a hovercraft and was trying to make it to the roof to assail into the air. But not today! I was coming for him with intent to kill for I'm sure this wasn't as personal to him as it was to me. So I was cutting those bends like a mad bat outta hell. Coming around the fifth level we finally met face to face. I had my gun in my left hand, positioned it out the window, aimed the antique Glock for his head and let it rip. The gunshots resonated in the enclosured space

445

like a bomb. He ducked and tried to returned fire. But I keep my guns loaded; I rattled off the stolen M-16. He put his car in reverse and tried to go backwards. What saved him was I let go of the steering wheel to maneuver the car with my knees. In that split second he was gone. That fucker teleported. That was the only way out. He had the ability to move objects. But not very far.

I heard the traffic below honking at him when he hit the streets, burning rubber from the sound of the tires screeching. I knew I had lost him but at least I had disabled the flight components of his car. But if I ever see him again his ass is mine. I give as good as I get. I hurried out the garage for I could hear sirens coming from above and below. I knew if I didn't flee they'd be hauling me off to jail. From the sound of the sirens, the cops above were at least two miles away but those inside were a few levels below. I knew I was taking a chance but it was a chance I had to take. I flew out the parking garage at at least 80 mph and gathered speed as I wove in and out of traffic; the slowpokes were blaring at me. But fuck them. As long as I could stayed ahead of the hover-cruisers I'd be ok. I kept out on the populous street to a dilapidated old suburban neighborhood. Cops hated these neighborhoods and avoided them at all costs. Well, a few dirty cops frequented them to exploit the residents. These people had enough problems of their own to worry about to wonder why I was in their neighborhood. Frankly, they didn't give a shit just so long as I wasn't there to fuck with them or make their lives harder as opposed to an upscale area; they'd have me on the cameras flying through their neighborhood. I slowed down and turned off onto a derelict lot, overgrown with weeds and littered trash where a house once sit perhaps centuries ago. The men standing around on the street corner sent a causal glance my way but basically ignored us for the rest of the evening and there we waited it out. I knew these people wouldn't call the police because most were probably like me. Wanted by the police themselves. So around 2:00 A.M. I got the hell out of San Antonia.

"Ain't that a bitch, my first time meeting another like myself. He's trying to kill me."

We made it to the Louisiana/Texas state line by sunrise and I stopped to rest and check the car. My extrasensory, blended with intuition, sprinkled with experience told me the money and jewelry were gone. I checked the hiding place in the trunk after stopping in the Delta and sure enough, everything was gone. Not only was the man a killer but a thief as well. So if he had already taken the money why was he waiting around to kill me? Perhaps whomever gave me the riches wanted them back. If so, all they had to do was ask.

Bender wanted a chip of the woman being killed. I didn't record it for I'd be nuts to give him more ammo to use against me. I walked around the old car after she and the kid got out and went in the hospital. You can tell a lot about a person by the contents in their car, I performed a serial number scan on the car and won the lottery. I used the tools of my trade to open the driver's door and popped the trunk. It had to be under all this junk because my scanner is going nuts. I felt along the formation of the trunk but found nothing but a spare tire. I realized it was one of the gas tank safes. The general public aren't familiar with them so Cargill must have had this done. But why would he put them out like that knowing there were threats on her life? He obviously still wanted her from the fight I saw him put up. Henninger is right. He is an immortal. I hid on a cafe roof and watched the whole thing before teleporting down the road to watch her. I believe he saw me for I stepped back through the realms but for the next day or so I sensed something huge and pernicious coming after me, tracking me like a lion tracks prey. I'd a feeling of impending death shall it catch me. So I leaped through loops of time and space for I knew it was him. I wasn't on the top of my game while aiming at her, three days with little or no sleep. I had to keep track of her and stay ahead of whatever trying to hunt me down and kill me. This is it. Bender and all the others can go to hell. I'm not killing for hire anymore. Now, I've something I can't see after me. It feels far worse than any hellhound. All because those nasty bastards touched the wrong man's wife now there's something trying to kill me but I sense something else keeping it at bay. This shit is getting too spooky for me. I'm out of the killing business. Bender is on his own.

In the grimy, sheet rock peeling room I counted the money; it and the jewelry was enough to live comfortably on for the rest of my life if that roaring thing didn't catch me and end it soon.

He arrived at the airport in Dallas, after ditching his damaged car at an all night eatery and calling a cab. That woman had torn the hell out of it with bullets. He kept a low profile for he noticed the police seemed to be looking for someone. They spotted him across the terminal and begun yelling for him to halt. He opened fire on them and
447

sprinted out the door and down the streets. Now he knew Bender had released the chip. Made it virtual, streaming live to the whole world for all who cared to look.

But his assumption was in err. What he didn't know was that Bender was dead is why the chip was being aired all over the world. He didn't know when Cargill's security team saw Ana on live national footage fleeing down the road Sewell decided to eliminate Bender. For it was Sewell's belief this was who sent the hit man whose equipment the police were collecting on the rooftop. The intonation switch was activated when his heart stopped beating. Now he had more killings under his belt. He'd killed two cops. He knew without doubt, his life was over now. He was a wanted man. But he'd enough cash to stay afloat a few years here in the USA but needed to trade this hot money in for random currency for the serial numbers tells where it came from and he knows who it came from; the man out to kill him. He knew how dangerous it is to leave a paper money trail. He walked the streets in the shadows on the rough side of Dallas knowing he had to buy or steal a ride, buying would be easier if he could convince an individual owner not to report the sale. At least there would be no alert put out for a stolen car.

Around midday the next day he found a woman named Stachhyus with a car for sale in her weedy driveway. He offered her ten grand for a car worth only two. He wondered as he drove if Stachhyus was her first or last name? Either way it was a peculiar name. He had to talk long and hard to convince her into selling to him for she didn't like him very much. The weirdest thing is he saw the same light in her eyes he saw in this Ana BuFaye's eyes when looking at her through the scope. He headed north back where he belonged and took many back roads getting there.

His heart froze when he pulled into a rest stop area with the intent to rent a rest booth and get some sleep. He had stopped because this one seemed pretty decent for it wasn't totally in the boondocks, not like the ones where serial killers and hee-haws roamed. His mouth went dry as cotton when he saw the same woman he was sent to kill. He'd give her some of her money back but she might make good on the attempt to kill him so he left without parking and continued on his way. Her skills were superior to his own and besides—she'd kill him about the Birkin handbag if nothing else. He'd been in this business long enough to know there was nothing more dangerous than a woman with a killer's instinct. It's said the male is the most dangerous of the human species but he

448

begged to differ. Whomever believes that has never met Ana BuFaye. She's the very epitome of "**Heaven has no rage like love to hatred turned**, Nor hell a **fury like** a woman scorned," and he scorned her badly. He saw that in the woman's spiritual eyes. So was she, too, was an immortal like Cargill? Or just a mad, pissed off mother? It's hard to distinguish the two.

Looking out the window from one of his hotels in Antofagasta at a calculi, rock formation, it's silhouette was that of a woman. It reminded him of someone but who? He can't remember. He knows his memory has been erased. He knows he has left carnage in his wake in the past few days, but why? He does not know. He know angels made him leave someone alone but he can't remember why he was even after this man? He clearly remembered seeing the man with a leather duffel belonging to him and wondered where he obtained it from? It was obvious money was inside the bag. He spread his left hand out a waist height. He's a wedding band on his ring finger. He cringed, he doesn't know who he married. He prayed it wasn't a member of his harem. He despaired he hadn't turned dumb enough to marry Dawn. There appears to be five-ten months out of his life missing.

He teleports to the residence of the one person who is bold and sassy enough to tell him the truth and rings her doorbell. Sewell and all the other staff members hid things from him. She doesn't know he is immortal so he walks instead of teleport to her as her staff led the way.

"Ming, when I last saw you did I say where I was going?" He turned and asked the petite business associate.

"No, you left in a hurry. You said something about a family emergency. You could've been honest with me and told me you were married." Ming Tekco said, sipping the champagne from the tulip glass. "I still would've sold to you. But I assume you're in love with Mrs. Cargill. That's so rare nowadays."

"Why do you say that?" He asked, trying to probe her to help him piece together the

449

last few months if not the last year of his life. It's obvious he spent it with someone he cared a great deal for or he wouldn't be wearing this ring. A dismissive chuckle escaped his lips.

"Whomever she is, she must be one hell of a woman to convince me to marry her," he said looking down at the diamond studded wedding band. Did he finally capture the one he had been chasing and married her? If so, then where is she? Why can't he remember anything about the marriage? He contacted the jeweler who made the band and they swore they had no record of making it. But he's positive this is their trademark.

The Sinkhole, Wyoming estate said they last saw a woman on camera ten months ago so where did she go after that? Why is there kiddie stuff all over the place? Where did the new horses and other pets come from? Now he is positive he married her.

Ming Tekco interrupted his thoughts saying, "No, love is what convinced you to marry her. However, I'm sure you didn't come all this way simply let me watch you ponder over your wife. I'm glad you came. I want to learn what's all the rave about you is all about. Do you measure up to your reputation? For you to gain my interest I expect action." As she spoke she glided her shapely, manicured hand over his strong, muscular thigh seductively leading up to his crotch.

"I'm not in the mood. Plus, I'm no woman's stud. But if you'd like dinner I'd be happy to oblige," he said testily. He only offered dinner in hope to pry her for information. Hoping she would relay more datum but he sensed her holding back. The truth was he was sick of Ming's air of authority. He was only polite to close the deal. Deal closed months ago so he had no reason to continue the facade.

Ming recollected what her mother, a former Japanese Geisha taught her how men use kindness as a cleaving device and sometimes as a weapon to get what they wanted.

So could she. "I understand you're upset about your wife and concerned for her well-being. But I can assure you had anyone taken her they would've sent you a ransom demand by now. Have you checked your in-laws? Perhaps she's there. Daughters, unlike sons, they always return home."

He smiled, mentally admitting Ming was very good at what she does. That's why she's the single richest woman in China.

"Yeah, I checked them, they haven't seen her." He lied. "But in the meantime I intend to remain faithful to her," he said, turning around to face Ming.

"I'm not asking you to betray your heart. I do not want any man's heart. It's a troublesome thing. To me sex is as basic as breathing and eating, merely a natural function having nothing to do with love. That's where you and I are alike. But shall you change your mind, you know where to find me," she said, rising from an original floral Louis XIV parlor seatte. She turned at the door and said, "There's a way to see what happened to you. There a Far East practice in getting around this pesky spiritual blockade. I can put you in touch with the specialist I use."

"Thanks, but I'm familiar with the practice. Looking that far into things you're likely to get your eyes burnt out if you survive at all."

"Why not give it a try to put your mind at ease," she purred coming closer to him, again, so closer he could feel her heart beat. She glided her tiny. shapely hand over his chest. He gently grabbed her hand to still it. And softly chuckled, for her small hands reminded him of someone else.

"Ming, no means no. I know every trick in the book and beyond. I wrote the books. *Kama Sutra, Taoist Book of Sex Positions*. Did you know there are over a thousand ways to make love? Do you even realize I know far more about a woman's body than you, I know how she'll move her body during the relation. There're the five major signs she's about to have an orgasm. How do I intend to help her? First: I'd kiss her passionately causing her to become aroused and then she blushes, now I can come closer to her. Pulling her to mold my body." He said moving close in on her, catching her by surprise. "Second, I watch for like visible signs, I know her nipples will become hard but I can't see that with her fully dressed. I know her nose may become humid, may flair or even quiver a little," he said in his most seductive voice, "then I slowly but patiently undress her and cover her with kisses and caresses so can I enter into her slowly. Third, her mouth becomes dry and she may or may swallow her saliva, but not always, it depends on the woman. Each woman is different. That's where mortal men make many mistakes. Believing that all women are the same. Then I begin to move very slowly inside of her. Fourth, I know her private parts will become wet, then I can penetrate her deeper. Fifth, the secretions of her private parts fall over her buttocks, then I can move freely as I wish. When she tense or grab me or the cover or arch or push from below or whatever her personal gesture maybe then she having an orgasm and there's many more to come." He goes on to describe in great lavish details the flying dragon, the tiger walk, the jumping monkey, the mating cicadas, the mounting turtle, and others she had never heard of.

Ming stood rooted to the floor and stared dumbfounded at him. A little embarrassed she had an orgasm without him touching her in a sexual way. Cargill always teased her or played the sexual cat and mouse game with her but he never outright described fucking and definitely never so seductively.

"Now that I'm fine, thanks for your concern." He knew that contrary to the western popular view, the *Kama Sutra* was not exclusively a sex manual. It's a guide to living a virtuous and gracious full life. Discussing the nature of love, family life, and other aspects relating to the pleasure oriented faculties of life

She smiled immodestly, slowly fanning herself with her well-refined hands. Wondering how did he do that with nothing but his voice and dirty talk?

"Yes, you're fine. I'm sure your wife and I both agree. But since she has forsaken her duty why should you suffer? As a friend, of course I was concerned about you. You dropped off the face of the earth for ten months not to be seen or heard from again. Even your girls had not heard from you. Dawn and Delores tried to give the accustomed annual Employee Appreciation party to which I was invited but it wasn't the same without you. It was a disaster. No one knew where you were and those who knew weren't talking." Ming explained.

She never liked Dawn Shepherd. She was a cheap, no-class floozy. Reminded her of the men who thought she'd be dumb enough to take care of them all because they were pretty.

To find a way to busy herself, to take her mind off what he just did she says, "I rounded the executive employees up and gave them gifts I thought you might. I thought your personal assistant did all that. Why do you hire these useless people, they merely suck up resources. I sent the bill to your headquarters and expect to be reimbursed. You knew better than leaving Dawn to host such important event. It was far above her misguided understanding."

He was amused at Ming trying to hide what just happened, he did it to make her leave him alone about sex. To show her she really knew nothing at all about sex. He was getting more ticked off by the moment. He remembered his wife doesn't lecture him (not that he can remember) and nor will he be lectured by a business associate. He grabs her firmly under the arm and half walked and half dragged her to the door and opened it and put her on the other side. She was one of the few women he considered a friend. He knew if you ever crossed that line, it's never the same.

"I'll personally see to your reimbursements. Thanks for everything," he said closing the door in Ming Tekco's unamused face. So what if this was her place? He didn't want to teleport in front of her. He was anxious to get away to enter Dreamland where the mystery woman sometimes comes to meet him and he couldn't go there wide awake. Exiting in one of his locations he lies on the bed horizontally and puts himself into a trance sleep. Almost immediately he finds her because she's asleep looking for him.

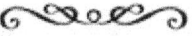

The pitch black swamp offers no consolations, only fear of the unknown. She can see the fireflies, prehistoric mosquitoes, and other life forms of the swamp. Occasionally she hears a human voice from afar. But then she heard a big splash. She knows all about alligators and crocodiles being from the South. She looks back and shushes Bea. The portable AC hums softly in the night, inhaling and exhaling through the car ventilation system. She doesn't trust leaving the regular AC on while they sleep. Then she senses something like a dog sniffling around the car. An awful big dog. But dogs don't make that kind of low, guttural growl. Only two creatures do. Alligators and crocodiles. It's unusual for one to be so far inland. But they're known to travel far at night on land from one watering spot to another; with the drought and all it's not unusual for them to travel. She slid down further, the sniffling beast was right on the other side of the door. It could smell her and sense her the same as she sensed it. Suddenly, the car rocked hard. She sensed it was trying to use its snout to flip them over. She had to scare it away so she reached under her seat and pulled out a short rifle. But when she looked around an eye the size of a baseball was staring at her. She wondered had it ever tasted human flesh? Something told her it had. She heard some develop a knack for human meat while others don't. She believe this one loves human snacks. She had heard of these giants but thought they were mere fisherman's tales. They were fishermen so telling epic tales was what they did. She remembered her glass was now bullet-proof. She had the one in the back installed in Flagstaff, the military had the ammo to break such glass and had broken the back one in Sinkhole. (How in the hell does she remember all that but can't remember who she was with?) When it opened its mouth she could sees a row of jagged teeth and a deep red tongue. She knew as a child sometimes she glowed if she was afraid but had no idea if she still did that. She saw its eyes widen as it started to back away.

"Yea, you go on now," she said mentally to the natural beast. "You scare my baby, I'll have to hurt you."

As the crocodile turned away she heard an agglomeration of shouting, yelling, and shooting.

"Damn yahoos!" She cussed under her breath. "I got it calmed down and here they came putting hell back in it."

The humongous beast turned its great head and focused its deadly attention away from them on to the shouting hunters. Agitatedly, I sucked in a sharp breath! I hadn't seen the smaller one on the other side stealing a peek in the back at Bea under the iron blanket. They were staring curiously at each other, I realized they both were kids and this was the momma over here on my side. The giant let out a roar and moved faster than expected toward the men. I was yelling for them to stop shooting and run like hell. Bullets were not going to pierce that tough hide.

An intrinsic reflex prompted me to get out and try to save these idiots. Who in the hell hunts making all this damn noise? But I was too late for one, I heard his anguished screaming as I ran in their direction, tripping and falling in the gelatine muck. I wanted to cuss but was afraid the glow would go away if I did, so I ignore my throbbing shin and picked myself up and talked to the mother who was sharing the man with the little ones the size of my car. Another big one was racing after the remaining four men.

"Go get in my car!" I yelled, causing the gigantic one to turn and look at me as if I were a traitor. It was as if her eyes were saying "All you humans are the same I thought you were different."

Behind me, I heard my car doors slamming but they still had those damn flashlights on. So I could see I was only about seventy feet from the car. I started glowing brighter the more scared I became. They started circling around me looking for a way in. My talking to them wasn't working. In their primitive minds I had betrayed them for my own kind. I saw the larger one quickly yank back out of my vision range and the others started behaving nervously. I saw a big man walking toward me.

"Lady, what in the hell you doing out here messing around with these monsters? These things are hundreds of years old," he said, holding the mother off as easily as one held a fighting, clawing kitten. Seeing the break I ran for the car. The four men were crowded in the front and back seat. I squeezed in with them. The big man's eyes gleamed in the dark like an animal's or pieces of jewelry. We didn't know which we were more afraid of, him or the monstrous reptiles. At least we knew what they were but him, we had no idea what he was. If he could sling those things around like a toy, what in the hell could he do to us? Everyone started screaming when he began walking toward us. I was shaking to bad I could barely start the car and try to back out. He was on us before I could press the reverse gear. The car had somehow stalled. Trusty never stalled when I needed her to move.

"Baby, be quiet. You know I'm not going to hurt you. You fuckers get the hell out of my car before you piss me off!"

"You know him?!" The man pressed against the windshield asked, reaching over and switching on the head lights.

"No," I stammered. "No, I don't think so. I-I don't know." We all heard the doors mysteriously unlock and we quickly locked them back. We saw him slightly grin as if this shit was funny. He held up his hand and pointed at a ring on it.

"Baby, look down at your ring finger," he smiled, bemused at all of us crowded in the car like a bunch of circus clowns performing their comedic see-how-many-of-us-a-car-can-hold stunt. The black man in the front with me shone his flashlight down at my hand.

"You're wearing a set matching his," he pointed out. I didn't know guys noticed things like that.

"That don't mean a thing!" the brown haired white guy in the back said. "If he can do all what he just did then he probably can easily make one to match hers. I'm telling ya, it's a swamp demon."

Ashton rolled his eyes, quickly yanked the door open, and pulled me out. The men fired at him. His eyes darkened and he was in the car with them throwing them out so fast none had time to react. Had not Bea been in the backseat I would've sprinted away with those men who hit the ground running. But I couldn't run and leave my baby. His big, swampy, gator smelling hands enclosed my face as he kissed me. I started fighting. He held up his hand again softly saying, "Baby, it's OK. We obviously are married. But what on earth are you doing out here?!"

"I don't know you, I owe you no explanation."

"Ok, whatever you say. Anyway, let's get out of this swamp before you two are befallen with swamp fever.", he said as Bea waved at him. "Daddy Ash, you come to take us back home?" She asked leaning out the window after I specifically told her not to roll it down. We both were startled that Bea knew him.

"Bea, who is he?" I asked, astonished. Standing in the darkness of the swamp, the damp scent of overgrown algae and Spanish moss was assaulting my nose while mosquitoes were setting my skin on fire. He was right, too many mosquitoes bites did lead to swamp fever or malaria. I knew couldn't find my way out of this place in the thick greenish darkness.

"That's your huggyman.", the barely three year old said, getting out the car smiling and wrapping her slimming down arms around his leg. He reached down and picked her up and tickled her belly.

Picking the child up brought back memories. It was like a lost memory rushed back into his head. The rush was so hard and brilliant he thought he was going to pass out. But didn't.

"Hey, my pretty Little Bumble Bea." He laughed, jostling her up and down on his forearm and taking her back to the car. They left me there standing in a swarm of mosquitoes staring after them.

"C'mon mommy. We going home." Bea said beckoning me over his shoulder to follow. I had never seen a real swamp at night and was unaware that my surroundings would be illuminated by a creepy, eerie green glow.

I saw Bea was happy to see her "Daddy Ash" as she called him but I don't recall ever seeing this man before in my God-given life. Watching the two of them, I began to vaguely remember him tickling her in a room somewhere. This shit was getting too weird. How can you have a recollection of someone but yet not remember them? I was as tired of the strange memory lapses as I was the life on the road. As if everything wasn't hard enough already. I wished whomever was messing with my head would stop. I can remember everything else except him and our life together.

I got in on the passenger side as he pushed the driver's seat back and folded his long legs into the car. He teased me about being short and having to driving right up on the steering wheel to reach the pedals. I kept looking at him as he backed out and turned the car toward the way out, down a dirt road I hadn't noticed coming in. The long gray

457

beards of Spanish moss cast ghostly shadows and set an unearthly scene as they brushed over the top and windshield of the car as we drove on an almost non-existent trail. The headlights turned eastward and shone on the monsters I thought were gone. Meaning the giants crocs had been watching us all along. Sensing something amiss, I looked to my right I saw a few disembodied, ghastly spirits roaming and rolling with the whitish, low fog coming in as if it were following us. I seriously wondered what possessed me to hide out here? I had experienced enough to know that was no natural fog. This was many spirits combined and coasting together as one. The macabre miasma of despair, death, and maleficence told me that these were the swamp demons my previous impromptu companion had spoken of. How in the hell did they manage to hide their true nature from me and blend in with the environment?

I guess he must had been ignoring my peculiarity for he reached over and grasped my hand and smiled at me. After we were back on the paved road I thought about what the man said about swamp demons and asked, "How did you find me? How did you know we were under siege by giant reptiles?"

He looked kindly over at me; his eyes freaked me out. They were so unsettling, far more luminous than the dashboard lights. Then I recalled him from my closet.

"You live in my heart as I live in yours," he said. "I can feel almost anytime you are afraid or hurt. No, I didn't know about the croc attack until I found you. But you were asleep, out of your body looking for me and saw the area you stepped from. I followed you back to where you abruptly went back to."

I nervously licked my lips, hoping this inhuman thing didn't intend to kill us. I've had something supernatural trying to kill me all my life. So why would he be different? Then I thought, wouldn't it be easier to kill us by feeding us to the giant crocs than take us someplace else to do it? Maybe he intended to take us to that man who kidnapped us about a year ago and performed some kind of weird black mass ceremony.

"Baby, do you really think I'd feed my girls to those monsters?" he asked, shocked by my private thoughts. He looked into the rearview mirror at the men following us to see what he intended to do to the woman who rescued them.

458

Having read her frightened, unconcealed cerebration he asked with a frown, "And who performed a black mass ceremony on you?"

"I don't know! I don't know who you're nor what you are. You could be a swamp demon for all I know!" I cried.

He chuckled. "No, I'm not a swamp demon. I hate swamps. Had not you been out here screaming like a banshee I wouldn't have dared visit this place. It stinks. Hey, do you've still a cognac coloured leather bag filled with money?"

"Well, I did. A man stole it from me and then tried to kill us. I was out here hiding from the police and him too in case he showed up again. He was obviously a hired hit."

In the dim blue dashboard light I saw his eyes darken and jaw muscles flex as he sucked his lower lip over his lower teeth.

"I thought so," he said as his anger brimmed at the angel who stopped him from killing the man. Hell, he recognized his own luggage and the man who had it. He didn't know how but he knew it was his. He just knew. But he definitely recognized the man simply known the "The Hitman" in the underworld circuit.

The day was forecasting to be even more blistering than the night and the prior day as the sun rose hot and fierce, breaking up the darkness as they entered a medium sized city called Gadsden, Louisiana. The four men were still behind them. He drove straight to a luxury hotel called The Gladstone. It seemed to be the only one of its kind in the area.

He sighed when he saw those four men were still right behind them.

"They aren't going away. Are they?" He asked, diverting from their conversation regarding what they can recollect of their lives in the past few months. Much of it felt like déjà vu. As thus they had been here before. Done this before, many times over but she was almost positive she had never seen this place.

Parking behind them the men got out of their truck and walked around to her side and asked were they ok.

"Yes, we are fine. Thanks for asking."

"We saw you go in there in the twilight a lil' bit 'fore dark but thought ya might had be some of 'em damn Wiccans who used that area for they ceremonies. They feed people to them damn things. Well, they and the mobsters, trying to get rid of evident. But when didn't no more come in behind ya we knew you were city dwellers who done got themselves lost out there and couldn't get out. So we came to get y'all but by the time we got there them gators had done surrounded the car. We tried to make them follow us for them damn things can flip a little car like this over," the black guy who was in the front seat earlier with her said as he eyed her driver in the subdued morning light.

"I'm terribly sorry about your friend. I really am," I said realizing that man wouldn't have died had not he been trying to save us. And we wouldn't have been out there had not the police and a psycho killer been looking for us. He was still after us. I saw him at the rest stop just in a different car so I figured he went down the road to wait for us is why I hid in that haunted, cursed area.

"Thanks you for your consolation," the white guy with the now stringy brown hair heat and sweated had plastered to his forehead said, taking off his cap and shaking my hand.

"But dad died doing what he was born to do. Protecting innocent people from the witchery folks who drag them down there to sacrifice 'em to 'em there gators. We're hunters. This is what we do."

My face must had shown my sorrows. The first man continued, "My dad used to take me hunting."

To cover up my feeling for these men didn't want sympathy nor pity, I asked. "How were y'all gonna shoot anything making all that fuss?" The second black guy smiled.

Seeing the woman didn't understand what his partner was saying, he pointed out, "Ma'am, we ain't that kinda hunter. We buy our food out the grocery store like everybody else. We hunt bad supernatural things. There are cells of us all over the place." He explained throwing an accusatory glance at my driver. I could tell Ashton was bored with our conversation. But was being polite for whatever reason. I guess for my sake.

"Gentlemen, thank you for saving my family. Would you do me the honor of accepting a few days rest here? I promise you, your friend's family will be well compensated." Ashton said in an attempt to end the conversation between them and Ana. The mention of money seemed to have deeply insulted these proud men.

"Money can not replace Mr. Alton. He taught all of us how to hunt. We'll not insult his memory. We can not accept pay or rest for the devil never rests as you very well know. We do not take pay for our service. It cheapens the dignity of our work," the man said rebuking Ashton's offer. Ashton also knew there was nothing left of Mr. Alton to bury.

"Please, don't look at it that way," I requested, knowing how proud southerners are and want nobody's pity nor charity. "But a man lost his life back there all because of us. Had we not been back there then y'all would've been home safe. It will affect his family. Had not I been running and hiding in the wrong place he'd be alive this morning." I said tearfully.

"Now, now, little lady. Ain't no needa all that. Dad did what he wanted. He used to always joke 'em damn gators was gonna be de' death of him. But if it make you feel any better and you promise to stop crying I'll take the money and gave it to maw. How 'bout that?" He said, reaching through the window patting my shoulder. I nodded I'd feel much better if they at least let me thank them properly.

"Whatever ya was running from is what really killed pa. Not 'em gators," the second white guy said before turning to Ashton. "Ya know, ya shouldn't scare your wife and kid like that. That's just plain ol' mean. Got her running over all the place, slab dab right in the middle of danger. What kinda husband and daddy are ya?"

"No, no, gentlemen," I said in Ashton's defense. "He isn't who I'm running from. I think I'm running from the same people you guys protect other people from. My husband has nothing to do with it." I tried to explain but they didn't seemed very convinced.

I watched Ashton get out of the car and take Bea with him. He shifted Bea to his other arm and pulled out several check cards and keyed in numbers while asking the men their names. I heard them say something. If they were being truthful. That? I didn't know but he keyed in the names they said. I got out and took the heavier Bea. I swear she weighed twenty lbs more than last year.

"I see she's a daddy's girl. Look just like her daddy," the obvious leader of the pack said. "Just like my sister looks just like our daddy."

"Are you two brothers?" I asked the two African American men.

"Yeah, we brothers. Our daddies were best friends from little boys. They married two sisters. Mr. Alton was really our uncle by marriage. We just called him mister when doing business. At home we called him uncle." I looked closer at the white guys and saw they weren't white.

"So all y'all kin? Cousins and brothers?" I asked, smiling, letting the southern drawl hang out. I was happy to see a family working together. The four men nodded.

Ashton issued the check cards saying, "Gentlemen, I commend your work but you can't do it properly without a sufficient cash flow."

The others urged the leader to take the card Ashton was handing him. "I'm sorry, I can't take this kinda money. The banks will swear to God we stole it. We're simple swamp folks. We don't live elaborately." By now Ashton was pulling me along with him and Bea who he had taken back from me and a tow truck was backing up to Trusty.

"Where are they taking my car?" I cried.

"To clean and fumigate it. Those men funked it up." he said without looking back but still walking. Bea was perched on his forearm looking straight ahead, too.

The hotel's main entrance was sheltered by a large awning of glass and cast iron. The magnificent grandeur of the main lobby was Art Deco designed. I hadn't realized truly how badly we smelled until we entered the cool luxuriant room and were surrounded by fragrant air.. That's when I smelled the fetid swamp muck I had fallen into last night compounded with sweat and humidity.

I was cleaning Bea up when someone knocked at the door. I opened it; there was a woman with fresh clothing for both of us. Even down to fresh underwear. I thanked her and closed the door. I put the nightgown on Bea and put her to bed and took loose my pinned up sweaty hair deciding it needed washing. But I needed more than a few minutes to do that for this hair was heavy when wet. Just as I got in the shower I heard Bea at the bathroom door crying she was hungry.

"Give me few minutes, Sweetheart, I'll be right out." By the time I dried off and came out Bea was sitting up in the bed eating a big breakfast as if she really were a Queen Bee. I had rushed and my hair was still very damp.

"I thought she might be hungry. Children can't deal with hunger as well as adults," he said from the chair and table in the west corner of the room. I pulled my robe tighter. I was naked underneath the robe.

As I thanked him, I noticed he was fresh as morning dew in clean light summer clothing. I saw the other side across from him was set up for a meal. I sat down; I didn't know I was so hungry until I started eating the delicious southern breakfast, the bacon was crisp and succulent. Most of the bacon I get on the road is hard and chewy. Like I might need dental work performed after eating it. I was surprised anyone knew what Redwood sausages were. I ate my full but was a little embarrassed at how I gorged the food down in front of a stranger named Ashton. I hadn't noticed the top of the robe had slipped open until I asked to see his ring. He slightly pushed it aside. I closed it back sending him an intrepid glance. He chuckled, "Apparently, I've seen more than that. She's living evidence," he said, gesturing toward Bea who was making a big mess in the

463

bed.

I said nothing. I took my ring set off and asked to see his. He abides my request and hands it over. I read the inscriptions inside. They were dedicated to each other. I saw they matched.

"Now, do you believe I'm your huggyman?" He grinned, laughed, mimicking Bea's inability to say husband.

"The heavens erased our memory of each other so you can do whatever they assigned you."

"Did they say what the assignment was?"

"No, but if it involves fighting genetically altered "gators" as your newfound friends called them then I vivaciously object."

"If they went to this degree to separate us then it must be something very important."

"I do not know nor do I care. All I know is I do not want you in the swamp fighting giant gators, or whatever in the hell else might be out in this world. You're my family. It's my job to protect you two."

He was treating her like a silly damsel in distress and she wasn't too thrilled with that but then again had not he shown up they all would be in the belly of a giant gator basking in the sun this morning. So swallowed her pride and kept her mouth shut. If he wanted to save them from giant gators, hitmen, Godzilla, King Kong, or whatever other monsters were out there, oh hell, let him. She didn't have a damn thing to prove by pretending she wasn't scared. She was tired of running and fighting psychos.

He knew the time he had to spend with them was very limited and also knew a lot had been wasted already. Which is why he was glad when the female security officer arrived to sit with Bea so he could talk to her mother privately. Well, talking wasn't exactly what he had in mind but he'd call it *talking* for now. Normally, he didn't date women with

464

kids. But when the kid was suspected to be his own what could he say? He loved the little girl and had to figure out a way to get her out of this chaotic misfortunate. He also knew Ana wasn't wearing anything under the robe. So what? They were simply going across the hall. Bea was engulfed in a cartoon and paying them no mind. She apparently remembered more about their life together than her mom. But sadly as she ages, she'll forget. The moment the door closed behind them he embraced her in a kiss, "My darling, I don't know if I can handle this separation from you." he said hoarsely, refusing to let her go.

Aggressively returning the kisses and hugs, clasping him with all my strength, "What kinda of cruelty is being played on us and why?" I mumbled wearily, leaning against his chest. He kissed the top of my head.

Not having an answer to her question and fearing the angel of time was closing in on them he opened the robe and begin kissing her all over. He wanted to savor the taste of her naturally fragrant skin, He moved down to her silky mound and pushed the hairs aside. She didn't intend to moan but she did. It was musical to him. She used his broad shoulders to brace herself for the ecstasy was building up in waves. He felt her knees giving away so he picked her up and laid her gently on the bed and proceeded to make love very tenderly and passionately to her. Hours later, lying in each other's arms he broached the subject of Bea living with him while she completed her mission.

"She'll receive the best of everything," he said softly as early spring rain. Knowing that wherever Bea is Ana will find a way to get there.

"No, I'm sorry. I can't just give Bea to you regardless of what she remembers!"

"Ana, she's my daughter too and she wasn't called to do anything but be a normal child." He argued.

"The blood test says otherwise." I snapped back. "She's Thaddeus' daughter not yours."

He didn't mean to lose his patience nor temper with her. He knew she was doing the

465

best she could with what she had to work with, which was virtually nothing. But he lost it. Last night upset him more than he was letting her believe. He had seen what creatures like those can do. "Stop being selfish and think of Bea. Let the child have a normal life, a normal childhood. You may get her and yourself killed out there doing whatever it is you're doing! Whenever the heck you remember what it is, do it, and then come home to us. And exactly what are you doing besides' running? Nothing you nor heaven have told me so far makes a bird's brain bit of sense!"

Calling me selfish really rubbed me the wrong way. I'd heard that so many times before. I wasn't taking it from someone who'd just said he loved me, "What will you do? Stick her with nannies while you do whatever in the hell it is you do!? Who will be there to talk to her as a parent?!"

"I've raised lots of children, half of the employees you've seen I had a hand in raising them and they aren't mine."

That stopped me cold. I didn't know about the employees. That explained their loyalty. But I don't care what he says. I'm not parting with Bea. Bea was not his daughter. If I didn't give her to mom or Helena, I definitely am not giving her to this man—if that's what he is?

"Ashton, exactly, what are you?"

"A person!," he snapped.

From his foul attitude it's hard to believe we just made love. His eyes and voice softened, "Ana, I've seen what happens to those like you. It's usually a very tragic end. That's why I'm upset. I do not want to lose you and Bea. Is that so wrong?"

No, I didn't think it was wrong to want to be with the ones you love. I paused a moment before speaking. "Honey, when this is over we can then be together."

"Ana, you don't understand. It's *never* going to be over until you're dead. That's how heaven works. There's no retirement.", he stressed.

466

"How do you know?" I asked cantankerously, sitting up to look him in the face.

"Because that's where I'm from! That's how I know. Heaven doesn't let go. There's no completion of an assignment and you go on to a normal life!"

I stared at him. I was baffled. "Are you an angel?"

He laughed aloud. "No, baby, I'm unquestionably no angel. I'm a son of God. I probably told you this before but it was erased from your memory."

All I could do was gaze at him. I had no idea my dream lover was a real live immortal. I thought...hell, I don't know what I thought. Half of the time, I don't know my own mind anymore.

"Ok," I said swallowing hard. "I don't believe God will do that to us seeing how much we love each other. There's so little love in the world. I thinks every little bit counts. I believe if we keep the faith we'll find a way to have a happy home and still do whatever God wants done. He created the institution of marriage so I don't believe He'll go against His Own creation. I can't say I know how it all will work out but I believe it will...somehow."

Unbeknownst to them both angels were watching. Raphael looked at Denziuel and smiled. "See, I told you they'd find each other even with a memory erase. Their love is chiseled in each other's heart and the heart remembers even when the mind does not. So I firmly believe it will be easier on everyone to simply let them be together. She goes out and does her job and returns home to him."

Denziuel shakes his head, disagreeing; he thinks Raphael still grieves for their lost brother by it was him who had to chain Draco/Azazel in the desert of Dudael and pile rocks on him. When Azazael was forced to help their brother Adam carry the burden of his world since he created many of the problems.

"How will she ever learn the things she needs to know to be successful at her calling?
467

No, they must be kept apart until the designated time. There's too much at stake for her to be allowed to be with him. We both know how stubborn and steel-willed Azazael is. You saw what happened a few hours ago. She'll never learn how to lead if he fights every battle for her. How about this? You do your job and I do mine. Mine is to see to it that this saint keeps the Law and does as called and yours is dealing with her romance and love, healing and mercy." Raphael agrees and closes the veil as the couple made up from their spat and begun to make love again. He was smiling because he knew love always won and if she could use Azazael's great power and wealth for the sake of the Kingdom, then all was good.

But he reached down and took the second duffel of money with him. Denziuel was right. Azazael would interfere.

⁓◈◉◈⁓

Travis had many aliases. At the place in Freeport Delaware he'd rented a sparsely furnished room under the name of Trenton Miller. He still felt he couldn't discombobulate the being after him. It was exhausting to sleep on high alert at all times. He had been home to Deland, Florida but the cops had surrounded the area looking for him. He ditched the leather duffel he felt belonged to Azazael and kept the murderous immortal connected to him. For about a week he didn't feel him and he used this to his advantage. To convert the money into smaller bills he needed help. He called some of his friends including his old girlfriend Jarretta and his partner in crime Henninger to help get rid of the sequentially numbered money in exchange for random bills.

He gave some of the jewelry in the bag to Jarretta. She was one of the few people who knew him before he turned to a life of crime. He also knew Jarretta was sort of racist. His entire hometown was. It had gotten better over the centuries but the underlying racism was still there. It was much more subtle than in the twentieth century.

"Can I have the handbag?", she asked from perched on the window ledge. He wished she would get dressed to sit there. She stood facing the window, watching the traffic below and the rain splatter and slide down the thick glass panel. She was wearing nothing but the rich woman's jewelry and handbag. Her long, straight dark blonde hair shielded her right breast from public display while the rest of her was exposed.

"Sure," he said he knew it was a custom made Birkin costing over a hundred grand but he also knew it would impossible to sell for what it was worth. He had forgotten he had the photo of Ana with her things.

"Is this her? The woman Ashton Cargill married?" Jarretta asked, holding up the old-fashion specialty photo. The skill to make those photo paper pictures nowadays was rare and expensive.

"Yeah," He said, glancing around at the picture.

"She's a negro. Why would a man like that marry a nigger?" Jarretta asked, frowning at the picture.

"I don't know. To each his own taste in women but Jarretta, be careful at what you say. He might be listening. I told you, he's not human. He'd kill all of us if he heard you call that woman a nigger. So drop the 'N' word out your vocabulary!"

Jarretta indifferently shrugged her lovely tanned shoulders and sulked at his rebuttal. She wasn't stupid. She'd never say that to a black person's face.

"But it's perfectly ok to say it behind their back?" A mellifluous, masculine voice asked from the far corner of the apartment. The three turned in unison and there sat a man in an expensive double-breasted suit. His handsome face was set off blue topaz eyes and lubricious wavy hair, the hair was like nothing they'd ever seen. It reminded everyone of a lion's mane. Travis knew without introduction this was Cargill/Azazael sitting in that chair in the corner. He had finally tracked him down, just when he thought the man/thing had given up. The three friends glanced at each other. The silence in the room was ominous. The funerary bleak air in the room felt as if a black hooded Reaper was dragging it direful sickle across the floor making a scrapping sound against the ancient hard wood floor. The three knew who this man really was. Death. Their death.

"Travis Rankin, that's your real name, isn't it? Who hired you to kill my wife? Your answer determines if you live or die," Ashton Cargill said, beckoning Jarretta to hand over Ana' personal effects.

"To answer your question about the woman I married. She's a nicer, prettier person than you. I'm not exactly attracted to white women." He said it to be insulting, while in truth the human race and it silliness mattered very little to him. Jarretta inched toward him; he waved his hand using his power, snatching Ana's items off the woman.

Jarretta knew he was lying, she had seen him in Monte Carlo with his main squeeze named Dawn, who was blonder than her. So she pushed his insult aside.

Azazael wrestled with the temptation. The urge to kill. He wouldn't hesitate to kill them all if he didn't feel it could lessen his chances in being reunited with Ana. Travis noticed the man's gestures and movement were deliberate, diligent, his body language was calm and free of the agitation burning in his eyes. It was in the relaxed mode of a confident person. Someone at total ease with his environment and himself. The movements of a killer.

"A special agent named Ralph Bender hired me to kill her." Travis said, carefully not looking at the immortal because he worrying about his own mortality.

"Ralph Bender is dead. I killed him. Just as I'm going to kill you if you don't hand over my money. I guess you figured out I'd it tagged to keep track of my wife spending habits by I see you and your buddies here have been converting it into untraceable bills."

Following Jarretta's instinct in dealing with this thing, Travis carefully handed the man the old, battered, dark olive army duffel.

"Where is the bag the money was originally in?" Ashton wanted to know.

"At a pawn shop in Atlantic City." Travis said, staring back into Cargill's cold unyielding eyes. He figured if he were to die, at least he'd die facing his killer. That's a luxury he denied those whose lives he took. Most never saw him.

"Two million is missing. If I've to ask you pieces of shit one more time where in the unholy fuck is my money it's going to get ugly real fast!"

"I spent it. It's very expensive living on the run from you and Bender." Travis honestly explained.

"I really don't give a shit. Come up with the remaining of my money or you all three of you are dead. It's bad enough you tried to make me a widower. And this worn out rawboned bitch here called my love derogatory names. But then you've the audacity to steal my money, too. So tell me why shouldn't I kill all of you? And this strange looking retard sitting over in the corner trying to stealthy draw a gun on me; this fucker over there wearing outdated Dracula's sunglasses must thinks he's fucking Werner Karl Heisenberg, Bram Stoker, or someone of the evil ass grand equivalent," Cargill said, referring to Henninger. "I'm trying real hard to be nice here and you three fuckers are making that real hard. Taking the advantage of it. Which is why I'm rarely nice."

"Because we haven't done anything worthy of death." Jarretta softly cooed, believing their only hope lies in her ability to tempt him with her femininity. "I mean, she isn't dead. Travis didn't want to kill her. Had he wanted to kill her she'd be dead. But for some reason he didn't." Jarretta argued. She rested her case saying, "Because you are merciful."

Azazel threw his head back and laughed a deep brass laughter that was almost musical, "You think so?!"

"Yes," She said, daring to walk closer upon him. He was violently fighting hard the urge to kill her. But didn't want to lose any Brownie points with Denzuiel. That stick to the letter, tight-arsed brother of his was worse than Mike, you could get Mike to see things your way some of the times. But Denziuel never budged no matter what was involved. Even Father had to tell him from time to time to show mercy. To chill the hell out. Denzuiel was always like. "You broke the Law therefore your ass shall pay dearly."

Azazel found it a little comedic how this woman thinks she can tempt him into not killing her. Had she lived in the days of the Gender War she would've been killed by

471

some crazed misogynist for this very act of temptation. How the war broke out was there started to be a global rash of murders. The complaint of female manipulation had been fostering for years. Out of it grew hatred, contempt, and prejudice against women or girls. Misogyny had outright manifested globally in numerous ways; social exclusion, discrimination, open hostility, androcentrism, patriarchy, the dumb ass ideas of male pregnancies, gender privileges, public belittling of women, violence against women, and viewing them strictly as sexual objects. There was a secret plan to eliminate them completely once they discovered a way to grow human children outside the womb. Of course it was nothing new but he had never seen it on such a global scale. For misogyny is found within all ancient texts and myths. Much of the so-called enlightened influential Western philosophers and thinkers ideology was very misogynistic. Even the foundations of early Christianity with its guilt about sex, its insistence on female subjection, its dread of female seduction. What led to the war was the killings started spreading world-wide. It was a bloody war and was won when the women's lovers, father, sons and other male relatives and female soldiers staged a massive invasion, a Normandic landing much like the allies during World War II. This demonic plot of Lucifer had been before in other worlds. But Adamite males wised up whereas the others didn't. A world filled with males is not a nice place to be. It's on a fast forward track to self-destruction. In the other worlds the males turned on each other after all the females were eliminated and destroyed themselves. These other worlds started out the same as earth did in 19th to 20th century. There were more gay men than straight so they thought they could eliminate the female gender and still survive.

The young spiritual world of Kryptico, succeeded about 200,000 B.C., for a while they did raise test tube babies born of male implants but there was something wrong with the kids and they didn't live very long. Being immortals, the women they killed were simply taken back into heaven. Seeing their error they asked for them back after the savage war waged on for many years. Father refused to give them back and even cut off the women' access to their former world. Well, to make a long story short, in the end the men destroyed their worlds and realm fighting each other and Lucifer was having a belly roll laugh. Today it's a massive wasteland defiled with all types of debauchery and creatures that were once men lurking in bushes waiting to attack.

The thing about Krypticoites were they were half flesh and half spiritual. They were a

472

young world. Older than earth but yet still young in the cosmic order of age. He remembers well when Father made him go to this world to make them stop fighting. He remembers how peeved off he was. He didn't give a damn if they killed each other off. The weaker males were turned on after the female genocide. The place looked like a level of hell and not one of the more civilized levels. He saw gangly men, covered with lankiness, everywhere. The mere fact one brushed against another turned into a big brawl. He was pissed off Father made him come him so he started kicking ass all the way up to their leader whom he found with a harem of drags. To him that was the most foolish thing he had ever seen. Why would you want an imitation of a woman when you had the real thing? Anyway, that wasn't his concern, Father sent him to kick their asses and make them stop fighting. Why Dad didn't just nuke them as He did everyone else who sunk this low was beyond his comprehension. He was glad to be out of there. The last he heard they were living like animals.

Bored and pulling his mind back to the issue at hand, "No, naked lady." He mildly chuckled. "You've me confused with my brother Raphael. The Angel of Mercy. Isn't that right? Heisenberg?" Azazel asked, looking over at the man staring at him over the realm of the dark tinted wire-frame sunglasses. "The only reason I haven't killed you is because of my wife but I expect my two million or I'll kill you," he said cold-cocking all three unconscious and disappearing.

Travis Rankin spent the next five years trying to replace what he spent. Before he died, Bender had put into motion a plan to bankrupt him on trumped up charges of tax evasion. His penthouse and other assets were seized and sold, plus he owed a supernatural killer money. But surprisingly Jarretta and Henninger stuck with him.

The three worked hard at trying to replace the spent loot but with the immortal or some of his henchman popping up whenever they felt the need to make a nuisance of themselves was making replacing it harder. One of the half humans ones hired him to kill for Cargill International. Paying him chicken feed in comparison to his prior earnings. He finally understood how so many people came to owe Azazel something, once he had you in his snares, he never let you go. But he had to find a way out of this trap. Cargill was no better than Bender and friends.

The incisiveness was they were holding his friends hostage to make sure he carried out their dirty work. The trenchancy of this life was wearing him down and he wanted out. This wasn't like working for himself where he took jobs as he pleased and turned down those he felt funny about after learning details about the intended hit. After a year of this it was bothering his conscience. Some of the hits made—in his opinion the person didn't deserve to die. He began plotting an escape and was wondering how could he execute it without throwing his friends under the bus?

Chapter 10
Wonders of the Past. Life is but a dream.
(The Present Day)

He traveled back in time. Eons earlier. He sensed he knew where she was. With an ancient god. Himself, one of his past personas. He wonders how this ancient god reached way into the future and found her when he can't find her and he's living in the present with her. Again she is gone by the time he arrives.

"Damn! That woman can move." Ashton Cargill laughed bitterly. He still doesn't know fully what she looks like. Something is keeping her image from him and pissing him off royally. He can't deny he's looking for her two reasons. First, to keep that fucked up ass wizard from her, he kills his spouses. And secondly, for sexually conquest. She sounded very sexy.

"Where is she?" He asked himself, his ancient persona, not very politely.

"Who? Ana? She was pulled back from me again."

"AGAIN??!" Ashton asked "How many times has she been here with you?" He asked, knowing the ancient god did not know who he was. He was looking at his future with distrust.

"Not often enough." Draco replied displaying suspicion as to why this immortal was inquiring about his woman. Well, one of his thousands. And most of all why he looked like him? He smiled, pleased with the result when it dawned on him this was him! But from the future.

"You appeared before her last night, how did you do that?" Cargill asked. Draco was watching him curiously."Why do you seek her? You're one of my brothers so I know your reason can not be good? She's not to be your toy." Draco said to test his future self. Hey, it's himself so no, he doesn't trust himself to have charitable intentions.

Ashton chuckled. Look at the kettle calling the pot black. "A warlock wants to kill her."

"WHAT??" Draco yelled and fluidly leapt up from the black marble throne. "I'll rip him limb by limb!!"

Ashton saw this was his opportunity to convince Draco to tell where he pulled her from. Time division kept him from accessing his own mind. He hated time travel especially knowing that these children of his now staring curiously at him are long dead. That's why he didn't want children; he was tired of them dying on him.

"You see, I'm trying to save her. And if I can find her first then I can protect her." Ashton semi-lied.

"Liar, you only want to find her for sexual relations. You do not love her." Draco says, seeing through his ruse.

Ashton laughed softly at how well he knew himself. Even time hadn't rusted that knowledge. "Ok, I'll admit I don't love her, I don't know her. That warlock, if he finds her first he'll mercilessly rape her and pass her around to his friends and then kill her when they're finished."

This caused Draco to forget the nude women on the huge bed nearby and start pacing the floor with everyone trying to watch him move back and forth. He was moving too fast for the humans to effectively watch him. He suddenly stopped and grabbed Ashton's arm, his own arm.

"Find her. I do not know what era she lives but you must find her. I'll cease to exist without her. You love her and have never stopped loving her. I do not know how I found her. The portal opened, I saw her. She looked very sad so I stepped through to her. Follow my path back to your era which she lives, she was sitting on a stone seat in a garden. There was huge house with strange lighting inside. Much like the ones we once created. There were strange carriages without horses. Much like those we used to drive. She fled me but later to came me." Ashton thanked him and followed the path Draco instructed him about back but he knew she was already gone.

He steps back in time again but merely a day back; he sees her. This is his first real good look at her. Without the divine illusions and cloaks created to protect her, "Wow! She is beautiful!" he lowly whispers an exclamation. "Almost too pretty to fuck." He thinks to himself, he feels a pang of jealousy slowing evolving into rage when he heard a neighbor trying to allure her to his place. *"Yeah! Righttt you wanna help her alright! Help her right into your bed. Motherfucker! Who do you think you're fooling?"* He reverses time travel and goes as far into modern era as allowed. He teleports into the man's apartment and waits for him. It's a simple place, neat, and clean. Nice furniture. "Ah! A military man." He said, looking through Charles' closet for clues as to who the man really is.

"Fortunately, she wasn't impressed." He cussed his difficulty in remembering some things from his past. Somehow the things he can't remember always involve her. Like he doesn't remember Draco being in love with a time traveling mortal. And definitely doesn't remember feeling jealousy pertaining any woman. There was no need to. There were too many available. He asked himself why was he here when he had a houseful of willing women in his French mansion and around the world? Nearly every palace he owned had its harem. Except those in the USA. America was still too Puritanical for such an arrangement. They all lived in separate houses. So why was he here chasing this lone skinny girl? His interest is ebbing away. He was tired of waiting for soldier boy to

476

come home to question him. He could beat the answers out of him or knock at the door pretending to be a dear friend looking for her. Nahhh! He wouldn't willingly reveal anything, so he'll beat it out of him. Usually this close to someone's trail he can track them like a wolf after a sheep but with her he's being blocked, he wonders why? He knows Who is blocking him. Only the heavens can so thoroughly block him, hell definitely couldn't.

He teleports to her old apartment. He touches the striped tucked mattress, he gets a flash vision. He's lying beside her in a room he doesn't know. It looks like her house in Boston from the outside. But he'd never been there before the night of Carole Cadwell's party, he's certain of that. Another reason he wants to find her is he needs her to help him repair his memory. Somehow he senses she can help him remember what's missing. He can't remember a lot about that night but he doesn't remember sleeping with her. Maybe he dreamed he did. Hell, he doesn't know. And definitely doesn't remember being affectionate to her, he isn't about the lovey-dovey shit. He fucks and move on to the next one and has no pity for anyone who falls in love with him. He doesn't lie and deceive anyone. Or build up their hope of getting love from him. She knows what he's about before she climbs into his bed. If she can't handle sharing him with others then they've no arrangement.

Strolling slowly through the apartment he visionized her milling around the small place doing daily things. He smiles against his will at the image in his mind. He shakes his head hard to clear it of the sappy whimsicality.

"The only thing love earns you is a broken heart," he thinks to himself. His watchphone rings while he is deep in pondering. It's his Washington D.C. office.

"YES!" he answer in an angry tone. He's peeved because they interrupted his thoughts. "Mrs. Carole Cadwell has some valuable information for you." the caller said.

"What is it?" He asked, getting madder by the seconds. Why does every other call have to be about bullshit? "She said she can only trust to deliver it directly to you, sir."

"Put her through," he sighs. She better not be calling him about another goddamn party. He swears, he don't know what he will do to her right about now.

A sultry, smoky female voice comes over the airwaves. "Ashton, darling, I know where Ana Wyett is hiding." Carole says, reading off the address over the phone. He really feels like teleporting to her house and killing her for the belated news.

"Stupid bitch I already know that!" He growls.

He watched her tiny face on the watch screen react negatively to his name calling. She quickly regained her compose as the actress she is, "Well, how about let's get together for a little sexual fun?" She says, point blankly revealing the real reason she is calling. "My friend Helga is here also." She adds.

"No, leave me the hellish fuck alone before you make me kill your whorish, trifling ass. And make James eat you as a pot of stew for dinner!" He yelled through the phone snapping the connection off.

He never encountered this kind of interference before—so why was everyone suddenly wanting to be his new best friend? This is Nikola's ploy to defer him from his quest. Doesn't that man know that pussy in a pretty package can't alter his quest? He's far too old for that ancient trick. He doesn't fully understand Heaven's reason for keeping him off Nikola but he intends to get to the bottom of it.

He quickly teleports back upstairs; Ana's old place is fucking with his mind. Making him nostalgic and sappy. He didn't like that. This entire shenanigan has grown the feel of being against his will

He heard feet trotting up the staircase, not hard, nor soft. The man who lives upstairs is now home about to sit down to a dinner. Without seeing him but acting purely on adrenaline the decorated soldier quickly reached for his service gun. But Ashton moves quicker than Charles can see and yanks the gun from his hand with such force the handle tears into his palm. Charles doesn't know what nor who this is man is but he knows he isn't human. He heard the immortals had returned to the earth and wondered if this was one?

478

"One of you talking monkeys has already pissed me off today. I can only be pissed off but only so much before I start killing. Now I'm going to ask you a simple question but you better not give me a simpleton, bullshitting answer," Ashton said; his eyes were now orbs of fire. He somewhat admired the man for not flinching or screaming as blood dripped from his torn hand and splattered on the floor. The soldier stared at him, right into his flaming eyes. Which was really a very foolish and dangerous thing to do.

"Now, where is Ana Wyett? I know you know where she is." Charles stands and begins swinging his clenched fists; deciding if he was going to die he was going down on his feet and swinging. Azazael quickly dodged him, grabbing the soldier pinning his arms behind his back. Charles immediately noted the man had no scent. Yes, this was one of the immortals, for demons stunk.

"I do not know where she's residing. She refused to tell me and if I knew I would not tell you," Charles vowed through clench teeth. Biting down pain and fear. Refusing to show either. This thing was pulling his arms out of their sockets.

Ashton moves at super speed and pushed Charles against the wall with his forearm on his throat. "I told you not to fuck with me, didn't I?" He grimaced, his face snarling, his upper lip curling, and punch him in the ribs at human strength. Charles groans, the direct punch deflates his lung, causing a nausea to rise in his guts. "You're who she's running from. You're who she's afraid of and always looking over her shoulder for. You should be ashamed of yourself terrorizing them. She's the kindness person you'll ever know."

"Them?" He thought she was traveling alone? "Who else is with her?" Charles realized this monster in a human form didn't know about Bea and Mrs. BuFaye, so he wasn't telling him. He'll kill them, too. "I asked you a question. Who else is with her? Is she traveling with a man?"

The word '*man*' gave Ashton away. Charles knows why he is acting like a lunatic. A very strong one but nonetheless, a lunatic."If you love her as you pretend to, you'd let her go." Charles said calmly as blood tickled from the corner of his mouth.

The subject of love rattles Azazel, he applies harder pressure to the man's thorax, gambling with the idea of compressing until he crushed it, "I didn't say a damn fucking thing about loving her. I'm trying to find her so the psycho who *is* after her doesn't fillet her like a fucking fish!" Ashton yells his fiery breath into the unperturbed man's face.

Charles' demeanor changes at these words. Charles knew the enemy could and would lie as easily as tell the truth, so this demon could more likely be lying.

"If you wish to help I'm sure you'll find a way." Charles' calm words made Ashton consider letting him go but before he does another thought crosses his evil mind. "Have you slept with her?" Ashton asked suspiciously.

Just as Charles suspected, this beast was fishing for a reason to kill him. He's behaving abominably jealous not to be in love. Then again, possessiveness and love aren't the same thing. They're far distant relatives.

"NO, I care about her and respect her too much to risk losing our friendship."

Ashton laughed a nasty laughter that was really one of relief. "Oh, so she shot you down. The very model of a modern major general!"

Now it was Charles' turn to get mad. He now fully understood why Ana was running from him. This man is nuts; mean and batshit crazy kind of nuts.

"Men and women can be friends." He cried, realizing this being had a very vile and perverted mind. Perverted or not he knew had he lied about their friendship and said they were lovers this being would kill him.

Close up and personal in his face, grinning a feverish, maniacal grin Azazel asked, "Are you gay or a faggot?"

"No," Charles replied but he didn't believe in applying degrading labels, "Sir, that's a highly, extremely offensive term for a homosexual man."

Ashton laughed that mean, menacing laughter again. "So?!? I've offended God so what do I care about offending a gay man? I don't give a damn who I offend. But you must be one if you could sleep every night above a woman who looks like her and didn't try to fuck her. So you expect me to believe you're straight and didn't try anything. Aw! C'mon son, I was born before earth's first sunrise. So tell me another bullshitting lie. C'mon, you can tell me the truth." Azazel baited in his most seductive voice. The one he uses to make others trust him. "I promise I won't get mad. I mean she's just a friend. She means nothing else to me. I'm just looking out for her well-being." His coaxing voice was almost hypnotizing. Charles shook his head hard to shake off the effect. He had stopped looking this thing in the eyes. Realizing that was a very bad idea. The stare down only works with other humans not immortals hell bent on killing.

Charles knew better than to know show the slightest hint of how distasteful he found the subject. This being was a mean, murderous bastard. He had no idea what peeved him off so greatly but he was remaining calm and determined not to be a contributing factor.

Azazel admired the man's stance. Not many can stand to look into his eyes and not break, go mad if he wish to drive them insane or induce night terrors. But before disappearing, Ashton erased Charles memory of him. Of his having ever been there. He was satisfied with the answer. But he knew the man wasn't gay. He just felt like messing with the man. He decided to let him live. Ana may contact him in the near future.

❦

Arriving at his L.A. home, his harem member named Dawn had just flown in from Paris. Figuring he was in the US. Seeing him materialize she was enraged when she asked him of his whereabouts for the last few days. His temper was already teeming and nerves tethering on the edge when he backhanded her. He meant to, it was no accident. "I told you years ago! Do not ask where I've been. You're not my wife. You've no right to question me."

Rubbing her face she decided not to tell him she may be pregnant; the last girl with them who got knocked up ended up getting kicked out. He didn't want kids. The others warned Mimosa not to tell him he would say the baby wasn't his and kick her out. You'd

481

to have an abortion or get out. He was right, their home was no place for a child when they had orgies nearly on a daily basis.

"I only asked because someone named Zeus came here looking for you."

"Oh, what did he want?" Azazel grunted, trying to shift back into the Ashton Cargill persona. When so angry the morpheme took a while.

"Money, as usual. He said you stiffed his son out of his pay. I told him he would've to wait until you came home." She said, astringently rubbing his neck hard to erase the tension out of his shoulder. His massive shoulders were difficult for her small hands to grasp. She knew what always made him relax when he was tensed up like this. She gracefully moved from behind him and seductively knelt before him, expertly unzipping his jeans and removing his penis through the unzipped slit and begun fellation. She'd heard about the woman he was chasing and they all knew if he became serious about her they'd have to leave this glamorous lifestyle of riches beyond comparison. Right now, every possible luxury was at their finger tip. Right now, she enjoyed whatever her heart desired. She didn't like the idea of a Mrs Cargill taking her place. He probably would still see them but it wouldn't be the same. If he cares enough to be out looking for this woman for days on the end, then he's growing serious about her and this bitch is a threat to them all.

He grabbed her hair and shoved himself into her throat, choking her. She fought him but he pulled harder and refused to let go, not before he ejaculated into her mouth. He knew, unlike some women, she didn't like that. She spat and cussed him, clawed at his legs. Finally, he let her go. She was angry when she raised her head, glaring at him. Her anger quickly dissolved; she saw it wasn't Cargill she was sucking but Azazel and he had read her thoughts about that woman.

The seven other main harems knew Dawn's group had called and had been discussing what they heard about Ashton and the mystery woman.

"I think she's merely someone new to him. We've seen them come and go but we're still here. The sooner he finds her and sleeps with her, the sooner he'll get over his fucking infatuation with her." Dawn dismissively said, sipping her champagne. She was tired of talking about that woman. No one else was in that room to see what he made her do for berating his so-called lady love. She championed herself to know every sexual position in the world by now. So she was going to let the others keep right on talking until he walked down on them and turned into fucking crazy ass Azazel.

"Oh, you mean fuck her." Delores cried, throwing her luscious Irish red head back, laughing. Dawn flinched. Delores' salacious language was pissing her off, it doesn't feel good to be fucked. She was wishfully hoping he came along right now and fucked the red dye job outta Delores hair for thinking it was funny. Maybe the bitches did know he did it as to why she had been in bed for three days. The problem was it wasn't painful but you stayed intoxicated on something when common sense told you it was high time to stop fucking. The others had been looking at her enviously all day because of all the expensive jewelry brought to her room. Fuck them. She was the one he rode for hours and damn near drove out of her mind with ecstasy for two days, so she earned it.

"Ashton doesn't *sleep* with anyone," Doris quipped. The other five laughed at Doris joke. *Dawn knew now they were laughing at her. Just you wait. She'd fix, fix them all.*

"Supposed he's really serious about this woman?! Why else would he be out looking for her?" Candy argued amidst the clamorous laughter.

Dawn had been with him the longest. She totally disagreed with Candy. She knew him better than Candy.

"Candy, there's always some new blood trying to take our place. I've been with him over 20 years and I'm telling you, we don't age. We still look fabulous. Keep him well sexed and we'll be alright. This beats working and wearing yourself out slaving away in an office or factory. A lot of heifers say they wouldn't do the things we do but they're lying. A lot of them are doing much worse for nothing. At least we get paid millions to suck his dick. There're pictures all over the place of dumb girls flashing themselves for free." Dawn argued, but she really didn't feel as secure as she boasted. Of their 20 years together she had never known him to literally *hunt* anyone down. Sure, he has brought hundreds home and kept them a few days before telling his people to get rid of them. Some made a scene not wanting to leave. But they always left richer than they came. But the witches say this woman is closer to what Ashton is. So she wonders should they really be worried about her? Whomever she is? She has seen her. She has failed to kill her. So is this woman really a Nephilim? Would that explains why she's next to impossible to kill.

Delores lazily stretches out her long, shapely, unfreckled legs saying, "I'm not worried about a Mrs. Ashton Cargill; by the time he finish taking her through a round of days on the end of fucking she'll be begging us to come help her out with him. Her ass will be so sore she can't walk!"

Everyone burst out laughing agreeing with Delores. "One woman can't handle him by herself. I know I've tried it." Dawn threw her glass hard at Delores' head. She wasn't talking about the mystery woman. She was talking about her. Delores dodged it and pitched a heavy lamp back at her. Dawn rolled off her sore rear, sprang up, and headed for her with all manicured claws bent into talons. She tackled her midriff and took her down with a loud crash as heavy antique furniture turned over and décor shattered to the floor. Saddled her and started beating her in the face. Dawn was long tired of Delores' thinking because she was bigger and taller she could handle her. Dawn hasn't reigned supreme in this household by being weak. She grabbed a heavy bronze sculpture to bash her in the head with it but someone snatched it away, so she continued with her fists.

Ashton entered the room to visit the others and pulled the two apart. Some days he's temped to let them kill each other. But the haunting image of the 1920's always surfaced of two of his harem members being executed. Hanging from a noose when he had the power to stop them from killing each other but didn't.

Some noticed the blood covering him and were distressed. They undressed and fondled him; he appeared disinterested for a while but eventually made love to the group. About 12 hours later he drops the bomb, "Everyone I'm sure you all know I may marry someday and it won't be any of you. When that day comes each of you will get 10 million; Dawn you'll get 20 million-you been with me the longest. I hope you all can
484

move on with your lives when that day comes. Don't act surprised I know each of you knew this day would come. All good things must come to an end. I've always shown you ladies transparency."

They each looked at the other. So the witches were right, he was looking for that woman to marry her. They had had this conversation before. He just doesn't remember it. So no one was telling him.

"Ashton, do you love her?" Candy asked.

He pauses a few seconds,"Love in a marriage is a very human concept. Immortals do not necessarily marry for love," he replied as he nestled among seven of them.

"Have you found her?" Doris asked, secretly deciding he leaves her no choice except to steal his sperm and freeze them. That way he would have to take care of her for life.

"When will all this happen?" Dawn asked angrily. Ashton doesn't hit much but everyone expected him to slap Dawn for her ornery attitude. "You'll be the first to know when I tell you to get the hell out of my house," he gently and over sweetly replied.

He knew he would soon revisit with Dawn's version of the meaning of "*Heaven has no rage like love to hatred turned,* Nor hell a fury like a woman scorned." He had pissed Dawn off and she wasn't the one to annoy. He knew she'd craft a way to get back at him for this conversation and for wildly fucking her for pissing him off. He tried to tell her was sorry but her eyes kept saying, "Sorry don't cut it."

⸎

Ashton Cargill had spend the last seven centuries building and establishing "Cargill International", his earthly empire. A lot has changed since Jesus came and went back Home. You can't force people to perform under duress anymore and take what you want or your ass will end up in Celestial Prison. Nowadays you've to actually work and build your wealth yourself. Nowadays his inner circle of demigods ran his empire. He was grateful they didn't need constant supervision. So he was free to roam at his leisure.

"That little satanic talking monkey actually hit me and guess what? It hurts!" He said to himself and chuckled. This latest one reminded him of a wizard of long ago. Everyone thinks Merlin was the biggest dog there ever was. But there lived an ancient one named Magnus. Who was greater than Merlin. It was Magnus who defeated Merlin and locked him away from humanity. The shame of it was Magnus was human.

But this young warlock named Nikola reminded him of another warlock named Faizon. He was powerful enough to fight him back and win for a while but mortals tire easily. That's when he moved in for the kill. But that Wizard was born that way, he didn't acquire it through satanic endorsement or worship. That's the worse kind. He heard Faizon made mince meat of Orman, the Grand Wizard. Had not Orman's student and lover Nikola jumped in to defeat Faizon, Faizon would've won. While they were in a weakened state, he heard Nikola took the three of them out. Oregon, Orman, and Faizon. From word on hell's street. He pretended to help Orman and Oregon fight Faizon but when he saw his two masters and the challenger were enervated he moved in for the kill and took over the rein and worn Vonderbilt's name so the dumb masses of satanic-glorifiers wouldn't know the difference until he cemented his stake in the empire. Smart move.

He followed Nikola right to where Ana Wyett was living. He knew the little trick knew where she was. But there's something divine about that house. Nikola knows it too, that's why he won't go charging in there and dragging her out. One of the resident's spiritual imprint...he's familiar with her. He fought her at least 3-4 centuries ago. That's impossible. Humans doesn't live that long! She must have traveled through time. Right now his expansion of pleasure did not included fighting a Nazarene warrior saint. It only included acquiring Ana Wyett, getting laid, and siphoning off her powers for healing. Repairing his memory that millions of years of imprisonment had robbed him of. And staying out of the hell or celestial prison.

Once face to face with her he intend to let his charm do the work. If he could allure Venus' rigid virgins out of their sacred temple, he most surely could beguile a scared girl out of a house. He'd no intention of tangling with a senior Nazarene warrior saint. They're like fighting someone with divine powers but yet hyped up on the old 20th century drug called crack. So he'll sit and wait, being immortal time is always on his side.

Nikola can sense him, he can tell by the way the man keeps moving his head. He blew a strong breeze at the elm trees shading the big rumbling house and watched the mortal man listen carefully. Then the wrought iron lattice door opened; an elderly woman of about 70 walked outside with her divine blade akin to Excalibur in her age spotted right hand.

"I know you're out here! And if you know what's best for you you'd leave us alone!" She calls out in the darkness coating her backyard. He teased her, he blew cold air, he knew his breath caused the temperature to drop. He saw the elderly woman pulled her sweater tighter around her regal shoulders. He saw Nikola's eyes narrow at the woman. He too is cloaked. He watched Nikola go to Ana's car and use his power to unlock it and pull out what appeared to be a scarf and sniff it. Satisfied it's hers he slammed the door shut and went down the street to the dark car waiting for him. Apparently, he's getting tired of holding up the cloak and plus daylight is coming. But Ashton remains and watches the three women and a child get in the car and go somewhere. The car disappeared. That damn warrior saint took them through the 8th day. Through eternity.

～～❦～～

Having other things to do Cargill put Ana Wyett out of his mind for a few weeks. His employee Bleeker informed him she declined the new position. So he fired him as promised. His main security line kept buzzing. He answers, thinking it's Dawn wanting more money.

"What in the hell you want now?!" He asked, almost snarling.

"Mr. Cargill, sir," a crisp male voice says. "The woman you had us tracking is dead. We believe Bjors, Vonderbilt's henchman, fire-bombed the place." Cargill's head of security informed him.

Ashton bolted upright in the chair and bellowed "That stupid, imbecilic cocksucker!

That cesspool crawling vermin! I'm going to pulverize his ass!"

Forcing himself to calm down somewhat, he quizzed Sewell. "Are you sure she is dead? I mean, her mentor is a warrior saint and they don't die easily. Maybe she got her out."

Sewell didn't want to quash his employer's hope but there no way anyone could've survived the still smouldering rubble he was looking at; the two houses next door were still smoking. The neighbors told him across town the same thing had happened to this Harris woman's children.

"Were there any survivors?" He asked the woman standing in the streets in a floral pink angiosperm tent dress. He hated those things, his wife loved hers.

"No, the fire department said there is no way anyone could've survived that. Those were military grade bombs used. But who would want to hurt Mother Harris? She was the kindest soul I've ever met," the woman wiped her eyes on the hem of the dress exposing her chubby knees. The woman he had pegged a busybody was now sniffling back tears. "Lord, what is this world coming to? People bombing saints! That's a crying shame."

Ashton having arrived at the fuming ground zero. The charred debris was wet from the firefighter's hover-trucks hoses. He saw a powerful weapon had been used to demolish the three properties. "I knew I should've killed the bastard that day," Ashton Cargill says mainly to himself while fighting to control his own emotion. A great sob caught in his thought like an angry frog trying to escape. He walked a short distance away leaving Sewell hanging among the mortals to go view the wreckage himself. Standing amidst the blackened remnants of the once backyard he scanned the spiritual air for departed souls. He smiled when he sensed none, at least none matching her signature meaning somehow the women had escaped.

"They aren't dead, Sewell. Find them while I go kill that slithering bastard." He disappears again. Sewell wished Ashton wouldn't do that publicly. Pink dress fainted. Being half mortal he had to attend her.

Sewell knew this happened months ago. So he sought to find a way to make Ashton know this had already happened. His best calculation was someone had pulled this area into a time fluctuation and was fucking with Ashton's mind. But he also knew Ashton Cargill didn't like being reminded of the periodical lapse of his mental faculty. Only a few knew this besides himself and the harem. In the world in which they moved, this knowledge would be pure ammo for the enemies, which are many. Whomever called wanted to get them out in the open. So where are they? He prays it isn't some fool trying to prove his strength by fighting. Azazael is changing back into Azazel and Azazel is always ready for a fight.

⌒✤⌒

The early thirties techie held his hand out for payment. The harem hired him to call Cargill on an untraceable network and tell him Ana was dead. They knew Sewell would protect him as much as possible. They used his memory lapse against him. Delores slapped the ten grand in the man's outstretched hand and when his back was turned she slid a small pistol out her 20 grand designer purse and blew his brains out.

"Pervert, you didn't have to be such a greedy little bastard. Charging me ten grand for a grand phone call." She said wrathfully, snatching tissue wipes from his hand sanitizer dispenser and wiping the blood and brain matter off the single currency note and re-pocketing it along with her pistol.

⌒✤⌒

He sensed he had been through this before but wasn't sure. Why is that building still smothering after all these months? Did they used a small nuke? No, even a small nuke would've taken out that entire neighborhood.

When he arrived at the haven, he was positive he had been there before. The heavenly realm was closed. There was nothing there but a brown grassy mountain side. He had to mentally bear down hard to figure out what was going on. Everything was a mirage but

489

nothing was an illusion. That he was certain of. Slowly it dawned on him, he was in a time loop. It was fluctuating like crazy. Someone had used his emotions, his grief to open a time loop. And if he wasn't careful he'd relive this painful day until the end of earth time.

He stood still as the loop swirled around him, closed his eyes, and listened for the wings of the angels of time. When they passed they left a nanosecond opening to the present, past, and future. But it was dangerous to try to the future. The present was always in the middle. He saw the blurry wings and leapt before the small time slot closed, exiting in the midst of a crowd of tourists who ran screaming after seeing someone jump out the thin air and hit the ground. He got up and dusted the dirt and detritus from his clothing. He chuckled softly, "Dad has many ways of controlling bad children".

Ignoring the tourists he scanned the spiritual atmosphere picking up her trail and stepped through the realms of time and space into another big crowd of humans. He hoped she wasn't among this drunken, partying crowd. He didn't want to have to break any bones. But he would after all he'd been through to find her. She better not be with a man. He'd had all he could stand for the last whom knows how long?

Chapter 11
You really don't want to tango with me.

He sensed her in an area that was once a night club. He knew she wasn't dead for he could still feel her but hasn't been able to find her. That was odd for he usually found someone in a matter of minutes. She disappeared after she left that safe haven in the mountains. He can remember that much. He hadn't been here in years but he remembers the beach houses, the fetes along the beach. Most are a sad remnant of their former selves and appear as if their residents now are a vastly different crowd than four hundred years ago when it was primarily college students. He summons one of the Cthulhus, mean, horrendous creatures made from divine condemnation of his flesh to thin out the crowd. But then reconsiders and tells the monster to go back to sleep. She might be here and get caught up in the panic and be killed or hurt in the trample.

He goes to the rental office to see if she works or lives here. He doesn't know which alias she may be using.

All the major universities continued the tradition of Spring Break which is now held at the end of the school year. So officially the student is no longer in school but out for the summer. The rental office manager was stoned as everyone else. He decided to search the crowd to see if he could detect her, several girls planked up beside him while the boys stared at him as a challenge.

"Hey, how long you all been here?" he asked taking the reefer from one of the girls. The other was smoking a cigarette. It and the joint were laced with something neither of the girls really needed and would dearly regret ingesting later.

"Hey, that's mine!" The college freshman cried.

Snubbing her he repeated the question and asked about the hot cleaning lady again. He knew that would get the stoned young men tongues waggling.

"Oh, you mean the red head with the hot ass." A blonde muscle head wearing bikini trunks asked.

"Yeah," he said, holding back his temper. "Oh, I haven't seen her since yesterday evening when she was making the rounds with the cute little girl."

"I heard she lived down on the beach in her car." Another guy added. "But she ain't down there. I went down there to tell her to come clear up the puke these assholes vomited all over my damn place. I didn't find her." Ashton could tell the boy had had gross pimples surgically removed. His face was still a little scraggly.

491

"Your friends puked it out so why in the fuck didn't your friends clean it up?" He asked exhaustedly, remembering his own mortal teens. Talking to this age group was wearying, especially if they were rich and never had to apply themselves in life.

"Calm down, old dude!" Another of the drunken boys said. "We just wanted a little fun, that's all. The woman never says hello if you say anything to her. She just keeps right on cleaning like you wasn't talking to her. That pissed me off."

"Every woman in her right mind knows don't go in a hut with a bunch of drunks!" The bikini wearing girl said, trying to jump to reach the joint he was holding above her head. *"Stop jumping! You're bouncing and these wolves are looking."* He mentally projected in her head.

"Hey, big guy! Come here!" The stoned man who was Ana's boss who had finally woke up called to him. He wondered how they ran this place if the owner was stoned all the time. But he strolled to see what the young man wanted. "You ain't no rags are you?" He had to think for a second or two as to what the young man was asking. "No, I'm not a cop." He saw the idea coggling in the man's mind as whether he could say anything or not.

"How much she worth to ya?" The young man said, holding out his hand for payment for his information. Ashton reached in his pocket and slapped a five thousand dollar bill in his hand. The man whooped and instantly pocketed it.

"Ok, here's the deal!" The not so clear headed young said leaning on the counter closer to Ashton to make sure he heard him. "My mother hired the cutie. She don't live here. She live further back in town."

Anticipating how high they could all get for the remaining of the evening off of five grand a young man wearing retro Bermuda shorts chimed in, "She lives up on Coconut Street in a little pink house. I think it's a boarding house or something. It got pink Spanish plaster stucco shit all over it."

He quickly disappeared from the presence of the Bermuda shorts and friends who burst out laughing. Believing it was drug induced illusion they just witnessed. He exited onto Coconut Street. Several loitering the streets in the soft summer breeze who saw this and were sober enough to run, they ran. They ran like the wind.

"Aw!! Fuck!" Ashton cried inwardly when he saw the golden head of flowing hair just above the hedges. He knew it was his brother Ralph. Ralph was obviously waiting for him.

"I see you found her." Raphael said telepathically. He knew it was going to be some obfuscate shit out of his brother, why else would he be waiting? "Raphael, why have you been keeping me from finding her. From remembering where I know her from? What gives, man?"

"What gives is you. You're the problem. She has enough problems without your madness. How many concubines, girlfriends, and causal lovers do you have? How many do you need? I'm putting my feathers on the line for you and you still haven't learned to be faithful. Being faithful doesn't mean you're true as long as you're with the person, fidelity endures in their absence."

"Hell, I don't know I guess about 56 harem members. I do not have concubines. You know the difference!"

Raphael had recently debated with Cassiel that Azazael loved the woman. If his memory was restored he'd be true to her. Cassiel called him a helpless romantic.

Losing his patience with Azazel's actions kicking him in the teeth at every conference. "See, that's the problem!" Raphael yelled, which was extremely rare. "That woman is a gift of love and not to be used by you for your pleasure. Glory isn't a drug. It's part of Father and you can't use IT whenever you feel like it with no regard for the person wearing IT."

What was upsetting him more was Azazel willfully ignoring him, looking back at the plaster peeling, orangey-pink house, and around the neighborhood for anyone he could ask about the occupants of the house. Seeing no one, Ashton was forced to answer his brother.

"I've never bothered those Hand Maids of God, they were always too damn boring for my taste. The women I sleep with know what the relationship is all about. I never lied to anyone. I confessed my love to this one but she up and ran away and keeps on running."

"Azazael, you've confessed your 'love' to millions but once the thrill was gone so were you. She doesn't need your brand of love. Now go away."

Refusing to give up, he plead, "Ralph, you don't understand. This one is different. I can't get her out of my head, out of my heart. I don't like the way she makes me feel. It makes me vulnerable."

"Azazael, love makes everyone feels vulnerable. It's not proud or boastful. It doesn't want its own way. So if you love her as you say then you will wait until the time comes. If she accepts you we shall see."

"What do I've to do?" He asked, resigning, surrendering, not quite believing he was asking that question. But added, "Give me her and I promise I'll give up the others. They I can live without; her, I can't. Why? I don't know but now that I know she exists I can not exist without her."

Raphael sighed, wondering could he believe Azazael? After all this is his brother who can lie as easily as he speaks. This is the one whom their Father asked what was wrong with him and told him he made Him sick. He was so determined to do as he pleased. "When and if the time comes it will be up to her to accept you. Then I'll tell you." Raphael said, side-eyeing the demons trying to slither up the wall and listen to their conversation.

"She loves me. I know she does. I can feel it. But is afraid to show or expression it. What have you heavenly guys told her about me?" He noted the pink and yellow gingham curtains moving the slightest in the left corner. He knew she was peering out at them and wondered how did he appear to her.

"Nothing. Your reputation proceeds you. It has told her it is wise to flee you." Raphael said, disappearing, taking Azazel with him.

⌒◯◯◯⌒

Although, her memory of him had been divinely erased Ana sensed the man from the Kennesaw mountainside. She intuited he was nearby. Close enough to touch. She knows she's playing a dangerous game to invite him in. But she loves him. She astrally soars to an area that she'd found years ago. An escape from the daily pain. The area sort of looks like her favorite spot down by a brook on the farm she grew up on but it was far more grandeur. She doesn't know if she is there body or soul or both. She tosses pebbles into the water and waits for him. He will come. At least she believes he will. She feels the heavy footfalls crushing the foliage that's carpeting the wood's ground. She knows it's him without turning around.

"Baby, why do you keep running from me? I'm not going to hurt you," he asked in the most beatific, yet sexiest voice she has ever heard. Maybe her sister is right. Maybe she is attracted to bad boys. This one, she knows in her heart, is as bad as they come.

"I do not wish another broken heart," she replied without turning around to look in his eyes.

"The only way that one can break your heart is you love him. Shall you give your heart to me, I promise you I'll do everything in my power never to break it," he said in that angelical, masculine voice that sent tingles down her spine. It's said the devil sounds very much the same.

"Yeah, that's what you all say." She chuckled sadly.

"Then why are you here?" He asked curiously, approaching her cautiously. She's like a flighty bird, if startled she'll fly away. The wind rustled the leaves above in this place of her own creation. Very few humans reach this potential. Many can create illusions but rarely do they reach the potential to create actual existential.

Now, he's in her's beside her. In her warm, sunny, bright land of perfect day, tossing pebbles along side her and watching them float to the bottom. To her, each pebble was a problem, pain, or heartache to be tossed away.

"A nice, calming place," he said, complimenting her creation. Guessing what she's doing, "Which of those pebbles are me?" He lightly teased.

She laughed at how easily he figured her out. "Neither. None of them are you." She said, still without looking around at him. She figured what was the point in looking at him? She wouldn't remember what he looked like once back in the real world. She would only have this memory. This was her ode to the memory of him. She didn't know why she tortured herself for a love and life that would never be. But if not for dreams and hopes she would go mad.

His heart quickened and pulse sped up. She just admitted she loved him but on the other hand was afraid he'd hurt her. "My darling, I couldn't hurt you anymore than I would hurt myself. You've visited me down through the ages. Many times was my sole comfort. My better angel, why would I hurt you?", he asked. She shrugged her thin, tired shoulders as they drooped into a pose of defeatism. He didn't want to see that.

"There's something about me that rikes others, peeves them off...it's like some sort of ancient rime or curse I can't escape. Eventually you, too, will grow to dislike me. You think you wouldn't cause you ain't around me enough to feel it. But it would affect you, too."

He turned her to face him. He knows all about curses, rimes, potions and all the bunk in between and she definitely isn't cursed. Only One can curse someone and it survives and that's God. He doesn't know why she is talking this foolishness but she is not cursed.

"Have you ever consider perhaps your goodness and the glory in you searches out and shows up the evil in the hearts of men? That no one likes light shed on their evil deeds?" He asked before kissing her. He didn't want to hear anymore of this madness. She was merely repeating what she had been labeled. He refused to let her belittle herself. He kissed until she stopped struggling, stopped talking, and kissed him back. He intended to make passionate love to her, hopefully to show her she isn't cursed. He wondered why Vonderbilt keep pursuing her as he made love to her. Brushing her hair away from her face, "Will you promise not to run away once in the physical world again? I want to make you mine."

"I do not know what life holds in the physical world. I can not make that promise. I come here for solace. I take a risk."

"What's the risk?" He asked. It was her own private space. Only she could invite one inside.

"I've left my child under a prayer shield. No one has broken it yet but there's a first time for everything. I means she is with my mom and a friend."

"You don't have to live like that. I'm a man of great means..."

She intercepted. "You are not a man. What are you?"

"I'm an immortal," he said without doubt he had told her this exact same thing many time before. He knew he had to be patient with her. If the heavens was jumbling his antediluvian mind, he can only imagine what was happening to her unweathered one.

"I thought so." She said, getting up and getting dressed. "It's a sin that I lie here with you as if you're a mortal man." She begun getting dressed. She was long weary of this constant circling around of memory loss. Not remembering a love lost. Meeting like passing spirits in the night. So why can't he see it's best they say their goodbyes and stop torturing themselves?

"Whether did you get that from?!" he asked curious as to what creed she were quoting.

"It's in the Bible." She cried, surprised he had to ask. He should already know that!

"No, it's not." he chuckled softly, for he had heard that one before. "Ana, I'm just as your father Adam, my youngest brother. Adam was immortal made mortal. He was once

497

just like the rest of us and is again. So all of humanity is a descendant of one like myself. The only different is I'm immortal and can not die. Adam was punished for his fall through death and I wasn't. I have seen many a times, death would've been a blessed relief."

Thinking of all those lost to death, she violently shakes her head. "You do not know what you are saying. Death is not a blessed relief. It's the end of existence as we know it. But I don't expect you to understand the pain it causes being what you are."

"Promise to stay and when I come physically, I promise to take you away from that drudgery way of life." He plead before she disappeared just as he heard a child's voice sleepy calling her mommy. He wonders shall that child be his own?

The area fades into the lowest level of Paradise, the celestial realm between earth and Paradise and the brightness of glory was painful without her shielding him. It hurts like hell. He quickly exited it. But he appears back in the bed with Dawn and the others instead of where he wants to be.

"Dammit!" He cussed and teleports back to the stucco house. She's gone according to the boarding lady. "Sometimes she stays down in one of them huts when they need her. I think that's where she is said she'll be staying tonight. Her mother left for the airport hours ago. Her health is bad." He had forgotten time moves much faster in the earthly plane than on the spiritual plane, well in most cases. Some parts of hell it moves at a lighting speed. An earth year can be fifty years in hell.

Frustrated with where he landed he teleported away once again, to find her. He wasn't finished talking to her. They always wait until he has something very important to say to snatch her away. The heavens are seriously cramping his style and he know they don't care.

He exited in the middle of a partying crowd down at the beach. There were police lights flashing, siren blaring, and ambulances wailing everywhere against the darkness of predawn. He hoped a Cthulhu didn't disobey him and come to this realm after he sent it back. His emotions are going haywire and completely off the chart. He reaches to the heavens and prays, which is something he hasn't done in eons. He prays that none are here for the woman or/and her little girl. He takes his ears off the spiritual world and then hears the clamoring of the large crowd pointing down at the last hut where the police are gathered, he rushed down there. In recognizance of who he is, several cops steps aside. The room he enters is a bloodbath. Blood is splattered everywhere. Blood and brain tissue decorate the grayish white crumby walls covered with cheap paint budging in awkward spots. Four cops are dead. A high powered gun was used and used very quickly. Each of these men died with their gun drawn. He takes down the bath towel which is still damp. He knows they were waiting for her, hoping to catch her off guard.

In the dingy sleeping part of the room he heard a deputy sheriff said. "This woman leaves dead bodies wherever she goes. I mean to catch her, dead or alive. We've tried being nice about bringing her in but she wants war. Then baby, you got it! She is a gruesome, cold bloodied killer. How in the hell she took down four grown men?"

"Leave her alone," Ashton Cargill icily said, staring down those who dare to question his order. The entire police squad looked at him.

The sheriff confronted him asking. "Who the hell are you? Get back over there with the civilians."

He did the wrong thing. All the seasoned veterans knew that. But this was a polished political sheriff who didn't know the hierarchic structure of the governing of politics very well nor who he was talking to. They all stepped back, for Mr. Know-It-All was about to find out and they wanted no part of what he was about to receive.

Ashton Cargill grabbed him by the neck and raised him as easy as arising his own arm. "Look here, little prissy. I said leave her the fuck alone! LOOK!" He shouted, pointing at the dead men's head and hands. Toward the glaring fact each of the dead men were still clutching their gun in their cooling, lifeless hands. Meaning the final death grip before rigor mortis set in.

"Your men all had their guns drawn? So it was they who were looking for a fight and they got one. Why would they've their guns drawn just to *talk* to a woman and child?

499

Since you want to act like you're in the days of the Old West then be prepared to deal with the consequences. The fastest draw always win. Call back that APB on her or I'll make you so sorry you were ever born." He drops the man like a sack of potatoes. His super keen ears could hear the sirens wailing throughout the city. He prayed they were safe.

"If anyone shoots her all of you fuckers and your whole damn families are dying, tonight." He promised before disappearing. He had gone to try and find her. He knew he couldn't trace her on the move. Angels were shielding her. He imaged her scared, frightened and alone, holed up somewhere in the dark, hiding...hoping for an opening for her to escape. Tonight he was making that opening even if he had to send a good number of souls to hell.

He stood in the night's air and watched the air traffic with flashing sirens and glaring search lights as he listened to the increased volume. He knew if they were close to her their melee would crackle over the air as badly as they wanted her. He moved in the night like a phantom to see which direction the hovercopters were headed and hoped he didn't find them in danger because only his Father would have mercy on them for he wouldn't.

⚬⚬⚬

"Who in the hell was that nut-job?" The grossly embarrassed sheriff abrasively asks his deputies who didn't come to his aid.

"The single most richest and powerful man in the world, Ashton Cargill. Sir, don't push it. That man can make or break your career or even take your life with just a phone call." One of the veteran deputies advised.

"Ok, I've heard of him but I've never seen him. So can any of you gossip columns tell me what in the hell he wants with a low-life killer like Ana BuFaye?"

A female deputy tells her boss to think it over. She sighed inwardly as she sees him thinking over the reasons why a man of such caliber would help out a killer?

500

Figuring out the man's motive, "Hell, there're millions, no billions of law abiding pretty women," the sheriff grunted looking down at the carnage of bloody bodies. Cargill had a point. Why were their guns out the holsters? But was puzzled as to how she did it?

"Law abiding women aren't sexy. This woman is. The badder they are the more you guys love them." The female deputy points out how she believes Cargill isn't the only male helping her escape. "How else does she slip through the crack everytime. Every road block, she escapes only to resurface and kill again. There are lots of guys in blue helping her." She said looking accusingly at her male counterparts. She had heard what the now dead ones said they intended to do before arresting her and if she hadn't fought back...then they'd kill her. But instead she killed them.

The female cop was like many other modern women. Many women won't admit it but they see this Ana BuFaye as some sort of folklore hero against the oppressive male dominance of society. She's sort of like a modern day suffrage heroine who did what she wanted, when she wanted, and told society to kiss her ass. There's a website dedicated to this woman run by a feminist group in New York. So secretly, everytime this BuFaye woman appears in the news, her fans are hoping she escapes to live another day and kill another chauvinist bastard or bitchy woman who got it coming. No one openly admits that but it's true. Whoever thought after the Gender War we'd still be dealing with the same age old adage?

The GBI had been alerted she may be headed homeward, they were at the Georgia-Florida state line expecting her. But all of a sudden their superior called them, calling off the watch. Saying shall you spot her let her pass. They same was done with the ABI. They saw her passing down near the swamp but had been ordered to back off.

Back at his Manhattan office, he paced the floor wondering how did they go from making love one moment to a deadly shooting the next? He had no idea where she was but felt her brothers may know is the only reason he agreed to meet them at this hour.

They said she hadn't made contact with them. Not that he expected her to. Theirs would be the first place Vonderbilt would look for her. He could see these men really didn't know their sister at all. They had an idea in their mind who she is but hadn't the faddiness idea of her true gentle nature. Her moral turpitude seemed to their only concern. Leaving their minds open when speaking with him was a dangerous thing. He didn't like the fact they were more concerned about their wives and kids and how these alleged murders would affect their families' standings in their community than they were that maybe a revengeful group of cops, or Vonderbilt, may have killed her and their niece and dumped the bodies somewhere never to be found. He gave them money for their sister shall they see her; Ana had mentioned her mother's health problems the last night they were together. But somehow, he knew neither Ana nor her mother would see a dime of the money. Letting this fact not bother nor defer him was a totally new side of himself, even he didn't know he had. He would let it go because it he was who called them. Sewell at least told him who her people were.

That's another thing. He needed to talk to Sewell about withholding information. He knows he's mentally slipping because there are so many mind swipes one can handle before it start erasing everyday things but he hasn't reached that point yet and hopes to save them before he does.

✦

They waited out the police, saved a truckload of girls intended for sex slaves, and made it as far Texas in one piece. She was considering u-turning back to Mississippi since she hadn't left any graves there. But then again that was still the deep south so she better keep west or north.

Five year old Bea was reading an article about bratty kids who didn't know how good they had it. Seemed as thus all the exciting stories were depressing as hell. She flipped through her ISPAN Pad for a story that wasn't deleterious nor depressing. All the movies were about the supernatural or cops and neither had it accurate.

Ana glanced to see what mode Bea's ISPAN was set on. Offline. That's ok. But dammit! Those idiots caused her to leave another paycheck behind. So she would have to look for a job soon. The money from the Janus job and retribution from that collector had ran out. It's very expensive to live on the road.

The police pull up the car's image, tags are useless. People always change them. The description fits that of a woman wanted for four cop's murders in Florida. A real killer would've stolen another car by now. The information glared on their screen, "classified." Meaning do not approach her or attempt to bring her in. He wasn't a fool, it says she single-highhandedly killed four so she would make him, alone, into a Tex-Mex barbecue. He raps on the window.

"Ma'am. You and the little Missy can't sleep here. There's an overnight shelter in Salinas for women and children traveling alone. I can take you there if you'd like but either way you gonna have to move on."

The rap startled her, she wonders how long that man had been watching her.

"Sorry, officer, we were just waiting for daylight. Its safer to travel in daylight." Ana said, smiling.

Tilting his hat back, looking in the car, he sees a sleeping child. The report mentioned nothing about the woman had a child. "I tell ya what, ma'am. I been watching y'all since 5:00 P.M., people around these areas are quiet, I ain't seen y'all eat a bite yet. I'm heading into town to the Griddle House, how bout I get them to fix y'all up a batch of their pancakes? That's little more than a toddler back there, growing babies need food."

"Ok," Ana said, nervously wondering if this wasn't a grave mistake? Did he intend to turn her in? She watched him disappear in the darkness in her side rearview mirror as he walked back in the direction he came. She hadn't seen a patrol cruiser alit that close to her, so maybe she had fallen asleep. Perhaps the branches concealed it. But still he was right across the road watching them since five and it's now 11:56 P.M.. Had he intended to call for backup he would've done so in the past 5 hours.

She pulls in the all-night eatery parking lot behind the cruiser and shuts off her headlights. He held the door open and helped her picked up sleeping Beauty Bea who was now rubbing her eyes wondering why were they at this place. But froze when she saw the uniform and looked questioningly at her mother.

"I ain't gonna hurt ya. Lil' lady." The blonde haired man said having taken the hat off, thinking perhaps the child and woman would feel less afraid of him. He carried Bea in behind her mom and sat them both in a booth beside her mother.

She notices immediately that everyone seems to know him and was looking perspicuously at her. She ruminated was this guy married as to why everyone was looking at her like that.

"Bring three Big Breakfasts, two tall O.Js., one short O.J., and a tall glass of milk, and two cups of coffee and no spit," he joked noting all the claws out on this girl.

"I'm just kidding." He said after the waitress left. Ana knew that it was no joke, she had worked enough waitress jobs to have seen it done many times. Bea knew to go sit at the counter and watch since they had an open griddle like grill. No one would suspect a child that young knowing to watch their ass.

"Ma'am, where are you headed?" The cop asked.

"To San Antonia to visit my sister," Ana lied. *If people didn't want me to lie to them then don't ask questions that are none of their business.*

The chef knew the kid was watching him. He turned and smiled at Bea who didn't return his smile.

"That's my cousin who brought you and your mother in. I tell you what. I'm fixing you my specials. Heart-shaped pancakes with strawberries for such a pretty lil' lady. I got a lil' girl bout your age, she just loves them." the chef said putting a grilled cheese sandwich in front of the well-trained child.

"Would you like some fries and a shake to go with that?" Bea shook her head no. *Although it sounded delicious, her momma had said some strangers like to give kids*
504

poison cause they're sick in the head. And a milkshake is an easy way to fed it to them. This man looked sane but momma said you can't tell by just looking at them if they are evil or just plain crazy.

The chef brought the new arrivals their meals. "Cousin, where you find this lovely lady that your ugly mug didn't send fleeing in terror?" The tall, muscular blonde guy wearing a grease smeared apron joked as he sat the meals in front of us and brought Bea's extra treats to the table.

"At the county rest stop. And cool your heels. The lady has enough problems without you and your women plaguing her," the cop said to his handsomer cousin Thor who Ana saw was wearing a wedding ring.

"Marriage don't mean you can't talk to women. I think you two would be cute together. Y'all looked like a real little family coming in that door."

"Hmph, Thor, mind your own business, OK. How's things down at the shop?"

"You know I don't like farming or fixing cars. The last I was there everything was fine. Your dad's still riding my ass about working at the shop with him." Thor said, making his cousin move over and brought the steaming coffee pot with him. The night was early and slow, plus he wanted a closer look at this woman, he was wondering who was she? Seemed to him he has seen her before, not in real life. But in the dream world.

"I forgot, your derriere is too pretty for good honest labor." His cousin guffawed, chomping on several of the thin, crispy bacon strips that Ana and Bea were devouring shamelessly. They hadn't eaten anything substantial in over a week. Pay day was always big eating day.

The country police officer sadly recognized that type of eating; it was that of a homeless person stocking up for they didn't know when the next meal would come.

"Man, working in a kitchen over a hot stove is hard work. Try it and you won't call it not working." The man named Thor challenged his cousin.

505

"Are you named after the Norse god of thunder?" Bea asked.

"Yea, I reckon so lil' lady, I think my momma watched too many 'em damn movies," Thor said, his cousin kicked him under the table to remind him ladies were present. He begged the ladies pardon for his expletives. He had another order to fill so he bid them a good evening and left to return to work.

"Miss, if y'all ready. I can get ya a foam plate for the rest of your food and take ya by the shelter. Sometime they have space for longer than one night. If ya ain't in no hurry I would look into that."

He knew they had to leave the shelter at 7 and it was 2:00 A.M. now. That's only five hours or four if they didn't fall asleep immediately, rarely do people do that in a strange place. "I tell ya what. I can see y'all are tired. There's a hotel about a mile down the road. How about y'all sleep there until ya rest up, cause I would feel rightly bad if you got out on that road 'morrow and had a wreck cause ya tired."

"No, the shelter will do. We need to be going in the morning anyway." Ana said. He understood why she declined. She was on the run and didn't want to get caught but he still can't figure out how a little lady like her took down four men his size or bigger. Maybe she knows karate or something.

"Ma'am, I'm an honorable man. The shelter only has floor room for a pallet and sheet, the regular residents have all the beds. I just think you and your kid looks like you bout ready to fall out from exhaustion. I don't know what you running from and ain't gonna try to make it my business to find out. But whatever it is ya gotta take care of yourself. Y'all will see all us cops aren't bad."

After they left the all-night cafe she walks around to back of the car with a gun behind her back. She was positive he didn't see it. He slowly followed her, sensing she felt threatened. He had unclasped his service revolver. He read the woman was considered mentally unstable. She sensed he had unclasped his gun, she had seen Helena do that too many time not to know what it meant. She turned and faced him, placing Bea behind her and pushing her toward the car.

"Let's not kid each other. You know who I really am—don't you?" She asked as her dark eyes gleamed in the night like an angry panther.

"Yes, I had a sneaking suspicion. But I don't know the whole story, you don't seem like the type of lady to just go around shooting people just for the pure heck of it."

Ana didn't know what to say. She never met a Texas police who wasn't a trigger happy Jack. And certainly never met one who knew she was and wasn't shooting at her.

"What's your name?"

"Myles, Myles Duke. Most people call me Duke. I'm the sheriff of this part of the county, it's a pretty big county so they got more than one department."

"Ok, Myles....uh, no one ever asked me my side of what happened. I didn't kill out of cold blood, I killed to survive. Somebody is out to kill me and is using anyone they can," she explained and afterward feeling like a fool. Supposed he was wearing a hidden body cam recording everything she said. She had stupidly confessed if he was.

"I know somebody like that. Folks been trying to kill him 'fore he could walk. My cousin back there at the diner....uh, you just met him. For some unknown reason certain people just don't like him. Why? We ain't never figured that one out. That's how come I became a police; to look out for him. Our mommas are twin sisters that how come we look so much alike."

"It's scary when stinkbug people you don't know want you dead and none of them ever tell you why? All they do is come after you like a radical psychopath and expect you not to kill them and when you do, it's you who the authorities believe is the psychopath." She cried almost with relief, finally someone understood what she was saying.

They check in a little after two A.M. He sat out in the parking lot for a while and watched. According to his cousin Thor if you watched around those like himself long enough you could see haints, ghosts, and demons. But he didn't see anything.

His personal phone rang, it wasn't his ex-wife so he wondered what Thor wanted? The ante meridiem hours were the worse for any police work. His shift was over but since he talked this woman into a room with no one but she and that baby child, it was his job to watch them. "Man, I think you better get here. There's a big shot here looking for that woman you brought in here tonight," Thor cautioned.

The man in the expensive sport car asked the diners had they seen this woman with a little girl? He slipped a few a hundred a piece to loosen up their tongues.

"Yeah, the sheriff, Myles Duke, took her to the women shelter a while ago." The waitress had told this big mean man before Thor could signal her to shut up.

"Where can I find this sheriff?" The man wearing a Patek watch asked.

"There's he right now." The waitress said, pointing at the cruiser just alighting in the parking lot, wondering why this fine looking man was looking for that skinny thing Myles dragged in here an hour or so ago.

Observing the big man from within the car through the windshield Duke recognized the man as Ashton Cargill. Damn, he had never seen him personally but the police fraternity president talked about him a lot as being one of the principal donors of the police fraternal as long that branch did as he wanted. If he had someone that size was on his tail he would run, too. He gets out of the cruiser and enters and pretends to be unruffled.

"I understand you just took this woman and child to a shelter?" Cargill said the moment he walked in.

"The woman changed her mind and kept on out of town, why?"

"If I found out you lied to me... so God help you," the rich man warned. Myles pushed
508

his hat back off his forehead, wondering does this man do anything else besides threaten people?

"Sir, you can't come in my town threatening people."

Cargill changed his tone but not his eyes. "I'm merely looking for my wife and kid, I don't want someone figuring out who she is and kidnapping them for ransom," Ashton lied, although it wasn't a total lie. "We had a little disagreement and she left home angry."

Duke knew he was lying.

"Look, man! I've no intention of harming her. I know she's still in town. So would you please tell me where is she," Ashton swallowed hard, pushing down the pride along with the bile rising in his throat. This facade was pissing him off he had to beg this man for information. Begging was something he wasn't accustomed to. It wasn't in his nature.

"I don't know where she is, she left the dinner and the last I saw of her she was headed west." Duke lied again.

"Stop lying!" The big man roared so loud the small diner shook. In the back of the small diner, Thor whipped out his blade. He didn't know what name this immortal wore but he was positive that's what he was. He's lying, that woman is not his wife. Ashton sensed a gifted nearby, preparing to attack, and it wasn't the woman he was looking for. He mentally projected. *"Whoever you are. Don't even think about it! If you enjoy living. "*

He heard the reshealthing of the metal blade as it slides down against leather. Out steps a man whom he wonders is a descendant of Thor, the Norse god? He scans him; he is...but from well over a 1,000 years ago. He doubts the man knows that. The immortal part has been so diluted since then, it practically nonexistent.

"Leave us in peace!" The Thor-resembling man said.

"I'll if you people tell me where is my wife." Ashton said shortly before one of his security team members called him saying they found them. She's at a local hotel.

"Thanks," he said into his watch phone. The volume decibel was inaudible for humans.

Duke knows he has found her, not that he needed to hear what was said but the fact this man has the manpower to find anyone he sets his mind to find.

He waited until the expensive sport car roared out the Griddle House parking lot to go back to the hotel. Thor halted him and jumped in the car. They followed at a safe distance. He parked across the street to watch for trouble. They watched her say a few words at the door and let him in. So there was nothing else they could do.

"Apparently, the big guy was telling the truth," Thor said, watching Cargill from the shadow of the cruiser go inside squat, boxy built old-timey motel room. The shadow from the roof hid the tall man's upper torso but his legs were clearly illuminated by the dim, yellowish fluorescent lights in the broken paved parking lot. They both saw her small silhouette against the inside lights when she cracked open the door and her face wore no fear of him.

"Seemed to me she's just mad at him about something and wanted him to chase her to prove his love or something or whatever crazy shit goes on in women's cute little heads. I love them to death but I swear I can't figure them out."

Myles half-listened to his cousin. He still watched with the scrutiny of a cop. He knew Thor had it all wrong for he more of her background than Thor. He knew who this seemingly harmless lady really was. She's Ana BuFaye, the notorious killer. Her callous, chapped hands, chipped nails, and rough-dried street clothing told him she didn't live in luxury with this man. Putting the puzzle together he now knows who has been helping her escape the death penalty and why. Now he knows why his governor put out a "do not approach or reprimand" warning pertaining this woman. The most powerful man in the world was in love with her. Oh well, she hadn't killed anyone in his county so he didn't give a shit. He knew she was easing her gun loose while talking to him. Before she admitted to killing those people in self defense. He saw the fear in her eyes when he rapped on her window. But he wasn't the type of man who enjoy scaring women or making them afraid of him. So he had no intention of antagonizing her into shooting him. This whole premise sounds and looks a lot like the things Thor has been dealing with his entire life. Why did those guys bust in with their guns drawn if they didn't intend to kill her?

⁓∾⦾∾⁓

Ana was asleep when a soft knock came at the door; it was around 3:00 A.M., give or take a few minutes. She had just gotten settled into a comfortable rhythm of sleep. A cyclicity she hadn't enjoyed in quite some time. The lumpy mattress wasn't very comfortable but was better than sleeping in a cramped car. Upon hearing the knock she immediately awakened, jumped up, grabbed her pistols, stood on the side of the door, and peeked out through the tawny draperies' slit. The man looked familiar but she didn't know him. She kept retrieving her memory. Trying to figure out where she knew him from? But something about him seems as familiar as the back of her hand. This wasn't the man who bombed them at Mother Harris'. She was certain of that.

"Yes, who are you?" She asked authoritatively through the door.

"I do not mean you any harm. I just need to see you. See that you're ok," he softly replied. His voice sounded familiar also.

"See me about what?" She asked firmly. She wasn't opening that door. It could be a demon trying to trick her but then again they aren't known for asking nicely to speak to her. This guy is awful big. He could kill them with one hand.

He remembered her brothers said her name was Ana. "Ana, remember we were in this private place of yours down near a brook, we tossed pebbles into the water..."

She remembered very well as to why she quickly opened the door for she was afraid he was going to say what else they did while Ms. Bea was awake listening. She quickly opened the door and pulled him in so he would shut up.

511

"How did you find me?" She asked curiously. Nervously evaluating the fact that if he could find her so easily so should Vonderbilt.

"Mind if I come in and join you?" He asked from near the door. He didn't quite remember her being so short and tiny. She seemed bigger in the spiritual world. Then again, it doesn't matter, by the time the heavens are finished with them he won't remember much about her anyway.

By now Bea is sitting up in the bed wondering who is this new visitor. It isn't the nice police guy. She remembers seeing this guy when she was younger. Ana invites him to sit on the first bed, nearest the door, while she sits on Bea's bed.

"Sir, what's so important you've to talk to me at this hour?" Ana asked.

"For a starter, everytime I leave you I forget what you look like. I can remember many things about you but your exact physique always eludes me."

"What do you remember about me? Why is it so important to you to know what I look like?" she asked, not sure of where this conversation was going. She was aware by now that she often didn't look the same to everyone. It served as a protective shield. So she contemplated was he someone sent by Nikola? She knew he had sleeper cells all over the world so perhaps the local one was alerted to her position.

"I remember I love you very much, so much that I've to find you again after each encounter. My heart will not rest until I find you again. Each encounter opens the window to my heart wider and wider. Your love is like a warm balm to my weary existence."

"What's encounters?" Bea asked from behind her mother's back. Ana really didn't feel like dealing with the two of them right now but she told Bea it was when people or things met. And to go back to sleep.

"I can't! *Your* guests keep waking me up!" Bea said obstinately and pulled the covers

512

over her head.

When she looked back around at the stranger who just confessed his love for her he looking at her as thus he were upset about something...if she wasn't mistaken...was that anger in his eyes? If so, why? He didn't know her and certainly didn't own her.

"I guess I can safely assume one of the Thor looking blonde guys were here tonight.", he said in a wry tone.

"I don't have to check in with you as to who I can see or talk to!"

He had a mind to tell her what he did to get her out of Florida alive, the money he gave her brothers, the security watch he had placed on her family in Long Island and other locations, the numerous other things he recorded doing to protect her. But remained silent on them. He sighed wearily when he looked up and saw the angel hovering over her head. He didn't know this one but it was clear the angel knew him.

"I suppose I'm wasting my time, the other night meant nothing to you," he said, rising to leave. For some unknown reason, she didn't want him to leave. She sensed she would never see him again shall she let him walk out that door. An unfound fear gripped her heart. It was like her inner soul was speaking and remembering something she could not.

"Please don't go! I'm just exhausted, the exertion of the past days, the past week has gotten to me."

"I understand, so why don't we all lie down and get some sleep," he said, hoping she was still here in the morning. Bea let it be known loud and clear no one was lying in her bed but her mommy.

He chuckled, "Very well. Duly noted." Bea kept her dark amber, blue speckled eyes trained on him until sleep peacefully closed them. They both were asleep within a few minutes of each other. Seeing them sleep jolted his memory.

Cassiel saw the recognition click in Azazael's eyes. That's when he revealed himself and stepped fully through into the physical.

"Azazael...don't go there. Let it go. She belongs to Heaven, not you."

"How can you all herald about love and mercy but yet are willing to separate a man from his family? Tear a family apart?!" Azazael telepathically hissed at him. He didn't like it that Cassiel hid his identity from him a few minutes ago.

Cassiel sighed and raked his hand through his heavy, dark brown, glowing mane. Micheala is right. Talking to Azazael is like talking to a stubborn broken record. He makes you repeat yourself until he drives you on the verge of madness.

"You don't know when to quit..do you? We've told you the same mundanely thing with dreadful repetition. But you keep coming. You keep ignoring us as if no one is speaking to you and don't tell me *it's* because you love her. We both know you're lying. What's in this for you? You don't serve heaven nor hell. You serve only yourself."

Azazael apathetically replies, "Cassiel, I'm not a demon anymore. I don't answer to you. Believe it or not. You are not Father. You've never had a wife and family so don't judge me on what you've never experienced. You say you understand the synonymic of Christ and the Church, but if you truly did then you wouldn't ask me that question. Why do I keep after her? Why I won't give up this pursuit? No man gives up on the woman he loves who in return loves him. I don't expect you to understand what I'm saying but take my word for it. There's more than one type of love. There's another type of love I wish you had the opportunity to experience. That's my other half lying there. My much better half. "

Cassiel wearily exhaled, it sounded like a breeze making treetops sigh. Ana stirred a little and pulled Bea closer. Cassiel waved his hand over her crinkled brow to give her peace. He closely observed his brother's face soften in love as he watched her sleep. He can't remember the last time he had seen Azazael looking this close to his original state. He decided it was either Azazael was truly in love or planning an outright assault against heaven, hell, earth, or who knows what? Who knows what really ticks through Azazael's mind but Father? He slowly vanished, leaving Azazael with his family, hoping he didn't

514

later regret it.

While mother and daughter slept he ordered from one of his local restaurants and from the exquisite one in Dallas. His expanded holographic ISPAN Pad told him he had acquired the local Griddle House a few years ago when the chain of diners was about to go under. His acquisition teams redid the old styled, low income diners that mainly catered to truckers and late night travelers. Now they were turning a marginal profit. He rarely visited an entrepreneurship in isolated areas like this, the regional managers handled such things. He only showed up if there was a major problem they couldn't handle.

The following day, around 2:13 P.M., Bea woke up to the smell of good food. She sat up and looked at him, blinking bewilderedly at him wondering where all the food came from. It smelt good.

"Awake, sleepy heads!" he said calling to both of them. "Wake up and eat."

The Cargill Restaurant in Dallas had sent out an entire array of a real meal, with table, fine china, silverware, and crystal. He ordered things he thought the child might eat from the Griddle House whose staff had never seen their employer and were a little shamefaced about bringing the order after their disgruntled behavior last night.

The array of exquisitely prepared foods looked fit for a queen. Ana eyed the formal setting of crystal glasses, fine china, linen napkins, and elegant silverware against the sober backdrop of this run-down motel room. It looked romantically out of place. He took the single rose from the vase and handed it to her. She looked up into his loving eyes (unashamed, not shielding the love he felt for her) and took it. Their hands touched, he hooked his forefinger around hers. She felt a charge of fiery passion exchange between them. She looked away and bashfully whispered, "Uh, thanks, but all this wasn't necessary."

"Yes, it is necessary. Your life on the road is over," he said as the man in a formal attire arranged the food on elaborately scrolled silver bed trays and sat one in front of each of them.

515

"Excuse me???" she asked, feeling they've had this conversation before. She got up to join him at the table then another plate was prepared, she told the man that wasn't necessary but to simply pass the one from the bed here.

"I said your days on the road, half eating, being chased all over creation are over. I'm not running all over creation to find you. You're exhausting yourself and everyone who loves you. Decide where you wants to live and then we're getting married," he said loudly and firmly looked across the table he was seated at to be sure she heard him very clearly.

She did a neck roll and looked squarely back at him. "Who do you think you're talking to?" She ardently asked.

"You, my dear. I'm talking to you. You admitted you loved me and I love you. So what's the problem?"

"Mister..."

"Cargill. Ashton Cargill," he completed her sentence.

"Mister, you're the most irritating, bossiest person I've ever had the misfortune to meet. You can't just tell women 'we're going to get married' anymore. It no longer works that way. That's so primitive."

He ignored Ana's pedagogics just as he ignores everyone else's, including angels. He turned to Bea, asking was she enjoying herself?

With waffle filled cheeks and maple syrup painted lips Bea nodded. And for a few seconds he saw himself in the child. It was so strong it stupefied him. Her spiritual essence consisted of a lot of his own. Their contiguity was nearly the same as any of his children down through the ages! He knew then, this was his daughter no matter what the medical results said. There was no way he was letting this girl's fate continue to be decided by her overly zestful, willfully opinionated, independent, strong-headed mother.

516

Who is determined to continue drag her all over hell. He was putting his foot down! And knew just how to do it.

"Miss Bea, would you like your own room, your own pony, and as many pets as your heart desires?"

"Yayyy!!!" Bea yelled and grinned up from her plate at her mother. "Momma, can I've a pony?"

"No.", she answered irascibly. "They crap all over the place."

"Daddy said I can." Bea sulked, pouted, and crossed her arms.

With my eyes moving disingenuously from Bea to him I indignantly bit into the food, believing he was putting things in Bea's mind. I diligently believe he was filling her head with things he knows we can't do on the open road.

His own words verified my suspicions as I irefully listened to their conversation. He was telling Bea she could have as many ponies as she liked while looking into my wintry eyes. His eyes were telling me he knows who this kid is and he wasn't having his child being chased and shot at! I looked away and focused my attention on my plate before this man made me stab him with this fork.

Now I was angry. Who in the hell does he think he is? Did he think I enjoyed the life we lived? I don't trust anyone else to keep Bea safe. I felt throwing this plate of food at him and would've...had Bea not been watching us and I wasn't so hungry.

"Sweetie, how old are you?" He so sweetly asked Bea who held up five fingers. He did the math while staring at me.

"Ahem, Ana, can I see you outside a moment, please?" He said politely. I knew the politeness for Bea's sake not mine.

"This man will attend to all the little lady's needs," he said, referring to the man

517

standing by with a white server cloth over his forearm. The man was so quiet I had forgotten he was there. I felt bad for forgetting the man was there. I had many times worked as a server. So I knew what it felt like to work for dickheads like Ashton Cargill.

I'd no idea where the plush bathroom and slippers came from the man placed in front of me. As he held up the robe for me to slip my arms into the sleeves he looked away. But Cargill didn't look away. Oh, how rude?! There's no way in hell I ever told this ill-mannered man I loved him. I must have been drunk, high, or stupid or all three at once to have told him I loved him.

I reluctantly followed him outside into the late evening dusk. I looked and saw Myles sitting in his cruiser and courteously waved. This seemed to infuriate him.

"*What didn't piss him off?*" I wondered as the sheriff politely returned my greeting.

Cargill conspicuously ignored the sheriff. He knew the man was watching. He directed her toward the limo right outside her door. A chauffeur got out and opened the door. She stopped and looked at him, deciding she wasn't getting in. But he was determined not to have a show down with her in front the man across the parking lot. He waited until she changed her mind and got in and was comfortable about being inside before climbing in behind her. The moment the door was closed he started his opening dialogue.

"When were you going to tell me that's my daughter in there? I don't appreciate the way you're forcing her to live like goddamn pauper. Putting her life in danger. I made the offer of marriage because I love you but either way – you aren't dragging my child through hell any more. So what's it's going to be? Are you coming with us or not? Because she isn't going back on the road with you," he said, reaching for the bumper bar in the back of the limo and pouring himself a generous glass of sherry from the cabinet, gulped it down, and poured another. He offered her a drink but she declined. Her, the satanists, heaven, hell, Nikola, and all else in-between was all getting on his damn nerves. He knew the jitters were because he was so relieved to have found them alive and unharmed and her lying wasn't helping him calm down.

For a few seconds Ana was lost for words. This man could change on you so fast your head spun. Nice one moment and like a pit of vipers the next.

"You aren't her father, Thad Wyett is her father!" She snapped back.

"You're free to hold on to the all the nostalgic bullshit about that as long as you'd like. The man who you believe is her father. As right about now, I'm through giving a fuck. But my kid is coming with me. If you want to go back on the road and get yourself killed, then...that's fine by me. Anyway, here are the keys to this crappy ass hotel. I bought it for you this morning while you slept. I knew there would resistance out of you," he said tossing the keys into her robed lap. The electronic keys bounced out of her lap and hit the black carpeted floor of the limo. He tossed them to land in the triangle fold of the robe.

Her eyelids fluttered in rage. She saw red. She tried materializing her blade as she did on the mountainside when she faced him; nothing happened.

"Darling, it's not going to materialize because I've a right to look after my child's well-being. I previously asked you about this a year ago, if memory serves me correctly, if that was my daughter and you consistently lied. Why? Oh I see, it's fine if you fuck me and even have my child but when it comes to commitments you bale out. I'll not be your cicisbeo."

"My what?" She asked, frowning at him.

"Never mind."

"You've no right to take my child! I won't let you!" She yelled, leaping on him, attacking him. He held her back as she kicked, scratched, bit his knuckles, and screamed at him. He grabbed her wrists and pinned her hands down.

"Ana, stop! I don't want to hurt you. You can barely move as it is from all the injuries! Why are you so fucking determined to get yourself killed?! You can't out run whomever forever!"

She broke down sobbing from sheer frustration. Anger swelled in her bosom, hopelessness was cutting off her breath. He was asking her to surrender to a death sentence. He didn't understand the peril of her situation.

"YOU!! Stupid! stupid, stupid man! Don't you see....Can't you see what I'm trying to do? Can't you see that whomever is after me will stop at nothing! You aren't taking this terrible, dangerous, unholy pursuit from the depths of hell seriously enough. They'll kill you, too! I can't leave Bea with you, they kidnapped her once and I barely got her back. You don't know how dangerous those after me are! We can never have a life together. They aren't going to let that happen."

He held her racking body tight, close. He knew he had to come clean with her. She doesn't remember anything about him or what he is. That's what mind fucks do to you.

"Baby, baby, listen to me. Nothing can kill me. But God Himself! They can't kill me. I won't let them kill you nor Bea," he shushed her but wondered was he getting through to her. She was still wailing. He waved up a sound barrier to keep Bea from hearing them. He knew Bea perhaps had superior human hearing and the ability to teleport and he didn't want to have to fight her, too.

"Don't you see, I keep her with me because I know they'll use her to make me come to them. If I marry you they'll do the same to you. That's why I must keep moving," she tried to explain wiping away tears. Hoping he understood the seriousness of her predicament.

"Ana, look at me," he urged much more softly. "Who or what do you think I'm?"

"Hell, I don't know, a rich man, a warlock—I guess?" she sniffed.

He dearly wished up above would leave their minds alone for he's certain he has told her these words. Their relationship was a maddening time loop. Restating the same details again and again.

"No, baby, I'm not a warlock. No warlock can do the things I do. I'm an immortal. I'm a son of God. This Nikola Machiavelli's hooligans can not kill nor harm me. Not even Lucifer can. While our memories of each other are fresh and attached let's go get married. That way we can't be separated again."

"What's your real name?" she asked carefully for an instinct was tugging at her psyche. She wasn't sure if was real. She believes she already knows his name.

"My real name, heavenly name is Azazael. But I'm better known as Azazel," he said. It broke his heart to see her flinch at his name.

"Oh well, you can't any worse than the devils I've already encountered nor anything I've already been through." She quipped, wearily flipping her hands dismissively. Surprising them both. She was thinking of all the evil she had seen and experienced in the hearts of humanity and demons alike. So how can he be any worse?

"What's the difference?! You're a devil, Nikola, Vonderbilt, or whatever he calls himself is an even bigger devil. Besides, I won't remember anything about us in a few days or months from now anyway. All I'll have left is a deep feeling that I know you. Let's do it."

His spiritual sight being more profound than hers he looked through the dark tinted glass of the limo and narrowed his eyes at the legion of demonic red eyes staring, unblinking, out in the parking lot watching them and awaiting their next move before he removed the diamond and blue topaz ring from his left pinky and placed it on her finger before they returned inside to make Bea go to bed. Once inside, while Ana was in the bathroom preparing Bea for bed, he moved to the window and drew the drapes aside to be sure they saw him as he looked through the middle space in ill-hanging, dingy, water stained curtains and narrowed his eyes at one particular pair of glowing orbs among the legion of demonic red eyes. Lucifer's narrowed his in return telepathically saying this was not over and far from it.

"You know, if I wasn't concerned about her and the baby getting upset from hearing you all screech and scream I'd come out there and beat the shit out of all you. Don't you

know I'm not Michael? You know better than to fuck with me this way"

"I know....but you can't." Lucifer mentally replied. *"That's what I was counting on."* Lucifer grinned.

He turned from the window just as bathroom door opened and the two he loved exited.

⸎⸎⸎

Since she agreed to the spontaneous marriage, he told the driver to call the local justice of peace and to take them to the courthouse. She seemed to have a vague memory of them doing this before. The other time there was a giant Christmas tree. Were they really in a hellish time loop? Or was she really one of those dead souls in hell who are cursed to relive the same thing over and over for all of eternity and the things chasing her are really the demons assigned to punish her? For she could have sworn she had married this man before...so was her punishment to remarry him again and again and lose him over and over?

As they walked up the ancient, dull marble steps that had been around since shortly after the Alamo, she was wearing the white plush robe and matching slippers. It didn't matter what she wore as long as they wouldn't be separated again. His agent had brought the judge to her chamber and pretty much made her officiate the ceremony.

Holding her hand as they ascended the ancient steps he felt he had done this before with her, many years ago. That's so crazy! All of this, the constant repetition. He feels he married her when he was the King of Azazaeland. Why do they keep having to repeat this? He knew there was a realm in hell where everything was a repetition. Were they trapped there and didn't know it?

The moment the woman said, "I pronounce you Mr. and Mrs. Anton Ashton Cargill, you may kiss your bride" Ana disappeared, the judge fainted, and Ashton roared so loud it shook the building; dust and debris crumbled from the ceiling.

"What in the hell more must I do?" He yelled heavenward. "Why can't YOU leave me alone?"

Realizing Ana is wherever Bea is, "The child is still in the room with the attendants." He quickly directed his people. "That's where heaven sent her."

The Texas branch of the Cargill Security agents arrived to find their coworker unconscious and the girl, woman, and her car gone.

"What happened?" One of the agents asked his coworker.

"I don't know. All I know is I saw a huge, blinding white wing and the kid was gone!"

"Shit, boss isn't gonna like this at all." The man standing in the doorway hissed through clenched teeth.

Ashton arrived and pushed the man aside. Looked wildly about the room. Bea's bed was empty. He sensed an angelic charge had exploded in the room. He was furious and roared like a fiery, caged lion.

"MICHAEL! RAPHAEL! GABRIEL! Whichever one of you all did this to me. I demand to know why!" Azazael bellowed, bringing the room down around him. Walls burst, glass shrapnel flew everywhere as metal buckled, leaving a gaping hole in the antique building's roof. He angrily kicked the debris out his way when his brother Raphael appeared. The agents of Cargill Security had seen this mood before and had cleared the area before he erupted like Mount Vesuvius.

"I demand to know where are *my wife and child*!" He yelled as Raphael leaned against the last remaining steel balustrade of the building. He was totally unflustered by his younger brother's tantrum. He was weary of Azazael trying to outsmart Father and his unwillingness to take no for an answer.

"I told you, she has work to do. Your temper tantrums can't undo the Will of God. I

523

told you when the time comes, you'll be given the conditions on which you can marry her. Be patient."

"I just married her, she's my wife!" Azazael roared. "Who knows what will happen to them with you guys doing such a piss-poor job of protecting them. Nobody can protect my little girl as I can. Somebody has to look after them! Lucifer himself was here last evening! He brought a legion prepared to fight!"

Raphael wasn't really in the mood to argue with his brother. He touched his forehead sending him home, erasing the memory of the ceremony from all who were in attendance or were aware it had taken place. This was for the best. Azazael would interfere with her every assignment and nothing would get done. It was either this or prison.

⸎

Feeling excessively drowsy, which was rare for him, Ashton looked around his bedroom. It seemed he must have fallen asleep. He yawned, another gesture he rarely performed. Sure, he did it to people when he was bored with them but rarely yawned from a natural reflex. He got up and looked in the garden under his window, it was very early morning outside of the romantic city of Paris. A place he could remember when it was a mere village with a few thatch huts. He looked back at the bed, he had been in a sea of naked, shapely arms and legs of every ethnicity. Whatever happened to him was so articulated it felt real. He shakes the woman nearest him.

"Hey, have I been here all day and yesterday?" He asked roughly.

"No, your ass hasn't been here in damn near a week," the woman of Persian descent said.

"Did you find her?" Dawn asked from the outer edge of the 16 foot wide bed.

"Find who?"

"That little skinny, no tits heifer you been dying and crying over the past five years," Dawn said aridly and chortled drowsily at her own joke, turning to lay back down. He used his phantasm hand and slapped her.

"That's my wife you're talking about." He said icily.

Holding her burning face, she angrily turns the cover back and gets up fully nude. She was sick of his insane shit about that woman!

She taunts. "I'm sick of every time something goes wrong with her you come take it out on me! How in the hell am I supposed to know where in the hell you've been when you don't even remember where you've been? Dream on, big boy. Dream on. A woman like that isn't going to marry the likes of you no matter how much money you flash in her face. I know that kind. I was raised by one like her! The only man they truly ever love is Jesus and you damn sure ain't him. You should be glad she's gone. They will drive you outta your goddam mind talking 'bout Jesus every day, all fucking day long!"

He stopped and glacially stared at Dawn as his face darkened and twisted in rage. Dawn had to have met her face to face to know all that about the woman. What did she tell her? Did she tell her about his living arrangement? He thought he made it clear to the harem they were to stay out of his personal life? He was sick of everyone telling him whom to love! Believing Dawn informed the woman of something very incriminating about his lifestyle he leapt up, grabbed her by the hair, and slapped her until the others woke up and struggled to put him off her. With the mere sweep of his arm the eight tuggers crashed to floor.

The Parisian harem is at a loss in what to do about him. He's getting abusive which is something he has never exhibited toward them. These tedious mental lapses were bringing out the worst in him. His behavior is becoming erratic and totally obscure. His cool, calm, and collected demeanor flies out the window every time he returns from dealing with that woman.

He let go of Dawn and quickly called a meeting, before the entire memory faded. He was holding on to the mental straws as a drowning man to a vilipend raft. All gathered in the magnificent sitting room.

Unapologetic, his cool countenance toward the nine harem members was something none had ever seen him display. His arctic eyes plainly stated he didn't care if they stayed or left.

"As you all knew from the contracts this day may some day come. I left the clause open shall I fall in love and marry. My marriage would nullify our arrangements." He said slowly and carefully for he couldn't remember anything about the woman except the white robe and slippers. Maybe she was getting ready for the wedding. Maybe he was being pretentious. Maybe nothing happened. Perhaps he dreamed it all. Either way, he was sick of it.

"When do we meet your blushing bride?" Delores sweetly asked. Several others disported their agreement with Delores. To sure he wasn't lying to nullify their written agreement.

He smiled a very mean smile and asked did she think he was stupid enough to bring his wife to meet them? "The day has come for you ladies to get out," he said and slowly faded from their sight with only the startling ethereally eyes remaining visible, returning to the last place he could actually remember being with his bride. He was positive of that for the time being.

He was so weary of the endless chase and the impossible psychogenic hostage situation, the memory erasures. His life was becoming like a dirge; a long slow mournful musical with short-lived stints of merriment before returning to the sad song of lamentations.

A small part of him wanted to give up and resume his life as before. He was happy, well at least pleased, with his harems. They provided all the joy of many wives but none of the responsibilities beyond that which he wished to bear. Telling himself if heaven doesn't want him to have her then screw this. Forget her and move on. His best remedy to forget a tragedy or heartbreak is a party but he doesn't feel like partying with the harem so he goes to an underground club in Singapore. He wasn't going to let his

526

personal ambivalence get in the way of his fun he thinks as he got up and strolled toward two beauties beckoning him with their index fingers. He knew he was an excellent dancer but he would rather be dancing with the faceless, dark auburn haired woman.

Ana looked around and finds herself and Bea in Trusty; she looks at the neon clock on the dashboard. It's past 7:00 P.M. She reads the road signs beside the highway as cars whisked by and it seems they are on the road headed toward Jackson, Mississippi. She wonders why is she wearing this silly plush white bath robe, it will easily get dirty. Bea is asleep but clutching a fine linen napkin. Where on earth have they been this time? Only very expensive places offer that kind of dining utility. She wonders did she foolishly check into a place they couldn't afford and haul ass to keep from paying the bill. She will look at the emblem on the robe when she finds a place to stop and look for housing. She seemed to be suffering from a memory lapse again. The feeling of looking down a long tunnel was surfacing. The sheer unknown ambivalency of the whole thing tells her something very important took place. But what? She wishes she could remember. She has long ago given up trying to figure things out. She lives and act only for the moment which always ensure their survival. She did not have the leisureliness to sit and ponder. While pondering someone could walk up and put a bullet in their brains. She glanced back to see if the traffic was clear and pulled onto the highway and moved on with the flow of others going her way.

She wasn't aware Bea had made a mental connection to the man. Nor was she aware that Bea sensed they were related but didn't know how. She didn't know Bea had an inherent ability that told her things about herself and him. And many other things she knew her mother preferred that she did not know.

Bea didn't like the feeling she got when around this guy. It wasn't a bad one. It was a puzzling one. There appears to be a recidivism with this man she can not explain. Every time she resolves to dislike him, she found herself liking him ok. She sees he isn't so bad after all. She wants to ask her mother questions but that can wait until mom is in a better mood. Mom gets in a sad, weepy, bad mood she tries to hide from her every time that guy comes around and leaves. What she doesn't understand is why don't they just get together and stay together? They both get in bad moods when they leave each other and it's getting on her nerves. *But it would've been nice to have a pony, thus. Her doggy B Girl is with Uncle Junior, so she doesn't see her anymore.* She sighed and looked out the window to find something to distract her mind from her dog.

Ana decided to turn off the main road onto a back road. It's usually easier to get in and out of a town via back roads. Up ahead, she sees what she believes to be a man walking the lone road in the moonlight but when her car headlights shone in the spot, no one was there. That was odd. Unless it was a ghost. They passed a few houses along the road. She looked in the rearview mirror and saw a man sitting in the back matching the description of the man she saw earlier in the moonlight.

"It's not safe to drive these roads at night." the man said, realizing she could see him.

"Considering my life...no road is safe." she wearily replied.

"It would've been safer had you stayed on the main road," the young black man's spirit warned.

To her left she sees what she knows is a vision of the past or at least hopes it is. She sees the fire of a huge cross' reflective glare on her window. The white hooded beings surrounding it aren't all human. Many are demons or demons wearing a human.

"Don't look!" The man in the back seat warned too late. A demon turned and saw her. It yelled something, points toward Trusty, and a truck load of Klansmen from a haunted distant past pulled away from the crowd and cut across the field at a high speed. These were phantoms that had somehow managed to cross the chasm of time. They were evil then and they are still evil. She woke Bea up and made her climb in the back and under the iron blanket. She knew the body burning on the ground was the young man in the back seat who had now appeared up front.

"I walks this road for untold years to warn others that they used diabolical activities to open a portal in this area so they can continue their evil deeds beyond the grave," he said, glancing back occasionally at the truck gunning for them. They were outrunning it

528

for the time being.

But I was growing angrier by the second, the animus was spreading like wildfire. These evil spirits are always invading my privacy. Intruding on my time. I'm sick of spiritual crap intruding on my time as if my existence on earth isn't important. It's all about them, them, them and what in the fuck they want. I don't give a damn what they want! I want lots of shit but it's all unattainable. The spiritual world has invaded and stolen enough of my time and I'm not taking it anymore.

"Someone shoulda closed that portal years ago!" I cried, materializing my sword. I wasn't sure how it worked against something like this. But I was mad as hell and sure as hell ready to find out. My life had been stomped upon enough as it was.

Everyone watched the Sword sail backward, passing through the material of the car without missing a hitch, without damaging it, striking the old-fashioned truck that had rammed them so hard from behind she nearly lost control while materializing her weapon. In the rearview mirror she saw the furious red, yellow, and blue tongues of fire leaping from one demon to another and travel on to one area to another. Long streaks sailed like a comet in the night's atmosphere as some tongues leapt ahead of them into the nearest city. She knew that meant someone was keeping this hateful tradition alive. It lit up the night's sky over the city like a Fourth of July fireworks. When she looked to her right the spirit of the young man who died long ago was smiling.

"For years, no one believed drivers who said they were attacked along this stretch of the road. A few have been killed but their deaths were always classified as a mere auto accidents. My job is done," he informed her before he started glowing and within seconds was gone.

Bea broke the unnerving silence asking. "Mommy, was that a dead man's ghost?"

"Ahem, yes, baby. He died over five hundred years ago," she replied as Bea climbed back up front. But if her history served her accurately the man's clothing and the truck's model were from the 1940's. So she knew there was a major coven up ahead to have kept a time portal that powerful for so long. She wondered what deeds they performed to keep it open? Perhaps she really didn't want to know.

"Those bad people who were chasing us killed him?"

"Yes, baby. Those bad people and the demons with them killed him," I replied trying to keep the sadness out of my voice.

Shortly before the break of the day flooded the dark, shrouded city they pulled into a motel's parking lot and checked in. The confusion of traveling through the 8th Day was weighing heavily on her mind. If she could remember the event in the past two days then perhaps she would fathom why they traveled through the 8th Day. The last thing she clearly remembers was escaping Florida after having to kill those killers who tried to ambush them and driving like mad along the Gulf coastal line and hours later crossing entering a small town in east Texas to stop and rest before the long trek across the vast state. How did they get from Florida to Texas in one night? Trusty wasn't a hovercraft?! At least she didn't think it was?

"I remember the motel by the road, a busy road. I think I rescued of some girls. But who knows? I probably imagined them, too." Suddenly, she was mentally exhausted, felt an emergent sadness she didn't understand. It felt as thus she had lost her last chance of happiness outside of being Bea's mother.

We slept all day, got up and found an affordable take out diner; returned to the room and watched a few movie chips. Cheap motels don't have fancy holograms. So we watched a regular screen. Eventually, I fell asleep, I felt I hadn't slept in days. I hated horror movies and didn't watch them. For us, real life was far scarier than any movie chip. But I didn't know Bea was still awake watching one on mute until I felt her tiny body jerk along with the covers as she yanked them over her head and moved closer to my back. I thought Bea was asleep. I turned over to see what Bea was watching. The demon in the movies was trying to make the woman come to him, love him, kiss, or whatever. The woman hit him and the demon squeezed out a meningeal, menacing laugh and then I had to sit up and look more carefully. I wasn't sure if I saw what I did. Weird shit started coming out the demon clouding out the screen reaching like teeming, wet, glittering tentacles made of many tiny horrible eviscerate beings floated out into the

530

room. The woman held her face and screamed bloody murder. Bea screamed and I screamed right along with her. I quickly reached for the remote and turned the screen off and it was gone. That shit was scary.

"See there! This is why I told you don't sneak and watch this crap. We can't afford to be sleep deprived because of some stupid movie. Now go to sleep, sugar," I said softly, pulling my five year old closer to comfort us both and saying a prayer my mother taught me long ago. Bea was sleep again within minutes. Now it was I who couldn't sleep, wondering had I gotten myself mixed up with something like the woman had in that dumb movie? Those things clamoring, pushing, and clouding, and pressing against the screen made my skin crawl like a bad case of hives. They were so disgusting. Eeeww!

After finding a new job, again, as a waitress the following day, that night I had to ask the closet man a few questions. I went to my special place and called him. He didn't show up. I called him several more times. He still did not come. I had no idea how to find him so I waited. Two hours later he finally appeared. But it wasn't in his usually friendly fashion, he was a little aloof, cool and distant.

"Didn't you hear me calling you?" I asked impatiently and a tad bit hurt.

"Yes, I heard you. What do you want?" He insouciantly asked.

"If you heard me why didn't you answer?"

"I was busy!"

"Busy doing what?" I asked warily.

"Look, lady, what do you want? I'm here. I was hoping you'd call soon because I wanted to tell you I'm no longer interested in playing this childish cat and mouse game heaven has thrown us into. So I've moved on."

I gasped, I couldn't believe after all his confession of love and blah, blah, blah he could move on so easily. I think he confessed he loved me?? Anyway, it doesn't matter whether he said so or not.

"My name is Ana! Dammit!" I screamed at him. I couldn't believe he was saying this. Settling down, I guess there was no reason for my question but I asked anyway.

"Don't you remember?!?

He shook his head.

"I called you here to ask you is there anything else in you?" I stepped back from him. I saw he didn't like being yelled at.

"What??" He asked, knitting his well-formed brows together.

I repeated the question.

"Like what?" He asked a little harsher than I ever remember him addressing me.

"Uh, nothing. Never mind, I'm sorry I called you."

"Ah no, you aren't calling me away from what I was doing to suddenly say 'never mind." He said, crossing his arms across his chest.

"Ok, I was wondering if there was anything gross inside that body? Like megascopic squiggle stuff?"

He frowned and leaned in and looked closer at me. "Are you all right? I think not from your line of questioning. No, the same things are in my body as in yours. Have you been watching some dumb horror movie?"

"No, I've not." I lied. "I was just wondering and what did you mean by you were no longer interested in me? You've moved on. Is there another woman?"

He suspected she knew already knew the answers to her questions. Of course there were other women. In the past day or so he had hooked up with an old girlfriend. She was who was partying with him now. They were making love when Ana called him.

"Look Ana, you seem like a nice lady and yes, I still love you and probably always will but let's face reality here. Heaven isn't going to let us be together and I'm tired of chasing you and us meeting like this but not remembering what in the hell happened. Why continue to torture ourselves with things we won't remember when we return to our permanence in the physical world? I mean, it's a waste of time if we don't remember what was done or said."

She felt unspilled tears stinging her eyes. "So you're pretty much saying let's go our separate ways although we love each other."

"Baby, sometimes—love isn't enough. This is no kind of real relationship. You deserve more than heaven is willing to let me give you. You deserve someone who will be here with you always. Not rumples in the sack and the man disappears. Do you understand what I'm saying?"

Tearfully she said. "Oh, I understand just fine. You don't love me enough to keep trying. You don't love me enough to protect me from Vonderbilt. Oh, I knew you were screwing some bitch is why you didn't answer me. The next time I'll return the favor." She said fighting back tears but saw his eyes darken.

"Fuck whomever you want. You don't owe me any explanation. That's probably very easy to do with all the traveling you do. Be sure to keep a supply of good condoms. The cheap shit bursts. Oh, I'm sure you can find plenty to screw. Like the cop who wanted to fuck you is why he didn't turn you in or arrest you. Why else would he have you gotten a motel room? I hope you weren't naive enough to believe it was out of charity."

She sucked in her trembling bottom lip to still it and lied to hurt him as much as he was hurting her. "I told Bob, you know, I was with somebody, we could only be friends. But now I see, I can change that status." She stood staring him stubbornly in the eyes.

"What's this Bob's last name?" He asked staring down angrily at her. He could kiss her ass for all she cared at the moment.

"Noneofyourdamnbusiness, that's his last name. I didn't ask you what's that heifer's name you just crawled out the bed with." She replied nonchalantly as thus who he slept with didn't matter to her any more.

"There's no *'heifer'* in my bed," he lied but it bore some truth with. He lied with a continuous but angry face. There wasn't a cow in his bed. There was a beautiful woman. "I asked because a woman has to be more careful than a man."

"I know perfectly well how to protect myself." She said, turning her head in the air and tilting her chin. That gesture triggered something about her. He remembers something vital about her...she isn't a good liar. She can't lie worth a nickle.

"Ana, I know there's no "Bob" or Robert," he sighed. "I'm trying to make this easy on both of us without all the tears and drama."

"Yes, there is," she vibrantly reassured him.

"So you gonna go fuck this stranger named "Bob" all because you're angry at me? Ana, you're a mature woman with a child. So don't behave like one. So is this *"BOB"* traveling with you?"

"What do you care? You don't love me anymore. Why could you care who I spend time with?" Now the tears were falling. Why did she always do this shit? She hated crying. To her crying meant you are a weak ass punk.

"Ana, I just left you a little over a day, anyone trying to move in on you that quickly is either one of those people trying to hurt you or a cad just after sex."

"What do you care? If you can remember the cop who supposedly got me a hotel room then you remember other things too. You made your point. You got what you wanted and now want me to quietly disappear. Don't worry, I won't call you again. I hope you enjoy the rest of eternity." Bits about him were returning also, somehow she knew he was an immortal.

He grabbed both of her upper arms so quickly it surprised her. She yanked out of his grip and stared at him with eyes ablaze with a roiling fire coming from her heart. She was perfervid and breathing fire, for she suspected he was sleeping with, no screwing, another woman when she called him as to why he didn't answer. "Woman, don't make me kill somebody with your absurdness. When I find you again, if I find anybody between your legs I'm snapping his head off like a bottle cap. Do you hear me?!" He asked through clenched teeth. "With all this flakiness of yours I can't believe I actually married you." His words and remembrance thunderstruck them both.

The apprehension that seizes him is based on the fact that if she can spiritually follow him, she will discover there's a woman in his bed and if she can react so melodramatic about this, then she will erupt like a volcano.

"I'm not your wife!" She said, struggling again to break his ironclad hold on her arms. "I don't remember marrying you or anyone else. You're lying to keep me away from Bob."

He laughed a nasty, evil laughter; it was a little creepy. "There better not be a damn Bob," He said; his anger and jealousy enabled him to break through the way she travels through realms to him. Bea was asleep. He could see the blue glow of the cover of the prayer barrier over the bed. He focused on a live body in the bathroom but it was empty. He was satisfied she was lying.

"Ana, don't play with me like that again. I'm a very jealous man. You know damn well I can't leave you no matter what!" Between her and heaven he was pulling his hair out by the roots. Which was the most annoying? It was hard to tell. But yet he loved them both.

"Well, why were you saying all those hurtful things?"

"I thought they'd force you to leave me, I don't have the strength to leave you. "

"Supposed I *had* left?"

"*There she goes with the craziness again. "* He hid a smile to make her believe he was still upset.

"Then I would've just hunted you down and won you back. I'm never letting you go," he said, hugging her. At least she had a justifiable reason for her insanity; nonetheless he loved her. He was actually relieved she hadn't picked up anyone. He teleports them both into the empty room next door, so he could hear if anyone came near Bea. They made vivacious, sweet, and passionate love; they both knew the time was limited. He knew when the changing of the guards of time arrived they would be separated again. But at least they got a few hours of togetherness or honeymooning if they are married. But just as predicted at the harmonious singing of the angels' wings, the change of guards by the guardians of time, they both went back to where they were the proceeding evening.

The separation returned him to where he was last night. In a room of the Cargill Hotel in Seoul. He looked about the room, realizing his bed wasn't empty. He quickly told his rekindled flame to get up and get out before his wife found them. He doesn't know how he sensed it but somehow he sensed Ana was developing and honing her spiritual gifts well enough to track and follow him in the physical world. With no real mediation required. All it took was the irrational motive of a jealous woman.

"You didn't say anything about you had gotten married," the supermodel angrily cried, getting up cussing him, snatching up her clothing from the floor. She was very upset. He had said he wanted to see if was there were anything real feelings between them. If so, let's they try again to make it work. He sent his jet to pick her up with champagne, flowers, and fine jewelry aboard awaiting her. She knew about the harem but they didn't count as an obstruction.

"You no-good lying bastard! You had no intention of trying to have a real relationship. I should've known your damn lying ass hadn't changed! You're still the same liar you've always been!"

"Ok, ok, I'm a lying bastard. But hurry the fuck up and get the hell out. My wife is on her way.," he agreed, looking in the empty air in the direction he sensed the realm about to open and all hell spilling in it with it. He accepts the name calling, hurriedly helping her search for her belongings for he can feel Ana coming. And she isn't coming happy.

"I don't believe you. You aren't married. You're lying to get rid of me," the woman scorned, slowly recollecting her clothing scattered about the room and slowly getting dressed. They were to attend a bash tonight and being seen with him would thrust her back into the spotlight as it did before they broke up about seven years ago. Now this! He hadn't changed a bit. She should've known better than to believe his lies a second time.

Seconds after the supermodel angrily storms out the elegant suite he jumps in the bed shortly before the realm opened and Ana appeared. He was right somehow...she had figured out how to follow him. She firmly believes he's lying to her about sleeping alone. He peeked from under his thick eyelashes, he sees her at the foot of the bed. Standing there, surveying the room, looking for evidence. She seems to think he's asleep. She tiptoed closer but didn't say anything but quickly inspected. His insides nervously fret she might see the long hairs on the pillow, but she doesn't get close enough to inspect the other pillow. She quietly opens his nightstand and closes it when she sees it's empty. She walks quietly to the bathroom and then the closet and inspects. Seeing nothing she comes back into the center of the bedroom with her fists on her hips while wearing a puzzled visage, wondering where had he tucked that woman? He sees the swirling of the portal opening behind her and blows her a kiss seconds before she is pulled back into her location and her memory erased. But the surprised expression in her eyes told him she didn't like the fact he let her run around the place looking for evidence of his infidelity while he lay there and pretended to be asleep.

He decided that for tonight he was safe. But it's for the nights in Paris and beyond that he desperately needed to arrange to start sleeping alone. That was too close of a call and he knew heaven wouldn't erase *that* memory from her mind. He quickly got up and wrote it down to so he wouldn't forget. No more communal bed sharing with his harems. While his head was down writing, out of peripheral view he saw a pair of female legs much like his own when he reclined in the bed. The garment told him she was sent from the celestial realms. Someone was resting against the headboard. He looked around in the face of his sister, Freedom.

"Azazael, you asked why we keep blocking your access to the woman. Things like this is why. You couldn't go a day without sacking someone else. That woman doesn't need this kind of grief. It will make her distraught and overwrought which can be dangerous with what she has been called to do...supposed she had caught you? This devilry of yours is not what my name means. Freedom doesn't mean you've a right to do whatever in the hell you feel like doing and damn the consequences. It's a privilege, a God given right, but it is to be taken seriously. You haven't proven to us you deserve a woman like her. You haven't proven you can respect her for who she is. So why should we give her to you when all you'd do is cheat on her every chance you get?" Freedom rebuked. "She deserves better than that. If you can't give her that then stop chasing her. Don't force us to lock you away again."

"I'm sorry. I'll work on doing better. I've to do better. I don't want to lose her," he humbly promised. This whole change in his demeanor shocked his sister. She came in ready to do a battle of words with him.

"You really do love her--- don't you?" Freedom asked, looking at her younger brother, the ultimate womanizer in a whole new light.

"Yes, I do. I wish I could remember what she looks like. She was just here but I have no recollection of her face or figure. I remember very well how she feels. She feels like love."

"Has it ever occurred to you that maybe heaven wants you to learn about a love other than that you can see? To learn to love the person's soul. That's how many love Father. They've never seen the Source of all things but they still love Him. Perhaps you've loved her soul, her inner beauty all these years."

Azazael ponders over the sisterly advice. He knows she is beautiful inside and out which is some-thing very rare outside of heaven. He finally says what he hasn't wanted to admit even to himself.

"I'm afraid I'll get hurt. My heart has been closed toward love for so long that to open it scares me. Suppose she finds another love, I couldn't handle it. Someone so beautiful, I know there are many others vying for her love and attention."

"Love is something mortals take a chance on everyday." Freedom replied. "They survive rejections and so shall you. But I hardly think what I just saw is rejection. Her trampling through the Neutral Zone to catch you cheating. She needs to remain focused and clear headed. Which is why we keep you from her."

He chuckled softly; mortals seem much better equipped to deal with emotional pain than immortals, who rarely experience it. Mortals can pick themselves up again and again after one calamity after another and rebuild better and bigger than before. They don't let pain stop them. That's one of the things immortals have always admired about them. Their spiritual abilities are almost nonexistence. That's why when one of them has any spiritual talent, it's such a very big deal to them. They've built civilizations, kingdoms and empires, strictly on their carnal abilities and grit of never calling quit. After a cataclysmic event they lie down and cry for a while, but soon they pull each other up and start rebuilding again. They even question their gods as to why should they do A, B, C, or D when they don't want to do it. If you try to restrict them, it becomes hell to pay. Sometimes all they want to do is go look out over the land but if you tell them they can't they want to know why not? He has seen one group of them consult with another group about what their god has requested. The nonbelievers may say; "Nah man, something about that ain't right. Don't do that."

"You know, that didn't sound right." The believers might reply and follow the advice "Keep the faith and keep your penis under control."

Freedom laughed. "I promise you more good things comes of their fellow humans than the command of their gods. When the gods return and asked them why they didn't do it? They'll boldly stand in your face and say. "My fellow man said you're jacked up. I'm not doing that. You can kiss my ass." *Never mind they are powerless to keep you from killing them. It hard not to be attracted to a species so brave and defiant.*

"She doesn't remember any more than you. When your appointed time cometh your hearts will rejoice. You will finally be happy."

"Ok, if you say so." He was skeptical, for heaven's appointed time could mean years from now. And the woman he loved didn't have years to wait. She pecked him on the cheek and disappeared. Then he remembered no more.

⌒◦◦◦⌒

The local satanists in Salinas, Texas's clerk office stumbled upon an official marriage license issued to Ana BuFaye and Ashton Cargill. They quickly forwarded the document to their coven head who forwarded it so forth to his superiors until it reached Vonderbilt who was furious out of his mind as to how the local imbeciles allowed this to happen. Deciding the Cadwells and Shervenport were all but useless but Lucifer wanted them alive was the only thing kept him from outright killing them. But he would surely show up and beat the hell out of them.

"By now, she's probably stuffed with Azazael's bastard. What part of she's appointed for creating a vessel for our lord you inbreds don't possibly understand?!"

Caroline Caldwell or Cadwell or whichever last name Nikola decided to use at the moment nervously frets. Nikola knew before she arrived how she felt about Ana. He also knew most women care less or nothing for each other's plight. Regardless of what's openly preached. He and every man on earth knew the truth. So why did she expect the Cargill harem members to be different? She knew those concubines were only interested in their own hides. They don't really care how much she suffers from their ineptness. Those 56 courtesans are only interested in how well they can shop, buy pretty clothing and jewelry, and their private homes. Their infelicitous brains can not grasp the concept that there's a new world order at stake here. That a golden age is attempted to be ushered in. Of 56 of them, they can't handle him?! Then what good are they? She wonders is the rumor true that Azazael doesn't have all of his mind. Hell, she would hate to see him if he did. He has instantly placed their greatest mortal enemy in a rank she would have never acquired no matter how hard she worked and followed the rules.

540

If true, she know just the remedy to erase that woman forever from Cargill's memory but she can not descend into hell but Nikola can.

Before attempting to call Dawn, Caroline decides to take matters in her own hand. Since it is her life at stake. She decided to attempt to summon the goddess Lethe, the dreadful underworld goddess. The goddess of the underworld river of oblivion. It's rumored that the shades or souls of the dead drank of its waters to forget their mortal lives. According to myth it formed the border between the gloomy realm of Hades and the paradise realm of Elysion (Elysium). She knows the Elysion is *not* a realm of paradise. It's a hellish realm of madness, a realm of illusions from what James told her. He said it was a realm of *pure* madness. The other four rivers of the underworld bordering her realm were the Styx, Akheron (Acheron), Pyriphlegethon, and Kokytos (Cocytus). Everyone knows about the River Styx. That's why she avoided the Elysium fields as much as possible when traveling through the spiritual worlds. No sane person could possibly be that happy.

She rushed to her spa-like bathroom and closed the door and run a tubful of water. The last time she tried this a mean water nymph showed up.

She closed her eyes and begun the incantation. The waters started to bubble and rise, the clear form of water slowly changed to that of a beautiful woman with water running through her irises. The river-goddess Lethe is sometimes called the daimona Lethe, the very one of forgetfulness personified. Caroline knew never to let her touch her. So she backed away from the waters spilling over the rim of the tub. She watched, mortified, as the goddess stepped out the tub with feet as solid as her own. The hem of her gown was pale, greenish-clear, blue moving water.

"You called, what may I help you with?" The watery eyed woman asked before solidifying her eyes after seeing the fear of her in Caroline's face.

"Uh, ahem. I need you to bottle some water from your realm. I need it to help
541

someone forget someone forever."

Lethe already knew who the woman was referring to. Nothing happens on earth and hell doesn't know about it. But she wasn't sure if she wanted to get involved. Sure the waters of the river bearing her name worked on immortals. But supposed Azazael broke the hold long after the mortal woman was dead? Lethe, knowing his temper, declined to aid the mortal woman beseeching her.

"You don't understand. If I don't do this, I can end up as a resident of your realm."

"I can help you forget the pain your husband's infidelity has caused you." Lethe said, walking closer as Caroline stepped back. "I can help you forget the cruelty of your father, all the pains you have carried buried in your heart."

Realizing her error, Caroline quickly turned and fled the bathroom with the goddess' laughter chasing her through the room like eerie, watery butterflies. She's hiding in James closet as she fearfully peeks through the small slit between the double paneled-louvre doors and sees the goddess walk out the room and out of her life.

⌁⌁⌁

She waits for the harebrained woman to come back to the screen before continuing. She hears a scuffling but doesn't see Dawn. Cargill wouldn't have her in his harem were not for those oversized tits. Which she think is scrofulous way to judge a woman. But who was she to disagree for James judged her accordingly.

"Where is he?" Caroline asked.

"The last I heard he was in the USA."

"I know that!" Caroline said impatiently, rubbing her brow and grimacing from the slaps Vonderbilt delivered a few minutes ago. "I mean where in the USA, is he?"

"I ain't his wife. He don't tell me where he is going." Dawn rebutted.

"Dawn," Caroline patiently explains. "In France and most developed nations...you're a common-law-wife so you need to learn to exercise that authority and question him more often. Anyway, look at the screen. This is an official marriage license. The skinny bitch is not dead. She's comfortably married to *your* common-law husband."

Dawn grows more infuriated the longer she looks closer at the screen. She sees the state seal and the signatures. *"Dammit! It's his signature. He's been lying all along. While she was performing fellatio which she is sure he wouldn't dare ask his precious wife to do. To suck his dick. The tessellation of his lies has no boundary. He found the bitch and married her. He had already married her when they all were fawning all over him and he didn't say a word. He pretended not to know he had married her. She even doubts he fucks her in the ass. Most likely he's gentle with her. She can safely bet he doesn't just roll on her and get his rocks off. Get his rocks off first and leave her high and dry."*

"That lying asshole!" Dawn screamed, pushing the screen and the manicurist away from her. "Send me a copy of that!"

"Gladly," Caroline Caldwell smiled satisfactorily, she knew that would wake the nit-witted bitch up.

"Now, it's time you stop acting like this is a damn fantasy and claim your authority as a common-law wife and nip this shit in the bud." Caroline knew Dawn had no real authority because men of Cargill's calibre wasn't binded by the common-law legalism as regular men are. She knew that this Ana bitch had the upper hand in being able to drag Cargill to the altar. But Dawn could definitely make them both miserable. That's one expertise Dawn Shepherd had. Making one miserable; for she was making her miserable right now just from talking to her.

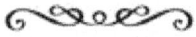

Immediately after her conversation with Caroline, Dawn calls a house meeting for the harem only. She made copies of the legal certificate and passed them around. Everyone is silent as they read the document again and again trying to masticate what this means for their life.

"At least he could've been honest about it." Kirba wryly said. "We all punctually asked him had he truly gotten married. We soporifically asked him to tell us the truth so we could make plans, but instead he willfully lied."

"Of course he lied. I doubt this Ana BuFaye knows about us any more than we knew about her, he's a man. They all lie." Delores added. "We need to figure out a way to maintain our way of life. Let her have him. We all know what she is in for."

Several laughed. For each knew of his sexual perversions. "After a few days with him by herself she will some be begging us to help her with him." Several more giggled, their cachinnations pealed through the ritzy room like lovely bells.

"It's the wife who fraught the small end of the stick with these rich guys like him." Karena reminded her co-workers.

"Hey," Dawn cried. "I'm a common-law wife and I've no intending of getting the small end of the stick."

Delores angrily sighed and lashed out. They were all sick of Dawn's claim as a common-in-law wife. That didn't really mean a thing anymore. This was merely Dawn trying to assert her seniority again and everyone was purely sick of it.

"Dawn, your common-law years don't mean shit over this piece of paper. Forget him and help us plan what we are going to do. First of all, if he had a memory lapse don't mention this to him. Pretend we do not know and that will buy us some time to get our acts together."

Ashton appeared in the room behind them, looked around at all of them huddled together, then remembered this is why he no longer had multiple wives and asked what was their meeting about? The women looked at each other and Dawn lied. "We were

544

discussing perhaps it would be easier if we took turns in different groups of spending the night with you." Wearing an off white, off the shoulders peasant style top she shrugged her lovely cream and sandalwood shoulders.

"Yeah, about that." He said, looking at the note he had written to himself. "I do not want anyone to spend the night with me any more. I want all of you out of here. See Hohenstaufen, the chief of house staff for your compensation. I'm terminating your service."

"You can't do that!" A young blonde cried as she stood up and confronted him.

"Oh really. Says who?" He asked, rather amused by her boldness. She hadn't been here long enough to know who he really was.

"Our written agreement says twenty years or should you fall in love. What proof have you presented you are in love? You behave the same. A man in love changes. You haven't." The 23 year old argues, dismayed by everything ending so soon. Several others agreed with the girl.

"Do not make this difficult. Just leave. Do not force me to bodily toss you out. I'd like to have fond memories of our time together." Ashton said softly. So soft all the women looked at each other. They were used to his authoritarian way of speaking. Not caring how anyone felt. They all watched him walk out the door and wondered who was that?

His identical brother Pascasiel appeared or rather stepped from hiding in the earthly ethereal and asked Dawn to speak with her privately. He followed her back to the sanctuary of her private cloistered bedroom. The room was modeled after the suite of Marie Antoinette. Ashton once told her some of the furniture belonged to the mistress of Louis XIV. That Madame de Montespan, who eventually became the king's chief mistress, gave birth to seven of the monarch's children was the one he loved most. He read her an ancient book about the flamboyant and often oleaginous king who had a queen, but always two mistresses and sometimes more. His household sometimes amounted to a royal harem. So she knew she was Ashton's Madame de Montespan and just as de Montespan won over her rival the queen of France and his other mistress,

Louise de La Vallière so would she win over Ana BuFaye. No matter what it took. That was the only way to spend a lifetime in luxury.

"I heard the news, but if you want to hold on to all this have a child for him. My brother is a patsy for his kids. That's why Ashley and Lavenica are lazy as shite." Pascasiel advised.

"If my father had his type of money, I wouldn't work either. Besides, Ashton always protects himself." Dawn volunteered.

"That's where I may be able to help you. Since he and I are identical. I'll father your child. The child will look like him. Our children have always looked alike."

"Won't Ashton know the difference?" She quizzed.

"Sure, he'll but his lady love won't. He'll do anything to keep the child a secret from her.," Pascasiel knowingly stated.

"Yes, that *any thing* could include killing me," she smartly quipped. Pascasiel dismissed her notion that his look-alike brother would kill her. Although, he knew there was always a possibility. It's true, she has a point. Azazael might freak out and kill her but it was worth it to stick the knife into his brother's perfect life and twist it with joyful revenge. A life Azazael thinks is under his control.

"Hashwash! You've been with him over 25 years, I know my brother. If he didn't gave a tinker's cuss about you he would've gotten rid of you years ago."

Dawn ponders over Pascasiel's words without a clue the brother had an ulterior motive older than the earth. They had been lovers for years while he let Dawn believe it was all behind Ashton's back. But Pascasiel knew his brother knew about their tryst. He just didn't care. They've always traded and shared women. Except their wives. Most people couldn't tell them apart. But he had a cud to chew with both Ana and Ashton. Those two don't care who they hurt just so long as it isn't each other.

I opened my eyes in the dimly lit room to the sound of a low cacophonous growling. Without rising my head off the pillow I carefully, slightly tilted my head to the left. I saw a figure blending in with the shadows of the corner. I saw red embers glowing in the far nook of the room. It wasn't the dim nightlight reflecting in its eyes. That was hellfire burning in those evil eyes!

The hell Doberman quickly rose off it hinds and swiftly, long-leggedly walked closer toward the bed, and leapt before I had a chance to materialize my blade. He was much heavier than he looked. The bed broke and crashed to the floor. I put my arm up and kept his mouth from my face, the human-like teeth were aiming for my pharynx. Suddenly he turned to ashes. I looked up at the headboard and Bea was standing in the corner rapidly throwing fireballs. Three more were leaping for us. She turned them into ashes in midair. Her hands were fierce gloves of flame. All I could do was stare. There was nothing else to say. I had to admit to even to myself what she was. She was a nephilim or at least bore the essence of one. I could no longer tell myself otherwise. Now, I understood why I was given such a child. In reality, a normal child would be dead by now. I was too late to defend her. By the tumultuous life I've been forced to live a normal child would be of little help or no aid to me in defense against what we must face.

After Bea rid us of the hell dogs I went into the bathroom to inspect the wounds. Avidly praying I didn't catch an infection. I grit my teeth to keep from screaming in anguish as I cauterized the wounds on forearm with my flaming short blade. As far as I knew, only Holy Fire could purify such a wound. I knew hell cooties were likely to be in the dog's saliva. A hellhound's bite hurts like the devil. I knew soap and water was useless against whatever they infected you with. It was 2:17 A.M. but it was time to get moving again; I knew would be more coming when those didn't return to whomever sent them.

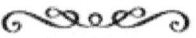

Swishing the rich red wine around in a wine glass, Nikola sat by the open fireplace with his cat resting comfortable in his lap. The black cat that was once a man; it lazily flicked its tail from side to side as he played with the neon green energy balls he floated in the air. Nikola had a cat like this the night his family was slaughtered. He loved that cat. He liked this warlock a little better than most so he made him into a cat rather than kill him.

"Ferdiad, do you think we were successful?" he asked, absently stroking the purring cat's back. The cat's eyes frosted and warlock in the cat became visible as he shrugged his shoulders. The frost returned for a second they were cat eyes again. Ferdiad didn't fight the change for it was futile. Which was something he learnt long ago. He simply let the feline instinct reclaim him and resumed his animalistic pleasure and actions.

It was long after breakfast so he was enjoying the robust fragrance of fresh wine. His dark eyes narrowed to deadly slits as he looked out the window at the darkness descending and covering the icy valley below. Nikola assumed his pets must have ripped her apart by now and angels were coming for him. What else would explain the eerie darkness descending on the valley at this later afternoon hour? The Lord of Darkness had arrived and he wasn't thrilled about what he had done. To come in such fury on clouds Nikola knew Lucifer was angry. He sat patiently as he heard the heavy threading on the thick stone floor. He don't know where the legend came from that Lucifer had hooves. It was Moloch who had hooves not Lucifer.

A huge shadow darkened the doorway. Ferdiad sprinted from his lap and hid under a heavy table seconds before Lucifer was upon him. He grabbed him by the throat and threw him across the room. The crash against the stone wall knocked the breath from his body. He tried to rise but Lucifer pushed him back down with his foot in his chest, slowly applying pressure, crushing the life from his body.

"What in the name of all that is unholy do you think you are doing?" Lucifer bellowed.

Nikola gasped for air; for the reek of the sulfurous air and the weigh of the huge foot was suffocating him.

"I hate you pricks born with your powers. You think you do not have to obey me. I do not care you are in love with her and she will not come to you. So you decided to kill to her in a jealous rage Of course you are in love with her! I do not want parents who aren't in love. That's the woman is to be the mother of my earthly vessel and you tried to kill her before my body is conceived?!"

Nikola's neon green shield is the only thing that kept Lucifer from killing him. He couldn't break the shield. But he pounded him in so much rage that the castle shook. When he was pulled back to hell he left the dreadful warning: Never to try to kill her again or he would kill him the next time.

Nikola knew there had been another born almost equal his strength. And he also knew Lucifer was planning to kill him once the young man had reached his full potential. But not if he kill the young warlock first. Those like himself didn't have to answer to the darkside for their powers. They were born with them and it was up to them how they used them.

⸙

Ashton Cargill sat with his back to the door. He was confident enough to do that. The two men and one woman wearing all black entered one of his many private sanctuaries. These are the places no one wants to be summoned to for very few, mortal or immortals, have entered and come out alive or were ever to be seen again. The trio stood with their hands clasped behind their backs while their boss enjoyed the marine life in the wall sized aquarium; they stool stiff as statues until addressed.

"Keep an eye on Dawn Shepherd and the others when the day comes to evict. Do not hesitate to kill if you must. According to this paper...," he paused to distribute the copy of the marriage license Dawn had sent to her by Caroline Caldwell onto Sewell among them.

"...I now have a wife so things are going to have to be more secretive. Shall she drop in unexpectedly be prepared to move the harem quickly and quietly. I know I won't remember all this so I'm counting on you three." He paused a few seconds more. "This paper most likely will disappear like everything else pertaining this woman." he continued, flicking on a life-like graphic image of a smiling Ana holding baby Bea. An image he had his people to steal from Thaddeus Wyett. It was the only one that remained visible. A fact that he deeply resented.

"Here is an image created of her based on her sister's photograph. She's being divinely moved so it's difficult next to impossible to keep track of her. She can be standing right in front of you and you won't recognize her because heaven will shield her from you. But when you do find her if you find any man around who is not a relative, showing personal interest... Kill him. Here is a photograph of Thad Wyett," he said clicking on the third picture. "If he attempts to use the kid to rekindle any affection eliminate him. I do not intend let anyone or anything to stand in my way. I've waited too long for her to let anyone stop me from making her mine."

The three knew when he stopped speaking it was time to give their report. One of the harem members wasn't whom the others thought she was. She was a Cargill agent. Had the others noted she always found an exit when the sexacades started they would've figure out quickly what she was.

"Sir, Dawn Shepherd is encouraging the others to stage a coupe. She intends to make demands that she remain on the premise longer under the jurisprudence of a common-law wife. She is presently with your brother. They plan to defraud you with a child of his to be passed off as your own." Sharaim said.

Ashton clicked on the screen showing Dawn's room. "You mean this?" He asked. "I already know that."

"Her brother-in-law in Long Island called the authority on our people posted outside his door to protect her mother. Shall we kill him? The man is quite a nuisance." Capolona asked.

"No, ignore him. To hurt her sister is to hurt her." Cargill replied. "Give him more work, he won't have time to annoy us. But keep a tab on him. People like him defect

550

easily to the other side. I need you guys to remember to protect her family even if I do not."

"Sir, it was Delores who placed the call leading you to the site of the demolished house." The third agent said. Ashton turned back to the aquarium to hide his anger. He suspected something odd about that phone call but was in too much hurry and concern over Ana's well-being to follow his instincts. He turned his back to the three to enjoy the aquarium life a little while longer before letting them know they are dismissed.

All of the hell dogs didn't return. Several were missing as those who did return sat on their hinds before him. He knew what had happened but he was certain they'd caught her off guard ;when he left her she was sleeping. He watched her sleep for at least an hour while trying to decided did he really want her dead. Sure necromancy could bring her back but a person was never the same. He had caressed her troubled sleeping face but when he sprinkled detective dust on her he saw blue handprints illuminated on her face, a man's hand print. He knew then she had to die and he couldn't kill her. So he sent the hounds to do it.

Nikola called Bjors into the room. He offered no explanation for his bruises for all already knew what happened. He gave him an address in Northern Ireland and instructed him to rid the world of the residents there. Kill them all. Bjors took the scrap of paper. When his back was turned he slowly smiled. Happy that Nikola had for once suffered at the hands of someone more powerful than himself. but he forgot Nikola had a mirror that showed what was done behind his back. The mirror revealed the smirk at the beating at the hands of Lucifer. "I'll deal with you when you return." Nikola said into the enchanted mirror. Bjors hung his head and continued on his way.

Chapter 12
The Killings

I value life above all else, the thrill of killing isn't in my nature but I will if I have to. It was an early spring night, not cold but not yet enough warm to truly call it springtime weather. This was her first real job since leaving Mother Harris and her mom. The snow had melted from the awful winter that year, making the sidewalks slushy and forming rivulets in the streets. Walking the street cautiously, being aware of her total surroundings, Ana was returning home from a late night job. Around 11:30 P.M. Ana's shift at the neighborhood's cafe ended. She tucked had away in her black canvas tote the ribs and barbequed chicken which was left unserved that night along with her colt 45 revolver. Her employer allowed the last shift to take home all the food left over. For the next day a new batch had to be prepared.

Ana knew she was being followed. The two men called her to their table and ordered two rare burgers, almost dripping with blood. She knew who and what they were from their spiritual aura. It was so evil, it made others shudder as they passed. She willed herself calm to keep from running out there to see if Bea was OK in their small rented room. Her screen ISPAD told her Bea was fine. She could see her on the tiny screen grinning at her with her front tooth missing. She had left her blade guarding her. She saw it swirling over Bea's head. Meaning anyone came near her was turned to ashes. She was relieved they hadn't found where she lived.

Untying and hanging up her apron for the evening her mind, body and soul were weary and raw-boned tired. No matter how far she traveled or how fast she ran she could not lose them, the sinister figures that followed her. All her life she been followed, spied on, harassed, and hounded by them. Maybe not these devils but a devil. No matter how many corners she turned or how many alleys she ducked through, they were always behind her. Hounding her, stalking her, driving her. Pushing her toward extinction. They had always driven her and this night she was tired and mean-tempered. She felt meaner than a hundred junkyard dogs. While running with all her reserved strength in her tired body to stay ahead of them she wondered; Was there a hole she could hide in or was there a peopled corner nearby, even the foxes and gophers had a place to hide if frightened and chased by a predator. But she had none.

Never once had she felt truly safe from them. They were everywhere. Always, always they had driven her and keep driving her with no mercy. Her legs were feeling rubbery and her breath was coming in raspy gasps. Her chest was hurting. Her lungs felt as though they were about to explode. She wasn't in the best of health. She knew she couldn't go on much longer. She had two alternatives in these streets- one was to fight, the other was to die fighting. They were close behind. There was no in-between. The heavy and swift footfalls of her chasers were quickly closing the distance between them. The zestfulness of their pursuit told her there had never been any in-between. They meant to kill her.

Feeling they were pausing to shoot, she started running, zigzagging, to make herself a difficult target to hit. She felt heat of the bullets whisking pass her head. So close they singed her hair but she continued to run. Coming to an alley that had no exit, she knew she was trapped. But for once, she felt anger growing instead of the usual fear when they were nearby or chasing her. Being trapped she was therefore forced to fight back. A feral, primitive instinct swelled in her. It completely overshadowed fear. A reckless danger took its place. Standing in the darkness she saw the dark silhouettes of her would-be murders against the wan, weak street lights when they turned into the alley. Expertly, she raised the big antediluvian revolver and returned the fire the men had issued. Something had snapped in her; she was determined not to let these thugs take her away from her loved ones and she fired upon them without hesitation. Relief washed over her that they were no longer trailing her, that they now lay dead at her feet. Perhaps she had put an end to the incessant hounding once and for all. At least by these two. But she knew there were many more. For these bastards, Lucifer or someone equally as evil purchased them a dime a dozen. Another thing, she was tired of her life always being under the auspices of a fine tooth comb. Never enjoying any real privacy.

She wasn't a killer. She never had the desire to deliberately murder anyone in cold blood but out of self-defense she had returned the fire of those who would have felled her. Having done it she was glad. She hoped she would put fear in the others, they'd

553

know from the news of these men deaths she was armed, way beyond tired of their stalking and hounding, and would fight back. The unbridled rage swelling in her chest made her wanted to kill more of them now. She felt she would never be completely rid of them unless she did kill. All of them she could find. So the only thing to do was to kill, kill, kill until her hands were dripping with their blood and then perhaps her heart would feel safe and secure.

She walked up to look them in the eyes to make sure they were dead. One was white and the other black. She was learning race, age, or ethnicity meant nothing to these people. For they often sent those who looked like you to befriend you. Like the neighbor who was stealing from them while she was at work. One day they came home earlier than expected and they caught the lady from upstairs coming out their front door loaded down with the supplies she had just purchased. The irony of this was the woman ran upstairs and when asked to hand over their much needed supplies the woman pretended she had no idea what she was talking about. Another time, she learned another she believed to be friend had been making malicious, slanderous phone calls pertaining her and caused them to lose an apartment. According to her next door neighbor "friend", the smell of Bea's dog, B Girl, fur was seeping through the vents triggering her allergies.

She picked up the casings and walked by the blinking, shiny eyed evil spirits, searching for a way to kill them too. She stopped and looked at them as hateful as they were glaring at her. Recalling what Mother Harris taught her she materialize her second blade and with a single clean swipe she turned them to ashes.

Hearing the sirens from afar, she knew someone had heard the shots and called the police. With renewed strength she sprinted out the alley and caught the oncoming bus. She went home and slept better that night than she had in a very, very long time. She had left her car parked out front so people would think she was home and Bea wasn't alone. She hoped it worked.

She remembered the next morning as she warmed up the cafe's unserved food for their breakfast; once behind a service station in Vermont she shot a man for trying to grab her as she tried to use the outdoor women' bathroom. She stepped over him and ran back to the car. Fannie asked what was wrong? She said nothing. She hated lying to her mom. She really did. She wouldn't have shot him had not he broke in on her sitting on the toilet. He was begging to get shot! She had yelled several times "Restroom occupied!" But the fool broke the door down anyway and tried to pull her to him. So she shot him in his oversized gut.

"Ana! I smell gunpowder!" Fannie cried. "What did you do?" Her mother reached behind her and forcefully pulled the still hot pistol from her jean's waist band.

"Ok, mom...I had to shoot a fool who broke in that nasty ass bathroom on me."

"Oh well, if the bullet don't kill him that nasty ass floor will." Fannie nonchalantly said. "Some-times, you gotta do what you gotta do."

She was surprised mom didn't lecture her on the Ten Commandments or something. Instead they exchanged mirthful glances and bust out laughing at her comment about the filthy bathroom floor.

"I swore I saw shit moving on that floor." Fannie added, laughing.

Mom knew about some of her kills, no one else in the family knew but her. Fannie and now 5 year old Bea knows. And now someone in that alley knows. For someone called the police.

Usually after a kill she gets a few days sometimes weeks of tranquility. She assumed the big dog was sending someone else crazy enough to go up against her. She will get her paycheck on the way out of dodge. She has no idea where these shooting skills come from. It's like someone else is firing the gun, giving her the courage to keep walking toward her opponent as she keeps shooting. That move unnerves them every time. That's their fatal mistake.

The man she killed in Maine was her first kill. She killed him because, again, she told the person to leave her alone. Ok, he said she couldn't park by the water that summer night. She was cool with that. She had parked by the water so her mom and Bea could keep cool from the damp air drifting off the sea. He said it was private property and they had to move. Mom had been driving the interstate all day and suggested the ocean scene spot for the night.

It was 2:00 A.M., so who in the hell is out casing their wooded property at such ungodly, diabolical hour. I had slept all day while mom drove so I was still awake when he came and banged on the driver's window, nearly breaking it. It was partially up to keep anyone from reaching in and grabbing us. When he banged the window 14 month old Bea woke up and started crying again. I had just got her back to sleep from crying because she was too hot. I heard mom telling me to get back in the car but I was too pissed off at everyone from Thad to my former boss in Boston, the sheriff dept who evicted us, James Caldwell with his lying ass, and my sister Helena who gave me grief about my life. I had a mile long shit list and this asshole was adding to it.

"Sir, I understand this may be private property but I promise you we'll be gone in a few minutes. When we parked here we thought by it was so far away from everything it didn't belong to anyone," I said calmly. Trying to hold my peace for mom and Bea's sake. I thought I was talking a reasonable person.

"Bitch! Now you know it's private property. I want y'all black asses off my property now!" He snarled at her with a police grade flashlight shinning in her eyes. While shielding her eyes from the painful glare she saw his eyes becoming angry black shiny globes. She knew then he had followed them, he wasn't an angry property owner. This was an indwelling. A demon wearing a meatsuit. Had not she moved her head quickly out of the flashlight's beam she wouldn't have seen it bearing down on her head and been able to duck out the way. She remembered what the cop in Boston told her about getting out the way when you see something coming for you. He struck the bony part of her left shoulder, knocking her down. While on the ground she reached behind her back and pulled out the antiqued Colt; she fired, hitting him in the center of the chest. They were only a few feet from the car. Fannie was running toward them with a crowbar but the man was already dead. Fannie helped her pull the body into the sparse woods and they emptied his pockets.

Hey! We weren't looking to kill nor take anyone's money that night. All we wanted was a cramped up, half-way decent sleep. We met his cohorts on the way back to the

556

main road. We took his gun for we felt someone else was nearby and this would be one less gun they had to shoot at us with. I placed Bea down in the floor of the car and covered her with the scrape piece of iron I had gotten from a junkyard after our first gun fight shortly after leaving Boston.

This time they decided to leave the eastern seaboard and head to the Heartland of America. I still wasn't able to cash in those strange gemstones. No one knows what they are. A jeweler in Cleveland, OH, he knew what they were but called the cops on me saying I had stolen them. They were priceless colored diamonds according to him. I had been on the road long enough to know when someone says, "Hold on, a minute I've to make a phone call" they're calling the cops. No, the man didn't directly say I stole them but he kept asking me where did I get them from? I told him twice a friend gave them to me and when I couldn't produce the *friend's* contact information that's when he said he had to make a phone call. At least I was able to sell one in East Chicago, Indiana. I knew I didn't get a fair price for it but something was better than nothing. It was getting too hot for Bea and mom to sleep in the car.

There was talk on TV on the local news channel now about the two men found dead on Farlane Street near a piles of strange ashes. Some speculated it was a satanic ritualism gone bad that killed them. I listened carefully to the woman who said she saw the shooter. She said she hear footsteps and looked outside after hearing gunshots.

"There were four men chasing this woman, they got her cornered up back yonder in that dead-end alley and she came out shooting like an assassin or a professional killer. I didn't see how she turned those two into ashes but it was very quick."

The news reporter anxiously asked the witness, "Which way did the woman go?" The woman with the bandana tied around her head, "I don't know. All I know is she ran up the streets."

Another female bystander took the microphone from the reporter and asked "If it had been a woman killed up here in this alley nobody would be saying shit now would they? Several women have been killed here and you guys didn't come down here with all the cameras and shit. Whomever you are! I salute you with your bad ass self!" They did a fist salute in the camera. Ana had frozen, she was certain the woman who saw her was going to identify her. So apparently there had been killings in that alley before, but all the victims were female. A horrible chill swept over her when she realized those guys knew exactly where to chase her so there would be inquest of her death.

With Trusty loaded, gassed, and Bea riding shotgun in her accustomed seat we headed out of town. Now that her grandma was in New York City with her Aunt Helena who said she wanted Bea to come live with her too, the front seat was vacant. Ana missed the adult conversations with mom.

Ana stops by her job to tell them she needed her pay now, she wouldn't be returning to work. Her boss's face turned pale and pasty when he saw her. He looked as thus he had seen a ghost. His face told her he knew she was supposed to be a ghost by now. He asked her to sign the check log and he paid her cash from the office safe. As she lean over to sign the check on his battered silver and puke pea green metal desk she whispered, "Sorry about your friends. Don't make me have to come back and kill you, too." The man was so lambasted he didn't where to rest his eyes. He had accepted a hundred to give her the night shift. He often did it for nothing.

She was relieved there was no drama about her pay. "Mom, where is my daddy? Why he doesn't live with us?" 5 year old Bea inquired out of the blue once she saw her mom had calmed down. Ana was watching for sirens to pull behind her to stop her before she was out of the city of DuPont, North Carolina.

"Sweetie, your daddy is away because he did something bad."

"Did he kill somebody? Bea asked innocently.

"No, he didn't...remember what I talked to you about. You aren't to tell what you see mommy do to bad people."

Bea screws up her face and says "Mom, I'm not stupid. I asked because the man in the hotel room said he was my daddy. The man who took me away to that big scary house."

Ana nearly slammed on brakes as her heart jumped in her chest and missed a few beats. She whipped her around and looked at her daughter, "Breanna, when did this man with black curly hair show up?" She asked very carefully to be sure Bea wasn't asleep and having nightmares about her kidnapping.

"A few minutes after you called and said you were coming home. Another scary man ran him away. He said you weren't coming home and he came to take me home because he was my daddy. I pointed my gun at him and he got mad."

Ana bit down hard on her lower lip; she felt like the worse mom in the world. Why didn't the blade kill him? What kind of mother gives a kid a gun and tell her to shoot people? What kind of mom teaches her 5 year old how to shoot? Unfortunately, this was the reality of their life. That explains why this job pitched such a double down fit about her bringing Bea to work. Nikola wanted her.

"No Sweetie, that's the bad man trying to hurt us. He's not your daddy. I showed you a picture of Thad. Look on your ISPAN Pad." she said encouraging her to look at Thad's picture. "There's a picture of your daddy. The scary man who ran him away...what did he look like?"

Bea frowned and paused a moment and said "I think he was the same guy who went in our closet when we lived in Augusta."

Ana had to keep her eyes on the road but she wondered what Bea knew she hadn't told her. "The morning before we left Augusta, this big scary dude with lots of hair came out your closet."

Ana wondered what was it with this spiritual being and fucking closets? She remembered waking up embarrassed, wondering if Bea heard her moaning and groaning because the portal to this world was left open. Now she knows she had. "You left the room and went with him through the closet. I was too scared to follow you." Bea added to her information.

"I did?" Ana asked surprised and feeling rotten. For years she thought all that was a merely dream. She felt even worse about Bea being too scared to follow her. "I'm glad you didn't follow me sweetie. Mommy don't know who that man is nor why she followed him."

"Yeah, he had on weird funny looking clothes, a long black beard, and a crown on his head. He even had on earrings and all kinds of rings on his hand. I think it was him again last night who chased away the bad man who took me through the dark house. But somebody else brought you back."

She contemplated if this the kind of things Saint Anne was trying to ask her had she experienced. She thinks the woman knew she was lying, that she was too chagrined to tell her. She pondered on how to stop these phantom visitations when she allowed herself at first believed they were dreams. Now she knows they aren't dreams. She is going to other worlds. She recalled when she was about Bea's age two strangers showed up in her room. One was a woman who was really nice to her.

"Sweetheart when you see things like this you must tell mommy. Sometimes mommy can't see them, sometimes mommy's head ain't screwed on right, so promise me from now and on when you see something that isn't supposed to be there you will tell me."

Bea giggled at the *"head isn't screwed on right comment"* and said "He screamed at the other man "YOU BASTARD!" and started chasing him, they both ran right thought the wall like ghosts in a movie. Oh, you mean things like the pretty lady who sometimes rides with us?"

Between her and her associates, Bea was learning an awful lot of bad words she preferred her not to know or repeat. Ana had always felt a presence with them but never saw anyone.

"I think that's a guardian angel. I think she is yours by you can see her." Ana smiled, happy they weren't alone. For very rare moment she felt was allowed into heaven's inner sanctum.

"No, mom she's yours; mine's a big muscular guy with wings." Bea corrected. "They

560

both sit in the back seat."

Ana couldn't resist looking backseat via the rearview mirror, she looked right into the face of the *pretty lady*. She knew then that's who was aiming the pistol.

"I'm going after that bitch myself!" Gianna Machiavelli roared at his alleged half-brother, Jarvis Jr. Now, Nikola had two spiritual beings on his trail about the woman. Why didn't he just kill her when he had the chance?

"My brother have lost his damn mind over that whore!" Gianna grunted. Jarvis Jr. didn't know what to say. Their childhood friend Baghid is dead. He was killed by the woman his uncle been after for years. Baghid and his partner were experts. They didn't miss whomever they was after. His uncle had just returned from the Vectorian realm and decided it was time to kill this woman. She had made his reign as Grand Wizard seem incompetent and blundering long enough.

"Gianna, its best to wait until Nikola comes back. The lord of darkness himself wants her for some rational motive."

"I agree with Gianna," Bjors says strapping on his guns. "The kvetch has killed five of our best North American hit men. That's no ordinary woman. I don't know what she is but I know where she is going. I'm bringing her home frozen or alive. Either way she is ending up in that basement. I hope to bring her and her little bastard in alive. That way we can gut them both screaming." Bjors said ravishing the idea of killing Ana and Bea. He was savouring of all the times he was close enough to touch her and was ordered to let her live. He was thinking of all the nights he went to sleep with a hard-on thinking of how he would kill her. "Nikola isn't here so we are who is the law right now." Bjors said, acknowledging Gianna's authority.

"What does Cargill have to do with all this?" Gianna wonders aloud as a servant straps on his guns. "I mean, she's a mortal so what does Cargill want with her?"

561

"That one isn't hard to figure out. It's obvious! He's fucking the whore. He can have her after we are finished with her." Bjors commented with a cruel snicker.

Jarvis Jr. isn't so sure that's the reason. "I believe he wants her for the same reason the Lucifer wants her. If we disobey Lucifer commands, won't his wrath rain down on us?" He questioned his uncle and best friend who it is said is really Nikola's son by one of the maids. Bjors is really about five years younger than he but no one knows that except the trusted staff. The two who men who shared strong resemblance asked Jarvis Jr. what was his solution to this very problematic woman? Jarvis Jr. meditates a few moments.

"Has anyone ever considered romancing her? Breaking through to her via the way of her heart? She's a young mother and alone. So I'm sure she must get lonely a lot. It would be easy to pretend to be romantically interested in her." He seriously asked the two whom he considered a little too bloodthirsty for his taste to comprehend the art of seduction.

The two looked at each other and guffawed long and hard. So hard tears rolled down their faces. They both fought to control their deep belly laughs.

"You'd come out better romancing a stone," Bjors howled and laughed. "At least a rock wouldn't blow your head off. Remember a few years ago, a guy named James Caldwell tried to court and woo the wild thing and somehow she convinced Nikola to bruise up the man really bad. So mark my word, she's a very powerful witch. You know she has to be very strong to play apparitional psychotherapist on Nikola."

Jokingly, Gianna makes a deal with Jarvis Jr. "I tell you, since you're so scared of the devil and punishment in hell, she's seen me and Bjors but she haven't seen you...how about you try and romance the stone-hearted bitch?" Both were surprised when Jarvis Jr. agreed to do so.

"You can't serious?!" Bjors cried. He wasn't complaisanting Jarvis Jr.'s utter foolishness in willingly facing this killer alone.

"Man, forget the pictures you've seen of her. She's nothing like how she looks. The men she killed in Omaha, Nebraska she walked toward them shooting assassin style and kept shooting until they were ridden with bullets. They had cornered her and her killer kid behind the store she was shopping at. She ran the moment she saw them. But when she appeared from around the corner she was shooting with a gun in each hand. I tell you, it was a beautiful thing to watch. Even the kid had a gun. I firmly believe whatever Cargill is, that kid is the same. I think he's that kid's real father. The child is too wise to be so young."

Jarvis Jr. hadn't considered the child might be Cargill's as to why he's so pissed off about their harassment of the woman. That makes more sense than he simply wanting to screw her. So why isn't Cargill supporting his kid and woman? If he loves them so fucking much? "So you two believe it's the kid telling him where they are?"

"Who else could it be? She doesn't have what it takes to hook him but his kid can somehow call him." Gianna confidently affirmed they had solved the mystery of why and how Ashton Cargill keeps popping up trying to kill Nikola.

In Oklahoma City, Oklahoma a man dressed in casual but rather expensive blue jeans and t-shirt with close cropped black hair showed up on the scene. He appeared among the working class who were migrating home from work. He knew exactly who he was looking for but didn't see her in the crowd. So he waited outside the hotel she is said to be employed.

Ana worked as a housekeeping technician at the Cargill Imperial Hotel downtown under an alias her brother Jack help set up to hide her true identity. She preferred working in hotels to cafes and restaurants because she could take Bea to work with her. Her direct supervisor told her that morning the owner was in the Imperial suite and everyone was to be precise and on time for the next few days. She worked the night shift which started at 6:00 P.M. The hotel was built to replicate the ancient Imperial Palace of China, it was almost like a step back in time. The least expensive rooms started at $1,550.00, so only the wealthy visited which is why she was surprised to see the man who asked her out earlier for a lunch date there at the door. But more careful observation told her he came from money, lots of it. He was trying to blend in with the workers. She started toward the huge decorated door to ask him not to come to her place of employment asking for her.

"Ms., aren't you supposed to be at work?" A security guard asked. She turns around as he beckons her to the thick glass panel. But she ignores him, she needed her job.

She gives Bea money for the vending machine and pull out Bea's books since she is being homeschooled and sits her in the employee's lounge. This hotel is too big for Bea to follow her until late at night.

Her supervisor vigorously enters the employee's lounge room, "Jan, the owner, Mr. Cargill, wants to see you in the main Emperor's Suite!" Mathis said excitedly.

Ana is puzzled, she heard the owner was here but why he would he want to see her? From her experience the boss only want to see you for one thing and that's to tell you you're fired. The head of her department had already warned them to be precise and crisp until he departs.

"Sweetie, eat your dinner mommy will check on you at 8:30." She says to Bea whose name is now Brittany. Bea has cast her school books aside and is already absorbed in the cartoons on the chips. She takes the staff elevator tube to the 125 floor. Usually it's only reserved for supervisors to use to go up to the Emperor's Suite. After walking down the long hallway after the elevator operator turns the key to open the door and leave her alone—key entrance is the only way to access this area- she isn't sure rather to knock or run. The Emperor's Suite covered the entire top floor. But she turned fully forward to face their future; she nervously smoothed out her already crisp uniform against her body, swallowed her pride, and rang the bell instead.

The woman who answered looks her up and down literally and openly ostracizes her. The woman's outfit cost more than she makes in a year.

"Come in. Ashton wants to talk to you," the beautiful bleached platinum blonde says. "The office is down the hall. She softly raps and seems as through to her something changes; she can't explain it but she is certain something changed. The stranger behind the desk looks vaguely familiar but yet again she has never seen this man before in her life. He is holding a paper folder, which is something rarely used anymore. Paper folders became obsolete centuries ago. She knows it's hers.

"Have a seat, Ms. Whitaker," He says rather indifferently. She sits as far from him as she can get. "I called you because we got several complaints on you, do you enjoy working here?" He asked as if bored with her, the interview, the whole shebang.

"Yes sir, I enjoy working here. Sir, I don't know what complaints there could possibly be." She said firmly. Now he looks directly at her and seems to have forgotten what he intended to ask her. He frowns and looks away and re-reads the report. He lays the report aside and looks point blankly at her, "Ms., I like to know who is working for me. So what's your real name? Nothing exists under the name Jan Whitaker nor the id number belonging to that name. You've no fingerprints, you are wearing silvernite contacts to prevent iris scans, we did a face recognition and came up blank. I don't care what you have done. Just so long as you are honest with me. Now, who are you really??"

Remembering what she was taught in the cave about shutting down, not allowing anyone to spiritually scan you, she rigidly shut down, "I have spent the last five years or so at home as a housewife until my husband and I divorced." This was the same story she told Libya, the head of housekeeping who took her on mainly because of Bea.

He sighed, rubbed his frowned brow in mild vexation and leaned back in the chair. "Ms. Whitaker, I'll give you three days to provide me with proper identification; if you can't or won't I'll have to let you go. If you like working here as you say then you'll be honest with me."

"What complaints are there, sir?" She asked knowing they'd found her again.

He hands her a complaint list, the list is endlessly long. "Some of these things are not my job requirements. I've no authority to check anyone in nor complete any transaction."

"I'm aware of that Ms. Whitaker which is why I'm asking you to be honest with me. I'm trying to find out why are you being blacklisted, blackballed? I hope you know what means?"

Of course she knew what it meant. She have lived it for years. Taking jobs far below her educational level and expertise. Ana knew from experience with hedonistic, hard-ass bosses this man really didn't give a shit about her no matter how sympathetic he appeared. She has been through this with countless bosses.

"Sir, I'm telling you the truth. If you can't believe me then I shall resign now for there's nothing more to say." He politely but indifferently pushed an electronic resignation board across the desk for her to sign; she doesn't sign it, signatures can be traced.

"Ms," he says more aggravated than before. "The only way I'm paying you cash is you sign the release form, after you sign I could care less who you are."

"He's one a rude, nasty ass bastard", she thinks as she takes the pad, scribbles her signature and accept the $1,000 dollar bill. He said he didn't have change. She takes it and hurries out. She nearly bumps into the woman who let her in. The woman trotted to the door in high heels with her and slammed it behind her. The door slam was completely and totally uncalled for.

Running down the hall to the main elevator she calls Bea on her phone, telling her to meet her downstairs in the lobby, don't go outside. She's no longer an employee here so she can ride any service she damn well please. So she rides down with the customers. She slows down walking through the lobby to Bea and the moment she's close enough she grabs Bea's hand and keeps walking. She knows they're out there waiting for her. She pulls a smaller gun out and holds it under her arm.

As she fled speedwalking she heard someone calls her real name. She pushed Bea behind her, turned quickly, and aimed; it was the man who invited her to lunch. He stopped and held up his hands.

"Ana, get out of here. They're coming to kill you. I don't want the same thing to happen to you that happened to my mother." he says, looking around for whomever. He stuffed an envelope of money in her tote and ran in the opposite direction.

Intuition told her to pack the car this evening because last night she was told the boss would be here today and she knew anytime a boss or owner shows up there is always going to be some shite about something. They jumped in the car and burnt rubber getting out of the luxury parking garage. She was prepared to ram that automatic guard bar to get out if the garage guards started any crap about paying a parking fee. She always studied every city to find the safest route out without drawing unwanted police attention. She is taking Broadway straight out to an old depreciated suburban neighborhood road; she hit the expressway detour ramp flying at about 95 MHP exiting onto the expressway about 5 miles from the downtown exit, she saw in her rearview mirror lights flashing behind her. She pushed the car up to 125 and expertly wove in and out of traffic like a weaver at a loom. She knew they were after her. It isn't those on the ground that worry her; it is those above in the sky. They love their spotlight shows ordering you to pull over. Horns are blaring at her but she refuses to let up. She pushed Trusty up to 149 and outran a semi who honked at her. She didn't know if it was good or bad and didn't have time to analyze the meaning.

About 40 miles down the road they were finally alone; she asked Bea how much they had? "$6,000" Bea quipped happily. Sensing the money was tagged she told her to put in the iron money case in the back under her seat. Not wanting Bea to unbuckle at this speed she pulled over and did it herself.

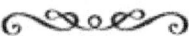

Ashton had gone back to the main part of the suite and was seated comfortably with his main harem when his wristwatch beeps telling him there's a match for the signature. He can barely believe his eyes when he reads it along with the photo. There must a mistake. Machines aren't perfect. He double checked. The handwriting, the calligraphic psychosomatic report comes back the same. It matches the sample he got from her brothers some time ago. Knowing she is next to impossible for him to trace spiritually he teleports downstairs. The security cameras show her tearing out the garage like a mad hellbat flying out of Hades. He sends his people in the direction she has gone.

Fuck! Why didn't he recognize her?? When he looked at her in person she looked like someone totally different. Heaven is fogging his mind big time. Why is it so important he stay away from her? He isn't the one trying to kill her....Vonderbilt is! So why don't they cloud Vonderbilt's mind on her identity? Dammit, he doesn't have wings anymore so he can't soar after her. He calls for a hovercraft.

While awaiting the needed aircraft to arrive, Dawn hurried downstairs, "Where are you going?!" she asked, very nearly hysterical. He realized Dawn knew who she was. Carole Caldwell had probably shown her her a picture many times. Dawn or Carol was who placed all the complaints.

"You knew who she was, that's why you wanted to come to this hotel. Did Carole or James Caldwell tell you where she was?" he asked grabbing and shaking her. "You better pray I find her or not be able to find you when I get back." He snarled, swiftly crossing the munificent lobby, taking the awaiting vehicle himself without awaiting a driver.

❧

Dawn re-entered the Emperor's Suite and burst into tears. She informs the others he's gone after that bitch, again. The forgetful potion Caroline gave them which she swore Nikola enhanced but Dawn doubted it, it worked but not for long. Somehow he still found out who she was.

"This is totally ludicrous." Delores cried tossing the thin glass against the wall; the fine shards splattered everywhere. "How did he possibly break through that easily?"

One of the others had grown weary of the game, it wasn't fun and games anymore. It was fun to poke fun at or ridicule the woman who was winning without even trying. Now, seeing herself back at her old job as a sales clerk the fun was deflated out of the game.

"We might as well face reality." Shaula says weary. "He's in love with that woman. We all need to start thinking about another way to support our lifestyles. Because if he comes back with her tonight we are all outdoors. There's no way he's letting her learn about us. We all knew the deal coming in."

Several grunt at the notion, especially Dawn. "I'm not going anywhere. I've been with him for over a quarter of a century. That little bitch is not putting me out of my home."

Shaula shook her head in disbelief at the absurdity of Dawn's claim. "Bitch, are you dumb, stupid, or what? We don't mean a bean pie to him. He probably has had thousands of groups like us. I hope you've saved some of your allowance in these last 25 years. I bought me a nice little house in Northern Nevada cause I knew this day would come. Dawn, you ain't never going to be his wife no matter much you think you'll be." Shaula laughed and Dawn slapped her. Shaula slugs her a good one before Superior and the others pull them apart although most agreed with Shaula.

Dawn calls Carole to tell her the potion did not work for long. "It worked long enough for him to fire her about your complaints." Dawn laughed but remembered he can be in the room and you not sense him. Carole blames Ana for what Vonderbilt did to them is why she agreed to help Dawn rid Ashton of his crazy fascination with Ana. He has been too close to finding and keeping her for the past three years.

Meanwhile, Ashton knows he's close, he can feel her but she is being hidden from him. "Ana, I'm not here to hurt you." He says softly as he walks in the area where he feels her. "I know you can hear me. So please step out of cloak so I can prove to you I'm nothing like Vonderbilt."

Still no sound nor appearance.

"Ana...I know who you're running from and why. I'll give you anything you want. Baby, you can't keep running like this forever. Eventually, they'll catch you." He doesn't know for sure if angels are cloaking them but suspects they are, nor does he knows he's right outside her window. He looks different again and that's one of the reasons she doesn't trust him.

An angel appears before him, "Leave my subject alone. I'll not let you defile her." He knows this is her guardian angel and guardian angels can be a violent, vicious bunch when it comes to their beloved children.

"Angel, you need to do something about that dead body she tried to bury in a shallow grave. I'm not the enemy here. You know as well as I she can't keep running like this. You know what will happen if Vonderbilt or Machiavelli or whatever he hell his is calling himself at the moment catches her. Unless you've been given authority to intervene, which I doubt you have. You know they'll kill her as easily as they've killed many before her."

Despite his true argument the angel of the Lord refuses to move from between him and Ana. "I know very well of your philandering and obnoxiousness." The glowing angel with varicolored beautiful features assured him.

Ashton throws his arms up in the air in frustration and yells, he feels like punching this guy. As if this is the time and place to bring up his shortcoming. Pointing at the body lying 500 years away he cries, "Glowhead! You've far bigger problems to worry about than if I intend to sleep with her or not or if I intend to be rude or if I'll break her heart. Get your head out the clouds. If the authorities catch her she's done for; she's wanted for murder, assault, thief by deception, you name it, she's wanted for it. There are several serious warrants out for her arrest. So right now, I surely think I'm the least of your concerns."

Another angel appears, he recognize from the statute he is from the order of realms patrol. They guards portal and the separation of heaven and hell or earth and other worlds and hell.

"I agree Ashton if that's whom you're called nowadays. You've made your point but the orders we were given are to keep you away from her." The brawny angel with sterling white wings said. The first one with feminine attributes agrees. Ana steps from behind the cloak and the multifaceted glowing one steps in front of her. He was right. This one belonged to Ana. Ashton chuckles, wondering what does this angel thinks he

570

plan to do to her?

"All I want to do is talk to her." Ashton pleas.

"Your talking usually leads to lewd things." The brawny one says. He didn't rebuttal the angel, he reaches out for her; her angel slaps his hand down.

"No touching," her commanded. The angel was upset that he didn't recognize her so that means he doesn't really love her. Ashton abides and laces his hands behind his back.

"Ms. BuFaye, I believe that's your real name. Vonderbilt is very dangerous man and is very angry at you right now. They believe you killed their top hit man. The authorities are looking for you for numerous crimes. I apologize for my behavior at the hotel. You and your kid can move into any of my hotels. I'll see to it that no one touches nor harm you."

Ana steps closer to him and asked, "And what then, when I refuse to sleep with you or if I do and you grow tired of me. You'll throw us out like old trash. And then I'll be at their mercy again. No thank you. I'd rather die at least with my dignity intact."

To him, her reasoning sounded so much like her prudent angel and made about as much sense. But then again, when has something not making sense ever stopped him? What good was dignity when you are hungry and cold or worse, dead? So he tries again to reach her.

"Listen lady, they know where you are, they sent someone after you. More than likely the person is chipped. They'll easily find him. While we're out here in these woods talking about dignity, honor, and righteousness they're searching for whomever that person is out there in that shallow grave. Like I told you back at the hotel, I don't care what you've done, I want to help you. You've a child to think about. All of this isn't just about you. What kind of life is this for a child, sleeping in a car a few yards from a dead body? She'll grow up so traumatized she'll never be able to function normally," he says, cognizing someone has offered her help in the past but demanded sex in return.

Reading her open thoughts while he dug a deeper hole with his hands to hide the body, since her angel was ignoring it. "Sorry, sweet cheeks-that's usually how it works. Even in the glorified institution of marriage. Stop sleeping with a husband and see how much financial support you get. People like to sugar coat everything which usually ends up causing more harm than good."

"What's in this offer for you? Nothing is free, everything comes with a price." She quizzed him face to face, her beautiful, angelic face turned looking him directly in the eyes. She was so beautiful in the dim moonlight filtering through the trees. He knew he was on sure fast-track to breaking down her ornery resistance. He could see the weariness in her blood-chapped eyes. He can also see she's tired and worn. Tired of running, tired of killing, tired of being a victim. His words are like an ambrosia to her. He felt an overwhelming desire to hold her, protect her from harm. The feeling stunned him he backed away. But he also knew that had to wait, airhounds were looking for her.

Suddenly, he heard from afar the whooshing of air pushed by a projector as of an approaching aircraft, then an authority hovercraft shines a brilliant spotlight down on them. "GET THE FUCK OUT OF HERE!" He yells at the patrol-hover. After realizing who is speaking they turn around immediately and head back to the city. When he looks around back at ground level Ana and the angels are gone. In a vindictive rage, he runs swiftly through the woods, breaking trees in his path and thunderously trampling foliage under his feet and when under the hovercraft he leaps and punches the belly of it, sending it spiraling out of control crashing in a fiery ball of metal and glass. He walks back to his own vehicle in a consuming rage. "The fumbling pieces of shit, the mentally devoid miscreants spoiled three years worth of work. I was breaking her down. Her free will to come to me would've trumped anything the angels had to say!" He screams to the emptiness surrounding him before roaring the engine of his vehicle to life and slamming the steering wheel with his palm, breaking it. He set it on automatic steering.

"UN-fucking-believable!" He angrily rants as he set the vehicle on autopilot steering to sail to it's designation. He's so blind with rage and fury he doesn't wait for the craft to land, he bails out over the hotel and punch a jagged hole through the roof. Cement and steel rains down around him. The occupants fled to another room.

"Those bitches better be gone when I get in there." His rage fogged mind thinks. He can hear sound of feet wearing heels running throughout the suite.

"DAWN! ALL YOU BITCHES GET YOUR ASSES IN HERE!!" He yells so loud the room quivered like a minor quake was afoot. Everyone is hiding, even the staff. "IF I HAVE SAY IT TO AGAIN, I'M LEVELING THIS MOTHERFUCKING PLACE! TAKING OUT EVERYONE WITH IT!" He yells, shaking the building again. Slowly everyone emerged from hiding. Dawn emerges last. She has seen him angry countless times but nothing like this. She didn't know he was capable of shaking the whole freaking building. He's on fire, none had ever seen his entire body on fire.

"All of you get the fuck out of my sight before I kill every single one of you," he growls a low, animalistic snarl. Everyone makes a stealthily exit out the destroyed suite. No one has ever seen his *eyes* on fire. Burning out of the socket.

When alone he thrashes the place, destroying priceless artifacts. He is angry at everyone including Ana BuFaye. He knew he remembered her from somewhere but could not conjure the knowledge of where. Had not she been so fucking paranoid they could be somewhere relaxing, discussing her and her child's future by now.

He was angry at himself for allowing himself to be stunned by her. She has this sweet magnetism that doesn't exactly inspire sexual arousal or attraction but is the Aura of Unconditional Love. He decided then and there he was going to make her his. His own voice of reason is screaming in his brain to give up the pursuit. You can't win against Heaven.

He was unaware his archenemies was watching and mirthfully enjoying the fall out, especially Nikola. At least he knew it was true. He now knew the water of Lethe at least worked for a while.

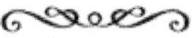

The seven huddled together in the limo headed to the L.A. palace to discuss their futures. The still vacillating of the powerful engine was all that was felt, for the seven, everything else was somewhat numb. Having to face the reality of their inadequacies in trying to hold on to a lifestyle with nothing substantial to validate their claims was slowly sinking in. Even Dawn had to admit she miscalculated the imperiousness of their predicament. She had never seen him like this. Her plan utterly backfired. Caroline Caldwell promised her Ashton wouldn't recognize her. But guess what? He did. Now Ana has ran away again like a loon and he's blaming everyone but her neourpsycahtic ass. Had Ana screwed him and he gave her a few millions, she'd be happy, he'd be happy. Everybody would be fucking happy. But noooo, she just knows she pulled some of that fucking church lady bullshit on him, crying out like those moronic damsels in those idiotic Victorian romance novels.

"I think we should go home, give him time to calm down." Dawn suggested.

Maleah asked, "After today, exactly where is home? If you haven't bought a house or condo, then you've no home. That woman might as well be here with us from the influence she has on how he behaves." Shaula nods and takes another sip of the champagne. This carrousel of emotions was utmost exhausting.

"What's his daughter's name?" Delores asked.

"Venice or Veniana or something like that," Dawn remembers. She snatches Dawn's ISPAD and hit the instance call button and a feminized version of Ashton's smoky sultry voice answers.

"Hello, honey," Delores says lacing her voice with grave concern making an arable agenda to approach her subject.

"Who is this?" Lavenica Cargill asked.

"This is your father's friend Delores. I'm calling because I'm worried about your father." The woman didn't hang up so Delores continues. "Your father has become very unhealthily obsessed with this witch. Uh, I mean woman. He has even gone to the point of tracking her down, fighting wizards over her; now he is destroying his own property. We fear he is losing grip with reality and may end up back in prison."

"Where is he?" Lavenica sourly asked.

"He's upstairs in the Emperor's suite of the Oklahoma City Cargill Imperial Hotel. He's raving like a madman."

"Thanks," Lavenica says teleporting to the given location, it probably nothing but him pitching a fit on his concubines. But she felt she'd better check on him.

Clinking off the phone Delores smiles, thinking, *"Mission accomplished."* But devilishly relishing a naughty thought, "E*verytime that bitch kiss him she'll be tasting my pussy."*

Every one was alert; intensively waiting, listening, and wanting to know what his daughter said. "She said she would take good care of papa, we all can go home." Delores lies.

Lavenica Cargill exited in the demolished suite; there were shards of metal and glass everywhere. Live sparking, bare wires which looked like exposed multicolored veins crackled with electricity as the morning dew dampened them. She stepped purposefully over the hazards and walked through the debris in the enormous Emperor's Suite remembering the last time her father went nuts he went on a debilitating path of destruction causing the angels to lock him away for years. She had to curb that for she may not be alive to see his return shall that happen again and all would fail. Her brother wasn't the business man their father was and she didn't care to deal with the outside world. She was remembering the pain of seeing the angel take him away after he killed a lot of people. It's said he killed an entire village. So yes, she had to reach him and make him understand.

"Father, where are you?" She calls out because he's blocking her connection to him. Fearing he had gone completely mad and the angels have chained him again, she hurries through the suite. She finds him in a back bedroom sitting in a chair facing the still standing glass wall staring into the dying night. The darkness beyond the wall reflected his face to her and it was like living stone. "I found her but she slipped right through my fingers." he said sorrowfully without turning to look at her.

"Found who, dad?" She cautiously, but tenderly asked. Times like this one had deal with him delicately. He was an explosion of emotions; the least thing, anything, could set him off again.

"The one I'm supposed to be with. The one I haven't been able to remember. There was a stronger connection between us than between your mother and I. No pun meant, for I truly loved Etula." Ashton explains. "I loved your mother very much but with Ana it's different. She's my other half as no one has ever been to me. I don't expect you to understand what I'm saying."Lavenica feels a pang of jealousy and betrayal of the memory of her mother to hear him say there's someone he loves more than MOM. So maybe this Delores is right perhaps a powerful witch has enchanted him.

Not sure of his mental state she proceeds with precaution. She sees the hard liquor by his chair. She knelt beside him and softly and carefully asked "Where is this woman?"

He throws his head back glancing sorrowfully up at the still integral ceiling, his hair falls in waves of curls behind the back of the chair as he stared absently at his destruction. "Angels took her away."

"Oh, Dad...I'm sorry, I didn't know your friend died." Lavenica says but was somewhat relieved.

"No, I don't mean that kind of "*taking away.*" I mean they took her away to another location. Hid her. As far as I know she could be on Mars by now." He said, downing the last of the dark brown liquid in glass.

Lavenedica hated to see her father drinking. He didn't get drunk in a mortal sense but it sometime affected his moods.

"Is she an immortal?" Lavenica asked, mistily remembering her mother cussing her father out about a woman she said came to him in the still of the night like an apparition. She came out of nowhere.

"No, she's mortal, but she's my better half. Whom I need in order to heal." He says, rising to refill his glass. Her dad isn't making any sense. How can a mortal who lived in the late 1700's-early 1800's still be alive today? Dad is losing it again. This is how it all started years ago.

"Dad, you need to go to *your* Father for healing."

Ashton laughed a cruel but small, sad laughter. "Yeah, righttt! My Father forsook me eons ago. Why go to Him? So He can throw my ass in chains again? No thank you, sugar. But I'm glad you still duly believe in your Grandfather."

Lavenica gently puts her arms around his shoulders and lays her head on his chest, he gently pats her head covered with dark thick hair so much like his own as he did when she was a small child. While listening to his doleful heart beat she says, "Dad, come home with me, to people who loves you." Without waiting for a reply she teleports them both out. She can clearly see he's on the brink of full collapse.

～∞∞∞～

They ended up in a decent hotel room in southern Oregon. The damp peacefulness of the Pacific Ocean moisturized the air, gentle breezes kissed their faces like a shy lover. The milder climate was what they needed. Their room wasn't half bad, at least cockroaches weren't 80% of the building's structure. She wanted to ask the angels questions before they disappeared. She hated it when they did that. It was like they sensed her questions coming and disappeared. Why do they always do that? Now she has a lot of question but no one to answer them. She can't even remember what the man, her boss, looked like nor why was it so important that she talked to him. But she felt his grief, it rips her heart into a sorrow too deep to cry. She stares out at the crowd of vacationers hoping to see him among them. She knows it's silly but what does she've left besides hope. And even hope was now a fleeting reminder of what once was and will never be. A lost fruition that will never reach it's crowning. One can survive with many things lost but hope is not one of them.

She slightly frowned looking out to sea; pondering. For she was trying to envision the man who helped her escape. She clearly remembers the man who asked her for a lunch date; she remembers him putting money in her open tote telling her to run like hell. She didn't have to be told twice. So this man's mother was one of those frozen people in that creepy ass basement? Why would he do that for her?! So, was he Vonderbilt's son? If so, he feared Nikola as much as she. It chagrined her for not seeing the resemblance, but too often her mind, body, and spirit are so exhausted she moves on autonomous rather than reasoning.

She sensed the buxom blonde woman she saw in that man's office suite (her boss) wanted her dead so badly she was salivating at thought of standing over her dead body. Why? She didn't know the woman. She acted more like a jealous wife listening at the door to see if her husband was going to hit on the new girl.

Here they are in a strange city she didn't get the opportunity to drive around and plan an escape route with a lot of unanswered questions and no one to ask. She couldn't call Mother Harris, she knows that line is tapped. They took their phones when they entered the cave and she doesn't know the new numbers. With the cost of living today this money on hand might last them a month so she better check out the local job market and if there's nothing here move on to the next largest city. Large cities offered a better chance to get lost in the crowd.

"C'mon Pumpkin, let's go get something to eat." Right then, looking down at Bea, she pasted on the happy face, portraying the idea she felt pretty good, the sun was shinning, she'd 6 grand and some in their coffer. Most don't know this but if you've ever been scared, tired, and weary long enough your emotions convert to physical pain and a mere few minutes absence of these constant companions felt like ecstasy.

Gianna Machiavelli industriously wanted to know how she escaped this time? "The police said Cargill was out in the woods with her." Jarvis Jr. explained.

Deeply pondering, Gianna was in a languorous inertia state, barely listening while Jarvis Jr. explains the details of his encounter with Ana.

"Great! Oh fucking great! He found her, again. Then we might as well forget it. No talisman or Lethe Waters in the known world or next can confine that crazy fucker. Look what he did to his own building. What did you say to her outside the parking garage?" Gianna asked suspiciously, staring at Jarvis Jr. hard and coldly. Wondering did he warn Ana? He knew Jarvis Jr. knew he was a Machiavelli. The mirror told him that. He also knew the younger man knows what happened to his mother. A Machiavelli or not shall he catch him lying, he will be laid to rest beside his frozen mommy.

"I was merely reminding her of our date and she pulled out a gun." Jarvis Jr. lied. He knew they were spying on him.

Boris laughed. "See! I told she was crazy but you wouldn't listen. Cargill killed our Oklahoma man and according to Cadwell, Cargill's whores says she isn't with him. Sooo, that mean we're back in business. The hunt is back on." Boris laughed and looked at Gianna for the signal to proceed. Jarvis Jr. flinched inwardly but remained outwardly unagitated. Cringing around his family was as dangerous as grimacing in front of a high officer of the old Third Reich.

"Yeah, y'all did say she was dangerous," Jarvis Jr. laughed weakly.

"And had you gone out with her, you would be who they're pulling out the dirt now. Jarvis, she's Nikola's opposite and just as wild and crazy. So next time, leave the dirty work to us, you just keep your nose to the running of the castle like your old man." Gianna advised.

Jarvis Jr. watched Gianna from his marginal vision in the back of the luxury limo and finally saw not only was Gianna his uncle but his blood brother. He long suspected Jarvis Sr. was his old man, too. No, that can't be right. The three of them looks like various versions of Nikola. Not that it mattered for in their covert world. Parentage wasn't important, only loyalty to the dark master is what's important. He has wanted out of that castle he was born into for years and has been secretly studying the bible. A book Nikola allows no one to dare look at. He wasn't alone. Many of their members didn't know their mothers, only their fathers if they knew a parent at all. Hmm, that sounds familiar. From what he records Christendom is the only major faith teaches the acknowledgment of mothers is important, too. So this stark fact makes him questions just who *really* found the others? When so many of their patriarchal practices are so similar to those of the faith of his birth. In secret he has questioned why are the practices so similar but serve different masters? They both are very misogynistic; the bible and other so called holy books eliminated nearly female name. Every female name is merely a womb of "begats" just the satanic structure does? Why is that?

"Jarvis J. I'm talking to you." Bjors said, shaking his shoulder roughly. Jarvis is secrectly said to have gotten the ability to trance out from Nikola. So what if he knew he was a Machiavelli. Half of the staff is.

"Yes?" Jarvis Jr. recollecting himself as Boris and Bjors stared at hard and mean him. Searching for betrayal. Grounds to kill.

"I said, the blood of a saint is sweet, what would you like to do to her when we catch her? I intend to savor her blood and make her suffer." Boris dreams.

"Make love to a woman for once." Jarvis Jr. said looking equally as frigid back at the two. His black eyes matching their own bored levelly back into their souls. Seeing he had more of Nikola in him than imperviously assumed the two back down a bit, knowing he wouldn't be as easy to kill as presumed.

"You two brutes ought to try it sometime. It's a lot more fun than rutting like an animal. Man was intended to make love. Only animals merely fuck."

Bjors and Boris stared at him a few seconds and guffawed, ribbing each other. Accusing him of having grown a vagina. But Gianna quietly watches the three from his corner seat, he knows what happened. Ana is what happened. He vows to never let that siren touch him. If she could make Nikola love her, then she can turn any of them into a melting puddle of emotions.

The ancient Orient stone castle was built in 457 B.C. but later converted to modern living. It sits high and lofty above the Yellow River. Occasionally, the yellowish mud tinted the waters, most mortals never lived long enough to see the waters run clear. Over the centuries the river changes, its gradual blend of orange to brownish yellow hue highlighted unusually moving tints and shades from light to dark before becoming clear. It was peaceful to watch as the sun sets and lends the waters a dazzling ombré shade.

From the late 1700's to the early 1800's this was the only piece of her father's vast estate the thieves hadn't stolen from them because they didn't know it existed. After her escape from slavery she caught a schooner on it's way to China in the 1800's and has been here since. Lavenica Cargill Hendricks was brought here as a child by her father, those were the days before the tumultuous affairs and distrust loomed in their household. Her parents were happy and in love. Her mother name her Dontella but she renamed herself Lavenedica but everyone called her Lavenica. Only her father and brother knew her birth-name. Her brother Ashley never changed his name. He looked like a white guy with a tan, so he didn't have to. Her mother was a raving beauty from a small village outside a place called Erienque, Ethiopia. A raving beauty she was not. She looked too much like her dad to fit that slot. Unfortunately she didn't inherit her mother's looks. Dammit, she even sounds like him. Everyone always said she was a daddy's girl. So she guesses she is. Her brother was always more attached to their mother. Whom she thinks he resembled a lot. But as he ages, he looks more and more like dad. Dad didn't exactly look like a Caucasian. His golden olive, brown complexion looked like no race she never seen among humanity. He always told them his features belongs to no race of Adam's children for he wasn't Adam's child as they were.

The few who knew what her father were often forced her to defend his name. People always spoke about her father's evil side as if they were sweet innocent little lambs and big bad dad just came out of nowhere and beat the shit outta them. She've seen and lived the depth of human evil and the evil within, it was all them, there was no spiritual influence. The only influence was money. The Middle Passage was literally hell on earth and slavery unbearable. She watched the weak perish and be thrown away like feces.

Being a Nephilim, which is really a derogatory term for her kind, enabled her to escape and bring the man she loved with her. He died centuries ago and so did their children, these here with her now are about 115 generations descendants of her original children. But five are her own children by latter husbands.

She isn't defending her dad's evil ways but if people knew he was evil what did they go over to where he was for? She knew the slave master was evil and you literally couldn't throw her in a room with the evil bastard. Like those heifers who lived with him now always calling her when he's beating their asses about something. She's even tried to help some leave him but they always go right back to him with some asininity about love and he didn't mean it. Yes, he did. It has nothing to do with love. They didn't want another woman taking their place. That's another thing she never figured out. Why do these stupid women line up to live with dad? Like the dizzy bitch, Dawn, that called her a while ago crying about dad and some imaginary woman. "He has made me have an abortion three times but this bitch he said if he knocked her up he would take care of her and their baby? That's not fair!" Going on and on about how long her dad rode her. As if she wanted to hear that?

Years ago, detesting her father's prurient pattern of courtesan concubines, lovers, and mistresses gathering (and some she had no idea what they were to him other than a bed or fuck buddy), she used to try and encourage them to leave him. Some even accused her of wanting to keep him alone in memory of her dead mother. All said he wasn't mean to them but just was never faithful. So nowadays, she is over seven hundred years old and people dumb down over the years. She let him and his harems be. She isn't going to spend her last few years dealing with his women. The red haired one included.

She didn't have the privation to but felt it was the right thing to do. She asked her why don't she leave him? Dawn acted like she had spit in her face. "I'm not going to work, I was not made for that life! To be getting all sweaty, dirty, and stressed out and be looking all old and bad." Dawn cried. She wonders what those 56 lazy heifers are going to do when dad run this woman down and if she loves him in return? It's plain as this radiant orange and yellow sunset he loves her. He has been here a week and barely said two words, the grave expatiation of his depression bothers her. He doesn't have to eat. But his drinking is getting excessive and he roams the spiritual worlds when drinking. In her opinion, that's as bad as drunk driving. He is an immortal but they can suffer depression just as mortals. She decided to walk his time-line to see if she could find this damn woman. It can't possibly be the same woman mom cussed him out about. That was well over 700 years ago! But the calamity to logic, she couldn't explain the strands of long kinky auburn hair she saw on his twin pillow the other morning. She had gone in to check on him and change his sheets and sensed someone incorporeal had been there. She picked up the hair to use it as a focus point, a finding device but sent the maid in to clean the room. She wasn't touching sheets her Dad had been rumpling around on with some woman. She remember her mother said the home-wrecker had long dark red hair.

She walks out on the stone imperial styled balcony towering over the ledge of the slow river's yellowish embankment and kisses her father on the cheek.

"How you feeling?' She asked, trying to hide her disapproval in his drinking.

"Much better, dear, thanks for asking."

She thinks "*I'm sure you're feeling much better...now that that homewrecker has visited you.*"

Having never been one to mince words; she bluntly asked her father did he have a visitor?

"No, no one has been here," Ashton relied, puzzled about his daughter's question.

"Dad, uh um, I think you have. The other day when I came to check on you. To make sure you were alright I found these on the other pillow. I also pulled these long strands from between your fingers."

She showed him but didn't tell him these weren't all of them. She kept some for finding this woman to tell her to love her father or leave him the fuck alone. To quit playing with his heart. To quit with these childish mind games. To grow up and behave like a grown woman.

Ashton held his hand out commanding her to give him the strands.

"No, dad. These mind games have got to stop! This woman came between you and mom, now she's back at her same old games. This isn't a person, this is some kinda demon, only a demon would do this to someone. And you of all people should know the games demons play!"

Listening to Dontella's intense ranting he knew Ana had been here. Had she found him and it wasn't a dream that he made consuming, sweet love to her? He remembers entwining his finger in her hair as he moved deeper in her. He remembers her clawing his back as she arched hers toward him. He remember her quivering as his tongue flickered her nipples playfully. He remembers her sweet, salty taste when she came as his tongue played between her legs. He remembered the shape of those beautiful legs spreading to receive him.

"Dad! I'm talking to you!" Lavenedica cried, noticing the nearly invisible, nearly healed welts on the side of his neck. She watched his hand move unconsciously to the love welts on his neck. She hated to imagine where else those marks resided.

"Dad, please! Listen to me! For the sake of your own sanity, please send her away the next time she visits. We all have our sins to answer for and I think you've paid for yours and many others, many times over; if this a punishment or test....resist the evil temptation. Stop punishing yourself."

He looks at her seriously concerned face and promised he would send her away if she visited again. Dontella was right, this couldn't continue or he would go mad. He would have to find the strength somewhere, somehow to resist her. Even as he said it he knew the memory of Ana's visit would fade and he would remember her no more. Her name, face, physique, taste, would all fade into the deep, dark abyss of time. It always does only to continue to resurface in a mockery of the cruelest kind.

Satisfied that her father was feeling better and out of the dangerous zone she kissed his cheek again and told him the kitchen had prepared raffin fish. She knew this was one of the few things he liked if prepared correctly. She hadn't told him she had those women put out those houses until he was better. She knew they'd plunge and raffle through all the papers and records...quite frankly she didn't trust the lot of them. Anyone willingly sell themselves as they've done in her opinion can not be trusted. It's all about money. There's a difference if a woman has to sell herself in order to survive but this isn't the case. They do it for fame, fortune and wealth.

Returning to her private living quarters she set out to find this wayward red haired temptress and put a stop to her playing with her father's mind and heart. Enough is enough! If it's the same immortal or timewalker succubus then it was she who started her family on the path to decline and destruction causing them to end up parentless and her to end up in slavery. So yes, she had an axe to grind with her. She calms down, takes a deep breath and concentrates on the owner of the strands of auburn hair. The Neutral Zone opens up, she steps through, and follows the silvery thread leading back to the owner. She steps out in a neat little room, it's small but tidy. The woman turns around quickly and pushes the dark-amber freckled eyed child behind her. The girl's eyes were a lot like her own. She sensed her father's essence in the child.

"Oh fuck! Dad didn't tell me I'd a little sister. Little wonder this woman keeps coming to him! Oh well, the palaces all over the world are filled of paintings of my long dead siblings. But this is the first alive one I've ever seen. How old is she? About five or six!!?"

"Who are you and what do you want?!" Ana asked holding the gun on the woman whose eyes looked like jewels.

"Can you send the child in the bathroom, what I came to say is not suitable for a child to hear." Lavenedica said icily.

Ana moved toward the bathroom still shielding Bea, placing her in the bathroom and closing the door. The amazonian woman stood her distance until Ana turned to address her again.

"I came to tell you to love my father or leave him the hell alone. In the very early 1800's you single-highhandedly wrecked my parents' marriage and yet you're still at your same infantile game of fucking and leaving him. I'll not stand by and let you do that again to him. Destroy him. Your desultory actions will cease on this day. Here is how I found you. You left a calling card," Lavenedica said, holding up the strand of hair folded in a fine embroidered linen handkerchief.

"I do not know who your father is," Ana said calmly.

Lavenedica laughed a grotty laugh. This woman is either wackier than dad or a little sweet liar.

"Obviously whatever you were doing with him was so aggravated he pulled your hair out and you've have a child for him and you don't know who he is??!! Lady, pleassse! You're either whack or a liar! Which one is it?"

Ana was getting mad. She didn't appreciate being accused of something when she had no idea what she was being accused of. She dreamed she went to a man. Is this is his daughter? Well, the woman called him father. So apparently....she is his daughter.

"Look! Amazon Lady, I don't know what you're talking about and right about now-- don't care. I"m sorry about your parents' problems but I wasn't alive in the 1800's to cause anyone any problems so you're barking at the wrong tree. And Thad Wyett isn't old enough to be your father."

Again, Lavenedica laughed and walked closer to Ana who raised the gun, leveling it at the woman's head, warning the Amazon she wasn't afraid to use it.

Lavenica had seen enough killers to know this woman was one. Boy, her dad really knows how to pick them! "How do you explain your child having my father's essence and your hair being in his hands *if* you don't know him. Oh well, you probably don't know his name."

"What's his name?" Ana asked, not liking at all what this gorgeous multi-hued hair Amazon is implying and avariciously calling her. The half-immortal woman was definitely of African descent just as herself but was mixed with something

586

unidentifiable.

"It isn't my place to tell you his name being that he obviously haven't told you. But I'm curious, tell me. Make me understand. How can you sleep with a man again and again and not know his name? For some unknown reason his care for you doesn't extend to him telling you his name nor supporting his child. But I see, you're just like all the others, only after his money. Apparently he isn't giving you nor his kid any if you're living in this dump." Lavenedica said looking around distastefully at the small common room comparing it to her lavish Oriental palace. She came prepared to hate the woman but seeing what sorry state she was in, she pitied her. This woman honesty believes her father loves her and sadly doesn't see he is only using her. He'll never do anything about her plight except summon her when he's aroused. And this woman is too gullible to see she means nothing to him. She's just like all the others. He's merely using her for sex which she sadly misdiagnose as love.

Ana fired above her head piercing the ceiling. The woman appeared surprised Ana would actually fire the gun.

"Don't you dare come up in my place calling me names! You know nothing about me!" Ana yelled quickly returning the aim to the woman's head.

"I know enough to know you destroyed my family, my dad was taken away, I was kidnapped and sold into slavery. What more I need to know about you! You *Timewalker*? " The woman said the word "timewalker" as if it was a vulgar word. This was Ana's first time ever being referred to by this word.

Neither heard the bathroom door open but both turned and looked when Bea said. "Mean lady! Leave my mommy alone or I'll shoot you in the gut." The child with perfect aim held her small pistol pointed at Lavenedica's midriff.

"Come on out, little sister, it's time you and I got to know each other." Lavenedica said kindly to the child standing in the bathroom doorway. She had a word or two to deliver her dad. Leaving this child in this desiccated life. What was wrong with him?

"I ain't none of your sister." Bea sassed, steadfastly holding her gun with her finger on the trigger. The meanness in the child's eyes reminded her of her father so she knew the child would pull the trigger. What kind of mother allow a child so young access to a gun? This child was too intelligent and accomplished to not be an Nephilim. This bitch has lied about about everything. The child bearing her father's essence is how he keeps finding this woman. Why is she running to and from dad?

"My father has every right to know about his child. You don't have the right to drag her all over creation without telling him. Oh, I see your game. Since he won't marry you you decided to keep this child from him as a punishment." Lavenedica snarled at Ana who opened fire just as she stepped back through the Neutral Zone, bullets waltzed passed her. Ana had had it with strangers and their hostile ass attitudes. Acting as thus she was obligated to accept it. She vowed a few years ago she would obviate all bad attitudes before they blossom into full-blown attacks.

Lavenedica timely saw the killer rage surface in this woman who could move at the speed of a Nephilim is how she avoided getting shot.

Back in China she found her father in the library sitting reading an ancient paper book. She made her grandchildren leave the sitting nook of the huge book lined room and closed the door. "Your wannabe girlfriend is the mother of my very violent little sister. When were you going to tell me I had a little sister who acts like you?" Uncrossing his long muscular legs, Ashton put the book down and says, "You don't have any siblings but Ashley."

Lavenedica was tired of them both lying. She resisted the urge to tell him this woman fired at her. Why? She wasn't quiet sure. She takes the seat opposite him, "Dad, the woman is lying to you. I saw the child. The girl is strong willed and hot-tempered just like you. I scanned your essence in her, how did that happen if she's not your child?" She wasn't letting him worm his way out of his parental responsibilities as a father. Even if he didn't love the mother.

"I don't think you really want to know." Ashton replied asking where did she see them?

"I just left them in a cheap room off the coast of Oregon. Those two crazies shot at me! Hell, that woman doesn't even know your name. How are you pining for a woman who doesn't even know your name? Dad, can't you see? She's a cyprian. Let her go."

He quickly threw the book aside and chastised Lavenedica for approaching them. Fear grips his heart. He adverts a few things about Ana. "She is not a lewd nor licentious person, and most definitely not a prostitute."

"Well, can you explain why she is living in a motel with weapons?" Lavenedica questioned. "That sounds like a lady of the evening protecting herself from johns to me."

Ashton sighs. He was hoping this woman and his beloved daughter would someday meet but not like this. "I love you sweetheart, but you shouldn't gone there. That was a foolish thing to do. When frightened Ana can be dangerous person. She has a lot of evil, corrupted people, malevolent spirits, and demons after her. She could've killed you in a heartbeat."

Lavenedica is seeing a side of her father she had never seen."Dad, are you genuinely in love with this woman? If so why?" She asked, looking him in the eyes, searching for the truth.

He sighs heavily, again, "After serious mediating and sorting through my tangles of emotions. No, I don't think so. I mean I like her, I'm rather fond of her and she has what I need..."

Lavenedica threw up her hands to halt him. "Way too much information."

Ashton chuckled "No, I'm not talking about that need."

"Well, you coulda fooled me." Lavenedica scoffed, disliking this Ana more and more by the minute. She can see plain as day her father is only kidding himself. He's in love with that cyprian named Annie Oakley.

"You see, after my atonement, I didn't walk the straight and narrow line for long. I semi-went back to my old ways. I need healing."

"Dad, the only healings you're going to get from that woman is sexual. She has hidden your daughter from you, so she isn't exactly an honest person."

"That is not my daughter. Had she been, she would here with you and my grandchildren. I stumbled upon the woman one night after heavy drinking and made love to her shortly after the child was conceived. That's how the kid has a small part of my essence. She thought I was her husband."

Lavenedica laughed a cruel laugh he recognized as cruel as his own. "Dad, she knew the difference, she just didn't care. Didn't that tell you something about her character? C'mon dad. Women do not make love to strangers who happen to wander into their bedrooms."

"No, she didn't know. When she saw me in the morning light she screamed, her husband came running." Ashton chuckled softly. Fully reminiscing that morning. "I sobered up quickly and got out of there."

"I'd scream too if I'd just screwed another man in my husband's bed and thought he was coming to beat my ass. Dad, if I know that old trick, surely, you must know it." Lavenedica chortled. Her father frowned, she corrected her face and held back her riant. He was giving her a variant paternalistic glare. Which always meant, "Keep it up, I'll spank you. You aren't too old for me still spank your bottom."

"Ok, she doesn't know who you are and you don't really know her. So let this be a lesson, don't go drunk surfing the spiritual realms and let this situation take care of itself. She obsequiously doesn't want anything but to time walk and occasionally sleep with you. I didn't sense any healing power in that woman. Now why Vonderbilt believes she has a gift...I don't know but I sensed nothing in her but a lot of rage and craftiness." Lavenedica said, remembering the woman moved exceptionally fast.

"Promise me you won't go looking for her again."

"I won't, sweetheart, I won't." Ashton said, meaning it at that moment, "Promise me, you won't confront her again? Many have gravely misjudged her."

"I won't if you don't go off on the deep end again over her." This was the best she could promise.

Ashton excused himself to his room. He felt it was time to go home. His mind wondered to where Ana was or may be. Unable to resist the temptation he traces Lavenedica's route through the Neutral Zone and exited in a small hotel room. He doesn't see her, the kid, nor their angels. She appeared to have left in a hurry. He looks out in the quiet parking lot; none of the cars are hers. He remembers hers' is an older model land car. He carefully inspects the fast food empty plastic containers. He wonders does she know leaving these behind with her spiritual imprint on them make it easier for a warlock to trace her? He remains still for a few seconds and listens. He's positive he senses someone else here but under cloak. He reaches into the veil of the cloak and pulls out one of younger brothers he doesn't know very well.

"What are you doing here?" He asked the young immortal. "What did you see and hear?"

"I merely saw a woman come through this portal and was arguing with another woman who left a few minutes ago."

Quickly he asked which way did the red head go?

"She went up the road and made a right onto the expressway." Forgiving he intended to beat his younger brother's ass for spying, he knew he was lying. He knew his flaming red haired brother had been there more than a few minutes. He probably watched her sleep and shower, too. Somebody needs to teach this woman how to set up sight barriers. Maybe Saint Anne's people were trying to teach her how to do these things but with Vonderbilt on your ass, it's difficult to learn anything new. He teleports down the road about 70 miles ahead hoping they haven't passed his location. He waits about 10 minutes and she doesn't pass. He teleports again and she doesn't pass. "That little piece of shit lied to me. She went another direction."

591

Now he had time to go kick his ass before heading home. He suspects the imp had a hard-on from watching her undress. Has he been trailing her and if so why? He teleports back to the room, his red-headed angelic looking brother is gone and has erased his trail.

Lavenedica checks on her dad before retiring for the evening and is disheartened, he broke his promise.

"I certainly hope she is worth it, dad, I really do." She said softly closing the door and ushering her grandchild out who had followed her to tell Big Papa goodnight. She felt betrayed his by lying so easily. But she assumed he had been lying for years; she just never knew it.

⚜

They packed the car and left 20 minutes after the Amazon left. Ana hit the expressway making a left turn headed further south. As if they didn't already have enough problems now some new woman with supernatural powers telling her to stay away from her daddy. How was she to love someone she didn't know? This one was new, who was that woman and what in the hell was talking about? So that man has children...she wondered which of those women were the Amazon's mother? She remember part of the hotel's name in Oklahoma City, it was Car-something. She was usually proficient with memory so why was she having such a hard time remembering anything about this man? She knows he's an immortal. That much is clear by now. But his sassy-ass daughter wouldn't tell her his name. What did the woman mean about Bea having his essence? So he's the immortal who visited her that night. But now even that memory of what he looked like is fading.

One gift that's developing is little scary. She can see from above. It's like she is in the sky looking down at people. She sees him now by the north side of the road. His face is obstructed from her view but his stance is familiar to her. At least he doesn't know where she is so perhaps they can get some sleep. She turns off onto a lone highway and pulls under low bushes, she doesn't know the one who sped along behind her is more dangerous to her than Cargill. The one she's hiding from in hope to gain her wit without interference. She doesn't sense nor see him as he stealthy follows her, moving through the outer realm furthermost from hell but closer to earth. Nor does she detect silicious ethereal activity when he cast a sound barrier over the car in hope of preventing her or the child from calling his older brother, Azazel. His report back to Cabiriel can wait. This is too luscious of an opportunity to pass up.

Caroline Caldwell invited the women of the Cargill harem on a lavish vacation at the Cadwell's pristine resort in the French Rivera. They had called her crying saying Cargill's daughter kicked them out and he was gone on a mad pursuit chasing that woman, again. Deciding to fight fire with fire, she and her coven sisters contact Cabiriel, another son of God. It is said he is the leader of the rebels who were imprisoned underground, though the evil machinations of dark sorcerers that practiced in a region now called Denmark and founded the very early practices of masonry with which Solomon and David would become familiar with. He may yet to this day seek to fulfill his plan of revenge on the offspring of that intermarriages between humans and immortals. She didn't care about all the ancient history. She didn't care that those sorcerers was said to be sons of Azazael.

"Do any of you've children with my brother whom you call Ashton Cargill?" Cabiriel politely asked the women. Everyone shakes their heads.

"Which of you are his wife?" Everyone looks at Caroline who is staring straight ahead. Mentally wanting to know why all the questions?

"None of us are married to him if that's what you mean!?" Shaula says, speaking for the group. This man is starting to creep her out. But he has a big shiny blade on his hip so she figured she better be cool and keep that opinion to herself. Just who are these spaced-out friends of Carole's?

"We're his harem." Dawn adds. "Can you help us find her and kill her?"

"So you're all his wives!" Cabiriel says causally, trying to figure out exactly what this

593

group of beautiful women wanted him to do? What was the real problem?

Cabiriel really wasn't thrilled about going up against his much older brother. Azazael was once a destroyer. He wasn't sure how much power Azazael still retained. But his thirst for revenge against those little warlock bastards of Azazael overrode his doubts and concern.

"I'll send scouts to look for her and when they find her I'll let you know."

Now Caroline speaks lewdly of Ana, hoping to increase Cabiriel's dying interest. "She's a real slut. I'm talking about a first class whore. She'll sleep with anybody and anything." The seven agree with Carole.

"Do you've a picture of her?" Cabiriel asked. Dawn produced her ISPAN pad and says "We believe her kid belongs to him."

Now his interest in Ana improves. "Oh really, she has a child for him? Well, that's a whole another agenda." Caroline smiles a big happy grin because she knows what Cabiriel does to his siblings' half-mortal offspring.

Cabiriel is informed by his group they've seen a woman fitting this description in a small town in southern Oregon and sure enough it is her. But angels are camped around and standing nearby. What's the meaning of this? So he waits and waits. He watches her showers and use the toilet.

"I sees why our brother is chasing her. She's beautiful but that's not Azazael's child. Maybe she's running from Azazael because she cheated on him with the child's father." the scout said.

Cabiriel tossed the ISPAN back to Dawn, "That isn't the point whether it is or not. The point is Azazael believes it is and that makes the pursuit all the more fun." Cabiriel grinned at the prospect of repaying an ancient debt long overdue.

"Be quiet or I'll slash your throat." Cabiriel hissed into Ana's ear, startling her awake in the front seat. His hand travels from her mouth to inside her top.

"You'll find me as great in bed as my brother," he whispered menacingly, holding her mouth in a steel grip. "Now, if you get out the car we can do business and my murderous brother will be none the wiser." She glanced around as far as she could see. Bea was asleep. She remembered Saint Anne said gun are useless against immortals, but they can hurt and kill some half-immortals but she could tell this man wasn't human.

"Don't even think about whatever you're plotting" Cabiriel said squeezing her right breast painfully. "Bitches like you're how many of my brothers lost their crowns." Cabiriel whispered. "Now, get out or I kill the kid back there." He nodded toward the back seat.

She obeyed and got out the car. She didn't know what he'd do to Bea if she didn't. Letting her guard down is how she ended up being ambushed. He pushed her to the ground and was on top her before she hit the ground, ripping her jeans as if they were made of paper. She tries to remember about materializing swords and dagger before he penetrated her. She thought it was supposed to materialize when under assault. But it didn't, now she was in full panic mode. She knows he intend to kill her when he finishes. She knew that the possibility of rape went along with the life she lived. But if this was a mortal she would stand a better fighting chance. She bears down with all within her heart and managed to will a blade into her hand and started trying to stab him in the back as he took his time moving in her. She managed to snick him on the shoulder. The blade goes in deep and singes his immortal flesh.

"What in Hades are you? Where did that blade come from?" He yelled tightening his grip on her neck, with that blade in her hand he can't snap her neck. It's protecting her. By now, Bea was awake, trying to see what was going on. She wiggled her hand aloose when he slacken his grip to attend his wound. She slashed at him again. She didn't have time to worry about her nudity. The emblem on the short blade started to glow. Saint Anne told her it was the Emblem of God.

"Recognize your Father's Seal?" Ana croaked, half scared, madly taunting him. She saw the wound wasn't deep enough for him to be screaming like a disembodied spirit. But something else did cause him to scream. A ball of fire shot from the car hitting him dead center in the back. When he turned and looked at Bea she rushed him, cutting and slashing. He was too skilled for her to take his head, and too late extracting his blade to fight back effectively.

Cabiriel eye's was watching through this one's eye. They gleamed an angry silvery light as he snarled at her, "This isn't the end, bitch." He grimaced and growled still holding his injured arm. She slashed at him cutting his clothing again for calling her a bitch. She hated that word. She didn't know there was another one watching.

"I'll get you yet, at least one of us will," he promised before disappearing.

"So there was more than one?" She whips around looking for the other. But is still puzzled why her main blade didn't appear. She was unaware the second one had weaved a talisman blocking her primary connection to the heavens.

She rushed to the trunk of the car and found fresh panties and jeans, picking up her shredded one and stuffed them in the trunk, slammed the lid and got back in the car. The bruises begun to burn but she ignored them and got dressed and drove out the woods as fast as possible. Bea was sniffling as she drove. She knew in her heart it could have been a lot worse had he taken his fist to her. He could've killed her had he wanted to. Why didn't he? He had the chance.

"Sweetheart, I'm so very sorry you had to see that." Ana felt utterly hapless and ashamed Bea had to witnessed something so horrible, being so young. All she could do was hold herself together and keep Trusty on the road and try to muster an explanation to talk to Bea about rape.

Once on the main road again, getting as far away from that spot as possible, Bea spoke first, "Mom, there's no shame in what just happened. That man thingy is who should be ashamed." Bea's words were wisdom far beyond her age. Ana looked at her and smiled and continued driving on down the dark lonely road with nothing but their headlight penetrating the deep darkness of moonless night.

Hours later we both watched the sun rise through Trusty windshield. I turned on the radio to have something else to concentrate on other than the rape but soon clicked it back off. I wasn't in the mood to listen to a local sunrise service broadcast. I think, *"People want Christianity in this neat, clean package, with the baby Jesus in a manager and everyone standing around worshiping Him. But that is the real picture? No, it's not. This truth of it is, Christianity had to fight a dirty low down fight to be stay alive and still does. I haven't had single Christian or religious person to help me beside Mother Harris. Everyone else simply wants to preach to me. I know better than most what Jesus said."* She angrily wiped away the tears finally falling now that Bea had drifted off to sleep.

⚬⚬⚬

Cabiriel arrived full of wrath back at Carole Caldwell's to find them all standing in a hexed circle against his wrath. A Chimera appeared beside him and walked slowly around him, it wasn't corporeal enough to attack.

"You deceiving backbiters didn't tell me she was a fucking Nazarene Warrior Saint! You lying cunts!" He screamed at them and the beast from Hell. He knew the only way to make the burning from her blade stop was to repent of what he had done.

"I hope she kills all of you!" He ranted, walking around the protective, hexed circle, looking for a way in.

"You bitches knew I'd return angry or might get sent to celestial prison, why else are you all in this damn circle? I'll get my revenge on you. Just you wait. All of you are dead!"

Growing bold Dawn taunts. "Ashton isn't going to let you kill us."

Cabiriel hacked and coughed from the anguish of the searing heat and laughed, "Don't delude yourself. Azazel doesn't give a damn about you whores. I saw him tonight with her," he deliberately lied because they lied to him first. Seeing hurt in several pairs of eyes he pushed further.

"When I arrived she was laying in his arms, he was kissing her passionately. You ladies, were the farthest thing from his mind."

Caroline, not believing him, asked. "Who cut you then if Ashton had her so occupied?"

"Azazael cut me! Who else? She helped. I went alone thinking she was a normal woman based on your pathetic lies and when I arrived he held me while she cut me. They worked together. So if I were you dumb bitches I wouldn't go home to him. When I found them together I told him who sent me. Why else do you think he let me go? Sorry harem, the gig is up! You lost the fight." He snickered evilly at his bold lies. Someone else had to hurt since he was hurting and they are the reason for his injuries.

"NNOOoo," Dawn cried out weeping. Not wanting to believe this immortal's words. He has to be lying. Ashton wouldn't do anything so devastating and harmful to her.

"Yyeess!!!" Cabiriel laughed, aggressively nodding his head, cruelly mocking, mimicking Dawn's distress.

"All the while he has been gone, he has been between her legs having a grand ole time. That's what I caught them doing." He laughed and disappeared. Everyone eyes were now on the Chimera which Carole conjured but willed to go away for it was materializing too solid for her comfort.

"Why didn't you send that thing after her?" Shaula asked. Inquisitive, had they gotten in over their heads dealing with these surreptitious witches and warlocks.

"She would've easily killed it." Carole answered. "And I didn't feel like dealing with Lilith had she killed her pet."

"What's a fucking Nazarene Warrior Saint!?" Another harem member asked.
598

One of the other coven members explained seeing that Carole was bored and wanted the harem gone. "It's a person who is killing machine. They're earthly members of the heavenly army. It's like a green beret but they fight with a sword that's aflame with the all consuming fire of God. This is why we must stop now her before she grows too strong to stop. With Azazael at her side she'll have too much earthly power and influence coupled with divine power she'll truly be to a majestic force. We must never let them join forces."

The lackadaisical harem wrote the witch's words off as witchery gibberish. They had no interest in learning more about whatever Cabiriel called Ana. They had bigger fish to fry than to worry about the heaven and its army.

Caroline reasoned; *"If what Cabiriel said was true, then I have no further use for this group of spoiled, overly pampered, useless whining women. But then again, I don't want to sever my connections to Ashton Cargill too soon and they are my only connection."*

"I suggest you ladies go home and put an end to this madness. As long as you all have been with him he isn't going to let some Johnnie Mae come lately kill you all." Carole cajoled the women. She knew her chthonian plan may not work but she felt it was worth a try. Frankly, she was beyond caring if it worked. She wanted them gone. "Screw what his daughter says. She isn't the boss of him nor his estate. If he hasn't told you all to get out, then why are you ladies crying foul? His daughter isn't the boss. He is. Now go home and reclaim your man."

⟨⟩

I've never been fascinated by the so-called charm of old houses for they had too many ghosts. This place was no exception, the first one I encountered was a lady dressed in 20th century attire who walked up and down the stairs all night causing them to creak. She did so until one night I was fed up with her creaking the damn stairs and went out into the hardwood floored hallway and told her if she creaked those stairs one more time I would give her something to cry about. She flashed a pale gruesome face, eyes missing from sockets in which insects squirmed in a blackish, bloody mess. I was sick of being scared. I'd no idea how my hand made contact with her dead, decaying face but it did and I slapped the scary right out of her. She looked at me as in disbelief I actually hit her.

"I don't know what happened to you and right now am beyond caring but you're scaring my baby therefore you made this my business. Creak those damn stairs one more goddamn time and I'm beating your ass all the way back to hell!" After that night I didn't encounter her again and I assume the others took the clue.

Two weeks later, it was cold and rainy that night so my mood wasn't very placid. I was tired that night for I had to work late helping the data entry department for one of the workers was sick and I didn't get home until eleven. I had worked for 9:00 A.M.-11:00 P.M., I was so glad mom had already cooked and fed Bea who was asleep on the sofa when I got home. I bent and kissed her. She didn't wake up. I ate my dinner-breakfast round 12 midnight after putting Bea in my bed and decided I would watch a little news. I hadn't kept up with current events in the past two months. I wondered would this be a three month stay, we are blessed if things stayed calm for 6 months to a year. I fell asleep on the sofa thinking of our next move and suddenly I felt a pull as thus something pulled me through the sofa, through the floor, soil-I could see the long dead skeletons of creatures who lived and died in that area but my descent continued until I hit a hot, sticky liquid.

I swum to the top of this dark water; I could hear creatures growling around me but couldn't see anything. I knew the liquid wasn't water, it had the thick consistency of blood. It stunk too, like long dead blood. It stunk like the blood of dead men. I felt a hand grab my ankle and try to pull me under but I called Jesus so loud, it let go and I could hear it splashing, swimming away from me. I began swimming in the direction I heard the others go. I felt or rather sensed something large swimming toward me at a high speed, it swum under me. The under current pulled me with it, I was being pulled by something I couldn't see. This felt like a real live night terror I couldn't wake up from. I could hear my mother calling me, asking where were I? I kept yelling I did not know. I don't think she could hear me. I believe I was in hell.

600

I came to shallower part of this river. There was fire shooting up as far as I could see. There were hideous, bulbous scintillations suspended from the roof of this cave that was glowing an eerie red, reflecting the fire in the water which was now bubbling or boiling. I wasn't feeling the effect of the heat. The light from the fire revealed the creatures that were in the water with me. And I wished it hadn't; it showed me the horrors I could not see earlier. They were huge orangeish red scaly, horned horrors snakes with rows of sharp teeth going down their throat. Their eyes were like huge, angry, dimly glowing lights. Their nostril flared and smoke wisp from them. There was something else moving inside the scaly hide, I didn't want to know what was pulsating inside for a blackish goo was seeping from beneath the scale. I saw they were talon tipped along the side, when it raised it's underside I saw seemingly millions of smaller creatures with humanoid faces squirming around in intricate knots inside the transparent underbelly I stifled a scream, an inner voice told me shall I scream they will attack.

"Jesus, help me." I whimpered. The moment I said that a moldy winged creature flying overhead threw fire and cussed at me telling me to shut the hell up. As it leathery wings beat the air it reached down and wrapped a talon claw around my head and pulled me out the river of blood seconds before the leviathan lunged for me. It dropped me in a fiery area. It felt warm but not hot. I saw several people standing around watching as I waded out the fire and blood. The creature came for me again. My head was bleeding where it talon dug in. I picked up rocks and started throwing them at it. It kept dodging and laughing but I kept throwing until one rock struck it in the head and it yelped like a dog and growled and flew for me at top speed. I tucked into a small cave and moved back as far as possible. The winged demon had lit on the ground and was reaching for me through the narrow fissure of the cave I crawled into. I was calling God at the top of my lungs but nothing was happening and I wondered why? I know He heard me. All of hell heard me screaming.

"Your prayers are being blocked." The demon snarled as it kept reaching it's gnarly claws through the opening too small for it's body to enter. Suddenly several arms wrapped around me and held me in a death grip, I struggled to escape.

"You're powerful in your world but this is mine." The voice of the woman from the staircase said.

"My Lord is Ruler of earth, heaven, and here below. I command you in His Name to let me go." I said, struggling against her.

She laughed a nasty dry crackling laughter, I was expecting her to hack up a lung. She quickly brought a black tipped nail to my throat and was about slice when one hand, reached out and grabbed her and the second hand pulled me out the crevice. I couldn't see the man's face, he refused to let me look at him but I felt I knew him. As I passed I noticed the woman's hand where the man had touched her had withered like a dead leaf and dropped off. I looked back; she was laying on the damp, stinky ground wailing and weeping, thrusting about and then stopped.

Everything in our path was scrambling to get out this man's way. Next thing I knew we were walking on air through a wall of pure light that had become solid. In the blink of an eye I was back on the sofa smelling fresh as roses in spring dew. Mom ran to me on the couch and grabbed and hugged me painfully tight.

"Thank you, Jesus." Mom kept saying over and over. Finally she asked. "Are you alright?"

"I think so." I said feeling my face and head. They felt normal.

"Where were you? Where did you go?" Fannie asked fanatically.

"Mom...uh ahem. I'm not sure but I think I was in hell. I think something pulled me into hell. I think that hallway spirit or something pulled me into hell, I think I was in the River Styx."

The dreadful ashen of Mom's honey toned face told me that's exactly what she suspected. She pulled me closer, almost in her lap. To ensure her I was alright.

"A man brought me back. Everything ran from him."

"That was the Lord, baby," Fannie said. "Don't you recall He led you out of a crypt when you were about eight? You disappeared from your bed. Your father and I could hear you but couldn't see you. You were telling us you were in a grave."

Oh, I remembered that scary trip very well. The incident she was referring to stuck with me for years. I was about eight years old and very sick. I had been in a coma from what I was told. I had gone to a birthday party of a childhood friend and someone poisoned the cake. The poison put me to sleep but killed two of my friends. While in the coma a man led me through a churchyard to the cemetery right outside the door and down a flight of stairs leading from a grave in this old church yard. I remembered hearing my mother crying and calling me to come back to her but the man pulling me was too strong, I couldn't break away from him. Suddenly a man in a bloodstained robe appeared and took me from the other man and led me back up the stairs where mom and dad were waiting for me. When I arrived back in my bedroom I saw behind them a beautiful city, all aglow. There were no words to describe its beauty. The lights of this city were like nothing earthly. Dad covered my eyes with his hands and held my face against his chest until I no longer heard the angels singing.

While leaning against my dad I heard the other man, the evil one said as clear as day. "I'll get you for that!" Then I knew this was no dream. But how was mom and dad in this other world with me? As far as I knew neither of them had the ability to enter the spiritual world. But somehow they were there reaching for me.

Over fourteen years ago Ana was at home in a coma in her room for the small town hospital refused to keep her in ICU by popular demand of the community, saying she was bad luck or a hex. Taking the higher road, Jacob and Fannie BuFaye went to pay their respect to their daughter's friend whose parents barred them from the wake saying, "How dare you two show your faces here?! The poison was meant for your little evil, strange, horribly creepy child but killed ours. At least your's is alive and we all hope she dies and then you shall know our grief! We begged you to keep that little witch home but you kept saying the girls liked each other! Look at those damn coffins! Your evil daughter did this!" A mother of one of the dead girls accusingly cried.

"Ana did no such thing!" Fannie screamed back with tears of great sorrow running down her face. "Why would she poison herself?"

"The devil needs no reason. When are you two going to wake up and see that's not a child but a demon? Your household was normal before that thing entered it! Now it's a house of horror!" Another dead friend's mother screamed back at Fannie, slapping the tuna casserole out her hand. The scattering of the dish brought others out to the front porch. They left without further confrontation.

⁂

After eight year old Ana woke up after a month of existing in a comatose state and regained her strength she wanted to see her friends. Her family deeply regretted they had to tell her the truth. Her little friends were all dead and the two which survived, their parents had moved away. Then she wanted to see their graves. Fannie took her to the small church yard where the girls were buried and eight year old Ana fell on the small graves sobbing she was sorry she killed them. Fannie found this unbearable and pulled her off the graves when she saw the church sexton watching them and frowning. They rode home in silence. Fannie stopped at the Dairy Hut for a sundae to cheer Ana up but nothing was working.

When school began for the following fall, the BuFaye children were constantly stunned. The older siblings had to protect Ana from attacks. Ana's older siblings lost their friends for nothing more than having a little sister whom the community said was really a demon not a child. They began to resent her.

The family of Jack BuFaye's friend from the farm across the road forbid their son to visit or play with ten year old Jackson. His friend's mother met Jack at the door one day he decided he was going to visit his lifelong friend, turned him around, and sent him back home. He loved his little sister but some days he wished she had died in infancy like the others between him and Helen. His young life had became a hell he didn't ask for nor understand.

⁂

Despite being one of the prettiest girls in Ford County, the stunningly beautiful sixteen year old Helena BuFaye's boyfriend, Cranston, (who was the son of local state representative), dumped her openly and publicly as he was advised by his parents to do. He did it in the school's cafeteria announcing: "I'm not dying for you! Your whole damn family is cursed"

The shame and embarrassment kept her from school until the state demanded she return or her parent pay a hefty fine for violating the state's ordinance on chronic truancy. When she returned to school her ex-boyfriend told her if she get rid of her creepy little sister they could be together. Desperate for his affection and reacceptation by the cool kids she takes the capsule he handed her under the guise of deep kiss in the high school hallway. She felt the only way back into her old gang was to get rid of this weird little stigma called Ana.

She didn't want to but Cranston kept pushing her and saying Ana wouldn't feel a thing. She would die in her sleep and when it was all over they could get back together. Even get married. So the following Saturday morning she told her parents she would fix Ana's breakfast. She emptied the capsule in a glass of chocolate milk, something Ana wasn't allowed until lunch. Lost in the daydream of her getting together back with her old gang she hadn't noticed Ana's dog Happy following her, when she got to the top landing of the stairs right across from Ana's room Happy came charging up the stairs like a mad bat out of hell with a fiery cross ablaze in her forehead and knocked her down, spilling the breakfast all over her and the landing and stairs.

The dog stood and glared at her with humanoid eyes, clearly telling her she knew what she was up and that wasn't about to happen. Fear made her screamed for her parents! This wasn't a dog. This was Ana's familiar! Everyone was right about her sister. Ana came to the door looking puzzled at her and the dog. Oh, how she hated that little skinny, long-haired buggy eyed freak! It ain't natural for a human to be all hair and eyes. Her life was over. She was going to be stuck in this hick town forever all because of that little skinny freak!

Nineteen year old Jacob Jr's girlfriend brought a bright red capsule on their date. While they sat and talked and listened to music, she lovingly took his hand turned the palm up and kissed it while looking deep into his dark amber eyes, thinking how handsome he was.

"Jacob, the only way we can be together is you have get rid of your little sister." Tisha said. "My parents censure me to see you as long as that little demon is alive."

Junior was flabbergasted, he didn't know Tisha was resentful about Ana. When true reality settled he became upset and looked down at the red capsule in his hand, looked down at the bright red pill and asked, "What in the hell is this?" Holding up the pill in the dim moonlight filtering in the backseat of the car.

"A poisonous capsule, the same toxicant used to kill those other kids." Tisha said beside him, leaning against his chest slowly arousing him while in the back seat of his nearly new hovercraft his dad bargained to buy.

"She won't feel a thing. She won't suffer, go into convulsions. Empty it in a glass of milk and she'll fall asleep to never wake up again." She rose lovingly and looked him in the slightly illuminate eyes,

"Jacob, if you love me...you'll give this to her. We deserve a life which isn't plagued by what she is. As long as she's alive evil will follow us. She'll fall asleep and never wake up again to hurt anybody else." Tisha Afanston pled desperately to make him understand the affect Ana would have on everyone's life.

"I don't know how she came to be but she isn't human. I don't know did a demon visit your mommy but that child is evil. She creeps me out. She looks at you as if she wants to kill ya. One of y'all gonna have to wise up and kill that thing before she kills someone else. One of her friends was my little cousin."

Junior unwound his arm from around her shoulder, "Are you crazy?! That would kill my momma, too. Momma would die of grief!" Junior cried, zipping his pants up and

606

climbing out the back seat. Tisha pulled him back to her. He sat back down and faced her.

"Sure, I love you and want to spend the rest of my life with you. But you're out of your damn mind if you and your siddity ass folks think I'm killing my sister offa bullshitting ass rumors. My Gosh! She's only eight years old! Ana can barely kill the gnats swarming around and pestering her let alone somebody. Fuck this shit! We're through!" He said, getting dressed. "Sorry, as much as I love you, I can't and won't do that for ya. My job is to protect the other three not kill them."

"So that's how it's going to be? Huh? You're choosing that demonic little sister of yours over me. The mother of your first born child." Tisha asked angrily.

"Bullshit! You aren't pregnant. I listened to my dad when he said always wear a condom. So if you are-send me the bill. I'm man enough to take care of what's mine's." Junior said, climbing over into the driver's seat and starting the engine. He began driving Tisha back home as she redressed in the back seat. Looking in the rearview at the girl he thought he knew and loved him he said, "Let me kill your annoying little brother and then I will give Ana the pill."

"Hell no! Are you crazy?!" Tisha cried, climbing into the front seat of the soaring hovercar.

"Just what I thought!" Junior snorted.

"What's that supposed to mean?" Tisha snipped, fastening her bra.

"What I mean is you think I'm so into you because of your fair skin and wavy hair I'll do any damn thing for you. You want me to kill my little sister but yet your little brother who is Damien incarnated is too precious to kill. You need to get your damn mind out of the old slavery-time bullshit that yellow black women and white women drive a black man like me to murder. Sorry baby, that way of thinking died out years ago. That shit is in the tar pits with the dinosaurs. I ain't your puppet. You can go hell for all I care. Just to think I had applied for a family grant at Yale! I can't believe I intended to take you with me when I left this hicktown. But tonight you just told me how you really feel about me. You don't give a fuck about me, not if you ask me to kill my baby sister. You see, if Ana dies...that's gonna kill momma. If momma dies dad may not die but who knows, he might just try to follow her. Either way, I'll be left responsible for Helena and Jack; that means two to eight years of responsibility while I'm entering my freshman year at college. They ain't going to stay with Aunt Gayle not with my being of legal age to be their guardian. But that don't mean shit to you just so long as you get what you want!" He said, alighting on the Afanstons' well manicured lawn that Mr. Afanston worked religiously to keep in immaculate condition. His heart was shattered. He had so many plans for them; to see them blown to the wind hurt like hell.

"Junior, you're ranting like a mad man! You know your uncle and aunt will take Helena and Jack in shall your parents turn suicidal. Besides, your parents are young enough to have another child. They're too close to that child to see her for what she is. Just as you're too attached to her. Somebody in your family has to wake up and see that something is seriously and abominably wrong with Ana and do the unpleasant deed. Save your family while there's still enough time. They say people like Ana grow stronger the older they become. I feel I've a voice and say so in your family matters since you asked me to marry you. In a few short years she will be strong enough to kill everyone!"

Without looking at her he got out, let Tisha out at the door, and walked her to the porch. He didn't kiss her good-bye. He knew this would be the last time he ever saw her. He blinked back the tears as he turned and walked away. He had loved her since he was eleven. He walked to his car wondering had the whole world gone mad?

The months following the summer birthday party deaths Jacob BuFaye's seasonal harvest wasn't accepted in the local Brunswick's farmer's market. He had to drive as far away as Jacksonville to sell his produce. Several farm hands had left out of the frenzy of the superstition that Ana was a witch as to why the poison didn't kill her. The Salem Witch trial from ages past had flown south and landed in Brunswick, GA.

Fannie was fired from her sub-teaching position, a school system in Fla accepted her based on her outstanding criteria; this meant driving over 200 miles when a regular teacher was absent. She gave up her teaching career. Two hundreds miles was too far. They had began discussing selling the farm to relatives and moving out West to start over. The Prescott farm had been in Fannie's family since the late 1870s.

Out of desperation to save his friend, Jacob BuFaye's childhood friend, Ted Costigan, suggested they give Ana up for adoption. Put her in an orphanage.

"Jacob, she's a cute kid. Somebody will adopt her. She won't be there long. She still young enough for someone to take her. If y'all wait until she's older...it will be hard to place her with another family." Ted argued, trying to talk some sense into his friend before the entire BuFaye family ended up broke and homeless.

"Ted, are you out of your freaking mind?" Jacob asked, sideying his long time childhood friend.

Ted hated to sound heartless but like everyone said, something was off or evil about that child.

"Jac, you gotta admit something is severely wrong with that child. You and Fan have had nothing but bad luck since she was born. I don't think that's a human spirit in that child. 'Member how her eyes used to shine like two little damn flashlights, she would got so bright one while she looked white. You see, sometimes that happens at conception; before the Lord could slip a human spirit in an embryo, the devil slips a demon in. Or maybe there's two spirits in that one body. I don't mean it's a fault of yours or Fannie. It just mean the devil is more clever than we think. I mean, let someone adopt that girl who can afford all the shit she causes. I'm telling ya man. She's bad luck. 'Member that time she threw that boy over the fence into the cow pasture with nothing but pressing her hands? I love her too but something is wrong. Things don't just fly through the air at normal people. "

"You want somebody to adopt a child, give up one of them little ugly rugrats of yours." Jacob retorted. "Cause my baby ain't going nowhere."

"Jac, stop being a fool, that man who threatened you was serious. I ain't losing you over no damn kid. Simple as that!"

"Costigan, get the hell outta my house!" Jacob said, glaring at his oldest friend.

"Who threatened Jac?" Fannie asked from the doorway, drying her hands on a dish towel. Both men looked up, wondering how much she heard.

"Ted, shut up!" Jac warned.

"I don't know, when we were at the market a man walked up to him and said, "Kill the little witch or we kill ya. Of course, Jac here beat the shit out of him but that's scary. Strange people have started hanging out in the woods around my house. You can see them moving in the woods at night. I set several bear traps. I caught some but the others helps them get away before I could get out there. I swore I heard wings out there one night."

Jacob and Fannie looked at each other. They know he spoke the truth. They too, have heard leathery wings at night.

"Ted, don't come back here anymore." Jacob said sadly. He felt deep in his heart that if Ted remained associated with him, they'd kill him.

"I ain't leaving you and Fan to deal with this spooky shit by y'all selves. I've seen enough to know there're some things out there that aren't good and some of it is worse than death. I know there are other planes and dimensions and I believe that's where all this shit is coming from. I ain't scared. I'm a man of God. God will protect me. I saw people step out of some kinda transponder the other night. They came out a hazy blue light and they wasn't nothing good. I sensed a dreadful sickness about them I can't explain. I'm telling y'all, something evil is afoot around here."

"Did they come near you?" Fannie asked, hiding the fright rising in her throat.

"No, they came to the edge of my yard and wouldn't come no further but there was lots of them, them traps were going off like crazy. The next morning I told Edie I was going out there to check those traps. I saw where the crazy fucks had sawed off their foot to get outta them traps. What kinda crazy son of a bitch can do that without hollering in pain? There was a foot left in the trap."

Ted Costigan and his family moved in with the BuFayes for a while, feeling they all would be safer in numbers since all the other neighbors and farmers nearby had moved away. Most without saying a word. The BuFayes and Costigans were the only two left out on route 27 heading toward Florida.

～⌒⌒～

Around Thanksgiving, which was still unseasonably hot, Jacob and Ted's third childhood friend named Plano Hayes came to visit. He hadn't seen Jacob and Ted in years. Immediately upon meeting him Ana didn't like him. This was his first time seeing Ana, so he handed her an old 2072 silver dollar and bent near her young ear and said, "Here is the payment for Charon to ferry your evil soul across the River Styx, away from my buddy."

To an average observer it seemed as thus they were merely talking but Fannie was watching Ana's little thin face and didn't like the changes in her young child's eyes.

"Ana, sweetie, come here." Fannie called Ana to her side but didn't hide her glare at Plano, they never liked each other.

"Hello, Fan. Where's Jacob and Ted?" The tall, cream complexioned black man asked.

"Out back. What in the hell did you say to my baby?" Fannie asked with Ana's thin arms tightly hugging her waist.

"Nothing, I was kidding with the child." He grinned. "The kid's just like you. Can't take a joke."

611

Ana tugged her mother's sleeve and said. "Momma, he said Charon is coming to get my evil soul and gave me this to pay my way back to hell." Ana held up the fine minted coin for her mother to see.

Fannie's slap sounded like a crackling whip. Leaving a bright red handprint across the man's face.

"Neither of us can take a joke when it ain't funny. She has been through enough without you bringing more sorrows."

With Jacob not at the home and Plano having never liked this pretty girl whom he always swore broke up their friendship, he decided to let her know his true feelings. He, Jac, and Ted had been friends since kindergarten and all that changed when Jac started talking to Fantasia Prescott. His long legs quickly took him out of Fantasia Prescott's reach; he walked further into the wide country yard. "Ted said them people gonna kill Jace if he don't give up that girl. One child ain't worth him, you, and the other three children dying for. I mean, whomever wants that girl bad enough to drive y'all into financial ruins, to kill for her, it has to be something from hell and if she was a regular child hell wouldn't want her. So I've to ask you?? Is that really Jacob's child? Or did you dance with a devil and passed it off as a friend's?"

Fannie stopped her in trek across the yard to hit him again for saying she was unfaithful to Jacob when she heard the shuffling of feet coming from around the house. Someone stepping in the gravel.

Coming from the east side of the house with ten year old Jack right behind, Jacob heard his wife and second best friend arguing, that was nothing new. They been arguing since they all were teenagers. According to Plano, Fannie took him from the gang and he wouldn't let him play with them anymore.

"Hey, hey, hey, what's y'all arguing bout now?" Jacob asked teasingly, slipping his arm around Fannie's perfect waist and kissing her upturned cheek.

"This fool gave this gal this ancient silver dollar talking about goddam Theron is

612

coming to take her evil ass back to hell." Fannie snaps, showing her husband the coin.

"Man, I was teasing the girl. It's Charon, not Theron. Fannie blew the whole things outta proportion but I guess that's expected considering the stress y'all been under." Plano said sympathetically but there was no sympathy in his eyes.

"Fan, baby, honey...we need as many armed men as we can get. I mean, Giles and Ted is here so Ted invited Plano. Plano have always had a dark, twisted sense of humor. You know that!" Jacob said, reaching picking up Ana and kissing them both.

"Daddy will kick Charon's ass if he show his face around here," Jacob said, tickling Ana.

"Daddy, Charon is bones," Ana giggles, playfully correcting her father.

"Well then, daddy will kick his bony ass." Jacobs laughed and tickled her again. He wanted to hear his children's laughter as often as possible for he had no idea the gravity of their fate.

Helena comes outside on the porch and hug Uncle Plano as the older BuFaye children calls him.

"Don't pay her no mind. My little sister makes a big deal of everything." She said, rolling her eyes before asking him about the university where he teaches but she was more interested in the wavy haired young male still seated in his car. He followed Helena's gaze to the car and said "That's David Wales, one of the junior assistant professors. He's studying for his PhD so I hired him out of the grant allotted my department to work for me. This is his last year." Plano explained, beckoning the young man out the cool, air-conditioned car. He didn't appear to be eager about stepping out in the furious heat. Not that anyone blamed him.

"I think the University scene will be a good change for Helena. I mean, she'll soon have to start thinking about college."

"How old is that boy?" Fannie asked, watching the feminine looking young man walk from the graveled driveway to the porch as if the crushed stones were hurting his tender city accustomed feet. "He looks awful young to be a professor."

"He has a very high IQ, he finished high school at age 14." Plano boasted.

"Well, I hope that high IQ tells him to quit looking at my daughter. That her papa is about to get this shotgun out," Jacob quipped.

Plano laughed but knew Jacob wasn't joshing. "Hey, I heard about you went to that state representative's house and called the boy's daddy out. You ain't quit fighting yet!"

"Hello, sir, ma'am." David Wales said politely, shaking the parents' hands but his eyes were on Helena. The girl had a perfect hourglass figure. Those jean shorts and tight sleeveless top didn't do her justice.

"Hey, boy! I'm over here." Fannie said ,waving her hand in his perspiring face.

"Well, there's a decent way to do anything. If he wanted to break up with her he didn't have to be an ass about it. That's why I beat his daddy's ass. He was too young for me or Junior to beat his ass."

"Well, Jacob- don't you see? That's who is trying to ruin you. You can't go up against people of that caliber without experiencing some serious retaliation." Plano lectured.

"Well, whatever." Jacob said, leading everyone into the coolness of the house where the remaining of the family and guests were.

The withering heat was hard on 22 year old David Wales. He was sweating profoundly. Being a Northerner, he had never been South. At least not to this area, he had never seen a girl so naturally beautiful. Her mid-back, thick jet black hair highlighted her heart-shaped face. He had watched her from the safety and comfort of the air-conditioned car. The girl was absolutely stunning. Professor Hayes didn't lie when he said the girl was a true work of art. Her slender, shapely honey toned legs were divine, leading up to a very magnificent ass and tiny waist flaring to at least a D cup on her chest. That girl was a stone cold heart breaker. Someone a nerd like him rarely talked to. He looked up the graveled road leading to the house when he heard a car coming. It tires crunching the stone. He wondered why these people hadn't paved the area. It would've been less dusty and rackety.

"Hey, Helena," a young man called as they leaned against the swing in a garden the west of the yard. He knew this jock type. They made him sick.

"Wanna go for a ride with us?" The second boy asked.

"Nah, y'all go on. We got company." Helena shouted her reply from the porch. Dave smirked at the boy who gave him a "I'm gonna whip your ass" look.

"Is one of them your boyfriend?" he inquired.

"Good Lord, no. I been knowing them since we were in preschool. Any girl would be nuts to fall for them. C'mon in the kitchen; I gotta help start dinner with mom and Aunt Gale." She said, waving him to follow her but he was having a difficult time taking his eyes off her figure. Where he's from people pay thousands to look as close as they can get to how she naturally looks.

But the men took him from the kitchen, from around Helena, and dragged him with them out into the woods checking the traps and talking about things they didn't want the women to hear. Jacob has already told Jack to watch that slick-headed boy from New York City. Jack had become Dave's constant shadow, even out in the woods. But the ten year old couldn't understand what all this ado was about nor how it all was about one little skinny kid.

"I'm telling ya, man." Ted argued. "I saw them step out some shit that opened up in the night's air. It's was neon green trimmed in purple. These ain't no humans."

"The *feet* prints you found were they humanoids?" Plano asked, humoring his childhood friend.

"Yeah, they looked human but there was other footprints around these and some of them were some type of hoofed animal."

"Perhaps they were on horseback." Plano continued to debate.

"Nah, man...even a Clydesdale foot ain't that big. It shan't been a horse" Ted said using his hands to emphasize the size of the print. "Besides horses don't have hooves like that."

"Maybe it was a Centaur or Minotaur." David said irritably, he was hot and cranky and tired of swatting flying insects. This heat is too insufferable to be out here listening to this old kook talk about UFO's.

"That's it!" Giles cried. "One was right outside our bedroom window about a month ago, we heard something walking around outside and Gale started praying. I heard it was clear as day when it told her to shut the fuck up! I grabbed my rifle and ran outside but it was gone, but like Ted said--those prints were huge and deep. To make that kind of impression on a lawn that thing had to weigh at least a ton. Upon examining them the next morning, I concluded it like this young man said: it was a Minotaur."

David Wales secretly rolled his eyes. He couldn't believe these seemingly sane, adult men believe that Minotaurs are real. He was being an ass when he made the suggestion and these backwoods men are taking him seriously.

Deciding to put a stop to this nonsense, "Sir, Minotaurs are mythical creatures. They aren't real." Dave pointed out. Only to find Jacob BuFaye watching him more closely.

"Young man to every myth there are many threads of truth. Today, people say Jesus of Nazareth was a myth. That he never walked on water. But we Christians know such a man once walked this earth."

"Sir, I do not believe Jesus of Nazareth and a Minotaur are hardly of a sound comparison." David said, trying not to alienate the man whose daughter he was smitten

616

with. But as a man of letters and science he couldn't let superstitions rule the day or mankind would sink back into the Dark Ages.

"I know perfectly well what a Minotaur is. An offspring between a fallen celestial child of God and a damn cow. Those fallen children of God once walked this earth as freely as you and I. The Great Flood cut off a lot of their access to this world but remember the Bibles says; what has been will be again. So who are you to say the creature saw was not as Giles and Ted say it was? I saw the tracks and Ted is right; only something huge and heavy could've made those deep impressions. We all know how to hunt by tracks and taught all our children how. Do you? Boy, do you know how to find food other than in a grocery store?" Jacob BuFaye lectured.

"No sir." David said, not looking at the man whom he sensed wanted to *hunt* him at this moment.

Dave was glad when he heard what the men called the dinner bell ring. He was glad to get out of this oppressive heat and away from the annoying gnats but one little gnat was still following him. An auburn haired little boy with eyes lighter than Helena's. He was itching like mad, everywhere, and wanted to scratch like a dog with fleas. Helena insisted he sit by her during dinner. He sat on one side, her gnatty little brother sit on the other. The joyful house full of people made dinner livelier than his parents would allow. At his family's gatherings there was no loud talking. No one asking anyone to pass the cornbread, no tall glasses of iced tea, and definitely no finger food. The fried pork chops and chicken was succulent and delicious. Helena made sure he knew she cooked it. He had never had food like this. Even the little kids were eating unhealthy. But they weren't overweight like city children are.

After dinner Helena asked him to walk up a country lane on the other side of the field. Jack, again, followed behind them.

"Mom! Make Jack stay home and leave me alone." Helena called to the adults sitting out relaxing on the porch after a big meal. Dave wonders how this family didn't go broke from their eating habits alone?

"Well, you taking one of them!" Jacob called back at the young couple. "It's Ana or Jack." Her daddy ensured her.

"Ok, Jack, come on." Helena said, surly. She was trying to hook this guy to get out of this hick town when she finished high school and she would never hook anyone not with her little tattletale brother in tow. She wanted Cranston to get wind of this older guy, a college professor was interested in her. Jack followed them to the stream and sat on the other side of Helena, looking not too friendly at David Wales.

"If I give you a hundred dollars will you go sit on that rock over there?" Dave asked bending down to young Jack's level.

"No," the boy said. Dave smiled and said. "There are amphibians over near that brook. I'll point them out to you in a minute if you take two hundred and go observe them for a while."

Jack agreed. He missed his friend who moved away and Helena and Ana were girls, they didn't like newts and frogs. They screamed at him for trying to get them to hold them. Sometimes his father came down here with him but since his big brother left he had no other male to follow around but his uncle Ted boys and their were just too violent for his taste. He preferred studying things to killing them. A gathering with them always ended in a fight. Ana always had his back when he was attacked by them. He records one day she threw one of the boy out in the cow pastures by doing something with her hands. The adults didn't believe it. But the kids saw her do it. The two brothers had double teamed him and had him on the ground. Ana jumped on the oldest one's back, he threw her a few feet away, he saw her stand up with a very angry look on her face and scream but no sound came out her mouth. She waved her hands in a sweeping motion and Tater went flying over the fence, out into the cow pasture, landing in a pile of cow pies. His crying and their laughing is what brought the adults outside. He had known Ana could do strange things since she was a little over a year old but he knew told anyone. He had seen her float her bottle to herself when she wanted it. He thinks everyone else knew it too but no one wanted to talk about it.

"Helena, I'd like to see you again. I know my boss is leaving in a day or so but I know

618

I won't be able to forget you. Which airport is closet here? Atlanta, Savannah or Jacksonville?" Dave Wales asked. He was totally smitten by this country girl. He never pictured himself falling for a girl like her. He always felt he'd fall for a Manhattan socialite. But all those women were boring, all they talked about was how much money so-and-so made or had, whose grandparents kicked the bucket and left them what, what type of car so-and-so drove, what type of shoes they wore or if they were last season. Most had slept with everyone in their social circle. He didn't want a wife every guy in town knew what she looked like nude. He knew this girl would make all the assholes droop.

"Jacksonville the closest. I was considering going to Uncle Plano's school next year when I finish high school. I mean mom and dad won't have any problems with that because they know him."

His heart quickened at the idea of her coming to his school. He preferred her at another. There was a policy against dating students. Especially freshmen. "I notice there's been a big uproar about your little sister. Does she talk? She's unusually quiet for a child so young."

Helena sighed, she has felt a pang of guilt ever since she attempted to give Ana that poisoned food. She loved her little sister and is now glad Happy stopped her. But there was something seriously off about the child which is destroying their family. She knew Ana could do magical things. She knew things visited her in the night. But all that was the trait of a witch and she wasn't admitting that to anyone that she suspected her baby sister was born a witch. She used to glow so bright you could use her as a night light in their room. But had she succeeded Mom and Dad could just have another baby to replace her. Maybe the new one wouldn't be a weirdo. But that dog of hers...what in the hell is that thing? She saw humanoid eyes in that crazy mutt.

"It's nothing, my little sister is spoiled, pampered to death. Mom and dad make too big of a deal out of everything she does or says. If they would stop it then Ana would quit making up stories. She makes them up for attention, she's an attention hog."

Dave told her about the conversation in the woods. Helena covered her face with her hands. She was so chagrined, she can't believe her father really believes there are monsters out to get Ana! How dare he embarrasses her with such foolish conversation.

"They're on a monster hunt, trying to find the fabled, alleged evil monsters supposedly after my crazy little sister." Helena confessed.

Dave chuckled softly. "You are kidding. Right?" He asked, smiling. He thought all this was a joke.

"No, they're dead serious." Helena said, shaking her head.

"But Professor Hayes knows there are no such things as monster so why would he go along with such an asinine idea?"

Helena turned to face her new interest to see if she can make sense of how this childhood friendship thing worked. "Uncle Ted is one of Uncle Plano's oldest friends. They're like brothers. Uncle Plano knows better. He said it to appease him. He came down here to set the record straight but Uncle Ted is a stubborn man and my dad is worse. Uncle Plano is the only voice of reason."

"It must be very difficult for you to watch your parents being manipulated by this clever child. I know all parents want what's best for their children but perhaps the child needs psychological help. Sometimes people can convince themselves there are monsters when there's none. The mind is a powerful thing. Perhaps the child's intent isn't to deceive, maybe, in her mind she really does *believe* she see monsters."

Helena shook her head."Gee, you don't know the half of it! But no, there's nothing wrong with my sister. She is exceptionally bright and very intelligent. She knows what she is doing. She is selfish and thinks all attention should be on her and that's her way of getting it."

He has two younger sisters and he remembers the stunts they used to pull to get their parent's attention but in his family such behavior wasn't rewarded. How he sees it..if the parents stop rewarding the little girl she will cease the absurd behavior.

Jack pokes his head up on the other side of the twin boulder they were sitting on, startling the couple saying he couldn't hear them talking anymore. Asking what were they doing? Helena swatted at him and missed, Dave handed him another hundred to go back to his rock a few feet away and play with the tadpoles in the shallow water. Anything, just leave them some privacy. He wanted the opportunity to kiss this beautiful goddess but her little bratty brother just won't go away.

⸙

A few months later Jacob and Ted are dead. Dave Wales returns with Plano Hayes not so much to comfort the family but to see Helena again. He helps her oldest brother Junior move them into a much smaller house.

Helena calls him again when her Uncles Giles is found dead. He returns again, much against his family's wishes. On the first plane ride to his best friends' funerals Plano Hayes says something that make Dave wonder did he know who killed the three men.

"I told Jac to give that girl to those people but he wouldn't listen. Ted always did whatever Jacob said and see where it landed him. In a grave yard with his ancestors! Those people are too powerful to fight. Sometimes you've to accept defeat and move on. There's a whole 'nothing system of things. An unseen system that's the true rulers of this world. There's an unseen power that runs this world. They're ruled by evil and darkness. All we see and believe we know is merely a front, a facade. There's a man named Orman or Vonderbilt, head of the Illuminati, I'm not sure which is what. But they don't take no for an answer," senior Professor Plano Hayes said before resuming his reading. Dave Wales swallowed hard and resumed his own reading. The words somehow agitated Dave. He heard something akin to this from his own father. As to why his father didn't want him mixed up with the BuFayes.

Plano Hayes leaned in closer to the younger man on the first class flight on Cargill's Aviation. His mentor's sapphire and brown eyes glittered in the bright sunlight flowing in through the aerodynamic designed window, the golden, bright sunlight above the clouds gave Plano's pale face a surreal glow. Dave knew they were unspilled tears in his

621

eyes, "My friends met their demise by not accepting it when they were beaten. That's the worse thing a man can do. Be brave until foolishness. Ain't no shame in accepting defeat. Jacob and Ted, let bravery killed them. Son, there's a time to be valiant and a time to be a coward and a wise man knows when to be which."

❧

He stood and stared down at the grave of Jacob BuFaye and slowly shook his head. All he had to do was hand the damn girl over so he could begin training her to be his bride. Orman told him this man was stubborn as a mule. The girl was born when he took over Orman's empire and name. Unlike Orman he didn't have time to haggle with this fool. But he had to give the man his dues, he put up a better fight than most. Now he had to collect the skull to use it to hex the girl. She would come if she saw her father calling her.

The BuFayes and Prescotts have been a thorn in the occult's side for years. Everywhere they went there was trouble. They didn't conform, bend, or follow. Every satanist worth their salt knew the legend of Joseph Prescott praying up crops in the dead of the winter on the Prescott farm in the harsh winter of 1888 after many crops failed that proceeding spring and summer. He made the entire place as holy as possible, it was harder to proceed on the ground the stronger you were in satan. It hurt but shouldn't the strength have died down some by now? It's 2474. Anyway, he came to collect the skull of Jacob BuFaye and had better hurry for there were houses surrounding the ancient cemetery.

He liked to collect his trophies in private. He took a steel-headed sledge hammer to vault's lid and it bounced back as if it had hit rubber not a hard marble top. He tried again and fire sparked from the white marble memorial slab.

"Fantasia was expecting you to try that as to why she sealed the grave with love and prayer." A male's voice said. Nikola's head jerked up and he looked around. One of the statues in the graveyard was talking at midnight. It wasn't a statue at all. It was a live angel. "I guard this cemetery from those like you. So that those like you will not desecrate the bodies of saints."

622

Nikola dropped the hammer and fled. He knew what that angel intended to do to him had he stayed.

Having made it outside the holy ground he turned looked back and the damn thing looked like a statue again. But the face was still animated, the angel smiled at him as if inviting him back on the holy ground. He looked carefully, he now remembers this angel. This is the one who stayed his hand when he tried to sacrifice the girl to Lucifer about two years ago. She was in a coma so he pulled her into the underworld. For some reason Lucifer wanted her body to be killed here, in this graveyard, so he took her back to the topside to the BuFayes' family mausoleum and this angel held him and Lucifer off so the girl ran further into the spirit world and fell in the river of blood, the river Styx but was able to open the sky of hell to the realm of heaven. Lucifer said Jesus pulled her out of hell, all he knew was Lucifer screamed for him to run. The King of kings was coming. Samahiel had the girl, leading her deeper into hell. The King took her from Samahiel and passed her through the door of life back to her awaiting parents. For a while there was a blue sky above her and a red river of blood below the child. That's when they knew just how powerful she really was and if she could open heaven's gate that wide at such a young age she was going to someday be the strongest one to ever live. She's the one mentioned in the unholy bible. The Unholy Bible spoke of a child to come after Jesus ascended who will hold the Cross in one hand and a flaming sword in the other and is said be even greater than Moses. Of course traditional Christianity had never heard of this prophecy and wouldn't believe it or accept it for the child isn't a boy but a girl. Orman and Lucifer are right, she is his equal.

Helena enters college the following fall after her father's mysterious death but isn't able to study as she should for she is always having to return back down south to attend her mother, and little brother and sister. She finds herself shopping for all three of them in anticipation of how well dressed they will look in high end designer wear. Being a student, she used her discount card all over the city and on airline tickets back to Jacksonville. Dave isn't stringy with helping her. For the first Christmas after dad's passing she get him to charge expensive gifts on his black unlimited credit card for the whole family. She intend to dress Ana and Jack to impress.

When she arrived home she found Jack and Ana guarding mom like two little pitbulls, they inspected even what she was handing their mother to eat.

Jack would ask Ana, "Do you see anything?"

Ana would say, "No, it's safe.

She had a local catering service to deliver their first Christmas dinner but they were eating what Ana cooked all because Ana said there were harpies on the white coconut cake. She was cooking one for mom. Helena tried to understand their fear of losing mom too being that dad had died less than a year ago but they were being ridiculous. No one was allowed near mom. When at school they were constantly calling back home looking at the screen to make sure no one was there. She was remorseful to see Ana's schizophrenia take over the entire household.

She updated Ana's wardrobe and heard from friends back home that the new look was helping a lot. People was still leery of the girl but they didn't quite see her as a witch anymore. She had the long hair clipped to a decent, fashionable length. Her mother was furious at her for taking Ana to have her hair dressed in a permanent style But she wasn't there to comb it and mom had slipped into a form of manic depression. Ana had no girlfriends to help with it, so something had to be done.

A lot of the guys on campus are sniffling around her. Dave returns to the south with her to keep the wolves away. To let every man who met his eyes know she's his and he wasn't sharing with no one. His dad warned him a woman that beauteous was nothing but trouble because every man wants her. But he was in love. He hadn't told his parents she was barely 18 and not so good a student. He talked her professors into passing her to keep her in school. He knew had she dropped out, her backward mom was going to demand she attend a school down south and there was no way in hell he was going down there to deal with the killer heat.

They had a lovely wedding at the same church entombing Helena's father's body. His parents weren't pleased. They wanted a St. Peter's Cathedral wedding or at least one in the Hamptons. But Helena refused to hear of it, citing her mother had to be there; her mother's health was too fragile to travel all the way to New York. He explained traveling to New York wasn't tedious as it was five hundred years ago. He knew he was in trouble when Helena refused to throw her bridal bouquet but instead left his side in the middle of the rice tossing tradition and went into the graveyard and knelt down in a ten thousand dollar wedding dress to lay it on her father's grave. He knew couldn't live up to Jacob BuFaye's legacy.

Chapter 13
Flight of the Wizard

Languishing in the castle, Nikola Vonderbilt aka the Grand Wizard ponders his next move. He knows he better decide quickly for that half-crazed immortal will surely show up now that his bloodthirsty servant has killed the woman he so desperately wanted. He wondered what did Cargill want with the woman? There were millions of beautiful women. So it wasn't her looks. He knew it was her gifts but what would Cargill do with them? How did he plan to activate them?

Appearing in the realm of Vector, ruled by a fierce half-man, half vulture race created by one of the fallen sons of God who was well known for his vile bestiality, the braggart leader Vulpine asked him what was he doing in his kingdom? Nikola knew they were capable of devouring him. Never mind they were part human themselves. Appealing to Vulpine that they and humanity were distant cousins didn't mean shit to this savage race. He looked around at all the beady vulture eyes in a humanoid face. Their faces were framed by plumes of vulture feathers. Their fingers ended in razor-sharp talons. He heard they had downy feathers all over their bodies but he didn't care to find out.

"Vulpine, have I not sent you truckloads of goods since you have known me?"

Nikola asked.

The vulture man stares at him as thus he haven't asked a question. "Yeah, but I want the good shit you earthlings are eating, not goddamn road kill!" Vulpine replied.

Nikola thinks, "*You're a damn buzzard. You're supposed to eat roadkill, garbage, and shit! Damn, even the damn vultures don't know their place anymore!*" But instead he says "I'll send steaks and lamb chops the next time. But right now, if you don't hide me, I won't be around to send you anything. One of your father's brothers are after me for killing some woman. She was a nobody so I don't know why he is bent all outta shape."

Vulpine listens as he gnaws on a bone, saliva seeps down his chin. "This here is mutton. I got this from Uncle Zeus." Vulpine says, pointing the leg of lamb at Nikola "I don't want no more of your people, they stink worse than roadkill."

Nikola nods; he had been sending those who displease him to be eaten by these creatures. He was a little ticked off to see one of his former female members sitting snugly under a Vectorian male's arm that could be flexed out into wings. She turned her head when he glared at her. Vulpine had cozened him. They weren't eating these people sent to them! They were mating with them. He saw several with hair, earth human hair not feathers on their heads. But he would deal with this betrayal later. Right now he needed Vulpine to hide him. They were expert at deception and hiding in plain sight.

"That's my daughter-in-law." Vulpine said, following Nikola's gaze. He had forgotten these birdies could read mind if you left your thoughts unguarded.

"You didn't say we *had* to eat them; besides they taste terrible. Taste like they're full of shit."

His fallen from his grace former member then sat up and stared back at him. Those beady eyed children of hers' glared hatefully at him "Vasaphod, take your wife and children elsewhere; we've business to discuss."

Nikola was glad to see the damn witch leave. The conniving bitch had wormed her

626

way into Vulpine's prince's heart. They'll be sorry they didn't eat her.

The walls of the palace started rumbling and trembling, those perched in the loft flew down and hid. Vulpine pushed him behind a door behind his seat. The force with which the portal opens sent atmospheric ripples and everything flying as Azazel steps through.

"WHERE IN THE FUCK IS VONDERBILT?! He bellowed in a loud voice shaking the palace.

"Hello Uncle Azazel, it's good to see you, too." Vulpine replied calmly, still tearing meat from the chop.

"Don't fuck with me, Vulpine, or I'll pluck you like the bird you are!" Ashton Cargill roared.

Vulpine shrugged his feathered shoulders and wisecracked "It's your brother's fault I got all these itchy ass feathers. He shouldn't had been fucking around with my vulture mother. Had you been doing your job, watching him to keep him from fucking around with her, I wouldn't be here. So my existence is partially your fault. So don't come in here hollering at me because you don't like the way I look. Go yell at your own brother." Vupline says, tearing off a piece of meat and feeding it to the large prehistoric vulture perched on a stand behind him. Ashton feels like kicking his brother's ass for creating such a strange creature. His own world was destroyed too but he didn't resort to repopulating it with weird ass creatures like this.

"I'm looking for his trifling ass too. He was supposed to have delivered me lamb chops instead of freaking roadkill. You see I've a human palate and like the finer things in life too." Ashton knows his brother is good at deception therefore so would his son be very deceiving. He scans the palace; he sense earthlings here but none of them are Nikola.

"Vulpine, lambs can't be raised here so where did you get a giant leg of lamb?" Ashton asked suspiciously.

"Uncle Zeus brought me these in exchange for some diamonds. I went to visit dad. He's doing well considering...Dad said don't give Zeus shit else. He can't be trusted."

Growing impatient with his nephew's chattering, "Shut up!" Ashton snapped "If you see that cocksucker you tell him I'm pressing his ass into a diamond and wearing him on my pinky. And buy the way, I'm not your damn uncle, you freak of nature!" Ashton said and roared out as loudly as he came in.

"Love ya too, uncle." Vulpine seraphically and sarcastically quipped behind Azazel's back. Wondering why all the immortals are so damn noisy? Can't they do anything quietly like a normal person?

⁓∾₰℮℘⌇

Nikola decided he better remain with the Vectorians for a while until Cargill cools off. He trembled when he heard Vulpine called Ashton Cargill by his real name. His God given name. So apparently neither Burdock nor Orman knew who he really was. They sent him on a suicide mission knowing the being was Azazel. But he bets they *now* regret fucking with him. Sure, Lucifer had said that's who Cargill really was but one can't put much stock in anything Lucifer says. He lies for the fun of lying.

"You can come out now," Vulpine said. "But here's our deal; I want pork chops, steak, eggs---nah, leave off the eggs, bacon, salmon, lamb chops, beef, deer, veal, bottled water, whiskey, and wine. I don't like vegetable nor worms. And bring me some of those pretty silver metal goblets you have. If you don't I'll call my uncle back." Vulpine says, training his ancient hard cold beady eyes on Nikola. Knowing he had the wizard by the nuts Vulpine amped up his ante, "I want ONE, no four of those battery powered cars my son's wife talks about, I want one of your best women. I don't want no witch covered with the scent of hell!"

The requests could easily be digested. No problems. The only problem was getting past Ashton Cargill back to the earthly realm. "I'll need you to take me through the realms so Cargill won't know I'm back to instruct my household."

Lazily, Vulpine fluffs his feathers, Nikola expecting him to start priming them, too.

"I'll cloak your telepathic message to your servants. I'm not going back to earth. Those people are mean to me." Vulpine says, pouting like a hurt child.

Already feeling ill-tempered and evil about Vulpine's demands Nikola smiles wickedly within, "Vulpine...earth is where your kind came from. Surely your mother here would like to see it again."

Knowing a con when he hears one Vulpine sticks to his guns and asks, "Do you want me to cloak your message or shall I call my uncle back?"

Knowing when to fold the game, Nikola submits to Vulpine's method and agrees to a mind-merge so he tells Jarvis what to send to Vector. He highly resents Ashton Cargill brought up his unfortunate past. Those acts were not done on his own free will. Those rich deranged, demented, bastards were forcing themselves on him.

Jarvis Jr. telepathically replied back *"Cargill has been here and terrified everyone looking for you. The hex against him didn't hold. Dad will serve as the conductor to send the items. We need to gather the others to open a portal large enough to send that many items."*

"Idiot! I already know the hex didn't hold against him. I just saw the immortal psychopath. Do whatever it takes to get the merchandise through." Nikola said, suddenly developing an intense headache, thanking the gods Jarvis Jr. didn't get his idiocy from his aunt. He got the stupid shit from Jarvis. But he knew the truth; inbred DNA caused the young man troubles. His mother and Nikola's father were brother and sister. He was another commodity of Orman's incestuous mating practice to produce gifted children through the Machiavelli family. They kidnapped his older aunt who had long ago married and moved to London and dragged her back to the castle and Jarvis Jr. was the result.

"Ok, Uncle Nik," his cousin/son says breaking connections. So he had to assume his mother was fine. Jarvis Jr. didn't say otherwise.

Vulpine relaxes now having ordered enough to last him for years until he finds another diamond buyer from earth. His feathered queen sister and their children had now gathered back around in the vast hall their father built for them before being haul off to celestial prison under the charges of bestiality.

"Nikola, a word to the wise. You should have left that woman alone. You never bother anything belonging to the ancient ones."

"Vulpine, she doesn't belongs to him, she's from the Christian sect. She is highly gifted and he merely wants her for a lay."

Vulpine looked in the loft ceiling, toying with an idea from something he heard his father say once when he was a young chickboy. "Nikola, what you want from her can only be activated through love not terror. Seems to me she is running from both of you. Perhaps he wants offspring. Isn't that what you want?"

"*The gall of this talking buzzard*," banteringly Nikola thinks, "Sure! She's my wife and I've a right to expect her to give me heirs."

Vulpine chuckled and asked? "Does she know she's your wife? If she saw what you did to your other wives, she's running like hell and I don't blame her!"

"Why does everyone keep asking me does she know she's my wife? As if I forced her to wed me?" Nikola snapped.

Vulpine's wife laughed and said, "I'm part vulture and I wouldn't marry you unless I was forced. So I know a gifted Christian woman didn't marry you on her free will. Plus, those like you have a sick sexual perversion about killing women."

"Warlocks do not hate women, women need to learn their place." Nikola gently replied but felt like biting her chicken-like head off. That mole on her nose was disgusting. Why doesn't she have it removed?

"Oh really??" Queen Xanthippe asked, raising her downy feathered brow "Well, then why nearly all those you and all the other Grand Wizards before you sent to us to be eaten are female? Rarely we get a male. I suppose every warlock does exactly as the big, bad Grand Wizard says?"

Nikola not liking this bird bitch's tone but needing her husband right now explains, "Women, witches, are harder to rule than men, warlocks. They're sneaky and backstabbing. All the females here are your daughters so you all don't have my problems."

Sensing the two plotting, he didn't like the template these two bird people were building against him. He didn't know exactly how strong they were in power; they were after all demigods. So he swallowed his pride and let Xanthippe's words roll over him.

They heard the eery, ethereal moans and groans of other worlds resonating through the palace and a huge portal open in a swirling fit of blackness sprinkled with stars of an unknown world. He saw scores of his people bringing the goods Vulpine requested. He hoped Jarvis was strong enough to hold open the portal for all products to clear and nothing got lost or trapped in an in-between dimension. He chuckled inwardly when he saw the crates of frozen chicken. He knew Jarvis sent it as an insult. How brilliant!

"Take those damn chickens back!" Vulpine roared, standing to his full height of nine feet tall. Nikola hadn't realized Vulpine was so huge standing up. His kids perched upon the high loft overhead had started moving around nervously at the sight of dead birds.

Vulpine looked up in the loft at his nervous offsprings, "Calm down, sweeties." He coos to them in a pigeon-like voice. Nikola realized those were the young ones up there. All the old ones were on the ground. Nikola half-hardheartedly scorned his servants for bringing birds.

"Your highness, Jarvis thought you might miss your favorite dish," the servant humbly said. The bird people up high in the loft gasped, a whining from up high was heard.

"Dadddy! He's gonna eat us!" They cried, referring to Nikola by the servant said chicken was his favorite food.

Nikola saw the amusement in his servant's face but pushed the man back through the portal. "No, not here, I must respect my host and hostess."

Jarvis can only hold the portal open for 45 minutes or less so the servants are working fast. Finally, they pushed a frighten woman through. Someone they apparently had kidnapped at the last moment. She was wearing a Sunday's church outfit and hat. She screamed and fainted when she looked around at the Vectorains.

"She'll do, at least she doesn't reek of sulfur and demon piss." Vulpine says, directing one of his sons to pick her up and carry her to an unseen location much to Nikola's relief. *"Good grief, of all the women to pick up the idiots had to go pick up a Christian".* But then let Vulpine deal with her when she starts crying and calling Jesus. He kept his end of the bargain.

The UNholy Pursuit of Ana continues:

Nikola was wrothful, vehemently outraged, and condemnatory of everything. Nothing was going as planned. Ana was being guarded by a warrior saint. He knows Cargill was out there last night. He was spiritually cloaked but he could still sense him. The immortal, cantankerous dickhead followed him. Nothing was going his way. Why?! He had planned every detail and now it was all falling apart. He was in an ireful modality that the man had the gumption to move openly on what was his. He was in an umbrageous mood one of the damn warriors was trying to return to their unit. Every damn time he turned around there was something up with angels or saints. He didn't know which were the biggest pains in the ass. Now his people are asking him to decide the fate of one of them. Can't they do anything without him?

He entered the grand room orating "We posses the power of great nations at our disposal. We can easily conquer them in the carnal realm but in the spiritual realm they are invincible!!" He was referring to the Nazarene warriors and warrior saints.

"Never forget that!" He cried

"No matter how haggard their physical form may appear. Remember, they all possesses what they call "the gift of endurance." Making it difficult, next to nearly impossible to kill them. Remember Sebastian, the bastardy saint, shot with 52 arrows and yet was still standing and talking. Their kind walked away from Hiroshima unharmed. Remember Catherine, the wayward woman who was dubbed a saint?!? Refused to be quiet even after her tongue had been cut out! To their lovable Margaret the same applies. These women just as women today refused to accept their place. And don't get me started on the wretched woman named Mary who got all this spiritual detritus started, had she just said "No." then we wouldn't be dealing with these holy Rottweilers of that Nazarene today!"

"Our coven was started pre-Noahian days. We were formed as an alliance to rule the world when ancient men and women of renown walked the earth. We predate Judaism, Christianity, Muslim, Islam, and all the other major religion. We are the only true religion of this world. We are the rightful rulers of the world".

"Our founding father Van, the wisest of the great sons of God, gave us clear and precise instructions never to fall in love with a warrior of God, they're incapable of truly loving anyone or anything except God and will slice your throat in the still of the night at His command".

"No matter how sweet their lullabies sound, turn deaf ear to their words or you will find yourself standing before Apollyon".

Walking around the council of 24 seated at the round table with hands clasped behind his back, as thus pondering what to say next. He stops behind the elegantly engraved chair of the USA Major satanic leader. Leaning over near his ear he says, "We retrieved this letter from the mail of James Cadwell. He wrote it to his lady love, who just happen to be the infamous Lady Ana." The rustling sound of the letter unfolding filled the room. Nikola appeared to be in a humorous mood but with him one never can tell for sure.

With him humor can be deadly. Holding the letter at reading level he says cheerfully "Now...let us all read it for we keep no secrets from each other."

The letter contained quotes from famous love letters of great men such as Bonaparte, Bryon, and Shakespeare. After the gleeful glances and soft chuckling of the others abated when finished he asked James to stand and slaps him hard across the face. James rubs the bruised cheek wondering how did his letter end up in the hand of his minor lord? Bowing to show respect he asks may he speak?

Waving his arm in a smooth manner, gesturing James the one chance to clarify his actions.

"Your highness. I've trailed her since age 12 and she've grown into a beautiful woman. I understand we aren't to love them but I must gain her trust as well as her heart. The only way to a woman's heart is to woo her with romance. When I completely gain her trust and she declares her love for me then she'll freely use her gifts for our cause. Please don't ask me to render this mission invalid. I've made contact with her but my present mate is jealous so what must I do?"

Nikola walks with his hands again laced behind his back and asked "I know you have actually communicated with her. I know you've lived next door to her but my question is have you fucked her yet?"

Caldwell quickly tries to calm his master down. "No, I haven't. I knew she was to be your queen. But I've help destroyed her pitiful marriage through our usual vices. The young man was no match for me."

Nikola gazes at the ceiling and asked "You are telling me you love her and haven't screwed her yet? Have she made any professions of affection toward you? If you haven't screwed her then what's wrong...my wife isn't good enough or white enough for you?"

He carefully considered his response. He knew The Grand Wizard was laying a trap. He was damned no matter which way he answered. He meticulously says, "No, she is very beautiful but the fear of you causes my penis not to be able to function." A roar of laughter erupted at this reply. James gulped for air and continued. " No, she has never shown any real interest in me. It you who she asked about."

Nikola knew he was lying but if lying would save his life so be it. Cadwell adds "We've gone out on several dates before she was your queen and I've showered her with many gifts but the conversation always comes back to you." Caldwell said as Nicola laughed, "I never heard I was so wrothful I literally scared the fuck out of a man's dick. But know this, she has always been my queen. I was whom was designated her for."

The others joined in with him in laughing at Cadwell. He beckon the man to stand, punches him hard in the stomach, and laughs, "I know you're lying regarding her talking about me while you two were dating; she hadn't met me then and nor does she remember me because the angels cleared her memory of our ceremony and other encounters. Saints are delicate, their nature is soft, their aren't callous like yours and mine. So heaven erases unpleasantries or shields them from the gall. But I like a good liar. Lying is good for the soul. Too much truth rots the brain and causes confusion."

He quieted everyone with a mere glance and asked "Do you think she suspects who you are and who she really is?" Seeking that he might stand a chance of living Caldwell quickly but informative says, "No, your highness, she hasn't a clue. We, our kind, aren't discussed in Christendom. We eliminated their teaching about our kind centuries ago and with the scientific age anyone who openly says we exist is virtuously ridiculed." James deliberately left out the meeting of Ana at the Janus Cargill's pool party.

"Hmm..." Nicola says, absently rubbing his chin as if in deep thought. Then fast as lighting he suddenly slaps James again and again roaring, "Fool, you've forgotten one thing! You aren't a Christian! Do you really think Christ is going to sat back and allow His handmaid to fall in love with you?! He'll eventually tell her who you are and what she is! And then what? She'll know too much about us by then."

James wonders why Nikola is beating up on him when everything he did pertaining Ana Wyett was at the warlock's command. He knows without doubt Caroline had his letters pulled from the courier. How else had they ended up in Nikola's hand? Rendered on his knees from the blows and from fear, James pleads, "I'm aware of all of that but her powers are worth the risk. I've kept tag on her for years. I've destroyed every avenue of income. I've destroyed her every residence and she'll eventually have to accept aid. She has a child to care for."

Nikola seemed to have calmed down a bit; his highness asked "What's your plan for your present Mrs. Cadwell if you win the love of this warrior saint of the Nazarene?"

James isn't sure what to say. He hadn't anticipated things that far but he replies "I'll kill her. Her gifts aren't strong enough for what I need to do."

The grand warlock grinned a pleasant but evil smile, "Now, you're talking Jim. You had me worried there for a moment. I was worried you had gone soft. You know what I do to softies?"

Nikola narrowed his dark eyes at the wisp of smoke rising from the center of the table. He hadn't opened a consultation to hell. A translucent angelic face appeared and addressed him in the divine language saying, "I'm tried of waiting. You haven't caught that woman yet? How did she slip through your fingers this time? The entire lot of you are useless." Nikola knew the others didn't understand what was said so he answered in a manner to make them believe he still had control of the room.

"My lord, we are working on the impending situation as you speak. She will be apprehended very soon."

"How soon are we speaking of? Orman failed, you are failing. So must I assign another your induction? My time has come and I will not let it pass me by due to human's inadequacy and incompetence!" The room rumbled.

"No, my lord. She will be ground into submission and perform as the ancient prophecies foretold." Nikola humbly replied as the twenty five men watched the smoke descend back through the hole in center of the table.

On a merrier tone Jim Caldwell is removed from the dinning chamber and locked away in his assigned room. He isn't surprised to see Carole there in the room assigned to

636

him. He hears The High Wizard announces."I've a surprise for you my honorable guests! We've managed to capture a regiment's 1st officer trying to escape us. He's in the dungeon for the living as I speak." Most of his guests have never been close to one and observe their ways.

"I ignores his constant calling his god. Apparently, God have ignored him too." Nikola laughed, this was the cue for everyone in the room to laugh also.

Holden, the leader of the middle United States region timidly asked "Your majesty...I know you know all things and you are all wise and all powerful, and you and your predecessors ruled nations from time immemorable but do you feel it is wise to have one of them here? Supposed the others come for their missing comrade?"

Nikola soothes their fear saying, "Ahh, dear child...that's the beauty of this hostage, I and your other royalty have discussed this matter already. We want his regiment to appear. A 1st officer, they're surely to come to his rescue! Then we'll be waiting. The talismans are waiting to entrap them and when powerless... we kill them."

Some wondered did the High Wizard have a death wish? They knew of no talisman able to hold that which is divine! Feeling their uncertainty, His Majesty angrily asked, "Do I sense fear among my council?!"

The regional leaders from the UK, Europe, India, USA, Russia, Ghana, China, Japan, and many other parts of the world shook their heads no. Although they had a simmering gut urge to run out the chamber screaming. Wondering had their lord lost his mind?! No one wanted to be around when and if that warrior bi-located out of that holding cell with his sword aflame, angry and screaming for their heads or their blood or both.

Sensing their fear the high wizard pressed a button and a 12 foot wall panel opened revealing a disgruntled, haggled man strapped to a torture table. Blood matted his hair and cheeks. Hands and feet were open wounds. He had been crucified. They collectively gasped when he looked into the camera knowing they were watching and saw his carnal pupils were no longer there. There were orbs of Red fire there instead. The high wizard sounded the alarm saying, "WE'VE A SAMSON ALERT. EVERYONE CLEAR THE

CASTLE!" Meaning the man had broken loose, reached his god and about to kill them as Samson killed the ancient Philistines. Amazingly, there are no teachings to what Samson really was. He was a warrior, not a warrior saint. And if a mere warrior can cause that much destruction just image the damage a warrior saint can cause.

Calling his advisers to him, Nikola asked, "I thought you imbeciles said this man didn't posses the gift of fire or any of dangerous gifts, especially the gift of bi-location??"

Rushing to their high wizard's side and bowing as customary to do, the advisers says, "He doesn't have the ability to remove himself from the torture table. He forfeited those abilities for wealth and the illusion of love of one of our sisters. He turned his back on his kind. But recently his wife caught him quietly praying; asking to be allowed back into the unison of his regiment and a report was made known to us. We strongly advised him he would lose all wealth, multimillion dollar home, and even his children if he didn't stop this nonsense. But he choose to keep trying to reach those who abandoned him so we had no other choice but to bring him here or kill him. His gifts are too valuable to destroy him. So please, everyone relax. He has been glaring at us in that manner for the past 24 hours. He's harmless."

Showing visible signs of distress the wizard roars "Bring his whore of a wife to me!"

An attractive woman is brought out weeping. Nikola raises from his seat and grabs her face. "Shut the fuck up! Or I'll give you something to cry about. You better get your husband under control or your ass is furniture polish." He said, roughly thrusting her away from him.

She is led away to the chamber as Nikola ordered. Although, he knows he really can't contain this once warrior saint if the man is given back his powers. He have heard there are such spells but he doesn't know them. Lucifer nor Orman taught them to him. So he needs her to calm him down.

Watching the uproar unfold through astral vision, Caldwell, whose real name is Cadwell, is thankful for once someone else is pissing Nikola off besides him. Taking the heat off himself for a moment. The ignominy of deprecating his manhood in front of his juniors was still burning. But he wonders how Nikola got those letters. They were written quite a while ago. At least two years ago before Nikola married the woman. He telepathically reached Caroline who swears she didn't give Nikola those letters. But he suspects she's lying.

The warlocks all watch on the large screen as the wife coos and coaxes her husband into calming down. The Nazarene warrior saint knows he made a grave mistake. But he has to find a way out or his children will die. They've already promised him that.

"Woodrow, darling you knew what you were getting into when you accepted the offer so why all the uproar now?" His wife gently asked with trembling hands wiping his wounds.

He couldn't tell her something big was about to go down in spiritual warfare. He had betrayed his kind enough already. "I had a horrible dream you and the children were about to be killed because of me." He lied.

She laughed dismissively at his claim saying, "The Grand Wizard is not a killer. As long as you behave yourself, the children and I will be fine."

In weary suspiration Nikola says "See everyone, this is a fine excellent example of why I teach against falling in love. Loving your children. It make you forget your focus, your goals which are only to love and serve me," he says, then instructs his servants to bring James and Carole back out and strap Carole to the sex chair. He carefully watches James reaction. The man shows no emotions. That's good.

The beautiful actress, Carole Cadwell held her face passionless and frigorific as the stranger plundered into her as if making a porn movie. Deciding this is better than ending up in the refrigerated basement. But she didn't expect the other male regional leaders to join in.

"This woman is your Grand Witch," Nikola explains, pointing to a cheerful picture of Ana. "You're to treat her accordingly. Only I've the authority to do what what you did."

639

Nicola further patiently explains while standing next to her, watching the salacious act. She see tears swimming in James' eyes as he stares at her face. She know then that he does love her and that love will cause a problem called disloyalty which he has the perfect remedy for.

Around midnight, Nikola instructed Carole to be removed from the chair and brought to him tired, sore, and bleeding. He instructed the female attendants to clean her up and put a nice, virginal white gown on her.

"You showed defiance and unresponsiveness to my punishment out there. I didn't hear you moan a single time. I do not appreciate your display of arrogance." He said as he pushed her near the sex horse Orman used to use on him. "You've given birth, haven't you?" He asked insouciantly.

"Yes, my lord." She replied nervously, wondering what he was about to do and what was that damn thing?

"How many times?" He asked in a softer tone. She was panicking big time now, this must had been like Jane Grey must have felt trapped in the house with Henry VIII.

"Three times." She honestly replied as he pushed her over on her stomach and strapped her hands and feet. He knew better than she how painful this device was. He endured it every night for a year. She feels him casually tosses the gown above her hips and feels a sharp pain in her anus as he roughly penetrate her. The painful copulation got the sound out of her he desired. He imagines she is Ana and humps harder until she is weeping and crying. When he is finished he leaves her tied to the torture device and the servants turn out the lights. She is scared shitless to be in his room in the dark. She heard he sleeps with a succubus. She hears heavy footsteps treading the floor. She wants to scream but she knows if she does someone will kill her. She feels hands that are too hairy to be human on her naked buttocks. Shortly before pure white pain blinds her mind her witchery sentiency picks up on an eutherian creature. "Carole, meet Taurus" She heard the Grand Wizard say before passing out.

James wonders how much more of this can he stand? These three succubus are driving him insane. They won't let his erection die. He knew Nikola was a diabolical, evil, masochistic cocksucker but why not just flog him? He knew some of other warlocks who are disfigured because of Nikola's childish rage. He never knew an erection could literally be painful. These demons are infected with succums. He know they are infested, he can see the black squiggly harpies crawling around their vaginas if that's what one would call the mawing twat between their legs. Succums cause atrocious, horrifying pain, they slowly kills the victim by crawling and digging through vital organs. There's no medical cure for them, only a priest or holy person can rebuke them. He feels his penis and scrotum swelling as those horrible creatures make their way up into his body via his his urethra. He heard Nikola telepathically say, "I thought I would help you out with your impotency since I'm the cause of it."

He threw up all over the bed when one of those things tried to make him suck her teats. She slaps and beats him all over the room with her clawed hands. They catch him and hold him down and force the bloody, milky substance into his mouth. He he no idea what it is but he starts hallucinating. Seeing them not as demons but as beautiful women. But the sense of intuition is still screaming wildly in his ear they are not human. He has no idea what else is done to his body; it takes over and he passes out.

The next day the badly injured couple is put on a plane with duly noted instructions on how to continue their work. Nikola is unavailable.

Everyone had left the castle and returned to their stations mindful not to upset the High or Grand Wizard or their punishment would be perverted and severe. Never mind he could change the rules on a whim and punish you for that which he personally instructed you to do. But the old-timers still punctually swear he is far more merciful than Orman, his predecessor.

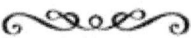

Back in the land of half-Vultures, Nikola is unsatisfied Lucifer wanted the Caldwells to live for future usage and wants that blossoming warrior saint kept in captivity to milk him for his blood. He swears the blood of saints is sweet. Knowing that Ana is alone and most likely weak he sends an aswang after her, which is a spiritual being, an element who feeds upon the soul of the helpless person. Had not she shown affection to Azazael he wouldn't be in exile from the earth and his empire. Had she simply come and preformed the duty she was created for, things would be well within his kingdom with no demonic immortal hot on his trail. He is satisfied the aswang will find her and give her a taste of her own medicine.

Chapter 14
I wish you didn't hate me so much.

His executives tells him the man named Tobias Jones is in. The man won't go away until he agrees to see him. Seems to him this morning it's one problem after another. Ana running off, refusing to tell him where she is living. Some fool hit one of his banks in San Francisco. And now, some second rate builder who thinks he's the next Frank Lloyd Wright is pestering him and won't go away.

"Sewell, any news on the bank robbery?" Ashton asked drying off but his mind is really still on Ana BuFaye.

"Sir, he got past the laser security. The only way I see possible is he teleported into the vault. Nothing is broken. But I've an image of him. Do you wish to see it?"

"No, that's ok. The poor sap only took six million. I will just claim it as a lost." Ashton says, getting dressed. Sewell is concerned about his boss' disinterest in things. Normally had anyone robbed one of his banks he would have them by the nuts by now. But now, he's this easy as Sunday afternoon in May, laid back person Sewell doesn't know.

"Sir," Sewell says into the wall phone. "I know this is none of my business but your behavior has been very lenient as of late".

"You're right, it's none of your business. Tell Mr. Jones I'll see him at 2:00, maybe he will go away after he learns he doesn't have what I'm looking for."

"Very well, sir." Sewell says promptly and waits for Ashton to break the connection. You never break connection first with him. At least, one thing he is thankful for.... when that woman visits, afterwards he is much easier to get along with. He doesn't hold your feet to the fire for every mistake.

Ashton tossed the tie on the bed, deciding he is pissed off and doesn't feel like wearing it. He has got to get that woman out of his head. She's making him soft. He chuckled at his own thought. *"Well...she doesn't me soften below the belt."*

He waits only a few minutes before his Norfolk, Va secretary escorts a pleasant looking, fairly attractive man in carrying a building blueprint under his arm.

"Hello, Mr. Cargill. My name is Tobias Jones". Ashton counts it against him he doesn't have it in a tube or an at least a briefcase. If one is to do work for him they had better be on their P's and Q's from start to finish. The man shivers when he spiritually scans him.

"Aw fuck, another one of those damn gifted humans. I am already dealing with one. My baby is a fruitcake and I know it." He smiles affectionately, thinking to himself he would kill them had anyone besides himself called Ana a fruitcake. Tobias returned the small gesture, assuming the man is smiling about his non-sophistication; in a way he is. Ashton is caught off guard in mentally referring to Ana as his baby.

"Sir, here's the design. I believe you'll love it!" Tobias said, unrolling the blueprint. He views it. He has seen this design before in another world. He had to admit it was quite impressive. But he wonders if he hires this man will he forget to come to work; the gifted are a whole another level of peculiar. Like this morning, Ana hiding under the covers to get dressed when he saw it all last night.

"Mr. Jones, thank you for coming but this is not what I had in mind." Ashton says to a disappointed man. Ashton remembers something else, *"Saints aren't good at hiding emotions. They're open books"*

"Sir, I can change the plan, the design, and build it anyway you would like." Tobias ensures him.

"Mr. Jones, I don't pay for a building until it's completed. Do you have 36 billion to build it?" Ashton asked, knowing the man didn't.

"No sir, I do not." Tobias admitted. "But I"m willing to borrow it. I know I can provide the best craftsmanship around."

Ashton has grown bored with the man. He looks at his family info record. He have a five kids and a wife named Star. He once knew a woman named Star, he wonders if she is the same person? She was one of those flings he had no intention of seeing again.

"How long you and your wife been married? How long have you been in business for yourself?

"I'm just starting my own business, I've been married about fifteen years."

"I see the company you presently work for is going under, there aren't many family homes being built in this economy. I wish you all the luck in the world but Cargill International can't use your service right now."

"Sir, I wouldn't be here if I didn't know I can build any design you want. I've five children, Truilla Construction is going under as you said. Everyone has to start somewhere."

Ashton pushed the silent button to alert his secretary. To bring her into his office to show this man out. *Oh yes, he remembers Star Madden, she was high minded and thought she was prettier than she actually was. He remember she wanted him to take her shopping in Paris. Oh pplease, her pussy wasn't that good. Oh! He forgot, he did put 25 grand in Ana's jeans pocket last night while she slept. He hopes she isn't crazy enough to come back and throw it at him. Shrieking she can't be bought or some lunatic nonsense like that.*

The secretary arrived and escorted Tobias out without a deal. Ashton knows Star isn't going to be happy at all. But that's just tough. He has enough of his own problems without financing an old lover's project.

Watching the disappointed, distressed man leave, Ashton feels a little something for the man. Something he rarely if ever feels for anyone. It's a rare blue moon he feels sympathy for anyone. But this man had his sympathy married to that skanky fishwife. He had to let the man walk for two of his kind (the gifted) had already fucked up his day. He wasn't in the mood to learn if Tobias would be his third strike for the day he thinks as he views the footage of a dark skinned, young black man walking around inside the vault, not sure how much to take. He believes he just discovered that ability. Grief may have brought it forth. He got a report the man paid cash for his grand aunt's funeral. So he guessed he wouldn't add insult to injury. But this boy better not try him again. The next time he won't be so nice about this shit.

He felt the emotions transpire across time and dimension; since they were in the same realm it didn't have to travel through another realm when she touched the money. That was a physical link between them. He sensed dislike, hurt, anger, disdain, despair, love, hate, uncertainty, fear, guilt, loneliness, joy, and an array of other all stirred together in a huge pot called her psyche.

"I didn't give it to you as payment for sex, I gave it to you to stay alive, to stay ahead of Vonderbilt, I gave it to you cause I love you. My little Silly Valentine. I wish you didn't hate me so much."

He heard her sigh before replying, he felt the portal closing that linked them within these next few minutes he said, *"Darling, my beautiful darling, I won't deny I've done a lot of evil but you're one person who has no need at all to fear me. I love you and always will, nothing will change that."*

He felt as thus someone had died when the link was broken and tears rolled down his cheeks. He angrily slapped him palm down on the desk where Tobias Jones had just unfurled his blueprint. He suddenly remembered those of the same kind can find each other. Why did he stupidly send the man away when this man is gifted in love and compassion just as Ana? He can find her.

He quickly disappeared back to the house where they spent the night looking for something personal of hers. He found her bra. "Hell no, I can't use that." He said to himself, pocketing it so no one else would find it. He looks at the glasses, she didn't drink anything. He removed the pillowcase, thankful this house didn't have a staff yet. So no maid had been here to clean up and then he teleported to Tobias' hotel. He exited outside the door. He reminds himself if he scares the man half to death, he will run like hell. The true gifted are a nervous bunch. They sprint at the first sign of one like himself showing up on the scene. They run, calling Father, and Father beats your ass for scaring them. So he knocked. He hears the man on the phone. He hears the man rise off the bed to come to the door and opens it wearing a puzzled expression.

"Mr. Tobias Jones, would you care to join me for dinner so we can further discuss our business plan?" He said charmingly, as he smiles pleasantly, pushing his normal scowl aside. The man is rather surprised he is here. "I believe I was a little hasty in my judgment."

Finding his voice Tobias says "Come Mr. Cargill. What a pleasant surprise!" Ashton flinched because this man sounds a little like Ana if she were a guy. "*They are even nice to people who treat them like shit.*"

.

"Sir, what can I do for you?" Tobias asked curiously.

"You can have dinner with me. We can further discuss the blueprints and a few other things." Ashton said with a smile linked to a motive. He watched the man's face light up. *Gosh, these people reminds his so much of his Father.*

"Sure, I was just telling Star I was going downstairs to the vending machine to get some chips and soda for dinner. My plane doesn't leave until 10:00 in the morning." Tobias says, still uncertain why the richest man in the world is inviting him, lowly, broke Tobias Jones to dinner.

"Nonsense, you are coming with me to the Stieglitz Cargill hotel. This hotel will deliver your effects to your room. I've reserved it for a week, you are welcome to invite Star. I'll send a plane for her if you like."

"*Effects*?" Tobias thinks, looking around. "*What effects? I only have one suit bag and a suitcase if that's what you call 'effects'?!*" But instead he replied, "Sure sir, I'm certain Star would enjoy that."

The two men rode pretty much in silence to dinner. Ashton ordered whatever Tobias wanted which wasn't much. A huge jet had been sent to pick up Star and his children. Ashton knew they would be at the luxurious hotel suite waiting. After dinner he led Tobias to his office. He prays it isn't too late.

"Mr. Jones...I know you are like my wife. I want you to touch this and tell me where she is." Ashton said, startling even himself in referring to Ana as his wife.

Tobias reaches for the expensive silk pillowcase and as touches it he hears a woman moaning in ecstasy. Embarrassed, he breaks the connection and hands the pillow case back to the immortal man. "This is from your matrimony bed, sir. Sorry, I-I can't look at that."

This gesture of chivalry impressed Ashton, a lesser man would have looked. "Understandable, I need to find her. Someone wants to hurt her. She got upset with me today and left home. I must find her before those who want to kill her find her." Ashton pled desperately.

Tobias sighed. He felt sorry for the man who had everything, even the love of a good woman but yet, still wasn't happy.

"Ashton", Tobias said, dropping the formality between them. "You need to get rid of those other women in your life. Your wife isn't fooled. She knows they're in your life. It's hurt as to why she ran away. She sensed their presence. A good woman is more valuable than gold. Behind every great man stands an even a greater woman. You built an empire

647

for her, you will give her all the wealth of this world. But refuse to give yourself to her alone. She is a handmaid of God. So treat her accordingly."

Ashton felt he didn't need a lecture, he already knew her value but needed to know where in the hell she was.

"Tell me where she is and we have a 36 billion dollar deal."

Tobias reached for the case again. Tobias sees Cargill's wife and child shopping at Target Mart, a store Star thumbs her nose at. He sees Cargill's concubines living in the grandest luxury money can buy, he sees his wife and child in passe, unpressed, rough-dried clothing while his harem is dressed like queens and movie stars. He sees his wife working menial jobs and running afraid for her and their child's life, he sees his child with the worry of adult. This is more than Tobias can bear when he sees the mother goes hungry, pushing the plate of food in front of the child.

"I do not wish to do business with you. A man is known by how he treats his family. Dogs on the city's heap pile live better than your wife and child. She was with your child, sick and weakened, trying to work to take care of your child already living. The Lord took back that child because she is weakened, it would've kill her." Tobias said against his wishes, as he stared in admonishment in Cargill's eyes.

Ashton was shocked at the news of the miscarriage. Ana never told him. Or had she told him and he doesn't remember?

"I know I'm a terrible, horrible person but this isn't about me. I don't care about me. I need to know where is she? Someone is trying to hurt her. So I need to know where is she? You don't understand the urgency in finding her before the darkside finds her," Ashton pleads again. The news of the miscarriage shook him very badly. "I really, truly had no idea."

Toshiba glared at him in the manner of the prophets of old, (Ashton hadn't noticed the name nor the facial change) and said "The Lord God Almighty instructed me not to tell you. You aren't ready to be the husband she needs."

Ashton realized quickly he was no longer talking to Tobias Jones but to his Father. "You aren't anymore deserving of My Daughter than Nikola who call himself Vonderbilt. Long ago, you sincerely asked Me for one of my finest daughters to help save your world. I gave her unto you. She came from the same order of the one which I chose the Savior to be born through. But did you appreciate My Gift? No, you did not! You dragged her before My Throne half dressed with your newborn child in her arms. Showing her nakedness to your brothers. All because she wasn't the neat and clean package you were accustomed to. Her kind bleeds, they were made from their earth, they aren't made from the same substance as you. You damaged her so greatly she married your brother to cover her shame. Yes, she is still your wife, that's why I plucked her from before the creation of her mother Eve and her father Adam to visit you when you became maddened with emotions while suffering your punishment. But until you learn to behave accordingly I'll not allow you to find and hurt her. Until you have suffered enough to give all yourself and all your love to her and none others you will not find her. Those whom I've bestowed My Love upon, LOVE IS ALL THEY KNOW. And like I, they're very jealous. She senses you share yourself with others. And that hurts her. I have erased her memory to spare her the pain and erased yours so you can not pursue her. Azazael, this is not a game. This is a reality you haven't shown Me you are serious about!"

"Father, I promise to do better!", he cried.

"Then why are those ill-reputed women still in her houses? All I've allowed you to accumulate was for her sake, not yours. When I atoned you I did it because she begged Me. She crawled and prostrated at the Throne and begged Me not to destroy you. I spared you for her sake, not yours."

All of this was new to him. He never knew who petitioned to bring him out of the chains, perhaps he once knew but had forgotten.

"Father, I understand all that but if I can not be with her then remove her memory of me! She doesn't deserve to be tortured because of me. She hasn't done anything worthy of her suffering."

649

"Love is the strongest of all the powers and principles. She would eventually remember you and go back to you and get hurt again. Her suffering has nothing to do with you. She is suffering because of Me. I blocked her and you for she will never complete the assignment I appointed her with you in her life."

"Father, I really love her. I've learned my lesson. Please, please, I'm begging You. Please tell me where she is."

"Son, your wife is a soldier just as yourself, she has a job to do. You would interfere with My Work. If you are serious about finding your wife practice on being the husband she needs." He watched in astonishment as his Father signs out and Tobias Jones returns. It had been a long while since he had seen that.

"Thank you for time." Ashton says leaving a $50 grand bill on the table between himself and Tobias.

"Mr. Cargill, I'm sorry," Tobias said, referring to the miscarriage.

"Don't be my Father always strong-arms people," Ashton telepathically replied and kept on walking.

"Sir, wait a minute." Tobias called after Cargill. Ashton stopped and turned around curiously.

"I feel you love her very much. I would be besides myself shall anything happened to Star or one of the kids. I felt your pains. Hand me the pillow again. I can call my own kind."

Ashton reluctantly pulled the silk cover from his pocket and placed it to the man's outstretched hand. Tobias takes it and they head to the elevator to the private sitting room of the restaurant's office. He isn't sure the woman will answer but it's worth a try. Those like himself have to be certain you aren't a demon trying to trick them before they will answer. Not that he blames them.

Tobias closed his eyes and mediated on finding the woman connected to the pillowcase. In his third eyes he sees her with a little girl of about 8 or 9. "Mrs. Cargill, please through the realm, I'm sitting here with your husband. Ma'am...he desperately needs to talk to you."

Ana stopped playing the electronic game with Bea and looked around. How was this stranger able to talk to her? For once it wasn't Nikola. But how does she know it isn't someone trying to trick her?

"What did you call me and how do you know me?" The reply came back. But then she remembered Mother Harris and the saints in the cave told her demons and satanists can not speak nor hear through the Royal Telephone as they call this method of communication.

"I'm sitting here with your husband. He needs to talk to you about something very important."

They both are surprised she actually came through holding an electronic game in one hand while the other held on to a child.

Cargill immediately rushed to them and held them both in a tight embrace. Tobias, seeing the emotional reunion, tried to slip away unnoticed but Ana wouldn't let him go without thanking him.

⁕

Ana was trying to decide whether to take a job or give her days solely to Bea. Now she had some breathing room. She had gone somewhere last night and met with Ashton and a client before being pulled back to her location. His client was like her. He had a third eye. She saw him look through the opening and frowned at how shabby her room was. They had argued the night before because she wouldn't tell him where they were and he was taking it out on this poor man.

651

Having substantial dough she figured she better spend it before angels take it. She knew just the thing to do. Go to an amusement park. She decided they were going even if she had to hurt a few people along the way shall anyone get in her way.

The carnival's fiesta atmosphere was contagious. It was lively and colorful. The day was a warm day. A great day for fun and that was what she was determined they was going to have today. The last time they were at such a place was at a Fall or Winter Festival in Canada and that was a number of years ago.

Bea was exhilarated to be in her favorite cartoons theme park, she hadn't had much interaction with children her own age. The Pocahontas character attracted Ana for some unknown reason. A little boy named Jude who had been running around with Bea all day runs up to the tall, elegant, true Native American princess, yelling, "Mom, I want tickets to run the space tea cups." She reached into a drawstring pouch and pulled out two tickets.

"Here's one for your cute little friend." The woman said handing Bea a ticket, too. Ana catches up with the two little speed demons

"Uh, sorry Ms, but that thing looks nothing like the pictures of their old teacup ride, that thing looks it will sling you into space." Ana chuckled handing Bea's ticket back "I appreciate your hospitality."

"AH! Mom!" Bea cried "Sacajawea is letting Jude ride." Ana was shocked; she thought the character was Pocahontas.

The tall woman introduced herself saying, "Hi, my name is Melinda Gilmore and this is my son Jude Gilmore and you are??" The several inches taller than herself woman asked with her hand extended, common courtesy prompted her to shake her hand and utter a fake name.

"Sorry, sweetheart but it looks dangerous. You can't ride that thing," Ana said watching a saucer sling the cups like an angry monster and another saucer catching it. The cups with screaming, laughing kids and teens were being passed from one saucer to another.

She was imagining some of Vonderbilt's goons showing up cutting the power as a cup separated from one saucer and moved to the next and children falling to their far too soon death.

The woman laughed and said, "Don't worry, the cups are attached to suspense cables. No one has fallen since I've been here. It's designed to look as thus they are moving unsupported in the air."

Bea pulls her new friend in front of Ana "Hey Jude." She giggled, "Jude explain to my mom how it works." The boy crosses his arms and surly said, "If you don't call me "Hey Jude" any more, Queen Bee!"

"I heard an old song on the car radio called "Hey Jude." I didn't implore your ridicule, my name is Breanna, and don't you forget it!" Bea said sounding like her Aunt Helena with her tiny finger wagging in the boy's face while her other hand was clenched into a fist planted firmly on her narrow hip and her neck dancing like an a Hindu goddess.

"You sound like a bee to me." Jude cried, buzzing around like a bee.

"Ok, you two old married people." Melinda said. seeing that Bea was about to punch her ornery son.

"Jude, you aren't supposed to call girls names. Y'all ain't been married but one day and about to kill each other already. Go get on that train off over there, I'm sure her mother would approve of it."

Watching her son and new friend (he told his mom he was going to marry Bea when he grew up) run off to get in line a few feet away Melinda chuckled. Ana did feel more comfortable with that ride.

"Boys are a handful." Melinda said behind her back, smiling and watching her son think he is protecting Bea.

"How old is he?" Ana asked.

"Seven but think he's seventeen. According to him you're his mother-in-law. He put that candy ring on your daughter's finger and said he would buy her a real one when he grew up. How old is your daughter?" Melinda laughed.

"Oh really?" Ana asked astonished. "Yeah, he'll have to get another one because she will have eaten that one by the end of the day. She's 6." Ana knew she lied about Bea's age but she wasn't thrilled about how Bea forgot to lie about her name so she felt she had to insert a lie somewhere in the scenario. Ana noticed the woman's eyes following a young couple dressed in all black as thus they were in Victorian mourning attire. Four more young men joined them and all six got in line to her show. Their looks were not very friendly. She recognize it very well. She clandestinely watched them as two moved surreptitiously to the side of the line to better watch Melinda. Ana stealthily moved her hand to the hidden gun in her lining of her handbag. She had sewn a thin lining of flat lead in bags she needed to take in public places for she suspected they would search her for weapons. Her hand was on the trigger, she was preparing to rise the bag and shoot through it if they as so much twitched the wrong way.

"You know them?" Ana asked, seeing that the three plainly didn't like each other. They were saying something to a man who appeared to be Melinda's manager. The man approached them and smiled politely at Ana but not so nicely at Melinda.

"Melinda, that couple said you were rude to them because they're white." The man said rather sharply. "You're to be nice to all the customer regardless of ethnicity. If you can't then hang up the costume. So what if they don't know Pocahontas from Sacagawea."

Stating the attenuation of her theme Melinda cried. "The baby on the back should've told them which was which." Melinda grunted and crossed her arms. "Had they paid attention in school they would know that."

Ana was behind the man shaking her head at her would be new friend. To be quiet if she doesn't want to get fired today.

"You are lucky there isn't anyone to take your place who looks authentic," the tall balding man growled lowly at Melinda. Surprising Ana with his aggressive attitude. She felt the growl was a little over the top and totally unnecessary.

"You can take this job and shove it up your ass! I'm not going to let those oily black-eyed fools insult my heritage!" Ana wanted to slap her hand across her mouth. This woman was worse than her about not knowing when to shut up. She looked back through the crowd at the couple and sure enough, Melinda was right. They had demons in them. It's not a total black out as they show in movies, it's more like another pair of shiny black pupils looking through the person's eyes. If it was a total black out, hell, the whole world would see them.

A tall man with the physique of a body builder who neither had seen approached them asked, "Ladies, what seems to be the problem?" Ana tells him the scenario but sees another man in the crowd wearing dark sunglasses.

"There is no problem, sir." The rude manager says to the strange man. Who acknowledged the man with a nod before turning address Ana.

"Ms. BuFaye, my name is Kortris, my employer would like to speak to you." Ana had been caught in her lie. Melinda looks at her, a little hurt.

"Sorry, lady you seem like a nice person but I've too much evil pursuing me to give my real name everytime someone asks it."

"Tell him to come in here. I don't meet strangers." she inauspiciously replied after pointing out the six people intimidating the woman named Melinda.

"Very well. I'll forward your message and handle the deplorables." The man named Kortris said with a slight bow toward both women and a look was cast in the manager's direction that meant leave them alone. Panic started kicking in, where in the hell was that damn train? She couldn't hide without Bea.

"If you are on the run, you didn't have to lie to me about your name. I know what it's

655

like," Melinda said, watching her crane her neck in search of the train she finally allowed Bea to ride.

"I"m sorry but telling my real name will get me killed," she replied still looking for the train to pull back in the depot. She had refused to let Bea ride the slinging cups so they settled for a train ride but now she was starting to regret it. A new wave of panic set in; supposed Bea has been kidnapped again? That man didn't say who his employer was. Tears started clouding her vision.

"Don't cry, she'll be out in a little bit." Melinda said, rubbing her back. "Oh no, here comes the Big Boss." Melinda sighed, knowing she was fired.

Ashton has never liked theme parks nor kids for that matter and this damn place is crawling with the little horrors. A child ran into him and bounced off and got up and kept on running to where ever he was in such a hurry to get to. Why does Ana have to make everything so damn difficult? When his reporter anchored the story about an hotel on fire and the fire burnt down the building and is still burning a week later he knew it was Ana who had attacked someone. He was right, she had been there. The money he gave her was electronically tagged. Fuck all who thought that was a dirty way to keep up with her. The manager at the Target Mart told him she had been in there, she also told him another older man had been there too looking for her. The man she described was Shrevenport. Another one of Nikola's murdering bastards. She had no choice but to tell him, her boss. He saw Ana and Bea running all over the store on the security camera like these munchkins are running all here.

He bought this place about 200 years ago for his several generations grand-children, his daughter Lavenedica's children so they would have someplace to play other than in his face or in his house when she brought them to visit.

He believed he made an error with Ana by sending Kortris to tell her to come to him. Who knows, she has probably waded the pond by now with Bea on her back. He spotted her auburn hair up in a bun up ahead in the crushing crowd but he didn't see Bea, so apparently Bea was riding something and she couldn't run.

She was talking to a taller Native American woman.

"Good afternoon, ladies." He said politely, carefully watching Ana's reaction.

Ana turns and her eyes widen. "H-How did you find me?" She stuttered.

"I have my ways." He replied a lot nicer than he felt at the moment. "May I speak with you a moment?" He asked, leading her away.

"Take care of the little girl when she gets off the ride." He instructed Melinda.

"Yes sir, Mr. Cargill." She replied, wondering how this Ana knew him, and what in the hell was he? He escorted her under a dark green eave covering a souvenir shop and asked, "Why are you doing this? Don't you know you'll soon be too heavy to keep jumping fences? I came to tell you, you may be pregnant." He knew he was lying but hey what else can he do to talk sense into her? He knew God had stopped the conception from occurring. She conspicuously grabbed her stomach.

"I hadn't thought about that! I can't afford another child!" She cried. Still watching out for Bea, he had instructed the carnival ride operators to take the child on a longer than standard ride so he could talk to Ana in private.

"Well, you need to think about it. How and where are you plan to have it and support it." *Father was going to haul his lying ass off to hell for his lies.*

"I hadn't thought that far ahead. I felt a little queasy a few days ago but I thought it was the food we ate, Bea was fine with her quesadilla." The *queasy* part caught him off guard, maybe Dad called his bluff to see what he would do. Maybe she is pregnant. Aw fuck! He didn't want any snot nosed brats. He only wanted her. Bea was fine. She's a big kid now. So he was prepared to deal with the one she already had, that one was plenty enough. He knew she hadn't been to a doctor nor used home kit because a pregnancy wasn't something she thought could happen.

"When your daughter gets off her ride we need to talk. I'm not letting you drag my

657

child all over creation with Vonderbilt shooting at him or her."

Ana felt trapped. She was in no position to have another child. She could hear Helena screaming at her asking was she dumb, stupid, or what? Having a baby while on the run?

She nodded, she agreed to go with him. They indeed needed to talk. She retrieved Bea the moment she and Jude got off the train.

"Hey, you're the dude from the closet." Bea cried.

Melinda gave her a knowing smile. "It was nice meeting you, Melinda. I hope we someday meet again." Ana said, hugging her new friend good-bye. It's hard to meet people you feel close to.

Ashton whisked them both out the park into a waiting limo being driven by the man she saw earlier.

To make conversation, she told him she hoped her new friend was alright, she has a mean manager.

"Her job is secured." Was all he said to her for he wasn't thrilled about her queasiness.

They arrived at a house, no a palace, in Beverly Hills. She didn't know there were palaces in Beverly Hills. Immediately upon arriving he called a woman to supervise Bea, not giving her a chance to protest. Saying Bea didn't need to hear what he had to say and they really needed to talk. He ushered her into a room and closed the door.

"For a start, they whisked you away before I got the opportunity to ask you about the miscarriage. You need to know that I'm not human. That I smelt you when I hugged you and if I'm not mistaken you are pregnant. But this one won't be like having Bea. The child could be a titan or even winged." He said, sipping a drink as he scares the hell outta her.

"Or there could be as many as 6-8 born at once." He knew he was scaring her.

"Six to eight at once." She moaned.

He chuckled inward but he wasn't lying about the large number of them nor about their physical characteristics.

"How do you feel about abortions?" He asked.

So, there goes the real reason he invited her here, to talk her into an abortion. She looked him squarely in the eyes and said, "I'm not aborting them, I don't care how many there are or if you like it or not."

He mentally kicks himself. This is what he gets for lying.

"Fine, I won't be the one having them." He retorted. "You will. But I just thought you should know what you're up against."

Feeling mean and hurt that he asked her to have an abortion she asked. "How do you know you are the father? I'm on the road all the time."

She saw his eyes darken; they literally changed color. Like a Mean Evil Spirit suddenly jumped in him. "When you came to me a week or so ago, you weren't pregnant, and if you are, it's by another man. He better had raped you and you couldn't fight him off. If they aren't mine I can be real ugly. So don't let this pretty exterior fool you. If you've fucked another man on your own free will and got yourself knocked up...you think Vonderbilt is hell on two legs, then you haven't seen nothing yet."

She stared back at him trying to figure him out and to how to get the hell out of here. That was a deadly threat if she ever heard one. The door was closed. His angry eyes followed hers to the door.

He shouted, causing her to jump "TELL ME, HAVE YOU BEEN FUCKING AROUND ON ME?!"

Regaining her pose, "I didn't realize we were in a relationship." She said meekly, not wanting to antagonize him further. She saw in his eyes he had killed many and she didn't plan to be next. "So, you track me down just to ask me if I have another lover?"

"I suppose you make midnight visits to a lot of motherfuckers whenever you get horny." He said in a rather nasty tone. "I never pegged you the type to sleep around but I guess I was wrong. How many motherfuckers out there feeling good off your pussy?"

She knew her mouth was open as she stared at him, his language was not that of a gentleman. *"What in the hell is wrong with this psycho? He looks sane but, in truth, he's batshit crazy. How can I ever thought I loved him?!"*

"Of course not!" She cried, after regaining her voice, she was shocked his language was so vulgar. "I don't even know why I make midnight visits to you. You're very rude and mean."

"Well, don't fuck with me like that." He said callously. "I'm trying to tell you this kid or children could kill you and you're bullshitting me."

"Ain't nobody but you. I ain't never slept with nobody but you and Thad and both of you son of bitches treat me like shit." She slobbered in her hands, hiding her face. She was tired, emotionally drained, and here he is yelling at her, "If I had any sense, I would get someone else. Somebody who ain't yelling at me." She was trying to find a way out. There was no way she was staying here and letting this bastard yell at her no matter how rich and handsome he was.

Now he feels like a real first class heel, like pure shit for making her cry. But he felt he had to get the truth out of her. He knew his way of finding out was grotesquely lacking affection and very much unprofessional but how else was he going to make her tell the truth? Oh Lord! She's about to get hysterical. But isn't this the same woman who just killed up a bunch of people, burned down the building? A woman who dared to defy the world's Grand Wizard's wishes? Who knows how many she has actually killed and now his mere words and yelling at her are making her brawl like a baby????

660

"Why you being so mean to me?" She unceremoniously wails. He knows the customary thing to do is hug her. But he approaches her carefully, she is after all, a divine assassin who is highly pissed off right now...

"Sssh, baby, don't cry. You're right we aren't in a relationship. I do care a great deal about you and don't want to share you with anyone else." He said, wrapping his arms around her. He was rather surprised she had only had two lovers. Hell, there are teenagers who have had more lovers than that! Little wonder she knows so little about pleasing a man. He thought she was disinterested not that she didn't know. He wonders has he taught her things in the bedroom and was that swiped away too along with everything else?

"What do you mean...we aren't in a relationship?" She asked suddenly sitting upright, wiping her eyes. "I don't give myself to just anybody! I'm a Queen and you better know it!"

Now he wanted to know what did *she* want to categorize them as?

"I know about your love life. All that I didn't know Carole Caldwell told me to be spiteful. I'll not be another one of your concubines. If I can't be your wife then I'll be nothing to you." She said angrily.

"Ana, I'm not going to lie to you, I'm not ready for marriage. If you're pregnant I'll take care of my kids but I'm not going to marry you."

Ana face becomes pinched and withdrawn upon hearing those words.

"So I'm just sex to you and supposed to ask for no commitment in return?"

"No, you aren't just sex to me. I care a great deal for you. I care about you a lot but just am not ready to see with just one woman."

"Well, I guess we've nothing more to talk about." She said sourly. "You want to see other people but was yelling a few minutes ago about the very idea of my seeing other people. Do you realize how very chauvinistic that is?"

Sure, he knew. But still, he had no intention of sharing her with another man. He didn't care what her argument was. That wasn't going to happen. "There's a doctor in the house, she can examine you and determined if you are pregnant or not."

"That's ok, I'll just work a little harder to take care of them. If we need anything I'll let you know."

He saw his plan had backfired with her. She was expecting a real proposal if she was pregnant. He sighed "Ana...if marriage is what you want then we can get married."

"Nah, no, nope." She said, holding up her hands as if they were shielding her emotions, her heart. "I been married once to a man who really didn't want me. I'm not going down that road again. I can take care of myself." She said rising from the sofa walking toward the door. He knew if he let her go she wasn't going to visit anymore.

"Where is my daughter?" she turned around and asked.

"Ana, I do love you," he said softly, forsaking his promise to himself and his daughter.

"Nah, nah, no you don't," she replied shaking her head as if the gesture would erase the pain in her heart. "You're just like Thad, I was merely a tensile challenge. You got what you wanted so now it's time to move on. But I've learned my lesson. Ring first and then sex."

He teleports besides her and tries to talk her into staying. He could see and feel the hurt in her blood shot eyes.

"No, I'm fine. I'm cool." She said, slipping out his embrace and calling for Bea. Who comes running.

"I'll let you know what they are." She said before Bea reached her. He calls the woman following Bea, telling her to take Bea back to the playroom. Bea has no problems returning to her playthings. When Bea follows the nanny out of sight, he tried to kiss away her tears. She pushed him off, "What do you think you are you doing?! You ain't nobody to me but baby's daddy and baby daddy don't get to kiss me!"

He let her go and sighed, "Ana, at least spend the night and sleep for once with both eyes closed."

"I've to go get my car." Ana said stubbornly, fumbling through her purse for her keys. She had to get out of here. She wasn't giving him the satisfaction any longer in seeing her cry. This is the last time she will shed a tear over a man. Mortal or Immortal. They're all alike.

"Your car is outside, in the garage. I had it towed here."

"Take me to my car. We're leaving. It wasn't very nice knowing you."

She couldn't deny she was exhausted. For knocking her up, he at least owed her at one good night sleep. She was hurt. Hurt that he only agreed to marry her if she's pregnant not because he loved her.

"Ok, we'll spend the night but I"m leaving in the morning." She said firmly.

"I'd appreciate if you at least let the residential doctor check you out before you go. I promise you I won't bother you."

"No, I'll visit a free clinic. It will do just fine." she replied thinking it was a little late to worry about not bothering her.

"They know nothing about these type of children." He said softly.

"Well, I guess it's high time for them to learn." She quipped, putting on a brave front.

His phone rung on the decorative table near the wall, he ignored it's shrilling for a while but it doesn't stop ringing an angry ring.

663

"Excuse me a moment." He said, taking the call. She strained to hear the caller whom he listened to for a few seconds, "I'm busy right now, don't call me again with stupid shit." He yelled at the caller. She wonders does he talks to everybody that way?

"Now where were we?" He asked politely turning back to her.

"On my agreeing to spend one night only because I'm raw-boned tired." She reminded him.

"Oh yes," He said, leading her to an elevator. "Right this way, please."

She followed him although common sense was telling her to get the hell out of this house. He had already told her how he felt. So what more was there to do or say? All the lovey-dovey shit she pictured and held in her heart for them someday to do was merely a fantasy she created in her own feverish mind to deal with a harsh, dangerous reality. But reality just up and bitch-slapped her Fantasy square in the face.

Suddenly the double door of the front foyer flew open and in came a woman wearing enough expensive jewelry to finance a nation while sporting a clinging, figure hugging jet black dress fully emphasizing her hourglass figure, outlined by tresses of blonde hair flowing and bouncing as she strutted sexier than a runway super model. Someone else came in behind her, a security guard, bursting through the front door, trying to stop her. The sultry woman's eyes popped fire when she trained them on her.

"What in the hell is she doing here?" The woman, who looked vaguely familiar, pointed at her as if she were a stray dog her husband had brought home and she had no intention of letting him keep it. Ana realized she was one of the women she saw in Oklahoma City.

"I asked you a fucking question...what is she doing here?" The beautiful woman asked again with her hands on her shapely hips waiting for an answer. Ana believe she would've slapped her had she been certain there would be no retaliation.

Little did she know she was facing one of her greatest enemies at the time.

"None of your goddamn business. I bring whomever I want to my house," he replied equally as abrasive. But to Ana's ears he didn't sound very convincing. He sounded more guilty than disenchant.

"Wow! These people really do speaks horribly to each other. She mumbled to herself, "Let me go find Bea and get the hell out of here. I don't have time for rich people's pettiness." She turned to walk away when the woman called her. Mocking her.

"What's the matter Ms. Goody-Two-Shoes?" The blond woman taunted her around him. "Why you so fucking quiet, looking about to cry? You got a bun in the oven? Well, if you do... He ain't gonna marry you. So you might as well march your little skinny ass up outta here. Did he send you to the abortion doctor yet? He ain't big on babies!" The woman jeered at her.

Ana looked at him as he pushed the woman into the room they just vacated. The expensively dressed woman laughed at the shocked expression on her face and mimicked, "Boo-hoo, she's about to cry." Ana heard the muffled sounds of their arguing behind the door.

"He's already married." She told herself. *"Let me get out of here. This is all a game to those two."*

She went looking for Bea, deciding she was getting out of here before he came out the library but ran into a maid who informed her she could show her the guest room if that's where she preferred to stay.

"Mrs. Cargill, Mr. Cargill will with you shortly" the crisply uniformed maid said. Ana felt like a fool for asking but she wasn't sure if this woman didn't just call her Mrs. Cargill.

"Excuse me, Ms., but is that blonde woman downstairs Mrs. Cargill?"

665

The woman laughed with a sparkle in her strange emerald eyes and said, "No, you are. He's married to you." Seeing the lost and puzzled look on Ana's face the woman realized her collective memory is absent.

"Come, I want to show you something."

Ana followed her into a room long out of usage, the maid pointed at a larger than life portrait of a beautifully dressed woman in a silken green dress decorated with many pearls and diamonds. The woman's hair is done in an upswept style with waves of auburn hair framing her dark bronze face.

"Normally, there's nothing there but the background when you come the image he painted long ago fades back in."

"Wait, wait, a moment. What do you mean...are you saying I'm Mrs. Cargill?" Ana asked, pointing her index finger at her own chest.

The maid seeing she may have said too much already, tries to leave Ana alone to figure out her place in this house.

"No, come back here." She cried, calling the retreating woman back to her. "Are you saying *that's* my husband and this is my house???" Ana nearly shouts as she points in the direction they traveled to arrive in this room.

"Why else do you think he keeps chasing you down? Sometime we all forget who you are and can't remind him but when he finds you, we old ones like myself who have been with him for many years remember."

That explains his extreme reaction to her comment about another man. But when did she marry him? She doesn't remember marrying anyone but Thad. And this ancient portrait??? She hopes it's not like the Portrait of Dorian Gray....

"So this blonde bitch is in my house raising hell with my husband? *I'm going to*
666

hurt both of them really bad."

The maid sideyed the door and vivaciously nods. Ana knew she was half crazy by now from Vonderbilt chasing her from here to hell. But what was their excuse? Right now, she didn't care. She was going downstairs and getting some answers. She marched downstairs and found him and the woman standing in separate corners glaring at each other like two bloodied prizefighters, sizing up their opponent.

"GET THE HELL OUT OF MY HOUSE!" She yelled, shocking them both. "Get out! Now!"

The woman walked up to her, towering over her in a magnificent statuesque, Ashton teleports between them. The woman looked nasty around him and asked, "Says who?"

"Say I, I'm Mrs. Cargill! I said get out of my fucking house and stay away from my husband!" Ana yelled.

The woman looked questioningly at Ashton, "Dawn, this is reason I can't marry you or anybody else. Like I told you. I'm already married. My wife is just remembering we're married." He rushed to her and hugged her; she pushed him off.

"Get the funk offa me." She growled, wiggling out his embrace.

"You finally remember." He smiled triumphantly. "I knew if I was harsh enough it would jolt your memory." He said, dismissing her shoving and elbowing him. She didn't feel he really wanted her to remember. He just told her he wouldn't marry her. This man is a real first class piece of work.

The woman stood and looked at them totally baffled. "I'll see you at home when you're through making a fool of her." Dawn said, turning expertly on the five inch heels and heading toward the exit, flinging open the doors and walking briskly out.

"Now what kinda sick game are you playing? What does she mean about see you at home? You live somewhere with her?!" Ana asked, walking around the room more confidently. Knowing that she had all rights to, this was her house, and she was about to tear her husband a new anus.

Ignoring her questions about Dawn and his living arrangements, "I don't remember all of it but I do remember we were once married and very happy. But I'm not sure if we lived here on earth or my on home world. I remember we had children. The most I remember is how happy we were."

She looks at him as thus he'd lost his mind. She couldn't resist slapping him. Slapping him for hurting her feelings. Slapping him for lying. Slapping him for seeing other women. She felt like slapping until her hand was numb. He was laughing and side stepping her swings at his face. To him this was funny, he was making her madder.

"Reincarnation doesn't exist. We mortals lives only one lifetime. So I don't know what you remember but it wasn't me! I've only been married once and that was to Thad Wyett. Do you know how crazy this sounds?"

He shrugged his shoulders and hugged her again. "Get off me. I asked you do you know how crazy this sounds?"

"If it weren't true how would servants from my home world know you?"

"They'll say anything *you* tell them to say." She snaps wondering. *"Just how old are these people?"*

"So you don't really remembers, do you?" He asked sadly.

"Hell nah, I don't remember being married to you. I wouldn't marry you. You're a liar and a cheater."

"Well, then why when I said I didn't want to marry you, it hurt you? If you don't love me? How do you find me time and time again?" He asked.

She couldn't explain all the whys. So she hauls off and hit him. "If I'm your wife don't
668

you ever bring a bitch up in my house again. Get rid of all of them and do it quickly. I'm not bullshitting you." She stops dead in the middle of her rant, seems to her they have had this argument before. She flew into an insurmountable rage and stabbed him with her dagger.

Horrified at what she had done, for she knew the destruction her weapon caused, "Have I ever stabbed you for cheating on me?" She asked barely above a whisper, trying to attend his wound. But he heard her just fine.

"I don't know. You tell me," he angrily replied, rubbing the nick on his arm.

"Seems to me we have had this argument before." She said, pondering the truthfulness of a memory of very vague flashback.

"I do remember you were extremely jealous. Always cussing me out about women. So you probably did stab me. I don't remember."

"What's your real name? I mean the name God gave you?" She asked cautiously.

"In due time, you'll remember, if I tell you now it will destroy all chances of us ever getting back together." He said seriously.

She peered at him and asked. "It's not Lucifer? Is it!?"

He bust out laughing. "No, no, but I'm sure you can find a lot on me. Lucifer is not a son of God." Now he remembers they talked about his name before and she asked him was it Lucifer?

"You mean, you're like the father of the Nephilim? Like in the Bible?" She was a tab bit shocked. Curious if now was the time to be afraid of him. "Did you travel to the future and kidnap me or something?"

"If I had I wouldn't tell you." He joked. "But no, I asked for a godly wife."

"So you're like Jesus and Michael's brother?" She asked, but deep in her heart she was afraid he would turn to dust as the demons she had stabbed or cut. Placing her hand over the stab wound, watching it heal. She can sometime heal others but never herself or close blood relatives. She was surprised it was working on him.

"Yes, something like that. Yes, I'm a son of God. I'm an immortal."

She had to sit down. She somehow already knew that. They have had this conversation before. Seems like many times before. This amnesia crap was getting to be a real royal a pain in the ass. A real drag. She was so sick of the repetition. She knew her amnesiac caused her to suffer the loss of memory and the causes of amnesia may be organic or functional. Organic causes may include brain damage through injury—well, she been through enough fights, assaults, and accidents to have brain damage or the use of specific drugs-usually sedative drugs. She knew that wasn't the cause. So obviously hers was trauma related. But that wasn't right either. Something else was causing her to forget.

"How you do remember so much more than I?"

"I'm older than this earth let alone you. I've had much more practice in remember things than you," he replied. "I've been told it isn't our time to be together again, yet. You've work to do and I would interfere. I probably would if it involves anyone hurting you."

"So you have no intention of trying to kill me and my daughter? Gutting us and using us as trophies." She asked auspiciously.

"Where did you get that idea?! He asked, astonished she would even consider him doing something like that to her. "I've waited over 265 trillion years for you, why on earth would I want to kill you after such a long wait? I won't deny I've a bad temper at times but kill you? Why? I"m not Vonderbilt. I'll admit sometimes my memory fades or is even divinely erased but I've always remembered how much I loved you. I was much better with you than without you."

She shrugged her narrow shoulders and said "Well, all my life when someone or something was pursuing me they usually were trying to kill me. That's why I asked."

He laughed and hugged her. This time she didn't resist. "Don't you think it's a little late to be worrying about if I intend to kill you? You didn't seem to think so the other night. For someone afraid you took a hell of a chance."

She couldn't explain why she felt comfortable with him when they made love. Maybe Helena was right. Maybe she did need professional mental health care. But where would she get it from where the people wouldn't poison or torture her?

He saw an angel standing in the corner of the room, he knew why he was there. He had come to take her away or erase everything he told her. He glowered at his unfallen brother over her head and hugged her tighter.

"You'll have to refresh my memory on your favorite foods. The kitchen will prepare whatever you would like. Would you please join me for dinner?"

She gave him a weak smile. "Sure, why not."

The meal was succulent. They hadn't had a full course meal in months. Not since they left the cave. At least, she didn't think so. Bea was more intrigued by the game room than by her mom and Ashton. They dined upstairs in a bedroom ;she'd have to be a fool not to know the meaning of this. Seemed to her the more she talked to him, the more bits and pieces of another life was falling into place. When she put Bea to bed in her room, she asked him to stay a little longer. She wonders why she did that? Is she buying this cock and bull story, well maybe not but she definitely could get used to living like this but she knew she had to leave. This was merely a wayside station to her true destination. She also knew all this was a fantasy to him. He dreamed up all that to tell her to make her stay until he was tired of her. But why? The woman who was here earlier was drop dead gorgeous.

Neither Ana nor Ashton were aware the satanic-glorified triplets who were watching the woman at the amusement park had reported to their superior who was with their target. None other than Ana BuFaye. Their superior informed James Cadwell who told his wife to tell Dawn Shepherd to go in and flush Ana back into the streets. They were certain upon seeing Dawn and seeing that Cargill was a womanizer she would flee the palace. They had posted their people within distant to catch her before she escaped. Surely, Nikola would reward them for such clever work.

The would-be captors sat and watched the gate open and it was Dawn exiting, not Ana. This can't be right. Women like Ana BuFaye are said not to be able to handle infidelity. It's said they live in a magical world in their minds where everything is right as rain. But they watched Dawn angrily get in the back of her limo and it rise and head eastward. So Ana isn't leaving.

Deciding she didn't feel like getting out the backseat and boarding a jet she told the driver to keep going, keep going on to Paris. Dawn thought the woman would be like her mother. A flighty bird, flee at the first sign of trouble. Caroline Cadwell said she was a Christian woman and they are so very easy to intimidated. But this woman had fire in her belly and a mouth about as bad as Cargill's.

However, she saw they had been arguing before she arrive. The woman's tear stained face showed that much. And she hit the nail on the head as to what it was about. Dawn sighs, and reclines in the plush leather seat and takes another sip of the liquor that was awaiting her. Her outburst didn't work. The woman wasn't easily intimidated as earlier perceived. With a weary, heavy heart not from loss of love but the procrastination of her bleak future she sighed. This shit is getting old and extremely exhausting. She didn't have the stamina to keep this up any longer. She had about eight million saved plus her severance package, that will have to do. Cargill is going to do whatever he wants to do regardless of what anyone says. She safely bets, even if God told him not to do something, he would still do it. She will just wait and see how things turn out. He will be back. He always does come back to her.

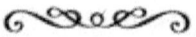

That one night stay turned into three months. He was right; she was happy. Bea was happy. He was happy. Everyone was happy until the day the angel showed up again and told her the story of Jonah and the whale.

"You've work to do. You've been neglecting your divine duty for your husband." So he really was her husband?!? She marveled.

"I don't want to go back out there." She whined tearfully. "Besides, all I've done on the outside is run from one psychopath after another. What use is that to me or whatever work I'm to do?"

"There's too much at stake for you to live in the lap of luxury and forsake your duties. There are many out there who need you. Their needs are much greater than Azazael's whims. However, like Jonah, you can make this hard or you can make it easy. Either way The Lord's Command will not go unanswered."

Ashton heard them talking and rushed to her side, he begged the angel to let her stay. "Cassiel, whatever Father wants her to do she can do it just as well here as she can out there in harm's way." He argued. "I promise I won't interfere."

"Does all you sons of God have a bad attitude?" she inquired.

"Only when we have to. When the servant is deliberately being disobedient. Yes, we all have *bad attitudes*." Cassiel replied, knowing she was stalling with questions.

"She is already behind schedule. She must come now or I'll take her." The angel replied.

The couple hugs each other hard as they try to override their fate. She hugs Ashton equally as hard not wanting to let him go, not wanting to say goodbye, apparently for the umpteenth time before asking the angel can she take her items such as jewelry and designer clothing? The angel shook his head saying she will have too much to aid her along the way. Citing the wealth will overshadow the Power of God working through her.

Ashton rebutted him saying, "I do not care. Take whatever you need. It's yours." He blatantly ignored the archangel's command and continued to plead with and adjure the angel to let her stay citing the danger she will encounter as soon as they know she is no longer with him.

"Can I've a few moments alone with him?" Ana asked with a heavy heart.

"One hour tops you are given to get your house in order." The angel of Law and Order said.

They walked hand in hand out to the vast garden out back. She looked at him and said "I do believe if our love has lasted through trillions of years it will last until my job is done. I do believe someday we'll be together."

His heart ached for he knew she didn't know what she was saying. An assignment by God doesn't end until the person dies and he knows he won't spend eternity in heaven. His sins are too great and too numerous. He can't promise he won't keep trying to steal her away as much as possible. He has done time for a whole lot worse than trying to be with the one he loves. He knew each time she wouldn't remember him nor he fully remember her. But now that he has found her, he can't so easily walk away and let her go.

"Wait for me, I will be back." She promised as the angel walked toward them.

He couldn't watch her drive away. He sent his security team after her. To at least follow and protect them. They reported an hour later she drove through the 8th day. He goes to the room housing her portrait he painted during the reign of Darius I, her image was gone, he teleported to an island resort to be alone with his thoughts before all memories of her faded. He remembers she disappeared like this during the time Babylon was being invaded and he was so distorted he didn't care if the invasion took place. He abandoned Babylon. To him this was crueler than being chained to boulders for eons. That, he could handle but this he can not. This maddening cycle of repetition was getting the better of him.

"I thought she would never leave." A female voice said behind him as he stood in the cool shadows of the room and he watched from the palace large bay window, the love of his immortal life drive away.

Recognizing the owner of the voice, he warned her without turning around.

"Ninsianna, if you knew what was best for you you wouldn't mess with me right about now."

The dark haired beauty walked up beside him and placed her blood stained hand on his shoulder; the dried, coppery scent of blood filled his nostrils. He shrugged her hand off. He knew where she just came from. A sacrifice.

"I told you years ago. I do not wish to be your mate nor Draco anymore. Can't you take a hint? Times have changed, it's time to move on. Our time has passed. Long passed. Xerxes saw to that."

She knew his thirst for blood and violence equaled her own, she was once married to him during his reign of terror as the ancient god Draco. No one could defeat her with him at her side. They were a great team then so they can be a great team again. When she returned to earth four hundred years ago he had grown soft and passive. He needed her to remind him of who he truly is.

"I tell you what darling, you can call me Ana, she inherited a suboptimal of my name anyway. Ann, Anna, Ana were all derived from Ninsianna, you know that." She cooed. "You loved me once so I know it's still there."

He didn't feel like giving her an explanation so he disappeared to be alone with his heartache.

The Archangel Raphael called another conference meeting after seeing how callously

Cassiel dealt with the couple. He knew law and order were important but so was love. Without love there's no desire to follow law and order. Once the divine conference gathered. Raphael said:

"I think they can work well together. For the first time in years Azazel was sitting somewhere behaving himself and acting as if he's in his right mind. In case no one noticed, her pull on glory became stronger and brighter. She was at peace with him. She sees something good in him that has eluded us. He really put his best foot forward with her. Look at how she spend his wealth on the poor. We all know Azazel couldn't have cared less about the poor and misfortune. But he pretended he did just to please her. Frankly, I think they balance each other out. We don't understand all the ways of Father but I think there's a reason He put them together long ago. There's a reason they keep finding each other. Time after time." Raphael said, looking at Cassiel and Denzuiel.

Denzuiel slowly rose with his monolithic, glowing black wings trailing behind him and took the floor after Raphael was seated, properly addressed Michael and Micheala, and said in a soft, patronizing tone, "Raphael, anyone can be nice for what? Three months? No matter what you say Azazael still hasn't proven himself. He's still fretful and easily enraged. He still has those harems' members. So what if he was nice a few days? Lucifer can be nice too if the mood suits him but that doesn't mean he won't pull souls into hell. That woman's attraction to Azazael is purely carnal. Physical desire is no reason to risk what has been in place before the creation of that physical world. I understand your position here for you see light and love in everything. But there's an ugly side to all of this and it's name is Azazael."

Both sides having their say they turned to the Michael and Micheala for the final verdict.

"I know a woman's heart." Micheala slowly said. "This one has a heart of an angel but the desires of a normal woman. I know she loves Azazael and I truly believe Azazael believes he loves her. But his lifestyle will render her tender heart asunder. As much as I'd love to see her happy with him... No, Raphael their time has arrived yet. When it does, I weep for her not rejoice."

Raphael dropped his golden head as the others left. Aurora touched her brother's arm. "Keep the faith, if their love has lasted this long a few more years won't destroy it." His hand covered hers on his shoulder. "Thanks, dear sister. Thanks for the encouragement."

⁓⁓⁓

Ana looked in the rearview mirror as she drove eastward on Route 66 wondering where she bought all that junk in the back seat. Where had it come from and why was she riding around with high end designer stuff peering at the public? "*I'm begging to get robbed.*"

She pulled over to a newer, modern rest stop in the arid inhospitable environ, got out, and looked among all the packages. She saw Bea was still asleep. Looking at the hologram map she was nearing Flagstaff, AZ. "I guess this is as good a place as any to stop and get a room for tonight." Referring to the fact that this was one of those centers where one could rent a room for a few hours. But she decided to keep going. Usually those rooms aren't very clean and she didn't have time to clean it.

She stopped at a Super Sleeper Inn. Unloaded a few things but was still wondering where all this stuff came from? She carried sleeping Bea inside with a tote on her arm. Once inside she checked their resources and they had $100,000 more than she remembered from yesterday at the theme park.

"Oh well, I didn't steal it. Those ninjas I fought didn't have anything on them not that I could see."

Settling in for the evening, eating Chinese food in bed, and watching the plasma screen but on high alert for an intruder as she flips through the channels. She stops when she come to a social media channel. "Trillionaire mogul Ashton Cargill is said to be married, ladies." The female host of the show said "Too bad no one has seen the new Mrs. Cargill except Dawn Shepherd." The host turns toward the woman she saw in Oklahoma City and said. "Tell us Dawn, what's the lucky lady like? We're dying to know."

The buxom blonde spoke saying "She ain't much to look at. " The woman named Dawn looks familiar to Ana from somewhere besides Oklahoma City but she couldn't put a finger on where else had she seen her. The show hostess laughed a cute laugh and said "She must be, she got him to the altar whereas you failed." Ana laughed at the hostess' joke.

Ana never cared much for these shows the host or hostess were always mean to their guests. But it's hard to turn on the television without fifty of them glaring you in the face. This area had limited channels.

"Oh! I wasn't trying to marry him. I was having too fun for that! I didn't want to tied to one man." The beautiful blonde woman smiles into the camera.

"But you were everywhere with him for the past—what? Thirty years and you weren't trying to marry him? C'mon Dawn, our audience isn't that stupid. Admit the lady bested you."

The woman named Dawn face twisted in rage. "He only married her because the dumb bitch got herself knocked up."

"Aw! C'mon, men don't marry for that reason anymore. You know that." The hostess smirked.

Ana thought this hostess was a really nasty piece of work. But for some reason she was glued to this program. Various pictures of this Cargill guy with Dawn was flashed on the screen behind the sofa they were sitting on. This Cargill guy looked familiar, too. Maybe she saw them at a hotel she worked at; she has worked so many hotels until they all sorta blend together. She flicks off the set and snuggles down under the covers in the well air-conditioned room and was sleep with in a few minutes. She clicked it off seconds before the image of herself that Dawn had obtained flashed on the screen.

She woke up around 3:45 because she felt the covers move. As if a snake was under there with her. Glancing up, something was plastered on the ceiling looking down at her. The horrendous winged creature was looking down at her jacking off it oversized dick. The face was so horrible she nearly froze. It was full of of blood and dripping something acidic on the bed. The cover flew off the bed. Something was pulling it. She saw the blood was changing into pus filled fat worms. One was on her leg. She kicked it off. The demon in the ceiling, its barbed tail flicked from side to side before it leapt down from the ceiling on her. She remembered Mother Harris called these beings an aswang.

"I heard you fuck demons, I'm as good as lover boy." It's foul breath made her eyes literally cross; at least she felt they actually crossed. It pinned her arms above her head and used it's free clawed hand to tear her oversized nightshirt open. She bucked and kicked wildly. He slaps her hard across the face. So hard it almost made her nearly lose consciousness.

"Be still bitch! You just fucked Azazael so why can't you fuck me!?"

She heard Bea struggling to wake up. "She won't be waking up anytime some." The fanged fetid mouth said.

"I command you in the name of Jesus to let me go." It laughed at her. It didn't move but instead kept trying to penetrate her with its barbed tail. She knew if it succeeded whatever that shit was could do serious damage to a human if it didn't kill her. She saw her Sword when it swung and vaporized the demon. There were no ashes, nothing was left. Even the fat bloody worms were gone. Bea woke up crying. She quickly grabs her robe and sits beside her. She needed a shower but sat there until Bea fell back to sleep. She decided since that one won't be telling anyone where they were, she would stay until check out.

Seeing what she was up against Ninsianna knew she needed to revise her plan. She knew she would lose if she attacked now. When she was married to Azazael his name was Draco, meaning the dragon. But the dragon had lost his fire and rage. But how can this be the same mortal who caused him to dump her years ago? This woman shows up and he changed his entire demeanor. He becomes civilized; stops the sacrifices, the wars, shuts down the prostitute temple, all he wanted to do was walk with her in the Hanging

Garden and talk about poetry, art, and bullshit of that nature. He became one big bore.

Ninsianna is known to the modern world as the Black Venus. The Babylonian Goddess is seen as the personification of the planet Venus and also as the goddess of war and strife, she held the high title Nin- kur-ra-igi-ga, translates "the queen who eyes the highland" meaning that other lands feared her. Her Battle Ceremony was called the "dance of Inanna' and she danced at the very heart of it. She was 'the star of the battle-cry.' Her symbol is the eight-pointed star. She was the ancient Babylonian goddess of sexuality and fertility, her worship included sacred prostitution. The demon she sent had failed to turn the woman's mentality into that of a prostitute. She knew Azazael would then leave her or perhaps kill her. This is the same woman who shut down her temple of sacred prostitution. Oh yes, she remembers the Timewalker.

⸎⸎⸎

Five hundred miles away from the place of the demon rapist the loud crashing sound of the door being kicked opened was deafening. The door swung open so hard the knob made a sizable hole in the stained wall of the already dumpy room. She was jolted awake and she started shooting with a Glock in both hands by survival instinct. One ancient and the other modern. The old one had a powerful blow. You don't kick in the door of a woman suffering from Active Traumatic Stress Syndrome and expect not to get shot. Not if you have a lick of self-preservation. When she was clearly awake she saw two officers lying face down at the foot of bed. She knew they were Vonderbilt's henchmen. Although they may be on the police force they also nonetheless worked for Nikola Vonderbilt. He had lots of officials in his back pocket.

Six year old Bea was already on the move, stuffing their few belongings in a duffel bag. Most of their artifices was well ingrained by now and most of their belongings were still within the car. She never fully unpacked the car. The cop's radios crackling prompt them to move faster. Throwing everything in the back seat they left the room like two she-bats flying out of hell.

She turned Trusty's lights off driving through the back streets to their hiding place she scouted out a few days ago. A lot of gangs hung out in these depleted districts. She prayed none was out and about tonight. She didn't want to draw attention to them. Attention was their enemy. Most of the street lights were out or broken in this neighborhood, working to her advantage. A rusted out metal and glass building came into view. She surveyed the area carefully to make sure no one else had her idea. Seeing that the way was clear she crept quietly to the derelict building. She had cased out the area and the old empty warehouse down near the dock when they first arrived as a hiding place in case she had to kill somebody and they had to run.

Four months later that prediction came true. She used the car to break the door open. The locks were rusty. So they gave away easily. She drove in and put the weak chain back on and set them up for the next few days. She was checking their supplies to see how long could they survive hidden in the belly of this old humongous building. The floor was littered with dust, mold, used condoms, fallen installation, beer cans, and rat shit. She kept a steady supply of camping food, can goods and utensils for times like these. Not much moonlight reached them so she decided to wait until morning before setting up camp. She put Bea to bed in the back seat just in case they were discovered and she had to drive like hell to get out here.

Ana had already believed their room was a killing room. The musty smell of long ago decay could be smelt seeping from the walls. The bulges and discoloration stains in the ceiling and walls told her exactly where the bodies were or still are lodged. She believed quicklime was used to cover up the odor of rotting flesh. When she saw the two ghosts the first night they arrived she knew her suspicion was true. She didn't want them following her so she ignored them. There was nothing she could do about whatever happened to them. Although she had a pretty good idea what happened in this begrimed environment. But they stood at her bed trying to tell her something every night around 2:00 A.M.. She knew their bodies were in these wall but she was too tired to care. She was almost delirious from exertion. She had driven a normal day's trip in 12 hours, taking the back roads down near the Okefenokee Swap. The swap was so haunted it was hard at times to discern the spirits from the living people. Both were getting on her already frayed nerves.

Earlier she was working down near the beach where they had rented a rundown shack, unfortunately someone broke in on them and she killed them too, so this room was the best she could find on such a short notice. She knew all the roads out of the state were barricaded looking for her so she laid low within the state until they gave up the search and if she makes it out alive, Florida would never see her again. That was if her wacky brain could remember not to come here again.

With nothing better to do than sit and listen she finally gives her attention to the two spirits who followed her from the room. "Ok, ladies I know your bodies are in that room. What do you want me to do about it?" She hadn't realized they were so young when they were killed.

"That entire place is a meat market. You are the only person who have been there who could see and hear us, what we want you to do is notify our families so they can come take us home and bury us with our ancestors." The oldest of the girls said. The other explained how they got caught up in the lifestyle, they were promised excitement and continuation of partying and drugs. Believing this man or pimp, they followed him from two different states. One, the oldest, was from Minnesota, the youngest was from South Dakota. "Darren runs a bar over on Ponce de Leon called "The Rave." Those two cops who broke in on you are some of Darren's friends. They know he's trafficking girls. They and many others get to do sick things to us in exchange for their silence and looking the other way." The girls give her their real names and addresses.

"There's a shipment of girls coming in to Darren' place tomorrow night, they'll be kept in the trailer out back of the club until brought to the hotel. We want you to let them out and tell them to go to the rape crisis center. Some of those porn freak porn bastards can't get off unless they're killing the girl. The porn industry isn't harmless as projected."

In case they wasn't watching Ana carefully explained her own grave predicament.

"We saw what happened, that demon who watched you all told them you were there, we weren't staring at you all night. We were staring at it. It was perched up on the headboard." Chills run down Ana's spine. "You have something they want. They let you stay there as long as you did because they want that little girl to sell.", the second girl added, pointing in the back at Bea.

"She just turned six!" Ana cried.

"That don't matter to these freaks. The younger the better." The oldest girl who said she was seventeen when she was killed six years ago. Ana had often been at truck stops and rest stops and wondered what was in those trucks. Some trucks she sensed humans in them and is now ashamed she didn't act.

"That's one of the reasons abducted children are rarely if ever found. They're sold and hidden by people like Darren."

Ana was indecisive on what to do. She knew this Darren Miller's sex trafficking ring had to be stopped. She looks up several local churches to report this to. Her brother had rigged her phone to appear as if she is calling from a location 100's of miles away. She called 60 churches, as Bea, who is wide awake by now, looks on. Several hung up on her, some wanted to know how she knew all these things. But lo and behold she finally reached a church, a Baptist Church, who had been trying to put that hotel and "The Rave" out of business for years. But they had always encountered roadblocks of having no proof of their accusations.

"I KNEW IT!" The female minister cried, "Too many non-local girls show up down there never to be seen again." Ana felt bad having to lie to a priest saying she was once one of their victims. The woman offered her free consultation, prayer, and shelter but Ana declined for she knew Vonderbilt would bomb that church to hell and back. The local news on her portable chip screen had a new hot story, it showed this lady minister and her congregation down at the hotel pulling the walls apart and next, breaking open the trailer the ghost girls described a few hours ago and sure enough about 50 girls, some as young as Bea, were back there. Some were in grave need of medical attention. She smiled as she watched this crusader on the breaking news story. Ana knew Baptists wouldn't mind raising the hell needed to get the public's attention and were not going to back down.

"In the cover of the night you two get out of here. The police department will their hands full pulling out all those bodies." The girls said. They all watched the news as the local coroner office informed the public some of the bodies were at least a hundred years old. They were primarily women and children.

When the night fell, the girls showed Ana how to get out and told her to head along the midsection of Alabama after leaving Florida. "The swamp cops are looking for illegal contra-brands." The oldest girl said.

"Drive normal so you don't draw attention." The youngest girl advised. The girls showed her the way out and roads she wasn't aware of. With no deferments, by sunrise they were completely out of Alabama.

"We must go back to heaven now that our job is done." The girls said, kissing Ana and Bea goodbye and disappeared.

Ana had long ago noticed aiding someone, living or dead, often went hand-in-hand with her travels. Once they were in Little Rock, she had to take Bea to the local hospital, her temperature had spiked 103. She had a terrible cold. Nowadays colds aren't tolerated, they are easily treatable. The last time Bea had a cold she was about three yrs old. It was Bea who spotted the man out of his body. Some shadowy things were attacking him. The man's disembodied spirit was trying to reattach to the body and fight them off. She left Bea on Fannie's lap and beckoned and taunted those demons into following her. They tried to claw her but couldn't. She runs out in the parking lot and looks up at the highrise hospital. It's full of those things, whatever they are; this was her first exorcism.

"I command all of you in the Name of Jesus to come out of there and leave those poor people alone! Go back to the depths of hell from thence thy cometh!" She said clear and audibly. She had no idea where those words came from. It was like Someone put them in her mouth and slapped her across her back to make her spit them out. An angry roaring wind was heard coming for her. They came out in such a fury and rage that she froze to the spot. She saw they had fangs and sharp white talons. Close up they were ghastly creatures. "Stand still. I'll fight this battle." A Voice said. She obeyed and a few seconds before reaching her a portal opened and sucked them all in. Even some kind she hadn't seen earlier. They cussed her ancestry all the way back to Eve as they were sucked back into hell. She quickly retrieved Bea and Fannie and Bea's medicine and

684

again got out of town. Temperamentally, she wonders why she's always encountering others who need help when she can't help herself. She then felt censurable for not listening to the girls before the other nights. "I'm only human." She utters.

It was late Spring, the birds were singing, the flowers were blossoming, pollination was everywhere in Central Park. Love was in the air everywhere but not for the men who sat in the overly expensive but impersonal executive-styled room waiting to speak to Ashton Cargill. They were determined to see him if it took all day. The secretary tried to defer them but they weren't having any of it. One was an auburn haired man of average height, muscular, handsome with a pretty girlish face. With eyelashes most women would kill for. Under the well-trimmed mustache was a heart-shaped feminine mouth which is why he worn the hair across his upper lip. This pouty mouth maybe cute and even sexy on a woman but on a man, he viewed it as a disaster. The second man, tall and muscular with some fat around the waist, little weigh gained over years of comfort and worrying. His 6'3" frame was carrying approaching 300 lbs. But doesn't show because he works out to keep himself fit. His deep dark amber, soulful eyes are what his wife says she fell in love with first. His demeanor is usually mild and laid back. but today he is mad enough to burn down hell itself.

They sipped the now warm Champagne served earlier by the lady who told them Mr. Cargill was not in office and wasn't expected in anytime soon. "Let me reiterate" Jack BuFaye said forcefully "We aren't going anywhere until pretty-boy brings his pretty ass out that office."

The pretty brunette was distressed to no fortuitousness, "I'm sorry, sir but he really is not in. Perhaps if would tell me the nature of your visit I could forward a message to Mr. Cargill."

The oldest of the BuFaye brothers asked, "Lady, what part of the anatomy of personal and private you didn't understand? Now get your skinny butt in there and call him and tell him Ana BuFaye's family demands to see him. I don't care what it takes to get his ass here."

685

The young woman huffs angrily and turns on her heels and twists back to her desk. The brothers were there for two reasons: One, it's believed their sister allegedly killed some cops in Florida and is being broadcast nationwide as armed and dangerous. There is a nationwide manhunt for her. And secondly, they want to know has he seen her and if so what are his damn intentions?

Finally, around 4:30 P.M. the massive engraved antiqued oak door opened and the young woman led the brothers in. The lavish carpet was firm not shaggy as they so often are in offices of big cheeses. The long walk to the main office left them wondering exactly what or who was this man the nun told them she saw their sister talking to. Finally, they arrived at an office even larger than the one they walked through. The decoration was dark and bellicose. Ancient suits of armors lined the walls, various battle axes hung crisscrossed in artful manners. J.J. already wasn't liking what he saw.

"Mr. Cargill, these men would like to speak with you." The woman said, seemingly exiting too fast after the introduction. The man standing near a wine cart pouring drinks was hard for the brothers to figure out if he were black with an olive and milk coffee complexion or white with a lot of ethnic in him. They had never seen anyone with seeming so many different ethnic groups blended together.

"He's a big 'un." Jack whispered to his older brother. "I believe the two of us together can take him. Why Ana always have to get the biggest sum-of-bitch round?"

Having heard Jack BuFaye, "That won't be necessary." Ashton said offering the men a drink which they both declined. "How may I help you?"

"We're sure since you own the network telling lies on our sister you must know she is wanted in a massive manhunt." Jacob Jr. said.

"News is reported as it told. If it's a lie, then the witnesses are lying." Ashton said, sipping his wine.

The man's cool demeanor was pissing Jack off. This man was behaving as if Ana's life wasn't in danger. "Nobody got time for your bullshit!" Jack snapped. "If the cops find her first you know damn well what's going to happen. She didn't kill those bastards, they're lying on her. Get your head out the fucking clouds and tell us where is she!"

Looking directly at Jack reminded him so much of Ana that it hurt. "Frankly, gentlemen...I do not know where she is. I last saw her approximately 9 months ago. We chatted a little while. She made it perfectly clear she wanted nothing more to do with me."

Jacob Jr. walks so close to him he could smell his cologne. "And so...you're going to let her die because she refused to be your plaything?"

Junior words angered him. He turned and glared at the big man, he saw enough resemblance to know he was Ana's brother, too.

"For your information Mr. BuFaye, I never wanted your sister for a toy. I wanted her for love but you can't not force someone to love you."

Jack chuckled, looked at his brother, "Oh, I get it. She hurt your feelings so now you are out to punish her. You're going to sat back and let her die. Well, hell no wonder she don't want you. She saw through your shit. When you love somebody you don't let shit happen to them cause they pissed you off. My wife piss me off all the time. She has made an occupation of pissing me off but I don't want anything horrible to happen to her. Junior, we need to teach this man how to rap. How to sing like Bryon with the determination of Marc Anthony."

Ashton shrugged his massive shoulders in the dark gray personal tailored suit that cost a fortune. He had already been to Florida trying to track her but those pesky angels covered her tracks. He felt broadcasting her perilous predicament would let her know just how badly Vonderbilt was out for tasting blood. He won't deny his interest in her had started to wan. He felt if she was so damn determined to keep running even after he told her how he felt then there was nothing else he could do.

Jack walked up to the big guy and reached up and put his hand on his shoulder as if they had known each other for years. Ashton didn't appreciate the move but Jack didn't care. "Women are finicky, they don't know what they want, you've to keep after them until they surrender." Jack advised.

"I'm going to be straight forward." J.J. said, standing in Ashton's comfort zone. "I want you to use your influence to tell the feds to call off their dogs. If she killed those men, they made her kill them. Our sister isn't a cold-bloodied killer who kills for thrills. Her life is troubled, she needs your help. If you ever had any real feeling for her now is the time to show it. Not at her funeral, that is if we get a body to bury." Jacob Jr. saw his sensible words had moved and reached the behemoth of a man when he saw pain flash across his his perfectly formed brow. Frowning, Ashton asked, "What makes you so sure I can get the feds to call off their search?"

"A man of your quality can get anything done he wants. Men like you are who actually rule the world not kings, rulers, princes, and politicians. They're merely figureheads." Jacob Jr. said with a deadly stillness that told Ashton this mortal knew he wasn't a normal, natural man.

Jack added, "We know she is eccentric or even erratic at times but I'm sure that's what attracted you in the beginning."

Ashton didn't know how to explain to these men who obviously loved their sister that she was a spiritual timewalker. She walks into his arms, into his life, and walks out as easy as a phantom. She is a night visitor who comes and makes mad passionate love to him and walks away. Yes, he loves her but he can't keep up this charade. He some days go an entire day without thinking about her and wham! She shows up in his arms at night and by morning is gone.

"Sewell, call the prominent agent handling the Wyett case," he said into a phone the brothers can't see. Within 15 minutes the Head of Homeland Security, the FBI, and CIA, and even the Oval Office call while the brothers waited. He spoke to all four at once.

"Call your dogs off, you all know those bastards made that woman kill them. What in the hell were they doing busting in on a helpless mother and child with cocked guns?"

Cargill roared in the phone somewhere hidden in the room. The man from Homeland Security said "She's been suspected in several other shootings. We just got in a report there has been another shooting near the gulf in Alabama. The witnesses describe the same woman. This woman is not hapless. She's either militia or terrorist group trained. It was reported the child fired a handgun at the men hitting them but not killing them. The mother is who said to have killed them."

Ashton watched the two men listen carefully as the G-man described their sister as a notorious, dangerous psychopath. He saw they didn't know about their niece's ability to kill.

"I don't give a fuck if she killed a whole fucking patroon. You better call off that search or deal with me. Because if they hurt her, I'm going crazy on everybody's ass. Have I made myself clear?" He growled in the phone, wherever it was. Several mumbles of "Yes sirs," were vocalized before Ashton cut the connection.

The brothers were dumbfounded and highly impressed with how this man merely made a phone to the top officials in the country and they obeyed.

"One more thing," Jack said watching this man eyes change back to the gemstone blue from dark as sapphires. "Who is this Vonderbilt that keeps calling us? He says he's a close friend of hers."

Ashton heavily sighed "Don't go near that man nor talk to him. He's who setting her up in these demoniacal innuendos. He's a warlock. I hope you guys know what a warlock is. Real ones are nothing like the sugarcoated chips' versions. This man is a very dangerous person. It's he who is trying to kill her because she rejected him."

Jacob Jr.'s instinct was right when intuition led him not to try and find this man. No matter how sweet he talked. There was something sinistral about him. The man was so evil he could feel it, even over the phone.

"Your sister is highly gifted, she's a born Nazarene Warrior Saint. Nikola believes by mating with her he can produce a legion of gifted children. When the child isn't born gifted he kills mother and child. So STOP talking to him!" Ashton says, frustrated her family had the gall to talk to Nikola. "A man named James Caldwell who used to live next door to her in Boston works for Nikola. He, too, is a very powerful warlock. You people need to start taking greater precaution in who you talk to. Everybody who calls you about your sister doesn't have your nor her best interest in their hearts. Just remember this, everyone who calls you with news about your sister is calling because she's winning. They aren't going to call you moments before they kill her."

The brothers clearly see this man is their only hope for their sister remaining alive. Reading their thoughts Ashton says, "I would marry Ana in a heartbeat if she stops running away." This is exactly what they wanted to know. He pulls a 100 grand bill out of his desk. "Shall you see her, give this to her or use it to keep her ahead of them, which ever one you see best." He says handing the bill to Jacob Jr. "Maybe one day she will come to believe I mean her no harm."

He calls his security team to escort the brothers back to their respective homes. For strange feeling settled over him. He feels these men may someday be his brothers-in-laws and uncles to his children.

Shortly before arriving home the brothers' memory had been divinely erased of the knowledge of Ashton's proposal. They both knew there's something else they intended to tell their bed confined mother about their visit to this strange looking man who for some reason was keenly interested in their wild, contumacious sister but couldn't remember what.

"Thank you Jesus," Fannie whispered a prayer of thanks for the man agreeing to help protect Ana.

"He agreed to help her?" Helena asked in astonishment. Jack was surprised and hurt to see jealousy in Helena's eyes. He had always idolized Helena and thought she was the better of his two sisters.

"Yes, he did." Junior replied. "We had to wait all day but he came through for her. He even got all the directors of the CIA, FBI, and the Oval Office on line."

690

"You're falsifying information." David scorned. "That's a federal offense."

"David, I don't boast about something this serious and what's your problem with Ana?" David's underlying discomfort told Ana's oldest brother something terrible happened between him and Ana and demanded to know exactly what it was. What happened between him and Ana?

David gathered a serious expression and looked squarely at J.J. and lied "She came on to me, she tried to play me, her own brother-in-law, the same as she is playing Ashton Cargill. She wounded my feelings, I've known her since she wasn't much older than my son. You don't mess around in your family. I know Mrs, BuFaye raised her better than that."

J.J. did not really believe him. But his ill mother had to stay in this man's house he said, "Ok, David, I'm sure she didn't mean it. Pain changes people. Pain can make people do a lot of things they normally wouldn't have done. Anyway, no one is to talk to that Vonderbilt guy anymore. He's who behind all these attacks on Ana. According to Cargill, the man is a warlock, he wants her for some sort of satanic mating ritual believing they can have more children like himself and Ana."

David and Helena exchanged glance, believing Junior's explanation to be false, dismiss it, and break out laughing, "He's as big of a loon as Ana! No wonder he's attracted to her. They're both crazy." Helena said, laughing as thus this was the funniest thing she had ever heard.

Fannie silenced them both with an angry glare. "Just because you don't believe something doesn't make it no less true. To go to the level this man is taking things there must be something to this claim. People don't kill and mercilessly hunt for something that means nothing to them. I was there, I saw him on camera materialize out the thin air, grab Bea, and disappeared. Which would've never happened had we kept Bea at home. It was you, Helena, whom Ana listened to and enrolled Bea in that school. Somebody told him Bea was there. So that man is something. If he ain't a warlock, then he is a devil, maybe he's both. Ana already told ya who he is."

691

David Wales couldn't believe his ivy-league, university educated brother-in-law was falling for his mother's superstitious crock of bullshit. This is the one person in this god forsaken family he was dumb enough to marry into against his mother's wishes he thought was a cut above the rest. He was disappointed to see that Jacob BuFaye Jr. was as superstitious as the rest. His mother warned him he was just fascinated with Helena's hourglass figure.

"You can't see anything but those big tits she has in your face. She is socially below you. I can't invite her to my Garden Club luncheons without her stopping traffic." His mother argued. His mother had great exert over his behavior and actions but when it came to Helena BuFaye she didn't win. If Helen of Troy looked ANY way like his Helena, he can see how she launched a thousand ships. Helena did have a great pair of legs. But he was certain was that Jacob BuFaye Jr. was above all this mambo-jumbo voodoo shit his mom was always spewing.

"I'm sure Cargill said that because they're both competing for the same woman. He said those things to impress you guys. To get an upper leg on the competition. All men lie in their cause to help eliminate their competition. That's what we do. We lie on them." David laughed as thus this assemblage is elementary. Fannie's dark brownish, dark sapphire eyes flashed fire at him.

J.J. wonders what is it really like for his mother living with these two? If they so easily belittle her in front of him, what must they do when they are alone with her? Helena talks about Ana being stupid over Thad, but Thad had much more respect for their mother than David. He'd heard Ana cuss Thad out in the kitchen about not wanting them to come over.

"Your family practically lives here, I see them every other day! Mine only comes once or twice a year and you are going to be nice to them or I'll go back home with them." Everyone heard Ana yell at Thad while slamming the oven door shut. Thad came out the kitchen looking a little sheepish a few minutes later greeting them, explaining Ana had been up all night cooking and was just cranky and tired. He offered the guys a beer and told Mom and Helena Ana was in the kitchen. Thad attempted to collaborate the account he knew they all heard saying, "I merely suggested to my wife, y'all sister to have the meal catered and that way she could sit and enjoy you guys but she insisted on cooking it so I suggested to buy a sweet potato pie since she said something didn't come out right in hers".

"Thad, we all know Ana can be a bit high strung at times and she inherited Mom's mouth. No big deal." He told his brother-in-law. Now had Thad made fun of Mom in front of Ana, there would've been a mile-wide cussing streak. But Helena ignores what David says.

"David, I respect Dianah Chantilly or is it Chalice, I believe that's her name, although I think she needs to pull that stick outta her behind. So I expect you to respect my mother, too. I better not ever hear you dis her that way again or Helena won't be able to save you from my fist because her ass will be mine, too."

Helena knew their oldest sibling rarely threatened anyone but she also knew he didn't deliver idle threats. He delivered promises.

"Calm down J.J., David was only teasing mom." Helena smiled at her brother.

"No he wasn't, he was calling her a stump in an off-handed way. Little wonder Mom prefers to live with Ana than you. She might have a lot of man drama but those men have to respect mom or they know she will leave them in a heartbeat."

To illustrate how well they get along and Junior is overreacting Dave flops down beside Fannie and hugs her. "Mom and I get along just fine. Don't we?" He said, flashing his perfect dazzling smile.

"We do alright." Fannie said drily.

Dave knew Fannie knew the truth about him and Ana and figure if he made her seem like a queer duck, no one would believe her shall she decided to come clean. She mentioned it to him one day Helena was gone, telling him he ought to be ashamed of himself.

693

The homecare nurse who stayed with Fannie every day and night at the height of her strange illness at J.J.'s expense eventually told him Helena and her family rarely visited Fannie. So he finally told Frances he was bringing his mother home. But he now believes Mom lied when she said everything was fine. She would remain at Helena's.

⮞⮜⮞⮜

He'd been anticipating a visit from her since the murders. He laughs at the cops now that they have their hand full dissecting an antique sex trade ring.

"Well, that's just like my Father, if you don't have enough to do, He'll find something tedious and constructive for you to do and usually it's so dull it leaves you exhausted."

He wasn't asleep when she showed up. He pretended he was. He watched her under hooded lashes crawl in the bed beside him and curl up into a tense, tight ball.

"I killed them because I had to," she said sorrowfully, laying down by his side of the bed hugging her knees but looking through time and space at Bea. He couldn't have cared less about those satanists but since she wanted to talk about killing them he would listen. "Ana, where are you?" He asked impatiently.

"I'm right here." She puzzlingly replied. He chuckled, he knew she understood the question.

"No, I mean where are you living? What state?"

"Does that matter?" She asked, leaning over kissing his neck. He holds her back at arm length.

"Yes, it does matter. We're going to have to stop meeting like this. I mean you show up, screws my brains out, and leave like someone cheating on their spouse. What's up with that? The last time I saw you, all I did was mention the birthmark near your pussy and you got all huffed up and angry. Now you are ready to give it to me because you feel like it. I'm not your toy, your sex machine you can come to whenever you've an itch. I've feelings, damn it!"

She kissed him on the mouth to silence him. She kissed him deeper and deeper until she got the response out of him she wanted. She wiggles out her top and bra. He feels her warm flesh against his side which kills his last ounce of resistance. Her hand glides down to his budge and she slowly undo his pants. All the while kissing him. He kicks them the rest of the way off. She stands up and step out her jeans and panties in one clean sweep. He pulls her on top of him and takes control. He lays her down gently where he just risen from and saddles himself between her legs, spreading them wide enough to see the birthmark. He bring his mouth down softly on her clitoris and pulls it in, she begin to moan and move. He flicks it with his tongue and her moaning grows louder. He knows she is having orgasms. He can feel and taste them. He knows she will try to crawl away from him when the pleasure get unbearable so he holds her hips. He usually lets go when she crawls away but not this time. He is still pissed with her for keep running away from him. He can't remember the last time they had sex this intense but he remembers her ways and responses. She tries to push him away from between her legs, but he applies the pleasure harder. He isn't surprise when she start screaming at him to let her up. He carefully guides a finger in her and he remembers that drives her wild.

"Baby, put it in." She gasped.

He grinned wickedly and replied. "Not yet darling, lay back and enjoy." He feels he is too fucking old to play this game with. Hell, he invented this game. But slowly he begun making passionate love to her. He also remembers his only weakness was he could never stay angry at her. And his kind possessed the ability to hold grudges for millenniums. With each thrust he bring them closer together.

"Honey, I wonder why we keep forgetting each other?" He wonders out aloud as she lays in his arms.

"I've no idea. Maybe it isn't our time yet and we're trying to force things beyond our control. It's sad but by tomorrow I won't remember how beautiful tonight was." She said, falling asleep, wishing she could stay here like this forever.

695

He's rather surprised she's still there the next morning asleep on his chest. He realizes she's totally exhausted and doesn't bother her, she wakes up and looks at him, frowning. "Don't scream. I didn't drag you here." He said, recognizing that expression in her eyes.

"You're Ashton Cargill...right?" She asked bashfully realizing she is naked under the covers.

"Yes, I am." he replied knowing to expect a different Ana. He wonders does she suffer from schizophrenia or a *dissociative identity disorder*?

"I must go, my daughter is alone," she said panicking as she quickly got dressed. At least he sees this time how she leaves, she goes through the 8th day. Soooo, this is a ploy of the heavens. What purpose does it serve other than pissing him off. He looked heavenward and said, "Ok, I get it, this is payback for all times I've played with people's hearts. I need to know where she is just in case she's knocked up." No reply came from up above, not that he was really expecting one. He cursed himself for forgoing to check her out before she left. He tried again:

"Ok, since You aren't going to answer. Why are You messing with her mind? The poor thing has enough problems without adding amnesia to the mix. She's barely holding things together. Don't You care?" He angrily turns back the covers, gets up, and showers. He's trying to shower away her scent, not so the harem won't know he been with someone else. He doesn't care if they know. But eliminating her make it easier to live without her.

Ana arrived back in their room in outside of Jackson, Mississippi in a panic. Bea is fine, still asleep. She tells herself she've got to stop this shit. Supposed Vonderbilt had shown up while she was out screwing around? Then she remembers she is single. Thad divorced her. But still, Bea was here alone. She glances up and sees Bea guardian angel standing by her head.

"Where were you guys when that mess went down in Miami?" She asked angrily, mainly to calm her guilty conscience for leaving Bea alone in a hotel room.

"We were there. Who do you think those two girls really were?" He asked a little sarcastically as if he were saying *'Don't be blaming me because you can't stay away from him.'* It dawned on her! The biggest of the girls was him and the smaller one was her own guardian angel. She decided to ask questions since this angel is visible. "Why do I keep forgetting that man?

"It's best to forget him, he is not a nice person." The angel replied. "He'll only break your heart. You must stay clear and focused to do what needs to be done."

His executives tells him the man named Tobias Jones won't go away until he agree to see him. Seems to him this morning is one problem after another. Ana running off, refusing to tell him where she is living. Some fool hit one of his banks in San Francisco. Now a second rate builder who thinks he's the next Frank Lloyd Wright is here and won't go away.

"Sewell, any news on the bank robbery?" Ashton asked drying off but his mind is really still on Ana BuFaye. So a fat lot of good the shower did in washing her from his constant thoughts.

"Sir, he got past the laser security. The only way I see possible is he teleported into the vault. Nothing is broken. But they've an image of him. Do you wish to see it?"

"No, that's ok. The poor sap only took six million. I'll just claim it as a lost." Ashton says getting dressed. Sewell is concerned about his boss' disinterest in urgent matters. Normally, had anyone robbed one of his banks he would've them by the nuts by now. Now he's like a gentle laid back person Sewell doesn't know.

"Sir," Sewell says into the wall phone. "I know this is none of my business but your behavior has been very lenient as of late."

"You're right, it's none of your business. Tell Mr. Jones I'll see him at 2:00, maybe he'll go away after he learns he doesn't have what I'm looking for."

"Very well, sir." Sewell says promptly and waits for Ashton to break the connection. You never break connection first with him. At least when that woman visits he's much easier to get along with. He doesn't hold your feet to the fire for every mistake.

Seemed to him he had read Sewell's mind saying this before.

Ashton tossed the tie on the bed deciding he's still pissed off and doesn't feel like wearing it. He has got to get that woman out of his head. She makes him soft. He chuckled at his own thought. "Well, she doesn't get me soft below the belt. She's right. I do have a dirty mind."

He waits only a few minutes before his Norfolk, Va secretary escort a pleasant looking, fairly attractive man in carrying a building blueprint under his arm.

"Hello, Mr. Cargill, my name is Tobias Jones". Ashton counts it against him he doesn't have the plan in a tube or at least in a briefcase. If one is to do work for him they had better be on their P's and Q's from start to finish. The man shivers when spiritually scanned.

"Aw fuck, another gifted human. He's already dealing with one. My baby is a fruitcake and I know it." He smiles at his private joke. Tobias assumed he is smiling about him, in a way he is. Ashton is mentally caught as guard off in referring to Ana as his baby.

"This entire day has started to feel like a huge case of Déjà vu. " Ashton thinks as he watched the man unroll the blueprint.

"Sir, here's the design. I believe you'll love it." Tobias said, unrolling the blueprint. He views it. He has seen this before in another world. He had to admit it was quite impressive. But he wonders if he hires this man will he forget to come to work; the gifted are a whole nother level of peculiar. Like this morning, Ana hiding under the cover to get dressed when he saw it all last night.

698

"Mr. Jones, thank you for coming in but this isn't quite what I had in mind." Ashton says to a disappointed Jones.

"Sir, I can change the plan and build it any way you would like." Tobias ensures him.

"Mr. Jones, I don't pay for a building until it's completed. Do you've 36 billion to build it?" Ashton asked, knowing the man didn't.

"No sir, I do not." Tobias admitted. "But I"m willing to borrow the funds to buy the supplies and hire a team. I know I can provide the best craftsmanship around."

Ashton has grown bored with the man. He looks at his family info record. He has five kids and a wife named Star. He once knew a woman named Star, he wonders if she is the same person? She was one of those flings he had no intention of seeing again.

"How long you and your wife been married? How long have you been in business for yourself?

"I'm just starting my own business, I've been married about fifteen years."

"I see the company you presently work for is going under, there aren't many family homes being built in this economy. I wish you all the luck in the world but Cargill International can't use your service right now."

"I'm positive I have met this man before. There seems to be some pieces missing in the original conversation." He shakes himself mentally.

Shaking out of the hold the vision he is seeing has roped him into, "Sir, I wouldn't be here if I didn't know I can build any design you want. I've five children, Truilla Construction is going under as you said. Everyone has to start somewhere."

Ashton pushed the silent button to summon his secretary to show this man out. Oh, he remembers Star Madden, she was high minded and thought she was prettier than she actually was. He remember she wanted him to take her shopping in Paris. Oh please, her pussy wasn't that good. These are the sort of things he wished he didn't remember but he does. Oh! He nearly forgot, he did put 25 grand in Ana's jean pocket last night while she slept. He watched Bea through the realms as always when she spent the night with him. He hopes she isn't crazy enough to come back and throw it at him. Screaming she can't be bought or some equally lunatic nonsense.

The secretary arrived and escorted Tobias out without a deal. He knows Star isn't going to happy at all. He delivers his piece before he leaves, that the man's mind wasn't really on the project. It was a million miles away. Cargill wasn't insulted when he told him he wouldn't build for him.

Ashton feels a little sympathy for man married to that swanky fishwife, but two of his kind had already fucked up his day. He wasn't in the mood to learn if Tobias would be his third strike for the day he thinks as he views the footage of a dark complexion, young black man walking around inside the vault. The nervous pacing tells him the young man isn't sure how much to take. He believes he just discovered that ability. Grief brought it forth. He got a report the man paid cash for his grand aunt's funeral. So he guess he wouldn't add insult to injury. But this boy better not try him again. The next time he won't be so nice about this shit.

He felt the emotions transpires across time and dimension since they were in the same realm now, it didn't have to travel through another realm when she touched the money. That was a physical link between them. He sensed dislike, hurt, anger, disdain, despair, love, hate, uncertainty, fear, guilt, loneliness, joy, and an array of other emotions all stirred together in a huge pot call her psyche.

He sighed for he knew how her high-strung mind worked, *"I didn't give it to you as payment for sex, I gave it to you to stay alive, stay ahead of Vonderbilt, I gave it to youcause I love you. My little Silly Valentine. I wish you didn't hate me so much."*

He heard her respond thought through time saying she didn't hate him. She loved him. That's why it hurt so much not being able to remember him.

He heard her sweet reply, he felt the portal closing that linked them for these few minutes he said, *"Darling, my beautiful darling, I won't deny I've done a lot of evil but you're one person who has no need at all to fear me. I love you and always will, nothing will change that."* He felt as thus someone had died when the link was broken and tears rolled down his cheeks. He angrily slapped him palm down on the desk where Tobias Jones had just unfurled his blueprint. He suddenly remembered those of the same kind can find each other. Why did he stupidly send the man away when this man is gifted in love and compassion just as Ana, he can find her.

He quickly disappeared back to the house where they spent the night looking for something personal of hers. He found her bra. "Hell no, I can't use that." He said to himself pocketing it. He looks at the glass, she didn't drink anything. He removed the pillowcase, thankful this house didn't have a staff yet. So no maid had been here to clean up and then he teleports to Tobias' hotel. He exited outside the door. He reminds himself if he scares the man half to death, he'll run like hell. The true gifted are a nervous bunch. They sprint at the first sign of one like himself showing up on the scene. They ran calling Father and Father beat your ass for scaring them. So he knocked. He hears the man on the phone. He hears the man rise off the bed to come to the door.

He can't seems to stop himself from going through this weird motion a second time. What is going on here? Has someone trapped him again in a time loop? He is positive this has happened before.

"Tobias, would you care to join me for dinner so we can further discuss your plan?" He smiles pleasantly, pushing his normal scowl aside. The man is rather surprised he's here. "I believe I was a little hastily premature in my judgment."

Finding his voice Tobias says "Come in, Mr. Cargill. What a pleasant surprise!"

Ashton flinched because this man sounds a little like Ana if she were a guy. *"They're even nice to people who treat them like shit."*

"Sir, what can I do for you?" Tobias asked curiously.

701

"You can have dinner with me. We can further discuss the blueprints and a few other things." Ashton said with a smile linked to a motive. He watched the man's face light up. *Gosh, these saints remind me so much of my Father.*

"Sure, I was just telling Star I was going downstairs to the vending machine to get some more chips and soda for dinner. My plane doesn't leave until 10:00 in the morning." Tobias says, still uncertain why the richest man in the world is inviting him, lowly, broke, contractor Tobias Jones to dinner.

"Nonsense, you're coming with me to the Jackson Cargill hotel; they'll deliver your effects to your room. I've reserved it for a week, you're welcome to invite Star. I'll send a plane for her if you like."

"Effects?" Tobias thought *"I only have one suit bag and a suitcase if that's what you call effects?!"* But instead he replied "Sure sir, I'm certain Star would enjoy that."

The two men rode pretty much in silence to dinner. Ashton ordered whatever Tobias wanted, which wasn't much. The huge jet had been sent to pick up Star and his children. Ashton knew they'd be at the hotel suite waiting. After dinner he led Tobias to his office. He prays it isn't too late.

(Ashton stops and looks around. He is now positive this has happened before. But who is doing it and why?)

"Tell me where she is and we've a 36 billion dollar deal."

"HELLO, WHOMEVER. I'LL FIND YOU AND WHEN I DO I'M RIPPING YOU TO PIECES." *He said, carefully getting up. These things must be handled delicately or the person can trap you for a very long time in them or in cases such as his, it can be forever.*

Tobias slowly reached for the pillowcase again and concentrated on the here and now.

"I do not wish to do business with you. A man is known by how he treats his family.

Dogs on the city's heap pile live better than your wife and child. She was with your child, sick and weakened, trying to work to take care of your child already living.

"Someone overheard this conversation and is now playing it back to him. But who is this good at illusion and time trapping?"

"Father, I promised to do better!" He cried in desperation.

"Then why are those ill-reputed women in her houses? All I've allowed you to accumulate was for her sake, not yours. When I atoned you I did it because she begged Me. She crawled, prostrated humbly to the Throne begging Me not to destroy you. I spared you for her sake, not yours."

"Father, I understand all that but remove her memory of me?"

"I have many times. She goes back to you and gets hurt again. With you she will never complete the assignment I appointed her."

"Father, I really love her. I've learned my lesson. Please tell me where she is."

"Son, your wife is a soldier just as yourself, she has a job to do. You'll interfere with My Work. If you're serious about finding her then practice on being the husband she needs." He watched in astonishment as his Father signs out the body and Tobias Jones returns.

"Thank you for time." Ashton says, leaving a $50 grand bill on the table between himself and Tobias.

"Mr. Cargill, I'm sorry....I can't..."

Their voices started to fluctuate and become distorted as if speaking from inside along deep tunnel.

"Don't be, my Father always strong-arms people." Ashton replied and kept on walking

703

not remembering doing any of the things he just heard. He knew his Father does not lie. So he really has been a terrible person to her. Which explains what ended of their marriage but it doesn't explains which of his brothers she married. He has more questions now than answers but knew better than to ask them.

He has managed to step outside the time warp into darkness, the culprit must had heard him coming for whomever it was had fled. He stands in the darkness for a long while trying to gather evidence of the spiritual trail. But he can't. Whomever it was knew very well how to erase their spiritual tracks.

Pascasiel barely got away. If he can help Dawn repay his self-serving brother he will. Plus, he has a very sharp axe to grind with Ana.

꩜

Changing into fresh clothing after showering, Ana stuffs the soiled clothing in a big plastic bag. They smell like his cologne, whatever his name is. She checks her pockets and something falls out. Bea grabs it.

"Mommy, we got lots, lots, and lots of money!"She cried hold up the money for her mom to see. "You can stay home with me today!" She adds.

There's a one hundred grand bill, something she have never seen before in reality, two ten thousand dollar bills, and one five grand bill. She wonders where can she get change for it in this small city. Usually retailers balk at something this big.

Ana is just as surprised as Bea. So she was right about him. That declaration of love outside the compound was merely a trick to get her to sleep with him. He lied saying she has had sex with him before. He paid her to let her know don't come back, he has done what he wanted to do. That angel is right; he is not a nice man, but hell, they can use the money. She wonders can she rent a small apartment? She have never lived this deep south.

Oh, if he doesn't want to see her again that is fine by her. She couldn't deny it hurt he paid her like a whore whom he had hired for her services. Why was she hurt? It was she who went to him. It was she who initiated the love making by lying on top of him. He tried to stop her but she pressed on. Any man, if you gave it to him he will take it. What was the incognito of her seducing him?

She had already groomed Bea for the day, "C'mon Bea let's go shopping! We aren't going to the Goodwill or Salvation Army, we going to Target!" Poor child hadn't been to any other store other than second hand stores in so long she just stared at her mom. Another bout of guilt bit Ana, even Fannie took her to Macy's when she was growing up and she can't even do that.

She plastered on a big smile and said "You'll see. I'm sure you'll love it."

"Yaaayyy!" Bea cried, jumping up and down. "We going to Target Mart!"

Ana thought after this we're going to Disney World or Land, whichever one in California even if Vonderbilt is the ticket puncher at the fucking gate. I'm sick of depriving my baby of everything fun because of those assholes. Hey, weren't we there some time ago? I can't remember but, if, so what? We'll just go again. What you don't remember don't count.

The time line manipulator didn't want her to go all the way back to the period she spent with his brother. So he tweak things a little to make them seems as if they are fresh, the present and not the past. Besides, with the heavens erasing her memory makes it all the more easier.

She takes the money from Bea to pocket it. She heard him talking to her, pledging his love to her. She was stunned at what he said; so stunned she looked around the room to see if he was there. She heard what he said. He said this was not payment for sex. He gave it to her so she can stay alive and ahead of Vonderbilt. He gave it to her because he loved her. He called her his Silly Valentine. Well, she didn't care for the "silly" part. She didn't know if he could hear her as well as she heard him.

"I don't hate you. I don't know what to think of anyone nor who to trust."

("I think I told him this before. I'm not sure for things aren't always clear with me.")

Ana instructs Bea to get in the shopping cart. Bea thinks that's for babies. She doesn't want to buy so much they have to lug a bunch of crap around and she want to buy enough to get the 5 grand bill broken. She buys Bea whole new outfit complete with matching shoes and a new portable air condition for Trusty. She doesn't like running the A.C. in the car to keep cool while they sleep. She is looking at the children's jewelry when a pleasant but stunningly beautiful young woman ask may she help them? The name tag read 'Regina Barnes.'

"Yes!" Bea cried. "I want that one!" Pointing to a child's costume ring with a butterfly on top. "I want the necklace and bracelet too. I want the red bracelet, too" Bea points through the glass showcase.

("I feel as if I have said this before.") Bea thinks, a little embarrassed at how dorky she thinks she sounds.

"Ooooh." Regina teased. "A diva in the making!" Pulling the pieces from the showcase. Bea beamed her winning smile at the sales clerk. Ana merely watched the two interact but was also watching for anyone paying them unusual attention. She saw no one seemingly singling them out but she knew that didn't mean a thing and it wouldn't last for long. Vonderbilt knew she survived the bombing and everything else he had thrown her way so he'd soon rear his ugly mug in some form.

"Will there be anything else?" The clerk asked, addressing Ana. "Yes, there is a blue topaz and opal ring in the adult jewelry selection. I'd like it in a size 5. And would like to speak to the manager, please." A puzzled look crossed the young woman's face.

"I'm the store's manager." The woman informed. Ana nervously licked her lower lip, "My husband doesn't understand it's hard to shop with large bills can I see you in the office please?"

"Sure." She beamed at back at Bea. "She's so pretty."

706

"Thank you." Bea beamed back. Ana pushed the cart behind the clerk while gambling rather to push her luck, ask her to break one of the ten grands bills instead. So she place the bill on the desk once the door was closed.

"We don't see these everyday." The clerk/manager chuckled. "How would you like the change?"

"Fifties and twenties."

"Ok, I'll be right back. I can ring up your sale back here if you'd like."

"Sure, that would be great!" Approximately 15 minutes later the woman returns. Another woman arrives and tries to see what's going on. Regina closes the door in her face and count the money out to her. She chats as she rings up the sale which came to $287.00. She politely hands Ana the change but leans in close to her, "I know you're running from someone or something, my advice... wear your old clothing while on the road and get out of this town as soon as possible."

Ana was startled. "You're gifted and so is she, your kid. I detected it the moment you two walked in; just like I detected it, so can they. You're safer in a large city."

Ana was flabbergasted at her cover being blown so easily. "Warning duly noted." Ana said.

This day and words feels familiar. She feels like they are going around in circles but isn't sure. This day feels a very bad case of Déjà vu.

Pascasiel cuts off the revengeful manipulation of the past before she returns to the motel room. Nikola's drama with her is none of his concern. Hers and Azazael's memory may had been erased but his wasn't. He remembers very well the days of her stealing away from his palace when she returned to his world. He followed her and found her in the arms of his brother. Both cared nothing for anyone else's feelings but their own. He has pretended to his triplet brother since time immeasurable that he was in the dark

707

about Ana seeing him after he married her.

She doesn't remember him but oh yes, he remembers her. He remembers the pain so vividly of seeing her back in his brother's arms. The pain of realizing she only married him to have legitimate access to the spiritual world. The agony of knowing she only married him to be near Azazael even after he so shamefully disgraced her was more than he could take. His stepping up and taking her as his queen despite her horrible condition, redressing the injuries, shame and humiliation his brother inflicted on her when he threw her out and restored, recrowned Paranorma as his queen. That was his mistake; Azazaeland would probably still exist today had not he taken Paranorma back but then that's Azazael's problem. Not his. Ana is his concern. He gave her access to the his world and this is how the Time Walker repaid him. His was what his brother did to people. Hurt you, humiliate you, and dog you out.

He watched them exit the vehicle and hurry into the new and present place. He stepped from the spiritual realm and called his wayward, adulterous ex-wife. Even out of the royal attires of a queen she was still beautiful. She looked haggard and tired about the eyes but then again dealing with his egoistical brother does that to you.

"Do I know you?" she asked curiously as she turned defensively to address the person who knew her name so intimately.

"Well, you could." Pascasiel said, coming closer.

He felt her scan him with no recognition as to who he is. She was searching for another soul. He saw her big eyes widen. Memory of Azazael had been erased but not memory of him. He had done nothing to deserved it to be erased.

"Bea, honey. Go inside, I'll be in shortly," Ana said pushing Bea in the room and pulling the door shut and then turning to address the familiar looking man, "Where do I know you from?"

"I at least hope you remember our wedding night." Pascasiel mildly replied. He wasn't intimidating as to why she didn't throw up a defense.

Knowing he is an immortal, she says, "Sorry, if I wronged you during a time walking adventure. I'm truly sorry but I can't say I remember you."

Pascasiel had a feeling she was lying. Her initial reaction stated otherwise. She divorced him in an attempt to remarry his brother and thinking that by she was from another world, at that time, not yet made she was safe from his wrath. Had she divorced him first and then slept with and remarried his brother he would have forgiven her but she didn't, she had an affair on him with his brother. And for that he hates them both.

Although Azazael was ridden with guilt for hurting him and even accepted the punishment for his anger, wrath being rained down on others because of his third wife's unfaithfulness. He was still angry at them for not considering anyone else's feelings but their own. Azazael decided he wanted her back after seeing her at the coronation of her queenship.

Knowing how she feels about the kid, he directed her to a stone bench under a birch tree populated by drunks and primary strung-out, hollow faced heroin addicts waiting for their next fix who also called this tatterdemalion place home suspiciously eyed the big stranger. The others, sensing something unusual about the man, quickly left the dirty, littered area. The hard-packed grey mud ground made their scuffling sound louder than it would have.

She looked before she sat for she knew people used drug pumps out here. The needles of the pump administered the fix and then dispensed itself and another needle took its place. The ground was covered with the hard razor thin plastic applications, but what choice did she have? She couldn't out run him and your sword doesn't appear unless there's a genuine threat. Talking to someone wasn't exactly a threat. Well, unless that someone was Nikola. Yes, merely talking to him was dangerous.

She watched him clear the place of debris and insects with the mere sweep of his hand. *Whoa! He is far more powerful than she guessed.*

After taking a seat on the bench beside her, he stared out in the parking lot for a few minutes before asking, "Ana, all I want to know is why did you do it? That's all."

"Do what?"

"Cheat on me with my brother Azazael." Pascasiel replied, now looking directly at her so she had to look at him, memorize his face. He and Azazael looked exactly alike, he was thinner and less muscular. Much more refined than his two older brothers. Azazael and Brustiel. "Did you ever love me at all?"

"Pascasiel, I'm sorry. At that time...I was going through a lot of things back here in my own world, era, and existence. I don't know all I did while in other realms. If I hurt you, I'm dearly sorry. I truly am. I did a lot of stupid shit back then that I now regret. I have grown up a lot since then. I 'm not the same girl I was back then."

He sucked in his breath hard and hastily; so she does remembers him and his name. To refresh her memory he tried to wave open the scenes from their lives and is surprised it is sealed. She doesn't know she left children behind in another world. Children who were destroyed when their father's worlds were judged. He tried to tell her these things but the heavens sealed his lips physically and telegraphically. He was unable to deliver what he felt she needed to know. He felt she needed to feel remorse for what happened.

"You asked did I once love you? Somewhere, something deep down inside tells me that I did," she said as much to her own surprise as to his.

"Ana, I loved you but not in the insane way my brother loves you. I would've appreciated it had you told me you wanted to go back to him and not crept behind my back."

She had no idea what he was referring to but it must had happened for him to feel so familiar to her. Knowing that time as humans know it isn't the same as time in the spiritual worlds, she carefully asked, "How many years were we together?"

"Time isn't the same there as here so we married about three hundred years."

"Oh, wow! That's a long time! But I'm so sorry I don't remember."

The archangel named Aurorael standing behind them rolled her eyes at Pascasiel's reemergence of the past. And in the blink of an eye she took Pascasiel away, erased most of his memory of their marriage and erased all of Ana's memory of him. This was not the time to take a trip down memory lane. That happened long ago and with the coming of the Antichrist emotional trips down through the past were the last thing Ana needed with Nikola so hot on her heels.

❧

"What in that bitch made of? Teflon?!" Vonderbilt shouted at closest aides. Who are hoping he doesn't start hitting and killing and blaming them for her escape, yet again.

"My spies in high offices said Cargill got them to call off the search." Cheng Toa said. Nikola wondered what in the hell was he doing here? He doesn't remember calling Cheng nor asking his opinion.

"Your highness, my request is we use martial arts on her. She can't be captured by normal methods." Cheng says. "Ninjas can easily capture and even kill her if you wish." Cheng had heard about those others who failed to capture her. He trained their teacher but a teacher never reveals everything to their students. So of course they could not defeat the witch.

"No, no I don't want her dead, you imbecile." Nikola said, slapping the world renowned martial artist whose performances are legendary. He has been known to defy nature by vibrating his molecules and walking through solids, run upon water without sinking. He has trained the deadliest ninjas to exist in the modern era. One had to be exceptionally good for him to take them on as a student.

"Very well, then capture her but if they fail me I'll have their nuts." Nikola promises. From what Cheng Toa heard of the Dark Dragon as his section of the world recalls about Nikola he would literally castrate you for failure.

"As you wish." Cheng says bowing and prostrating before his real master.

Having left the Grand Wizard, the thirteen ninjas and Cheng settle in a lotus position starting the spiritual preparations in the Oriental style Bìnàn dìdiǎn. They go into deep meditation so they can astral travel in the physical realm since her whereabouts are unknown. It would be useless to use the spiritual realms. He knows she is divinely cloaked. One ninja speaks in Mandarin Chinese saying "She is in a place in America called Jackson, Mississippi."

None realized Nikola followed them under a secretive dark cape until Vonderbilt hits him on the crown of his head, causing his spirit to be yanked back quickly. Nikola knows the danger of what he just did but doesn't care. He knows he could've triggered a heart attack.

"ENGLISH, Swedish, or Italian; anything but damn Chinese when in my presence. Cheng, you better teach your fools respect if you want them. What in the fuck did he say about Jackson, Mississippi?"

"She is at store in Jackson called Target Mart, your Highness."

Nikola laughed, "She is a damn target and is shopping at one. Women will die to go shopping."

No one else laughs because she is, after all. the Grand Witch and the Grand Wizard does not appreciate anyone laughing at or mimicking her. He has proven what happens if you do by using Carole and James Caldwell as his examples.

Nikola has a gun behind his back and quickly fires at one of the ninjas in a lotus position. The man reaches behind and catches the bullet before it enters his nape. Nikola is impressed. "You are going to need to be able to catch a lot of them if you plan to go after my wife. Get to it!" He stalks out leaving the men to devise their plan. He calls the Louisiana regional warlock Shrevenport and relays the ninja's information.

"No, I don't want you to go after her. She'll you kill before you get out the car. If she escapes them more likely she'll be headed your way, be on the look out for her."

"Yes, your Highness," Shrevenport nods via screen phone, lowering himself on the floor before the screen. He hopes she does come this way. He'd like to meet her and show her Cajun style sex. Nikola would never have to know.

They rushed back to their room and were giving it one final sweep so that nothing incriminating nor personal was left behind. Nothing that a practitioners of dark arts or a demon can use to find them to track them when they suddenly hears a strange vibration that isn't machinery. It was an odd sound she'd never heard before. More like if nature itself was vibrating at a high, rapid speed.

"Bea, go in the bathroom and climb out the window if no one is out back waiting for you." Ana said quickly as three men of Asian descent literally step through the door as effortlessly as phantoms. She fires at them; they easily dodge the bullets as ten more enters. Another drops down through the ceiling. She can't understand what they're saying but their eyes tell her it's not good and it has something to do with her and one of those beds. She semi-rolled her eyes wondering with men...why does everything always have to involve a damn bed?

She remembered her three months of training where Saint Anne made her move faster and faster; she could never move fast enough for her mentor. Saint Anne one day made her vibrate so fast her hand passed right through a boulder. Her arm tired out and her hand was stuck. It was very painful to have flesh stuck in stone. St Anne disinterestedly looked at her from her seat, perched on another rock with her palm cupping her chin and asked how did she plan to get her hand out? The pain forced her to start vibrating again. After freeing her hand the saint told her there were evil ones could do this also and so she had to move faster than they. And here they are. Live, in living color.

"Someone trying to kill isn't going to give you time to build up speed or friction. You must start out with it!" Saint Anne stressed every time she slowed down.

In a nanosecond she willed her uniform on and her sword slid into her right hand, on fire, while the shield appeared on her left arm. She see wonderment in one of the men' eyes speculating did they totally underestimate her. She certainly hopes they did.

She remembered you charge the enemy first with intent to kill. She leaps and runs sideways along the wooden panel wall to position herself in the center of the group to swing in 360 degrees. Cheng smiles at the girl thinking she can defeat him. But first, he would like to have some fun with her. When she leaps to land in the midst of them, Cheng grabs her midriff and slams her hard to the carpeted floor but she leapt up again swinging the fiery blade. She slices through four of his men before reaching standing position. Cheng wonders what master trained her? She is moving at an unnatural speed. Three more launch into assault; she throws fire at them. This fire was of no nature origin, it can not be quenched. By now Cheng is angry, he feel he has played with her for far too long. She is a master of these arts and a powerful witch. He wishes to test her hand to hand combat methods; she blocks his every blow while that Sword floats suspended in air and swipes at anyone who comes near them. She finds an opening and goes for his throat and lands a deadly blow obstructing his air passage.

"Have mercy," he croaked clutching his throat, dropping to his knees. She stops and looks at the five remaining ninjas. "Khwarizmi! Nüwa, and Fuxi, warisome but warmongering demons! I call you forth in the Name of your real Master, Jesus Christ the Nazarene, the Son of the Living God!!"

A greenish black wisp of smoke began drifting from Cheng and the others. The twin snake tailed demon with a man's body glowered at her. The smoke was assembling from the even the beheaded, burnt, and halved ones.

"I command you to go back to hell in the Name of Jesus!" She shouts.

At first Cheng laughed, he does not serve her god. Her god has no control over him. He watches her grow brighter and brighter; the flame from her sword is incinerating the ceiling. Sparks are starting to float down around them. He swiftly strikes a death blow. She grabs his fist and he isn't able to take it from her. As he stares into her eyes they are

714

literally fire in her small face. He can not ignore the fact he isn't dealing with anyone earthly trained. Cheng remember his grandmother taught him that a saint must show mercy if asked for it.

"Nikola lied, this woman is no witch. She is a warrior saint" was Cheng's last thought before passing onto eternity as the hand not holding his fist took his head.

The sword stood between them and Cheng's remaining men as she retrieved Bea from the bathroom and walked out the burning room. As she passed them she said "If you follow us I'll stop and finish you off." She knew if they attacked again that would void the plead for mercy.

She exited the room into the daylight with Bea at her side as divine smoke which was harmless to them billowed from the doorway and windows, melting the room. Again, they were untouched.

She opened the door placing Bea under the iron blanket without looking into the room again at the sound of the men's agony. As she was backing out she did see one try to escape through but a hand of smoke pulled him back into the burning room.

On the road heading out of Jackson she wondered how did the woman at Target know they were coming? How did this woman know Vonderbilt was so close? She noted she has met several like herself in their six years of travel.

She headed northward, not toward Louisiana. She was aware of a major coven there. This coven's membership is in the hundred thousands. The saints in the cave gave her a map showing the satanic Pentagramic affect on the nation; it showed crossroad towns and cities and lay over areas. And what areas in major cities and even small to mediums towns to avoid.

Each point of star was the location of a regional leader which meant hell on earth for those like herself who lived there. She decided Bea was going to have some fun if she had to kill a legion of these motherfuckers. Orlando, Florida was out of the question so she headed north and decided to go around Louisiana and Texas and get to California via Nevada.

Shrevenport's people forwarded the news to him of the ninjas' demise, of their utterly being slaughtered. He in turn forwarded the news to Nikola about Cheng and his men's deaths in the now burning motel off of Interstate 20.

"My people are following her north."Shrevenport informed of Ana's known direction taken. "The motel is on fire, the fire department is at loss in how to put out the fire."

"Castrate all the overconfident bastards still alive." Nikola irefully instructed. "I specifically told them she was not to be underestimated. I know they went in all cocky and macho and she turned it all into a blood party." Nikola said and cut the connection.

Frustrated, he throws an antiqued. decorative ceremonial skull at the ancient Luigi Frullini craved wooden wall panel, smashing it and yelling at the top of his lungs "I HATE THAT MURDEROUS, CONVIVING BITCH!!! When I catch her, I'm pulling her teeth one by one and enjoying it."

⟲∞∞⟳

Ninsianna refused to be dismissed so unceremoniously. The ancient beauteous Mesopotamia goddess of sexuality, fertility, marriage and prostitution is accustomed to getting what she wants and doesn't see the present day as any different from the past when thousands loved her. The immortals once ruled so they shall rule again.

"Silly men." She thinks, watching the motel burn in unquenchable fire for a few minutes before soaring to find the woman and talk to her woman to woman. She's Azazael's rightful wife and mate. He and all he owns is hers. He belongs looting and plunging the lands with her not trying to live like a fucking Seraphim which he'll never be again.

She stands suspended in the air and scans, she know the woman will have to come uncloaked at some point. One of her expertise is finding lost objects or people. From far

716

above the earth she, floating in icy space, sees the little car pull into another motel in southern Arkansas. She waits until the woman settles in. She watches them drive out to a greasy dinner she wouldn't dare visit. She goes inside the motel room and waits. Seeing what this woman can do, she knows it is not wise to antagonize her.

Ana and Bea are still shook up from the Jackson, Mississippi motel assault so she tells Bea to stay in the car while she goes in to check and make sure nothing is waiting for them. Highly trained instincts tell her someone is inside waiting and it's not her lover.

She finds a woman wearing ancient Mesopotamian style clothing and jewelry reclining on the bed against the headboard.

The bitch got her funky ass on our pillows. I don't like people sitting on my pillows.

"Come in and close the door." The ancient goddess said as if she was who paid for this room and I was the uninvited intruder. That ticked me off. I see this woman likes to come in and take over.

The exotic looking woman with blood stained hands sized me up and sighed a long tedious sigh, "Ana, save yourself a major heartache and leave Azazel alone. Dear, I'm his real wife, by the way, my name is Ninsianna. The name which your name is deprived from. Dear, there have been millions who loved him but with him being a god he isn't capable of returning love. People used to give their lives in hope that could gain his love. Human life is nothing but a short blip on the Timeline for those like my Azazel and myself. You know, how a fruit fly is to you. That's what your lifetime is to us." Ninsianna kindly explained the allegory without an iota of warmth in her eyes or voice.

I wasn't sure if she called him Azazel, the fallen heavenly prince or not but I wasn't going to let her know I didn't know his name. I was tired of people ridiculing me for not remembering his name.

"I assume you've been spying on me as to how you know about me. If you've seen me why didn't you make your claim if he's already married to you?"

Again Ninsianna, sighed as if I were retarded and cretinous and again slowly but carefully explained. "We immortals do not view love and marriage the same as mortals. I saw you but in our mateship he has always been free to bed whomever he likes. But I felt sorry for you believing he loves you. As I said, save yourself a lot of heartache and realize you're into an agenda far above your mortal comprehension. Get out before your attachment to him grows too strong and destroys you. Get out before your love for him consumes you and you can think of nothing else but him. There's a magnificent city in hell filled with woman like you and their offspring".

"Ninsianna, if you don't get out my room and your ass offa my pillow you'll be the next resident of this fabled city."

Ninsianna ignores my threat and summon Azazel. She called him twice with no reply; finally growing impatient she angrily cries, "I'm here with your precious Ana!"

He appeared in so much rage he was literally on fire. We both stepped away from him. His back is turned to me. I decided right then and there I wanted nothing to do with whatever they had going on, I was running like hell. This man is literally on fire! I turned toward the door and it slammed in my face. The fire around him and which he seemed to be made of was slowly extinguishing.

"Ana, please don't leave."

The door was jammed. I couldn't get out. I didn't think to vibrate out. I can't think of everything to do when in a tight spot. So I turned and asked him to be truthful with me. "Is this your wife or not?"

He rakes his hands through his thick mane and mentally debates before admitting the woman is right.

"Yes, she is an ex wife. We were a couple over twenty thousand years ago."

That was all I needed to hear. I headed for the door again. I had plenty enough trying to kill me, I didn't need a crazy ex-spouse who happens to be a blood-stained goddess after me, too. I pulled on the door with all my might and it wouldn't open. I placed my foot against the door frame and pulled with all my might. It didn't budge.

"Ashton, let me out of here. I'm not playing with you. I'm not playing her stupid, infantile game! I don't have time for your marital disputes."

"Ana, wait. Ninsianna is jerking you around and she knows it. She knows when our kind are imprisoned that pretty much severs the vows unless the other partner is willing to renew them. She knows I didn't pledge a unity to her after she was imprisoned for her bloodthirsty liturgies. I would've been mad, beyond crazy, to renew them with her."

He wanted to behead Ninsianna so badly his hand twitched but seconds before he did sound reasoning stayed his swing. Telling him shall he do it Ana would draw the conclusion if he beheaded one wife he would do the same to her. Ana won't see it as this woman being his ex and a bloodthirsty she-devil. She'll only see that she wants to see.

By now I had both of my feet planted on the wall near door, pulling. I glanced back at him and I saw her smirk as if something were funny. I guess I did look sort of stupid with my feet off the floor pulling on the door knob but that was a victory smirk not a humorous one. I planted my feet back on the floor and turned to face them both.

"I don't care what's the status of you two, I want both of you out of my room. I'm tired, sleepy, and very pissed off. So pissed off I can taste it." I said, extracting my blade. This was my room and I intended to get some sleep. First, I was bringing in my pillow from the car. There was no way I was sleeping on that pillow. I doubt there was an earthly antiseptic in existence that worked on whatever was on her. I shot fire at them both, a humming chorus of agonizing screeching rose from whatever those things were around her. She hastily disappeared. He tried to explain their connections but I didn't want to hear it. I held the door open and he lowered his head and left. I went to the car and got our covers and purified the bed and let Bea in. I didn't sleep a wink; I sensed him outside all night. I was hurt but I wasn't going to let him see me cry.

"Damn! How many women has he had?!" was my last thought before exhaustion pulled me under but I found myself waking up again still pissed off.

Before he returned to the motel he tracked Ninsianna down and beheaded her. She may have forever destroyed his one chance at happiness. Now that Ana knows his real name.

I couldn't sleep knowing his real name, a name he worked so hard to hide from me. I tossed and turned, wondering why I couldn't just go the fuck to sleep? It was he who lied. Not me. He knew my real name. I got up and went to the window. He was outside in a black antique muscle car. Those things are priceless today. Was he fucking with my mind, persuading me to let him in? Doesn't this man realize I'm human and have to go to fucking sleep?! I don't have an endless supply of energy. The shadows inside the car were obstructing his head, I could only see his chest and those strange luminous eyes. I saw the burning ember of the cigar he was smoking. Turning from the window, I went back to bed. I needed my rest, I didn't have the time nor energy to deal with his shit. Determined to get some rest, I drifted off and unexpectedly found myself sitting in the car with him. "*Dammit! How did I get here? My damn heart is gonna get me killed.*"

"Baby, my love. Why are you being so harsh?" He asked, pulling me close to him across the gulf separating our seats. I didn't resist when he teleported us to the backseat and we made tender, sweet love. I cursed myself afterward for being too weak to resist him.

Laying in the cramped backseat on his chest and stomach, I asked myself, "*Why do I forgive people who aren't deserving of my forgiveness? I don't even know where he lives. He could be living with someone for all I know and yet I don't have the strength to resist him. And it's like he knows I can't resist him.*" His eyes were closed but he wasn't asleep. As she rested he read her surface thoughts and smiled in the darkness and mentally projected. "*That makes two of us. I can not resist you either.*"

Chapter 15
The Empire Ascends

For reasons unknown to her for once she wasn't tired, feeling jilted, nor scared. Normally, she got up and gathered their few belongings and ran like the wind when something attacked. She felt more confident than she had apprehended in years. A fescennine devil such as the one the Sword just vaporized usually sent her fleeing in terror. She decided it's time she marketed her own brand. Vonderbilt has marketed his. Her motto from now and on will be "*If you fuck with me, I'll pulverize you. If you don't start none, there won't none. But if you start something I'll finish it along with you. I'm going to give as good as I get!*" That's a little long-winded for a marketing slogan or shibboleth but it's a start. They'll soon get the idea.

Like, shortly after vowing to herself she was determined nothing hurt her again, it was like something was watching and decided to test her. It waited until she was asleep and pounced on her. But she was determined that thing didn't fuck her because that wasn't "what" she wanted. She was doing her levelest best to kick its dick off. She got one painful kick in the groin, that's when it slapped her. By gosh! Pure, unadulterated hell fire rose in her bosom. She was seeing red. She's going have to teach these adamant motherfuckers---no, means no! She slapped it back with her solid gold enclosed wrist brace, knocking it backwards onto the floor. This time she was who did the pouncing; she leapt out of the bed and started kicking and kept kicking and stomping and kicking some more until there was nothing left but an ectoplasm stain on the floor. She must had stomped for at least a good ten minutes after there was nothing left. She was sick of everything and its evil ass mother thinking she was a toy. By now Bea was sitting up looking at her. She calmed down.

She wonders where did all the sheer unadulterated rage and attitude come from? Of course, she've never been a coward but she's always tried to walk away from troubles if she could. But she found out walking away from a fight only works if you're dealing with a pretty decent but sane person. It doesn't work when dealing with pure evil.

Looking with perplexity into the mirror, she still wonders what on earth was she thinking buying a diamond necklace? Damn! How much is this thing worth? She hadn't noticed her fingers. There's a rock on there the size of her thumbnail. Did she blank out and mug someone? When she touched the rock, the diamond on her left hand, she experienced a strong flash out of nowhere. A male voice said "Baby, you want that one, well that one you shall have." A middle age woman was lollying around about waiting on her. The woman literally looked down her nose at her. She was dressed nice for once unlike the clothing she had on last night.

"Baby, you don't have to be nice when you are who is spending your money. You're only obligated to be nice to people who are nice to you. Now assert yourself."

She looks up at him but can't see his face. "Miss, excuse I would like to see that set." She politely calls the woman who is ignoring her.

"Lady, get your ass over here and show her the damn ring before I pull your tired ass from behind that counter!" The man whose face she couldn't see said curtly.

"Sir." The clerk said, irritated. "That ring costs sixty million, why doesn't your (blank) look at something you can afford."

The man grew wrathful and hissed "I, (blank), own this fucking store. You're (blank)!" She hates it when visions have so much censorship. Another woman, who is slightly older, comes over and gets the ring and necklace too for her.

In the back of a limo, the same man poured her a fresh glass of sparkling champagne and said "Baby, you're (blank). You don't have to take shit off no one. If they don't do what you say, cuss their ass out." Whomever this person is he builds her up like no one has since her parents built confidence into her while growing up.

So, she knows she didn't steal it or mug anyone for it. Somebody bought it for her. Who thinks she's worth *this* much? Suddenly, Thad's hateful words echoed in her head; she had asked him to go the store and get something she was craving while pregnant with Bea and he snarled "*Your skinny ass ain't worth feeding. The only thing growing on ya is your big ass belly.*" She shakes it off and looks back at the still sleeping Bea. The best thing he ever gave her. "Fuck you Thad, you ain't hurting me no more. Somebody thinks I'm worth it!" She spread her fingers before her and smiled at the ring.

Moseying over to the phone, she calls the front desk "I'm paying for two more days." She said then hung up.

"Sweetheart!" She said, calling her daughter. Bea slowly sits up, sleepily rubbing her eyes. She noticed Bea has put on weight. She doesn't look so much like a waif anymore. Now dressed, she stops and looks at her own figure in the mirror. She had no idea she had such curves. Wherever they have been has certainly been good for them. Upon paying her tab, she looks causally at the bill but gasps when she sees the date. Nearly four months of her life are a blank. Where in creation has she dragged Bea off to? Were they with some magnate or mobocrate who paid a psychiatrist to erase her memory of him? The last she remembers they were in California. That thing said something about her having sex with a demon named Azazael. She remembers St. Anne mentioning that name. She stops by the car to look at her notes. He's in them. According to the saints he is worse than Lucifer. He once fought for the heavenly army but no one knows where he turned bad. Was this whom they had been living with for the past 3 1/2 months? Googling him wasn't much help. All she saw was a bunch of fearsome demons roaring and doing bad things. The person she saw was humanoid. Nothing like these gruesome images online. Why did he let them live? Obviously whomever wrote these accounts have never met a Grand Wizard.

She finds another account. An older account appearing to be written by someone who knew what in the hell they were talking about. In this one, he is said to be extraordinarily handsome and maidens have thrown themselves off cliffs pining away for his love and affection, some have walked into the sea and drowned because he refused to love them in return. She loved Thad but she was not jumping off no cliff or drowning herself for him. Another account says he is known to be a great womanizer. A great lover. She see they have never met Thad Wyett. Thad thought she didn't know about the night he thought she was gone to Helena's and brought a woman home and screwed her in their guestroom across the hall. She was too hurt and mortified to move, plus she was heavy with Bea and wasn't fooling with him and lose or hurt her baby. Why in all the so-called great love stories did somebody have to die? Hell, it's easy to idolize them once they're dead. They aren't there to fuck with you anymore, or get on your nerves. Where are the great love stories where the couple fight, cuss at each other, and get on each other's nerves but always have each other's back and still stay together and stay romantically in love for years? To her that's reality. Throwing yourself off some damn cliff about some damn man is downright stupid. That's the dumbest shit she'd ever heard. Maybe he did cause the others to do dumb shit like that but she'd be damned if she was going out like that! She scoffed and signed off the room provided computer.

They both were unable realize or remember Azazael had taken them with him for a second time in less than a year. That night from the backseat of the 2017 Mustang, he took them with him. Kept them in a palace off the coast of Monaco in the Condamine until the angels made him let them go.

He found himself wondering why was he in Monaco with a house filled with toys and a closet full of women clothing? None of the staff could answer his questions. Returning to the bedroom to search for clues, he found her torn red panties among the tangled silk sheets and smiled. They faded in his hand just as she faded from his memory.

$$\sim\!\infty\!\sim$$

Lounging on the beach connected to his estate in Monte Carlo reading a 4,000 year old book about King Minos and the Minotaur and the ancient maze he wished what's-her-name was here. Minos, he knew him. He was a sick bitch just like Vonderbilt. The man was involved in bestiality and cannibalism. All that has circled back around. It's perfectly legal nowadays to marry your pets. Fuck them, too.

Reminiscing the last 4 months, he knows what other men feel when they speak of love and romance. Wanting to be with only one woman. No one else could take her place. He used to think these men were punks who loved a woman so much she could do no wrong in his eyes. Here he was on a beach full of half-naked beauties, normally he would've five to ten lined up for the evening. But here he is thinking about her steamy kisses and the feel of himself inside her, her breasts in his hands, her clitoris in his mouth. Her jokes were funny not corny. She was very intelligent. He definitely doesn't remember ever carrying around an article of any woman's clothing to feel close to her. She has such a beautiful body and doesn't even know it.

When he touched the thin silk camisole in his bathing trunks' pocket a vision flashed before him. He tossed the book aside and hoped it would show him where she was. He saw himself positioned between her legs, not for sex but for birth. He was coaxing her lovingly to push. The labor was hard on her but finally they had a black haired, winged son. That can't be! He can't produce winged children anymore. It flips to another scene, again another birth, this time there are several of them. He counted 12. He sees himself changing diapers, holding bottles, holding and talking to the infants who smile at him; some even pissed on him and he didn't pitch a fit. *"That will be the day."* He chuckles to himself. The scene switches again. He sees lots of children. Sons whom aren't wrestling with him for control of the wealth. He doesn't have to kill these sons for attacking him. The woman teaches them to respect him. He sees sons and daughters helping him and this mysterious woman enlarges their global empire beyond his wildest dreams. He sees them as kings, queens, presidents, prime ministers, and business tycoons. He is flabbergasted when he sees himself in the king's attire of his now destroyed world escorting this woman whose face he can't see to sit on a throne more elegant than Panorama's throne was. The thousands of people surrounding them are their offspring.

"Hello Big Boy can I help you with that?" a sexy, savvy female voice says. He looks up and her eyes guided his down to the tent in his trunks.

"No thank you." He snapped, aggravated the woman interfered with his vision that's now gone.

"Heard you were off the market. Nobody seen you on the party circuit or scene the last few months. But don't look to me like the mistress is handling her business." The stranger cooed, sitting her curvy figure beside him, rubbing his penis through the shorts. He pushed her hand away. Normally he would have it in her mouth by now.

"Aw!! Don't be like that, sometimes the wifey needs help." She said, rubbing his nipples. He disappeared. The woman screamed; she thinks that was Ashton Cargill but how did he do that!?

Exiting at another beach he had forgotten was a nudist beach he says. "Okk Father, I know I'll have to do what You say to get her back. What will You have me to do?" Again he receives no response.

"So typical." He sighed.

He smiles, his words became truth. Nikola predicted when Cargill grew tired of Ana Wyett he'd send her packing. He said this months ago when Cheng's people informed him she had been whisked away from the big theme park Cargill owned. Had been at his Beverly Hills mansion and a little while later to the palace in Monaco, Monte Carlo. One good thing about demons, they're everywhere and work well with everyone. If one doesn't see her another will. There's no hiding from him with legions of spies at his disposal.

"Caldwell, do you really think Cargill married that woman?" Nikola asked his real second in command.

"I've no idea. He might have to spite you. Your Highness."

"Horseshit! Like hell he did. He probably brainwashed her into believing he married her. But as soon as he's bored with her she'll resurface on the streets."

Nikola gratingly disregarded the fact jealousy was creeping into his heart, avariciously gripping it with its ugly green fingers. He focused on observing the ninja's testicles in jars of preservatives consisting of a mixture of formaldehyde, glutaraldehyde, methanol, and other preservatives. These were his latest trophies next to Orman's heart and penis.

"Her breasts or vagina would complete my collection. I told her, very well, *punctually* instructed her not to fuck Cargill. He won't want her in the future without those parts. She's a very hardheaded woman. So she must bear the consequences for defying me. She can still be able to give birth without those parts. Did you know there is an African custom where they cut off the woman's clitoris to keep her faithful? No self-respecting man will marry a woman still possessing one. Of course many organizations have tried to banish the practice but it's still done secretly. Actually, it's not African at all, an old Mesopotamian custom. An old Canaanite practice that was ingrained in the African society when the people were conquered. I can see why. A woman with one is hard to control."

Caldwell really preferred not to know all that but Nikola likes grossing people out.

"You see that giant cask over there?" Nikola points to a glass case filled with the same preservative. "That's where I'm keeping her once I finish with her. I want to keep her so I can see her and talk to her. Keep her so she can see what she made me do. I tried to be good to her. But there are just some women you can't be good to no matter how hard you try."

Caldwell always suspected Nikola was crazy as fuck but now he *knows* he is. How in the hell will she will know anything if she's dead? Who wants to sleep in the room with a dead body floating in formaldehyde?

"Cargill was just spotted on his part of a private beach in the South Pacific and she wasn't with him. His improvised singleness tells me have dumped her." Nikola jeered.

Caldwell seriously doubted he had. Carol had informed him that Ashton's harem said he married her. The main woman of the harem named Dawn had called Carole crying.

Eager to keep away from Nikola and his peculiar collections and quaint thoughts, "Your Highness, let me call Caroline to see has Cargill returned home?" Nikola waved his hand in dismissal, approving the call.

When his wife Carol answers James Caldwell asked "Have those women said Cargill returned home yet?"

"No, he hasn't. They say he won't allow them near the Beverly Hills mansion. It was Ana who kicked Dawn out eight months ago. Dawn said when she pushed pass the doorman he told her she couldn't go in there. Mrs. Cargill was home! He was trying to hide her from Ana who came back down stairs like a battle axe and demanded she get out of her house and leave her husband alone." Caldwell ends the call in the middle of Carole's sentence. He don't have time to gossip. He'd listen to her gossip when he got home.

"That's laughable, impractical, and definitely perfidious," Nikola cried. "She's married to no one but me. Cargill is lying to all of them. If he was out alone, he was out scouting for a new playmate." Vonderbilt promised. "Men like him, whether mortal or immortal, never give their heart to anyone. If what Carole says is true then we must find a way to wrestle her from him. With her, his Empire will ascend to a height, we'll have no chance of keeping him in his actual second place. Collectively, right now we're the richest in the world. If he marries her...the lord of darkness will be furious. According to Lucifer, Cargill can transmogrify into his former glorious self. No one wants to nor is prepared to deal with that. He'll be far too strong. Lucifer said he knows this, as to why she's so important to him. It's about regaining what he lost."

Inwardly, Caldwell was meretriciously glad to see Nikola's ego and confidence take a bruising for once. Now he knows how his subjects feel when he lord his powers over them.

"Those incapacitate fools!" Nikola said, throwing a dirty fireball bursting the liquid filled jar that was prepared to someday house Ana's feminine parts. Caldwell had no clue who was Nikola referring to him or the ninjas? The man seems on a fast collision with straight up dementia. But being nuts has nothing to do with his powers. If anything, his mental condition seems to fortify them.

"My mother-in-law...how is she?" Nikola asked pleasantly, changing the subject.

"Still confined to her bed according the report of the nursing agency. But Cargill still has his people posted outside her door." Nikola nods, he remembers the family would at least speak to him when he called about Ana's welfare. This was before Cargill warned

728

them against him.

To take Nikola's mind off Ana he mentioned the acceptance of a shoo-in or secondary Grand Witch.

"Pashane Norton would make a great Grand Witch, she has guts to carry out what Ana never will. Plus, she is a white witch." Caldwell said, not sure if Nikola is listening so he continues. "I know this is inconsistent with the usual hierarchy of the Order but we've been chasing the real Grand Witch for nearing seven years. Pashane is no Ana Wyett but she is the Superior Witch of North America and the mother of your daughter. Even Lilith approves her of her as a substitute until Ana is captured and made perform her dark duties."

"Where is she from?" Nikola asked, disinterested. He isn't thrilled about another American. They're all proud and stiff-necked. Their genre of dark art isn't as seasoned as the Old World's. They mix too much shit together like this fucker sitting before him.

"Pensacola, Florida."

"Oh great! Another fucking American. I need another American Grand Witch like I need another hole in my ass. What is it with you damn Americans? You're all so arrogant, stubborn, and think you're oh so freaking special."

"We're damn special." Caldwell thinks under shrouded thoughts too deep for Nikola to read.

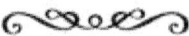

He's tired of their home appearing to be under house arrest when no one here has committed a crime. Through the early morning light fog David Wales whom everyone called Dave peered out the upstairs window. He could see the huge black military-like vehicle still stationed outside of his Long Island home. In the same position it was last night when he came home and went to bed. The neighbors have asked who are they,

729

these people have been there for at least four years. He and his wife Helena have tried everything to make them move. Helena has reported them several time to no prevalence. Even their tags can't be trace. There are usually four to six in the darkened vehicle. He was tired of appearing as thus they are illegal substance dealers and the Feds have them under surveillance. The neighbors are talking but Ana doesn't care. He has a reputation to maintain. They have explained numerous times they have no idea why those people are out there by the curb. To make matters worse, these people even inspect packages arriving for his family. Helena said some even follow her on the force. He knows this is Ana's paranoid doing. Everytime she goes crazy, some officials are at his door. Jack and Jacob complain about the same. One of Fannie's nurses ended up in a terrible accident. Her lawyer blamed those mysterious people outside. He peeked again through the heavy forest green curtains and tan valiance blinders.

"I've a mind to offer them poisoned coffee." Dave said, watching the vehicles they can't get rid of. "Rats are fed cyanide when can't rid of them in a humane fashion.

"Tried that, they won't bite the bait." Helena said dryly. "I know this is Ana's doing. She got her rich boyfriends watching mama." Helena scowled. Every since Ana killed those cops in Florida her co-workers have been her giving her a cool shoulder. People are talking before she enters the room and stop when they see her. She knows they are talking about her unbalanced sister.

Guessing that Fannie was slowly improving he'll be gladsome when she's well enough to leave his house, again and this time---stay gone for good. Not come back when Ana gets herself in another bind and can't support her mother. Fannie didn't like him and he didn't like her. But he knows she has ammo to destroy his marriage.

"I'm going out there to see can I talk to them again."

Helena sighed, "Dave, baby sit down. They aren't leaving no matter what you say. Even the cops are afraid of them. I think they're some sort of mafia or something. Who knows what kinda underworld my sister has crawled into?"

"How would Ana know anyone with this kinda pull?"
730

"I haven't a clue. Ana been a mystery to me since the day she was born." The 34 year old policewoman said. Dave ignore Helena's rebuttal and ventures outside on his lawn and approaches the dark windowed vehicle. He can heard the A.C. softly humming as he stood near the passenger door knocking. A stony-faced, black man slides down his window.

"Mister, I'd appreciate it very much if you all would move your tank. We've discussed this before to no resolution." Dave said politely. Much more nicely than he was feeling. "The neighbors are talking. They believe we've committed a federal offense and are trying to figure out what is it."

The man replied. "Sorry, Mr. Wales. Your neighbors need to find something better to do than watch your house. Their assumption is their problem, not yours nor ours." The dark window glides back up in his face. He can see his light coffee complexioned face in the reflective glass. He hates it these people knows his name but he knows virtually nothing about them. Seeing that the man has no further intention of talking to him he turns angrily and strides back to his house mumbling complaints about Ana. He doesn't see the men behind the dark windows finding his frustration amusing.

∽∾∾∾∽

The remnants of Ashton's harem led by Dawn Shepherd hired another world renowned assassin whose service did not come cheap but at the price tag of $50 million to rid themselves and the world of Ana Wyett who claims to be the true Mrs. Cargill. This was Dawn's second attempt to put Ana in the ground and she don't intend to fail this time. Four pulled out the deal and left the harem saying this is not what they signed up for. 31 of the remaining 52 consulted the man well known among the upper crust for his sniper skills. It's said he can easily hit a mark from as far away as the length of three football fields.

Dawn and Delores secretly met with the man at a small, local infamous cafe located near the Champs-Elysee. The grotesque showdown with Ana at Ashton's Beverly Hill mansion was still fresh in Dawn's faculty and she wanted revenge. Never in the history of the world would it taste so sweet. Not only did he take her into the Beverly Hills Palace, she got reports they were in Monte Carlo, too! One of her favorite spots for tanning and he knew it.

"We want her dead. Dead as dead can be, Ashton has lost his damn mind over that woman," Delores said after discovering her allowance had been discontinued, her charge accounts closed, and there would be no more free jetting all over the world. Now they had to pay a fare as everyone else. The limo service refused to take her home she had to call a cab. The chef refused to prepare her selected dish. The height of the humiliation was in the high-end store. When the clerks treated her like a commoner. It was next to unbearable. The maids refused to clean their bathrooms and the laundress refused their clothing, even the house doctor refuse to prescribe medication directing them to a local clinic in town. The gall of the Cargill French restaurant to bring them a bill to be paid after their lavish meal since the house refused to serve them! They all disgruntledly paid their tabs but vowed to eat elsewhere.

"I've been eating here since time immemorable." Dawn said in a serious tone, her Americanized accent was reaching back to her ancient Scandinavian roots. That told everyone she meant business.

"Sorry, mademoiselle, the line of credit has been discontinued. Pay or I will be forced to call the police." The Maître d said. The women paid their tabs and left complaining.

"What's happening?" Patty cried. She was highly upset because a much anticipative high-end designer's store refusal to bring her the latest spring fashion.

"Ana is what happening. This is the kind of shit only a woman would pull." Delores assured the others. "That's what happening. He cut off everything to appease her."

"I'm telling, y'all. The only way to things back to normal is to kill that woman." Dawn said. Several others agreed.

The tall, elegant, fortyish, stylish man looked nothing like a killer. He looked more like a count or baron than a highly paid killer. The super rich use him when they wish to off a spouse, client, ungrateful child, or business partner. The sophisticated, elegantly dressed man listened carefully to his prospective clients.

"Half now and the other half when you show us her body." Delores said, sliding the briefcase under the table to the killer.

"You must leave no connection to us." Dawn reminded him. Braddock never ceased to amazed at how his clients' gullibility makes them believe he can erase their motive for the kill. He simply does the kill, their reason rests on their shoulders not his.

Viewing the photograph of Ana BuFaye Wyett, the assassin isn't so sure she'll be an easy target. She's the alleged wife of multitrillionaire Ashton Cargill. Braddock Veese's, refined chisel features always deceive people into believing he isn't dangerous. Many have let him into their lives, their homes. Invited him to social functions because of his good looks, sex appeal, and elegant composition only to regret it a few hours or minutes before death. He's clever. He always thoroughly researched his target. He finds virtually nothing on this woman worthy of death but sees she's had lots of run-ins with the law enforcement in America. That's usually a signal to back off. Why is she still free with so many pursuing her? He wonders. The target is too risky. He can't deny the target this time makes him a little nervous; she's the said wife of mogul Ashton Cargill whom he believes may be able to put the dots together and come after him. His girlfriends wanted her dead. That's a no-brainier as to who hired the killer. He tries to decide whether to take this one slow or just keep the 25 million for his time and call it a loss. Curiosity made him want to see what kind of woman was this woman who has managed to stir the scorn of all these beauties. This is proof 'hell has no fury like a woman or in this case women who have been scorned.' This woman intrigued him. How has she managed to evade the law for so long with so many alleged murders under her belt? Was she like himself, a professional?

Through the high powered binoculars Braddock Veese watches Cargill, his woman, and a child enter a children's store with an army of guards befitting a king's entourage. One killer knows another. He knows Cargill is a killer and as protectively as he is hovering over that woman and child he'd easily kill him or anyone else who tried to take them from him. Being a man, he knows that stance and what it means. Continuing to

733

observe the family through his high powered digital binoculars he sees the big man turn and looks directly into the lenses before entering the store as the child runs ahead and woman runs to catch up with the girl. No one can possibly see him clearly at this distance nor know his nefarious plan. But the scowl on the big man's face tells him he know he is there and if he wishes to keep on living he had better abandon his deadly mission. Several of the killer guards are now looking in his general direction as Cargill converses with them. He knows it's humanly impossible to see him at this range and under cover. He is nearly two miles away. He quickly vacates the perimeter, he knows they're coming.

Resting in his downtown L.A. hotel room enjoying a cool, liquor laced drink, thanking the God he don't serve for getting out of that surveillance area before those killers arrived his calm was suddenly shattered.

"Who hired you?" A male voice asked from behind his chair.

Veese quickly glanced at the door and saw it's still locked. He slowly turned around and was confronted by Ashton Cargill's angry, unusually bejeweled eyes. Another code of honor for a hired killer is never reveal your client.

"If you feel they are worth dying for, then hold on to your silence." Cargill said and asked where was the briefcase of *his* money?

He was puzzled as to how the man knew his harem hired him but Cargill answered his curiosity. "Did they or you think I wasn't having them watched?"

Braddock quickly bounced from the chair and delivered martial art blows that have been known to bring down or kill a man; the blows had no effect on this monster. Who caught his leg and grabbed him around the neck and started to squeeze, "Last chance to speak before seeing hell." Cargill delivered an ominous warning.

Veese reached in his pant's pocket, pulled a gun out, and fired at close range. It should've blown a fist size hole in the man's abdomen not a nail size hole. The man didn't flinch. He acted as if he wasn't in pain. This wasn't a man. He doesn't know what

Cargill is but he isn't human. Feeling his life drain away knew he should've pulled the trigger the moment she came into his scope view.

"Your mistresses hired me." Veese wheezed through his narrowing trachea. "The money is in the closet." Veese normally doesn't carry his retainer fee with him but he's glad he followed his instinct to bring it along this time. Ashton angrily punched the man, shattering his innards. Killing him. He retrieved the millions from the closet and presses the button on his financial ISPAN draining all 56 members of his harem's accounts. He watches as the vengeful spirits of an evil life lived guide the dead man's soul before the Throne.

Ashton strides angrily in heavy footsteps into the room he had his people to herd the harem into. He vivaciously slammed the briefcase down on the baroque ornamented table. "I ought to kill every single one of you," he growled. "This is the last fucking time I'm telling all of you to stay the hell out of my life. You knew when you came here what the deal was. Had that assassin fool succeeded each of would be dead. If any of you wish to leave there's the door. It was I who cut off your monies, my wife doesn't know you ladies exist."

"I had left!" Shaula cried. "You drug me back here!"

"Just because you'd left doesn't make you an innocent!" Ashton snapped. The only reason he hadn't killed them all is that he has a very strong feeling if he kills them the heavens will forever forfeit his chances of getting Ana and keeping her. His rage is certainly great to clear out the entire harem. But by he brought these women into his life they can't be dealt with in his same customary manner as everyone else. "I cut off the gravy train because why pay for services I'm not receiving?"

"Whose fault is that?" Dawn yelled back at him. "You left us, we didn't leave you. You have been gone over four damn months playing house with your fake wife. I need my money, it takes work to look like this everyday!"

"You need money? Then get a fucking job, that's how other women live!" He snarled. "By the way, when I bring her around for a tour of the properties I want you ladies gone and this time there will be no return. I hope you've used you time here wisely." Patty began crying, saying she had only been there five years. She hasn't saved up much.

"At a million a year, that's more than most people make in a damn lifetime. If you haven't made other arrangements that's not my problem." Ashton said, taking the briefcase with him when he left the room.

Halting him before he reached the door, one who had left asked what about her exit severance package? "See the house office with your contract." He said over his shoulder.

Emeer, who along with three others whom had left and were dragged back to face the consequences of their plot advised those so radically determined to stay, "You ladies need to find yourselves other benefactors and give this shit a rest. Y'all gotta realize to him, sex is no more personal than the interior decorators who design these rooms. This is a job not a relationship! Sure, it paid well if you were willing to sacrifice every ounce of your dignity but y'all need to accept the fact this house belongs to his wife, he belongs to her, his money belongs to her. The sooner you all accept that the easier it will be to move on."

"Guru Emeer." Fresence mocked Emeer's words asking "Who else has this kind of money? And you aren't willing to fight for your *job*? Lowly secretaries put up a better fight than you."

"No, the labor unions protect secretaries. We don't even belong to the sex workers' unions." Shaula spoke up, outlining their true situation. "I'm not willing to die for it. If he kills any of us about that heifer nothing will be done about it. So, no. But I'm stoked you ladies think so highly of me. The getting was good while it lasted but didn't you nutty ladies see he had murder in his eyes? I say take the ten million and split."

Dawn Shepherd thought the four leaving were cop outs. Wussies. The women had vowed to stick together. "We don't need them. I've invested over half of my life in that man. I didn't tell the little skinny thing to up and marry my man! She's a fool if she honestly believes she's the only woman in his life."

Dawn's family had been begging her for years to come home. Earlier that day she and her mom had an argument when Mrs. Shepherd heard on the social network that Dawn's rich boyfriend was recently married.

"I told you years ago that man was playing games with you. It didn't take him no damn near thirty years to marry that woman." Mrs. Shepherd argued.

"Mom, he just married her because she was dumb enough to get herself knocked up."

Nuila Shepherd laughed and ask Dawn was she really dumb enough to believe that? Dawn vowed she wasn't going back to that rattan matted house in Hawaii she was raised in. She built her mother a modern house. Mom and the rest of her family had no problem with her being with him when the money was flowing in. She told him when she met him at a Bel Air styled Hawaiian party she was Norwegian. But he'd known for years that was a lie. At first, he told her parents she was a movie star as to why she was seen in so many glam party shots. She came clean when her mother came to visit and had been telling all her friends Ashton Cargill was her son-in-law and her parents discovered Dawn was one of his sex employees.

"So she's your personal prostitute?" Nuila asked in disbelief.

"Mrs. Shepherd, don't you think that's a little harsh? It's nothing like that. It's the same as your sleeping with Dawn's father for comfort, love, and support."

"B-but Midas loves me, you don't love my Dawn. All these others are your playmates, too?"

"Mother!" Dawn chastised.

"Mother, nothing! He has turned you into a whore."

"Mrs. Shepherd, you are delusional if you think Dawn was sweet, innocent, and

737

virginal when I met her. The man she was living with, his father was a well known pimp. Despite the construction business he ran in Honolulu. In due time, he would've bullied his son into putting her out for the tourist money. I pay a lot more than some family guy would have paid, vacationing there with his wife and kids."

Nuila glowered at them sitting side by side as if they were a real couple. The gall of this man to act as thus nothing was wrong with the life he was leading Dawn into!

"No, he was not. The boy was a fine young man. His father owned a small construction. They were in love and happy until you came along and filled her head with foolishness." Nuila turned to her daughter asking, "Dear, where did I go wrong with you? I took you to church every Sunday. I taught you the ways of God. So where did I go wrong?"

"Mrs. Shepherd, the construction company was only part of their business. Why do you think every major company with prime waterfront property hired them to 'fix' things? Where do you think all the beach beauties came from? Have you seen that many beautiful women walking around on an everyday occurrence who looks like them? The boy's father had been running a ring for years to get bored tourist's money. Every major tourist area has them. I don't see how you could not have known that when they weren't very good in construction, so what else were they doing? Sure, the son believed he loved Dawn and perhaps did. But that's the truth about his family business and has been so for years. Besides, it's Dawn's life to live, not yours nor his."

"Ah, mom, come off the religious bandwagon. I lost my virginity at twelve. I got tired of being broke and poor. You and dad think praying for things you'll never get is living. If prayers were pennies you two would be richer than Ashton by now. I got tired of your "Can I get an AMEN?" When I saw none coming. How is your getting up in the morning a blessing? Evil, non-praying people got up too this morning." Dawn cried, coming out the closet with her unknown lifestyle.

Reminiscing on her past twenty five years of her life, now that her mother is nagging her again, times like these make her glad she doesn't have children. This is why she doesn't like those damn church ladies like her mom and Ashton's new wife. They nag the fuck outta you. Mom is who Ana reminded her of. They suck the pure joy out of life with their bible quotes and silly, outdated do's and don't's.

⌒◟◝◞◜⌒

No one told her things would fall apart so soon. The others lied. They said life here was a dream come true.

"I can't deal with all the extra security. We used to go where we wanted, now all these people follow you. I can't deal with that." The nineteen year old who was brought in a few months ago thought this would be fun but found it's more like living in a royal palace with a backstabbers in every nook. She observed the older ones like Delores and Dawn, they're 40 something and still have no life of their own. They all came here about her age and look at how they behave now? Like spoiled children and act like Ashton is their daddy. She can't see herself stuck in this same juvenile mentality and situation 25 years from now. The others watched Adele leave.

"Good riddance" Dawn laughed. "She thinks she'll get ten million for a nine months worth of service but she'll be lucky if she get 500 grand. She doesn't know he keeps count of how many times he has had sex with you." Several gasped, for they didn't know he kept count.

"What??" Corosa asked genuinely, greatly surprised. "I thought it was by your years?"

"Read the fine print. If you leave before 5 years the pay is reduced. It's by the number of times. This is a business to him." Delores elucidated. "Five years, 5 million, and so on. But the catch is he can terminate the contract if he gets bored with you. These young ones are so convinced their pussy is so much the bomb that's he's gonna be so fascinated by it they can screw him a few months and walk away with millions. With Ashton Cargill it doesn't work that way."

Dawn and Delores watched the under ten years of service crowd gasp again. "That ain't shit in comparison to what his wife is getting out of him, plus we are helping her do her job for free." Cadence said, inching toward the door. The two devilish D's see their plan to eliminate the others is working. To make him sorry he fucked over them. So far nine have left. But they weren't lying about he kept count and the paid by the number of times, if you left or he terminated the contract within five years.

The nine former harem members stood outside waiting for a cab; most charged a very deceitful, inflated fare to come this far out.

"How long ago did we call them?" Shula asked.

"At least an hour ago." Adele cried. "I think it's mean they won't even give us a ride to the airport!"

One of the house securities sees a strange, dark tinted vehicle slowing near the ivy covered wall. They're canvassing the area to see who they can hit. The guard suspects it's a hit.

"Ladies, get in." Warfield said, pulling up to the curb piled high with the women's personal effects. He knows Vonderbilt is royally pissed at Ashton right now and would kill them simply for the flex of power. Driving to the airport he says, "Ladies, there is something going down right now between Ashton and another man, a very powerful, dangerous mad man. My advice to you is this stay in your secured chateaus until all this calms down."

"We've terminated our employment." Adele cried from the back of the luxurious Rolls Royce.

"He has an apartment in Paris, it's guarded. I suggest you ladies stay there until this storm blows over." Warfield advised, taking a detour to the Parisian place. Vonderbilt would knock these women off all in one night all because he's mad at Ashton. Warfield has seen the warlock's handiwork and it's not jolly. But how would they have known the women were leaving unless an insider told them? He knows there are plenty of traitors in the palace but he wonders who?

Caroline (Carole) Caldwell's report from Dawn was accurate; Gianna Machiavelli saw the women at the curb. Gianna had been interested in the one named Shula for years. He's sure Cargill doesn't care where they go. Maybe he and Bjorn can have some fun. Damn, the guard is picking them up. He calls his people to follow the limo, he wishes to know where the driver is taking them. This development has an intriguing premise, a very fascinating protagonist. He and Bjors follow the Cargill Rolls Royce through the Parisian streets. Why is Cargill still protecting them? His informant tells him they exited to another secured location. He can see that.

Adele unbeknownst called her would be killer, she called Dawn and informed her Warfield is taking them elsewhere. Dawn knows the place so she in turn calls Bjors revealing the women's whereabouts.

"Damn, my older brother lust for blood makes it hard to get a date with anyone other than a witch." Gianna sighed and detoured for the Parisian nightlife.

Warfield called Ashton and told him where he had taken the nine and why. He wasn't surprised Ashton showed no emotions. Warfield wasn't there to know that Azazael showed none when Michael clipped his wings. But Warfield knew the chilly, heartless truth. He knew Ashton was capable of letting Nikola kill them to keep Ana from learning about them. Sometimes he wanted to yell at his boss to, for once in his miserable life, show care and concern. To stop being such a cold-hearted bastard but that would result in a serious ass kicking and Ashton loved to fight. Ana was only person he had seen who could yell at him, hit him, and he didn't up and pulverize them.

"That's fine but they must be out before I take Ana to Paris." Ashton said, adding, "I want all new decoration in all the houses."

"Confirmed, sir" Warfield said.

Nikola held the bottles and looked at them. He could see the tiny faces of captured spirits in multiples colored bottles as the old man had shown him it could be done. He had never visited Shrevenport's area and was always curious about American witchcraft. The most he knew about it was from the elite of America.

"You can snatch her soul and hold it in this bottle to keep her alive but put another, more willing soul in the body." The old wizard said. It was a privilege to be visited by the grand master wizard as he was called in this part of the world.

"What happens if I break the bottle?" Nikola curiously asked. For he was well trained in the art of necromancy, summoning souls from hell was one of the few things Orman taught him, but this way was new to him. He decided to learn something new while he made Shevernport sweat. Sweat for disgusting himself and disgracing every warlock for miserably losing a fight with Ana. It was reported to Ana damn near killed him. Only teleporting and fleeing through the realms saved him. So yes, he intends to make him swither, wondering what his punishment will be.

But from the dozens of reports he has been receiving, Shevernport is right. She is different. Stronger. Since her last stay with Azazel she has become rather ornery. She baits people into fights just to kill them. She throws her sword at road and hover freight trucks she suspects are following her. Walks down the middle of the highway shooting at those trailing her. She has taken to tracking down covens and slaying the entire nest. It's like....like she is being him, turning into him, and the world isn't big enough for both of them. So yes, he has to confront her or lose his credibility. She is headed this way going west so he will wait until she reaches here and put a stop to her madness.

"The soul goes free. That person died years ago. Go ahead and see," the old man probed him to open the bottle. Nikola crashed the antique bottle to the floor and watched the soul of the man long dead float out in a thin, wimpish smoke. It's as if the man was tired. Nikola bet he was. After all, he had been used as a spiritual battery for years to help power spells, conjurings, and portal openings. Nikola had seen other variations of these spirit traps before; such as the colored glass bottles hanging from trees out front on people's lawns. Some used thick, heavy round crystal balls to trap spirits. The pros amped up the pull of their traps with bones such as those from chickens, goats, or cows. But he found nothing in the ancient libraries explaining this conjuration as to why he decided to let the old man teach him how to capture spirits.

"You are free to go." the old man said. The spirit appeared to be confused as to where to go. But he eventually turns and walks through the closed door into the world. A different world. For the one he knew had long passed.

"He will be back, he's a lost soul now. The time to have made it into heaven, hell, or paradise, or where ever he was designated has long passed him by. You don't want to do that to your lady. They'll turn into vengeful spirits you can't control. It's best to keep her soul inside her vessel and imbed a stronger spirit to control her. Make the Grand Witch more submissive."

"Can't you lock him back up?" Nikola asked curiously, thinking of those he encountered in the islands who were producing zombies. That is not what he wanted done to Ana. She'd be ineffectual as his partner in that lachrymose, stuporous state. He had enough idiots around him. He need not create more.

The old man shook his head. "No, you've to catch the spirit when it exhales the body in death or sleep. There's no organic structure to hold it still anymore. To capture it."

"Will he try to kill you?"

"Yes, when he sees how long he has been held and how much the world has changed. Although, I wasn't who did it but to him to yes, nonetheless, he'll come for me when he can't find the one who imprisoned him. Yes, he will come back and keep trying until he succeeds."

Nikola didn't plan on this happening with Ana. He wasn't dumb enough to let her out. He'd let whomever find her centuries from now let her out. He leaves the musky room darkened by heavy embroidered drapes at the windows. He was glad to be outside again. Even with the air conditioner on was the place was hot and stuffy.

His subjects in Baton Rouge spared no expense in making him comfortable but he wanted to stay at the Cargill Hotel downtown. For nothing more than his greatest nemesis owned it. As soon as he is informed of Ana's whereabouts he teleports to the shabby place outside of Baton Rouge and waits until he assumes she's asleep. It shouldn't be long considering she drove all day.

He teleports inside with the enchanted bottle intended to be her soul's final resting place. They are both asleep. Looking so peaceful and serene. He sprinkle the witchery power in the air the old man gave him to see her soul. The faded blue light is seen in her slightly open mouth and nostrils. He quietly leaned near her and uncorked the bottle. Her spiritual eyes flash open while the physical ones are closed. They roll to her right and look directly at him. He has never seen anyone do that. It looks nothing like the glow in her nose and mouth. It looks like her. She smiled a wicked grin as her eyes twinkled as evilly as that smile. The phantasm mouth relays how nice of him to visit her before in a split second she is out of herself fighting. The bottle thunks to the badly stained carpeted floor, the physical Ana doesn't wake up but turns over and pulls Bea closer as she somewhat puckers her lips and falls back into a deep sleep. She is kicking, scratching, pulling his hair, punching. She can make contact with him but he can't with her. His hands and blade are passing right through her spiritual existence.

Finally, he see an opening in her whirlwind of attack and rushes for the door. He makes it outside and she steps right through the wall and tackles him again, taking him down hard in the old pot holey parking that has more dirt than pavement by now. Hurling all kinds of obscenities and expletives at him with every blow. She picks up a piece of broken asphalt and raises it high over her head and is about to smash his brains out seconds before an angel pulls her off him and takes her back through the solid wall, kicking and trying to get aloose. Shrevenport is right. She has gone mad!

Sitting upright in the deserted parking lot with her car and a sparse few others he watched in amazement. For that was something he had never seen nor heard of. The soul defending the body. It's usually the other way around. He realized at that moment it has

744

been her soul attacking people. Azazel has tainted her very soul.

He was glad he came alone. No one witnessed the fight. He was furious that old kook didn't tell him the full danger in doing this. He teleports back to the old man but finds a knife already plunged in his chest. He watches the knife seemingly coming out unaided with a slurping sound and fly through the air at him. He knew the man released from the bottle earlier had returned as a revengeful spirit. He quickly teleported out again. Seconds before the knife is thrown so hard it drives deep into the wall singing and vibrating. This was turning out to be an all around bad night.

He teleport into Shrevenport's room and holds the bottle to his nose and captures his soul. This is his punishment. He doesn't summon another spirit to animate the body. He leaves him in a comatose state. He might change his mind and return it to the body or just be a bastard about it and keep it as a trophy. At least he learned something new today.

Five months later Ashton still had not made his regular visits to the remaining harems who disregarded his order to vacate in an attempt to emasculate him. He deliberately stayed out of their reach. Although, he still had no idea where Ana was and her image had faded from his memory. Even the photos of her were blank. He felt that was a little extreme in the task of erasing his memory of her. But the vision pertaining their family inspired him to take seriously the responsibility of expanding his empire. Apparently, she was going to be allowed to come back to him during her reproductive years for those children he saw to be born.

Right now Vonderbilt's collective wealth surpassed his own. He carefully reviewed his financial records and saw trillions was needed to surpass Nikola. He needed to cut expenses and put aside for their future. He has spend the last 600 years since his last release from celestial confinement, in the late 1800's, partying, keeping harems, and living the good life with no responsibilities. He decided it was time to settle down again. He wondered could he truly be faithful to Ana? If being faithful was the only way to keep her, then he believed he could do it. How hard could that be? The thing he dreaded most was humans didn't live very long. He may have only 50-70 years with her and then she's gone. And the only way to see her again is accept his Father's rules in Heaven. He laughed and shook his head.

"Dad is always a million steps ahead of you before you even get started. To make me do the right thing. To make me come Home He dangles a beautiful saint, whom I love very much, in my face. That's not fair!" He cried, laughing aloud. This time he got a response, he heard his Father laughing. That he finally wised up and caught the message. That was the last thing Azazael heard before his memory was erased more profoundly than that which the angels had done.

෧ঞ෧෧

Nearly a year had passed since they lived in Monte Carlo and nearly two since Beverly Hills but they had no memory of living in either. They had long ago left Arizona and worked their way farther east. She veed back across the country again, headed northwest. Her motto seems to be working. She hasn't had to kill anyone in several months. While working in a hotel in Nebraska she sensed someone in a room with her and Bea but saw no one. She kept looking for a presence but couldn't see anything but she knew someone was there, the group across the hall in this luxury hotel seemed determined to screw with her for no reason. She had taken them towels twice and they still demanded more. They now want the bathroom cleaned and they've left filth all over it.

She had a mind to just walk out and live off their stash but she knew had to be careful, if this was going to last the rest of their life. Bea would definitely not be scrubbing toilets when she grew up. She's now six nearly seven. She'd find some way for Bea to attend college. She didn't how but Breanna Wyett ain't scrubbing no shit even if she had to go Shaka Zulu on somebody's ass. And if anyone wishes to take it in a racist context that's their problem, not hers. But either way Bea's life is going to get better than hers.

"Stay here sweetheart, mommy will be right back." Ana said, answering the call for the third time from room 578. Groaning, what in the hell do they want now? She wants them to leave but they aren't leaving. So you don't always get what you want.

"We ain't got no toilet paper." A blonde said when she answered the door. Ana was positive she replenished the bathroom. This was her first time seeing the man. But he looked vaguely familiar and so did this annoying ass blonde.

"Dawn, leave the girl alone and you all quit messing up the bathroom." He said, smiling at her. "Ms. Driver." He said reading her name tag. "Here's extra for your troubles." He said handing her a thousand dollar bill.

"When will you be in here to clean up the kitchen?" A tall redhead asked, loudly complaining this hotel was a dump and so beneath them.

"I don't know, when would you like?" Ana asked ,telling herself these aren't witches they are just plain ole bitches.

"Let her go." The blonde said. "We'll call you when we need something else."

They didn't have to tell me twice I was glad to get out that room. The blonde shoves me out, the door literally caught my ass on the way out. So I go back to the room just cleaned and continue Bea's lessons.

The banging on the door, forcing me to look up and out; away from the paper books. Which are very expensive nowadays. "Ms. Maid, I know you are in there!" The annoying voice says.

"Damn! There go those aggravating bitches again." I said, straightening up the bed where we were sitting. She followed the annoying women back to their place.

While doing the dishes he came and leaned against the counter and he asked me out. I thought he was here with his lovers? And if he wanted to help me? Grab a drying towel and dry some dishes. But I told him no, I've been through this routine countless times with traveling business men.

747

"You know, you're fine as can be." He said before one of the women wearing a teddy pulled him back into the living quarters telling her she is free to go. She had no idea what kinda master and concubine sexacades shit they had going on but she wanted no part of it. She wondered why she felt rage and jealousy when that woman pulled him away. She didn't know him.

The women immediately noticed the 2.60 carats, full cut round, brilliant clarity: VS1 Color: F sapphire surrounded by 3 carats of diamonds set in an antique cathedral style platinum band the maid was wearing. Who would wear such a ring to scrub toilets?

The first time the maid came over he wasn't there. But the second time he was. Damn, she had a fine ass on her. She looked familiar, too. He watched her behind through the open bathroom door, wiggling around in the air, leaning over in the tub briskly cleaning it. He had to have that ass. He wondered if she would be interested in being a girlfriend? Not a harem member but a real girlfriend? And he also wondered why the women kept deliberately picking on her? He didn't have to wonder for long when turned around, her face was like an angel, he saw her move, she had the move of pure seduction, watching her move like a temptress, a siren. He is enchanted.

"Ladies, that's the newest member of my life." He said softly.

"NO!" The seven cried, almost in unison. "No, sweetie she couldn't deal with this lifestyle." Delores sweetly explained. They looked at Dawn for it was her idea they come here to taunt the woman. Now that his memory of her is gone.

He excused himself to the freshly cleaned bathroom, closes the door and teleports across the hall. He watches her. He feels sorry for her having to drag her child to work. His interest began to wan when he saw the child. But she looks familiar, like someone he loved long ago. Maybe she would accept an offer to be a girlfriend if she believes she's the only one. Either way, he intends to screw her.

He hears the ladies from across the hall banging on her door. She jumps and hides the books and quickly instructs the kid to sit on a chair. He sees it's Dawn and Delores. They appear to be looking for something; him. He chuckles.

"You can come clean the kitchen now. "Delores said as her excuse for barging in on the girl.

Upon returning to their room the cleaning girl was there. He doesn't care for the cramped space here but he did promise he would experience something different. He walks in the kitchen again and leans against the counter, she looks up at him.

"Sir, can I help you?" She asked without a smile. He can feel the anger brimming off her. She just cleaned the kitchen less than an hour ago.

"What are you doing after work?" He asked.

"Going home."

"Care to join me for dinner?"

"No, I can't." She said surly to defer him.

He was actually pissed at her for screwing whomever baby daddy was. He knew this was crazy. He didn't know this woman from Eve so why was he pissed off at her for her personal life? Somewhere in the in the depths of his psyche an image comes forth. In his anger he asks her, "Do you have a birthmark shaped like a heart on our inner thigh? Near your coochie." The woman is shocked, appalled, and angered all in one emotion. She doesn't know where to look but looks down and briskly continues to rub the counter the group of women had made a mess of. She is flabbergasted he's bold enough to ask such a private question. He intended to shock her stiff, rigid disposition. He doesn't take rejections kindly. Delores rescued the poor woman from his scrutiny and sent back her to her maid life. But he still truly believes he knows her. He'll have dinner with her to learn who she really is. If her name is Ms. Driver then his name is Jesus.

But it seemed to him they had moved ahead in the future, spent some time together. He has quit trying to figure out which way things were going with them. There seems to be no set formation to anything in the past year. He knows with his Father nothing is impossible! But c'mon. This is a little overkill. It's confusing even him. So he knows it's confusing to her. Poor thing is probably confused and scared right now. By the time he made it back across the hall she was gone. He looked out the window and saw her little blue car high tailing down the road. He is too mentally exhausted to chase her.

Caroline Caldwell had been ensured according to the lore of Azazael's punishment; soon he wouldn't remember her. Nor would she remember him. He finally came home after 9 months of this foolishness. Carole informed them Ana was at subsidiary family hotel in Nebraska. To punish her for the scare and disruption she caused they suggested coming there to rough her up. But now they believe this was a mistake. They think he remembers her after dashing out the door after standing still as a statue for a long while and then going into the bathroom.

The two D's looked at each other and rushed to the bathroom. He doesn't have to use the bathroom as humans do so where in the hell is he? Ana was over here doing the dishes. Opening the door slowly he asked. "What did they want?" He doesn't care for the cramped space here but he did promised he'd experience something different than the high end suites. Dawn was determined to pay the bitch back in full. She couldn't hide behind Ashton anymore and be spiteful; he didn't remember her. But now Dawn wasn't so sure. The look that passed between them, the outrageous tip, his asking her about a birthmark, and his making them leave her alone all were not good for their plight, these were indications that perhaps he did have some obscure memory of her...

Seeing their interaction Dawn decides the fun of screwing with and taunting Ana is over because if he recognizes her they are screwed.

"Let's go to the Beverly Hills palace," Dawn cheerfully after Ana left. There were a few employees in the Bel Air palace due payback as well. Due payback for daring to get uppity with her. She was deeply disturbed when he said no, they were staying here in these damn boondocks.

I wished could talk to my good old college friend Gena. We were close roommates throughout college. But I don't want to drag Gena into all this mess. I know without doubt Gena's phone is bugged. Plus, Gena and Tony got married a few years ago and they both know Thad. Oh well...Thad probably has heard about my woes by now. I haven't seen Gena since her wedding shortly after Bea's birth. I was her maid of honor, Gena probably would say maid of dishonor by now. Gena was a lot more street wise than me; maybe she would know why those women were deliberately being mean to me and why that man had a such a filthy mouth and what kind arrangement those people had. Why did the man with the filthy mouth and all seem so familiar? I looked him up the other day when we returned to our new room after leaving the hotel in a hurry. Vonderbilt's people had struck again. That wasn't a surprise. Now we are heading back east across Kansas. I hate to keep regurgitating the same issue but those four months missing from last year still scare me. How much of my mind is clear? These are the kind of things I could talk to Gena about. Even if she only told me to quit acting like a nut that was better than having no one to talk but a six year old. Bea was smart but still she was only a child.

Last night I had a dream. I dreamed I was happily married to someone I couldn't see very well. (Oh lord, here it goes again. I remember thinking in my dream, that is if I was actually dreaming.) The voice was distorted in the dream. I dreamed we lived in a house so big it looked like a palace. I dreamed we had lots of children but the children had wings like angels. Several looked like no one I knew. While several looked like me. But I clinched at the remote possibility of having that many children; despite the advancements in modern medicine childbirth was still painful.

I think it was merely a dream induced by the fact I'm sick of this road life and courting wishful thinking. People with that kind of money don't marry people like me. My inner voice asked. "Well, where did that necklace and ring come from valued at over $250,000? It's a wedding set." Shaking the inner voice out of my head, I sighed. *"Hell, I don't know. But if I had such a place I certainly wouldn't be out here."* I nearly said aloud.

It was a sunny but windy afternoon when they pulled into the Salina, Kansas local motel parking lot. They had never really stopped in this state. The desk clerk seemed pleasant enough. From her years of travel she learned the attitude of the first person you meet is a good indication of area. The personalities and mannerisms of individual locals in an area are usually reflections the general attitude of the entire area.

"Two days." She said, filling out the general registration form. The higher end hotels and motels asked your entire life story before telling you no so she avoided them as much as possible.

The security lights showed them the way to their room; it was early in the night. All the food joints were closed by now. Settling in for the night, food eaten, baths taken, teeth brushed, hair brushed and replaited, she decides to watch the screen to see what happened while on the road. While watching the news a woman about her age appeared beside her. Bea was asleep; she usually fell asleep after her bath.

"I see nothing has really changed." The woman beside her sighed, watching the gloomy news with her. All Ana could do was stare at her.

"Excuse my poor manners, dear." The woman said, extending her hand. "My name was Gilda Eastmore. I lived in the very late 21st century."

"You didn't die in here, did you?" Ana asked, trying to figure out how someone who lived four centuries ago could be as solid as herself?

"Oh, nah. I died at home," Gilda laughed. "Well in a hospital. I lived back before World War III, back when there was a black female president. Back when crimes against black women were overlooked by everyone even the black community. I was sent because you said you needed somebody to talk to that would understand what you are going through."

The scene of the room changed to beautiful, peaceful home sitting in the middle of a garden with Bea sleeping on a gargantuan rose petal.

"I brought your bottled water because I can't serve you tea from the water here. If I do I'll get in serious trouble." Gilda said, pouring the bottled water into a white porcelain tea kettle with tiny roses encircling the top.

"This is Damask Rose tea. It will help you to relax." She said, sitting the beautiful decorative cup in front of Ana. She turned to check on a stirring Bea but she was still fast asleep in her floral bed.

"I've truly, finally cracked."

Gilda laughed at her thought and assured her this was real. She wasn't imagining things.

Ana got up and looked around, the garden lead to wide, broad streets unlike any she had seen. They were golden, glassy, seemed iridescent. The familiar lyrics resounded in her head:

"Casting down their golden crowns upon the glassy sea."

Gilda smiled for she heard the song, too. "That's the choir, they never cease, they sing forever." Gilda said. "People like that Vonderbilt, they'll get what they got coming, don't worry he'll only last a season. Evil never survives very long before evil destroys itself, it always does. You'll outlast him. And about men, all are silly and childish whether mortal or immortal. But your man is heaven's ultimate bad boy and that's why your memory of him has been erased. When the appointed time comes, you'll remember him. Right now he has to get his house in order before he can claim his bride. Oh, he tried to get around that part because that's what bad boys do. That's where you were for intervals of three to four months."

Recalling a few things about her dream lover, Ana grinned and asked. "Does he have a potty mouth?"

"Potty mouth doesn't begin to describe his mouth. He's mean, ill-tempered and loves to fight because he knows he's one heck of a warrior. He was once a general in the heavenly army, I don't know the full reason he was kicked out. But I can safely assume it was probably because of his mouth. You and God are about the only two he won't cuss out. Everybody else is fair game. The heavens don't feel you can deal with who he is right now. And I agree, you can't."

"Sooo...my dream wasn't just a dream, wishful thinking?"

"Do you want it to be wishful thinking?" Gilda asked.

"No, I'm tired of this life on the road thing."

"You make your own dreams come true, if you can deal with Mr. Bad Butt, then go for it! I do believe despite all his horrible traits he truly loves you. But ain't nothing wrong with your mind. Been through that. It's nothing new. Everytime a black woman stands up and says she's tried of everyone stepping on her and starts kicking butt and taking names they always say there's something wrong with her mind, they been saying that since 1619. There ain't nothing wrong with your mind, there's something terribly wrong with your accusers' hearts. Proof of that is they want you to take their abuse quietly and don't speak up. Being a saint doesn't mean being so timid you'll let people walk all over you. It was Satan who came up with that definition of sainthood. Take for example; The students of St. Anthony, they cussed Lucifer so badly one day out in the desert that he showed up that night to ask Anthony to make them stop cussing him." Gilda laughed.

Why was I not totally surprised? I always felt something amiss about the tranquilly, submissive definition of sainthood. What good are you to anyone if you are dead?

Ana sipped her tea, it was quite delicious. There was an insistent, curious urge to get up and walk down those beautiful streets that led to the place the singing was coming from but Gilda forbade it. Ana thought this kind of thing was reserved for the perfect saints like those described in the bible and she definitely was not like the others she read about. She had forgotten some saints could read your surface thoughts.

"It is." Gilda said, sipping from the fine ornamented cup. "What make you so sure you aren't one of them? Honey, I want you to stop putting yourself down because there's no one written about those like you. You want to know why? Men wrote mostly what they wanted to write and all that which didn't suit their misogynist egos they erased it. In most cases, they killed her and erased her name from record. Daring anyone to mention her. Shoot, they even effaced the names of female archangels. So that pretty much tells you how far they were willing to go to make sure everything the world knew about God and His love was all masculine. But to sensible people that never sounded quiet right. There's more one type of saint. If everyone was the same how would the Body of Christ ever get anything done?Somebody has to watch the back of those who are trying to administer to the less fortunate or the darkside would kill them as surely as they'd you."

"Did you've children?"

"Yeah, I got two---they around here somewhere. Honey, another thing....don't worry so much about Bea. She'll do well in life. She is getting experience most people never encounter. I know it's natural to want a good home for her. You wouldn't be a loving mother if you didn't. But Breanna will take these experiences and apply them to her adult life and will do stellar. I'm not downplaying what you are enduring. I went through something similar to this is how I know how you feel. But unlike you, I never learned who was behind my troubles nor why until I arrived Here. They murdered my husband and all my friends. It's wise to stay away from your family and friends to keep them alive."

Ana quietly absorbed Gilda's advice. "Those women in that hotel room were jealous of you because you're prettier. It's sad such a thing is still important among some women. But it is. I passed away from earth at seventy six years old and it was till going strong during my life time and I hadn't been back until I was sent to keep you company for a while."

She asked a question knowing a heavenly saint can not lie. "Was the man with them, him...I mean heaven's bad boy?"

Gilda paused a moment before replying. "Now do you see why you can't be with him yet? He would only distract you from your work and break your heart and you've work to do for God's Kingdom on earth. Had you known that's who he was that hotel incident would have turned out a whole lot different."

She knew Gilda was right. She did suspect it was him, he confirmed it when he asked her about the birthmark. From there they talked about everything and anything but him. She learned Gilda was from Brunswick too, just only about 400 years earlier. She wished they had lived in the same time period. She had a feeling she wouldn't remember everything they talked about but only that she needed to know.

"My final words of advice, be patient with your older sister. She loves you but doesn't know how to show it. She hasn't had it easy, either. She pretty much carried on the family after your father died, your mother became gravely ill, your oldest brother was away in college so Helena had to take over. She sort of finished raising you and Jack. That's why she acts more like your mom than the sister you need. Plus she was only 8 when you were born. You had things trying to kill you so your parents devoted a lot of time to you and the focus was taken offa her. She resented you for that. It was no one's fault but merely devilish circumstances created by the darkside designed to tear a family apart."

Ana promised her she would try and get along with Helena better. Try to curb the frequency of their silly disagreements.

Eventually, Gilda instructed Ana to lie down and rest beside Bea but Ana wanted to explore her surrounding. "Maybe another time. You aren't getting rid of me anytime soon. I'll be there anytime you need someone to honestly talk to." Saint Gilda said, "Sleep well, my friend, your empire is ascending."

Drowsily, Ana wondered what did she mean by the last statement? When Ana opened her eyes they were back in the hotel, it was late evening going into twilight. She was well rested and went out and bought their supper. Deciding to try something different she stopped at a local steak house. That was something they hadn't had in quite a while. While they ate Bea talked about the smell and feel of sleeping on a giant rose petal.

"That was from a Rose of Sharon." the wise, austere child said with certainty. Bea's vast inherent knowledge never failed to fascinate her. *There was nothing macabre or ghostlike about Gilda. She was as warm as a living human. Suddenly her astral vision kicks in, she saw two men at the motel ice machine watching her car. She also learned they had spend two days with Gilda not one night. She armed herself and waited. She knew they would bust in at nightfall.*

She watched them leave but knew they'd be back when they assumed she had gone to bed. The bedside phone rung. She knew not to answer it. She knew it was them testing to see if she was still awake. She turned off the ringer and shortly after doing so there was a soft rap at the door. She looked through the peephole and a stranger was at the door. The woman appeared to be in distress. But again, that's another common deploy of theirs.

"Ma'am, may I come in?" The woman called out as if she knew I was at the door.

"What do you want?"

"My husband and I were in this room this weekend. For a weekend get away. You know how that is." The woman softly chuckled.

"No, I don't know how that is."

I sensed the woman smiled at my not understanding what she was saying. Oh, I understood perfectly well, I just didn't care. I was sticking to my motto. So she continued. "I believe, I left a serpentine gold necklace behind. One my grandma gave me. I would be grateful if you let me look around for it. Housekeeping say they haven't seen it. I know exactly where I hid it but forgot it."

"I tell ya what. Stick around until I leave; then you can come in, look around all you like but if you come in now... you won't be leaving." I heard feet fleeing up the walkway. *"Just what I thought."*

They pulled a stunt like this woman's right after they left Boston. They were in a place called Clarkston, Indiana. The moment she, her mother, and Bea checked in a woman came to the door saying she left an antique wallet her grandmother gave her in the room. Saying if we find it we may keep the money, all she wanted was the wallet. Yeeahh right! They got no rest that night for the local police banged on the door in intervals of thirty minutes telling them to open up or they would break the door down. Knowing our rights we didn't open the door.

By the next morning the parking lot was filled of law enforcement officers. We politely repacked our car and they searched it looking for the woman's wallet. That was an awful lot for just a lost wallet. They spilled the personal contents out in the parking lot for the world to see but Mom kept signaling me to remain silent and let them search.

"You better be glad we didn't catch you ladies lying." One sour faced officer said to me and mom leaving our clothing on the ground as other motel patrons came out to gawk at what was going on. I had all the jewelry, money and valuables I was able to save sewn in the underside of the car seat.

Chapter 16
With her pistol and sword her side.

Looking disapprovingly around the sparsely furnished motel/ apartment with depressing molded warped, bugling walls, Ana knew the environment wasn't healthy for Bea, who kept constant case of sniffles in places like this. She tried keeping air filters in the ventilation grates hoping that helped. Looking at the scary walls she wonders was it a mother's love or selfishness as to why she insist on dragging her young daughter across the country?

Her conscious mind refreshed her memory as to why she had to drag Bea with her. To keep her alive. A chill as thus someone had walked across her grave was felt when her mind went to back to that fateful day. Remembering a terror she prays she someday forgets. The reason she left Mother Harris comfortable haven is a man named Vonderbilt destroyed it. It's been over two years since the kidnapping but to her the terror is still raw. Vonderbilt was a man she had never seen before in her life prior to his kidnapping stint.

At that time, she with her own training, there was still much to be learned. Mother Harris said much of it would come naturally. It's already spiritually encoded into a warrior. But she had no idea what to do after he magically entered Bea's pre-school and took her. She later learned he moved through the fifth dimension through quantum magic or powers he already possessed which works by paralleling one's alpha brain waves in sync with the universe as Mother Harris explained to her. It work by mentally and spiritually *paralleling*, extending yourself in the same direction as the present flows, with equidistant at all points, and never converging or diverging from your goal. It's was more like concentrating on an area or place you would like to go and then zap yourself there. But how she followed him was different and much easier.

She took her stance by the door with her back flattened against the wall, peeking through the slot the drapes made hanging naturally from the rod above the window. Bea knew the routine, go in the bathroom and crawl out the window if she must. She watched the men walk around her car, kick the tires while she held her pistol and sword by her side; she definitely did not intend to go a-courting.

At this moment I'm burning alive in a fire of insatiable rage. I didn't create the fire nor do I kindle it. Others created it and keep it alive. Most times I feel nothing but rage when forced to kill. In this still moment, I'm not a woman but an insatiable, destructive rage. Rage exalts my will to survive, my right to live. It seduces me into deciding the God-given breath of life, no one will take it from me except God Himself. Anyone else who dares to try shall taste my blade.

Patience is not a satanic virtue so she knew they'd soon bust in shooting. And being impatient, the men who had waited days for her to return restlessness coupled with the feeling of over confidence they could easily take her down added fuel to their egos.

"Kick rocks, you satanic minions." She whispered, watching them kick her car until it shocked them. She quietly chuckled. She knew Trusty would do that.

Recovering from the shock both men headed back toward the motel lobby but she knew they intended to come through the back way or the window. They weren't gone. They wanted her to believe they were. She rushed and grabbed Bea and put her in the closet and placed the iron shield over her she had fashioned from a junkyard piece, this was for in case bullets fly all over the room. She had willed her uniform by now and stood in the middle of the room and waited, and sure enough she heard the roar of a big truck's engine shortly before it's chrome grill crashed through the window exactly where she stood a few minutes earlier. The headlights shone blindingly on the walls and their beds and nightwear. They cocked their guns and hiked up their pants getting out the truck. But she stood still waiting. The gun was in her left hand and the sword in her right. She switched hands as they came around the front of the big pickup truck. She saw them jeering as they expected to find her injured or dead in the debris. Their facial expression changed from jovial to fearful when she seductively asked, "Boys, y'all looking for me?" And opened fire. Hitting them both in the manhood area. She wanted them alive to question them. But she knew she had to be quick for she knew sirens always sounded when she did something in their defense. They never sounded when others were shooting at her or trying to run her off the road.

Dragging them further into the room, she punch and kick the injured places as Bea loaded the car.

"Who sent you?" She asked menacingly. She wanted a specific name besides Nikola. One was so enraged he tried to fight back by reaching up to grab her breast but the hard divine leather protected her; she slapped him hard across the face. Sending him crumbling back to the floor.

"Cadwell...Carole Caldwell." The whimpering man who was still conscious said.

"Thank you," she said rising her blade over her head, beheading them both. Bea had the car running. She sprinted outside and jumped in and hauled ass. Going the opposite direction of the sirens. She knew they'd follow for they'd seen her tail lights. She put the car up to 135 MPH on the narrow, winding, two lane road. The darkness of the night was their only cover. She turned off the headlights and drove by astral vision. The air police were about 5 miles behind, she could see their lights and hear the siren blaring. "I'm not going to jail for killing somebody who tried to kill us first." she vowed. Pushing the car until it felt as thus they were flying over the asphalt she came to a deep bend; she saw through astral vision a cliff in the middle of the bend, knowing it would take expert skills to make it at this speed she cried out. "Lord, help me to make that turn!" She sobs in the darkness. Another Pair of Hands covered hers, unseen Hands, and steered the car in a smooth motion around that bend at 140 MHP. She heard several crashes behind her but kept on going. When she finally dared to look back the road was littered with the flashing lights of the official vehicles. She knew some were now going to continue the pursuit from the air. Her lights were still off so she pulls over onto a lone, off-beaten single lane road. Underbushes scraped against the car as she drove under an old oak with branches spreading out like a Joshua tree. She saw them fly by overhead and on the road.

The unexpected sound she heard about 30 minutes after being parked were dogs barking. She knew she could talk to her pets but she'd never tried it with angry, barking K-9's. Deciding nothing beats a failure but a try she projected,

"Sweeties y'all go back the other way, those bad people are trying to find a good person. They'll kill me if you help them find me." She sensed the dogs listening; saw them turning around and begin barking in the direction she just come from.

"What in the fuck are you doing?" A guff male voice asked the dogs. She saw the German shepherds pull them away like huskies pulling sleds.

"Maybe she turned off further down. I mean the search team say she ain't down the road, she's somewhere up here in these here woods. Maybe she went over the cliff, that's a hard turn to make and she was driving at a suicidal speed.", the man who appeared to be a deputy said. They stood only 50 feet from her. The dogs saw them even under cloak. One dog looked her and she's positive he winked and started pulling the men again back down the weedy road.

When she was positive they were gone she finally exhaled and said. "Thank you, Lord." She knew she was going after this Caroline Caldwell but not yet.

Before the morning sun revealed their hiding place she crept onto the highway and drove at a normal speed, hoping not to attract attention. Taking another country road going past Manhattan toward Wichita. They had a long way to go before they hit the Missouri state line, not that Missouri would be any help from her experience. She knew another coven would be waiting so she instructed Bea to stay in the back under her iron blanket as she nicknamed it when Bea was small. A man driving a late model black sedan pulls up beside her at the red light staring unblinking at her, she refused to look around at him. She checked the mirrors. There were hundreds of them. She wondered how many bullets she had left.

"Oh fuck, they're blocking the detour I need to exit upon." They were trying to herd her onto a road she didn't wish to travel. They succeeded. It took all day to do it, with they all constantly circling the city, they blocked her every turn off. Waited nearby if she stopped to gas up. It was a tedious ride but by hell's command they succeeded. Flying down this lone, two lane road she saw several eighteen wheelers flying behind her. The low riding hover freights caught up with her in a matter of minutes and begun ramming the back end of her car. She nearly lost control twice. Her heart stopped when headlights of another shone in her face, it was in her lane! Meeting her head on. The only way to escape it bearing down on them was to go over the narrow shoulder which ended in a steep dead man, drop down cliff. Believing she had ran her last mile she prayed. "Lord, it's all in your Hands."

Next she heard the deafening, grating sound of huge metal machines grinding and scraping against each other. A herculean figure had pushed the one meeting her head on into the one on her right side. The winged giant with red crosses marked on his face and chest pushed the attached truck with such a force that fire was sparking back on them, on Trusty's windshield. Behind them was a huge, billowing, glowing robe equally the size of the figure in front of them. A blinding light engulf everything. The last thing they saw were the three trucks going over the ledge as muscle man pushed them like toys. In exaltation she realized these were their guardian angels.

They rode right between his legs as he stood askew the road daring anyone brave enough to follow. To face death twice in less than 24 hrs and win left her knees weak and legs rubbery. There's truly a God in heaven who answers prayers.

"MOMMY, THERE GO MY ANGEL!" Bea cried happily from the back seat pointing at the colossal size angel as they drove pass. My mouth was bone dry. I was too shocked to speak. I merely looked in the rearview mirror and smiled at Bea. I was even too tired and relieved to lecture her for poking her head above the iron blanket.

The remaining of the way was uneventful. Ana had to stop, the stress was more than her human heart and body could bear. They made it to Kansas City, Kansas that night around 10:00. She found a cheap room. She did manage to pull herself together and go through a drive-thru and pick up their dinner. Seeing she had been riding on pure adrenaline and fumes she stops by a service station before retiring in another cheap room. She liked the couple who ran the station. She saw he was gifted like herself and decided not to tarry. She didn't want to lead those after her to this nice couple. He insisted on working on her car. Trusty didn't shock the man named Devon when he looked under the hood and changed the shock plugs and performed a few other minor tasks.

"They came here looking for you," the stranger said as he busied himself with her car. This shocked her. She didn't know this man.

"They been circling around this station like vultures all day," his wife who was smitten by Bea said. "I know you two are hungry, what hotel you staying at, if you haven't already paid for a room you can stay with us." Delita said.

Normally Ana wouldn't have divulged this kind of information to a stranger but it was hard not to see God in this couple. "We're staying across the expressway at the Royals Motels in RM 316."

In reference to their room number, Devon quoted "For God so loved the world He gave His only begotten Son so whomsoever believe shall not perish but have everlasting life."

Ana hadn't thought of that when the desk clerk told her the room number. "Hey, I've often gotten the room 333. What does that mean?" She asked.

"GOD in Three Persons. The Blessed Trinity." Devon replied, closing the hood giving Trusty a clean bill of health.

He saw her looking at the billboard dictating the store hours. According to the digital store sign they were normally closed about an hour ago.

"I was told to wait for you. The car needed work," he said, adding. "Rooms with the 111 means the same. Some say it means you're being followed by a ghost. It may mean that for some but not for those like us. I'm going to pray your car a different color and model so you can get some rest tonight. I don't know how long it will seems dark blue to them but I pray it will be long enough for you two to get far away from this coven."

Once inside with their food eaten and bedtime routines handled, Bea's angel showed up. "I'll watch Breanna. Go get her!"

He must had read her mind because she was pondering how could she go kill that woman and yet leave Bea? She had no worries, he had already proven he'd kill for Bea. She still had a lot to learn about tracking but she figured the hellfire in her belly and grim determination in her will would lead the way to this woman.

Caroline Caldwell was creaming her face, preparing for bed when she saw Ana's angry face in the mirror. Knowing how to stop a warrior saint was to beg for mercy, she did. She screamed, begging for mercy bringing several people running into her large, luxurious bathroom including James. Who turned to run when he saw her.

"STAY! Don't make me run you down." Ana warned. She tried to swing the blade but it flew out of hand unaided and went right through the witch. She pointed her pistols but an unseen Hand knocked her aim toward the ceiling when she fired the bullet hitting the glass ceiling.

"Ana, I swear it was Pashane who ordered that hit." Caroline pleaded.

"She is the secondary Grand Witch, Nikola's second wife." James informed.

"WHY??" Ana asked, trying to make sense of this whole attempted murder scenario.

She didn't record meeting anyone named Pashane. But then again, she rightly didn't know any of these psychos trying to kill her.

Carole shrugged her shoulders. "If you're dead she officially becomes the Grand Witch, plus Nikola is in love with you."

Ana laughed. "If this is love I hate to see what he would be like if he hated me."

"Believe us, you don't want to see what his hatred is like." James said.

"As if you're any better." She snapped. Caroline looked warily at him wondering what Ana was referring to.

Deciding since she can't shoot them, she would shoot up the place; Ana unleashed her fury upon everything in sight. She shot lamps, windows, furniture, and the walls. She took special pleasure is destroying their closets, knowing what labels whores people like them were. All of their electronics were reduced to glittering shrapnel. Those who surrounded Carole ran for cover and their lives. She randomly shot everything as she walked through the house, finally realizing these two were behind the theft in her and Thad's dream home. Since these motherfuckers had destroyed her home she was glad to let them know what that shit felt like. Before disappearing she said, "As surely as the sun rises I'll get both of you someday."

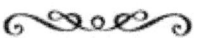

She finds Pashane Norton strapped in that strange chair in Nikola's bedroom. Why would anyone enjoy that horrendous thing is beyond her understanding or caring.

"Get dressed Pashane and prepare to meet God." Ana said from behind the unabashed couple. Nikola moved and she could see all the woman's secrets.

"I see you've come to your senses and returned home. Come and join us, dear." Nikola said, standing in the nude with a full erection. He laughed when she looked away. Quickly, she remembered her teachers told her no matter they show you, don't ever look away. Out of her peripheral vision she saw a ball of dirty fire coming; it slammed her in the chest knocking her down, and the woman was on her before she could rise into a sitting position let alone a standing one. Her strong black-tipped fingers entwined into Ana's hair. Pashane quickly took advantage of the other woman being down and started banging Ana's head on the marble floor. She materialized a lasso of blue energy and wrapped it around Ana's neck, almost choking her unconscious. Somehow she was getting beyond the protection of the uniform. The white witch willed the rope to rise, pulling Ana with it. Ana knew if this witch got her suspended in the air she was finished. She had failed to protect herself. She hadn't realized her hands were tied too until she felt the rope tighten behind her back.

"Did you think I'd be stupid enough to leave your hands free?" Pashane taunted.

Ana felt her eyes burning and herself being lifted from the floor. But she was *determined* she wasn't going out like this. Nikola was gleeful she was being killed before him. She quickly raised her legs, moving her arms from behind herself to form a hoop to step into, the strain on her neck was murderous. Remember an old trick as a child she bared down, moved her hands to front by stepping through the loop created by her binded hands. She decided if she had to die so will they. With hands still bound she wills her Sword to the white witch's surprise and beheads her with a clean sweep. The thump of the head hitting the marble floor was sickening. She dropped to the hard floor beside the woman's unbleeding, cauterized body. She quickly rose looking for Nikola. He was gone. She was so crazy with rage she started taciturnly singing and humming while looking for him;

A saint went a-huntin and she ain't playin. Hmm, Hmm. Mmm,Hmm

A saint went a-huntin and she is mad..

With her pistol and sword by her side. Hmm, Hmm. Mmm,Hmm

She's huntin for the Grand Warlock! Hmm, Hmm. Mmm, Hmm

She's huntin for the Grand Warlock!

She intend to have his head! Hmm, Hmm! Mmm, Hmm

She sees him in the darkness up ahead, he was quickly opening and closing portals creating obstacles to escape her. Running through cesspools which parted for her, the creatures swimming in the malodorous muck wanted no part of the package she was delivering to Nikola. Suddenly a colossal red horned creature reared up and blocked her way. She was mad as all of hell and then some and definitely wasn't in the mood to play patty cake with this red hunk of snot. She swung at it, slicing its shin, taking a boulder size chunk out, causing it to howl in rage and pain. Its fist came slamming down with the intent to smash her like a bug. She brought her shield upfront just in time to catch its powerful blow. The blow burrowed her into the ground. She charged the gargantuan, rushing out of the hole at top speed, running behind her shield and rammed its uninjured leg, bringing it to the ground with a mighty crash. Grayish dust fans out in great clouds and covers every thing. Leaping on top of the stupendous demon she started wildly hacking away in blind rage because she'd lost Nikola fucking around with this thing.

"Which way did that motherfucker go?" She screamed at the audience watching. The much smaller demons hiding didn't reply. She searched relentlessly but he was gone so she had no choice but to retrace her steps and go home.

When she returns it's daylight but Bea is still asleep and her angel still guarding. She promises herself as she tries to shower away the unpleasant feeling of being in the face of evil: "Just you wait. I'm going to get you too someday! I intend to finish this." She was speaking to whatever evil in her jurisdiction.

But Ana had no idea her and Pashane's fighting had made a highly gifted infant a motherless child.

The woman is poison

Ana takes an unwanted job at an eatery outside of North St. Louis, this was as far as their money would take them. She hated stopping here for something bad always happened but their resources are nearly non existent by now. They had to stop. They needed money to keep moving. She sat across from Bea reading and eating during her lunch break. She usually packed her own lunch. She never ate at the places she worked. Not for hygienic reasons but the fear of poison. People may laugh at her paranoia but let them. She knew without doubt those like Nikola's followers could easily encourage someone to lace your food. All they needed was a well orchestrated lie.

She wasn't aware that when she placed her sandwich in the refrigerator the junior chef was watching to see which container was hers. The American Grand Witch had offered a large monetary reward for anyone who succeeded in killing her. The short, pale cream complexioned man with long silky, black hair had a friendly smile to offset his huge Roman nose made it a mission to befriend Ana when they first arrived. She was a little cool at first but begun to warm up after a week of teasing and joshing her. He watched her as he had been watching for several days. The weather had been a little cool so she had not been using the refrigerator. Most days she left her food in the car. Caroline Caldwell had said poison the kid too if you must but didn't offer any money for the kid so he would let it slide. The kid was very pretty so she should fetch a high price on the sex trade slave market. Carol didn't make any claims on the child so the kid was free game. He made arranged meetings with several contacts who were willing to pay a hefty price for a girl so beautiful.

Adell sat with them on the outside wooden picnic table at lunch, knowing what he had done. He laughed and talked with Ana as always but intensely watched and wondered what would the mephistophelian substance that was sprinkled on her food do? He was told it was a form of screw worm. But he saw nothing in the glass tube. The woman told him be sure not to let anything touch his skin once he uncapped the tube.

They crawl very quickly. He flinched inwardly with her every bite but was somewhat glad. She had turned him down as a lover, because he was married was her excuse. So yes, the uppity bitch was getting what she deserved. He savored every bite she took. This was for all the good, hardworking men who tried to talk to her and she turned them down. Caroline Caldwell said she was used to rich and powerful men like Ashton Cargill and now that Cargill had dumped her she thought she was too supra for lowly men like himself. That's another reason that girl would fetch such a high price. Carole aforementioned the girl's father was Cargill and there wasn't hardly anyone alive who didn't want to stick to him. But since he was unattainable, untouchable, his daughter would do just fine.

Bea wanted piece of her mom's ham and cheese sandwich but he put a plate of french fries sauteed with melted cheddar in front of her. Ana refused to let her eat them. She didn't trust Adell. There was something sneaky about him. Normally, Ana would've broken the sandwich in half and passed it on to Bea even thus she had eaten her tuna sandwich but something within her maternal instinct stayed her hand. She gobbled it down to make Bea stop whining about what she wanted.

"I'll get you something on the way home." Which meant, "*I'll fix it for you.*"

After lunch Ana started to feel a little squeamish. She put it to swallowing the food too fast. But by 2:00 P.M. excruciating pains were gnawing her innards. She concluded she was coming down with a stomach virus and went to Trusty and swallowed a few of Bea's anti-virus pills. She felt better for a while but then the pain vehemently became worst. Unable to work she told her boss, Danie, she was going home. By the time she made it to Trusty she could barely walk. Blessed for her Bea was bigger and stronger than the average child her age. For she definitely had to lean on her to make it to the car.

Driving back to their motel room her vision became blurry. The sun light hurt her eyes. Her head was pounding as thus a thousand hammers were inside, hellishly banging away. It felt as through something were inside, screwing and crawling its way through her body. Bea was completely steering the car by now while she did the footwork. She was positive the traffic was deliberately trying to hit them but she kept onward while clutching her stomach.

"Mom, we need to go to the hospital." Bea said worriedly, watching her mom flinch as rivers of sweat poured off her in buckets. Remembering she saw a hospital sign when they were on their way to work she turned off and headed there. Ana was too sick to tell her not to go to the hospital. They weren't going to help her.

Pulling in the hospital parking lot Bea got her mom. This was the first Ana knew she could lift her. Bea was only seven and three quarters and able to lift 109 pounds?

Bea took her mother inside and demanded a doctor to see her. The personnel walked by them as if they weren't there. Bea sat her mom in a hover wheelchair and grabbed a passing nurse. The woman looked down at her, frowning. But soon erased it when she saw Bea had a far worse frown than her. Thin circles of fire were growing around her pupil. Ana saw her hands slowly change into transparent gloves of fire. She was too sick to care about the morality of where it came from.

They rushed her inside an examination room. By now Ana was seeing heaven's streets of gold and her surrounding was turning into crystalline, glassy gold. Everyone started backing down as they watched the room changed. Bea knew that meant her mom was dying. The nurses who prepped her laughed when they saw what was going on.

"Do something!" Bea yelled in an authoritative voice that was not that of a child.

"Little girl, no one knows what's kind of venereal disease your mother has. No one never seen anything like this! No one knows what to do. That's what happens when you're a nasty ho." The nurses whom had friends in the occult hilariously laughed. Bea threw fire at the cluster, causing third degree burns, and asked was the fire funny as they were being wheeled out to the burn unit with their uniforms burnt into their skin. The room slowly started returning to its normal state, giving Bea hope.

Looking around at all else for anyone who dared to laugh, she duly promises. "If my mother dies all you motherfuckers are going with her! And let God decide whether it's to heaven or hell cause I don't give a fuck!" Bea vowed and everyone could see she was serious for her hands and eyes were now pure fire.

The doctor looking at the IM images was flabbergasted at what he saw. "Get that child out of here!" he yelled at the nurses and orderlies. Taking an even closer look at the Internal Magnetic images, he could hardly believe his eyes. He saw the patient's internal organs moving seemingly of their own volition. He saw no internal parasites, it was as if an invisible force was spearing the organs, causing internal bleeding.

No one moved to touch her for the girl was literally on fire and had proven she didn't mind using it. Bea firmly grabbed her mother's hand. "Momma, fight it. Mom! I know you can fight and beat it. Can't nothing beat you. Mommy, don't leave me!" Bea begged, sniffling snot back as tears flowed down her cheeks.

Ana returned Bea's grip with as much strength as she could muster and turned her head from the City, she remembered her dad said, don't look at It. It will allure you in. "My little Bumble Bea, mommy ain't going no where. It ain't her time yet. You ain't getting rid of me this easy." But she wasn't sure of that for she felt her life draining away. Slipping, departing as easily as smoke.

There was a young Hindu doctor on staff who had seen this before. She knew nothing would show up in conventional tests. She pushed through the throes of others to Ana and Bea. This was once quite common in her part of the world, especially among rural people if a woman or girl became "uncontrollable". She was secretly killed in a manner that was undetectable. In a medical seminar she had heard of a doctor who saved a woman sickened with this same affliction about 15 years ago. Quickly looking the medical logs she found her. She called the dishonored heart surgeon named Dr. Angie Cotten.

The young doctor knew it was succums. They are ectoplasm, not carnal. They were demons. Not terrestrial parasites.

The areas they traveled to told her it was done by a man angry at this woman for something sexual. A lot is revealed by what areas succums attack.

"Where are they concentrated?" Dr. Cotten asked the young doctor.

771

"In the womb and vaginal area. The kid say she ate something which made her sick. But we both know that isn't the case." The young doctor replied. Dr. Cotten hissed and cursed. She knew, too, knew why it was there. It had something to do with sex. Some guy had done this to control or punish her and since he couldn't control her he'd rather kill her.

"Go to the hospital's chapel and get holy water. Rub it around her chest to keep them from her heart. That's where they are headed next."

The young doctor did as told but doubted it would work. She doubted any real holy people had been in their hospital's chapel. Her superiors asked what was she doing? She didn't reply. She simply rubbed it on Ana's chest. They all heard muffled squeaks and popping within the woman's body. They looked at each other and took the basin from her and started bathing Ana in it. It seemed to calm Ana down enough that she was no longer crashing.

Ana was stabilized and sent into a room for the night. They wanted to keep her for observation. The young doctor tried to explain to the others what happened and that it was far more commonplace than they realized. "All illnesses can not be explained by the medical field. The occult world is real!" She argued. Others told her to be quiet for she was talking herself out of a prestigious medical position.

Caroline Caldwell heard what happened and the young doctor's heroic feat. She demanded Ana be put out that hospital tonight. Not in the morning but now! The chief of staff, not wanting a liability suit on his head, told the powerful woman he would order her release in the morning. This powerful woman whom had had his state senators and even the governor call him saying the woman was burden to the state, he had done all he could do. So yes, he would be glad to get rid of her. The child playing with fire, the woman infected with something even the CDC has no idea what it is... But he was keeping her the legal tenure to avoid a lawsuit in case she died. All the attending physicians had given the same medical prognosis; they doubted she would make it through the night.

He didn't know what to make of the circus people were turning his hospital into. People were downstairs clamoring for the girl who keeps saying they aren't her relatives. He didn't like the troupe created at his upscale hospital. But he was dismissing her in the morning. She was leaving alive or under a sheet. He was once an avid fan of Caroline Caldwell, thought she was truly the most beautiful woman in Hollywood but now, he begs to differ.

⌒〜〜◦◦〜⌒

Ana was relaxing but the things were gearing up again when Caroline walks in her hospital dimly lit room. Wearing a floor length polar bear fur, she stopped at the door and stared. She heard about Azazel's kid's feat and wanted her skin and fur. So she pretended to come in charity and hospitality, meaning nothing malicious. But the child wasn't buying what she was selling. The woman's very presence was malevolent. She need not speak the words.

"Mom, do you know her?" Bea asked, thumbing at the Hollywood living legend.

"Yeah, I know her," Ana weakly replied. She was too weak to go into details.

"Hush, Ana," Caroline cooed in her native Western Virginian accent. "Don't try to talk. You're too weak."

The money she had was laced with another lethal dose. She extended her thick white gloved hands and offered it to Ana to help out with her expenses. Ana raised her eyebrows. She knew it was laced. She could those see them on the folded bills reaching their glossy, black, ghostly tentacles for her, to unite with those already inside.

"Bea, light her ass up." She whispered and grimaced. She didn't have say it twice
773

before Bea was slinging fire at her, setting off the sprinklers. Caroline threw up a shield to protect herself from the inexperienced child. But not before Bea incinerated the bills and the succums in the gold money clip and painfully scorched her hand through the soft white glove. She fled the room in genuine fear for her life. No one told her how dangerous the child was. Not even Nikola.

Caroline sat in the limo's butter soft leather seat oozing rage and wrathfully watching. She watched from her limo parked in the dark outside the hospital and smiled as she saw the two leave the hospital after the fire alarm broke the silence of the night. Ana was holding onto Bea who put her mom in the passenger seat and she got in the driver's side.

"Mission accomplished. The bitch needed to die in the gutter like the she dog she is," Caroline thinks before telling her driver to go to the nearest luxury hotel. She was spending the night as far away from this place as possible. For she heard angels came for those like Ana and she wanted to be no where in the vicinity.

Back in the motel room Ana turned gravely for the worse. She was too sick to know what the doctor at the hospital did to ease her suffering. She knew only one Person that could save her if she was not leave Bea motherless. She also knew this was no natural illness so it had no natural cure. Bea was anxiously watching, helped her as she rolled over out the bed onto her knees. Mother Harris and the saints in the cave had taught her how to go into deep contrition. Faster than she already knew. That's where she needed to be right now. She needed to leave this body and let Another dwell here who was able to handle this pain for she couldn't.

On her knees she hoarsely mumbled; "Pass me not, Oh Gentle Savior, hear my humble cry, Whilst on others, I'm calling. Please don't me by, I'm begging You. Please, don't pass me by."

Bea held on as her mother head started to bleed, blood started running down her face, dripping on the bedside. She saw blood rising to the surface of her clasped her and seeping through the t-shirt but she held on and helped her mother pray. She had to be brave and not cry. Now wasn't the time to be a baby. She knew her mother was in excruciating pain. She saw how bloody she was becoming but somehow knew this wasn't her mom's blood. It was Someone Else's Blood. It was the Blood of the Lamb of God. That frightened her more for she remembered what her grandmother told her happened to Him.

A horrible screaming, a terrifying squeaking coupled with sloshing and squelching was emitting from Ana's body and throughout the entire room. Even the walls were infected. Bea watched the things in it rise to surface and teems all over the room. Some were ghastly shadows, others were tall thin men, and some she had no idea what they were. All types of creepy crawlers were on the wall, floor, and ceiling. But they stayed down, ignored the demonic manifestations that had blotted out all light in the room and was trying to reach them but couldn't. They huddled together in a circle of light. They hugged and held on to each other no matter how bad the pain became. Even as Ana cried out in earsplitting pain, they held on to each other. Bea didn't know which was causing the most pain, the Stigmata or the demons.

Her mom started glowing so brightly all around them were turned to ashes and swept away by an Invisible Hand; the antiqued lamp light returned to the room and all were gone. They thought it was daylight it was so bright outside. So they went to the window to peek outside and stepped back when they saw outlines of hundreds of dead demons with their ghastly faces sealed in the agony of death plastered against the window. Ana gasped when she recognized some of the faces, one was the local sheriff, another....a believed to be friend or acquaintance of hers. It was only 3:30 A.M. so where were all the light coming from?

Ana recalled the centuries old song she used to hear sung in churches back home, *"He's the Lilly of the Valley and He's brighter than the Morning Sun."*

They watched in unbridled astonishment as the outlines faded as the mysterious glow grew brighter and brighter. The brilliant glow started to fade and then the deep darkness of the natural predawn returned.

I guess He *really* is *"Brighter than the Morning Sun."* Ana said, looking over at Bea for she knew Bea knew the song too. It was impossible not to know it with her granny singing it all day some days.

Looking carefully at her mother, Bea asked. "How you feel?"

Ana smiled, "I feel great, better than I've felt in a really long time. Let's get out of here."

Bea refused to let her drive, she was taking precautionary measures. Parents have a tendency to lie and say they feel better than they are actually feeling like crap. She knew the old Route 66 and that's the way out she was taking. While her head was down helping her mother pray, she saw Adell had done this horrible thing to her mother and she intend to make him pay. Bea knew she had grown that night and would never be the same. Now, she knew why she was different. She was the way she is to protect her mom. Had not she been able to make those people listen her mother would be dead by now.

Ana sat and watched the sunrise peak over the road, casting its soft yellow fingers far and wide. A sight she thought a mere few hours ago she would never see again. It was illegal for Bea to drive, but a lot of things were illegal but people still did them. She was finally at peace about how she caused Bea to be different from most humans. She now knows it was no mere coincidence Ashton showed up the moment of her conception to endow her with a portion of his powers. It was all planned. She knew this knowledge would fade from her memory but she savored it while it was lucid and clear.

"Bea, how long have you been able to do that to such degree?"

Knowing full well what her mother was referring to, Bea said. "All my life. As far back as I can remember. It only comes out if I'm upset, scared, or frightened. Uh, mom, I've known since I was about three I'm unlike other people. Perhaps I inherited a lot of your abilities." Bea knew that wasn't true but didn't give a rat's ass. She was too blissful to have her mom sitting over there happily looking out the window to wonder about her life before she was born. Nobody is fuckin' perfect and she knew her mom was far

776

better than most. Their lives were tragic, frustrating, wildly majestic, and bewildering at best but at least they lived to witness a miracle and another day.

To her, her mom is a priceless jewel and she intended that everyone knew it. Killing the enemy made no difference to her. She squinted her eyes from the pain of morning glare, staring hard and cold at the long, lonely white lines of the highway leading to nowhere in particular. A darkness was taking over. A long held within hatred boiled and churned in her young heart. She was taught to forgive others of their sins and God will forgive you of yours. But in her young eyes what these people are doing to them is unforgivable. She decided that day she would send as many to God as possible and let Him sort them out.

Complacent with her daughter's reply, Ana snuggled down in the seat with the promise Bea would wake her up if any trouble arose and let her know when they reached the nearest rest stop so she could take over the driving again. Bea promised she would but knew she wouldn't. They needed to put as much distance between themselves and St. Louis as possible. Everytime they unfortunately ended up there something bad always happened. She glanced in the rearview mirror and saw their two guardian angels in the backseat. She intended to have a dear conversation with those two at the earliest opportunity. She wanted to know why didn't they stop what happened?

Adell Mandigo walked down the lone country lane in the dark to meet with the strange woman down the road from his home. He knew this road like the back of his hand. His family bought the land years ago but none of them were ever successful enough to innovate it. Someone always had a problem as to how he and his wife got it and kicked his good-for-nothing cousins off the place.

He had never met a witch and didn't believe they were real. He thought they were merely folklore. Sure he had heard about the crossroad demons that supposedly resided down the road, in the crossroad. He had seen the fresh strange potholes in the pavement

777

and even obdurated when he had to drive over them everyday headed to work but old people will say anything to scare the bejesus outta you.

Getting closer to the nominated location he saw the woman with whitish blonde hair standing afar. She impatiently raked her fingers through that magnificent mane swept back in the manner of the glamorous stars of old. The pale moonlight shimmered on her great beauty, lending her the allurement of a goddess. Sure, he recognized her. She was every man's and boy's sexual fantasy. But he was curious and he wondered why couldn't the woman pay him at the diner? Why this lone spot at such iniquitous hour? He had kept his end of the deal. He had no control over Ana refusing to die. He had no control over kid rebutting their claim. They showed up at the hospital and asked social services to retrieve the girl but they said the mother was still alive and the girl said they weren't her relatives so they would have to go through a legal procedure to adopt her shall her mother pass. All of these things were out of his hands.

The morning dew scent had started to settle on the grassy fields of dead hay. A scent Caroline never hoped to smell again. She came from an area like this in Virginia and was hoping the hillbilly hurried the fuck up so she could wrap this shit up and go home. You never leave loose ends and Adell Mandigo was a loose end Vonderbilt could track back to her.

Ana had gone nuclear and killed everyone in the occults within a ten mile radius. All she left behind to watch them were dead. Luckily, she was out of town long before the hotel lit up like day time. She shuddered to think what would have had happened had she followed them.

"Hello," Adell said, curious as to why the espionage angle, why was she being so secretive about their meeting? Other coven members had already seen her talking to him.

Caroline Caldwell didn't return the greeting. She was used to men becoming tongue-tied in her presence. She pushed the briefcase to him with the toe of her designer shoe, the hard case, containing a cool 10 million made a loud grinding sound as it moved on the rough pavement. The price of a life. The fair price for a kill. Adell bent and picked it

778

up. So what if he didn't have the kid for an additional million? He planned to leave this area and never look back.

"Baby, you forgetting something." Caroline said in her famous sultry voice. Adell smiles and asks what's that?

"My kiss. Aren't you going to thank me for taking you out of this hellhole?"

He hadn't thought of that but guessed a single kiss couldn't hurt anything. He walked across the harmless pothole in the middle of the road and grabbed her and titled her backward in his arms as he had imagined doing many times and planted a very seductive kiss on her deep wine, red full, luscious lips. Caroline was a little surprised he was such a great kisser.

A thick, flimsy grey smoke rose from the pothole behind Adell Mandigo while he was trying to seduce Hollywood's great star. Seeing the demon she screamed, Adell stood upright and turned to protect her. The hellish beast morphed its hand into a blade and rammed it through the man's midriff and pulled hard upward, filleting the man as Caroline watched from the other side of the road.

"Ok, I've done it. Now say the incantation to free me from this area." An eerie, ancient, raspy voice said.

Caroline knew what the deal they made required of her but didn't care; it was stuck there. She knew it couldn't follow her so she turned and begun walking toward her Mercedes, merrily swinging the briefcase.

"Witch, you heard me! I said free me! That was the deal!" The demon called after her. But she kept walking down the lone country road in her four inch designer heels, stopped a few minutes, turned on her high heels, looked at it bellowing at her like a fool, and got into her car. She turned the ignite and soared away into the cool night air. Hoping never to see this place again. She was blonde but she wasn't stupid. She only asked it to kill in exchange for setting it loose on earth. She didn't ask for talent. She already had that. So she owed it nothing and there wasn't a damn thing it could do.

"Oh no she didn't." The crossroad demon said.

"Oh yes, she did." A nearby imp replied. "If you want me to? I can go tell Nikola what she tried to do to his bride," the greenish hobbit volunteered.

"Oh yeah, I forgot that woman is said to be Nikola's bride----making her that bitch's superior." The aphotic abyss of a mouth smiled. "Yeah, go tell him. Bring him here. I know he can reverse what these yahoo's did over 700 years ago. I don't get many offers nowadays since no one believes in us anymore." A country preacher trapped it in this Stygian hole over 700 years ago after learning the locals were summoning him to make deals in exchange for their souls. While others were using him to avenge a perceived wrong committed against them.

The imp found Nikola in a sordid, tenebrous mood but that was nothing new. He's always in a bad mood. He replayed his account of what he witnessed but didn't know the full details Nikola wanted.

"What are you telling me for if you don't know exactly what happened?"

"Your Highness, all I know it was something to do with your beloved and the dead man at the crossroad. When I arrived the kill was in progress and Caroline Caldwell was walking away. You have to talk to the roadside demon to get the full story."

Nikola got up and told the witches sharing his bed they were to stay put until he said they could leave.

He stepped through the realms and asked the crossroad demon about the deal. The black bleary eyes stared hard and coldly at him. He wasn't saying anything until Nikola got him out first.

"I asked you what happened to Ana?" Nikola hissed between his teeth, scarcely able to restrain his anger. How dare this thing not answer him?! Seeing he wasn't getting any result, he relinquished the threats and said the incantation to free the demon but held it in his neon fist made of energy. His powers.

"Your Highness Caroline Caldwell attacked your bride. Had this man to poison her. Allured him here and I killed him in exchange for freedom. She.."

Nikola halted him, he thought they had had an earnest talk about no grave attacks on Ana unless he authorized them.

"Attacked her how?"

"This man fed her succums." The crossroad demon replied. Nikola kicked the halved corpse and cussed it.

"That serves you right." He guffawed, hawked mucus, and spat on the dead man. Looking up the road he saw a house with a few lights still on. He knew this was perhaps where this dead man once lived. The demon who had seen Adell Mandigo since birth confirmed he did indeed live in the house with brown sidings that appeared gray in the moonlight.

Nikola telepathically called the local covens to come out and kill the entire family since this man had the audacity to try and take Ana from this earth. Away from him. If he isn't killing her then he will be damn if anyone will kill her. He might can't kill Caroline without Lucifer's permission but he intends to put a serious hurting on her and James as well. James will be hurt because it's his job to keep Caroline under control.

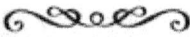

Ashton arrived in the spiritual realm of Discord after feeling Ana's distress to a big pile of goo that was once a colossal demon.

"Which way did she go?" He asked the imps and hell worms. All knew they had better tell the truth or they would be the next ones beat into the dust. He followed her fading trail. He arrived in Nikola's bedroom and watched several morbid, disgusting men have sex with a headless corpse. The act was still repugnant no matter how many times one has witnessed it. One of the men noticed him.

"Wanna hit?" he asked. "At least you don't have to listen to her mouth." The man joked and the others laughed.

He found the men so repulsive it was difficult to talk to them to ask what he wanted to know. "Which way did Ana go?" They pointed toward the door.

Last night he had heard on the American national news about an eight police car crash in Kansas about 60 miles outside of Wichita, and another where witnesses said a giant man picked up a semi and tossed it into another semi seemingly trying to pass a light blue car. So he knew this involved Ana. But couldn't pick up on her trail at either sites. When he viewed the headless bodies in the morgue he touched them to see the last thing they saw and it was her legs and her Sword coming down on them. He's angry and frustrated because she shouldn't be going through all this alone. If she was home where he could protect her all would be well. From the wreckage of the room, it dawned hard and forcefully on him she could've easily been killed.

He feels he has made great progress so why were they still keeping her from him? He'd cut his women down to only the 10 which now live in the palace outside of Paris. The other houses and palaces he has closed them. Saving himself billions on them and the lavish parties he once gave. Even cut down on the ten expenses, no more outrageously expensive salons and trips. He pays them their salary so whatever they want they had better buy it out of that. With this harrowing incident he plan to cuts the women down to 7. He makes it no secret soon they all will be gone and to make other arrangements because his wife will be coming home. Ok, he admits he isn't where he ought to be but living in a palace somewhere with him certainly beats getting killed. Was heaven making a martyr of her?

Upon returning to one of the empty houses after a futile search for Ana he appeals to his older brother, the Archangel Raphael. "Ralph, I'm really trying here. I, I mean they're going to eventually catch her and kill her and you know what those indecorous, penurious imbeciles will do to her body."

The graceful, beautiful Archangel looks sadly at his younger brother whom he once had to punish and says "Brother, the time hasn't arrived yet; for you yes, this is a great progress. Her life is in Father's capable Hands. When she is to be your bride? I can't say if you'll know her when you see her again but your heart will."

Ashton grows angry. He's so sick and tired of the half-clues, the frustration, and the talk about the appointed time malarkey. It wasn't like he was asking that the mysteries of the Heavens be revealed to him. All he wanted a straight answer for once. Without the mysticism surrounding it. Were they planning martyrdom for her? For it sure looked that way to him. He took in a deep breath and gave his questions another try. "I know you all are allergic to straight answers so for once...! I beseech you to give me a straight answer. Will she survive this ordeal?"

Raphael lovingly pats Ashton's broad shoulder and looks him kindly in the eyes. "I don't know, but if she doesn't. You'll know where to find her."

The answer only frustrated Ashton more, added to his fears not calmed them. He was hearing his worst case scenario.

He off-highhandedly says to hide his fear, "You've never loved a woman the way I love this woman so you've no idea how I feel. Every time I hear something horrible, I think the most pessimal thing has happened to her."

"No, I haven't. I love them all. I love everyone."

"No, Ralph, to love someone carnally and spiritually is a lot different from simply loving everyone."

Seeing that there's no relief for his brother's agony Raphael says. "Be still and be patient, you've waited this long what's a few more years? I know you'll repent and come Home even if Father doesn't allow you to be with her There."

"You see, that's what I'm afraid of, He might hold things off until she dies. And you know He isn't to let me near her once is with Him. What makes you so sure I will follow her Home?"

"I know you love her enough to come Home if that's the only way to see her. And have you ever consider truly cleaving unto her? Leaving all those other women alone to show Him you are serious?" Raphael asked.

"Well, who am I supposed to sleep with?" He asked, astonished, as thus this was the most ridiculous thing he had ever heard.

"By yourself, Azazael! How would you feel if she was sleeping with 10-7 men every night behind your back?"

Ashton didn't like the image Raphael was painting. The very thought of that many guys pawing her at once infuriated him. "I would've to kill them all and end up back in prison."

"Don't you think she feels the same way?"

"Nah, women are different. They can handle sharing better than men."

"Says who?" Raphael asked. "You and all other unfaithful men? They've been forced to handle it because they're the weaker vessels but their hearts hurt the same as men. They feel the same anger and jealousy as men. But I warn you shall she catch you being unfaithful she will use that same pistol and sword by her side on you."

Ashton didn't want to hear Raphael's lecture on fidelity. What did know, he was still a virgin. Well, at least as far as he knew. His sex with those women had nothing to do with his love for Ana. Those were two totally different things. Hey, wait a minute...didn't they have this conversation before? Damn it, Heaven and its lessons!

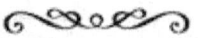

They stopped for the night to get some rest. Bea didn't wake her mother as she promised. She kept on driving and turning off on back roads she remembered seeing her mother turn off onto. She kept watching the sky all day. She knew the birds circling above were really harpies and not natural birds. They had been sent to watch which direction they traveled. But that was all right. She would get them later. She had encoded their spiritual imprint in her mind so she could someday find them just as she would someday find the woman in the white fur coat. Right now she had to get her mom someplace safe before night fall. Mom always said all the monstrosities come out at night.

The archangel Raphael was deeply saddened in what he knew had to do. He knew he had to utterly and totally erase all remembrance of this love from Azazael's mind to set him free. This couldn't continue. This maddening cycle of remembrance was defeating the very purpose Ana was created and called for. Azazael truly loves this woman and isn't going to stop until he has her in his arms forever. He has hurt many, even his own younger brother ,while in pursuit of her and refuses to give up until he reaches her. She is all which matters to him. He gently reached over with a sorrow laden heart and hugged his brother. Absorbing the love for Ana within himself. The force and strength of it was far greater than he suspected. It bored into his being like a beacon of splendiferous light. He knew even then there was a chance that Azazael still might remember her for love. Because after all, love is the strongest force there is to exist. Secretly, he hoped he did remember a love so strong. It definitely was remarkable and truly unforgettable.

Once he asked Father why was she born so late in time? Wouldn't it had been better had she been born much earlier in time?

"By now, she would be long dead and here at Home and he would still be crying. You know how loud he is. I didn't want to listen to that all these years. I didn't want to listen to Azazael cry outside My Walls until the end of time, until the judgment of all yet unjudged worlds. Sure he would go away for a while but he would be back the moment he longed for her and I didn't want to deal with her sneaking off to see him, going to areas a heavenly saints shouldn't tread. And mostly she has a job to do. This is her era."

What had been a greater mystery was why was she seemingly cursed with the love of Azazael of all the heavenly princes?

Father answered saying, "I didn't choose him. She did. She chose him on her own free will. That's why I sent you to bring her over the Great Chasm. He fitted the criteria of what she wanted and needed. Knowing what she would be up against she needed someone who would stand by her side no matter how stormy life became. She needed someone who was stubborn and persistent as hell itself. I answered her prayer; shortly after her first marriage she started to realized she had married the wrong man. Her husband loved her but had fallen out of being *in* love with her. She was watching his love for her dwindle. So she asked me to give her someone who would love her the way she needed and wanted to be loved. Not someone who takes her for granted".

Dawn felt she did what she had to do. The woman was gone and things were returning to normal. Ashton is back around the house enjoying parties as if the nightmare never happened. She is finding out the hard way a half immortal child is nothing like a full mortal child. Ashton isn't mean to her nor her son but has as little to do with her as possible. She loves it when everyone comments on how much he looks and acts like his father. Sure, Ashton has told her numerous times the boy isn't his. He knew about the liaison between she and Pascasiel but just didn't care.

But as she explained duly to Cargill, "The world doesn't know that Pascasiel exists. The world only knows you and the boy looks like you so that's all that matters."

Seeing things her way works better for everyone. Her, him, the company and even the other harem members. Accounts have been turned back on, shopping and buying resumed. So yes, she accomplished what she had to do. The others should appreciate her sacrifices but they don't. They think he had a change of heart all because he cares about them. Ha! How laughable.

She even put her foot down when he tried to bring in a new harem member who had an uncanny resemblance to Ana.

He has quietened down a lot. He isn't as vigorous as before. But with his age, that's expected. These last six months have been like old times. That little skinny thing is disruptive no matter where she goes and what on earth made that girl think she could handle Dawn Shepherd?

Sure, the sorry ass media still lynches her saying that love is what makes the world go around. That's bullshit and they know it. She hasn't seen love walk in any office and pay a bill. Those who preach this shit have never been broke.

And all the tired ass wives with five babies hanging off their teats who have been condemning the harem for years know they don't stand a chance of gaining one of these positions. They aren't pretty enough. But they do the same things with broke men she does with Cargill but it is said to be done for love. Oh, that supposed to make all the difference in the world? Sound like some brainwashing bologna to her.

That sounds like the same load of shit mother tried to feed me growing up but thought I was eating it up with a spoon, saying, "A good woman doesn't ask for much, all she wants is a man's love."

I told mom, "I will take the wallet he can keep his love." This are lines from broke men trying to get a pretty woman on a low budget. Mom fell for that with my dad. Mom was once very beautiful but she married dad and he didn't upkeep her and she started having all of us and her looks faded.

How many can say they don't have cook for their families if they don't own an automaton maid? And those things are expensive and can dysfunction and harm you. So fuck them. How many of their men hand them a million bucks like it's a single rose? None, she bets.

Nikola had Ana herded to one of the many apartments he owned which was already rigged with cameras for remote viewing. He was well acquainted with her extraordinaire perceptibility to seek them out. But the extreme micro ones she sometimes missed. From someone or somewhere she had obtained an illegal bug sweeper. He believes it came from high tech brother Jack. The scanner is definition military or spy grade. Or perhaps her supernatural abilities are sharping so that she can now scan electronic or even plasma devices. He began using these when he discovered she was learning how to throw up prayer barriers to keep out spying demons.

He watched the local coven members enter and switch the furniture around, mess with the food in the refrigerator, go through her personal affects to make sure she had nothing of value. He watch them do other little petty things to gaslight her. The idiots don't know Ana has been through this so many times she is immune to gaslighting. But he does know if they know what's best for them they would get out of there before she arrives. But what can he say? Fools never learn. In every town there's some overconfident fool whom Lucifer or some other demon has convinced he or she is strong enough to take on Ana who ends up dead.

He watches the group exit out the back door seconds before she and her daughter come in through the front door. He believes Ana heard them for she dropped the packages and ran to the back door. She sees the hover car full of happy simpletons rise into the air and take off. Knowing her car isn't a hover, the imbeciles think they are in the clear. But do know she can track them and kill every single one of them shall she take the notion to do so? She probably won't for they haven't done anything worthy of death in her book but in his they have. Several took a pair of her underwear after sniffing them.

He watched her go in the kitchen and start dinner. He was hoping she went in the bathroom first so he could see her finish what she started this morning. Watching her shower or bathe leaves him so excited it feels like his penis is going to rocket off and burst through his pants. He doesn't care to watch the other functions nor watch the kid.

His predecessor Orman messed up with Lucifer by not choosing a High Queen. Lucifer wanted that Eugenia Harris woman for Orman's queen, his High Witch but Orman kept decrying he was born gay. Lucifer didn't give a shit rather you were or weren't. But Orman was like himself born with his abilities and kept right on poking pretty boy Oregon. But lo and behold, he forgot what he was dealing with, the Prince of Darkness. Some things Luc will let slide, some petty things, but things of that magnitude of importance... you had better do as he said. Unwilling to conceive a child the old fashioned way as Lucifer demand, with a woman, Orman and Oregon decide to kill the family and kidnap a gifted one, him.

To Orman's dismay, Lucifer knew of another, younger, stronger warlock named Faizon and sent him to eliminate both Orman and Oregon. Lucifer doesn't run a democracy. Homosexuality is forbidden among those on his level for it deprives Lucifer of members who may be strong enough to carry on his kingdom. He remembers the fight like yesterday. Orman and Oregon against the power craving Faizon. They put on a spectacular show for the world of witchery. The fight began in the castle and spilled out into open. With energy balls and dirty fire flying everywhere the household and villagers fled for the mountains. Several balls missed their targets and turned items in creatures like the hell rabbits he had to eliminate some time ago.

Orman was over confident. He was so certain he had beat him down into a slave, he would fight for him. The three and all of the kingdom against Faizon. But this unknown warlock was fast. He was blitzing the hell out of Orman and Oregon and there was no way he was going to interstice himself in all that. Cedonna Machiavelli didn't raise no fool. The fight raged on into the night, lighting up the sky like a Chinese New Year celebration. When they all moved back indoors, he saw all three were weakened from taking constant blows. That's when he saw his chance. He took Faizon out first for the man was the strongest, whom he showed mercy. Faizon hadn't done anything to him. He didn't know the man. And seeing his ability Orman congratulated him, believing he killed Faizon for his master. He then lassoed the too weak Orman and moved on to Oregon whom he wanted Orman to watch die. He saved Orman for last. He wanted him to suffer as much as Orman had caused him and his family to suffer.

He dragged an incompetent Oregon down to the ice cellar housing his sister's body while he floated the lassoed Orman behind. Showed him the frozen body and asked him did he have to do that her? Oregon gave him the traditional rant and raving about Orman was in love with the beautiful woman and wanted the child. He wasn't losing his spot in the world's satanic hierarchy because of her.

That wasn't what he asked the murdering psycho. He asked did he have to kill her so horribly or any at all? Her gifts were minor. She was no real threat to him and Orman. Then he rammed the same blade left in his sister's corpse into Oregon's abdomen and pulled upward with all his might. The man's innards splattered out on the floor, all over his shoes. The catacombs were too good for Oregon, he dropped the body there and left it, he would feed it to the wild dogs later. That was the fitting ending for a Jezebel like Oregon. Now...it was time to deal with the big dog, Orman Vonderbilt. He floated the sobbing, enraged, struggling Orman to his mother's room. Pointed at the skull she was kissing and at the two other she was patting. While the two dark haired boys, little more than infants named Bjors and Gianna looked on wide-eyed and frightened. They had enough wits to know something dangerous was going down. His mother didn't. She was totally oblivious to the death match.

"That's my family!" he yelled pointing at the skulls of children. "Those are my little siblings whose slaughter I was powerless to stop. You cared nothing for my pain and tears. So now I care nothing for yours," He said, letting Orman go so they could duel. But it was no real fight. Orman knew he was defeated just as he defeated the warlock before him.

What those who write their glamorized tales of witches and warlocks fail to include is few warlocks, powerful warlocks such as those on Orman's level live long enough to become old and gray with a long white beard and pointed hat. Oh well, the idiots probably don't know that for this is, after all, a secret society.

After he chopped off Orman's head he kept it as a trophy. He pretty much dissected the entire body and kept it as a trophy, especially the dick. This was his first castration of many.

Later that night he dragged Oregon's disemboweled body through the castle escape tunnel that was once a home to Grand Warlocks centuries ago. This cavern palace led to a mountain exit; he left him on the mountain side for the wild dogs that roamed the high valley.

For his first five years in power he banned all the books and movies glamorizing witchery and wizardry agenda until Lucifer forced him to lift the ban. He did it because bastards like those cost him everything and there was nothing awesome or glamorous about it. They didn't play with people in reality as they do in the kiddie books and fantasies. They are truly very frightening and atrociously evil people.

Unlike many before him, he didn't volunteer to fight another warlock for control of the kingdom. He was pulled and forced into this sickness.

Many, having never seen Orman didn't know he and Orman were not the same man. He killed all who knew they weren't. He killed all who showed up in his peaceful village that fateful night. Those left knew if they knew what was best for them they would keep their mouths shut. So that's why he wears his predecessor's name. Which isn't uncommon. Popes do it all the time and to those of the world of the occults esteemed leaders like himself and Orman are considered pretty much the same as a pope.

Growing up, he used to believe that people like Orman were nicer and better than the general population. They seemed more refined and polite. At least the ones from his village were. But now he knows sexual preference has nothing to do with a person's character. It's what's in their heart which does.

He turns his attention back to the wine in hand and the camera. Ana doesn't shower again. She flops down in the bed and falls sleep from exhaustion. That's a disgusting habit he will have to eliminate. One showers before going to bed.

He sat in the garden and looks at the puzzling note he wrote to himself in Azazaelese. It said things about Ana may catch him, to stop sleeping with the harem.

Oh well, that's a life he will never have. He isn't so sure he ever really loved the woman. Maybe it was merely an infatuation.

Ghosts are part of old building, so he wasn't surprised to see the ghost of the child staring at him. This original place was built in the 1920's when the movie industry took wings and soared. The child must has been the son of a staff member from the clothing he's wearing. Ashton wonders what happened to him? Why did he die so young? But doesn't ask. That was long ago. Nothing can change the past and doesn't seems like much can change the future.

Being an Immortal death has always been a mystery to him. He remembers many mortals swearing he doesn't want to experience it.

Easing up beside him and sitting on the garden bench surrounded by fragrant roses the boy peered at his note, "What's that?" asked the child who was once African American during his life on earth.

"Nothing much, just a bunch of nonsense I wrote to myself."

"Why?" The boy asked. He had forgotten when souls returns to this side they are the same age they were when they left. So he's a child and children ask unnecessary, unwanted questions.

"What happened to you?" He asked the boy to defer answering something he preferred not to

"I got really sick and died." The boy said.

The reply satisfied Ashton, he was wondering was the child killed. They both turned in the direction of someone wailing, "Daddyyy!"

A pale girl, rather a young woman with flowing locks of deep platinum blonde hair spotted him and started a toddler trot with her arms extended while hiccuping tears was headed his way. He thought she was little too old to be performing this stunt.

She saw the ghost which seemed to upset her more. She didn't ask could she slobber all over him. She just did. He and the boy were puzzled as to where did she come from?

"Daddy, momma won't talk to me. She never liked Chris. The only Chris she likes is my brother Chris. Anton is gone to kill him and I can't stop him. Daddy, you have to stop Anton!"

Ashton is totally puzzled as to why this platinum chick is calling him daddy. He freezes. *"Oh fuck, he tripped up and married Dawn or one of the others who look like her. Dawn finally wore him down!"*

He is confused now more than ever. Who is Chris? Who is she? Who is her mother? Who is Anton?

"Dad, you know how momma can be when she doesn't get her way," the platinum blonde with his eyes said. Ignoring the skin color---she looks like someone else, not Dawn. Someone he knows very well.

"No, I don't know how your mother can be. So why don't you fill me in."

The woman sniffed and dried her eyes on his new shirt. He looked at the wet spot on his shirt and frowned at her and she started the tear work anew, saying no one loves her. Even he doesn't love her.

He pulled her back to his shoulder to make her shut up, she was getting on his nerves. What difference did it make? She had already fucked up his silk shirt.

"Sssh, honey, hush and tell daddy what happened."

She straighten up and look at him with gemstone blue mixed with speck amber eyes just as his own and someone else. He looked closer and saw little specks of gold in them also which greatly complimented her golden undertone. And that's when he knew she was from the future and had wandered back in time looking for him. So where was he in her life as to why she had to come to the past to find him?

"Dad, Anton is mad because Chris filed for divorce and drained my billions you gave me when I finished school. Mom is mad because she told me not to marry the iggglo as she called him. So, I came to get you to make Anton stop. Mom won't make him stop."

"You mean gigolo."

"Yeah, that's the word mom used."

"But back up a minute, who is Anton? And why did I give you a billion for doing what you were supposed to do? And who is your mother?"

Christina Cargill playfully slapped her dad's massive chest as she has seen her mother do millions of time. Laughs for she believes her dad to be joshing as he sometimes does. "Daddy, stop playing this is serious."

"I'm serious, too."

"Dad, your wife Ana, my mother---can be mean at times." Christina slowly explains. "I'm your beautiful daughter Christina. Anton is your damn momma's boy of a son. He's always on mom's side no matter what... Well, Chris is my third husband whom mom hates."

"Hold on? Wait a minute... how many of you all are there?"

Christina laughs for she thinks her dad is still kidding around. "I don't know. There's lot of us."

"And I give each of you a billion???"

The young platinum blonde woman nods.

"For doing what???" He cried, astonished.

"For being us! Because you love us." Christina said, leaning against him again.

"Ok, Christina, I hope you know you are in the past. This is me in the past. Where am I in your time?"

Christina looks curiously around. The place does look different. Her mother's flowers aren't where they supposed to be. Everything looks passe to her, even her dad's clothing looks old-fashioned. "What year is this?"

"2491."

"Oh My God!!" Christina gasped and slapped her hand over her mouth. "I'm so sorry for messing up your shirt." She tries to wipe it clean. "I'm from (blank). I was looking for you. Mom said you weren't home so I set out to find you."

"You need to calm down. Your emotions opened up the past. Apparently, we both were experiencing the same deep emotions at the same time and that led you to the past."

She eyed him curiously wondering why was he upset?

"It's best you go back to your time so you won't get lost." He said, rising to lead her as far into the future as he was allowed. He comes to a great Granite Wall he has never seen before. "What's behind here?" he inquired of the woman.

"This is (blank) where we all live. Well, I don't live here anymore. I live in New York City."

The wall was forboding and forbidding to him but not to her. It easily slide open for her; that's when he saw inside a pristine city. But not for long for an unseen force peddeled him backward. When it closed the Granite Wall started moving in his direction in a rather threatening manner as if attempting to drive him away. He slowly stepped back the way he came. The Wall followed. He picked up speed and so did it. It folded

795

itself and moved effectively through the mazes and realms of the Netural Zone, something like inherent knowledge told him it would crush him shall he stand in its path. When he exited into his own time peroid it stopped and disappeared.

He turned many questions around in his mind after exiting from the obvious danger. He walked back to the bench pondering over the mysterous moving wall and where did it go and what was that place he saw behind the wall as he returned to the stone bench. The ghost boy who had been silent throughout his strange, wailing, future daughter's visit reappeared on the bench beside him.

"I guess I need to hold on to this after all," he smiled within, looking at the note. "And I guess I need to write another one. Telling my future self not to listen to my wife and give a bunch of pampered, crying, children money they can't handle. But it seems I'm going to need all the help I can get if all of them are going to be sobbing and screaming like the one that just left." he joked.

The boy smiled.

"Son, what did you die from?"

"I had a little bird whose name was Enza, I opened the window and in flew Enza....." The boy said.

He had seen Dawn with her baby standing in the upper window watching him and the young woman. So he turned and looked at her and their eyes met. Not knowing who the woman was Dawn frowned and stepped away from the window. They both knew it was all over.

Gradually his memory faded, he remembered Ana, the city, the moving wall nor the platinum blonde woman no more.

Chapter 17
A Love born of Fire and Ice.

The East Coast annual gala affair for executives was to be held in New York City at the famous Cargill ballroom. The place screamed of excessive wealth, it was well known for the extricate chandeliers of crystal and diamonds.

It was late October when Dawn decided to sponsor the ball at the urging of Caroline Cadwell. Who was viewing whatever slump Cargill was in was a blessing in disguise. At least he wasn't chasing that God-awful woman for once.

"Come on, honey. You have to get ready." Dawn pleaded with Ashton who was still sitting in his underwear while his top employees were arriving from all over the world. She was getting tired of his no-energy, don't-care attitude. She worked hard to put this event together. With the help of Caroline she had managed to snag some of the biggest names in the world and here he sit in his drawers like no one is coming.

Pointing the finger of his hand holding a glass of Scotch at her, he said, "I don't have to do anything. This is your party. Not mine. Those coming in are my employees, I'm not their's!"

"Ashley is going to wonder what's wrong with you if you don't show up."

"So, let him. I'm his father. He isn't mine." Ashton quipped and started at her icily. "Do you want to know what's wrong with me? Huh?"

"NO, not particularly." Dawn thinks.

"Well, I will tell you. I'm sick of everybody thinking they know better than me how to live my life. I sick of everything. You, your kid, the harem, my kids, this damn company, and even Heaven has worn out my patience." He threw the glass against the wall so hard

797

it shattered and stuck to the wall in an interesting, complex pattern of glass and liquor.

She looked in the mirror at him and his eyes had started to look feral. Like a wild animal. She hoped he wasn't turning into that lion thing again. He has been doing a lot of that lately. She hated to give Ana any credit but he was easier to get along with when she was sleeping with him. Now, he is back to his same old nasty self.

"Get the hell out of here before I change." he growled.

He didn't have to tell her twice, she hurried out the room and hoped he didn't come trampling downstairs looking like a hellish lion.

She met Ashley in the hall way. She invited him because Ashton has been uncontrollable lately. Nothing no one did suited him.

"Where is dad?" Ashley asked as he approached her in the hallway.

"In the room losing his mind. He's changing." Dawn warned. Ashley had an idea what she meant.

It had been ages since Ashley has seen his father change but he knew his dad wouldn't hurt him. He pushed open the double doors to a scene he had never seen before. A creature whose huge majestic head was pressed against the ceiling. The long flowing mane had a human-like appearance. This is not the thing he saw as a child. The huge clawed feet looked at least five feet wide. The creature looked somewhat human and then again it didn't. The smooth, blackish-brown fur looked more like hair than a pelt.

"Son, what do you want?" The deep bass, rumbling voice asked.

"Dad, uh, why are you doing this?"

"Because I feel like it."

Ashley had been trying to find that woman. He looked everywhere for her but it was like she dropped off the face of the earth. His dad was turning mean as hell. He even cut him and his children off the gravy train. He cut his sibling off, fired people. He heard he was terrorizing people again. If he kept this up he was going to be divinely arrested again.

The way the big creature was watching him was unnerving. It was almost as if he were stalking prey. He moved to the liquor cart, the creature moved with him but from the other side of the room. The heavy steps following him were breaking the floor underneath the expensive carpet leaving a deep indentation in the rug. He was hoping his father didn't go into a rage and bring the building down on all of them. His dad's arctic blue, icy eyes were very intense and following him as primitively as a lion in a jungle pursuing quarry. This was creeping him out big time. He sensed if he ran some primeval inherent aptitude was going to surface and this creature just might kill him. He held his nerve and pretended everything was fine. But instinct was telling him he dad was angry at him. He had found out the woman lived with his son Janus for three months. And was furious with them for lying to him, knowing he had been looking for her for months.

"Dad, Lavenedica is supposed to be here. She doesn't need to see you like this." Ashley lied and gulped down the liquid he didn't bother to identify. He needed something to calm his nerves. He didn't know if his sister was coming or not but was hoping she did so his dad didn't kill anyone tonight. Starting with him. His father had that hunger to kill look in his eyes.

"Well, it's about time she sees this side of me. So she will know some of the things said about me are true."

"Dad, stop it. You're scaring the shit outta me!"

"Why? You've seen this form before." Azazel said nonchalantly as the flowing, thick mane fell over Ashley's face. The hot breath exhaled on his head felt like air on fire.

"Yeah, but not like this."

In a second Azazael morphed back to his humanoid size. Ashley kept his back turned for his father was naked. He heard his dad take a seat in an unbroken chair. That's when he turned around.

"Dad, your people bust their butts for you all year long. Don't you think they deserve some of your attention?"

"No, I don't. None of them does it for free."

Meanwhile downstairs Dawn had hired new help at the recommendation of Caroline Caldwell. She looked across the ballroom and almost spit the champagne into the face of the woman whom she was talking to. She peered through the crowd, it can't be. It just can't be who she thinks it is! That damn walk was unmistakeable. She rushed to Delores who was entertaining some Asian executives and pulled her aside.

"Look through the crowd there. How in the hell did she get in here?" Delores turned to see who Dawn was referring to and frowned.

"I think she may have come in with the new catering company from her uniform. Let me get rid of her before he comes downstairs."

Seeing the tall redhead making a beeline for Ana, Caroline cut Delores off before she reached Ana.

"No, let her stay. It's time to get revenge for all the trouble she caused. Since he doesn't remember her, I arranged this job for her when I learned she was in the city to see her mother."

"That's too big of a chance to take. Someone might tell him who she is. Someone like his damn son for instance." Delores whispered. By now, several of the harems members had joined the group. They too had noticed and recognized the woman serving from the other side of the ballroom.

"Have you all put the Lethe water in his liquors?" Caroline asked.

800

"Yeah, but he broke it's hold before. So he will probably do it again." Delia reminded Caroline.

"I doubt it. Lucifer prepared it this time. Not Nikola."

The group moved like a pack of hyenas to the end of the ballroom where Ana had been assigned to serve. As soon as they standing, surrounding her they begun making demands. One pointed out an invisible stain on her uniform saying it was tacky she came to work dirty.

Ana didn't know these women but she knew they were ganging up on her. Helena was demanding rent so she had to hold on to this job. Her sister said they stayed no where else for free so why did she expect to stay with her for no rent? So yes, she had to keep her cool and not let these women get her fired. The job was paying a $1,000 per gig.

"What may I get for you, ladies?" She asked with a pasted on smile.

"You can refill my champagne glass." Caroline said. "And don't throw anything this time."

Ana nodded and retrieved a fresh glass of champagne, taking the half empty one on her tray. When she turned to leave Caroline's foot shot out from under the evening dress sending her crashing to the marble floor. The fine champagne glasses shattered, sending shards of glass everywhere, even hitting some of the partygoers; the silver tray landed hard making a loud clunking a noise she found rather embarrassing. Pearls of laughter were heard in the background. When she tried to rise someone put the heel of her foot against her ass and pushed her back down into the glass, cutting her knee. Ana turned around furious, her eyes were white fire. Now, she remembers Caroline Cadwell from the pool party in Virginia. While still on the floor she kicked her hard in the knee, causing the leg to buckle, bringing her down to the floor with her. She quickly grabbed her, placing her in a headlock and started pounding her in the head with her fist. Dawn has wanted to do this for years...she grabbed the plait and pulled as hard as possible. Ana turned and punched her so hard in the stomach, air was nosily exhaled. Ana knew she

801

wouldn't get paid tonight so she was taking her pay out their asses. She swung her leg in a low round kick and swept Dawn's legs from under her. She was on her with her strong fingers interlaced in the thick hair, banging her head against the floor almost immediately upon the woman hitting the ground. Another grabbed her around the neck from behind. Many demons as she had fought employed the same method. She reached behind herself with her free hand and flipped a redhead she had never seen before over her shoulder. The woman slid a few feet on her back after crash landing hard on the black marble floor.

Now she was kicking Caroline with her right foot while sitting on the other woman's chest. Everytime she time she tried to get up Ana knocked her back down.

She sensed someone in the crowd coming for her head from the left; she ducked and turned a tall sultry black woman cold cocked her hard in the jaw with the rings she was wearing adding power to the punch. Ana was dazzled, but she was going to give them the ass whipping she wanted to give her big sister for talking shit. She stepped into the woman on the floor's, who was trying to get up, for she knew it was already sore and started walking upon the one who cold cocked her, landing punches like a man on the woman's face and upper body.

She was sick and tired of these massagonistic women and their pettiness. They hate every woman they see and doesn't bother to find out why? It's high time someone whooped their asses. Maybe then they will learn to sit it down. She kept pounding, kicking, stomping and punching anyone in her way without the strength to stop her. She had nothing else to lose. A person with nothing to lose is a very dangerous person. She'd had it with these damn city slickers who haven't never hit a lick at a snake but yet think they are strong enough to whip her ass.

With Jack and Helena as her first teachers, she definitely learned how to fight. Helena always quoted, *"Never let your mouth write a check your ass can't cash for I don't excuse insufficient funds."*

Several black tied guys tried to stop her only to end up being kicked in the groin or with a bloody, broken nose. If she had to fight for the next hour she was gearing up to do it. She was sick of these skanks always fucking with her. Enough was fucking enough!

Someone from behind grabbed her fist in mid-swing. Halting the trajectory of her next blow. She turned and looked in the eyes of an angry man. Fuck him! She was enraged, too. She swung at him. He seemed surprised her impact stung. He caught her next blow in the palm of his hand and pushed her fist down. They both stared at each like two champions coming out the corner to duke it out again. It hurt like hell to punch him, it was like hitting a face made of stone but she swallowed the pain, ready to deliver another blow to his face. He stared down wrathfully at her in the suddenly fallen silent room as she glared up equally as umbrageous at him.

He looked around at the hair, shoes, spilled hor d'oeuvres and champagne, shrapnel of glass, busted furniture, bits of fabric, blood, teeth, and broken jewelry scattered about the place and then looked back at this little furious woman in front of him, staring up at him in total defiance. Was she crazy or just one hell of a fighter? He recognized it as the fighting of someone very upset, feeling they had nothing to lose.

"Miss, I don't know what's your problem but it's best that you leave. I do not permit such savagery, such scandalous behavior at my functions," he said.

"They attacked me!" Ana shouted, turning from looking at the mess they made to fully to address the black tux wearing man who said this was his function. "I do expect to be paid for the full six hours I have worked this evening."

"Take that matter up with the company who hired you." The man said, dropping her clenched fist and trying to walk away. Ana followed him and pulled the back of his coat. He turned around furiously and looked down at her again as if he had no idea why she was following him. He tapped a button on his watch for security to usher her out.

The woman who hired Ana was busy trying to melt into the walls. She was utterly embarrassed. So, so sorry she ever hired Ana. Ana came with high recommendation so she thought she was a sure bet for the most important party of the year. People placed bids for this slot a year ahead of time. This was a $250,000 gig. But the waitress was right. Those high society women started the fight. One was Mrs. Cargill, the woman who hired her. Of course everyone knew Caroline Cadwell. The others she didn't know.

Ashley was gone and these security people didn't know Ana. Two men planked on both sides of her and politely but firmly asked her to follow them.

"I'm not going anywhere until I get my money. I ain't no damn slave. I don't work for free," she informed everyone standing around watching the event unfold.

Cargill beckoned for the men to carry her out if necessary. The one to her right reached for her upper arm, a move she has always hated. In rage and fury, she materialized her short dagger and snicked his hand. A muffled clamoring broke out in the room full of the world's movers and shakers. Everyone was wondering where had that weapon come from?

Azazael called off the second man when he saw the Emblem of Heaven on the dagger. He quickly crossed the room, much to the harem's dismay. Dawn glowered at Caroline, she knew something like this would happen. She knew they should have gotten rid of that woman when they had the chance, before he came downstairs.

"Miss, will you follow me?" He asked rather short tempered. He knew what she was, that was a divine military weapon she materialized.

She followed him but dared anyone to put their hands on her or she would let them have it. He walked through the vast ballroom to the glass elevator, she followed and so did Dawn. He angrily stabbed the button to take them upstairs. When the glass door slid opened he gestured for her to step off first. She returned the gesture. She wasn't letting him walk behind her. Who knows what he had in mind? He angrily exhaled but right about now, she just didn't give a fuck about anyone being pissed off. She was royally pissed. She just lost a month's rent over those pampered bitches.

She followed him to an office. It greatly advertised his vast wealth. Overhead hung four giant mesh chandeliers in the gold hued vaulted ceiling which were all diamonds and precious gemstones. She looked up and saw paintings of Renaissance masters in the ceiling. The unique frame added depths to the painting. The gold and white trimmed creamy furniture was made on a queen Anne design. The four, (two on each side) white, silver veined marble pillars framed the a full outlook on the world's largest city. The intricate design and patterns of the light beige nearly white carpet highly complimented the furniture and the entire room. The room looked familiar but she knows she has never been here before.

He turned and locked the door, she suspected something like this would happen. She materialized her entire uniform, he seemed somewhat surprised she had the entire ensemble in all its spangled glory.

"What regiment do you command?" He asked, crossing the room to the desk and pulling out a bill and handing it to her.

"None." She replied as icily as he asked her.

"Someday you will. By the way....what's your name? Your real name?"

"I'm not obligated to deliver that information."

He shrugged his tuxedoed shoulders. She was right, she wasn't obligated to abide his request. "If I were you I would be more careful about displaying what you are. That makes you a walking target for the darkside and there are plenty of them out there tonight."

"I was a target the day I was born."

He recognized that warrior's stance she had taken. She was preparing to fight him if that was the only way out of here. Just then the phone on his wrist rung. He hesitated to answer it. He was curious about this woman. One doesn't see a Nazarene Warrior Saint in full armor every day. The people downstairs, he could see them any day of the week. They can wait.

"You can disengage, I didn't bring you up here to fight. I brought you here because that weapon reminds me of someone I once knew. Would you care for a drink?" He asked approaching a wall. He pressed a button and a small bar appeared.

"No, thank you. But thanks, I must be going." What she meant was she knew once out of this uniform the glass in her knees and shin was going to be quite painful. Not to mention the pain in her knuckles and the glass in the heel of her hand.

"What's the rush?" He politely asked, handing her a glass of liquor anyway. She stood unmoved like the solider she was and still declined it. He placed it on the counter near the decanter. His phone was ringing like mad. He still refused to unlock the door. So finally, he answered his aggravating ass phone. "Dad, don't let her get away. It's her. She is in the room with you right now! A friend of mine called me saying what this waitress did at the gala. I'm telling you it's her!"

Sensing someone at his side, Ashton turned slowly and looked at her right beside him. He found himself looking at the tip of her blade. She had crossed the distance between them in a matter of seconds. Ana believed someone was telling him of her misdeeds and he was stalling and holding her for the police to arrest her. "Cut the connection. I don't want to hurt you but I will."

"Is your real name Ana?" he asked. The uniform was preventing a spiritual scan to identify her.

"No, it isn't," she said through hard, clenched teeth, pressing the blade's invincible sharp tip harder to his under chin, drawing a speck of blood. "Now, cut the connection and open the door and forget you ever saw me. That would be the wise thing to do."

Determined to learn if this angry woman really was her he raised his head and took a chance. He bared his neck to her. He saw her eyes flicker with precariousness in what to do next. He didn't know if it was her but the gesture was one of surrender and submission. He knew the blade did not kill unless one was threatened. This was a much more honorable blade than the one his own. She lowered it and asked what did he want?

"My memory of a lady whom I loved very much has been erased. I'm trying to learn

806

are you she? Your real name is Ana...isn't it? I know you lied for the gleam of your uniform became less radiant when you answered my question," he said, willing forth his own uniform.

She quickly stepped back and put up her gold and silver shield. She watched the man in the silver and gold breast plate with a uniform a lot like her own. The skirt was plated with silver along the strips of black leather. She carefully took in the majestic deep wine cape descending to the floor, she looked up at the towering, open faced headdress decorated with some sort of stiff plumes equally dark red as the cape, the knee protectors, the poleyn, the cup-shaped armor knee-guards, fan-plates, the heart shaped guards for the side of the knee extending from the poleyn were silver also with the image of a lion upon them.

"What are you?" she asked from behind her shield.

"I was once a heavenly version of what you are," he said, dissolving his uniform and the tux returned. To let her know he had no intention of fighting her. Unable to keep his emotions in check any longer, he beseeched her, praying that what happened tonight hadn't besmirched his chances of convincing her to unguard.

"Ana, I know it's you. Please let your guard down. You stopped visiting me. I was unable to find you."

"How do I know you are not a demon trying to trick me into accepting your surrender and you rearm yourself the moment I disengage?"

"You don't but your heart knows me. Listen to it. I don't remember much about us but I do remember I love you."

"And that is supposed to make me trust you because you say so?" She asked glacially. "Unlock the door or I'll blast it down."

"Ana, it's me. Think hard, concentrate...you can break through it. I know you can. Try. Just try. Trust me enough to try to remember at least our love if you remember nothing else," he said, walking toward her with open arms.

"Don't come any closer," she warned, turning and blasting the door down. She was gone in a matter of seconds. She didn't go through the 8th Day for Glory didn't open up so he took off after her. He wasn't letting her out his sight. Who knows when, if ever, he would see her again if he didn't break through to her? That was something he couldn't live with. Knowing she was walking the earth unaware of who he is and how much he loves her was more than he could bear.

Quickly entering the Neutral Zone, he saw her up ahead, running at a super human speed. He wasn't sure if he could catch her. But it was worth a try. Teleporting would take too long as fast as she was moving. He braced his legs and pushed with all his might and started flying through the zone in powerful leaps and bounds. He hates to tackle her but that seems to be the only way to make her listen. While she was looking behind for him, he was soaring under cloak. He flew overhead and she ran directly into him. He grabbed her, forcing her arms down before she had the opportunity to materialize a weapon. He hated holding her so tight. So tight he could feel her fragile bones through the exposed parts of her uniform.

"Let me go, I told you I'm not who you are looking for!"

"Ana, I know it's you," he said bring his mouth down hard and possessively on hers to make her shut up. She kneed him in the crotch, it hurt like hell but he refused to let her go. He held on as she struggled and twisted and turned, trying to break his hold. He was glad she hadn't come into her full potential yet or he might not have been able to hold her. The uniform was repelling his effect on her.

"Ana BuFaye, I'm not letting you go until you acknowledge me. We can tussle all day and all night. I'm immortal so I've plenty of time to do so."

Something about *the way* he said that resonated in her. Somewhere deep down inside she had heard his voice before. She stopped fighting and calmly asked what did he want her to do?

"Dissolve the uniform so we can talk."

She remembered St. Anne told her some demons will try and trick you into letting down your defense. She looked around at the area thick with the yellowish fog floating around them and wondered exactly where had she run into? It looked like a community of very old-fashioned houses with lantern lights burning inside of them but she saw no one.

"Where are we?" she asked with some intrinsical knowledge that he was familiar with this area.

"Somewhere you don't need to be." he said, gripping her hand leading her back the way they came for he didn't where to teleport them to for she hadn't told him where she was living. But he knew these houses were not unoccupied as they seemed. The occupants were watching from the windows and waiting for the victim to be alone. This town was once a lovely place before so many towns and village along this road fell prey to the persuasion of hell. This wasn't a realm of hell but from the violence the immortals here carried out it was hard to know that.

"Is this a part of hell?" she asked, looking back at the incandescent shades moving in the thick fog, the assembling of the slow moving, but strange people was forming in the sickly yellow density. More and more were venturing from the old houses watching them in a not so friendly manner as he led her out.

"No, it's a fallen world that it's best you do not take a wrong turn and enter again." he said, leading them back onto the main path of the Neutral Zone. He recognized the two main inhabitants of this world from his days of riding with Michael. He was whom they were staring at with eyes burning of hatred, not her.

He pulled her through a portal leading to an extravagant apartment. "I think you need to see about the injuries you suffered."

He wasn't sure if her uniform healed or not. She slowly dissolved it and the prick from the fine glass was felt in her knees, the heel of her hands, and left shin. She knew glass shards are difficult to remove.

He beckon her to a seat while he went into another part of the apartment to get a first aid kit, a towel, and a waste basket. She wondered what the waste basket was for but asked no questions. She was wearing a knee length skirt so it was easy to reach the issues. She also know she was wearing latex shorts under the skirt in case any of the guests had a grabbing problem. She wasn't expecting to fight, but with her life you can never tell when you might have to fight so she always dressed prepared.

He broke open a package of disinfectant with his teeth and begun cleaning her wounds. He asked her about the scars. Some she didn't want to talk about so she simply said they came from many accidents. He accepted her reply but he knew she wasn't telling the truth. No one has this many *accidents*. While holding her hand he noticed how callous they were despite the fresh manicure for the job. Hands tell a lot about a person's life.

He turned his attention to the wounds on her knee first. She was looking for the splinter remover in his kit but saw none.

"I'll make it as painless as possible," he spoken in a melodious voice that projected authority but yet was filled with compassion and love.

He lowered his head over her knees and begun sucking the wound. The strong suction felt strange at first but she soon relaxed. She wore a tasteful ensemble of a white blouse and knee length black skirt so it covered everything modestly. He blouse was torn and she hadn't realize he could see her bra until she looked down at her front and saw the fastening was missing. It was a barely noticeable peek.

He noticed plastic silver hair combs that was still attached as they glinted enigmatically in the soft lighting of the room. He thought she looked beautiful even if she did look a little disheveled.

She watched curiously as he raised his head from her knew and spit a mouthful of blood and glass shards in the waste basket. He wiped his mouth with the towel. She had never seen glass removed from wounds this way.

He slightly squeezed her knee asking did she feel any more tiny silvers of glass inside?

She shook her head that she didn't. He went to the other knee, her shin and then her palms and repeated the same process.

Anyone willing to take glass in their mouth for her she assumes must really love her as much as he said he does

"Does, that hurt?" she asked, for it seems like it ought to be painful.

"No," he shook his thick mane and tossed about his broad shoulder. "You hold it with blood and saliva and spit it out. I wouldn't advise humans to do this for their flesh is easily penetrated. "The worst part are the very fine silvers which fine fine glassware produces."

Feeling a little guilty about her behavior earlier tonight, she sought for a way to explain and apologize for it, "I'm, uh … hiding?" said Ana, unable to think of a lie.

"Hiding," he nods and continues attending and bandaging her wounds. He laid his hands on them and they felt better. Much of the sting was leaving "Well, you haven't chosen the most secluded city. People who are hiding usually avoid this city. It has cameras everywhere."

As he worked on her Ana looked around and inspected her surroundings for the first time. The luxury apartment was accented with much fine and famous artwork. There was one in particular which interested her. It rose several feet against the wall into the dark interior decorated room. This room was larger than many houses. The woman was wearing what looked to be a 1920's lace cream flapper dress complete with a long strand of white pearls and a burgundy plume in her auburn hair.

"Who is that?" she asked. She knew it was stupid question when she saw clearly who

811

the woman was but he must remember she had been running for her life for years and may not always ask the most sensible questions..

"Don't tell you don't know her." he said turning to look at the picture. "I knew it really you when the image returned. At long last, I've lived to see it come to life again. I painted it in 1925 after you visited me and left. After you left the image faded. This is the first time it has reappeared in nearing six hundred years."

She got up and hobbled, walked to the larger than life painting with his aid. He held her up with his arm around her waist. The colors were so alive and vibrant that her smile in the painting was identical to her fleshy one. The merry twinkle in the woman's laughing eyes was giving every impression she was experiencing a marvelous time.

"Of course I recognize myself," said Ana, a little offended that he thought her so ignorant. "Just that I didn't know you painted portraits of me..."

"Yes, I do. I always paint them so I will never forget your face. But the image fades when you leave. I'm the painter and proprietor of all the paintings of Ms. Ana BuFaye." he teased her and kissed her bandaged hand.

Her bronze skin had a cool and delicate feel. She flexed her fingers, he found they were surprisingly strong. She held his hand tightly as her sharp, but soft amber eyes turned from the picture and looked into his. Her pupils appeared to grow larger and more intriguing in the soft light of the apartment. Her eyes were as if two tiny pots of dark golden honey were slowly swirling around inside him, tugging and reaching for his deepest thoughts, searching for his love for her inside his mind and heart.

And then she released his hand. She blinked of embarrassment for rudely staring at him and returned her gaze toward the larger than life painting on the wall to have something to look at other than him.

In his eyes, her shy smile by far eclipsed that of the Mona Lisa's and was far more mystifying, beguiling, and prepossessing. She has a lovely, charming personality when she isn't pissed off. She is delightful, definitely more appealing. This woman is far more engaging; winsome, with a ravishing figure! Even making faces she was gorgeous. He watched her tonight before the fight broke out and saw she was stunning and arresting. Truthfully to him....Mona Lisa has always been butt ugly. He knew the actual woman and she wasn't a great beauty, at least not in his eyes. Then he realized that perhaps Da Vinic saw Mona as he sees this woman he's kneeing before. Beauty in the eyes of the beholder. Nah, that wasn't it.....the woman just didn't look that hot but she had a beautiful personality. Why is he being mean to Mona?

He picked her up without dissent and carried her back to the chair and eased her into it. "If I told you you're magical.... Would you believe me?"

There was no trickery in his words. "Yes, I believe you. I have been called many things but magical isn't one of them." She lightly joked.

She seemed to understand what he was thinking, gently nodding for him to continue. To continue complimenting her. She needed a few kind words for today. For she had had a very rough day, starting this morning with her sister urging to take this horrible job saying she had put in the application and the company needed extra help for tonight. She didn't want the job when she learned where it was. They called for her on Helena's private line and told her sister she had declined the offer. Helena huffed downstairs saying she and Dave could not take care of everyone. That Bea was bad and tore up things that she needed to get a job if she intended to stay here a few weeks to look after mom. Aunt Gayle's death set mom's health on collision course again.

He handed her the drinks saying it would help with the pain. She reached for it, but she pulled back with quicker reflexes than he expected.

"You swear you are not trying to get me drunk?"

Ashton chuckled mildly. "I don't know why you would think that? But I think you need to eat something in case you haven't already eaten."

"For one thing...we are alone in an apartment with what looks like bedrooms back there..." she said, gesturing toward the hallway. "No, I haven't eaten. I had planned to eat after serving tonight with the other staff members."

"Then I promise you nothing will happen, you do not wish to happen." he said, calling the kitchen and ordering her dinner.

"Azazael, tell them I want fried pork chops...." she said much to her own surprise.

He froze, he was very confident he had not told her his real name. He dropped the phone and ran and scooped her up and swirled her around. "Put me down." She objected.

"Honey, do you realize you remembered something I thought was lost to you forever?"

From there they discussed as many things in segments as they could remember them as she ate, well more or less as he fed her which he took pleasure in doing. She had nothing else to wear so she put on one of his many shirts in the closet.

The main thing we discussed is we both remember fragmented pieces of a wedding ceremony, but they appeared to be different ceremonies. Then we laughed that there was no need to add another one for we needed to figure out which one was our *original* and set an anniversary date. We went heavy on the kissing and caressing but didn't make love for I had fresh wounds.

During our talk tonight, we made peace with the fact that by morning we may be divinely separated again and not remember each other and to cherish the time we had. We vowed to ourselves we would stop worrying about that which we didn't remember and started taking more time to cherish that which we did.

We spooned and talked this way until around 3:00 A.M., then I reminded him I had to go home. Mom and Bea would be expecting me and become very worried if I didn't show up.

We went downstairs holding hands to a garage housing a 1925 Isotta Franschini Tipo 8 A S Roadster, at least that's what he told me the ancient car was. He said this was one of the cars he owned when I stepped back in time to him in the Roaring 20's when he owned a club called the Cotton Club. This was the car he wanted to take me for a ride in the next day but by morning I was gone. So according to him 500 years late is much better than never. I guess you would have to be an immortal to see things that way.

Looking at how happy she is made him happy. Elated. He watched her look around the car interior, inspecting it as he started the car. Rolling toward the door and waiting for the slow moving garage door to open, he knew she wasn't incapable of love, he felt that the moment the uniform was removed. Although, according to the scars he could see she had been through hell and back, she still had much love to give. She simply needed a man capable of giving her real love.

I always do this when riding and someone else is driving. It's an old habit that's became much keener in recent years. I make a mental map of the directions. He said that was the gift of navigation. Which meant I would have a hard time getting lost. We headed north on West St toward Fulton St, made a U-turn at Murray Street, kept right to continue on NY-9A S/West St which turned into going through Battery Park Underpass, and then onto FDR Drive taking exit 8 toward I-495/E 34 into St/Midtown. I got a little confused with the directions for he was making the turns on certain streets very fast. I laughed and said neither of us needed to be who taught our children to drive. He agreed, laughing, saying we can't have them out here driving as we drive. We were both speed demons.

She didn't tell him but she was seeing different versions of the city, different eras. It was like the people, their clothing, and car models were changing as they drove through the city. She has experienced this before but not very often. Once in a city, she saw all the way back to the days of horse and buggy. She was expecting to eventually go that far here. She has no idea what purpose this ability serves other than to enlighten her about the past.

The mighty roar of the powerful engine of the ancient roadster caused many to stare and point at us as we made turns and picked up speed and flew down the road. Very few modern people had ever seen such a beautiful car, including myself. My heart leapt with joy every time he looked over at me and smiled. I could feel his love for me from across the seat. I decided to move under his arm. I felt it was my rightful place. For once I felt I had no worries, no demons, no satanists, nor Nikola to worry about. I knew he loved me for that was all that mattered. Anyone willing to take shards of glass in their mouth for you must love you very much.

I was mentally taking notes as we cruised with the top down through the city that never sleeps. Some turns I had missed but that's OK, I didn't panic for I felt safe. Safe that at least one of us knew where we were going.

He was holding my hand with his right hand while driving with his left. The cool night air was a little chilly but I didn't complain. He let go of my hand long enough to pull a blanket from a compartment and spread over me. Now I was warm and toasty and snuggled closer to him, laying my head on his shoulder. It all felt right as rain.

We took exit 22A-E heading toward Interstate 678, Grand Central Parkway onto the old Van Wyck Expressway, keeping on right at the fork, following the signs for Grand Central Pkwy eastbound, and merged onto Grand Central Pkwy. He slowed up a bit when we came to Northern State Pkwy to prolong the ride back to my sister's. I knew he was going around in circles but I didn't care. What started out as hellish evening was turning into an exciting evening. It had been ages since I had this much fun just riding around.

I called mom and told her I was on my way. I didn't have to worry about Trusty for she was parked outside Helena' home. Helena had taken me to work to make sure I went inside. That now worked out to my advantage.

When we were finally on I-495 E, I was tempted to tell him about the fight Helena and I had this morning, since if memories served us correctly, he is my husband so it was OK to tell him why I was in the city. But I didn't want to taint his image of my family and didn't want talk about it for the next fourteen, 14.7 miles. I didn't want to return to reality. I wanted to enjoy the ride for once. He explained the route hadn't changed much in the last six hundred years. He talked about how things were when he at first returned to earth in the late 1800's and how much the world had changed and yet remained the same.

Finally, we took exit 57 toward NY-454 on the Commack/Patchogue and merged onto Express Dr headed south to the Long Island Expressway South Rd turning right onto NY-454 E, turning left onto 5th Ave and within the next fifteen minutes we were in Long Island.

He saw a vehicle from his own security team members parked outside the upper middle class, three story Tudor styled house with a neat lawn and a wide, four car driveway. Trusty was parked beside the street because Dave complained I wasn't getting up in the morning to move her so she would block his way, according to him he just had to use the car parked behind the last door.

He recognized the vehicle for he purchased them custom made by fleets. But he can't remember posting a guard here but was glad this local team remembered. He felt he was finally coming to the end of this maddening cycle of intermissions. He couldn't explain it but that was how he felt. She looked up at him smiling as thus she felt it, too. He kissed her long and lovingly.

They sat outside and talked as demons spied on them for Nikola and Lucifer. He had noticed demons following them long before they reached Long Island but he was happy. So fuck them, just so long as they didn't bother them. He would let them be. He had waited over 500 years to finish this date and they wasn't messing it up. He gently took her into his arms and hugged her and kissed her. To the hell with who was waiting and watching. This moment belonged to them.

"Thank you for allowing me to complete a date I believe we started over 500 years ago and never got to finish." Ashton said, raising her hand to his lips while looking her lovingly in the eyes. "My love, my sweet Ana, I can't get you out of my mind, heaven knows I've tried," he paused just to look in her amber eyes reflecting the silver tint of the late night moon and kissed her harder and deeper,;he groaned, drawing in slow gasps of air, his lips planting feverish kisses all over her face and neck before retuning to her mouth.

"Many a times down through the ages I've tried to forget you but failed. I'm totally obsessed with you. I think about you every moment I'm awake and dream about you when I go to sleep. I am often even in the Realm of Dreams searching for you. I must confess the remembrance of you have made me smile many times with great joy. It has gotten me through some terrible times. I haven't always remembered what you looked like but I have never forgotten how your love felt."

She felt much of the same way but didn't know how to put it into words as elegant as he.

"What I admire about you more than your beauty is that you have overcome so much that was meant and planned with malicious intent to destroy you. It would have been so much easier to have let your enemies win. But you didn't. It would have been so much easier to taken so many dishonorable routes out but you didn't. Like the job you were working tonight. Most women as beautiful as you wouldn't have taken it."

"Ashton, that's ok. I know I'm no great beauty. My sister inside is who is the great beauty." She said although she was enjoying his praises.

"I do not know about all that but I know no one has ever told you how beauteous you really are. You have a regal beauty that princes and kings look for when choosing a wife."

Meanwhile inside, Helena was complaining to their mother, saying when she arrived to pick Ana up tonight the woman who hired her said Ana got into a fight with Mrs. Cargill and her friends then went upstairs with Mr. Cargill and no one has seen her yet. That Ana utterly utterly embarrassed the woman in front of the entire city.

"No, *he* embarrassed her in front of the entire city. It was he who took Ana upstairs in front of his wife." Fannie corrected. Although she intended to give Ana holy hell for that stunt, she didn't tell Helena that. But the words of Mother Harris came to mind. "*To listen as to why Ana beat up a bunch of people Ana wasn't a violent person. But if you start something with her she was going to finish it.*" But the truth be told, in her opinion it didn't sound like the husband cared very much to disappear upstairs with the woman who just beat his wife up?! But it also sounded like this guy was used to women fighting over him and would someday treat Ana the same when a newer face come on the scene. So yes, as a mother---it was her duty to make Ana understands that.

Fannie knew Bea wasn't asleep beside her, she knew Bea was listening and had heard everything Helena said. She also knew Bea would encourage her mother to leave in a few hours and they just arrived less than 48 hours ago. Helena knew she didn't have to be so hard on her sister. She knew she treated her friends much better than her own sister. But her friends wasn't always embarrassing her.

Hearing the powerful engine outside their home the Wales look out the window and it's Ana in the car with some man driving and showing off in their opinion in a very ancient looking but beautiful car. They just knew the neighbors were going to start calling about the excessive noise. That car was breaking the natural sound barrier let alone the city's ordinance sound barrier. Things like this is why Ana's siblings doesn't want her around. They are trying to live respectful lives while Ana is wild and wind blown as autumn leaves. They watched them kiss for a few seconds before leaving the window.

Recognizing the man as Ashton Cargill and it's nearly 5 A.M. Helena heavily sighs, "My sister has no shame at all. I'm seriously worried about her. Those women have enough money, power, prestige and connections to have her killed and nothing will be done about it."

Helena goes downstairs with Dave right behind. She see Ana gets out wearing an oversized shirt reaching her knees for a dress. She all hugged up on the married man like he's hers. At least the man should have the common decency to buy her a real dress and not bring her home advertising what they have done. Her teenage daughter Rachael doesn't need to see that and neither does Bea. Thanks God they are both asleep. Dammit! Ana is so damn irresponsible it's a crying shame. But mom and dad made her like this for making excuses for her odd behavior growing up.

Ana didn't have a key so she had to ring the doorbell. Dave answered and scowled at her. "Your sister wants to see you in the kitchen."

Ana turned and invited Ashton inside, creating a deeper lour in Dave's face. With the wool blanket draped across her shoulder she walked through the living room into the kitchen to face the music, but their mother was calling both of them.

Helena ignored Fannie summoning them both to her bedroom. The moment they entered the kitchen, Ana saw her big sister at the breakfast table with a cup of coffee. She didn't greet her sister's guest before she started in on her. Like Ana, Helena doesn't remember the wedding in the Hamptons a few years ago.

"Miss Hot Ass, we need to lay down some ground rules if you are going to stay here." Helena said in a temperament hotter than her coffee. "One, people around here when they get off from work they come home. They don't go around street fighting like bums. Two, keep the noise down, this is a working community. Everyone here has to go to work in the morning. Just because you don't doesn't mean everyone else don't. While here you will conduct yourself respectful manner. I don't know what you were doing in the streets but you are back to civilization and you will act accordingly. Three, I want my rent money today. Four, make Bea stop acting like little Conananna, the little barbarian. She has been terrorizing her cousins, tearing up and breaking things since you two hit the front door...."

Ashton interrupted saying, "I don' know how you are used to talking to your sister but in front of me you will not speak to her that way."

Helena cracked her infamous evil grin Ana has seen all her life. "This is my house, my kitchen, my sister so I will talk some sense into her however I damn well please. Who in the hell are you to think you can come up in my house and tell me what I can't say to my sister!!!" By now Helena was out of her chair glaring up at him with Dave at her side. So Ana pulled closer to Ashton signaling to her sister she was defending him.

"She may be your sister, I do not know. But I know she's my wife and I will not have you or anyone speaking to her in such degrading tone. All the things you listed as a problem can very easily be fixed. Ana, go get your child. You are getting the hell out of this dump. How much damn money does she owe you?" He asked, reaching in his front pocketing out a slim pocket size checkcard puncher.

Helena looked at Dave and laughed, "This fool is being taken for a ride by my slick talking sister and don't even know it! There's two more fools always calling here talking about they love her. One used to call here crying saying Ana ran away." She taunted him for peeving her off.

But Helena was a little surprised when he flipped her off with, "Whatever, and I'm supposed to worry about some fools in love with her when she is right here with me??? As I asked, how much does she owe you?"

"Everybody sit their asses down, no one is going anywhere." Fannie said from the door walking with the aid of Bea and a cane as her assistants. "I'm sick of every time the two of you get together you are always after each other. I would give anything to see Gayle one more time and you two don't have sense enough to know what you have. No man, friends, children or I even can substitute for the bond of sisters. Young man, put your wallet away. I'm going to enjoy my daughter for as long as I can."

"Daddy Ash, when did you get here?" Bea asked drowsily from the doorway beside her grandmother.

"DADDY??!" Helena cried, quizzing Bea how she knew him?

"A few minutes ago, Bumble Bea." Ashton replied. "I came to take you and your mommy home."

The three adults looked puzzlingly at each other.

"Ok, let me get this straight--- if Ana is your alleged wife, why is she always struggling, out on the road?" Dave inserted in the conversation. He held a deep animosity that Cargill had so much disposable income to burn but he had to work every

821

day. Plus he had the nerve to pick the worst possible person to spend it on, his nut job sister-in-law. A woman as refined as one of his sisters would be far more suited for someone of his status. Ironically, Dave did not see the hypocrisy in this line of reasoning; his own parents had told him as much about the same thing regarding Helena years ago.

"Mr. Wales, since you are quick to point out the errs in my affairs why don't you tell your wife you tried to sell me her homestead?" Ashton asked looking down at the shorter, smaller man whom he dearly regrets is his brother-in-law. Dave blatantly denies it, calling the accusation absurd at worst and laughable at best.

From her seat where Bea and Ana had led her Fannie whops all three of them hard with her cane, for she thought she told everyone to shut the hell up. Apparently, they thought she was playing when she wasn't. (Ana learnt years ago how to avoid the switch, well in this case a cane, by keeping your mouth shut when mother was tired of their bickering.) This may be Helena's house but Mom was still the Matriarch of the BuFaye Clan.

Seated at the head of the table, Fannie asked Ana why was she bandaged up? Ana relayed the account of the evening. Then Fannie wanted to know if Ashton is married to her why isn't he taking care of her and Bea?

Ana did her best to explain the supernatural elements surrounding their marriage. That perhaps even they have met Ashton before and don't remember. The only person who seems able to remember much about anything is Bea.

"You are saying angels have been swiping all of our minds?" Fannie skeptically asked. Ana nodded. Helena giggled. Fannie shot her a "shut up" glance.

"Did they say why?" Fannie further quizzed her daughter, for Mother Harris had said something akin to this.

"No, not really. All I know is I'm supposed to do something---uh, without him. The saints in the cave didn't know the fullness of it or weren't telling. All St. Anne said was

I'm to lead a great army, a division of the heavenly army."

"Oh! For crying out loud!!!" Dave exclaimed, raising his hands to both sides of his head to demonstrate the insanity of Ana's story. He wasn't willing to sit here and listen to any more of this absurdity, this madness. Fannie quickly hit the top of the table where he sat, the loud thump echoed in the modern kitchen filled with the golden rays of early morning sunshine. Her slam meant. "Don't make me throw this stick at you."

"Excuse me, Mrs. BuFaye, but how is Ana supposed to lead anything if she can't remember anything? Ana can't lead herself straight let alone anything or anyone else!"

In the blink of an eye Ashton had a strange blade clinched between his teeth, choking Dave from behind. No one knew how he got over there from beside Ana so quickly other than Ana. Ana jumped up and tried to pull him off Dave. Ana was afraid Ashton was going to kill him when Dave's eyes rolled up in his head, revealing nothing but the white of his eyes; he was growing blueish and limp. Helena rushed for her service revolver and opened fire. The bullet pinged off Ashton's chest and ricocheted in the kitchen embedding itself in a cabinet door. But Bea telling him to stop made him stop and look up at her frightened eyes.

"Daddy Ash, Uncle Dave is always saying stupid, inconsiderate things. The family doesn't pay him any mind."

Helena was wiping Dave's face with a damp dishcloth as he coughed and gagged for breath. Ana was furious her sister actually shot the man she loved, supposed he had been human? He would be dead by now. She did something she had never done before. She slapped her sister so hard she staggered against the sink. Helena caught herself and lunged for her baby sister. Ana balled her bony fist up and let her have it again, before they both were being hit over the head with Fannie's cane.

"How dare you take side with a man over your own sister?" Helena screamed, she knew that last punch would leave a nasty bruise. "Especially one you don't know a damn thing about?! He is not fucking human. That shot should have killed him!"

823

All the Wales were on one side of the kitchen and the Cargills on the other. Only Fannie was in the middle as both sides glowered at the other.

Ana and Bea left with Ashton that morning around 9:30 as Fannie stood in the doorway with a heavy heart wondering where she went wrong with her two daughters. She hated to see this man load them and their car up and take them away. She had not seen them in nearly two years and most often she news she got about them was dreadful. Ana promised, she didn't know how or when but she was coming back for her mother one day. Fannie told her to not worry about her just keep themselves safe.

Helena watched from her upstairs bedroom window with a cold cloth compressing her face as her sister got in the hoverlimo called to pick them up. She saw the tears falling when Ana looked back and up at the window, eyes saying she was sorry. But her achy jaw hardened her heart against the perceived crocodile tears...

When Trusty, being driven by a member of Cargill Security, pulled out the driveway onto the lane leading from the Wales' home and made the turn left to head to New York City someone exhaled. "Good riddance," Dave quipped from behind his wife.

No one knew Fannie had collapsed downstairs in the doorway.

Looking at her Bulgari Serpenti Tubogas watch, curling up her arm, she waited impatiently for Ashton's return. He had deferred her from following. After 30 minutes, she knew he had broken the spell and he wasn't coming back. If she didn't slightly fear Caroline Cadwell she would kick her ass worse than Ana kicked all of theirs. But she would find her revenge. Caroline may be a witch but she was about to learn she is an even bigger bitch than she is a witch. Caroline did that on purpose. She's glad Ana kicked her ass. Had Caroline let them gotten rid of Ana when they first spotted her Ashton would be here now dancing and having fun instead of wherever the hell Ana has led him. The security pretends they have no idea where he is. She make her way across the pavilion to Ashley where he spent the night with someone new. Gosh, he is just like his father. Can't stay faithful for two seconds.

"Have you seen your father?"

"Yes," he grins mischievously, looking even more like his father. Dawn doesn't trust that grin. With Ashton it always means something evil so she safely assumes with Ashley it means the same.

"Well?"

"Dawn, give it up. You can't win. It's over. The gravy train has gone bye-bye. Wave at the steam engine's puff clouds before they fade into the obsolete." He grinned even more largely.

"Come off it, Ashley, you hate Ana."

"True, very true but I hate you more. Trying to pawn that kid off as my brother. Woman, I'm over seven hundred years old, did you really think that was the first time someone pulled that number with dad?"

"Ana's daughter isn't his child."

"I know but she didn't profess the girl ever was."

"Stop bullshitting me and tell me where is that no-good, lying father of yours?"

"Certainly, he's at the old mansion in Hyde Park. But if I were you. I wouldn't go there. Ana is there playing little wifey and dad is eating it up like sweet ambrosia."

"That's not true. They aren't married."

Ashley shrugged his broad shoulders. He sees this as an opportunity to get rid of both Ana and Dawn.

Dawn arrived at the estate just as the new family was settling in. Security refused to let her pass. She can not see beyond the wrought iron fence, but she knows he is in there. After an hour she gives up and tell the chauffeur to take her across the sea. She was going home. She knew their tryst wouldn't last and Ana would soon be gone as always and then he would come home. The driver turned on the vehicle's flight gears and slowly rose and soared above the mansion; she looked down and saw Ana entering with Ashton's arms around her. The pain was too much to keep watching. She saw Ashley was right. Nothing was working. Perhaps she should simply pack and be gone when he returns. Nahhh, that's exactly what he wants.

✸✸✸

The first rain of the season had started to fall, she decided it was time to head to a warmer climate. It was late November, as a matter of fact it was Thanksgiving Day. A time when normal families were sitting at a banquet with their loved ones gathered around thanking God for the prosperity of the year and praying it continues into the next and for many years to come. But they weren't a normal family. They were merely a small family, a unit of two. Here they are driving in the cold late November rain with the bluish black night sky matching her mood, and icy water drops pelleting the car feels like the poisonous darts that have pierced every inch of her life. She has given up hopes of their lives ever being anything other than what it is.

She glanced over at her sleeping daughter whose beautiful face the dashboard's neon green light was illuminating. She saw her mom in Bea. Bea inherited her mother's great beauty that skipped over herself. For Bea's sake she rescinded the feeling of hopelessness. With renewed valiance she lifted her head higher, rolled her shoulders, thrust her narrow chin out into the night's air in firmer determination and stared obstinately at the lone winding road which is now taking a beating from the ice falling from the sky. She had to keep and hold on to hope for her daughter's sake if not her own.

She reflects on these things before they are taken away. Ana know she has encountered a man who is inhumanely fine, sophisticated far beyond her few short years; who can be somewhat intimidating but to her he wasn't threatening. She knows she is unworldly

826

wise in some areas but in others she has had to become wise to survive. She finally admits to herself she wants this man more than she ever wanted any man; perhaps it's because she can't have him. Despite his genteel manners, incomprehensible coolness, and properness lately. Despite she has had a memory erase several times she keeps finding herself yearning to be in his arms. She finds her way back to him again and again. She finds a sweet gentle recourse in his arms when they embrace her. When his kisses cover her they rejuvenate not only her body but her soul. Even if she can not remember his name nor his face. She remember his love.

Ashton has never been to resist Ana. Her strong, serene beauty, her sometime dark witticism, and autarkic spirit makes him want her all the more. Ashton doesn't want to admit he wants her but on his own constituents. He isn't used to getting a woman on anyone's terms but his own.

She smiles thinking of him, she knows she is secretly amused by Ashton's erotic love making. Sometimes but not very often she is reluctant and hesitates when in his arms. But with her he has always been respectful and loving.

What she doesn't know about him is for all the accoutrement of his immortality, his multinational empire, his unequaled wealth, that Ashton Cargill is an immortal man tormented by nothing but his loss of her. He knows his to need and desire to control everything has come at a terrible price. When they are in each other's arms as a couple all is well. For together their firework is pure legendary. She knows there much about him she still doesn't know, she wish to uncovers the real man. The real Ashton Cargill's secrets. Things like; what's his real name? What was his world like prior to their meeting? What makes him who he is while exploring her own needs and desires? Which is something she had never done. She needs to learn who is she as a woman? This is an area she never had a chance to fully explore. A lot of it has to do with her rigidly strict upbringing. But she wants things to be different between them shall they ever get together for good.

Together, they know they're sexy, amusive, and a force to be reckoned with but apart they are lost. They need each other to be whole. Both know they're obsessed with the other, want to possess the other for they intend to stay together forever. But they know

827

only time will tell if this is possible for even a love great as theirs. Will theirs continue to withstand the test of time? The burden of the grinding affronting of everyday life? But as with every couple... both believe it will.

Watching the lightening of the gray overcast sky on this bleak November morning, her memory of him is slowly fading into the shroud of the passing night but before it's gone she knows whatever her feelings may be, she has to keep on moving. Like a shark swimming through waters. It's said if the shark stops it will die. This is how they swim through life, if she stops; they die.

.

www.ingramcontent.com/pod-product-compliance
Lightning Source LLC
Chambersburg PA
CBHW080941020726